D0180362

ALSO BY SHARON KAY PENMAN

Devil's Brood
Falls the Shadow
Here Be Dragons
The Sunne in Splendour

THE RECKONING

SHARON KAY PENMAN

St. Martin's Griffin
New York

This is a work of fiction. All of the characters, organizations, and events portrayed in this novel are either products of the author's imagination or are used fictitiously.

THE RECKONING. Copyright © 1991 by Sharon Kay Penman. All rights reserved. Printed in the United States of America. For information, address St. Martin's Press, 175 Fifth Avenue, New York, N.Y. 10010.

www.stmartins.com

Library of Congress Cataloging-in-Publication Data

Penman, Sharon Kay.
   The reckoning / Sharon Kay Penman. — 1st St. Martin's Griffin ed.
      p. cm.
   ISBN-13: 978-0-312-38247-6
   ISBN-10: 0-312-38247-2
   1. Llywelyn ap Gruffydd, d. 1282—Fiction. 2. Great Britain—History—13th century—Fiction. 3. Wales—History—1063–1284—Fiction. I. Title.
   PS3566.E474R4 2009
   813'.54—dc22

                                                                 2008050579

First published by Ballantine Books, a division of Random House, Inc.

10   9   8   7   6   5   4   3

To my parents

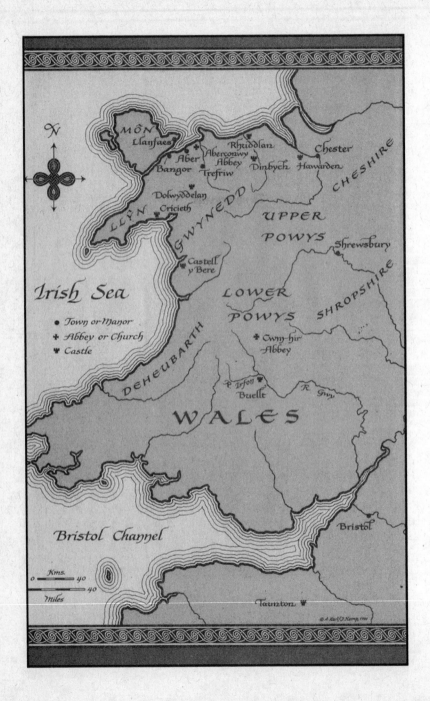

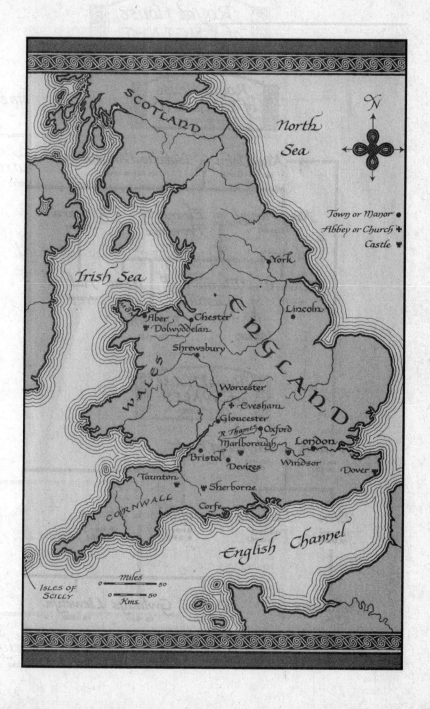

Royal House of ENGLAND
(as of 1271)

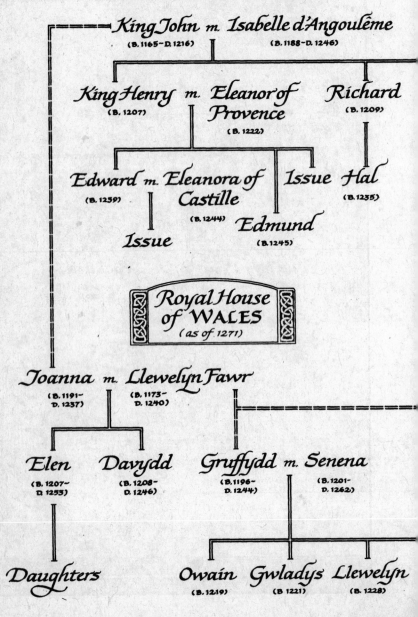

King John m. **Isabelle d'Angoulême**
(B. 1165–D. 1216)   (B. 1188–D. 1246)

King Henry m. **Eleanor of Provence**
(B. 1207)   (B. 1222)

Richard
(B. 1209)

Edward m. **Eleanora of Castille**
(B. 1239)   (B. 1244)

Issue   **Hal**
(B. 1235)

Issue   **Edmund**
(B. 1245)

Royal House of WALES
(as of 1271)

Joanna m. **Llewelyn Fawr**
(B. 1191– D. 1237)   (B. 1173– D. 1240)

Elen   **Davydd**
(B. 1207– D. 1253)   (B. 1208– D. 1246)

Gruffydd m. **Senena**
(B. 1196– D. 1244)   (B. 1201– D. 1262)

Daughters

Owain   **Gwladys**   **Llewelyn**
(B. 1219)   (B. 1221)   (B. 1228)

House of
MONTFORT
(as of 1271)

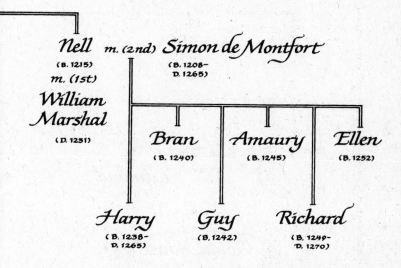

Nell
(B. 1215)
m. (1st)

m. (2nd) Simon de Montfort
(B. 1208–
D. 1265)

William
Marshal
(D. 1231)

Bran
(B. 1240)

Amaury
(B. 1245)

Ellen
(B. 1252)

Harry
(B. 1238–
D. 1265)

Guy
(B. 1242)

Richard
(B. 1249–
D. 1270)

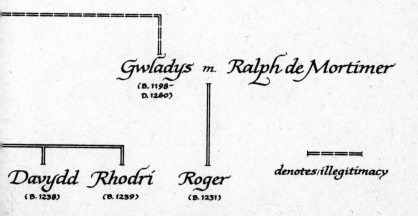

Gwladys   m.   Ralph de Mortimer
(B. 1198–
D. 1260)

Davydd
(B. 1238)

Rhodri
(B. 1239)

Roger
(B. 1231)

denotes illegitimacy

© A·Karl/J·Kemp, 1991

1

EVESHAM ABBEY, ENGLAND

January 1271

THERE were no stars. The sky was the color of cinders, and shadows were spilling out of every corner. Brother Damian was truly content with his lot in life, but border winters were brutal, and he sometimes found it hard to reconcile his monk's vow of poverty with his subversive yearning for a woolen mantle luxuriously lined with fox fur. Folklore held that St Hilary's Day was the coldest of the year, but he doubted that it could be as frigid as this first Friday in January, a day that had begun in snow and was ending now in this frozen twilight dusk, in swirling sleet and ice-edged gusting wind, sharp as any blade.

He had reached the dubious shelter of the cloisters when a snowball grazed his cheek, splattered against the nearest pillar. Damian stumbled, slipped on the glazed walkway, and went down. His assailants rushed to his rescue and he was soon encircled by dismayed young faces. With recognition, the boys' apologies became less anxious, more heartfelt, for Damian was a favorite of theirs. They often wished that he, rather than the dour Brother Gerald, was master of the novices, as Damian was young enough himself to wink at their indiscretions, understanding how bumpy was the road from country lad to reluctant scholar. Now he scolded them roundly as they helped him to his feet and retrieved his spilled candles, but his rebuke lacked sting; when he tallied up sins, he found no room on the list for snowball fights.

His duty done, Damian felt free to jest about poor marksmanship before sending them back to their studies. They crowded in, jockeying for position, warming him with their grins, imploring him to tell them again of the great Earl Simon and the battle of Evesham, fought within sight of the abbey's walls. Damian was not deceived, as able as the next man to recognize a delaying tactic. But it was a ploy he could never resist, and when they entreated him to tell the story "just one more time, for Jack," a freckle-faced newcomer to their ranks, he let himself be persuaded.

Five years had passed since the Earl of Leicester had found violent death and martyrdom on a bloody August morn, but his memory was still green. Evesham cherished its own saint, caring naught that Simon de Montfort had not been—and would likely never be—canonized by the Church. No pope or cardinal would antagonize the English Crown by sanctifying the Earl's rebellion as the holy quest he'd believed it to be. It was the English people—craftsmen and widows and village priests and shire gentry—who had declared him blessed, who flocked to his grave in faithful numbers, who defied Church and King to do reverence to a French-born rebel, who did not forget.

Evesham suffered from no dearth of de Montfort partisans. Some of the more knowing of the boys had concluded that if every man who claimed to have fought with the Earl that day had in fact done so, de Montfort would never have lost. But Damian's de Montfort credentials were impeccable, for all knew he had actually engaged the great Earl in conversation before the battle, that he had then dared to make his way alone to Dover Castle, determined to give the Earl's grieving widow an account of his last hours. Damian not only believed in the de Montfort legend, he had lived it, and the boys listened raptly as he shared with them his memories, his remembered pain.

So real was it still to Damian that as he spoke, the cold seemed to ebb away, and the boys began to breathe in humid August air that foretold a coming storm. They saw the Earl and his men ride into the abbey so that the captive King Henry might hear Mass. They experienced the rebel army's joy that salvation was at hand, for the Earl's second son—young Simon, known to friends and foes alike as Bran—was on his way from Kenilworth Castle with a vast army. And they shuddered and groaned when Damian told them that Bran had tarried too long, that through his lack of care, his men were ambushed by the King's son. Flying Bran's captured banners, the Lord Edward had swept down upon Evesham, and by the time Earl Simon discovered the ruse, it was too late. Trapped between Edward's advancing army and the river, he and his men had ridden out to die.

"Earl Simon knew they were doomed, but his faith never faltered. He told his men that their cause was just, that a king should not be accountable only to God. 'The men of England will cherish their liberties all the more,' he said, 'knowing that we died for them.' " Damian's voice trailed off. There was a somber silence, broken at last by one of the younger lads, wanting to know if it was true that the Earl had been hideously maimed by his enemies. It was a question Damian had often been asked, but it was not one he found easy to answer—even now. He hesitated and a young voice came from the shadows.

"They hacked off Earl Simon's head and his private male parts, dispatched them as keepsakes to Roger de Mortimer's wife. His arms and legs were chopped off, too, sent to towns that had favored the Earl, and his mangled corpse was thrown to the dogs. Brother Damian retrieved what was left of the Earl's body, carried it on a ladder into the church, and buried it before the High Altar. But even then the Earl's enemies were not satisfied. They dug his body up, buried him in unhallowed ground. It was only after Simon's son Amaury appealed to the Pope that we were able to give the Earl a decent Christian burial."

It was a grisly account, but none thought to challenge it, for the speaker was another who had reason to be well versed in the de Montfort mythology; Hugh de Whitton's father had died fighting for Simon on that rain-drenched Evesham field.

Damian gave Hugh a grateful glance, then sent them off to wash up before supper. He was not surprised when Hugh lingered, offering to help him carry his candles to the sacristy. Of all the boys who lived at the abbey, both novices and students, none were as generous, as open-hearted as Hugh. Damian was very fond of him, and he grieved for the bleakness of the boy's future. For a lad of fourteen, he'd had more than his share of sorrows. His mother had died giving birth to a stillborn son when he was just four; he'd been but nine at the time of his father's battlefield death, and there were none to redeem his sire's forfeit lands. A cousin was found who'd grudgingly agreed to pay for the boy's education, but now that he was in his fifteenth year, the payments had ceased. Damian knew that the Abbot could not keep the lad on indefinitely. Nor would he stay once he realized his presence had become a charity, for Hugh was as proud as he was impoverished. Damian was by nature an optimist, but even he had few illusions as to what lay ahead for Hugh. Landless orphans did not often prosper, even in the best of times.

As they headed for the church, Hugh shortened his stride to match the monk's. He might lack for earthly possessions, but not for stature; he was already taller than many men, and his long legs, loose-gaited walk, and broadening shoulders gave promise of even more impressive growth to come. Now he studied Damian through long, fair lashes, blue eyes shadowed with sudden doubts.

Nothing he'd heard this eve was unfamiliar; he knew the history of the de Montforts as if they were his own family. The Earl, a highborn lord who'd championed the commons, a legend even in his lifetime, arrogant and gallant and hot-tempered and reckless, a man who'd preferred death to dishonor. His Countess, the Lady Nell, forced to choose between her brother the King and her husband, forced into French exile after Evesham. Their five sons. Harry, who'd died with his father, and Guy, who'd survived only by the grace of God. Bran, who had to live with a guilt beyond anything Hugh could imagine. Amaury, the priest, and Richard, dead in France. Ellen, the only daughter, who was to have wed a Prince.

Hugh felt as if he knew them all. But his thoughts now were not of the beguiling, tragic de Montforts; it was Damian, his friend, for whom he feared. "The old King hated Earl Simon as if he were the veritable Antichrist," he said hesitantly. "And all know how wroth the Lord Edward is that men have taken the Earl's memory so to heart, that they make pilgrimages to his grave and speak of miracles, of children healed and fevers broken. Is it not dangerous, then, Brother Damian, to speak out so plainly? Not even the Lord Edward could deny Earl Simon's courage. But when you talk of his desire for reforms, when you say he was right to seize the government, is there not a risk that evil-minded men might missay you, might even claim you speak treason?"

Damian was touched by the youngster's concern. "There is some truth in what you say, lad. But King Henry is no great threat these days, addled by his age and his failures. And the Lord Edward, whilst undeniably formidable, is absent from the realm. Crusades can last for years; who knows when he might return to England?"

"I was thinking of a danger closer at hand—the Earl of Gloucester. Who hates Earl Simon more than Gloucester? A man always despises one he betrays, does he not?"

Damian gave Hugh an approving smile; the lad was learning fast. "You are right. That Judas Gloucester does indeed harbor great hatred for his former allies, for all who bear the name de Montfort. I may well be foolhardy for speaking out as I do. But I cannot keep silent, Hugh. That is all I can do for Earl Simon now, seek to make sure he is not forgotten."

Ahead loomed the abbey church, a massive silhouette against the darkening sky. The nave was lit only by Damian's lantern, but as they detoured around the rood screen, they could see a glimmer of light coming from the choir. Damian was not surprised to find a man standing before Simon de Montfort's grave stone; rarely a day passed without pilgrims to this illicit shrine.

"I am sorry, but you must go now," he said kindly. "It is nigh on time for Vespers. You may stay for the service if you wish; lay people are permitted in the nave."

The man did not answer. He was uncommonly tall, shrouded in a long, snow-splattered mantle, and there was something disconcerting about his silence, his utter stillness in the shadows. Damian felt a faint prickling of unease. To combat it, he stepped forward boldly, raising his lantern. His candle's flame flared, giving Hugh a glimpse of a dark hawk's face, cheekbones high and hollowed, eyes the shade of smoke, not a face to be forgotten. But then Damian's light faltered; the lantern slipped from fingers suddenly numbed, would have plunged to the ground had Hugh not snatched it up. He turned, wondering, close enough to hear the monk's ragged, indrawn breath.

"My lord Earl!" Damian stumbled backward, groping for his crucifix. The man took a quick step forward, reaching out. Damian recoiled from his touch, then whirled, fled the choir.

Hugh was no less frightened. He believed implicitly in spirits and the supernatural, but had never expected to encounter an apparition himself. He was ready to bolt, too, when the man cried, "Wait!" The voice was low, husky, managed both to command and to entreat. Hugh hesitated; although he did not think the Earl's spectre would do him harm, there was terror in any confrontation with the unknown. He had begun to back away when his lantern spilled light onto the tiles, onto the crimson droplets trickling down Earl Simon's grave stone. It was an eerie sight, fraught with sinister significance, should have triggered headlong flight. But Hugh's superstitions were diluted by a healthy dose of country common sense. Ghosts do not bleed. Unthinkingly, he blurted that out aloud, and the corner of the stranger's mouth twitched.

"No," he said, "they do not . . ." Hugh darted forward, catching him as he staggered, sank down upon the altar steps. "The monk," he gasped, "stop him from giving the alarm . . ."

"I will," Hugh promised, "I will!" There was blood now upon his own mantle, too. He gently disengaged the other's hold upon his arm. "I'll find him, never fear!"

Damian's panic had taken him only as far as the nave. Once he realized that Hugh had not followed, he was nerving himself to return for the lad when Hugh lurched into the rood screen. "Brother Damian, hurry! He needs our help, is bleeding badly!" Grabbing Damian's sleeve, Hugh tugged urgently, impatiently. " 'Tis no ghost, I swear! Not Earl Simon, his son!"

Damian was greatly relieved, but discomfited, too. Flushed and breathless, he bent over the injured man, devoting more attention to "the remarkable resemblance, verily Lord Simon's image" than to the makeshift bandage, the blood welling between Hugh's fingers. Fortunately for Simon's son, Hugh had a cooler head in a crisis. It was he who reminded them that Vespers was nigh, and, at his suggestion, they assisted the wounded man into the sacristy. Damian's embarrassment had yet to fade; it manifested itself now in a reluctance to be alone with his spurious saint, and when Hugh moved back into the choir, he made excuse to follow.

There he found Hugh dipping an altar cloth in the holy-water font. He should have rebuked the boy. Instead, he whispered, "Which son?"

"Bran," Hugh said without hesitation, although he could not have explained how he knew, only that he did. Wringing out the cloth, he hastened back into the sacristy, Damian at his heels.

Bran was slumped upon a wooden bench, eyes closed. He didn't move, even when Hugh began to unwind his bloodied bandage. Much to the boy's relief, the wound he exposed did not appear life-threatening: a jagged sword slash across the ribs. "You've lost a lot of blood, my lord, but the cut should heal well enough as long as no proud flesh forms."

Bran opened his eyes at that. "You are young to be a leech," he said, and smiled.

Hugh blushed, mumbled that he had oft-times aided Brother Mark in the infirmary. Then, realizing that he was being teased, he relaxed somewhat, and ventured to ask how Bran had come to be wounded.

Bran shrugged, winced. "My ship dropped anchor in Bristol harbor three days ago. I had no trouble until I reached Tewkesbury, where I had the bad luck to be recognized by two of Gloucester's knights. I fought my way free, but . . ." He shrugged again, then glanced from Hugh to Damian, back to Hugh. "I was more fortunate at Evesham, for here I found friends," he said, and Hugh flushed anew, this time with pleasure.

Damian held up a hand for silence. "I thought I heard footsteps in the nave. My lord, you are in grave danger. By now Gloucester's men will have raised a hue and cry, and it would be easy enough to guess where you were headed. You dare not stay here, lest you be taken."

Bran nodded. "I know. But I had to come . . ."

Hugh nodded, too. He understood perfectly why Bran should have taken such a mad risk, and was ready to perform miracles in order to save Simon de Montfort's son. "Mayhap we can hide him in the stables," he implored Damian, but the monk was already shaking his head.

"They'd find him, lad. No, he must get farther away, but I doubt he can ride—"

"I can ride," Bran interrupted, with a grim resolve that carried such conviction that they no longer doubted. "If I can reach the border, I'll be safe enough in Wales."

"For certes, Wales!" Damian marveled he hadn't thought of it, for the powerful Welsh Prince, Llewelyn ap Gruffydd, had been Simon de Montfort's most steadfast ally, betrothed to Simon's daughter, Ellen. Llewelyn had disavowed the plight troth after Simon's defeat, for royal marriages were based upon pragmatic considerations of statecraft, not sentiment. But Llewelyn had maintained his friendship with the de Montforts, and Damian was sure he would willingly extend his protection to Simon's son. How could Bran manage so perilous a journey, though, weak as he was?

That had occurred to Hugh, too. "You'll need a guide. Let it be me!"

Bran sat up, studying the boy's eager face. "I accept your offer right gladly, lad, but only if you understand the risks."

Hugh's grin was radiant enough to light the way into Wales. "I do, I swear I do!" Whirling upon Damian when the monk gave a smothered sound of protest: "Brother Damian, do not object, I beg you! A fortnight, that is all I'll be gone!"

Damian knew that to let Hugh go was madness. But when he started to refuse, he found the words wouldn't come. Mayhap this was meant to be. "I shall pray for you both," he said. "May you go with God."

TWELFTH NIGHT at the court of Llewelyn ap Gruffydd promised to be a memorable one. The Prince of Wales had spared no expense, and the trestle tables in Dolwyddelan's great hall were heavily laden with highly spiced dishes of venison and swan and salmon; rush lights blazed from every wall sconce, and haunting harp music floated out onto the snow-blinding alpine air. The wind carried its echoes for miles, occasionally interspersed with the distant howling of Welsh wolves. Beyond the castle's walls a blizzard raged upon the peaks of Eryri, aptly named "Haunt of Eagles" by the Welsh and "Snowdon" by the English. But Dolwyddelan's great hall was a citadel of cheer, defying nature to do its worst, offering warmth and light and pleasure to all fortunate enough to be sheltered before its open hearths.

The Welsh held poets in high esteem, and as Llygad Gwr approached the dais, he was accorded an enthusiastic reception. He strummed his harp until the audience fell silent, waiting expectantly for his latest composition. They were not disappointed. His song was a lyric tribute to his Prince, and Llewelyn heard himself acclaimed as a "chief of men, who rageth like fire from the flashes of lightning," heard himself lauded as another Arthur, as the Lion of Gwynedd and the Dragon of Arfon. Llygad Gwr concluded with a dramatic flourish, with a final paean to the "lawful King of Wales," and the hall resounded with exuberant applause.

Llygad Gwr was beckoned up onto the dais. People were discussing what they'd just heard, and few paid heed when another bard took center stage, for Llygad Gwr was the star and this man not known to them. His first verse, therefore, was all but drowned out by the clatter of knives and spoons, the clinking of cups. Only gradually did the hall quiet as men began to listen, heads swiveling in astonishment, mouths ajar, for if the bard was unknown to them, his song was not, a tribute penned by Y Prydydd Bychan to Owain ap Gruffydd, Llewelyn's brother, Llewelyn's prisoner.

A ruler bold is Owain, resolute
Round him the ravens flock,
All praise him bold in conflict,
From ancient kings descended.

By now there were no sounds to compete with the singer, but rarely had a poet performed in such strange isolation; every eye in the hall was riveted, not upon the bard, but upon the man on the dais. If Llewelyn was as astounded as the audience, it didn't show upon his face. Whatever his initial reaction, he had his emotions well in hand, and his face was impassive as he listened to this seditious eulogy to his elder brother, imprisoned at Dolbadarn Castle for the past fifteen years.

Men expected Llewelyn to interrupt. He did not, and the bard's rash assurance began to falter. He rushed through the final verses, no longer meeting his Prince's cool gaze. Only then did Llewelyn turn away. Ignoring the puppet, he sought the puppeteer, knowing that but one man would have dared such an outrageous affront. Across the width of the hall, his eyes linked with those of his brother Davydd. For a long moment, they looked at each other, and then Davydd slowly, deliberately, raised his wine cup high.

"To the Dragon of Arfon," he said, poisoning Llewelyn's peace with a smile as dazzling as it was dangerous.

Men followed Davydd's mocking lead, drank to their Prince's health. Conversation resumed. It was almost as if the incident had never happened—almost. There were few in the hall who did not understand the significance of what they'd just seen, for there were few who were not familiar with the history of Llewelyn ap Gruffydd and his brothers. Owain had been the firstborn, but in Wales that counted for naught. Unlike the English, Welsh sons shared their patrimony—even a kingdom. In theory, at least; in practice, the ancient Welsh laws fostered fratricide more often than not. Such had been the case for the sons of Gruffydd, the grandsons of Llewelyn Fawr, greatest of the Welsh princes.

Llewelyn Fawr had seen his country too often convulsed by these winner-take-all bloodlettings, had decided there must be a better way, even if that meant emulating their English enemies. He had dreamed of a united Wales, bequeathing that dream to his favorite grandson and namesake. And in time it had come to pass. Llewelyn ap Gruffydd was the first Welsh ruler to claim suzerainty over the realms of Gwynedd, Powys, and Deheubarth, to accept the homage of the other Welsh lords, to be recognized as Prince of Wales by the English Crown.

His was a great accomplishment, achieved at great cost. Owain, underestimating the power of his brother's dream, had led an army into Llewelyn's half of Gwynedd, and paid for his folly with his freedom. Rhodri, the youngest brother, prudently kept to the shadows. But Davydd was not one to acknowledge defeat and not one to be over-looked.

Twice Davydd had rebelled against Llewelyn's dominance. The first time, he was sixteen, riding at Owain's side. Unlike Owain, he had been forgiven. The second time, he had not. After an abortive alliance with the English King's son, he had fled into England. His exile was to last four years. But under the terms of the Treaty of Montgomery in 1267, he had been permitted to return. The Lord Edward had insisted upon it, for he saw Davydd—the discontented, the aggrieved—as the Trojan Horse in the Welsh Prince's camp. Edward, for all his shrewdness, had not yet realized that Davydd did no man's bidding but his own.

Dancing had begun, and the hall was soon aswirl with color. Llewelyn did not join the carol; he remained on the dais, absently sipping from a brimming cup of hippocras, ignoring the curious stares of his subjects. After a time, he felt a hand touch his elbow. Einion ap Caradog had watched the byplay between the brothers with a sad sense of inevitability. Uncle to them both, their mother's youngest brother, he had often sought to act as peacemaker, usually to no avail. He understood divided loyalties, understood the danger in loving where there can be no trust, and he knew that Llewelyn did, too. There had always been bad blood between Llewelyn and Owain. But with Davydd, it was different. Theirs was a more complex relationship, one of tangled need and rivalry and wary affection, and Llewelyn bore the scars to prove it. Einion suspected that Davydd did, too, although with Davydd, one could never be sure of anything.

Einion had often thought that Llewelyn seemed alone even in a crowd. He smiled now, but there was a distance in his eyes. Survivor of a turbulent childhood, a war-ravaged youth, he was, at forty-two, a man who'd learned to deal with pain by denying it, a man who shared few secrets of the soul. Einion moved closer, and as soon as no others were within earshot, he said quietly, "I thought you and Davydd were getting along better these days."

"I suppose we are . . . when compared with Cain and Abel." Llewelyn smiled again, briefly, without humor. "After I offered to make

Davydd my heir, I thought we'd finally found a path through the marshes and onto secure footing. I told him I did not want to see him shut away from the sun—like Owain. But neither did I want to spend my days wondering how long he'd be loyal this time. And so I held out the promise of a crown. Only Davydd grows impatient. He has never been one for waiting, has he?"

Einion sighed. "You're not being fair, Llewelyn," he said, and the younger man gave him a quick, searching look.

"You think not?" he asked, and Einion slowly shook his head.

"Davydd is not utterly to blame. You restored to him his former lands, but you have kept a heavy hand on the reins. Knowing Davydd as we do, is it so surprising that he is balking?"

Llewelyn was silent, dark eyes opaque, unrevealing. Einion dared hope he'd planted a seed, but he was not sanguine about it taking root, for he knew that whenever the needs of the Prince came into conflict with those of the brother, the Prince prevailed. Llewelyn always put Wales first. And Davydd always put Davydd first. Was it so surprising, then, that they were once again on a collision course?

"My ears are burning. Might you have been talking about me?" Davydd had appeared without warning; he had a sorcerer's flair for dramatic entrances and exits, and he grinned now at Llewelyn's involuntary twitch. "Your nerves are on the raw tonight, Brother. Could it be that the entertainment was not to your liking?"

"On the contrary, Davydd. It never hurts to remind men of the high price of treason."

For a fleeting second, so quickly they might have imagined it, Davydd's smile seemed to flicker. But then he laughed. "Not very sporting of you, Llewelyn. After I went to so much trouble to vex you, you might at least give me the satisfaction of a scowl or two!"

Llewelyn's smile was one that Davydd alone seemed to evoke, half-amused, half-angry. But before he could respond, a voice was calling out, "My lord Prince!" The man was one of the gatehouse guards, bundled up against the cold, well-dusted with snow. "Two men seek entry to the castle, my lord."

"For God's pity, bid them enter. I'd not turn away a stray cur on a night like this."

"We knew that, my lord, admitted them at once. They're half-frozen, for certes, although one of them is soaked with sweat, too, burning with fever. We thought you should know that he claims to be a highborn lord."

Llewelyn and Davydd exchanged interested glances. "An English lord, I'd wager," Davydd drawled, "for only an Englishman would be crazed enough to venture out in weather like this."

The guard grinned, savoring the revelation to come. "You're half right, my lord Davydd, for if he speaks true, our guest is but half-English. You see the lad with him swears by all the saints that he is Simon de Montfort's son!"

BRAN did not at once remember where he was. His bed was piled high with fur coverlets, and as he started to sit up, he discovered that his ribs were newly bandaged. Obviously he was amongst friends. His eyes were adjusting to the dark now, and he found Hugh asleep on a nearby pallet. The sight of the boy brought back memories of their harrowing journey into the mountains of Eryri.

Hugh's name was forming on his lips, but he caught himself in time. No, let the lad sleep. He reached for a flagon by the bedside table and drank gratefully. They seemed to be in a corner of the great hall, screened off for privacy. He wondered what time it was, what day it was. He was drifting back toward sleep when the screen shifted; a shadow flitted through the opening.

The intruder was a child, slender and small-boned, with a tangled mane of reddish-brown hair that hid her face. She moved over the floor rushes as silently as a cat, paused by the bed, where she stared solemnly down at Bran. He watched her through half-closed eyes, drowsily amused by the intensity of her scrutiny. He judged her age to be about seven, and he wondered what had drawn her to his bedside. When she reached out, put something on his pillow, he smiled at her, asked her name.

She froze at the sudden sound of a human voice, as a wild creature might, not so much timid as wary. Bran had spoken without thinking in Norman-French, the language of the English upper classes, and he laughed now at his own foolishness; how could he expect this Welsh wraith to understand an alien tongue? But then she said, in flawless French, "I am Caitlin. Bran is a Welsh name. Are you Welsh?"

"No, but I had a Welsh nurse when I was a lad. Bran was her pet name for me, and it stuck." He genuinely liked children, and usually they sensed it; Caitlin moved closer, tossing her hair back to reveal a thin little face, well smudged with grime, eyes of a truly startling green. Not pretty, perhaps, but appealing in an ethereal, fey sort of way, a fairy child to be conjured up by fever, or an overwrought imagination. Bran laughed again; should he ask if she were real? "What did you bring me, Caitlin?"

"Holly. You must keep it close whilst you are ailing, for it will ward off evil spirits," she said gravely, and he promised no less gravely that he would. The holly leaves pricked his fingers, fell into the floor rushes. Soon he slept again.

When he awakened, candles had chased away some of the shadows, and Hugh was bending over the bed. "How do you feel, my lord? Well enough to sup with Prince Llewelyn?"

Bran nodded, and with Hugh's help, managed to dress. His lingering weakness was a source of unease; for most of his thirty years, his body had done whatever he'd demanded of it. "I owe you a debt, Hugh," he said, but the boy shrugged off his thanks with a smile. Hugh seemed preoccupied, and after assisting Bran in pulling on his boots, he said abruptly:

"My lord, may we talk? Now that your fever has broken, I . . . I thought I ought to be starting back to the abbey. But what of the horse you bought for me? I need a mount for my return journey, but I could sell it in Evesham, send the money to you if that meets with your approval . . ." Hugh struggled to sound matter-of-fact, not wanting to reveal how reluctant he was to see their adventure end. He had fantasized a few times that Bran might permit him to keep the horse, but logic told him that was too extravagant a reward. Hugh had long ago learned to ride his expectations with a tight rein; he was less likely to be disappointed that way.

Bran sat back on the bed, gesturing for Hugh to do the same. During their days on the road, Hugh had talked freely about himself and the father who'd died on Evesham field. It had been easy enough for Bran to fill in the blanks, and as he looked now at the boy, he felt an impulse stirring. Hugh had done him a great service, and he was a likable lad; why not? "Hugh, let us speak plainly. Do you truly want to go back to the abbey? From what you have told me, there is not much for you there."

Hugh frowned. "What choice have I?"

"You could stay with me. I've need of another squire, and—" Bran paused, for Hugh was staring at him in wonderment. He had never seen such joy in another's eyes, and he said hastily, "Wait, lad, think it over ere you decide. It would mean exile, Hugh, mean leaving England—"

"My lord, I would follow you to the outer reaches of Hell!"

Bran smiled, because it was expected of him. But in truth, he was neither amused nor flattered by the boy's hero-worship. He did not deserve it. "No, not Hell," he said. "Italy."

BRAN had just proposed a graceful tribute to his host. As he set his wine cup down, it was immediately refilled by a solicitous servant.

He was not accustomed to mead, the honeyed malt drink so favored by the Welsh, but he gamely took a deep swallow. "I had a right strange dream this afternoon. I was being tended by a most unlikely nurse, an Irish sprite who spoke French as if she were Paris born and bred, an elfin little lass—" He got no further; Llewelyn had begun to laugh.

"That can only be our Caitlin. My niece, my brother Davydd's daughter."

"Yes, she did say she was called Caitlin. The lass's mother was Irish, then?"

"No, she was English. Caitlin was born during Davydd's years in exile. Since he was in no position to care for her, and her mother had died giving birth, he sent her back to Wales, to my court."

Bran drank again to conceal a grin, marveling at the sheer audacity of Davydd's act, expecting the brother he'd betrayed to rear his bastard child. "Why, then, 'Caitlin'? The name is Irish for certes, and if she's not . . . ?"

"Davydd fancied the name, and my brother," Llewelyn said wryly, "has ever been one to follow his fancies."

"Now why is it that you make 'following my fancies' sound only slightly less depraved than the Seven Deadly Sins?" Davydd queried good-naturedly, materializing as if from blue smoke. Bran started visibly, but Llewelyn was unperturbed; this time he'd noticed Davydd's circuitous approach.

"Eavesdroppers rarely hear good of themselves," he pointed out, gesturing for his brother to join them upon the dais. "Tell us," he said, glancing back toward Bran, "of the news from France."

Bran did, and they discussed the August death of the French King at Tunis, and its likely impact upon the crusade. The talk then turned to England. Their political affinities were quite compatible, for they shared the same enemies. Bran and Llewelyn would both have bartered their very souls for a chance to wreak havoc upon the Earl of Gloucester, and they passed an interesting half hour dissecting Llewelyn's recent raid upon the Earl's Welsh castle at Caerphilly.

"Gloucester has been awaiting his chance to disavow the Treaty of Montgomery. Now that Edward's off chasing Saracens, he and that Marcher whoreson, de Mortimer, are doing their utmost to encroach upon Welsh lands again. After all, who is going to rein them in—Henry?"

Llewelyn's sarcasm was bitter; all knew of the English King's deteriorating mental faculties. Bran nodded in grim agreement. He and his cousin Edward had once been friends, and, even now, memory blurred the harsher edges of their enmity. He could not truly blame

Edward for his father's death, not when he blamed himself more. But—unlike Edward—his uncle the King had been vengeful in victory, had treated his sister, Bran's mother, with a singular lack of Christian charity, and that, Bran could not forgive.

Davydd signaled for another round of drinks. "We heard that your brother Guy made a brilliant marriage last summer with an Italian heiress. Gossip . . . or gospel?"

"Guy wed Margherita, daughter of Ildebrandino d'Aldobrandini, Count of Sovana, in Viterbo on August tenth," Bran said and smiled. "I daresay you know that Guy is Vicar-General of all of Tuscany. But you may not know that in September, he was also named as Vicar of Florence. A comely wife, a father-in-law who holds Tuscany in the palm of his hand, rich lands of his own in the kingdom of Naples, and a King's favor—all in all, I'd say it was a good year for Guy."

It was nothing obvious; Bran's smile was steady, his gaze even. But Davydd had a sophisticated, exhaustive knowledge of brotherly jealousy in all its guises. Recognizing a kindred spirit when he saw one, he gave Bran a look of amused understanding, faintly flavored with sympathy. It was never easy, trailing after a brother whilst he blazed across the heavens like a flaming comet; who should know that better than he? A pity he and Bran could not commiserate with each other over their shared affliction, but he'd wager Bran would deny with his dying breath that he begrudged Guy's bedazzling success. Christendom was full to overflowing with those stricken by envy, but he alone seemed willing to admit it, that he was so jealous of his brother he was like to sicken on it. He laughed softly to himself, and at their questioning glances, said, " 'Tis nothing, a private jest."

Llewelyn was asking about Bran's lady mother, offering his condolences for the loss of his younger brother Richard, who'd died unexpectedly that past spring. Bran's face shadowed; draining the last of his mead, he beckoned for more. "The doctors said it was a rupture. He was just twenty-one . . ."

Davydd did not care for the morbid turn the conversation had taken; he saw no reason to mourn a man he'd never met, and after a moment of tactful silence, he posed some innocuous questions about Amaury de Montfort, who might not interest him overmuch, but at least was still alive. Amaury, he now learned, was thriving, studying medicine and religion at the University of Padua. But he soon grew bored with Brother Amaury, too, and giving Llewelyn a sideways smile of sudden mischief, he asked, "And how is your fair sister, the Lady Ellen? By chance, might there be a husband on the horizon?"

Davydd was not motivated by malice, just an irresistible urge to bedevil Llewelyn a bit, for his brother still felt a sense of responsibility for Ellen de Montfort. She'd been not yet thirteen when her world fell apart, and although the Prince knew he'd had no choice but to disavow the plight troth, the man could not help feeling that he'd failed an innocent in her time of need. Davydd knew this well, for he knew his brother was at heart a secret romantic, however pragmatic the Prince might appear. What he had not anticipated was the response of Ellen's brother.

Bran was looking at Llewelyn as if the question had been his. "No," he said slowly, never taking his eyes from the Welsh Prince's face. "She is not yet wed. She's of an age—eighteen last October—and beautiful. I daresay there'd be men willing to take her for herself alone, so fair is she to look upon. She'll not lack for a marriage portion, though, even if I have to beggar myself on her behalf. She'll want for nothing; we'll see to that. But she was cheated of her rightful destiny, for she was to have been a Prince's consort. You should have married her, Llewelyn. You broke her heart and for what? Christ, man, you could not have done better for a bride, in this world or the next!"

Llewelyn had stiffened with Bran's first words, listening with disbelief that soon flared into fury. But as he studied Bran, he saw what had escaped him until now, that his English guest was drunk. Not a loud or belligerent drunk, just an honest one. And his anger ebbed away in a surge of pity for Simon de Montfort's son.

Bran downed two more cups of mead before his speech began to slur, his eyes to glaze. Hugh had been hovering close at hand, and as Bran mumbled his excuses, the boy waved away Llewelyn's servants, insisting that he be the one to help his lord to bed. Llewelyn and Davydd watched in silence as Bran stumbled from the hall.

"Five years is a long time to grieve," Llewelyn said at last, and Davydd shook his head.

"Grief heals," he said. "Guilt does not." He saw Llewelyn's brows shoot upward and the corner of his mouth curved. "Jesú, what an easy face yours is to read, Brother! You wonder what I should know of guilt, do you not? I'll grant you it is not an emotion I've ever taken to heart. But a man need not be born in a country in order to speak the language."

"No," Llewelyn agreed, "mayhap not." After another silence, he said softly, "We ought not to be so surprised. For who would cast a longer shadow than Simon de Montfort?"

2

MONTARGIS, FRANCE

February 1271

Montargis was ensconced within a bend of the River Loing. It was also crisscrossed with canals, Bran told Hugh, putting him in mind of Venice. And even as Hugh nodded, it came to him that he would soon be seeing Venice for himself, a thought so preposterous that he burst out laughing.

It had all happened too fast. In four fleeting weeks, his world had expanded beyond all borders of belief. He, who'd never even set foot in a rowboat, suddenly found himself in a swift little esneque under sail for Rouen. He hadn't liked the sea voyage; his stomach was soon heaving in harmony with the pitching waves. But then their ship reached the mouth of the Seine. Three days later, they docked at the Grand Pont, and before Hugh's bedazzled eyes lay the city of Paris.

Nothing had prepared him for this. The largest town he'd ever seen was Shrewsbury; country-born and bred, he'd been very impressed by its size, for it had more than two thousand people. But now there was Paris—with perhaps a hundred thousand inhabitants, with paved streets and formidable stone walls, with so many churches that the city seemed a forest of steeples, with a river island that held both a palace and a cathedral, with sights to take away Hugh's breath and noise enough to rouse Heaven itself—Paris, pride of France, glory of Christendom.

In just one day, Hugh saw more beggars, dogs, prostitutes, and friars than he could count. He saw his first water clock, watched in morbid fascination as a man accused of blasphemy was held down and burned upon the tongue, nearly went deaf from the constant chiming of so many church bells, ate the best sausage of his life at the market by St Germain l'Auxerois, and met a Queen.

The Queen was Marguerite, widow of the saintly Louis, who'd died on crusade five months past. Marguerite had valid reasons to dislike the de Montforts; her sister Eleanor was wife to King Henry. But affection and reason were not always compatible, and Marguerite had become Nell de Montfort's staunchest friend, doing all she could to soften the rigors of Nell's exile. Bran bore one of her letters in his saddlebags as they rode toward Montargis, for if he was an outlaw in England, in France he was still the scion of a noble House and welcome at the French court.

When he had impulsively offered to share Bran's flight, Hugh had expected danger and adventure, both of which he found in full measure. But he had not expected to have his life transformed as if by magic; he had not expected Paris. He could feel his joy rising again, and he twisted around in the saddle to look upon his young lord, laughter about to spill out.

What he saw froze the smile upon his face. It was not yet noon and Bran was already reaching for the wineskin dangling from his saddle pommel. Hugh hastily glanced away, and they rode on in silence.

Hugh had often heard lurid tales of the young de Montforts' hell-raising. The three elder sons, Harry, Bran, and Guy, had been notorious for their whoring and carousing and ale-house brawling, in decided and dramatic contrast to their austere father, for Simon, a crusader who'd twice taken the cross and adhered to a rigid code of honor, a moralist who'd worn a hair shirt into that last doomed battle of his life, had been utterly devoted to his wife.

Like most youngsters, Hugh was intrigued by scandal, by these colorful accounts of Bran's turbulent past. It puzzled him, therefore, that the Bran of legend was so unlike the Bran he now knew. For a man reputed to have such a blazing temper, Bran seemed surprisingly equable. Not once in these four weeks had Hugh seen him angry; even the inevitable vexations of the road were shrugged off with admirable aplomb. At first, Hugh had much marveled at Bran's unfailing forbearance. Only slowly did he begin to suspect the truth, that Bran's patience was actually indifference.

Bran was not taciturn, and he and Hugh had often whiled away the boredom of the road in banter, filling their hours with easy conversation. Hugh had confided his entire life's story long before they'd reached Wales. And Bran, in turn, had shared with the boy memories of his own youth, of the two brothers they would soon join in Italy, of the mother and sister awaiting him at Montargis. But not once did he speak of Evesham, or of the father and brother who had died for his mistake. And Hugh came gradually to realize how deceptive was Bran de Montfort's affability, how effective a shield. Bran remained a man in shadow; he might lower the drawbridge into his outer bailey, but there would be no admittance into the castle keep. Even after a month in Bran's constant company, all Hugh could say with certainty was that Simon's son was generous, utterly fearless, and that he drank too much.

When Hugh first comprehended the extent of Bran's drinking, he had been dismayed and alarmed. All he knew of drunkards came from overheard shreds of gossip: an ale-house stabbing, garbled accounts of cupshotten villagers taking out their tempers upon wives and children. He had observed Bran's drinking, therefore, with some trepidation. But his qualms were soon assuaged, for Bran did not act like the quarrelsome drinkers who'd so enlivened Evesham folklore. He did not become bellicose, did not bluster or swagger or seek out fights. Drunk or sober, he treated Hugh with the same casual kindness. But drink he did, quietly, steadily, beginning his day with ale, ending it with hippocras, taking frequent swigs from his wine flask with the distant, distracted air of a man quaffing a doctor's brew. Hugh could only watch, bewildered; if drink brought Bran so little pleasure, why did he seek it so diligently?

A small castle overlooked Montargis, but it was not there that Nell de Montfort and her daughter had found a haven. The woman born to palaces now lived in a rented house upon the grounds of a Dominican convent.

Hugh was eagerly anticipating their arrival; his curiosity about the Countess of Leicester was intense. Like her husband, she was a figure of controversy, both loved and hated, for she had never been one tamely to await her fate, as women were expected to do. This youngest daughter of King John and Isabelle d'Angoulême had been a royal rebel. It was said she got her beauty from her mother, her willfulness and her temper from John. She had been wed as a child to the Earl of Pembroke, widowed at fifteen, and in the first throes of grief, she had sworn a holy oath of chastity, thus condemning herself to a lifelong widowhood. But then she'd met the young Frenchman, Simon de Montfort. Simon was not the first man to look upon Nell with forbidden desire. He was the first, however, who dared to defy King and Church for her.

Their marriage had scandalized Christendom, but they never looked back, forging a passionate partnership that was to survive court intrigues and wars and her brother's obsessive jealousy of Simon. Nell's loyalty to her husband never wavered, even when it meant forsaking the brothers she loved. She bore Simon seven children, saw him raised up to undreamed-of heights of power, for fifteen months as England's uncrowned King. And when he fell at Evesham, she lost all—lands, titles, even England—but not her faith in him. She sailed into exile as proudly as any queen, and if she had regrets, none but she knew of them.

To Simon's enemies, she was a dangerous, maddeningly presumptuous woman, who deserved all the grief that had befallen her. To those who had believed in Simon, she was a fitting mate for one who'd soared so high, and they embellished her story until it took on epic proportions, until no one—perhaps not even Nell—could distinguish the woman from the myth.

The sun was high overhead as they rode into the convent garth. The nunnery was small and secluded, an incongruous setting for a woman who'd lived most of her life on center stage. Their arrival stirred up immediate excitement, and by the time they reached the stables, Bran's squire was awaiting them. Hugh knew all about him; the sixteen-year-old son of a Norman knight, Noel de Pacy had been in Bran's service for two years, had been sworn to secrecy about his lord's hazardous mission in England. As their eyes met, Hugh smiled, but the other boy did not. Without saying a word, he was conveying an unmistakable message, one of jealousy and suspicion, and Hugh realized that his entrance into Bran's household would not be as smooth as he'd hoped.

Noel acknowledged the introductions with a formality that just barely passed for politeness, and at once began to assail his lord with questions. Bran fended him off good-naturedly, quickening his step, for his mother stood framed in the doorway of the hall.

She was smaller than Hugh expected. He'd instinctively cast Simon's lady as an Amazon, larger than life, and he was vaguely disappointed to find only a handsome woman in her mid-fifties, so simply dressed she might have been a nun. The stark black of widowhood suited her, though; she had the coloring for it, fair skin and blonde hair, scattered with silver. If she no longer had the light step and the svelte waist of her youth, the additional weight was still becoming, rounding out her face and sparing her that brittle tautness, that look of gaunt, attenuated elegance too common to aging beauties, those unable to make peace with time. As she and her son embraced warmly, Hugh decided he liked the way Nell de Montfort now looked, although it was difficult to imagine this matronly, sedate widow wed to an eagle or holding Dover Castle against an enemy army. But as the embrace ended, so, too, did the illusion. She stepped back, and suddenly those serene blue eyes were searing, filled with fury.

"Have you gone stark mad? Jesus God, Bran, why did you do it?"

Before Bran could respond, a shame-faced Noel began to babble a garbled apology; they could catch only "had to tell" and "my lady made me . . ."

Men were wilting before Nell's wrath, backing off. Hugh was staring, open-mouthed, awed by how swiftly the matriarch had become a valkyrie. Bran alone appeared unfazed by his mother's rage. Grinning, he cuffed Noel playfully on the back. "You need not fret, lad. It would take a foolhardy soul indeed to face down my lady mother in a temper!"

"I am glad you find this so amusing, Bran," Nell said scathingly. "Does it amuse you, too, that I lay awake each night till dawn, seeking to convince myself you were still alive?"

Bran's smile faded. "I know the risks I took," he admitted quietly. "But I had to do it, Mama."

After a long pause, Nell nodded. "Yes, I suppose you did," she conceded, no less quietly, and to their sympathetic spectators, the moment was all the more poignant for what was left unsaid. Nell hugged her son, clung tightly. "I should warn you," she said, "that if you ever scare me like this again, your homecoming will be hot enough to be held in Hell Everlasting." And although she laughed, none doubted that she meant every word, least of all, Bran.

As they entered the hall, the rest of the de Montfort servants and retainers surged forward, engulfing Bran in a noisy, chaotic welcome. One young woman in particular seemed so happy to see Bran that at first Hugh thought she must be his sister, Ellen. But a second glance quickly disabused him of that notion, for Ellen de Montfort was said to be very fair, and this girl was as dark as any gypsy. By the exacting standards of their society, she was no beauty, for not only was her coloring unfashionable, she was short and voluptuous, and theirs was a world in which the ideal woman was a tall, slender blonde. But Hugh could not take his eyes from her, perhaps because her allure was so very exotic, so alien. She looked verily like a wanton, like a Saracen concubine, he decided, and then blushed bright-red when Bran introduced her as Dame Juliana, his sister's lady-in-waiting.

Suddenly face to face with the object of his sinful lust, Hugh found himself hopelessly tongue-tied. At times it seemed to him that his male member had a life—and a will—of its own; he'd even given it a name, Barnabas, in rueful recognition of its newly independent ways. But never before had it focused upon a woman of his own class, a lady. Unable to meet Dame Juliana's eyes lest she somehow read his mind, he averted his gaze from her face, only to find himself staring at her very ample bosom, and blushed anew, this time as high as his hairline.

"I suppose I ought to have warned you, Juliana, that the lad is a mute!"

"Bran, hush!" Jabbing Bran with her elbow, Juliana held out her hand, and it took no more than that, a touch and a smile, to vanquish Hugh's discomfort. He smiled too, shyly, as the bedchamber door burst open.

"Bran!" At sound of his name, Bran swung about, then staggered backward under the onslaught. The girl in his arms was the prettiest creature Hugh had ever seen, with burnished masses of reddish-gold hair, emerald eyes, and flawless, fair skin. She was tall for a woman, as lissome and sleek as a pampered, purebred cat, and when Bran called her "kitten," Hugh thought it an inspired endearment. If Juliana aroused male lust, this girl stirred gallantry in even the most jaded of men, and as she spun in a circle, heedless of her dishevelment, her flying hair, Hugh fell utterly and helplessly under the spell of Simon de Montfort's daughter. Watching as Ellen laughed, sought to smother Bran with sisterly kisses, Hugh could think only that Llewelyn ap Gruffydd must be one of God's greatest fools.

THEY passed that first night at Nell de Montfort's small house, Hugh bedding down in the great hall with the other servants while Bran stayed up till dawn, talking with his mother and sister. He'd slept late the next day, then startled Hugh by insisting that they take up lodgings in the village. The move made no sense to Hugh, and he was still puzzling over it several hours later, while helping Noel to unpack Bran's belongings in an upper chamber of Montargis's only inn.

"If we'd stayed at the nunnery, it would have been easier for our lord to visit with his lady mother and sister, so why—"

"Jesú, what an innocent you are!" Noel slammed a coffer lid down, giving Hugh a look of withering scorn. His initial wariness had congealed into open hostility, all chance of rapport gone from the moment he overheard Bran telling the women that he owed Hugh his life. "What would you have Lord Bran do—couple with a wench under his lady mother's own roof? That might be the way it is done by you English, but the French have more style!"

Hugh swallowed the insult as best he could. "You mean he has a whore in the village." He sought to sound knowing; nothing less than torture could have gotten him to admit to the supercilious Noel that he was still a virgin.

"A whore? Well, the priests would call her that, for certes, though she lays with no man but Lord Bran. I daresay he could tumble her in a church if he wished, so hot is she for him!"

"You are describing a mistress, not a whore," Hugh objected. "She lives in Montargis, then?"

Noel's smile held a glint of mockery. "No . . . the convent."

Hugh stared, and then flushed. He was not easily provoked, and had been willing to overlook Noel's snide barbs, his lordly asides, for he had no false pride, knew that he was a green country lad with much to learn in the ways of the world. But enough was enough. "I am not so simple as that," he snapped. "Did you truly think I'd believe so outrageous a lie? Lord Bran would never seduce a nun, for that would be a mortal sin and he'd burn in Hell!"

Now it was Noel's turn to stare. But after a moment, he roared with laughter. "You dolt, I was not talking of a nun! I was talking of the Lady Juliana!"

Hugh gasped, then took a threatening step forward, "Liar! Take that back!"

Noel jumped to his feet, suddenly aware that the younger boy was four inches taller and twenty pounds heavier. "Make me," he said, and grabbed for the nearest weapon, a brass candelabra. But Hugh was surprisingly fast for his size. He got to the candelabra first, jerked it out of Noel's reach, and flung it across the room, where it crashed into the opening door, missing Bran by a hairsbreadth.

For an endless moment, Bran looked down at the candelabra, then back at the horrified boys. "Playing catch with a candelabra? My brothers and I always used a pig's bladder football," he said lightly, and Noel's relief was such that he almost made a serious blunder.

"It was Hugh's—" He choked the accusation back just in time, as Bran's head came up sharply. Noel knew that Bran did not give a fig for what his squires did between themselves, was not likely even to notice unless the blood began to flow in earnest. But he had only contempt for those who tried to divert blame onto others. "Nothing, my lord, nothing," Noel said hastily, chalking up one more debt to Hugh's account.

Bran's smile was sardonic. "Well, if you lads are done with this game of yours, you'd best be off, Noel. I told Juliana you'd be there by Vespers."

"I'll have your lady here in a trice, my lord," Noel promised, shooting Hugh a look of triumphant malice as he headed for the door.

Bran moved to the table, poured himself ale. "There are some sugared quinces here, Hugh. Help yourself if you fancy any," he said, and the boy mumbled his thanks. Sugared quince was a rare treat, but he had no appetite for it now. He was genuinely shocked that Bran should be bedding a woman of good birth; it was not seemly. As he busied himself in tidying up the chamber, he tried not to look at the bed, tried not to imagine Juliana and Bran sprawled naked upon it. Thinking now of Juliana, of her sultry smile and midnight-black eyes, he realized that some of his indignation had been fueled by his own guilty lust. And it occurred to him, too, with a jolt of dismay, that he was going to have to offer the loathsome Noel an apology for having called him a liar. Honor demanded as much.

JULIANA was a light sleeper. Although Bran's moan was soft, muffled by the pillow, it was enough to awaken her. Sitting up, she pulled the bed hangings back, groped for the bedside candle, and held it over her lover's face. It was as she suspected; Bran's breathing was rapid, uneven, his mouth contorted, dark hair drenched in sweat. She placed the candle in a niche of the headboard, then touched him gently on the cheek. "Bran?"

He jerked upright, eyes wide and staring, chest heaving. "You're all right, beloved," Juliana said soothingly, "you're awake now." After a moment, he reached for a corner of the sheet, wiped the perspiration from his face, then swung his legs over the side of the bed. She watched as he crossed the chamber, moving barefoot through the rushes so as not to awaken his squires, snoring on pallets by the hearth. When he returned to the bed with a wine flagon, she was touched to see that he'd remembered to bring a cup for her. No matter how much he was hurting, she thought sadly, his manners never failed him.

After Bran propped pillows behind his back, Juliana rolled over into his arms. She knew better than to ask questions, for in the three years that they'd been sharing a bed, only once had he been able to share with her the dream, too. But she had no need to hear it again. She could still recall each and every word he'd uttered, haunted by that one harrowing glimpse into the desolation, the guilt-ravaged depths of Bran's soul.

She knew that bad dreams came to all men, dreams of demon spirits, a dread of the unknown. But not for Bran such phantom fears and shadows. For him, reality was the nightmare. It was not enough, she thought bitterly, that he must live with the knowledge that he'd failed his father and brother when they'd needed him the most. No, the fates had decreed that he must also reach Evesham in time to see his father's head on a pike.

Her anger was unfocused, futile, for whom could she blame? She loved this man so very much, and yet that love was tearing her apart, for she could not help him. She could do naught but break her heart trying.

She knew Bran would not be able to sleep again; he never could after one of the Evesham dreams. She sought now to banish drowsiness, to keep him from dwelling upon his own dark thoughts. "Tell me more about Ellen's Welsh Prince," she teased. "What does he look like? Is he handsome? Would I be smitten at sight of him?"

That coaxed a shadowy smile. "Well, I cannot say that he set my heart aflutter, but I suppose women find him pleasing enough to the eye. He is tall for a Welshman, and dark, of course. Ah, and he is clean-shaven, save for a mustache, after the Welsh fashion."

She leaned over, touched her lips to his cheek, for he, too, was clean-shaven. Most men wore beards, but not Bran, for Simon had not.

"Why do you think Llewelyn has never married? Passing strange, is it not?"

Bran shrugged. "In earlier years, I suspect he was too busy fighting his brothers for control of Gwynedd, then defending what he'd won against the English Crown. I suppose he would eventually have taken a wife had he not been compelled to make peace with Davydd. Scrape away the gilt from Davydd's promises and you'll find naught but dross. Llewelyn knew that as well as any man, knew he had to imprison Davydd for life or else make it worth his while to stay loyal. And so he offered to make Davydd his heir, which is either an act of sheer inspiration or one of utter desperation."

"Which do you think it is?"

He shrugged again. "You'd best ask Ellen that. When it comes to Wales, she is the family sage, not I." He drained his cup, set it down in the floor rushes. "You called Llewelyn 'Ellen's Welsh Prince.' Was that a jest, Juliana? Or does Ellen still harbor false hopes? She always did dote on those foolish romances, those minstrels' tales of love unrequited and eternal. Does she still see Llewelyn as one of those gallant heroes, a Tristan or Lancelot?"

Juliana did not respond at once, pondering his query. She felt no conflict of loyalty between her lover and her friend, for she knew how much Bran loved Ellen. She sometimes wished he loved his sister a little less, for she knew, too, that each time he looked at Ellen and his mother, he could not help thinking of all they'd lost, lost because of him. And neither Nell nor Ellen nor Juliana had been able to convince him otherwise. Indeed, it seemed to Juliana that the less they blamed him, the more he then blamed himself. Amaury de Montfort had once told her of a powder made from the opium poppy, a strange powder that men craved more than food or money or women. Juliana occasionally found herself wondering if grieving, too, could possess a man's soul, become a habit impossible to break.

"Juliana?"

"No, I think not, beloved. Oh, I grant you that Ellen did spin fantasies once, pretend Llewelyn would one day send for her, honor the plight troth. She had to have hope, something in which to believe. But you're talking now of a woman grown, not a lass of thirteen. I think she will always take an interest in Llewelyn and in Wales, but no more than that. You need not fear for her, Bran. Our Ellen was never a fool, and she is no longer a starry-eyed child."

Bran's relief was obvious. "Last year, when she balked at Guy's offer to find a husband for her, I feared she might be deluding herself about Llewelyn."

Juliana felt no compunctions at breaking a confidence, for she was sure Ellen would want Bran to know; Ellen would do almost anything to give her brother peace of mind. "Her reluctance had naught to do with Llewelyn. It was partly because she did not want to leave your mother, not so soon after Richard's death. And partly because she was loath to live in Italy."

Bran showed neither surprise nor indignation, although women were rarely given a say as to whom they were to marry. He had, in the anguished aftermath of Evesham, promised Ellen upon the surety of his soul that he would never allow her to be wed against her will. "Well, now that Guy's prospects are bright enough to blind, we ought to be able to do better than an Italian alliance. I'll talk to Guy."

"Bran . . . how long can you stay this time?"

He gave her a sideways look, alerting her that his answer would not be to her liking. "Two more days," he said reluctantly, and then, "Ah, sweetheart, do not look like that! I cannot help it, in truth. I promised Guy I'd be back by the first week in March. Philippe and Charles have abandoned the Crusade, are on their way home. Guy thinks we ought to be on hand when they reach Tuscany."

Juliana bit back her disappointment; she was wise enough to realize that Bran would shy away as soon as she began to make demands. She smiled, said with forced cheer, " 'Philippe and Charles.' I presume you mean the King of France and his uncle, the King of Sicily?"

"Who else?" He sounded faintly bemused, and she hid a smile. To Bran, it was perfectly natural to refer to those powerful monarchs by their Christian names, and he could never understand why the familiarity sounded so strange to her ears. But then, he was the grandson and nephew of kings, not likely to be over-awed by crowns or the men who wore them. She sighed at that. How different were their worlds and how distant, for all that she lay within the circle of his arms, legs entwined, so close she could feel his breath upon her breast.

Having emptied his own cup, Bran now reached over to share hers. "I'll be back soon," he murmured, "mayhap even by Whitsuntide," sealing his promise with a lingering, wine-flavored kiss.

She nodded, knowing he would if at all possible. She doubted that he truly felt at home anywhere after Evesham, but for certes, not in Italy, for there he was starved for sun, stunted and chilled in his brother's spreading shadow. Raising up, she kissed the pulse in his throat. So often had she heard Ellen's childhood stories that she sometimes felt as if she'd lived them herself. It had always been Harry and Bran, Bran and Harry, two halves to the same coin. They might have been twins, so closely attuned were they to each other's moods; it was a family joke that if Harry were cut, Bran would bleed. It was not surprising that Guy had come to resent a comradeship so intense, so exclusive. With the plaintive clarity of hindsight, Ellen could see that now, see how Guy had sought in vain to impress, to belong, as young brothers have done since time immemorial.

And then, Evesham. Harry had died that day, and Guy almost did. He lay for weeks near death, a prisoner with nothing to do but to relive those last bloody moments, to watch his father fall again and again, and to wonder why Bran's army had not arrived. He cheated death, to the surprise of all, and then escaped, which should not have been a surprise, not to anyone who knew him. Fleeing to France, he set about finding his brother, with murder in his heart. But when he did, he'd discovered that he had to forgive Bran, if only because Bran could not forgive himself.

And now, Italy. A brilliant battle commander, Guy had won a King's favor, won a future full of promise. Whilst Bran, Juliana acknowledged, had naught but a past, one full of pain. And it seemed to her that, even with the best will in the world, Bran and Guy were yoked together too tightly, shackled by too many memories, too many regrets.

Bran leaned over, deposited her wine cup in the floor rushes. As he did, Juliana trailed her fingers along his chest, hovering over the new scar that zigzagged across his ribs. So much she'd wanted to do for him, to keep him safe from harm, to heal his wounds, to ease his pain, to stop his drinking. And she'd been able to do none of it. The only comfort she could offer was carnal, the only kind he seemed to want.

"Make love to me, Bran," she whispered. "Make love to me now."

3

SIENA, TUSCANY

March 1271

Hᴜɢʜ did not see how they could get to Italy in time to rendezvous with Bran's brother. While couriers had been known to travel from London to Rome in just twenty-five days, such couriers often covered close to fifty miles a day, and most travelers managed less than thirty. Hugh soon discovered, though, that Bran's will could be as steely as that of his formidable father. He rode fast and he rode hard, and the knights of his household were pressed to keep pace. By the time they reached the Mount Cenis Pass, they were averaging forty miles a day.

A winter passage across the Alps was every traveler's nightmare. Bran and his companions were more fortunate than many, for they were spared the most lethal perils of alpine crossings: blizzards and avalanches. Even so, their journey was a daunting one. A local guide was killed when he ventured ahead to mark their trail with wooden stakes. It was so bitter cold that the men's beards congealed with ice and Bran's wineskin froze solid. At one point, the slope was so glazed that they were forced to bind their horses' legs and lower them down on ropes. When they finally made their way to safety, Hugh was vowing that he'd live out the remainder of his days in Italy ere he'd face Mount Cenis again.

Bran had laughed, mercifully forbearing to remind the boy that ahead of them still lay the mountains of the Italian Apennines. They crossed at La Cisa, took the ancient Via Francigena that led toward Rome, and rode into the city of Florence on March 2nd, just twenty-six days since departing Montargis. There they were greeted by Guy de Montfort and the powerful Tuscan lord who was his wife's father, Ildebrandino d'Aldobrandini, Count of Sovana and Pitigliano, known to all as "il Rosso" for the auburn color of his hair. Three days later they took the road south, reaching the city walls of Siena by midday on Saturday, the 7th of March. It was a day to banish their bone-chilling memories of those alpine glaciers, to evoke forgotten echoes of spring, a sundrenched noon under a vivid sapphire sky—Hugh's fifteenth birthday.

ALTHOUGH Ildebrandino had a house in Siena, they accepted the hospitality of the Tolomei, an influential local family in uneasy alliance with the Count. Once they were settled in the Tolomei palazzo, their host suggested that they might enjoy watching a game of elmora, and in consequence, Hugh soon found himself riding through the steep, twisting streets that led to the Campo, listening to the applause of townspeople as they recognized il Rosso and his dashing son-in-law, the Vicar of Tuscany.

Hugh suspected that the welcome was politic, for he knew by now that these Tuscan city-states were profoundly suspicious of powerful, predatory neighbors like the Count. And Guy de Montfort was the Vicar, or Podestà, of Siena's great rival, Florence. But even if they were motivated more by expediency than heartfelt enthusiasm, the cheers still echoed buoyantly on the mild, sunlit air, and Guy acknowledged the salutations with grace, with the polished poise of a man accustomed to public accolades. Just as his father had once been acclaimed in the streets of London, so was Guy acclaimed in the streets of Siena, as Hugh watched and marveled that this de Montfort son should have found his destiny in a land so far from England.

The fan-shaped Piazza del Campo was the converging point for the city's three hills, the heart of Siena. Here markets were held, livestock penned up, fresh fish kept in huge wooden vats. Here fairs were celebrated. Here were played the rough-and-tumble games of elmora, in which young men formed teams and did mock battle with quarter staves, and pugna, in which weapons were barred, and palone, a boisterous form of football. Here stood the baratteria, a stockade roofed in canvas that served as the city's gambling hall. And here were clustered the citizens of Siena, eager to take what pleasures they could in a bleak Lenten season, unwilling to squander such a spring-like Saturday on mundane matters of work.

Hugh was enthralled by it all—the noise and confusion and merriment, the circling doves and pealing church bells, the sun slanting off the red roofs and rich russet-brown bricks of the houses fronting upon the square, even the clouds of dust stirred up by the brawling elmora players. Siena seduced with practiced ease, and as he elbowed his way through the crowd, following Bran toward the baratteria, he decided that Italy was verily like Cockayne, that legendary land in which night was day and hot was cold, so completely had his own expectations been turned upside-down. For he had been utterly certain that he would dislike Italy, and just as sure he would like Guy de Montfort, his lord's brother.

Italy was a term of convenience. Hugh knew there was no "Italy" in the same sense that there was an "England" or a "France." The independent city-states of Tuscany and Lombardy were part of "Italy." So were the Papal States. So, too, was the Kingdom of Naples and Sicily, which was ruled by a Frenchman, Charles of Anjou, uncle to the French King Philippe, and Guy de Montfort's powerful patron. They were not linked by language, for each region had its own dialect, its own accent, its own idioms. Even in Tuscany, the Sienese speech was notably less guttural than that of their Florentine neighbors. Nor were they bound by political affinities. People were "Guelphs" or "Ghibellines," the distinction part of an enduring quarrel that had its roots in a forty-year-old breach between the Pope and the Holy Roman Emperor. Cities like Siena and Florence and Venice minted their own money, adhered to their own systems of weights and measures, even their own calendars. And their rivalry was known the length and breadth of Christendom; men spoke of Siena and Florence or Venice and Genoa in the same breath with Rome and Carthage, Athens and Troy.

So even before they reached the Apennines, Hugh had judged Italy and found it wanting; a veritable Tower of Babel, an alien land of bandits and blood-feuds, a region notorious for its "pestilent air," its "Roman fevers and catarrhs," a foreboding world of droughts and earthquakes, volcanic mountains that "belched forth infernal fire," and Lombard money-lenders almost as unpopular as the Jews. It was the true measure of Hugh's devotion to Bran that he'd not balked upon learning that Italy lay at the end of their journey.

He was to discover that the Italy of his imagination was not a total distortion of reality; the roads were indeed bad and fevers were rampant and he had trouble remembering that the lira was not a coin but still worth twenty silver soldi, the same as a gold florin. He'd not expected, though, that Italy would be so beautiful, a land of alpine grandeur and icy mountain lakes and deep valleys and burnished, bright sunshine. The Tuscany hills put him in mind of his native Shropshire; he took pleasure in the vales and woods of chestnut and cypress, the olive groves and vineyards, the snow-white oxen and the lingering twilight dusks. And he had not expected that the people would be so friendly, so quick to offer assistance to wayfarers, so tolerant of the peculiarities of foreigners. He liked the zestful, genial citizens of these Tuscan highlands, and he was impressed by the prosperity of their cities, by their paved streets, formidable walls, spacious piazzas, lavish palazzos, and elaborate public fountains, centers of privilege and vitality and beguiling worldliness.

Within a noisy circle, men were casting dice, and Hugh squirmed closer, trying to see. Treading upon someone's toes, he quickly murmured, "Scusatemi," for he was determined to learn as much of this Tuscan language as he could. The man smiled; in the flow of words that followed, Hugh understood only "inglese" and acknowledged that "si," he was indeed English. There was a growing undercurrent of resentment directed against the French, for Charles had won his crown by the sword and there were many who begrudged him his battlefield sovereignty. But the English bore no such taint, and the Sienese grinned, told his neighbors to make room for the young inglese.

Hugh came forward shyly, warmed by the crowd's friendliness. He could hear snatches of conversation, the name "Guido di Monteforte." To Hugh, it sounded like a brigand's name, conjuring up visions of bandit chieftains and Barbary pirates. It was Hugh's secret conviction that it suited Guy de Montfort perfectly. It had come as a shock, the realization that he distrusted Guy, for he adored Bran, was in awe of the Lady Nell, bedazzled by the Lady Ellen. And Guy, too, was a de Montfort. So why, then, did he harbor such qualms about Bran's brother?

Shifting, he gazed over at the Vicar of Tuscany. Guy was a magnet for stares, a man to turn heads, tall and dark, with a rakish grin and a soldier's swagger, the only one of Simon's sons to have inherited his battlefield brilliance. But he lacked his father's honor, flourishing in this world of tangled loyalties and tarnished allegiances as Simon himself could never have done. One of Count Ildebrandino's squires had sworn that Guy had accepted four thousand florins that past year, money offered by the Florentines so that they could plunder their rival city of Poggibonsi. Hugh had been shaken by the revelation; how could a son of Simon de Montfort accept a bribe? But he did not doubt the accuracy of the squire's account; it rang true.

He had watched Guy ride through the streets of Florence, Lucifer-proud, blind to beggars, with a tongue sharp as a Fleming's blade and an eye for the main chance. Even Hugh could not help but see how utterly Guy eclipsed his older brother. The more brightly Guy burned, the more shadowy Bran became, and the more he drank. Hugh could only hope that they would soon reach Viterbo, hope that after they answered Charles's summons, Bran would then be free to blaze his own path. He might head south to Avellino, the fief given to him by Charles that past December. Or he might choose to go north, toward the city of Padua, where Amaury de Montfort dwelled and studied. Hugh didn't care which road they took . . . just as long as they didn't ride it in tandem with Bran's brother Guy.

Guy had more than three hundred soldiers in his service, most of them mercenaries of the Guelph League. But there were some Englishmen among their numbers, supporters of Simon de Montfort unable or unwilling to come to terms with the English Crown after Evesham. One of these exiles, Walter de Baskerville, had made his way to Bran's side, was murmuring intently in his ear. Their whispered colloquy caught Guy's attention. Sauntering over, he poked Bran play-fully in the ribs. "And what sort of devilry are the two of you plotting?"

"I was telling Bran that Pietro di Tolomei swears Siena has the best whorehouse in all of Tuscany. Just two streets away, La Sirena."

"The Mermaid?" Guy's interest quickened. "I've heard of it. And you were going off without me? What am I of a sudden—a leper?"

"I think you've forgotten someone, Guido," Bran gibed, and Guy's brows rose mockingly.

"God save me, not a lecture on fidelity and the sacred bonds of wedlock!"

"I did not mean your absent wife, Guy. I meant your wife's very-present father. Or do you plan to invite him along?"

Glancing across the Campo at the sturdy, redoubtable figure of his father-in-law, Guy conceded defeat with a wry grimace. "Your point is taken, Bran. Be off with you, then. Enjoy yourselves, wallow in lechery. But for Christ's sake, try not to catch the pox!"

They laughed, beckoned to Pietro, and began to thread their way through the crowd toward their horses. Bran remembered his squires just in time. Noel and Hugh were engrossed in a contest of zaro, a dice game similar to the English favorite, hazard. They came in reluctant response to his summons, but before he could speak, Noel asked plaintively, "Do you have need of us both, my lord? Hugh is willing to go in my stead, if that meets with your approval?"

This was apparently a surprise to Hugh, who looked distinctly taken aback to hear he'd volunteered on Noel's behalf. Bran studied the two of them, a smile hovering at one corner of his mouth. "Actually, I was going to tell you both to stay. But I think your suggestion has some merit, lad. Can you find your way back by yourself, Noel? Just remember that the Tolomei palazzo is in the Camollia quarter, close by the church of San Cristoforo."

Trapped, Hugh could only aim a muttered threat at Noel, sotto voce, before trailing dutifully after his lord, his unhappiness at leaving the Campo stoked by the echoes of Noel's jubilant laughter.

Their arrival at the brothel created a stir. Pietro de Tolomei and the brother of Guido di Monteforte were customers to be catered to, and the men immediately became the center of attention, surrounded by flirtatious, scantily clad women, flattered and fawned upon and plied with the finest red wines of Chianti. There was much bawdy joking and laughter as Bran and Pietro and their companions drank and swapped raunchy stories and conducted increasingly intimate inspections of the prostitutes brought forth for their scrutiny and selection.

Hugh sought to keep inconspicuously to the shadows, struggling with two conflicting emotions: disappointment that Bran should be betraying Juliana, embarrassed excitement at sight of so much alluring female flesh. Pietro di Tolomei had not exaggerated; La Sirena was a bordello for men with discriminating tastes and the money to indulge them. The women were much younger and sleeker and cleaner than the usual inhabitants of bawdy-houses, and wherever Hugh looked, he saw curving bosoms, trim ankles, glimpses of thigh. After a time, he began to attract glances himself. It flustered him, and he retreated into a corner, to no avail; still they giggled and whispered among themselves. It was only when one of the women came over, ran her fingers through his hair, and murmured, "Che biondo-chiaro!" that he understood; they were intrigued by the uncommon flaxen color of his hair.

Noticing the boy's discomfort, Bran looked about for Pietro. But the latter was nowhere in sight. He hesitated, then decided he'd try to make do without a translator; after nearly three years in Italy, he'd picked up enough of the local dialects to make himself understood. La Sirena's bawd was an unusually elegant woman in her forties. She came at once when he beckoned, ready to promise all the perversions known to man, so determined was she to please this free-spending English lord, kinsman to il Rosso.

"What I want," Bran said in slow, but comprehensible Tuscan, "is a wench not too seasoned or jaded, one young and gentle in her ways, not brazen. You understand?"

The woman thought she did. "An innocent," she said knowingly. "You are indeed in luck, signore, for it happens that I have a rare prize. Thirteen she is, with skin like milk and her maidenhead intact. Of course the price—"

But Bran was already shaking his head. "Too young. And I do not want a maiden," he said, politely masking his skepticism, for he equated whorehouse virgins with unicorns and like mythical beasts. "I am not seeking a child. I want a whore who does not look like one, a lass who knows how to coax a man along, to keep him from spilling his seed too soon."

She hastily lowered her lashes so her surprise would not show. She prided herself upon her ability to size up a man's needs, and for this inglese, she would have picked Anna, who boasted she could set a bed afire without need of flint and tinder. Rapidly reassessing, she said thoughtfully, "I do have just such a one. She was christened Lucia, but we call her Serafina, so sweet is her voice, so angelic her smile."

"A seraph?" Bran echoed, amused. Even allowing for the inevitable exaggeration in any sales pitch, Serafina still sounded promising. And when the girl herself appeared, slim and graceful and very young, he nodded approvingly. "Yes, she will do. But she's not for me. I'll take Anna, the wanton who was sitting on my lap. Serafina is for my squire." And reaching for the girl's hand, he led her across the room to Hugh.

"Your birthday gift, lad," he said, and could not help laughing at the astonished look on the boy's face. Serafina was not as diffident as the bawd claimed; linking her arm in Hugh's, she sought to steer him toward the stairs. But he resisted, grabbing Bran's sleeve and pulling him into the stairwell with them.

"What is it, Hugh? Is she not to your liking?"

"No, she . . . she is very pretty. But my lord, the monks at Evesham Abbey taught us that whoring is a mortal sin!" Hugh had not meant to blurt it out like that. He bit his lip in dismay, for he did not think he could bear to be laughed at, not by Bran. But Bran did not laugh.

"Well, it is hard to dispute that, Hugh. The Church does indeed hold fornication to be a sin. But to be honest, lad, few men could endure an entire summer of drought; we all need a little rain in our lives. For what it is worth, I think there are very few sins that God could not forgive. Now I would suggest you follow Serafina above-stairs; you'd not want her to lose face before the others, would you? After that— follow your conscience." Bran turned to go, then swung back, his grin at last breaking free. "But whatever you decide to do, lad, I hope you'll brag about it afterward to Noel!"

THE chamber was so cramped that the bed seemed to reach from wall to wall. There was one shuttered window, a trestle table, a washing laver, a chamber pot, and a wick lamp, sputtering in a bowl of pungent fish oil. But the bed linen looked reasonably clean and there was a large flagon of wine cooling in the laver. Serafina sat down upon the bed, kicked off her shoes. She knew some of the other women wasted no time, began by bluntly instructing their customers to wash their privy members, but she preferred to ease into it, to pretend she was being seduced, not sold; she was fourteen and still in need of illusions. She smiled, asked Hugh to help her with the laces of her gown, before remembering that he didn't speak Tuscan. He had not yet moved from the door, looked as if he might bolt at any moment. She was perplexed by his behavior, and hobbled by their lack of language. She had been proud that she'd been chosen for this young inglese with the bright flaxen hair, but it no longer seemed such an honor. What was he waiting for? Most men pounced upon her ere she could even get her clothes off. She'd never bedded an inglese before; were they all so shy? She sighed, lay back on the bed in a seductive pose, and looked at him expectantly.

Hugh was discovering that Serafina's silence spoke louder than any voice of conscience. His brain and body no longer worked in harmony, were suddenly at war. His head was filled with thoughts of sin, but Barnabas was throbbing with urgent need, caring naught for hellfire or the monks of Evesham. Jesú, she was so pretty, with dark eyes like Juliana and a mouth that needed no lip rouge, as soft and red as strawberries. He must not do this. But his legs received another message; they took a hesitant step toward the girl on the bed.

She had an expressive face, had been regarding him in puzzlement that was slowly turning into impatience. But then she cried out and clapped her hands together. She had a light, pleasing voice, and her words pattered about him like raindrops, an assault of musical notes.

He seized upon a familiar word, the one she kept repeating. Primo. First. He nodded slowly and pointed to the bed. "Si," he said softly, "primo."

Serafina was delighted to have her suspicions confirmed, delighted that she was to be the one to initiate this young inglese into the mysteries of manhood. It was great good luck to bed a virgin. Rising, she came toward him, took his hands in hers. "I know you do not understand me. But I will teach you all you need to know. You shall find joy in my bed and you shall remember me, English. You shall remember me even when your hair has greyed and your bones ache with age. For a man never forgets his first." Raising up on tiptoe, she kissed Hugh on the mouth, then drew him toward the bed.

When Hugh would later acquire the experience that allowed for comparison, he'd realize how well Bran had chosen for him, how fortunate he was to have found a Serafina. She was patient and tender and she made him forget the sordidness of their surroundings, forget the fire-and-brimstone sermons of Evesham's parish priest, forget that she was a Sienese whore. They might have been two youngsters out in a meadow, under a haystack, alone in a world whose borders ended at the bed's edge. Serafina was right; she did give him joy and he would remember her.

Hugh was awed by his body's explosive response to Serafina's caresses. He understood for the first time why the Church looked upon women with such suspicion, for lust did indeed allow them to exercise great power over men. But then he thought of Juliana, risking pregnancy and scandal and damnation for Bran. Mayhap women, too, burned with the same fever. If so, it seemed unfair to blame them for the cravings of men. After a moment, he began to laugh. "I cannot believe that I am lying in your bed and thinking of theology!"

Serafina did not understand a word he said, but she laughed, too, and he bent over, kissed her cheek. They were both very pleased with themselves, Hugh proud of his performance and Serafina proud of her tutoring. She was no less gratified by his attentiveness afterward, for she was accustomed to men who lost interest in the time it took to roll off of her. But Hugh continued to hold her in his arms, to murmur "bella" and "tesora." Men often told her she was pretty, but none had ever called her a "treasure." No man had taken her brush and combed out her long, dark hair, either. She was so delighted with Hugh's gallantry that when his hand slid from her shoulder to her breast and his mouth sought hers again, she did not rebuff him. Instead, she broke an iron-clad house rule, gave a customer two tumbles for the price of one.

Fetching the wine flagon, Serafina offered Hugh the first swig. "For a man's work, a man's thirst," she said coyly. Hugh accepted the flagon, but when she called him "Barnabas," he burst out laughing again.

"Ah, no, lass, that was a joke! My real name is Hugh—Hugh," he repeated, thumping his chest. But she merely giggled. He was still trying to break through their language barrier when a knock sounded on the door. They both stiffened, not yet ready to have the real world intrude, to have Serafina claimed by her next customer.

"Chi è?" she called out warily.

"Sono io." A singularly unhelpful response: it's me. But then the door swung open and Bran entered. His eyes flicked to the clothing strewn wildly about the room, but he kept a straight face as he said, "I thought I'd best look in on you, lad, make sure you were not being held hostage by that conscience of yours."

Hugh did not reply, made mute by a sudden realization, that behind Bran's banter lurked a genuine concern. He might never admit it, but he'd been worried enough to investigate, to make certain his birthday gift had not done more harm than good. Hugh was enormously touched by this evidence of affection. No more than Bran, though, could he have acknowledged such emotion. He sought, instead, to match Bran's playful mockery, saying with a bit of bravado, "Well, at least I shall have a right interesting sin to confess on the morrow!"

But that was not his true voice, flippancy not his style. He hesitated, losing his smile. "My lord . . . I can confess and promise to repent. But . . . but what if I sin again? In all honesty, I suspect I will."

He looked so solemn and so trusting. Not for the first time, Bran wondered if he'd done Hugh a wrong by plucking him out of the peace of Evesham Abbey, putting him down in the midst of the de Montfort maelstrom. "Do not fret, lad. Priests expect you to keep on sinning, do not care as long as you keep on confessing, too. In fact, I think they prefer it that way, for if there were no sinners, why would we need them?"

Hugh grinned; if he was tormented by remorse, he was hiding it extraordinarily well, and Bran had not been impressed by the boy's acting abilities. Picking up Hugh's hastily discarded belt, still holding a sheathed dagger and money pouch, he dropped it onto the foot of the bed, while fumbling for his own pouch. "When my brother Guy was fifteen, Harry and I took him to the Halfmoon, the best bawdy-house in Southwark. He always swore afterward that it was our fault he'd developed such a taste for carousing, claiming that if not for us, he'd likely have become a priest!" He laughed softly, then shook several coins onto the bed. "Un' altra volta per il ragazzo, signorina Serafina."

Even Hugh could follow that without translation. As the door closed quietly behind Bran, he shook his head regretfully, giving Serafina an apologetic smile. "I doubt that I'm up to a third joust, lass," he began, miming a yawn to get his point across. But Serafina paid him no mind, and when she put her hand on his inner thigh, he discovered—to his own surprise—that mayhap he was not too tired, after all. It was only later that he remembered what Bran had said about his brothers, realized that this was the first time Bran had mentioned Harry's name. It pleased him very much, for he could not help thinking that this was a sign of trust, proof that Bran was coming to understand how absolute was his loyalty, a bond beyond breaking. Or so he believed on that Saturday afternoon in Siena's best whorehouse.

HUGH's first glimpse of Viterbo was a disappointment. It was an important town, a papal residence, site of the current cardinals' conclave. But they arrived at dusk, and all Hugh saw through the gusting rain were streets narrow as any maze, churned up with mud, and shuttered, overhanging buildings of dark tufa stone, black and wet and foreboding.

Viterbo was filled to capacity, struggling to accommodate the entourages of two Kings, and the cardinals assembled to elect a pope. But a cousin of one of Count Ildebrandino's brothers-in-law had a palazzo close by the cathedral. Lodging as many of their attendants as they could in the great hall, they managed to find beds for the rest in neighboring inns. It was a tedious, protracted process, though, for men who'd been riding all day in a steady downpour, and by the time they were settled in, tempers were raw and patience in scarce supply.

The palazzo cooks did their best to feed so many mouths, but the meatless Lenten menu did nothing to raise rain-dampened spirits. In the fourth week of this somber season of fasting and self-denial, most of the men were heartily sick of fish, yearning for forbidden foods cooked with butter and milk and cheese. While their host was able to provide stewed eels and fresh pike for the Count, Guy, and the fortunates seated upon the dais, those at the lower tables had to make do with the most disliked of all Lenten dishes, smoked red herring. Hugh usually had an appetite to put a starving wolf to shame, but tonight he could muster up no enthusiasm for the salt-embalmed fish on his trencher, and he was poking at it listlessly with his knife when Niccolò di Tavena generously offered to share the last dollop of hot mustard.

"Senape," he said, "e pesce morto," for Niccolò never missed an opportunity to increase Hugh's Tuscan vocabulary. His own French was quite good, but he magnanimously forbore to laugh, no matter how Hugh mangled his native tongue, for he'd met numerous French and English knights since Guy de Montfort had wed the daughter of his lord, and Hugh was the only one who showed a genuine interest in the language of Tuscany.

Hugh dutifully repeated the words. "Senape—mustard, right? And pesce morto—herring?"

"No—dead fish," Niccolò said and grinned at the face Hugh made. "I have another one for you, so pay attention—figlio di puttana. This is for Noel—whoreson!"

Both boys laughed, for Hugh's relationship with Noel, fractious from the very first, had soured beyond redemption once Noel learned of Serafina. "Fair is fair, Niccolò. Let me teach you a blood-curdling French oath, one you—"

Hugh got no further. Voices were rising; the table rocked suddenly, and a bench overturned with a loud thud. Hugh swung about just in time to see one of the Florentines draw a dagger upon his neighbor. Evading that first thrust, the second man snatched up a table knife, slashed his assailant's sleeve. By now the hall was in an uproar: men shouting, shoving, dogs barking, other daggers being drawn. Into the very center of all this turmoil strode Count Ildebrandino. His own sword never left its scabbard, for his was the authority of blood and privilege, authority that took compliance for granted. Moving between the combatants, he quelled them by the very arrogance of his assurance, by his obvious disbelief that they would dare to disobey.

In minutes it was over, the transgressors rebuked, banished from the hall. As calm returned, Niccolò explained to Hugh what had driven the men to daggers. "They fought over a past wrong. Florence and Siena have often been at war. This time the Florentines won, and after plundering Siena, they took a number of the city's young women back with them to Florence."

Hugh was instantly on the side of the Sienese. "That is an outrage! Women are to be protected, not treated as spoils of war!"

"Easy, lad, I agree. But ere you offer to lead a rescue mission, you ought to know this—that abduction took place more than forty years ago, before either man was even born!" Niccolò laughed at Hugh's look of bemusement. "You see, Hugh, we Tuscans nurture our grievances, tend them well from one generation to the next. Forget not, forgive not; we live by that."

Hugh nodded slowly. "The Welsh live by that creed, too." Within the hour, he was to be given disturbing, dramatic proof that so did the de Montforts.

The quarrel set the tone for the night. Once the food was cleared away, men settled down to drink—and to trade stories of other war atrocities, of kingly cruelties and crimes of statecraft. It was a macabre game, but the men—bored, restless, stranded indoors by the storm—

entered into it with gusto, sought to outdo one another, and Hugh and Niccolò and the other squires listened in appalled awe to sagas in which soldiers raped nuns, stole from the dying and from God, melted down church chalices and candlesticks, sold false relics to gullible pilgrims, and broke each and every one of the Holy Commandments.

As the evening advanced, the tales grew grimmer; men dredged up gossip steeped in blood. The Tuscans told of wars in which entire towns were put to the torch. The French countered with accounts of the siege of Castle Gaillard, in which citizens who'd taken refuge within were expelled by the garrison, only to find themselves trapped between the castle walls and the besieging French army; huddled in this hellish no-man's-land, the wretched villagers began to die of hunger and cold and plague, and so desperate did they become that they seized and devoured a newborn baby. That reminded the English of their King John, who had cast into a dark dungeon the wife of a rebel baron, then starved her to death. Hugh thought that last story was rather tactless, given that King John was Guy and Bran de Montfort's grandfather. But they made no comments; they had so far taken no part at all in this grisly contest of griefs.

Someone then brought up John's brother Richard, the King called Lionheart, who had put to the sword at Acre more than two thousand Saracens, most of them women and children. Others were quick to point out, though, that infidels had no souls. Walter de Baskerville mentioned John again, this time for hanging twenty-eight Welsh hostages at Nottingham Castle, many of them mere lads. But as with the Saracens, the nationality of the victims diluted audience sympathy; Wales was too foreign to the Tuscans and French, and too familiar to the English, to stir up much pity for its murdered children.

Count Ildebrandino now came up with a crime so cold-blooded that Hugh involuntarily crossed himself, for this was a brutality not safely shrouded in the past. Twelve years ago, Michael Palaeologus was chosen as regent for his six-year-old cousin, rightful heir to the Byzantine Empire. Michael insisted upon being crowned with the boy, but swore a holy oath that he'd relinquish all authority once his young cousin came of age. Instead, he ordered the boy blinded, thus effectively rendering him unfit to rule.

Men murmured among themselves. For the moment at least, the Count seemed to have won the bloody laurels. Glancing toward his son-in-law, he queried, "You've been curiously quiet, Guy, for a man who has seen so much of war himself. What say you? What wrongs do you judge beyond forgiving?"

Guy raised his head, and there was something in his face that silenced the conversation in the hall. "That," he said, "is a question I find very easy to answer. What more despicable, cowardly act can there be than the mutilation of the dead?"

Hugh instinctively looked toward Bran. He'd made no outcry. Nor had he moved. But there was an unnatural stillness about him; he scarcely seemed to be breathing, his eyes riveted upon his brother's face. All other eyes were upon Guy, too, as he shoved his chair back. "Let's drink to that," he said loudly, "drink to the victors of Evesham. May they not be forgotten!"

Walter de Baskerville was also on his feet now, rather the worse for wine. "To William de Mautravers and Roger de Mortimer, sons of perdition, spawn of the Devil!"

Others were raising their wine cups, echoing this bitter toast. Hugh leaned over, whispered to Niccolò that de Mautravers was the man responsible for hacking Lord Simon's body into bloody pieces. "And de Mortimer sent Earl Simon's severed head to his wife—as a battlefield keepsake! They put it up over the gate of their castle at Wigmore, left it there till it rotted . . ."

Guy reached for a wine goblet, held it aloft. "And what of his God-cursed Grace? Edward Plantagenet, my father's godson, my kinsman who would be King! Why do you think scum like de Mautravers dared to butcher my father as he lay dying in the mud of Evesham? Because he knew—they all knew—that Edward would approve, that Edward wanted it done! No, give credit where due, Walter, to my cousin Ned, may we meet in Hell!"

And with that, he flung the goblet into the fire. Hissing flames shot up wildly, ashes and embers rained into the floor rushes, clay shards ricocheted off the hearth stones, and men watched, mesmerized.

Later, when Hugh had time to think upon what he'd witnessed, he would decide it was the unexpectedness of Guy's fury that was so frightening. Lightning searing a sky without clouds. A sudden burst of flame in a doused hearth. It was over almost as quickly as it began. Guy glanced at the clay fragments, said in a normal tone of voice that he owed his host some new crockery—as if that flare of killing rage had never been. Others did not find it so easy to forget. Hugh in particular was unsettled by what he'd seen, for it made him doubt his own judgment. He knew that Bran still bled, but Guy had seemed impervious to the past, so much so that Hugh even resented him a little for it, wondering why Bran must bear such deep scars when Guy bore so few. Now he knew better and wished he did not.

THE one most affected by Guy's outburst was his brother. Bran began drinking in earnest even before the broken crockery was cleared away.

By midnight he was well and truly drunk, and was still badly hung-over when he stumbled down to the great hall the next morning. Christians were expected to abstain from breakfast during Lent, but even the devout often found appetites overcoming obedience, and a number of men were helping themselves to tankards of ale and chunks of bread, soothing their consciences by eschewing butter. Others, those who had followed Bran's example, slumped on benches looking greensick, sipping ale or herbal potions supposed to cure a morning-after malaise.

Waving aside Noel's offer of hot bread, Bran drained a flagon of wine much too quickly, and, to the dismay of his squires, demanded another. Hugh had attempted to coax Bran to bed the night before, and in consequence, got his first taste of the fabled de Montfort temper. He was not eager to sample any more of it, but he watched Bran with growing unease, for they were meeting that forenoon with Charles and the King of France. In their months together, Hugh had never seen Bran publicly drunk, except for that night in Wales, when fever and mead had proved to be such a potent mixture. But he'd never seen his lord start drinking so early in the day, and he hovered about anxiously until Bran curtly told him to help Noel in saddling their horses. Even then he retreated from the hall with reluctance, with backward glances that Bran was determined to ignore. As fond as he was of Hugh, he was in no mood this morning to bear the burden of the boy's devotion.

Noel was worried, too, about Bran, but he and Hugh were well past the point where they could share anything, even a mutual concern, and they headed for the stables in sullen silence. Friday the 13th was believed to be a day of ill omen, but after yesterday's torrential rains, the morning seemed off to a promising start. The sky was an infinite, azure blue, and the air was cold but very clear, as if the night's storm had washed the world clean.

Niccolò di Tavena was already in the stables, tightening the girth on the Count's flashy white stallion. He beckoned hastily at sight of them. "Who is Henry of Almain and what is he to the de Montforts?"

It was an unexpected question. They exchanged quizzical looks, then answered almost in the same breath, Hugh saying, "Their cousin," and Noel, "Their enemy."

Niccolò frowned. "Which is it?"

"Both." Before Hugh could elaborate, Noel seized control of the conversation. "He is the eldest son of the English King's brother Richard, which makes him a first cousin to the de Montforts and the Lord Edward. They're all roughly of an age, grew up together, and he was once a fervent supporter of the Lord Simon. He claimed to believe in the Earl's reforms, but then he renounced his allegiance, at a time when Lord Simon most needed his backing. The de Montforts saw it as a betrayal, and there has been bad blood between them ever since. Why? The last we heard, he was on crusade with the Lord Edward. What put him in your mind this morn?"

"He's here—in Viterbo. It seems he arrived four days ago, with the two Kings. A couple of the English knights saw him in the marketplace. I heard them a few moments ago outside the stables; Walter de Baskerville was vowing to tell the de Montforts, and the other man was arguing against it, right vehemently, too. So I wondered who he was—"

"De Baskerville? We just passed him in the courtyard, headed for the hall!" Hugh spun around, started to run, with Noel and Niccolò right on his heels.

They heard the shouting even before they reached the hall. Guy was gripping Walter de Baskerville by both arms, shaking the other man in his urgency to get answers. "Are you sure, truly sure it was Hal?"

"Guy, I saw him, crossing the piazza bold as can be! It was him, I swear by my very soul!"

Guy seemed stunned. "That God would deliver him into my hands . . ." He swung away from de Baskerville, looking about for his squire. "Ancel, fetch my sword! Bran! Where in Christ did he go?" His eyes were sweeping the hall, singling out English exiles. "Walter, Geoffrey, Alan, you fought with me at Evesham. Are you with me now? Bran! Damn him!" Snatching up his scabbard, he buckled it with shaking hands. "Ancel, get to the stables, saddle my horse! What of the rest of you? Who rides with me?"

It was like watching a fire blazing out of control. Some caught the contagion, too, began to shout for their own swords and horses. Others were backing away, as if the very air around Guy had become hot enough to singe. But when he turned to his father-in-law, the Count did not hesitate. "Of course I go with you," he said, quite matter-of-factly. "A man must avenge his own." And it was then that Bran emerged from a corner privy chamber.

He paused, blinking in the surge of sunlight, looking puzzled and a little wary to find the hall in such turmoil. Grabbing Bran's scabbard from the back of a chair, Guy strode forward, thrust it at his brother. "We've no time to lose, Bran. Hal is here, right here in Viterbo! I still cannot believe it, cannot believe God could be so good to us. But Christ, why could it not have been Ned?"

Bran had always believed the folklore that a sudden shock could sober a man. He discovered now that it wasn't so. No matter how he tried to focus his thoughts, to banish the wine-fumes from his brain, he could not cut through the confusion. Drink did not numb as easily as it once had, so why now? Why now when he had such need for clear thinking? He looked at his brother, seeing not Guy but Harry, his constant, unseen companion, for who was more faithful than a ghost? Who understood better than the dead that there was no forgiveness, in this life or the next? What did Guy know of remorse, relentless and ever-present, goading a man toward madness? What did Guy know of that? And he must not ever learn!

"Guy, listen to me!" Why did his voice sound so slurred, echo so strangely in his own ears? Why could he not find the right words? "But it *is* Hal, not Ned. Hal. And he . . . he was not even at Evesham!"

He saw at once that he'd not gotten through to Guy; the look on his brother's face was one of disbelief, not comprehension. "Why are you so set upon destroying yourself? What will it change? You cannot even say that Papa would want this, Guy, for you know he would not!"

It was a cry of desperation, honest as only a plea utterly without hope can be. But Guy reacted as if he'd been struck a physical blow. His head came up, breath hissing through clenched teeth, eyes narrowing into slits of incredulous rage.

"You dare to talk of what Papa would have wanted, you who killed him! He and Harry died because of you, because of your criminal care-lessness, your God-cursed folly! Where were you when we most needed you? Camped by the lake at Kenilworth Castle, out in the open so your men could bathe, by God, so Ned could come down upon you like a hawk on a pigeon! And Papa never knowing, keeping faith in you till the last! Even when we realized that Ned had used your banners as bait, we assumed you'd fought and lost, not that you'd let yourself be ambushed like some green, witless stripling, never that! Does it comfort you any, that our father went to his death still believing in you, never knowing how you'd betrayed him? I watched him die, damn you, and Harry and all the others. Not you, Bran—me! And mayhap this is why I did not die that day myself, so I could avenge our father, avenge Evesham!"

Sweat stood out on Guy's forehead; his chest heaved as if he'd been running. He drew a deep, constricted breath, then said, more calmly but no less contemptuously, "You can come with me or not as you choose. But is it not enough that you failed Papa at Evesham? Are you truly going to fail him at Viterbo, too?"

Bran's throat had closed up, cutting off speech. But he had nothing to say. No denials to make. No excuses to offer. Every embittered ac-cusation that Guy had flung at him was one already embedded in his soul, five years festering. He could not defend himself. Nor could he save himself. All he could do was what he did now—reach for the sword that Guy was holding out to him.

❧

THE church of San Silvestro was only half-filled with parishioners, it not being a Sunday or a holy day. As the bell rang for the Consecration, they knelt upon their prayer cushions, began to chant in unison with their priest, "Jesú, Lord, welcome Thou be, in form of bread as I Thee see." They got no further; the door, barred to keep latecomers from interrupting the Mass, was struck a shuddering blow, splintered under the steel of thrusting blades.

Bran was still blinded by the sun from the piazza; at first all he saw was blackness. Voices were rising from all corners of the church, bewildered, angry, alarmed. He could barely make out a shadowy figure standing by the altar. "Who are you that dare to intrude upon God's service?" A priest's voice, fearful but indignant, too.

"You need not fear, Padre. We are not here for you." This voice Guy's, a voice like a knife. It cut through the murmuring protests just as surely as his sword had pierced the door, frightening to them all, familiar to one. He was on his feet now, his face a white blur, dark hollow eyes in a death mask, doomed and knowing it, for he'd recognized Guy. Their prey, their enemy, their cousin Hal.

"What . . . what do you want?" he cried, beginning to back away, and again it was Guy who answered for them.

"Retribution," he said, bringing up his sword. People would later ask why Hal had made no attempt to defend himself, why his attendants did not come to his aid. They were questions without answers. All that the eyewitnesses could report was what they saw, that Hal never drew his own sword. He fled, instead, to the altar, as if seeking sanctuary, and when Guy loomed over him, he was heard to gasp his cousin's name, to beg for God's mercy. Guy's reply burned itself into so many memories that parishioners would later be able to recall it word for word. He had said, they all agreed, "You shall have the mercy you showed my father and brother," and splattered San Silvestro's altar with the blood of his kinsman.

Guy's second thrust split open Hal's skull, but still he clung to the altar, clung to life. The priest sought to intercede, and paid dearly for his courage. When they saw their priest struck down, the people panicked, tried to flee. A mêlée broke out; other swords flashed.

Bran saw it all, every gory detail imprinting itself upon his brain, to be relived again and again: the blood pooling in the chancel, caking on his boots, darkening the priest's cassock, even saturating the Host itself, for the holy wafers had spilled out when the pyx overturned. Guy finally broke Hal's death-grip on the altar, severing three fingers in the process, and grabbed the dying man by the hair, began to drag him up the aisle, into the clear. Bran saw it all, the fingers still clutching the altar cloth, the candlesticks scattered underfoot, and always the blood, so much of it, more than he'd ever seen on the battlefield, or even when pigs were butchered for Martinmas. How could one man's body hold so much? But he was forgetting the priest. And a parish clerk had been injured, too, was crumpled, moaning, by the sacristy door.

Bran saw it all. But he felt none of it. For the rest of his life, he would be able to recall the murder scene in San Silvestro's church merely by closing his eyes. But he could never remember how he'd felt or what he'd thought as it was happening.

The sunlight in the piazza was dazzling, hurt his eyes. He shielded them with his hand, looked down upon the body sprawled at Guy's feet. Fair hair trailed in the mud; it, too, was turning red. Bran's sword-arm hung at his side; when he started to sheathe the weapon, he saw blood on the blade. Passing strange, but he could not remember how it got there. Why could he not remember?

Guy, too, was staring at their cousin's body. He was panting, drenched in blood, and soaked in sweat. "I have had my vengeance," he said, and spat with difficulty into the dirt.

"Have you forgotten what they did to your father's body? How they hacked him to pieces, then threw him to the dogs?"

The speaker was an English knight, one of the few survivors of Evesham. Bran knew him well, but now he found himself unable to recall the man's name. Guy whirled, and for a moment it looked as if he might turn upon his tormentor. But then he jerked his sword free of its scabbard again, slashed open his cousin's belly. Intestines spilled out in a gush of clotted black blood; a dreadful stench pervaded the piazza. As Guy swung a second time and then a third, a man fell to his knees, began to vomit. Bells suddenly echoed across the square; one of the parishioners was ringing the sanctus bell, sounding the alarm. Count Ildebrandino stepped toward his son-in-law, grabbed Guy's arm.

"We are done here," he said. "You have avenged your father. Now it is time to go—and to go quickly, whilst we still can."

The Count's warning broke the spell. The men scattered, running for their mounts. Sheathing his sword again, Guy swung up into the saddle, raked his spurs into his stallion's flanks. The horse leapt forward, began to lengthen stride. But then Guy jerked on the reins, for as he looked back, he saw his brother still standing by the body. "Bran, you fool, what are you waiting for, the hangman? Get to your horse!"

Bran turned at sound of his name. As their eyes met, Guy felt a queer chill, for Bran looked at him without apparent recognition. "Come on," he shouted. "Hurry!"

Bran didn't move, continued to gaze down at Hal's body. Footsteps sounded suddenly on the muddy cobblestones; he looked up to see Hugh standing beside him. The boy's face was streaked with tears, and not once did his eyes meet Bran's. But he was holding out the reins of Bran's stallion, and after a moment, Bran took them, mounted, and rode after his brother.

People now emerged from hiding places, approached the body. Someone produced a blanket, draped it mercifully over the mangled remains. A woman in widow's black dropped a rosary into a maimed hand. It was all done in an eerie silence, as if the murder had shocked them beyond speech. But then a wailing began in the church, and an elderly merchant sent a servant to the Franciscans, where the Kings of Sicily and France were attending Mass.

Hugh and Noel stood frozen, heedless of the activity beginning to swirl about them. Noel had started to shiver; even after a sympathetic spectator wrapped a mantle about his shoulders, he could not stop trembling. As if rousing himself from a trance, Hugh knelt on the cobblestones, made the sign of the cross over Hal's body. Straightening up, he moved toward the hitching post, untied their mounts. But Noel recoiled, looking at him in fresh horror.

"Have you gone mad? We cannot go with them! They've doomed themselves this day, will be hunted down like outlaws, with every man's hand against them!"

Hugh did not dispute him. "I know," he whispered, and shuddered. And then he mounted his gelding, sent it galloping across the piazza at a pace to outrun pursuit, but not memories of the murder.

4

MONTARGIS, FRANCE

April 1271

Tʜᴇ placid predictability of daily life in Montargis was shattered by the unexpected arrival of the French Queen. The villagers abandoned their chores, deserting ploughs, churns, and looms in their eagerness to glimpse their sovereign's mother. Even the nuns could not resist the turmoil, peeping surreptitiously from the windows of frater, infirmary, and almonry as Marguerite and her entourage rode into the priory precincts. The Prioress hastened out to greet their royal guest, having already sent a servant to alert the de Montfort household, for all knew it was Nell whom Marguerite had come to see.

By the time Marguerite reached the de Montfort lodgings, Nell was awaiting her in the doorway. If her curtsy displayed the deference due a Queen, her smile welcomed a friend. "Madame, what a joyful surprise! I'm sorry my daughter is not here to greet you, too, but Ellen has been away for the past fortnight, visiting her de Montfort cousins at La Ferté-Alais. I expect her back today or tomorrow, though, and . . ." Nell paused for breath, and only then did she become aware of the other woman's silence. "Marguerite? Is something wrong?"

Marguerite nodded, her eyes filling with tears.

THE church was very still, sun filtering through diamond-shaped panes of emerald- and ruby-tinted glass; the faint fragrance of incense hung in the air. Breathing in the perfumed scent, enveloping herself in the silence, it seemed to Nell that this shadowy chapel was her last refuge in a world gone mad. She did not approach the altar, though. In her despair, she turned not to God, but to Simon, and knelt by her husband's memorial stone. "Beloved," she whispered, "how unquiet is your grave . . ."

Another woman might have fumbled for a rosary; Nell reached for a ring. A sapphire set in the shape of a cross, it had once been Simon's, worn since Evesham on a chain around her neck. Fishing it from her bodice, she balanced it in her palm, then watched as her fingers curled around it, clenched into a fist.

"Was ever a man so ill-served by the sons who loved him? If Harry had not allowed Edward to escape, if Bran had only understood the urgency of your need at Evesham, if only . . ." Her voice wavered, then steadied. "How I hate those words! If only. What if. And the worst one of all, Simon—why."

After a while, she tried to pray, first for the soul of her murdered nephew, and then for her doomed sons. The prayers didn't help, for she had lost more at Evesham than her husband, her eldest son, and her country. She had lost, too, her faith in God's justice. From King's daughter to rebel's widow—it was a free-falling plunge into depths not yet plumbed. She had in time made her peace with the Almighty, but after Evesham, she no longer truly trusted Him, and she no longer believed that heavenly prayers could ease earthly pain.

"And now this," she said softly. "And now Viterbo. Simon . . . Simon, I do not understand!"

It was an involuntary cry, one that seemed to echo on the hushed chapel air, lingering until dispelled by a slamming door, by a familiar voice. "Mama? Mama, we're back!"

Ellen and Juliana were hastening up the nave. "There you are, Mama!" Even in such dimmed light, Ellen looked radiant. "We had a wonderful time. We went to Paris for a few days, heard Easter Mass at Notre Dame, and Cousin Alice took us to the apothecary who makes that jasmine perfume you fancy. Then, once we were back at La Ferté-Alais, they gave an elaborate feast, with dancing and jugglers and even a trained bear!" Ellen paused long enough to shoot a mischievous look in Juliana's direction. "Oh, yes, and Juliana made another conquest. One of the knights was so smitten with her that he followed her about like her own shadow, even—"

Juliana jogged Ellen's elbow. "She makes much ado over nothing, Madame. Can you tell us if it is true about the French Queen? She is here in Montargis?"

"Yes." Nell had risen at sound of her daughter's voice. For a moment, her fingers tightened around her husband's ring, and then she said, "Come here, Ellen. You, too, Juliana, for this concerns Bran."

The two girls exchanged startled, guilty glances, and Juliana flushed darkly, wondering how she and Ellen could have deluded themselves so easily, how they could ever have believed that the Countess knew naught of her liaison with Bran.

They moved forward, losing all joy and laughter in the few brief steps it took to enter the chapel, looking tense, anxious, and young enough to break Nell's heart. "Marguerite came to tell me, Ellen," she said abruptly, "that your cousin Hal is dead."

Ellen's lashes flickered, no more than that, and Nell felt a sense of weary wonderment that she and Simon could have bred this beautiful, impassive child, so unlike her volatile, impassioned parents. But Ellen had not always been so guarded. Growing up, she, too, had followed the de Montfort credo of no emotion denied, no thought left unspoken, for Simon and Nell had both prided themselves upon their candor, their willingness to speak out before the most exalted of audiences. After one of Henry's many battlefield blunders, Simon had even dared to tell the English King that he belonged by rights in an asylum for the deranged of mind, an audacity Henry never forgave and other men never forgot. Now, as Nell looked at Ellen's profile, so perfect and yet so inscrutable, she felt an old ache stirring, for Ellen's reticence was not hers by birthright. It was a painful, learned response to a lesson no thirteen-year-old should ever have to master. Evesham had scarred her daughter no less than her sons.

"Mama . . ." Ellen took her time, choosing her words with care. "I understand why you grieve for Uncle Richard. Indeed, I am sorry, too, for his pain. He is a decent man, and I know he truly tried to help us after Evesham. But please do not ask me to grieve for Hal. I cannot mourn him, Mama, for I cannot forgive him. If he had kept faith, Papa and Harry might still be alive. No, I can find no pity in my heart for Hal. I regret only that God gave him a crusader's death, for that is an honor he did not deserve."

There was no easy way to do it. "No, Ellen, you do not understand—not yet. Hal did not die in the Holy Land. He died in Italy."

Juliana's expression did not change; she continued to look puzzled and somewhat apprehensive. But Ellen's eyes widened; the mask cracked. "Italy," she echoed, and then, "Oh, Mama, no!"

Nell nodded grimly. "For reasons known but to God, he directed Hal to Viterbo. There what you fear came to pass. As soon as your brothers learned of his presence, they . . . they seem to have gone stark mad. They burst into the church where Hal was hearing Mass, murdered him as he clung to the altar, and then Guy . . . Guy mutilated his body ere they escaped. Marguerite says they are believed to have taken refuge at Sovana, Count Ildebrandino's castle in—"

Juliana gave a smothered sob; Ellen caught her arm as she swayed. "No, Juliana, it is not true! Guy . . . yes, for he's like one crazed when it comes to Papa's enemies. But not Bran, not a killing like that. Juliana, will you stop weeping and pay heed to what I say? It is a mistake, it has to be. You know what happened at Evesham, you know that Bran got to the battle too late, that he . . . God help him, but he saw our father's head on a pike. I cannot even begin to imagine what the ride back to Kenilworth must have been like for him. But the day's horror was not yet done. When the castle garrison heard, they went mad. My uncle Richard was being held at Kenilworth as a hostage, and they attacked him, would have killed him right there in the bailey if not for Bran. He stood over my uncle's body, sword drawn, and faced them down, just hours after seeing what Richard's allies had done to our father. Now you tell me, is that a man who'd murder during a Mass?"

But Juliana continued to sob softly. It was Nell who reached out to her daughter, laid her hand gently on Ellen's arm. Ellen's mouth trembled. "Tell her, Mama. Please tell her it's not true . . ." Pulling away when Nell slowly shook her head. "My God, Mama, how can you believe that of Bran?"

Nell did not flinch. "Because I know Bran's pain," she said quietly. "Because I know that he has spent the last five years looking for a way to punish himself. And I very much fear that he found it at Viterbo."

Ellen could not speak. "What will happen to them?" she asked, once she was sure her voice would not betray her.

"They have been outlawed, their lands forfeit, and they'll be excommunicated as soon as there is a new pope to do it, to damn them. Then no man will dare to help them . . ." Nell leaned back against the altar. "Child, there is more. Marguerite says suspicions have fallen upon Amaury, too."

"But why? Amaury was not at Viterbo . . . was he, Mama? Even if so, I'll never believe he took part in a church killing, never!"

"No, he was not in Viterbo. He was hundreds of miles away at Padua, had naught to do with the murder. But his blood alone convicts him in the eyes of some, and Marguerite says there has been talk of charging him with collusion." With an obvious effort, Nell pushed herself away from the altar, straightened her shoulders. "I must return to our bedchamber now, for I have a letter to write. I do not know where I shall find the words, though. How do I tell my brother that I am sorry my sons murdered his?"

Ellen's breath broke on a shudder. "Mama, I am so sorry! You do not deserve this!"

Nell's mouth twisted. "If we got what we deserved in this life, Simon would be in Westminster and Henry in Hell. Look after Juliana, and Ellen . . . do not despair. We'll get through this somehow. You are Plantagenet and de Montfort, and a sword made from that steel is too finely tempered to break."

Juliana sank to her knees, and Ellen knelt beside her, holding the other girl as she wept. Her own eyes were dry. She'd once cried easily: for a sorrowful song, a beggar's hunger, a homeless dog. Now she knew that tears availed for naught.

"Where will he go, Ellen? What will he do?"

"I do not know."

Juliana shivered, crossed herself. "What greater sacrilege can there be than a killing in God's own House? Do you think God could ever forgive him?"

Ellen bit her lip. "It is not God's vengeance that they must fear now. It is my cousin's. Ned will follow them to Hades if need be."

THE ship carrying Edmund Plantagenet, Earl of Leicester and Lancaster, second son of the English King, entered the port of Palermo at mid-day. Edmund was awed by his first sight of Sicily. He'd been told that it was a beautiful land, and he found it so: mountains soaring into infinity, harbors of translucent turquoise, a landscape on fire with flowers. He knew that it was a rich land, too, blessed with iron and salt mines, sugar cane, cotton. And as he looked upon this exotic island city, Edmund felt a sharp stab of regret, for it might have been his.

Although he had little interest in the past, Edmund was well-versed in the history of Sicily. He knew it had been settled by the Phoenicians a thousand years before the birth of the Lord Christ, that it had been conquered by the Greeks, the Romans, the Saracens, and then the Normans. After the death of the Emperor Frederick, his empire had split asunder, and the Pope sought English support for his feud with Frederick's son by offering the throne of Naples and Sicily to Edmund, then a lad of nine. Henry had been thrilled by the prospect of obtaining a crown for his younger son. But the English barons balked, unwilling to fight a war and drain the Exchequer in order to make Edmund ruler of a foreign realm.

It had been a bitter disappointment for Henry, just one more grievance to tally up against Simon de Montfort's account. But Edmund soon came to terms with his loss. It was not that difficult, for his was an equable, genial nature, not given to grudges. Moreover, he might lack a coronet, but he did not lack for lands; Henry had bestowed upon him Simon de Montfort's estates, and those of Lancaster as well. Young, healthy, with a doting father, an elder brother he adored, an heiress for his child-bride, and two earldoms, he was indeed blessed, but it was his saving grace that he knew it—even on this April afternoon in Palermo harbor, gazing upon palm trees and flowering mimosa and lemon groves, a sight sure to beguile anyone accustomed to the cool grey mists and recurrent rains of England.

Edmund had been told that his brother was staying at La Favrah, a Norman palazzo a few miles southeast of Palermo. He was looking forward to his reunion with Edward, eager to fulfill his crusader's vow. But he was also somewhat apprehensive about his brother's frame of mind, for upon landing at Naples, he'd been told of the murder in Viterbo.

Edmund had not been that well acquainted with Hal, who was ten years his senior. He was shocked, though, by the circumstances of his cousin's death, and he knew that Edward would not rest until the de Montforts paid a blood debt. His brother had a temper to rival the eruptions of Sicily's Mount Etna. As little as he liked to admit it, he could see Edward, too, raging into a church in pursuit of an enemy, blind to all but his own fury.

But no . . . they said Hal had not resisted. Ned would not have struck down a defenseless man. A foe crossing swords with Ned had one chance of saving his life: surrender. In that, Guy de Montfort was utterly unlike Ned. Unlike his own father, for Edmund was sure that his uncle Simon would never have shed blood in a church. An ugly business, for certes. Poor Uncle Richard; it was his ill health that had been bringing Hal home. Sad, so sad. Well, at least Hal would be avenged. That was a certainty. He knew his brother.

La Favrah was the most magnificent palace Edmund had ever seen. It was surrounded on three sides by a vast man-made lake that stretched to the foot of Monte Grifone. The grounds were crisscrossed with fish-ponds, planted with oleanders and orange trees and cypress, and barges gilded gold and silver floated upon the waters of the lagoon. The residential part of the palace encircled a large courtyard. The walls were of bright Spanish tile and white Parian marble. Red mosaics lined the pathways, and wherever Edmund's eye alighted, he saw cascading fountains, strutting peacocks, and graceful arcades adorned with honeycomb tracery. It was beautiful beyond compare, but in an alien, Arabic sort of way; Edmund had the uneasy sensation that a mosque would look more at home here than a chapel.

A tall, elegantly gowned woman was walking by one of the fountains. She smiled at sight of him, held out her hands in welcome. Edmund did not begrudge his brother the English crown—not often—but he did occasionally envy him his wife, for not only was Eleanora an alluring beauty in the dark Spanish style, she was utterly devoted to Edward, pledged to him heart, body, and soul. The best proof of her devotion was that she had left their three small children behind in England, knowing she would not see them for years, rather than be separated from Edward. Of course that could just be common sense, Edmund acknowledged wryly. Ned might be a loving husband, but he was not always a faithful one. Better to keep him close, lest temptation beckon. Kissing Eleanora's hand, he began to laugh, having belatedly become aware of her swelling silhouette.

"Ned did not tell me! When is the babe due?"

"Mid-summer, or so the midwife says. Eduardo tried to persuade me to remain here whilst he returns to the Holy Land. But I prevailed upon him, and we expect to sail for Acre within the fortnight." Eleanora had come to England as a child-bride of ten, but her voice still held echoes of her native Castile. "Edmundo . . . do you know?"

When he nodded, she sighed. "Never have I seen Eduardo so wroth," she confessed. "He is in council, making plans for his campaign against the infidel. Come, I shall take you to him." And linking her arm in his, she led him across the courtyard toward a spacious south-west hall.

Edmund was not surprised by the raised voices; his brother's strategy sessions tended to be turbulent. The men with Edward were well-known to him: Thomas de Clare, Erard de Valery, and William de Lusignan, Earl of Pembroke. The first was a friend, the younger and

more amenable brother of the Earl of Gloucester. The second was a
French knight who had the dubious distinction of having once saved
Guy de Montfort's life. And the third was a kinsman, Henry's half-
brother and their uncle, a man detested by virtually every Englishman
who'd had the bad fortune to cross paths with him.

They were all arguing with Edward, each in his own fashion—
Thomas reasoning, Erard joking, and William de Lusignan blustering—
but Edmund knew none were likely to prevail. His brother might not
yet have a king's crown, but he did have a king's will. So imperial was
his bearing, so regal and forceful his demeanor, that people sometimes
forgot he was a king-in-waiting, forgot the frail, aging shadow who
blocked Edward's emergence into the sun. It saddened Edmund that
their father's last days should be so meaningless, that he should be
reduced to the status of a caretaker king, or worse, a ghost lingering
beyond his time. Despite his manifest failings as a monarch, Henry had
been a loving father, and Edmund ached for his twilight impotence,
while understanding why England yearned for Edward's reign.

Not that it had always been so. Edmund knew there'd been a time
when men dreaded the day that Edward would be King. Edmund had
no memories himself of his brother's lawless youth; he'd been just a
child. But he'd heard the stories. Edward's escapades had gone far
beyond the usual hell-raising expected of young men of rank. Galloping
through villages at midnight, making enough clamor to awaken the
dead. Appropriating wagons and abandoning them in cemeteries. Playing cat-and-mouse with the City Watch, getting drunk in Southwark
whorehouses. Edward had done it all. But then his games took on darker
tones. The brawling was no longer in sport. There was an ugly incident
at Wallingford Priory, where monks were beaten and wine casks looted.
There were reports of women being molested. And then a young man
who'd somehow incurred Edward's displeasure was cruelly mutilated
by Edward's servants, at Edward's command. And as these accounts
were bruited about, people began to cross themselves and shiver at the
thought of Edward wielding the manifold powers of kingship.

But such fears had been—for the most part—laid to rest during
those tumultuous months between the battle of Lewes, in which Simon
de Montfort scored a stunning victory over the forces of the Crown, and
the battle of Evesham. Held hostage while Simon vainly sought to win
him as ally, Edward had contrived a daring escape, and brought Simon
to bay after a campaign brilliant in conception, flawless in execution.
Men had called Simon de Montfort the "greatest soldier in Christendom." After Evesham, they began to say the same of Edward. It was
Edmund's belief that the civil war had been for Edward a crucible, a
trial by fire in which the sins of youth were burned away and his true

manhood emerged from the ashes, as it was meant to be. For others, Edward's renowned skill with a sword was enough; much could be overlooked in a battle commander of Edward's caliber.

As Edmund stepped forward, Edward was the first to glance up. "Well, now," he said, "if it is not the prodigal sheep!" The other men looked understandably baffled, for that was an old family joke, the result of Edmund's childish confusion between the biblical prodigal son and the proverbial lost sheep. Edmund was not surprised that Edward had remembered; his memory was as sharp as his sword. He grinned, moved to embrace his brother.

Edward's bear hug took his breath. He was five feet, nine inches, the same height as their father, but Edward stood several fingers above six feet, so tall that men called him "longshanks." They were as unlike in appearance as they were in temperament. In childhood, Edward's hair had been as fair as Edmund's, but it had later darkened, was now a brownish-black, although in full sunlight, his beard still showed red-gold flecks. His eyes were a pale, clear blue like Henry's, and like Henry, one eyelid drooped drowsily. A slight speech impediment—a faint lisp—which would have put another man at a distinct disadvantage, was in Edward an irrelevancy, so impressive was his physique, so dominant his personality. White teeth flashed now as he laughed, throwing his head back, enveloping Edmund in another exuberant hug.

"By God, lad, it's glad I am to see you! What word from England?"

"I have a casket full of letters for you. Mama is thriving, as ever. But Papa is still ailing, and so is Uncle Richard. When he hears about Hal, it's like to kill him, Ned."

"You know, then." Edward's voice was flat. "All of it?" Edmund nodded quickly, hoping thus to avert a gory reenactment of the crime. He would rather not dwell upon the brutal details of his cousin's death, although he was unwilling to admit this, lest the other men think him squeamish or soft. Edward had begun to pace back and forth, taking long, sweeping strides, every line of his body communicating his outrage. He had yet to notice his wife, who seemed content to wait until he did.

"What I cannot understand," Edward said suddenly, "is why Hal did not fight back. If it had been me . . ." He shook his head, then gave Edmund a look of such searing intensity that his brother was thankful he was not the real recipient. "I would have bartered my very soul for a chance to cross swords with Guy de Montfort," he said, and none doubted him.

Moving to the window, Edward stood for some moments, staring out at the silver-sheened lake. "I would that I could lead the hunt to track them down. But my army awaits me at Acre. Charles has promised, though, that he'll see them brought to justice. Christ pity him if he does not, for I've sworn a holy oath that the de Montforts shall pay for Hal's murder, every one of them, and I—"

"Every one of them? Surely not Aunt Nell, too?" Edmund blurted out uneasily, and Edward gestured impatiently.

"Of course not. Aunt Nell would not have countenanced such a killing." After a pause, he said grudgingly, "And neither would Simon." An acknowledgment to an enemy did not come easily to Edward; moving back to the table, he reached for a cup of sweet red wine, swallowed to take the taste away. "There was a time, though, when I would have said the same of Bran . . ."

William de Lusignan laughed. "I hear he has not drawn a sober breath in years. He was probably so besotted he thought the blood-letting to be some quaint Italian custom, part of the Mass!"

Edmund and Thomas and Erard looked at him in distaste, the first two because they detested him, Erard because he had been Bran's friend. But then, so had Edward—once. He was staring out onto the lake again, eyes narrowed against the white Sicilian sun. "It was mainly Guy's doing," he said. "I know that, for I know Guy, God rot his misbegotten soul! But the fact that his guilt is greater does not excuse Bran or Amaury. They, too, have a debt to pay, and I shall see that they do."

"Amaury, too?" Edmund gasped, horrified that a priest might have taken part in a church killing. "I heard naught of Amaury at Naples!"

Erard shifted uncomfortably in his seat, wanting to speak up for Amaury, but loath to remind Edward of his friendship with the de Montforts. Thomas was reluctant, too, to intervene, but he'd been bur-dened with an innate sense of fairness. "Ned, you know there is no proof whatsoever that Amaury was—"

Edward spun around. "Proof? He is Simon de Montfort's spawn, is he not? What more proof do I need? When I think of all that man has to answer for, the evil ideas he brought to England like some noxious French pox, the way he tried to cripple the God-given powers of king-ship, I know he must be burning in eternal hellfire!"

By then the others had realized he was speaking not of Amaury, but of Simon. "He would have torn asunder the very foundation of the realm, dashed us down into hellish chaos and darkness! Look at the allies he drew to him: the London rabble, Oxford students, unlettered village priests, Welsh rebels. But not men of good birth, not men of the peerage. And yet there are people who still hold his memory dear, who have made him into a martyr, who bleat that he died for them and their precious Runnymede Charter, for their 'liberties.' If Simon de Montfort is a saint, then I'm the living, breathing incarnation of Christ Jesus the

Redeemer! But fools flourish in England like the green bay tree, and still he wreaks havoc upon us, even now from the grave."

None had dared to interrupt. When Edward at last fell silent, Eleanora crossed to his side, wiped away with gentle fingers the perspiration that trickled down his temples. He looked exhausted by his outburst, by this continuing struggle to defeat a phantom foe five years dead.

"Do you know whom I truly blame for Hal's death? Simon de Montfort, for it was he who led us to the cliff's edge. He's beyond my powers to punish. But his sons are not, and I shall see them in Hell. This I swear upon the surety of Hal's soul."

5

TALAMONE, THE MAREMMA, TUSCANY

May 1271

OTHER men might envision Hell as a subterranean underworld, an abyss filled with flames and rivers of boiling blood. But to Hugh, Hell would forever after be the bleak, low-lying marshes of the Maremma.

Hugh was not alone in hating it, this vast, barren swampland stretching north from Viterbo, south from Siena, a haven for snakes, wild boar, and pestilent fevers. Men who'd remained loyal to Bran, even after Viterbo, balked at the Maremma, and their numbers dwindled daily.

None knew exactly what had passed between Bran and his brother; Bran said nothing and not even the bravest man dared to breach his frozen silence. That the rupture had come surprised no one, for Guy had taken a bitter satisfaction in his act of vengeance, and Bran, once he'd sobered up, was sickened by it. Most of their men made the predictable and pragmatic decision to remain at Sovana Castle with Guy and his powerful father-in-law. But a score of knights had elected to follow Bran.

These die-hard loyalists had not bargained upon the Maremma, though, had not bargained upon endless, empty days under a searing sun, a landscape of windswept desolation, muddy bogs, reed-choked ponds of stagnant water. The impoverished port of Orbetello, the shabby coastal village of Talamone, the inland town of Grosseto, then back to Talamone—theirs was an aimless wandering without purpose or plan, and to the disgruntled, uneasy men, it began to seem like the accursed odyssey of Cain. Bran shrugged off their queries, ignored their protests, and as their patience waned, one by one they slipped away. By this hot, humid Whitsunday in late May, they had all forsaken Bran but two— Hugh and a French knight, Sir Roger de Valmy.

Hugh had risen early, eager to escape the oppressive atmosphere of their inn. He'd meandered about the harbor for a while, practicing his Tuscan upon obliging passersby. Out of sheer boredom, he stopped to help the blacksmith shoe a recalcitrant filly and then drew well water for an elderly widow. When several youths invited him to join in a rough-and-tumble game of palone, he was quick to accept.

Hugh was still surprised by the continuing friendliness of the Tuscan people. They were unabashedly curious about the Viterbo murder, but he found none of the hostility he'd expected. While he encountered no one who condoned the killing, he met no one who did not understand it, either. Blood-feuds were too familiar to shock. A pity, all agreed, before pointing out that it would not have happened if the Earl's body had not been so foully abused at Evesham. Two sides of the same coin, no? Men crossed themselves, then shrugged.

For several hours the boys tossed a football back and forth. By the time the game broke up, Hugh was sweaty and out of breath and limping from a particularly energetic tackle, but happier than he'd been in weeks. His conscience was beginning to prickle, though, and he headed back toward the inn, in case Bran might have need of him. Reaching the stables, he detoured to check upon their horses, and it was there that he found Sir Roger de Valmy, saddling his stallion.

Hugh could not conceal his dismay. "You are leaving?"

The Frenchman nodded. "I ought to have gone weeks ago, but I kept hoping Bran would come to his senses." Buckling the saddle girth, he stepped from the shadows. A dark, stocky man of middle height, his most notable feature was an ugly scar, one that twisted his mouth askew, into a sinister smile that could not have been more deceptive, for he was by nature affable, generous, and perceptive. "Look, lad," he said slowly, "I like Bran. But he is drifting into deep water, and I am not willing to drown with him."

Hugh saw there was no point in arguing. "Where will you go?"

"South. Charles keeps his court at Naples. I mean to seek him out, offer him my sword. I've fought for him in the past; he knows my worth."

"But . . . but are you not afraid to face him? After Viterbo . . ."

De Valmy smiled. "Have you not wondered, Hugh, why there was no pursuit? Why no efforts have been made to track Bran and Guy down? Oh, I daresay Charles disapproved of the killing. But no king willingly loses a good battle commander, and Guy de Montfort is one of the best. I'd wager a thousand livres—if I had it—that Charles is going to wait for the furor to die down, for men to forget, and then, lo and behold, Guy will turn up in his service again."

Hugh was shocked by de Valmy's cynicism. "But Guy and Bran have been outlawed, their lands forfeit!"

De Valmy shrugged. "Yes, but you did not see Charles laying siege to Sovana Castle, did you? No, if Charles does not in time restore Guy to favor, it'll be only because he could find no way to appease Edward, not because of his moral outrage over the murder."

"What of Bran? Does he know you're going?"

De Valmy nodded again. "He did not even blink," he said, then swung up into the saddle. "You're a good lad, Hugh, and I'm in need of a squire. Come with me."

"I thank you, Sir Roger. But I cannot."

De Valmy did not look surprised. "No, I suppose not. But I did want you to have a choice, lad," he said, and rode out of the stable.

His leaving sent Hugh's spirits plummeting. What would happen now? What were they going to do? He could not bring himself to face Bran, not yet, and he followed de Valmy into the blinding, white sunlight.

The rest of the day passed in a blur. He spent much of it sitting on a secluded, rocky beach just east of the village. Lying back upon the hot sand, he stared out to sea, watched gulls circle and squabble overhead, flung shells into the surf, and sought to convince himself that a happy ending was still within Bran's grasp. He had in fact devised a plan, but he'd so far lacked the courage to broach the subject with Bran, for never had Bran been so unapproachable as in the weeks after Viterbo. As always, he kept his grieving to himself, and thus made it impossible for others to offer any sort of comfort. Hugh could only look upon his silent sorrowing, his daily drinking, and hope for a miracle.

He dozed for a time, awoke with a start, with the guilty realization that this was Whitsunday and he'd not yet attended Mass. But what came to him next was worse. He'd been gone nigh on all day. What if Bran thought he'd ridden off with Sir Roger? Jumping to his feet, he started to run.

Their room was the best in the inn, but that wasn't saying much. The chamber was cramped and cluttered and stifling, for Bran had not bothered to unshutter the lone window. A reeking tallow candle was burning down toward the wick, a tray of untouched food had been dumped by the door, and several empty wine flagons lay scattered amidst the floor rushes. Bran was sprawled, fully dressed, upon the bed. Gaunt and unshaven, he looked like a stranger to Hugh, looked unnervingly like his brother Guy. The narrowed eyes were bloodshot, unfriendly. "So," he said, "you're still here, are you?"

He sounded like a stranger, too; there was a harsh, mocking edge to his voice that Hugh had never heard before. "Of course I am here, my lord."

"Why?"

Hugh blinked. "My lord?"

"A simple enough question, I should think. I asked why you did not go with Roger."

Hugh had been poised to begin removing some of the litter. Instead, he straightened up, eying Bran warily. Drink had always acted as a buffer for Bran, isolating him behind a moat of ale and wine, not as fuel for an erratic temper, as Hugh had once feared. He did not know how to handle this sudden wine-soaked sarcasm. After glancing down at one of the empty flagons, he said, "I would not leave you, my lord."

Bran gave a hoarse, rasping laugh. "Faithful to the grave, eh, Hugh? But did it ever occur to you that I do not want it, that steadfast, suffocating loyalty of yours? Christ, do not look at me like that! The truth is that I needed a squire, instead got a wet-nurse, and am heartily sick of it."

Hugh didn't speak; he couldn't. His silence seemed to spur Bran on. Sitting up, he said impatiently, "Do you not understand what I am saying? Go home to England, Hugh, where you belong." And when the boy just stood there, staring at him, he reached for a leather pouch, flung it at Hugh. "For services rendered, a debt paid in full. Now what are you waiting for? I no longer want you with me, am bone-weary of your infernal hovering. How much more plainly can I speak than that?"

Hugh caught the pouch, but it was an unthinking act. He looked at Bran, then kicked aside the flagon at his feet, turned, and bolted from the chamber. He went down the stairs so fast that only the reflexes of youth kept him from taking a headlong fall, and he did trip over the inn's aged dog, sound asleep in the doorway. The animal awoke with a snarl, its yellowed fangs snapping at Hugh's outstretched fingers, grazing his thumb. Hugh never felt the bite, did not notice the blood on his sleeve until hours later.

He would have no recollection of saddling his horse. He took the road toward Grosseto, but that was not a conscious choice, either. Grosseto was only fifteen miles away, but Hugh did not reach it until dusk, for he'd allowed his horse to set its own pace. He was half-way there before he remembered his belongings, back in Bran's chamber. But nothing on earth could have induced him to return to Talamone.

The first inn he tried was full, but the inn-keeper offered to let him sleep on the floor of the common room for a reduced rate. There were other inns in Grosseto, but Hugh didn't bother to check them out. The inn-keeper's wife made supper for the guests, but Hugh had no appetite. He'd left his bedroll at Talamone, bought a blanket from the inn-keeper, and passed the longest night of his life, listening to the snores of nearby sleepers, the yowling of stray cats, occasional bursts of barking, the wind rattling loose shutters, the creaking on the stairs as men stumbled down to use the outdoor privy.

He awoke soon after dawn, so tired he ached. During those endless hours in the dark, he'd sought to summon up anger, resentment, outrage. But it was still too soon. All he felt was a stunned sense of betrayal.

The smell of baking bread reminded him now that he'd not eaten for fully a day. As he sat up, stiff from a night on the floor, his brain, too, seemed to be stirring at last. It was a foolish move, going to Grosseto. He ought to have headed south, sought to overtake Sir Roger. Did he want to stay in Italy, though? Bran's taunting words came back at him, "home to England." Home. But what did England hold for him? His father's grave and lands no longer his.

It occurred to him suddenly that even if he wanted to, he might not have the money to return to England. He'd forgotten about Bran's pouch, paying for his lodgings out of his own meagre funds. As he unfastened it now from his belt, he frowned at the unexpected weight. For a moment he balanced it in the palm of his hand, and even before he pulled the drawstring, he could feel the hairs beginning to rise along the back of his neck. The pouch was crammed with coins, too many to count, more money than he'd ever seen.

As Hugh dismounted, the Talamone inn-keeper burst through the doorway, waving his arms, gesturing back toward the inn. His speech was so rapid that Hugh could understand little of what he said. But the man's agitation only confirmed the worst of Hugh's fears. Handing over his reins, he hastened inside, taking the stairs three at a time.

The room was in darkness. Striding to the window, he jerked open the shutters. One glance at the man on the bed and he whirled toward the door, shouting for blankets and hot wine. Snatching up his forgotten bedroll, he covered Bran with blankets, then added Bran's mantle. But Bran's chills showed no signs of abating. He was shivering so violently that the bed itself was shaking, and when the inn-keeper brought up the hot wine, his teeth were chattering too much for him to manage more than a swallow or two.

There was no doctor in Talamone. But Hugh did not need a doctor to diagnose Bran's ailment. Some called it ague, others tertian or quartan fever. Hugh was familiar with the symptoms; Brother Mark had enjoyed tutoring his young infirmary helpers. But he'd never before seen anyone stricken with the ague, as it was much more prevalent in the English Fenlands than in the Evesham vale. He understood now why tertian fever stirred such superstitious fears in men, for Bran did indeed seem possessed, so intense were the tremors convulsing his body.

The chills continued for almost an hour before giving way to fever. As Bran struggled weakly to escape the coverlets, Hugh hastily bent over the bed, jerking the blankets off. "Here, my lord," he said, "try to drink this."

Bran swallowed with difficulty, then lay still, watching the boy as he began to soak cold compresses. "You were a fool to come back, Hugh," he said huskily.

"You're a fine one to talk about foolishness!" Hugh snapped, then almost dropped the water laver, so astounded was he by his own words. But the corner of Bran's mouth was twitching. Bringing the compresses to the bed, he put one of the wet cloths upon Bran's forehead. "When did you have the first attack, my lord?"

"On Saturday, whilst you and Roger were in Grosseto."

"It is a tertian fever then, for the quartan fever recurs every fourth day. If we can only find some cinquefoil leaves—"

Bran reached out, caught Hugh's wrist. The boy could not suppress a gasp, so hot was Bran's skin. How could the body be freezing one moment, on fire the next? "Tertian fever, quartan fever—does it matter? What does is that it is contagious, Hugh! Do you not realize the risk?"

"We do not know that for certes, my lord. Anyway, I've had it already."

"Did you now? Doubtless due to all that time you spent in the great swamps of Evesham. Hugh, this is no game!"

"I know that! I do understand the risk, and I accept it. Now you can insult and mock me again, but it will avail you naught, for I'll not leave you. My lord, I have to say this straight out. What you did was brave, but it was crazy, too." Hugh paused for breath, amazed by his own daring. "I've had my say. Get angry if you will. But when your anger's done, I'll still be here."

He waited tensely, soon saw that the emotion Bran was fighting was not anger. Perching on the edge of the bed, he carefully checked Bran's compresses, while mentally polishing the plea he was about to make. "My lord, I know this is not the best time, but we need to talk. This is what I think we must do. As soon as your fever breaks, we must go to Grosseto, find a doctor. Then, once you have recovered, we must go to Siena, must—"

The corner of Bran's mouth twitched again. "Missing Serafina, are you, lad?"

Hugh refused to be distracted. "My lord, I am serious! I ask your pardon for speaking bluntly again, but I know no other way to say this. Since the . . . since Viterbo, I have been remembering what I learned at the abbey school about the murder of the Archbishop of Canterbury, Thomas à Becket."

He heard Bran's indrawn breath, and hurried on, before he lost his nerve. "I expect you know the story, my lord, how four of King Henry's knights decided to kill the Archbishop after hearing the King cry in a fit of rage, 'Will none rid me of this turbulent priest?' But did you know that after the deed was done and the Archbishop lay dead before the Cathedral altar, one of the knights, a man named de Tracy, set out at once for Rome, where he sought absolution from the Pope?"

Bran had not interrupted, and Hugh took heart from that. "Do you not see, my lord? Why can you not do the same? Since there is no new pope yet, I propose that we go to the Bishop of Siena, that you confess your sins, tell him of your remorse, and ask him to impose a penance upon you. Then you do as he directs, whether it be a crusade, a pilgrimage, whatever."

Hugh almost blurted out his belief that the Bishop would be sure to absolve Bran, for his contrition was beyond doubting and the greatest guilt lay with Guy, but he stopped just in time, knowing that Bran blamed no one but himself. "You must agree, my lord," he pleaded, "for it is your only chance. Once you satisfy the Bishop's penance, you'll be at peace again!"

Bran knew better. But he could not bring himself to deny the boy this last shred of hope, for Hugh's eyes were shining with certainty, with the affecting innocence of unquestioning faith. "I agree," he said wearily. "We shall go to Siena, seek out the Bishop. But not later; now, as soon as I am able to ride . . ."

Hugh started to object, thought better of it. "As you wish, my lord," he agreed, rising to change the compress. Bran's forehead was searing to the touch, and he could tell Bran was in sudden pain by the way he averted his eyes from the light, tangled his fist in the sheets. Remembering that severe, blinding headaches were a symptom of the ague, Hugh hastened to close the shutters, then went to find the inn-keeper, seeking chamomile and rue, herbs said to ease head pains.

For the next four hours, Bran's fever burned higher and higher, then broke as suddenly as it had begun. Bran was soon drenched in sweat, almost at once fell into an exhausted sleep. Hugh pulled a chair up to keep a bedside vigil and to plot strategy.

They'd have to pass through Grosseto on the way to Siena. Once they were there, mayhap he could coax Bran into remaining till he was fully recovered. But what if he could not? Men oft-times went on holy pilgrimages barefoot, their bleeding footsteps trailing painful proof of their devotion, their willingness to suffer for God's favor. Bran might well see his quest in the same light, might think that a fevered trek would mean more to the Almighty.

If so, at least they'd be able to get medicine from Grosseto's doctor ere they set out. Siena was about fifty miles away. With Bran's attacks coming every other day, they ought to be able to cover fifteen or twenty miles on his fever-free days. The weather was no threat, warm by day, mild by night, so camping out would present no problem. And if Bran did take a turn for the worse whilst on the road, there was a Cistercian abbey at San Galgano, about half-way to Siena, and monks were adept at healing.

Hugh smiled at that, thinking fondly of Brother Mark. No, however he looked at it, their prospects seemed promising, and for the first time in more than two months, he dared to let himself hope. Men did die of tertian fever. But it was not an inevitable death sentence, not like consumption or cancers or spotted fever. And Bran was young and healthy. Why should he not recover? Hugh was getting sleepy himself, but he thought to add a drowsy "God willing," lest the Lord think him impertinent.

THE doctor in Grosseto did not inspire Hugh with confidence. He seemed as old as Methuselah, spoke no French, and was taciturn even in his own Tuscan. After he tried to bleed Bran and botched it, puncturing Bran's arm repeatedly before he was able to find a vein, Hugh was not all that disappointed when he refused to accompany them to Siena.

The malarial fever struck on schedule, the day after their arrival in Grosseto. At Bran's insistence, they set out on the following morning for Siena. Because Bran had to stop and rest so often, they were not able to cover as much ground as Hugh had hoped; he guessed they'd made only about fifteen miles by nightfall. The next day Hugh built a bonfire to ease Bran's chills, meticulously measured out doses of the doctor's herbs, betony and sage, which he then mixed in strong ale. He had not tried very hard to dissuade Bran from starting for Siena, for he was half-afraid that if they loitered too long in Grosseto, Bran might change his mind about seeking absolution.

Hugh was faintly ashamed that Bran's illness should give him so much hope. But he'd begun to despair that Bran would ever come back from wherever he'd gone after the killing in Viterbo. Now those dark silences had been banished by the ague. On his fever-free days, Bran was no longer a stranger; he listened, joked, even laughed occasionally. And soon they'd be in Siena, where Bran could confess to the Bishop; then all would be well. There was no reason why he could not visit Serafina again, too, whilst they were in the city.

That Friday eve optimism was not to last, though. By the next day, Hugh's cheerful assurance had begun to falter. He'd not anticipated how rapidly these assaults of chills and fever would sap Bran's strength. He tired so easily that they managed to travel less than ten miles. On Sunday his seizures were more severe, more prolonged, than any that had come before; his fever burned out of control from noon till dusk, and, for the first time, he was stricken with bouts of nausea. On the following day he was weaker still. Each time he dismounted to rest, he found it harder to get back into the saddle, and by early afternoon, he was so exhausted that they had to halt, thus losing precious hours of daylight.

That night they both slept badly, and they awoke on Tuesday to a sky marbled by clouds. Bran's chills began in mid-morning. In vain Hugh stoked their fire higher, piled blanket after blanket upon Bran's trembling body. He found the chills more frightening than the fever; it seemed to defy the very laws of nature, that a man could be shivering so under a summer sun. They had camped beside a shallow stream, and when Bran began to throw off the blankets, Hugh soaked compresses in the clear, cold water, fought the fever as best he could. This was the worst day yet; for a time Bran was delirious, drifting in and out of fevered dreams as Hugh desperately doubled the doses of betony, and clouds continued to gather overhead.

Hugh kept an uneasy eye upon that darkening sky, for they'd left the Maremma behind, were in the highlands now, which meant that nights would be much cooler. What if it rained? If Bran got soaked in a downpour, could he survive a night out in the open? A distant rumbling of thunder stirred him to action, and he knelt by Bran's side.

"My lord, can you hear me? I must leave you for a while, must find us some shelter ere that storm breaks. There is a wineskin right here. I'll not be gone long."

Bran's world was shot through with hot colors and swirling mist. It was not unpleasant, though, a slow spiraling down into the dark. But someone would not let him be; he could hear his own name, oddly muted, as if echoing from a great distance. He didn't want to heed it, to come back. But a hand was gripping his shoulder. His lashes seemed sealed with stones; he struggled to raise them, to focus on the white, tense face floating above him.

"Thank God! I was so scared when I could not wake you . . ." Grabbing the wineskin, Hugh tilted it to Bran's lips. "My lord, listen. I found a shepherd and he says there is a castle not a mile from here. Lord Bran, can you try to stand? If we can just get you onto your horse . . ."

The lad might as well ask him to sprout wings and fly to Siena. The mere thought of moving was enough to give Bran a queasy pang; he wondered, with impersonal curiosity, if a man could get seasick on horseback. But Hugh looked so earnest, as if the world's fate hung upon his answer. A pity to let the lad down . . . He made an enormous effort, said faintly, "Why not?"

THE shepherd's "castello" was a small manor fortified with a weed-choked moat. As they approached the drawbridge, an unseen sentry ordered them to halt. A moment later he appeared in the doorway, a tall, rangy youth, hand on sword hilt. He lost his swagger, though, as soon as he got a good look at Bran. Shaking his head, he began to back up, waving them away from the castle. Hugh dismounted in dismay and started onto the drawbridge, entreating the guard to wait. But the man had already disappeared. Hugh was still on the drawbridge when the portcullis dropped down, barring the entrance.

For a moment Hugh stared at the portcullis, and then all the fear and tension and strain of the past weeks exploded in a wild rage, unlike anything he'd ever experienced. He could see the guard through the portcullis bars; had he been within reach, he'd have flung himself at the man's throat. "You must give my lord entry! He'll die without shelter!" But in his fury, he'd forgotten his Tuscan. The surging torrent of French meant nothing to the guard; he shrugged, started to walk away.

Hugh slammed his fist against the portcullis bars. "Damn you, wait!" A Tuscan curse came back to him then, obscene enough to spin the guard around in outrage. "Tell your castellan that Sir Simon de Montfort, Earl of Leicester and Lord of Avellino, seeks admittance!" Hugh shouted, in an uneven mix of French and Tuscan. At mention of his father's forfeit title and his own confiscated Italian fief, Bran laughed suddenly, a sound that chilled Hugh to the very bone. "My lord is kinsman to Ildebrandino d'Aldobrandini, Count of Sovana and Pitigliano! Turn him away and, by God, you'll long regret it!"

His threat had not yet died away before lightning stabbed the clouds above their heads, followed by a resounding crash of thunder. Hugh whirled as Bran cried out, reached him just as he started to slide from the saddle. Fortunately, Bran's stallion was well trained; it stood its ground as Hugh struggled to lower his lord onto the grass. Lightning blazed again, and Bran saw the sky through a blinding shower of blue-white sparks. He could feel rain upon his skin now, a blessed relief, so cool it was. Hugh's face was wet, too, although with tears or rain he couldn't tell. The boy's anguish was his last regret; he yearned to make Hugh see that it was all right, that there was no need to grieve so.

Cradling Bran's head in his lap, Hugh began to stammer whatever assurances he could think of, vowing to find the shepherd's hut. But he knew better, knew Bran was going to die there, out in the rain by the castle's mud-churned moat, a stone's throw from safety. It was then that he heard it—the sound of a windlass, straining to raise the portcullis gate.

He did not dare to move, afraid to let himself hope. But several hooded figures had now emerged onto the drawbridge. Heedless of the gusting rain, the man in the lead strode toward them, knelt by Bran's side.

"You are the Earl of Leicester's son, in truth?" he demanded, in accented but understandable French. His eyes searched Bran's face, found what he sought. Straightening up abruptly, he beckoned to his reluctant servants. "I apologize for my man's conduct. When he saw you were ailing, he feared the fever's contagion. You are welcome at my hearth, for as long as you wish."

"Why?" Bran whispered.

"I knew your lord father," the castellan said simply, as if that explained all, and ordered his men to assist Bran into the castle.

Hugh had been stricken dumb by the sheer intensity of his relief. But then, to his horror, he heard Bran say, "No . . . wait. I must tell . . . tell you first what I did . . ."

He had no breath for more, but the castellan understood. "You do not take advantage of my hospitality. I know about Viterbo. But that is between you and God."

They were all drenched by now. Sheets of rain were blowing sideways, sharp as needles. Lightning split a cypress tree upon a distant slope, and an acrid, burning odor hung upon the air. Men were bringing a litter from the castle, and the castellan was instructing one of the guards to ride for Siena, to fetch a doctor from the hospital of Santa Maria della Scala. Now that Bran's fate was in more competent hands than his,

Hugh was content merely to watch, to relinquish a responsibility too burdensome for any fifteen-year-old. Salvation come so suddenly had left him dazed. He could think only that Simon de Montfort had somehow managed a miracle in his son's hour of greatest need.

HUGH stood at an open window, gazing out upon sunlit hills and dappled olive groves. A night's sleep in a real bed, a huge breakfast, and the reemergence of the summer sun had been enough to send his spirits soaring, and his step was light, jaunty, as he mounted the stairs to Bran's bedchamber.

The room was shadowed, peaceful. "Does he still sleep?" Hugh whispered, and the castellan nodded. They stood for a time in silence, watching the man on the bed. Hugh was still marveling that they owed their deliverance to Simon de Montfort rather than Count Ildebrandino. "May I ask how you knew Earl Simon, my lord?"

The castellan beckoned him away from the bed. "We fought together in Palestine. In fact, we sailed on the same ship for the Holy Land. His lady had accompanied him as far as Brindisi, doubtless would have gone on crusade, too, had she not been great with child! Thirty years ago, it was, but I remember him well. A remarkable man, in truth. Did you know the citizens of Jerusalem asked him to be their governor?"

Hugh nodded, and then laughed. "I just realized—that was Bran his lady mother was expecting! He told me once that he was born in Italy."

An indistinct murmuring drew them back to the bed. "Ought the doctor to be here soon?" Hugh whispered, leaning over to smooth Bran's blankets. He straightened up almost at once. "Why is he so hot? This is one of his fever-free days . . ." He looked pleadingly at the castellan, had his answer in the older man's averted eyes, his sympathetic silence.

THE doctor came slowly down the stairs, sank into the closest chair. Looking over at the castellan, he shook his head. "I've done all I can. I even bled him again, but . . ." He shrugged expressively.

The castellan was gazing across the hall, searching out the boy amidst the shadows. Hugh had not moved for hours, refusing food or drink, all attempts at comfort. "I'll have to tell the lad," he said reluctantly, and the doctor pushed himself out of the chair.

"I'll tell him. You'd best fetch your chaplain."

Hugh did not look up, even when the doctor squatted down beside him. "I'm sorry, lad. He is in God's hands now. But as weak as he is,

I do not see how he can survive the morrow's onslaught of chills and fever . . ."

Hugh said nothing, hunched his shoulders when the doctors patted his arm in an awkward gesture of condolence. "I do not believe you," he said, almost inaudibly. The doctor sighed, did not argue. Hugh had his face against his drawn-up knees, clinging desperately to his disbelief. There was another strained silence, and then the castellan was coming swiftly toward them, trailed by a flustered priest.

"No!" Hugh was on his feet. "He's not dead, he's not!"

"No . . . not yet." The castellan was too agitated for diplomacy or discretion. "But he's gone stark mad, refuses to see my chaplain, refuses to be shriven!"

The doctor swore softly. For a long moment, they looked at one another, and on each man's face, shock warred with appalled awe. As horrified as they were by Bran's refusal, they could not help seeing it as the ultimate gesture of atonement, for what greater sacrifice could a man make than to deny himself salvation? The chaplain shivered, hastily crossed himself.

Hugh had been slow to comprehend the meaning of the castellan's words. When he did, he shoved the men aside, started for the stairs at a dead run.

Bran's chamber was lit by candles. They flared up as Hugh flung the door open; several guttered out. Hugh did not hesitate. Approaching the bed, he said, "You cannot do this, my lord. The fever has clouded your wits. But there is still time—"

Bran started to shake his head and gasped, for the movement triggered a blinding flash of pain. Black hair fell forward over his eyes, but he had not the strength to brush it back. He'd begun to think of the bed as a boat, in his feverish imaginings, envisioned its moorings snapping, one by one, until only a solitary line kept it from drifting out to sea. For hours, he'd been waiting for that final hawser to fray enough to break. But now he sought to hold on for a while longer, for the boy's sake.

Hugh sat on the edge of the bed. "Do you not remember what you told me in that Sienese bordello? You said there were few sins so great that God could not forgive. God will pardon your sins, too, my lord— if you'll but give Him the chance."

Bran's lips moved, and Hugh leaned forward, caught only, "God might, he'd not . . ."

Those few words had come with such obvious effort that Hugh grew alarmed. "No, my lord, just listen, save your breath for the priest." Reaching over, he smoothed the hair away from Bran's forehead. " 'He'd not,' " he repeated. "Do you mean . . . your lord father?"

Bran's lips parted again; they were cracked and swollen, blistered by fever.

Hugh was beginning to understand. "You think your father would not forgive you for Evesham or Viterbo. That I do not know, my lord. But this I can say for certes—that Earl Simon could never forgive you for the sin you are about to commit!"

Bran was struggling to speak, and Hugh grasped his hand. "What of your lady mother and your sister? Is it not enough they must mourn your death? How could they live with it, knowing your soul was damned to Hell for all eternity? If you inflict pain like that upon women who love you, Earl Simon will not be the only one unable to forgive you. Neither will I!"

Bran's lashes quivered. His eyes were as dark as Hugh had ever seen them, a fever-glazed grey. "My father . . ." Hugh bent over; Bran's breath just reached his ear. "He'd have liked you, lad," he whispered, and Hugh bit his lip, tasting blood. A creaking hinge warned him that they were no longer alone, and he turned, saw the priest hovering anxiously in the doorway. Hugh reluctantly released his grip on Bran's hand, but made no attempt to wipe away the tears streaking his face.

"I'll leave you now, my lord," he said, as steadily as he could, "so you may make your peace with God."

LAMMAS DAY, the first of August, was one of the most popular festivals of high summer. At Morrow Mass, the priests of Montargis had blessed the loaves of freshly baked bread, offered thanks to the Almighty for another bountiful harvest. Later, a Lammas feast would be held in the Countess of Leicester's great hall. The Prioress and village elders had been invited, and Nell's cooks had created an elaborate castle out of marzipan, glazed with sugar. The enticing aroma of baking gingerbread and plum bread now wafted out onto the morning air, and Durand's mouth began to water in anticipation.

Durand was looking forward eagerly to the feast, to the delicious drink known as lamb's wool, warm, spiced cider with baked apples floating on top, to the boisterous games and dancing, and lastly, to the candlelit evening procession that would bring the Lammas festivities to a close. Today's celebration would be the week's only joy for the members of the Countess's household, for they were approaching the anniversary of the battle of Evesham. Certain times were always harder for the Earl's women, but none more so than the day of Simon's death, and Nell's retainers and servants ached for her resurrected sorrow, while dreading her inevitably fraying temper. August 4th would be a bad day for all at Montargis.

But that was yet to come. Ahead lay a day of proven pleasures, and Durand was whistling as he emerged from the stables, only to halt abruptly at sight of the dog. It was one of the Countess's pampered greyhounds, but its sleek sides were heaving, its muzzle smeared with saliva. Durand's hand dropped to his sword hilt. He'd never seen a mad dog before, felt his muscles constrict in instinctive fear. People called them wood hounds, and their bites caused certain death. Had it been a stable or village dog, Durand would have slain it on the spot. But all knew what a store the Countess set by her greyhounds, and this white one was the most cherished of all, a gift from her husband in happier days. Slowly drawing his sword, he gestured to a youth standing by the door of the great hall. "Warn the others to stay inside, and tell the Countess that her greyhound is frothing at the mouth!"

The boy gasped, ducked back into the hall. Durand kept a wary eye upon the dog, yearning to strike and have done with it. Within moments, Nell was hastening out into the courtyard. To Durand's horror, the dog shot forward at sight of its mistress. He shouted, lunged, and missed, sprawling onto the hard, sun-baked ground. By the time he regained his feet, Nell was kneeling by the dog, seeking to pry its jaws apart.

"Christ, no! Madame, get back!"

Nell paid him no heed, and a moment later gave a triumphant cry, holding up a small bone. "Blanchette got it wedged between her jaws. That is why she was slobbering so. The poor creature could not close her mouth." Before rising, she hugged the panting dog, then beckoned to one of the spectators. "Raoul, fetch her some water!"

Durand was panting, too, and feeling rather foolish. "I am sorry I caused such an uproar, my lady. But when I saw—"

"This has happened before to Blanchette. But how were you to know?" Nell smiled suddenly. "I am glad you kept your head, Durand, did not do anything rash!"

"I always try to think ere I act, my lady," Durand said virtuously. Inwardly, he was shaking. What if he'd run the damned dog through? Sweet Jesus, her Ladyship would have dismissed him from her service then and there! She was a fair mistress most of the time, and handsome for all her years. But if she had any of the mild, womanly softness that was supposed to characterize those of her sex, he'd yet to see a trace of it. Men said the old Earl had possessed Lucifer's own temper. He and his prideful lady must have had some scorching fights, for certes! Durand glanced balefully at the greyhound, frisking at Nell's side as she started back into the hall. How close he'd come to disaster, and all because of a coddled cur that ate better than most men did!

Now that the excitement had subsided, people returned to their interrupted activities. Nell's scribe held out a parchment sheet for her inspection. "This is the letter we'd just begun, my lady, the one to Prince Llewelyn of Wales."

Nell scanned it to refresh her memory. "Write as follows, Baldwin: 'It gladdens my heart to be able to tell you that my son Amaury has succeeded in clearing himself of any complicity in the Viterbo murder. The Bishop and chapter of Padua, the doctors at the university, and the friars all gave sworn testimony that Amaury had not left the city since October, and that on the day of the killing, he was confined to bed with a raging fever. This satisfied Charles and the French King, would have satisfied all reasonable men. But friends at the French court tell me that Edward is still not convinced, is still vowing to exact vengeance upon Amaury, too. I cannot say this surprises me, Llewelyn, for—' "

"My lady!" Durand reeled to a stop in the doorway, gasping for breath. "That English squire of Lord Bran's—he's riding up the road from the village!"

Nell's hand clenched upon the table's edge. "And my son?"

Durand shook his head. "No, my lady. The lad is alone."

HUGH had traveled more than a thousand miles, including a rough sea crossing from Genoa to Marseilles. But the last hundred yards of his journey were the hardest of all. The Countess was awaiting him in the priory gateway, flanked by Ellen and Juliana, and the hope on their faces pierced Hugh to the heart. For weeks, he'd been rehearsing what to say. But now that the moment had come, he found himself utterly at a loss.

Nell watched as he reined in, slowly swung from the saddle to kneel before her. He was deeply tanned, tawny hair shaggy and windblown, seemed years older than the eager-eyed boy who had accompanied Bran to Montargis six short months ago; she could even detect the beginnings of a shadowy blond beard. He looked up at her in mute misery, and Nell knew what he had come to tell her. Without need of words, she knew.

"My son is dead," she said softly.

HUGH had been wandering about the priory grounds like a lost soul, not knowing where to go, what to do. For nearly two months, he'd had his quest to sustain him, his determination to bring word of Bran's death to Montargis. It had served as a lifeline, something to cling to even in the depths of despair. Now it was gone, and he felt bereft all over again, felt like a compass without a needle.

He would have liked to offer up a prayer for Bran's soul. But Nell was in the church, and he was loath to intrude upon her private grieving. Nor did he want to return to the great hall, unwilling to run the gauntlet again of so many curious eyes. He ended up on a bench in Nell's garden. The air was heavy with honeysuckle, the sun hot upon his face. He could not summon up energy to seek the shade, though, sat there as the afternoon dwindled away, aimlessly shredding rose petals and dropping them into the grass at his feet.

He supposed he ought to be thinking of the morrow, making plans of some sort. But he could not rouse himself from this peculiar lassitude. He felt numbed, so hollow it hurt.

"How far away you look." He'd not heard her light tread upon the grass, and he jumped at sound of Ellen's voice, scrambled hastily to his feet.

Ellen waved him back onto the bench, and then startled him by sitting down beside him. She looked pale, but composed. They sat in surprisingly companionable silence until, as if reading his mind, Ellen suddenly said, "I cannot cry. Mayhap it's because I'd be crying for myself, not for Bran." She saw his head swivel toward her, and smiled sadly. "How could I mourn on Bran's behalf after what you told us? How could I wish him back in such pain?"

Hugh could not argue with that. "Will your lady mother be all right?" he asked shyly, acutely aware of Ellen's perfume, the silky sweep of her lashes; he'd never been so close to a lady of rank before.

"Grief is an old adversary of my mother's, too familiar to catch her off guard. It is Juliana I fear for, Hugh. She loved my brother very much."

Hugh nodded, not sure what she wanted from him. She was regarding him steadily, and he found himself thinking that she had beautiful eyes, not green as he'd once thought, but an uncommon, gold-flecked hazel. "Hugh . . . Juliana has been weeping all afternoon, is like to make herself sick. She needs comfort. I hoped you might be able to give it to her."

"Me? How?"

"Can you not think back, try to remember something Bran might have said? A word, an act, anything to reassure Juliana that she was in his thoughts. If you but prodded your memory . . ."

"My lady, I . . . I do not know. Lord Bran was so ill in those last days . . ."

Those hazel eyes were fastened unwaveringly, hypnotically upon his face. "Not even words spoken in fever?" she suggested, but Hugh reluctantly shook his head.

"No, nothing like that." He frowned in thought, then grinned. "Wait, I do remember! On our second day in Siena, he bought a moonstone brooch in the Campo, asked me if I thought Juliana would fancy it. Of course it got left behind when we had to flee Viterbo, but it was very pretty, shaped like a heart. Do you think it would console Lady Juliana to know that?"

"Oh, yes, Hugh, I do!" Ellen cried, and then embarrassed, astounded, and delighted him by kissing him on the cheek. "Come," she said, "I'll take you to Juliana now." Catching his hand, she pulled him to his feet. "A heart-shaped brooch—that is perfect, Hugh! Is it true?"

"Lady Ellen, of course it is!" Astonishment was giving way to indignation. "I would not lie!"

Ellen knew there was less than four years between them, but at that moment she felt old enough to be his mother, older in ways she hoped he'd never learn. "I did not mean to offend you, Hugh," she said soothingly. "If not for you, my brother might have died alone—" And then, to her dismay, tears were clinging to her lashes, and she could not blink them back in time. "I'm going to be selfish, after all," she said and spun away from him.

Hugh's instinct was to follow, to try to comfort. But she was too proud to cry upon his shoulder as Juliana might have done. He thought of her mother's solitary church vigil, thought of Bran's conscience-stricken silences. Ellen had said grief was a familiar foe to the de Montforts. It was also one to be fought in private, and, understanding that, Hugh stood where he was, watching as Ellen fled the garden.

HUGH hesitated, then moved into the chapel. "Madame? You sent for me?"

Nell nodded. As she stepped into the light cast by his lantern, he felt a surge of pity, for she looked ravaged, her eyes puffy and shadowed, her skin ashen. "I wanted to see you alone," she said, "for there is something I must know, and only you can tell me. Hugh, did my son truly die in God's grace? Did he agree to be shriven, to—" She saw the shock on his face and her breath stopped. "Jesú, no!"

"Ah, no, Madame, you need not fear! He was shriven, I swear it! You just took me by surprise, for he did indeed refuse at first. But he did not persist in such madness. Madame, I would not lie to you."

Nell had caught the altar for support, and Hugh waited until she regained her composure. "My lady . . . however did you guess?"

"It was not second-sight, Hugh. That is the one crime my enemies have not accused me of—witchcraft." Her smile was so wry, so like Bran's, that Hugh winced. "I knew my son, as simple as that. Bran was ever one for doing the wrong thing, always for the right reasons."

Sifting through his own memories, both the good times and the bad, especially those last doomed weeks, Hugh had to agree with Nell's assessment of her son. "He tried to send me away when he was first stricken with the ague," he confided, and Nell drew back into the shadows.

"You have told me how my son died, and I thank you for that, Hugh. Now I would have you tell me why. I would hear about Viterbo." She saw him flinch and said swiftly, "No, lad, I do not mean the killing. I only wish I knew less of that, not more. I want you to tell me what happened that morn, ere they found Hal in that church."

Hugh did, as conscientiously as memory's inevitable distortions would allow. "Bran made no attempt to defend himself," he concluded quietly, "not even when Guy accused him of killing Earl Simon and Harry. That was so cruel; I'll never forget the look on his face, never. Then Guy demanded to know if he would fail the Earl at Viterbo as he had at Evesham, and held out his sword. Lord Bran . . . he took it, Madame. He never said a word, just took it . . ."

In the silence that followed, Hugh began to have qualms about his candor. In his indignation, he'd almost forgotten that Guy was Nell's son, too. But then she said, very low, "Guy has much to answer for."

With that, Hugh was in heartfelt agreement. He thought of what Ellen had told him about Amaury, and thanked God that Bran had never known. He thought of Nell, whose sorrows had only begun with Evesham. She'd borne seven children, and now four were dead and one was outlawed. And he thought of Ellen, who was once more a dubious marital prize. Just a few months ago, her prospects had seemed almost as bright as in the days of her father's glory. But it would take a brave man, indeed, to wed Ellen now, the sister of Edward's mortal enemy.

It was not until Nell repeated his name that he came out of his reverie, hastily offered an apology. "You did ask me . . . what, Madame?"

"Bran told me that you'd been educated by the Evesham monks. I assume then that you can read and write?"

"Yes, my lady, I can," Hugh said, with pardonable pride, for that was not so common an accomplishment. She was looking at him expectantly, and so he continued self-consciously, baffled by her inexplicable interest in his education. "I studied arithmetic, too, but in all honesty, I'm not good with numbers, cannot seem to keep them in my head. But I am better with languages. In addition to French, I speak English and some Latin, and I picked up a useful amount of Tuscan during our months in Italy."

Nell nodded approvingly. "You obviously are familiar with horses."

"Yes, my lady. I learned to ride whilst my lord father was still alive."

"I do not suppose that Bran had a chance to begin teaching you how to handle a sword?"

"No, my lady. He gave me a few lessons on the road, said my schooling would begin in earnest after we'd met with the two Kings at

Viterbo . . ." Hugh faltered, so great was his regret for what might have
been.

Nell came toward him. "We shall remedy that forthwith. I have
spoken to Sir Olivier de Croix, the captain of my guards, and he is
willing to take you on as his squire, if that be your wish."

Hugh's eyes widened. "If I wish? Oh, my lady, I—"

"Wait, Hugh, hear me out. Ere you decide, I want you to know
that you have a choice. If you would rather return to England, I will
arrange for your passage and give you a letter to take to a Yorkshire
knight, Sir John d'Eyvill. He was a friend of Bran's, and if I ask it of
him, I am sure he will accept you into his service. Or you may stay here
at Montargis. Sir Olivier is an exacting taskmaster, but a fair one. Give
him but one-half the loyalty you gave Bran, and he'll be content. Let
him teach you what you need to know, serve him well, and when you
come of age, I will see that you are knighted. If then you wish to remain
with my household—"

"My lady, nothing would give me greater joy!" Hugh was staring
at Nell in awe. No one had ever been kinder to him than Bran. And
now this! He yearned to pledge her his honor and his life, to swear to
serve her and her family as long as he had breath in his body, but he
feared to make himself ridiculous, feared that she might laugh at a raw
boy making a knight's vow.

Reaching out, Nell took his hand, her fingers cool and smooth in
his. "You did not forsake my son," she said, and he saw that her eyes
were brimming with tears. "How, then, could we forsake you?"

6

ACRE, KINGDOM OF JERUSALEM

June 1272

ALL day the sky had shimmered in a haze of
heat, a bleached-bone shade neither white nor blue. Now the sun was
flaming out, a fiery-red sphere that looked as if it were haloed in blood.

As Edward watched, it sank into the sea. For a moment, the waves churning shoreward were capped in sunset foam, and then the light was drowned, dusk settling over the land with breathtaking suddenness, a curtain rung down at play's end. Where there had been smeared crimson streaks, Edward could see the first glimmerings of stars.

But twilight had not cooled the air. It was sweltering, almost too hot to breathe; Edward felt as if he were inhaling steam. Sweat was chafing his skin, stinging his eyes, and even the luxury of wine chilled with Lebanese snow could not assuage the desert-dryness of his throat. This Thursday in mid-June was Edward's thirty-third birthday; so far it had brought him little joy.

The royal castle known as the Citadel was situated in the northern quarter of the city. Acre lay spread out below him like a chessboard, for all the roofs were flat, and many of the narrow streets were vaulted in sun-shielding stone. At this height, he had a spy's view of the inner courtyards of Acre's wealthy merchants, could see the silvery spray of private fountains, the silhouettes of palms and other tropical trees, and beyond, the darkening sapphire of the bay, the superb harbor that was the city's lifeblood. It was a sight alien and exotic, vibrantly alive, seductively compelling to most men—but not to Edward.

Acre was a busy port, the capital of the Kingdom of Jerusalem. It was also, by all accounts, one of the world's most sinful cities. Prostitutes sauntered brazenly along its dusty streets, competing with beggars and vendors for the attention of passersby. Pickpockets and thieves were more discreet, but just as numerous, for Acre was a penal colony of sorts; foreign criminals were sometimes given the choice of prison or service in the Holy Land. But it was not the presence of felons and harlots that irked Edward. It was the sight of infidels mingling freely with Christians, for thousands of Arabs dwelled within the walls of this crusaders' city.

The "Franks," those native-born Christians of European descent, were disturbingly complacent about such fraternizing. It was Edward's opinion that the torrid climate had sapped their crusading fervor, made them indolent and too receptive to Saracen guile. How else explain their willingness to let the enemy live in their very midst?

Edward's sojourn in the Holy Land had been a disillusioning experience. Although he was neither a romantic nor an idealist, he had still believed in the chivalric myths of a holy quest, had envied men like his celebrated great-uncle, Richard Lionheart, and Simon de Montfort, men who'd worn the white crosses of crusaders, fought the infidel in the cradle of Christendom.

But upon his arrival in Acre, those epic sagas of gallantry and Christian martyrdom soon lost their lustre. Reality was far grittier, far less heroic. Edward found a land in chaos, a handful of seacoast cities clinging to precarious survival in the shadow of a deadly foe, the ruthless Sultan of Egypt, Rukn ad-Din Baibars Bundukdari. Political rivalries flourished and corruption was epidemic; Acre's Venetian and Genoese merchants traded openly with the enemy, supplying Baibars with the weapons and slaves he needed to carry on his jihad, his holy war against the Christian kingdom of Jerusalem.

These months in Palestine had taught Edward some sobering lessons, that few men were willing to die for the greater glory of God, that few princes were willing to empty their coffers for yet another crusade. The French King and Charles of Anjou had long since sailed for home; even Edward's brother had abandoned their quest. Edward found himself bereft of powerful allies, with less than a thousand soldiers, and his requests for additional money only brought pitiful letters from his ailing father, begging him to come back to England.

More than three weeks had passed since Hugh de Lusignan, the young King of Jerusalem, had signed a ten-year truce with Sultan Baibars. Edward knew it was a sensible act, one that might buy the beleaguered kingdom some precious time. But boyhood dreams die hard, and there was a corner of his soul that cried out in protest, that had yet to accept the inevitable. Disappointment and frustration and stifling summer heat were flammable elements, and when a sudden knock sounded at the door, he spun away from the window with a snarled "What?"

Erard de Valery showed no surprise; those in Edward's service soon grew accustomed to such flashes of temper. "I thought you'd want to know," he said impassively, "that a messenger has come from John de Montfort. He arrives in Acre on the morrow."

Edward's response was obscene, imaginative, and predictable, for John's sins were twofold. He was a cousin to Simon and thus tainted by blood, and a stalwart friend to Guy de Montfort, which made him as welcome at Edward's court as the Saracen Sultan himself. But John was also the Lord of Tyre, brother-in-law to the King of Jerusalem, a man too powerful to be snubbed, to be treated with anything but icily correct courtesy—and Edward well knew it.

So did Erard, who waited patiently as Edward stalked about the chamber, damning John de Montfort to smoke and sulphur and hellish flames. "He dares to defend Guy even now, as if Viterbo were merely a lapse in manners! Fifteen months, Erard, fifteen months since Hal lay dying in the mud of that wretched piazza, and Guy is still free, living quite comfortably, too, I hear. Well, not for long, by God! When I get back to Italy, I'll see that murdering whoreson run to earth, even if I have to lead the hunt myself."

Edward's anger soon burned itself out, though; it was too hot for such intense emotion. Gesturing for Erard to pour them wine, he flung himself down upon a couch. Erard followed with the cups and they drank in silence for a time.

"It's nigh on two years since I left home," Edward said at last, "and all for what? I had a daughter born dead at Acre last year. My firstborn son died in England, half a world away. So did my uncle Richard, and that death, too, can be laid to Guy de Montfort's account; my uncle never got over Hal's murder. My father is ailing, and there's turmoil throughout the Marches, for that hothead Gloucester and Llewelyn ap Gruffydd are at swords' points again. I cannot help thinking that I ought never to have left England. Two years of my life and what did I gain? A ten-year truce that was not even my doing!"

"My lord, that's not so! Baibars would never have agreed to the truce if not for you. Have you forgotten your raid into the Plain of Sharon? Granted, your siege of Ququn Castle failed, but you then took Nazareth—"

Erard bit off the word in mid-sentence, but not in time; Edward's mouth tightened noticeably. His capture of Nazareth had been an undeniable military triumph, but it had caused the first serious rift between Edward and his brother, Edmund. After taking the city, Edward had allowed his men to slay the Arab townspeople, a bloody act of reprisal for Sultan Baibars's massacre of Christians in Antioch and Jaffa. But Edmund had not approved, had argued in vain that at least the women and children should be spared. Edward's knights had been baffled by Edmund's objections, concluding that England was fortunate Edward was the firstborn, as Edmund was plainly too soft-hearted to wield a king's power.

Erard was sure Edward did not regret the killings; they were infidels, after all. He knew, though, that Edward did regret the falling-out with his brother. They'd eventually mended the breach, but it had left a sour aftertaste, and he was sorry he'd reminded Edward of it.

Conversation lagged; again Edward was the one to break the silence. His tone had changed; to Erard's surprise, he sounded almost wistful. "I've been thinking about my great-uncle Richard. At the battle of Jaffa, he fought so bravely that when his stallion was slain, Saladin sent out a horse under a flag of truce. Jesú, what a gallant gesture! It would have been no disgrace to lose to such a foe. I came here seeking another Saladin, found instead Baibars, who adorns his castle at Safad with Christian skulls . . ."

Erard nearly blurted out that Edward had once faced a Saladin— Simon de Montfort. He gulped down the last of his wine, shaken, for he knew Edward would never have forgiven him for that.

"My lord . . ." A servant hovered in the doorway. "A messenger has arrived from the Emir of Jaffa. Should we bid him enter?"

Edward nodded, then glanced toward Erard. "I want you to fetch my wife," he said, for his conscience was beginning to stir. He'd been very curt with Eleanora that forenoon, was now regretting it. It was only a month since she'd been brought to bed of their babe, Joanna, and it had been a difficult pregnancy; she'd conceived a scant two months after the death of their daughter.

The Emir's messenger was familiar to Edward; this was his fifth visit. Beckoning him toward the couch, Edward reached for the letter. They'd been corresponding for weeks; the Emir had even hinted he might consider converting to Christianity. Edward was skeptical, but the Emir was worth courting, for he'd make a valuable ally. Sitting up, he broke the seal, began to read.

The man was quick. In one smooth motion, he drew a hidden dagger, plunged it toward the Englishman's heart. It would have been a lethal blow had Edward not been blessed with a soldier's reflexes. From the corner of his eye, he'd caught a blurred movement and instinctively flung up an arm, deflecting the knife. But the blade sliced deeply into his flesh, slashing from wrist to elbow; blood spurted wildly, splattering both men.

The assassin recovered swiftly, lunged again. Edward was just as fast, though. Rolling off the couch, he snatched up a footstool as he hit the floor, threw it at his assailant. The man stumbled, and by the time he'd regained his balance, Edward was upon him. He took a gash across the forehead before he was able to immobilize his attacker's knife hand. Locked in a death embrace, they swayed back and forth, until they lurched into the table and Edward saw his chance. With his free hand, he grabbed for a candlestick, thrust the flame into the other man's face. As he recoiled, Edward slammed his wrist onto the table, and then he had the dagger, burying it to the hilt in his enemy's abdomen.

Jerking the blade free, Edward prepared to strike again. But there was no need. The man sank to his knees, his face contorted. Edward reeled back against the table, gasping for breath. During their life-or-death struggle, it had not even occurred to him to call out for help. Now he looked in horror at the blood staining his tunic, the couch cushions, the tiled floor, his blood.

Beginning to shout, he jerked the tablecloth loose, sending objects flying about the chamber. A glass flagon shattered in a spray of red wine; cups went rolling across the tiles. Candles flared, guttered out as the door burst open. Men were gasping, cursing, questioning, and a woman was screaming. It was not until she flung herself into his arms that Edward realized it was his wife.

Suddenly there were so many people in the chamber that they were bumping into one another, slipping in blood as they elbowed and jostled to get closer, staring open-mouthed at the dying assassin. Edward had been attempting to wrap the tablecloth around his wound, but his left arm hung, useless, at his side, and Eleanora was clinging like a limpet, sobbing in Spanish.

"What are you fools waiting for?" he raged. "Till I bleed to death?"

That galvanized them to action, too much so. Fully a dozen hands reached for the bloodied tablecloth. Edward was getting light-headed, and it was with real relief that he recognized the voice now shouting down the others. A good man, Erard, one to keep his wits in a crisis. Within moments, Erard had justified his confidence, steering him toward the couch, sending for a doctor, turning the tablecloth into a makeshift bandage, and emptying the chamber of superfluous spectators.

"I've sent for the Master of the Templars. I know you have no liking for them, my lord, but the Templars' hospital is the best in Acre."

Edward nodded grudging agreement, patted his wife soothingly if absent-mindedly, all the while watching the man sprawled upon the floor. "This was no act of impulse. He waited until the guards knew him as the Emir's man, no longer bothered to search him."

Erard moved away from the couch, stood staring down at the assassin. "Hashishiyun," he said, and Eleanora shuddered, for the Hashishiyun, also known as the Assassins, were a Shiite sect infamous for political killings.

Edward looked thoughtful. "Yes," he said, "that makes the most sense. And I know whose gold bought that dagger. I'd wager the surety of my soul that this is Baibars's doing."

At the mention of the Sultan's name, the assassin stirred suddenly. Lying in a pool of his own blood, he must have been in intense pain, yet nothing showed on his face; he seemed to be listening to voices only he could hear. But now his eyes opened. He turned upon Edward a look of chilling malevolence, and then he laughed. It was a dreadful sound, a strangled cough that ended on a broken breath. Erard was bending over, for the man's lips were moving. Looking at Edward, the man laughed again, then choked. A bubble of blood formed at the corner of his mouth.

"Well?" Edward said impatiently. "You know I do not speak Arabic. What did he say?"

Erard straightened up slowly, and Eleanora gasped, for his face had gone grey. "He said . . . he said that you are a dead man, that he poisoned the dagger."

AT sight of the man being ushered into the Citadel's great hall, the Templars' Grand Master beckoned hastily. "Reynard, thank God!"

Reynard wasted no time on preliminaries. "When did it happen?"

"Thursday eve. At first we gave him centaury and fennel powder in wine, and then we tried nettle seeds, for men say they ward off the effects of hemlock, henbane, and mandrake. But I very much fear it was a poison unknown to us."

"Is he fevered?"

The Templar nodded. "The cut on his forehead seems to be healing, but the wound on his arm has begun to fester. It is swollen and discolored, first red, now yellow, and there is a foul smell."

Reynard drew a quick breath. "It sounds," he said grimly, "as if you sent for me too late."

EDWARD'S bedchamber was in semi-darkness, drawn curtains offering a feeble defense against the noonday heat. Eleanora sat on the bed, wielding a fan as if Edward's air supply depended upon her efforts alone. She did not look up as the two men approached the bed, but when the Grand Master introduced Reynard as a physician famed for his healing arts, she turned toward her husband with sudden, hungry hope. "Querido, did you hear?"

Edward struggled upright. There was nothing prepossessing about the man before him—at first glance—for he was thin, stoop-shouldered, hair and beard a muddy, grizzled brown, while his clothes proclaimed him one utterly indifferent to fashion; he wore an Arab kafiya upon his head, a too-short tunic, and monk's sandals. But he seemed unflustered by Edward's scrutiny, met the younger man's eyes with rare composure, heedless of the impression he was making, intent only upon those ugly blisters, that puffy, bruised flesh.

"If I may," he said brusquely, and without waiting for permission, began a thorough inspection of the wound. His fingers were surprisingly deft, but even so light a touch brought pain; Edward bit down on his lower lip, bit back a cry.

"Well?" he demanded. "Can you help me?"

Reynard straightened up slowly. "There are remedies we can try. A poultice of darnel, a powder made of black hellebore—"

"Will these poultices save my life?" Edward asked bluntly, and sucked in his breath when Reynard shook his head. "What are you saying? That nothing can be done? I'll not accept that!"

"I'll not lie to you, my lord. Yours is a grievous wound. There is a chance, but it will cause you great pain, mayhap for naught. I can cut away the putrid flesh—"

"Dios, no!" Eleanora was on her feet, a hand jammed against her mouth. "Eduardo, that would be certain death. I remember a young page back in my brother's palace at Seville. He fell on a rusty nail, and the doctors cut out the flesh as this man would do. That child died in agony, Eduardo! There must be another remedy . . ."

She might as well have been speaking in Spanish for all the heed they paid her. Edward did not even glance her way, kept his eyes riveted upon Reynard's face. "Do it," he said at last, and Eleanora gave a muffled scream.

The Templar looked questioningly at the man on the bed, and when Edward nodded, he gently but firmly grasped Eleanora by the elbows. "Forgive me, Madame, but you must come with me. Better you should weep than all England should mourn."

IT was over. Reynard had given Edward a smooth piece of wood to bite upon, and the Templar and Erard de Valery stood ready to hold him down. There was no need, though. He'd quivered at the first cut of the knife, but after that, he'd lain remarkably still. Erard was astonished by his own queasiness, for he was a soldier, knew death in its goriest guises. But somehow this was different, and when Reynard heated the knife blade, began to cauterize the wound, this man who'd seen bodies beyond counting found himself sickened by the stench of burning flesh. Edward's impressive control failed him at the last; he'd jerked convulsively, then went so limp that Reynard reached hastily for the pulse in his throat. Having reassured himself that his patient still lived, he sagged down upon the nearest footstool, blotted away so much sweat that his sleeve was soon sopping wet.

He was certain Edward had lost consciousness, was surprised now to see his lashes flicker. As he leaned over the bed, Edward's eyes opened. They were sunken back in his head, so swollen and bruised that they were little more than slits, but they were lucid. Edward tried to spit out the wood, failed, and Reynard gently pried it loose; it was bitten all the way through. Edward's chest was heaving. Reynard didn't like the sound of his breathing, not at all. But when he brought a cup to Edward's lips, he managed to swallow.

"Tell my wife . . ." The words so faint that Reynard had to put his ear almost to Edward's mouth. "Tell her that . . . that I shall live," Edward whispered, and the corner of Reynard's mouth softened in a sudden smile.

"By Christ," he said, "if I do not think you will!"

7

CASTELL Y BERE, WALES

December 1272

THAT year winter was late in coming to Wales. The first storm of the season did not hit until early December, and even then, it was not a full-blown tempest. The top of Cader Idris was glazed with snow, but Llewelyn ap Gruffydd's stronghold on the lower slopes escaped with a mere dusting, and those traces were washed away by the next day's rain. By dusk the sky had cleared, and the moon was soon rising above the last lingering clouds. But a freezing wind had driven all the inhabitants of Castell y Bere indoors, vying for space before the open hearths.

The south tower keep had been partitioned off to provide its Prince with a private chamber. Cadfael and Gwilym were standing by its door, casting wistful glances toward the fireside bench and their cooling drinks of mulled wine. But the Lady Arwenna was not one to be denied, and they'd been trapped for the past quarter hour as she laid out her instructions in meticulous, numbing detail.

"You understand, then? As soon as Lord Llewelyn's scribe leaves his chamber, you're to see that no one else is admitted. The cooks are preparing a special dinner, and I want it served precisely half an hour after I enter my lord's chamber. But I want that sweet wine from Cyprus served first. And remember, we are not to be disturbed—for any reason whatsoever. Is that clear?"

They nodded glumly, and she was off to intercept one of the wine bearers. She was a graceful woman, quite curvaceous, and Gwilym could not help admiring her sensual walk even as he yearned to see her fall flat on her shapely rump.

"We serve our lord, not his doxy," he said indignantly. "Why did you not tell her so, Cadfael?"

Cadfael chuckled indulgently. "My God, but you're green! That is one fine-looking woman, as ripe as they come. And our lord has only been bedding her for the past fortnight. There's a lesson you'd best learn fast, my lad. If you want a man to share a flagon, you wait till he's drunk his fill."

Gwilym had begun to bridle. "But Lord Llewelyn is not a man to let a woman meddle where she oughtn't—"

Cadfael was laughing again. "Gwilym, Gwilym, you've much to learn. A wise man lets a woman have her way in minor matters, a cheap price for household peace."

Arwenna heard the laughter, could feel their eyes following her. She'd have been surprised if they didn't stare, for she was accustomed to attracting male attention; men even said hers was a beauty worth dying for. She was twenty-eight, twice widowed, and each of her husbands had died in her bed within a matter of months. Her mournful marital history had given rise to predictable lewd jokes about her potent sexual charms. Arwenna knew of these jokes but was not offended by them. In fact, she rather enjoyed the notoriety. Men's desire and women's jealousy were the coins of her realm, and she was a lavish spender.

Tonight she had taken particular pains with her appearance, had mapped out her strategy with a military precision utterly at odds with her sultry image, for men dazzled by her beauty often failed to see the steely ambition camouflaged as feminine vanity. To be a Prince's concubine was no shame, and she'd settle for that if she had to, but she saw a chance for more, much more. She was the luckiest of women, for God had given her a lovely face, a voluptuous body, and a very fertile womb. Both of her husbands had been well past a man's prime, and yet with each she had conceived, giving birth to two healthy sons. If she could give Llewelyn ap Gruffydd a son, he might marry her.

The strength of her plan lay in its very simplicity. She need only please Llewelyn, in bed and out, until, God willing, his seed took root in her womb. It was odd that none of his bedmates had gotten with child, for his wretch of a brother spawned like a salmon. But each of her husbands had been past sixty and Llewelyn was only forty and four. For once, time was on her side.

She smiled at the thought, deliberately deepening her dimples, a smile she meant to use upon Llewelyn. She could arouse his lust easily enough, but could she ensnare his heart? He was not a man to be bewitched with sugared words, seduced with flattery. There was a wariness in the way he viewed the world; even in bed, he held back. Well, he need not love her, he need only marry her.

A child crossed into her line of vision, that bastard get of his brother's. Davydd, the heir-apparent . . . for now. How she'd enjoy denying him a crown. She had not always disliked Davydd, although his indifference had rankled. She could not understand why he had never even flirted with her, for if only half the stories told of him were true, his conquests were approaching legendary proportions. Not that she'd have yielded; she set a higher price upon herself than he'd have been willing to pay. She had still wanted him to try, though, and had been irked when he had not. And then, a few months ago, she'd overheard several men teasing him about her, urging him on. But he had merely laughed, saying he preferred a challenge, and for that insult, Arwenna would never forgive him.

The sight of his daughter brought back that memory, took the smile from her face. She did not like to be reminded of Davydd, did not see why Llewelyn must be burdened with his brother's brat. Well, not for long, not if she had her way, and she would.

Llewelyn's scribe had finally departed, but as Arwenna started for the door, so, too, did Caitlin. Quickening her step, she headed the child off just in time. "Lord Llewelyn is not to be disturbed. Go on now, run along."

Caitlin stood her ground. "But it is urgent," she said, and Arwenna's annoyance flared into active dislike. What an odd creature she was! How many eight-year-olds used words like *urgent*? No wonder she had no playmates. Mayhap Davydd was not so much to blame, after all, for not wanting her. She'd seen several of his other daughters. Pretty little lasses they were, beribboned and well-mannered. What a contrast to this bedraggled waif; did the child even own a comb?

"Lord Llewelyn has no time for you. You'll have to wait," she said coolly. Even then, Caitlin did not move, stood watching until Arwenna closed the door.

Llewelyn was rereading a letter he'd just dictated to the English government, yet another letter of protest. Not that he expected much from it. More fool he, for ever believing English promises. He'd had Gloucester's Caerphilly Castle at his mercy. But the Bishops of Lichfield and Worcester had begged him to lift the siege, swearing that Caerphilly would be put under royal control. In a moment of madness—how else explain it?—he'd accepted their assurances on behalf of the English government. And no sooner had he withdrawn than Gloucester retook the castle, set about making it the most formidable stronghold in all of South Wales.

Llewelyn's hand tightened upon the parchment. Their double-dealing over Caerphilly only confirmed his worst fears about their good faith. He could still hear his father's words, echoing across so many years. He could still see his father's face, the prison pallor, the haunted eyes, the bitterness of betrayal. Gruffydd ap Llewelyn, who'd deserved better from life than he'd gotten. He'd loved Wales with a doomed passion, but he'd died on alien soil, plunging to his death from the Tower of London's great keep in a foolhardy escape attempt. Yet he'd left a legacy worth more than gold, a cry from the heart. "Never forget, Llewelyn, that the world's greatest fool is a Welshman who trusts an English king."

When the door opened, he glanced up with a preoccupied frown. At sight of Arwenna, though, he smiled, and she found herself marveling how easily he shed years and cares. "I'm glad," she said, "that you smile so seldom. I only wish you saved them all for me." She'd thought that was a well-crafted compliment, but saw now that it was a wasted effort.

"Do I smile so seldom?" he echoed, sounding surprised, and she nodded, then very ostentatiously slid the door latch into place.

"If I'd known it was so easy to capture a Prince," she murmured, "I'd have done it long ere this."

Llewelyn's face was impassive, but she knew him well enough by now to catch an amused glint. "What are your terms?"

"An entire night alone, just the two of us," she said, and as she moved within range, he rose, drew her to him. She came eagerly into his arms, lifting her mouth to meet his. But after a few moments, she stepped back, laughing up into his face, smoothing her gown.

"Ah, my love," she said ruefully, "we've no time, for the dinner will soon be served: venison frumenty and marrow tarts, a fresh pike."

"You feed your prisoners well. Those happen to be my favorite foods."

"I think you'll find me to be a very generous gaoler," she said, and as he laughed softly, she turned to open the door for the wine bearer. After pouring the wine, she moved behind him, began to massage his shoulders. "How tense you are, sweetheart!" Leaning over, she kissed the nape of his neck. "I happened to see your brother's Caitlin earlier this eve. Davydd has quite a few baseborn children, does he not?"

Llewelyn grinned. "So many, in fact, that I've heard men claim it would be easier to find the Holy Grail than lasses who'd said Davydd nay!"

"I would," Arwenna said righteously, but Llewelyn looked more amused than impressed by her avowal.

"Did he ask?" he said mischievously, much to Arwenna's irritation. She was too clever, though, to lie.

"No," she admitted tersely. "To get back to Caitlin, I do not understand why she does not live with Davydd. Does he not take care of his other children?"

"He claims them as his, sees that they want for nothing. But I doubt if it even occurred to him to take any of them under his roof. Davydd's not one for rocking cradles. With his other children, it matters for naught; they live with their mothers' kin. But Caitlin's mother is dead."

"Why you, though? Why not Davydd?"

He shrugged. "She'd passed her first three years at my court, so why uproot her? The little lass has had a hard enough road to travel. Being born out of wedlock is no shame in Wales, but being half English is. Mayhap if her mother had been highborn. . . . But she was a serving wench, and Davydd never made a secret of it. Then, too, Caitlin is . . . well, she's not like other children. She goes off by herself for hours at a time, is so quiet that strangers have asked if she's mute. She has a remarkable way with animals of any sort, and after people saw her playing in the meadows at Dolwyddelan with a wild fox cub, they started saying she was fey."

Llewelyn set his wine cup down. "No, she's not had an easy time. Children can be cruel to those who're somehow different. I remember a few years ago, overhearing them taunting her, making fun of her Irish name, calling her 'catleek' and 'catkin.' Later, I took her aside, explained that there was a Welsh form of Caitlin, and suggested that she might like to call herself Catrin. She thought about it, keeping those great, green eyes on me all the while, and then she shook her head, said very solemnly, 'But Caitlin is who I am.' "

He laughed, but Arwenna did not. Lord God, he was truly fond of the chit! She'd have to mend that fence and right quick. Now, though, she'd best tell her side first, ere Caitlin came whining to him.

"I have a confession, love," she said and gave a light laugh. "I had my heart set upon being alone with you this eve, was not willing to share you with anyone else, and that included Caitlin. You do not mind, do you?"

"No, I suppose not. But what did Caitlin want?"

"She did not say, just mumbled something about it being 'urgent.' " Arwenna laughed again, indulgently. "Children—how they dearly love to make mountains of every molehill!"

"No," Llewelyn said slowly, "not Caitlin." Arwenna could not hide her dismay, and he smiled reassuringly. "You need not fret. A few moments for the lass, and the night for you."

By the time he'd sent a servant in search of Caitlin, Arwenna had regained her confidence, and when dinner arrived, she insisted upon serving him herself, buttering his bread, hanging on his every word, promising enough with her smiles to blot Caitlin's very name from his memory—or so she hoped. But the servant soon returned, reported that the child was nowhere to be found.

Arwenna stood watching in disbelief as men fanned out, under orders to search all of the buildings in the castle bailey. Waiting until no others were within earshot, she said coaxingly, "My love, the dinner grows cold, and for what? No harm has befallen the girl. I'm a mother myself, remember? I know children, believe me. Caitlin is off sulking somewhere, will come out when she is ready."

"No," Llewelyn said again, "not Caitlin," but this time in a very different tone, and Arwenna hastily changed tactics.

"Llewelyn, you told me yourself that she oft-times goes off to—"

But Llewelyn was turning away, for there was a sudden commotion by the door. Arwenna followed, inwardly seething; if that wretched child was not found soon, the entire evening would be spoiled. And then people were moving aside and she saw. One of the stable grooms stood in the doorway, holding a small limp body in his arms.

"I found her in a stall," he said hesitantly. "At first I thought she had been kicked by one of the horses, but then I heard the cat. Trapped up on the rafters, it was, my lord, and I'd wager she tried to climb up after it . . ."

Llewelyn reached out, took the little girl carefully into his arms. Her eyes had rolled back in her head and her long, loose hair was matted with straw and blood. But as he lifted her, she made a small whimpering sound, and he took heart from that.

"Llewelyn . . ." Arwenna plucked at his sleeve as he passed. He gave her one glance, no more than that, but what she read in it caused her to shrink back, watching helplessly as he carried Caitlin into his bedchamber. She was soon able to convince herself, though, that he'd forgive her once his anger cooled. She'd not yield her dreams so easily, would not be thwarted by a moonstruck, misbegotten foundling and a flea-bitten stable cat.

WHEN Caitlin was four, she had fallen into a pond. She still had bad dreams about it sometimes, reliving that slow-motion struggle to reach the surface. She was trapped in that same dream now, thrashing about in terrifying blackness, drowning all over again. Gradually, though, she could detect faint glimmerings of light, and she swam toward them, up out of the depths and into the shallows where it was safe.

At first the light hurt her eyes. She squinted until things came into focus, until she recognized her surroundings, realizing, with a sense of groggy astonishment, that she seemed to be in her uncle's bed.

"So you've finally decided to wake up, have you?"

The voice was familiar and only added to her bewilderment. "Papa? What are you doing here?"

"I just happened to be in the neighborhood." Davydd watched her eyes roam the chamber, to the oiled linen that shielded the window, back to his face. She seemed confused, but coherent, and he reached over, took a small hand in his own. "Do you remember what happened, Caitlin?"

She started to nod, then winced. "I fell. But . . . but it was night and I can see sunlight . . ."

Davydd laughed. "Sweetheart, that was nigh on three days ago! You've been sleeping much of the time since then. We'd wake you up to swallow the doctor's potions, and off you'd go again. I'd heard that bears and hedgehogs sleep through the winter months, but I never knew that Caitlins did, too."

That would have sent any of his other daughters into fits of giggles. Caitlin's gravity never failed to baffle him, so unchildlike was it, so alien to his own nature. "You truly did come here because I was hurt?" she asked, sounding so surprised that Davydd felt a faint prick of guilt. That was not a question she should need to ask.

"Of course I did, sweetheart," he said, with unwonted seriousness, and was dazzled by her sudden smile. It was a stranger's smile, a flash of pure joy, and Davydd was unexpectedly moved by it. But then he realized that her gaze was aimed over his shoulder, and turning, he saw that her smile was not meant for him at all, was for his brother.

Leaning over the bed, Llewelyn kissed his niece upon the forehead. "Welcome back, lass. You gave us quite a scare."

"I'm sorry," she whispered. "But when that lady would not let me see you, Uncle, I did not know who else to turn to . . ."

Both men were momentarily silent, Davydd struggling with what he recognized as an unworthy attack of jealousy, and Llewelyn stricken with remorse. Jesú, how alone she was, far more than he'd ever realized! And yet she was so pitifully grateful for his few crumbs of attention, his few scraps of affection. Looking into her eyes, he saw for the first time the true depths of her love and was awed by it, that she gave so much, asked for so little.

"You need not worry, lass. That will never happen again. The next time you need to rescue a cat, you'll have more allies than you can count," he promised. Her lashes were shadowing her cheek, but she was fighting sleep, and he knew why. "Yes," he said, "we did save your cat," and she gave him a drowsy smile, a contented sigh.

They stood there for some moments, gazing down at the sleeping child. Then Llewelyn beckoned his brother away from the bed. "Come over to the window. I've just had news from England."

Davydd was in no hurry to hear it; news from England was invariably bad. "Who was that 'lady' standing guard over your bedchamber?"

"No one of importance. Davydd, listen. The English King is dead."

Davydd did not even blink. "I'm surprised that anyone noticed. Evesham was Edward's coronation and all knew it—all but Henry, who had the bad taste to linger on for another seven years. I daresay Westminster was the only English palace haunted by a living ghost!"

As always when dealing with Davydd, Llewelyn ended up laughing in spite of himself. "I wonder if Edward knows yet. The last I heard, he'd finally left Acre, sailed for Sicily. It took weeks for his injury to heal, but it's a miracle he recovered at all. Not many men win against a poisoned dagger."

"Had I been in Acre, I'd have wagered all I owned that he'd survive. Edward has the Devil's own luck—though of course he thinks it's God's favor. I know him, Llewelyn, better than you do. For three years, I lived at his court. We plotted together, fought together, even went whoring together. He can be a surprisingly good companion for an Englishman! None can deny his courage, and his wits are sharp enough, for certes. Hard to believe he could have been sired by such a milksop. If Henry's Queen was not such a cold-blooded bitch, I might suspect her of some furtive fun beneath the sheets."

Davydd's grin slowly faded. "But whatever else Edward is or is not, only one fact truly matters—that he is not to be trusted. Bear that in mind, Llewelyn. For your sake, always bear that in mind."

"I well know I cannot trust Edward," Llewelyn said quietly. "So it is fortunate, is it not, that I can trust you?"

Davydd was momentarily caught off balance. Had Llewelyn learned of his secret meeting with the lords of Powys? Their plan was as ambitious as it was dangerous, involving nothing less than Llewelyn's overthrow. He had not committed himself in any way, but his mere presence at such a meeting was akin to treason, at least in Llewelyn's eyes.

He hesitated, then fell back upon a familiar tactic. "You can trust me with your very life, Llewelyn—on every other Thursday during Lent."

"I cannot tell you how that eases my mind, lad." Llewelyn's smile was wry, but somewhat sad, too, and Davydd found himself at a rare loss for words. They looked at each other as the silence spun out between them, a web sticky with all they dared not say.

8

MELUN, FRANCE

August 1273

Nᴇʟʟ ᴅᴇ ᴍᴏɴᴛꜰᴏʀᴛ approached Melun with some trepidation, dreading what lay ahead of her. She'd never understood why her Church held humility to be a virtue, had never sought to curb her prideful nature, and as a result, she'd had little practice in cultivating the modest demeanor, the demure bearing that her society demanded of its women. Born a Plantagenet Princess, wed to a man just as hot-blooded, she had gloried in the tumultuous passion of their life together, matching Simon's reckless candor with her own brand of forthright boldness. Those were traits that had stood her in good stead during her years as the Countess of Leicester. They availed her naught now, on her way to Melun to entreat an enemy for aid.

Upon her arrival at the French King's manor, she was personally welcomed by Philippe and his mother. Marguerite needed but one glance to detect Nell's inner agitation; Nell had not had such a perceptive woman friend since the death of her niece, Elen de Quincy. "Are you sure you want to do this, dearest?" Marguerite asked quietly, and when Nell nodded, the French Queen sighed, slipped a supportive arm through Nell's, and led her toward the solar for her audience with England's King.

But Edward made it surprisingly easy. The mere fact that he'd chosen the private solar over the public great hall showed a sensitivity she'd not expected, and there was a genuine warmth in his greeting, in the cheerful informality of his "Aunt Nell." Mayhap not so surprising, though; she knew he'd always been very fond of her. She'd been fond of him, too—in another lifetime. Eight years had passed since she'd seen him last, the day she'd surrendered Dover Castle to his besieging army, with Simon two months dead and her world in ruins. Yet he'd been kind, then, heeding her plea on behalf of her household retainers.

He'd even argued against her own banishment, sought in vain to soften his father's heart toward her. She'd truly tried to be grateful, but she could not forget the brutal mutilation of her husband's body, a mutilation Edward had permitted. Eight years were not long enough to blur a memory like that. She was in no position, though, to scorn his truce, however fragile or false it might be. And he, too, seemed to be trying; if "Evesham" did not pass her lips, neither did "Viterbo" pass his.

"Ellen did not come with you?"

"No," Nell said hastily, "she's been ailing," for although she was willing to treat with the enemy for her children's sake, they were not. It was a transparent falsehood; she'd never been good at lying. But Edward let her save face by pretending to believe her, then launched into a dramatic account of his encounter with Baibars's Assassin.

Nell listened with unfeigned interest, even admiration; in her hierarchy of values, courage headed the list. But when Edward described how Eleanora had been banished from his chamber by the Master of the Templars, her eyebrows shot upward and she exclaimed indignantly, "And she let herself be shunted aside like a wayward child? It would have taken a sword at my throat to get me from Simon's sickbed!"

And then, hearing her own words, she drew an audible breath. Simon's name echoed in the air between them, and their truce hung in the balance. Edward had stiffened, but after a taut, suspenseful pause, he relaxed again. "I wonder, Aunt Nell, if you realize what good friends you have at the French court? Since I arrived in Paris, Philippe and Marguerite have done naught but bedevil me on your behalf, urging me to right my father's wrong."

Nell was taken aback that he should broach the subject first. "You said they were persistent," she murmured. "Were they also persuasive?"

Edward grinned, amused by the obliqueness of her approach, so unlike her usual devil-be-damned directness. "Yes," he said, "they were," and saw her eyes widen. "My father did indeed wrong you, Aunt Nell. He had no right to claim the dower lands from your first marriage. I cannot make amends for all your lost income, but I can make sure you suffer no further losses. I will order the heirs of your first husband to answer to the Exchequer for what they owe you. I will also take measures to restore the lands to your control." And because Philippe had confided that Nell's income had dwindled dramatically now that Guy was excommunicate, his estates forfeit, Edward added, "And since it might take a while, I will order the Exchequer to advance you the sum of two hundred pounds. Will that be enough?"

Mute, she could only nod. To restore her lands was simple justice, although she'd been afraid to hope for even that much. But he'd gone beyond that, had responded with a generosity she had not expected. A lesser man would have made her beg. "I will repay your loan," she vowed, "without delay. I thank you, Edward. I could not bear that my daughter . . ."

She did not complete the sentence. As grateful as she was, she could not bring herself to confide in him her fears for Ellen's future. He did not seem offended by her reticence, though, saying with a smile, "I remember Ellen well, remember the letters she wrote to me at Kenilworth, seeking to cheer my confinement. She was all of what . . . twelve? Thirteen? I daresay she's grown into a beauty by now?"

Nell nodded, marveling that they could be talking so easily of a time in which he'd been her husband's prisoner, as if it had somehow happened to other people. "You are making this difficult for me, Edward," she confessed. "You have been more than fair, and now I must risk seeming greedy and ungrateful, for I have yet another favor to ask of you!"

They surprised themselves, then, by sharing a laugh. "Go ahead," Edward said, still grinning. "Do you not remember that folk wisdom, the one about striking whilst the iron is hot?"

"Now that the Pope has pardoned the Bishop of Chichester for having supported Simon, he yearns to end his exile, to spend his last years in the land of his birth. Surely that is not so much to ask, Edward? He wants to come home . . . and to take my son, Amaury, with him."

"No," he said abruptly, tersely.

"But Edward, why? Chichester is an old man, and Amaury . . . why should you hate him so? He was not even at Evesham, bears no guilt for what his brothers did at Viterbo—" Nell broke off. She'd never seen eyes as cold as Edward's. A vivid blue but moments before, they were now as colorless and chilling as ice, eyes that accused, judged, and damned her son without a word being said.

"Amaury de Montfort will never be allowed to return to England, not whilst I draw breath. You tell him that, Madame. Tell him, too, that should he be foolhardy enough to disregard my warning, all his prayers and papal connections will not help him. Nothing will."

NELL was frowning over the chessboard, her competitive instincts fully engaged. Across the table, her chaplain watched with a complacent smile. No matter how she studied the board, she could see no escape. Ellen's interruption came, therefore, at a most opportune time.

"The fair begins today, Mama. Juliana and I thought it worth a look."

Nell felt a pang that her daughter should have no better entertainment than this, a paltry village market, she who'd attended Winchester's famous St Giles Fair and London's equally celebrated St Bartholomew's Fair. "If you go," she said, "be sure to take an escort—Durand or Roger."

Ellen and Juliana exchanged grins. "We'd rather take Hugh," Ellen said, then lowered her voice to confide, "He's smitten with the apothecary's daughter. Have you not noticed how eagerly he offers to run errands in the village?"

Hugh was cleaning Sir Olivier's saddle, conscientiously dipping a cloth into a jar of foul-smelling sheep's tallow. When Ellen's summons came, he jumped to his feet as if launched from a crossbow, to a chorus of catcalls and hoots. But although every man in the hall would have welcomed a chance to attend the fair, there was no malice in their railery. They might enjoy teasing him about the apothecary's daughter—an open secret—but none of them seriously begrudged the lad an afternoon with his girl. It had not always been that way. When he'd first joined the Countess's household, there'd been some resentment of his privileged position, for it was obvious to all that the Countess and the Lady Ellen took a personal interest in his welfare. But he'd won them over by never shirking the dirty jobs, by deflecting their taunts with unassuming good humor, and by pitching the most persistent of his tormentors into a horse trough. Now, as he grinned self-consciously and buckled his scabbard, they shouted ribald courting suggestions after him, and he, Ellen, and Juliana departed on a wave of laughter.

It had been a hot, dry summer. For weeks on end, the skies had been as empty and vast and daunting as the uncharted seas that lay beyond Greenland. But September brought reviving showers of misty silver rain, perfect autumn days of mellow sun, the last flowering of village gardens and wild meadows. The River Loing flowed through Montargis like a swirl of moss-green ribbon, forking into two streams, winding and twisting and spilling over into a shallow lake, the site of the fair.

Montargis had more shops than most villages, enriched by the presence of the castle and the convent. But they offered only those necessities people could neither provide for themselves nor do without. There was a cobbler to repair shoes, a farrier to shoe horses, an apothecary to mix healing potions, a tanner to turn hides into leather. The villagers baked their own bread in the Lord's oven, mended their own tables and wagons, spun their own flax, grew their own food, and slaughtered their own livestock at Martinmas. Theirs was a world self-sufficient and sequestered, a world in which choices were a luxury reserved for the highborn.

On this sunlit Saturday, though, they were confronted by a range of choices, just as dazzling as the jugglers who moved through the crowds with sure-footed grace, tossing apples and balls skyward as they sauntered past. There were merchants selling olive and almond and linseed and poppy oil. There were peddlers with needles, mirrors, razors, and combs carved of bone, not wood. There were stalls draped in silks and fine Flanders wool. There was a booth filled with fragrant perfume vials of jasmine and rosewater. And there were the even more enticing aromas coming from a cook-shop tent: roasted joints and meat pasties and enough candied quince to satisfy the greediest sweet tooth. Hugh was not surprised that every man, woman, and child in Montargis not in need of the Last Rites had turned out for the occasion.

The jugglers were not the only performers drawn by the lure of a large crowd. There were brightly clad tumblers and a woman rope dancer and a man leading a bear on a chain. But as soon as Ellen and Juliana had begun to exclaim over the silk merchant's selections, Hugh sped sure as an arrow for the booth of Mauger the Leech.

Mauger was not really a doctor; that was merely a courtesy, recognition of his valuable services to the village, the castle, and the convent. He had spread out his spices and herbs and ointments upon a trestle table draped in burlap, but Hugh never gave them a glance. She was standing behind the table, her glossy brown hair demurely tucked under a white veil, a robust, big-boned girl, too tall for most men, but not for Hugh; at seventeen, he'd reached the same formidable height as England's King, two full fingers above six feet. Emma's dark eyes, dimples, and swaying walk had captivated him at first sight, and she seemed equally taken with his flaxen hair and good manners.

"I have a token for you," he said, holding out a hair ribbon he'd bought from the silk merchant just moments before.

"How pretty!" Reaching eagerly for the ribbon, she whispered, "Take care. My father is watching."

"Ah, good morrow, lad." Mauger's smile was friendly, for he was genuinely fond of Hugh. But he was worldly enough to know that young men like Hugh did not wed girls like Emma. Occasionally an impoverished knight might take a wealthy merchant's daughter as his wife, but he could provide no marriage portion large enough to tempt a man into marrying beneath his class. If there'd be no wedding ring for Emma, he was determined that there'd be no tumble in a hayrick either, and he hovered close at hand, keeping his daughter and Hugh under his benevolent, paternal eye—much to their mutual frustration.

Soon, though, customers began to crowd around the stall, wanting to consult with Mauger about their various ailments. Hugh took advantage of the confusion to seize Emma's hand. "Are you not going to show me your wares?"

Emma giggled. "Well . . . this is calament, a remedy for chest colds, best drunk hot. And this is sanicle, a gargle for those poor souls with throat ulcers. And over there are leeks, which ward off lightning, and wormwood, which kills fleas. But here is our most costly restorative, powdered unicorn horn from Cathay. Men say it protects you from poison." Casting Hugh a seductive sideways glance, she murmured, "They also say it does wonders for your manhood."

Hugh's mouth twitched. "Do you think my manhood needs help?"

Emma laughed low in her throat. "Jesú forfend!" But then, to her dismay, Hugh spun around. "I'll be back," he cried over his shoulder, before disappearing into the crowd. Emma's bewilderment was not long in giving way to vexed understanding. By the rood, if he was not off to defend the Lady Ellen's honor again!

Hugh was swearing under his breath, shoving and pushing against a wall of bodies. He ought never to have left her, not with so many strangers about, men ignorant of her identity, for if her dress was plain, her face was not. He'd developed a keen eye for potential trouble, had spotted the man almost at once, mounted on a blooded palfry, a fashionable mantle flung carelessly over his shoulder, just the sort of prideful young lordling to see a pretty village lass as fruit ripe for the picking. And this one was more brazen than most. He'd drawn rein, staring quite blatantly at the Lady Ellen, then slid from the saddle, tossing the reins to his servant. By then, though, Hugh was in motion, cursing himself for having allowed Emma to distract him from his duties.

Ellen was laughing at the antics of a small trained terrier; it was dancing on its hind legs in time to its master's tambour. Her attention focused upon the dog, Ellen was unaware that she was about to be accosted, not until the man grabbed her arm. She whirled, giving a surprised cry that turned into a scream as Hugh came barreling through the crowd, sent the man sprawling. It was one of his better football tackles; his target reeled backward, sat down heavily in the dirt.

Even before he regained his feet, Hugh sensed that he'd made a mistake. Revelers at a fair were a boisterous lot; nothing was likely to please them more than a brawl. Yet now he saw shock and disapproval upon the closest faces. "Are you daft, lad?" an elderly man remonstrated. "Whatever possessed you to clout a priest?" And it was only then that Hugh saw the well-tailored cassock beneath his victim's stylish mantle.

As the young priest got to his feet, he was jostled again, this time by Ellen, who flung herself into his arms with a joyful "Amaury!"

Hugh's chagrin chilled into consternation. "I am so sorry! But I thought that . . . that you were annoying my lady . . ."

Amaury was not mollified. "Priests do not often ravish women at village fairs," he observed coolly, dusting himself off with some care, and Hugh could not help thinking that he was not entirely to blame for the mishap. For certes, this youngest de Montfort son could not be more unlike his reckless, dark, and brooding elder brothers. He was only of average height, compact and sturdy, with curly chestnut hair, a neatly trimmed beard, and Ellen's hazel eyes. He looked elegant and urbane, and not amused in the least by Hugh's blunder. Although his anger was under restraint, it was real, nonetheless.

Hugh started to stammer another apology, but Ellen forestalled him. "I do not blame you, Hugh," she said, struggling gamely to suppress her laughter. "I've been warning Amaury for years that he looks more like a court fop than a servant of God. Little wonder you suspected the worst!" Turning back to her brother, she embraced him again. "I'd wager St Francis of Assisi was never once mistaken for a rake on the prowl! You might even take it as a compliment of sorts." When Amaury started to speak, she put a finger to his lips. "Ere you say something you'll regret, I think you ought to know the identity of my champion. Amaury, may I present Hugh de Whitton?"

Amaury's eyes cut sharply to Ellen. "The lad who was with Bran?" When she nodded, he glanced again at Hugh. And then he smiled. "Well, I'll say this for you, Hugh de Whitton. You make quite an impact upon a first meeting."

Hugh, smiling back shyly, could only marvel that his loyalty to Bran should have proven to be such a golden key, giving him unconditional entry into the very heart of the House of Montfort.

NELL found it difficult to forgive Guy for the havoc he had wreaked at Viterbo. He had committed the most profane of murders. Her nephew had not deserved such a death and well she knew it. Her brother Richard had never gotten over his son's murder, suffering an apoplectic seizure that proved fatal. Amaury had almost been sucked into the mire, too, splattered with the guilt of a blood-bond. Ellen had forfeited all chances of making a marriage that would be her salvation. Even Simon had not been spared, for now the proud name of de Montfort would evoke more than memories of his martyrdom. It would evoke images of a blood-stained altar cloth, a church defiled, a dying priest. And Bran—a grave on a lonely Tuscan hillside, eternal exile for an anguished, unquiet soul.

But Guy's April excommunication had sent shock tremors through all her painstakingly constructed defenses. An excommunicate was to be shunned by his fellow Christians as a man with "leprosy of the soul." None could break bread with him, pray with him, even acknowledge his existence. He was legally dead, with no rights under the law. He was denied the solace of the Sacraments, and if he died with the Church's curse still upon him, he could not be buried in consecrated ground. And an excommunicate—her son—was damned forever in the fires of Hell Everlasting.

Nell had yet to take her eyes from Amaury's face. "You have news of Guy," she said, bracing herself for fresh grief.

Amaury nodded. "I'm sure you've guessed that Ned was the one who finally prodded the Pope into action. When he reached Tuscany last February, he set about hunting Guy down. To his fury, though, the citizens of Siena and Florence balked. The Podestà of Siena even pleaded on Guy's behalf, and arranged for Guy to meet secretly in the city with Charles. That," he added, with a grin, "Ned never knew—else he'd have suffered a seizure for certes!"

"Guy met with Charles?" Nell was no innocent; she was King John's daughter. But even she was startled by the extent of Charles of Anjou's cynicism.

"Guy has not been forsaken, Mama. His father by marriage has stood by him, and his wife even appealed personally to the Pope. But with Ned in Tuscany, breathing down his neck, Guy thought it prudent to put some distance between them, and withdrew to the Count's castle at Monte Gemoli in the Cecina Valley. Once Ned realized that Guy was out of reach, he prevailed upon the Pope to excommunicate him, as you know."

Amaury paused. "It was then that I decided it was time to talk some sense into Guy; the stakes were just too high. It was no easy task, for Guy is Lucifer-proud. My arguments about the salvation of his soul fell on deaf ears. But I eventually convinced him that his defiance was playing right into Ned's hands, that Charles would not dare to restore him to favor as long as he was accursed by God. I also pointed out that nothing would enrage Ned more than if Guy reconciled with the Pope."

"Are you saying that Guy has made his peace with the Church?" Nell asked incredulously. Ellen, too, looked astonished.

Again, Amaury nodded. "On July sixteenth, as the Pope left Florence, Guy met him on the road, barefoot as befitted a true penitent, with a rope halter about his neck." Amaury smiled thinly. "The Pope was impressed by such a spectacular act of contrition, and I did my best to convince him that Guy's repentance was heartfelt." Another hinted smile. "Being a papal chaplain does have its advantages; having the Pope's ear is most decidedly one of them. The result was that the Pope declared Guy a prisoner of the Church and put him into the custody of that gentle gaoler, Charles of Anjou. Charles promptly sent Guy to his castle at Lecco on Lake Como, with servants and fine wines to ease the burden of confinement."

"But I met with Edward at Melun in early August, and he made no mention of this!"

"He'd not yet heard. When he does, he's like to declare war upon the Holy See," Amaury joked, but neither his mother nor sister laughed. A silence fell, broken at last by Ellen.

"I want to tell Juliana," she said, rising. "And Hugh has a right to know, too."

As the door closed behind her, Nell reached out, entwined her fingers in Amaury's. "She knew I wanted some private time with you. Where the two of you get your tact, the Lord God only knows; for certes, not from me or Simon! Amaury, I must tell you of my meeting with Edward. He was far more generous than I'd expected, has agreed to restore my Pembroke dower lands. But he refused to allow you or the Bishop of Chichester to return to England."

Her hand tightened upon his. "I do not know why he bears you such ill will. Mayhap because you refused to disown Guy. Or because you persuaded the Pope that Simon should be reburied in consecrated soil. He may even still believe you were implicated in the Viterbo killing. But this I do know—that his hatred of you runs so deep a man might drown in it."

Guy would have sneered; Bran might have shrugged. Amaury knew only a fool would make light of an English king's enmity. "I doubt then," he said, "that I shall be making any pilgrimages to English shrines. Mama, I want now to talk about you. Ellen wrote to me that you've been ailing."

"Ellen is fretting for naught. Sometimes if I am too long on my feet, my ankles swell, and I get out of breath if I exert myself too much, but surely such minor complaints—" Nell stopped abruptly, too late. So accustomed was she to underplaying her ailments that she'd forgotten Amaury would not be as easy to reassure as Ellen. Amaury had studied medicine at the University of Padua, and it was obvious that he'd at once comprehended the significance of her symptoms, making the same diagnosis as Marguerite's physician had done, that she was suffering from dropsy, an illness that was slow-paced but eventually fatal.

"Ah, Amaury, do not look like that! My dearest, death comes to us all, and in God's time. I do not fear it, for I am nigh on fifty-eight, have had joys and sorrows enough for any two lifetimes. I have no regrets for myself. They are all for Ellen."

Amaury was still in shock. But the son's need to hope was proving stronger than the doctor's diagnostic instincts. He could be wrong; it need not be dropsy. With an enormous effort, he focused upon what she was saying. "Ellen? What do you mean, Mama?"

"In less than a fortnight, your sister will be twenty-one, well past the age when young women of good birth are wed. What is going to happen to her, Amaury? A woman without a husband, without a male protector—"

"Christ, Mama, I'd give my life for Ellen!"

"My darling, I know that you would! But it is the sword men fear, not the psalter. Because you are a priest, there might well be fools who'd think that Ellen would have none to protect her or to avenge her, not with Bran dead, Guy in disgrace, and her cousin John in the Holy Land. That is just the way of men, those without honor. I need not tell you, Amaury, how often women are abducted, raped, forced into marriage against their will. Jesú, it nearly happened to my own grandmother, Eleanor of Aquitaine—twice! Ellen is no longer a great heiress, but she is beautiful, and I fear for her, fear that lust-blinded men might see her as fair game."

Hugh's protectiveness suddenly made sense to Amaury. "Then we must find her a husband, Mama, and the sooner the better."

"You sound like a sailor—any port in a storm! Would you have Ellen wed to some aged widower with foul breath and penny-pinching ways—our Ellen? Yes, I want a husband for Ellen, but he must be worthy of her, must be a man who'd protect and cherish her, who'd not try to break her spirit. I know how marriage is for most women, Amaury, but it was never like that for me, not with Simon. He let me speak my mind, trusted my judgment, confided in me. Growing up, Ellen saw that, saw how your father treated me. And I realized early on that we must take great care in choosing her husband."

Nell sat back in her chair, smiled sadly. "That is why I was so much in favor of the match with Llewelyn ap Gruffydd. Because he was a Prince, of course. But also because he was Welsh. The Welsh pamper their wives, lad, in truly astonishing ways. Their women cannot be wed against their will, as ours can. They cannot be beaten at a husband's whim. Under Welsh law, they can even object to a husband's infidelity! I'd seen how Llewelyn Fawr treated my sister Joanna, and I felt confident that his grandson would do right by Ellen. But it was not to be, and I regretted much more than the loss of a crown . . ."

"Well," Amaury said, after some moments of thoughtful quiet, "there is an honorable alternative to marriage. Ellen could take the veil. With a handsome corrody and the de Montfort name, who knows, she might end up as an abbess one day."

Nell was shaking her head. "Our Ellen's faith is deep, but we both know she has not the temperament for convent life. She'd find no contentment as a nun, no more than I could honor my vow of chastity— not after I met your father." She hesitated only briefly, for she knew his piety existed in harmony with a strong secular streak. "It was not," she explained playfully, "that I loved God less, but that I loved Simon more!" And Amaury justified her confidence by laughing softly.

"Ah, Amaury, how glad I am that you are here, that I can talk to you like this. I once asked—nay, demanded—so much from life. If it be true that ambition is a grievous sin, then grievously did Simon and I suffer for it. They're all gone, those old hungers, those high-flying dreams. Now I ask but one thing—that ere I die, I can see my daughter settled and safe. And yet I very much fear that is a wish beyond my grasp."

Amaury was silent. As much as he wanted to confort her, she was the one person he could not lie to, and he, too, feared for Ellen's future.

9

TALERDDIG GRANGE,
POWYS, WALES

January 1274

O<small>F</small> all the granges owned by the monks of Ystrad Marchell, Talerddig was the most isolated, sequestered deep in the mountains of western Powys. The monks and lay brothers were astonished, therefore, by the unexpected arrival of Gruffydd ap Gwenwynwyn, his wife, and son. Gruffydd was their lord, and they made haste to welcome him, wondering all the while what had brought him to this distant corner of his realm. Gruffydd did not enlighten them, and soon after dark, their cloistered quiet was broken by yet another arrival, a mystery guest muffled in a hooded mantle, accompanied by a small escort of armed men who rebuffed all attempts at conversation. Their lord was no more forthcoming, demanded to be taken at once to Gruffydd, and although his identity was hidden within that shadowed hood, his voice carried the steely inflection of one born to command. The lay brothers did not think to challenge him; instead, they obeyed.

Davydd sometimes suspected that he had a love of intrigue for its own sake. When he'd plotted with Edward against his brother, it had amused him enormously to insist upon a midnight meeting deep within the Welsh woods. Now he found himself relishing his clandestine role, and he wondered if men would be so quick to conspire were it not for the seductive trappings, the opportunity to play these high-risk games of espionage. He was still laughing softly as he entered the chamber of the Powys Prince.

That was not a title Gruffydd could still claim, although his forebears once had. But Gruffydd had the misfortune to be born in the lifetime at Llewelyn ab Iorwerth, known even to his enemies as Llewelyn Fawr, Llewelyn the Great. Gruffydd's father had challenged him, and died a broken man, a refugee at the English court. Gruffydd had grown up in English exile, not regaining the lost lands of Powys until Llewelyn Fawr's death in 1240. But another Llewelyn was soon to overshadow Wales, for the grandson had become the keeper of the grandsire's flame. Once again Gruffydd was forced to flee to England, and when he was eventually restored to his heritage, it was at a high price. This once proud Prince of Powys now held his lands as a vassal, swearing homage to his powerful neighbor to the north. Llewelyn's highborn countrymen recognized him as Prince of Wales no less reluctantly than did the English Crown. Their jealousy was Llewelyn's Achilles' heel—or so Davydd hoped.

Gruffydd seemed content to sit in silence, to let his son, Owen, and his English wife speak for him. There was no flash to the man; he was not one for shouting, for theatrical rages. Even his appearance was muted. Greyed and stooped, he showed every one of his fifty-eight years. But his hatred ran deep. Davydd knew that not many men would dare to defy Llewelyn.

Owen, his firstborn, had all the panache that Gruffydd lacked. He'd inherited his mother's English fairness, her sense of style, for Hawise was, at fifty, still an undeniably elegant woman. She'd been born a Lestrange, and Owen kept in close contact with his Marcher kin. He'd even adopted an English surname, calling himself Owen de la Pole instead of Owain ap Gruffydd. This misplaced pride was baffling to Davydd; he'd admit that English blood was no shame, but it was for certes nothing to boast about.

Owen had been holding forth for a good quarter hour, talking fast and tough, his the self-confident swagger of youth and privilege and an untested manhood. That, at least, was Davydd's acid assessment of his would-be ally. He listened, unimpressed, as Owen damned Llewelyn to eternal hellfire, vowed to reduce Dolforwyn to rubble.

Davydd marveled that one rock-hewn castle could so obsess men on both sides of the border. For Gruffydd, Dolforwyn's presence on Powys soil was one affront too many, was enough to push him into rebellion. And the English Crown had reacted with equal alarm, unwilling to allow a Welsh castle so close to their border stronghold at Montgomery. Acting in the absent Edward's name, the regents had even forbidden Llewelyn to proceed with its construction.

The bait was too tempting for Davydd to resist. "It sounds to me, Owen, as if you've been stricken with the same malady that infected the English court: Dolforwyn fever. They demanded that Llewelyn raze the castle, as I'm sure you know. But did I ever tell you about Llewelyn's response? He pointed out that he had every right to build castles in his own principality and, since Edward knew that full well, he could only conclude that the Chancery's letter must have been written without Edward's knowledge!"

Owen was not amused. "Are we here to plan Llewelyn's overthrow—or to commend his sardonic sense of humor? Are you with us, Davydd, or not? If we must look elsewhere for aid, better we should know now."

"And where would you look? My brother Owain? I daresay he'd be interested, but prisoners do not make ideal conspirators—do they? Ah, well, there's always my brother Rhodri. His grievance is real enough. Alas for you, though, Rhodri could walk across a field of newfallen snow and not leave a single footprint."

Owen was accustomed to being treated with the deference due a prince's son. He at once began to bristle, and his mother made haste to intercede, saying smoothly, "You are right, Davydd. We do need you. But you need us, too. Twice before you sought to overthrow your brother. Your first attempt gained you a year's confinement; your second, four years in English exile. Our support will make the difference, and I think you know that, else you'd not be here."

She paused. "The terms of our offer are straight-forward enough. In return for assisting you to claim Llewelyn's crown, Owen agrees to wed one of your daughters, and you cede to my husband the cantrefs of Ceri and Cydewain. That's more than fair, Davydd. You want what we do—Llewelyn's downfall. We are in agreement as to our aim. We need only agree upon our method."

Davydd's smile was razor thin. "I believe the method you had in mind was murder."

"And since when does killing make you queasy?" Owen demanded. "It's not as if we were asking you to do it yourself. All you have to do is get me and my men past Llewelyn's household guards. I'll take it from there. Damnation, Davydd, we told you that at our last meeting!"

"Yes, you did," Davydd said, "and I walked out."

Gruffydd stirred within the shadows. "But you came back," he said softly.

Davydd rose abruptly. "When I was nigh on seventeen, my brother Owain and I set out to claim my share of Gwynedd, led an army into Llewelyn's lands. He was waiting for us in the Bwlch Mawr pass, and in less than an hour, our men were in flight and all our hopes were bleeding away into the Desoch marshes. Owain and I were both taken prisoner. Owain was sure he was a dead man. But Llewelyn just looked at him and said, 'I am not Cain.' "

Gruffydd and Hawise exchanged glances. When Owen would have spoken, she shook her head. Gruffydd got slowly to his feet. "Your brother is too dangerous to let live. You and I might chafe under his high-handed ways, but too many Welshmen see him as their last and best hope of holding off the English. As our prisoner, he'd be a magnet for every rebel and malcontent in Wales. And if he ever got free . . . I'm not willing to risk that, Davydd. Alive, Llewelyn becomes a martyr. Dead, a memory."

Davydd did not answer, moved, instead, to the window. Hawise followed. "How old are you, Davydd?"

He gave her a bemused look, a terse "Thirty-six."

"You're Llewelyn's heir and likely to outlive him. But what of your brother Owain? He's been Llewelyn's prisoner for nigh on nineteen years, and he's well past fifty, is he not? You can wait. Can he?"

Davydd ignored her, reaching out and unlatching the shutters. The sudden blast of icy air caused him to gasp. The wind was raw and wet, coming from the east. The red wind of Shrewsbury, his people called it, gwynt coch Amythig. He'd begun to shiver, but he did not move until Hawise touched his arm. Only then did he close the shutters, turn again to face them.

"You were right, Gruffydd," he said. "I did come back."

Owen and Hawise could not conceal their jubilation. Gruffydd permitted himself a small smile. "I understand that Llewelyn will be at Cricieth Castle in late February, hearing appeals from the commote courts. Why not then?"

Davydd shook his head. "No. Toward the end of this month, he'll be staying at Llanfair Rhyd Castell, a grange owned by the monks of Aberconwy. It's closer to Powys, and we'd not have to deal with the Cricieth Castle garrison, just his household guard."

Gruffydd nodded approvingly. "You're right. I wonder I did not think of that myself. Let it be the abbey grange then, on Candlemas."

Owen smiled, too, but with an edge to it. "Are you sure you can gain entry for me and my men?"

"Yes," Davydd said, very evenly, "I am sure. He trusts me, you see."

THE rain had begun to fall on Candlemas Eve. When dawn came, the darkness lingered. All day long the skies were the color of slate, and so torrential was the rain that the lay brothers of Llanfair Rhyd Castell began to worry that the river might rise. To ease their fears, Llewelyn set up a flood watch.

The vile winter weather had not deterred petitioners, and Llewelyn had spent the better part of the day presiding over the llys uchaf, his high court. He'd taken a brief break for dinner, but he then withdrew to a quiet corner of the guest hall, began a low-voiced, intent discussion with Tudur ab Ednyved, his Seneschal. Davydd was not surprised by his diligence; his brother's work hours were legendary.

At Davydd's approach, Llewelyn looked up with a distracted smile. Tudur was less welcoming. His father, Ednyved ap Cynwrig, had been the greatest of Llewelyn Fawr's ministers. Tudur was the third of Ednyved's sons to serve as Seneschal to the Prince of Gwynedd. Like his brothers before him, he was blunt, shrewd, and not easily surprised. He'd never liked Davydd, had never bothered to hide it, either. At the sight now of those narrowed dark eyes and that thin-lipped mouth, Davydd had to reassure himself that Tudur's suspicions were nothing out of the ordinary, that he could have no inkling as to what the night would bring.

"Over the years, I've managed to offend, at one time or another, the Church, the Welsh lords, and my own tenants. Well, we now have a chance to offend them all at once, in one fell swoop," Llewelyn said wryly. "We've decided to impose a tax upon cattle, three pence per head."

Davydd whistled soundlessly. "That has never been done."

"I know," Llewelyn conceded. "But the money is trickling in, Davydd, and gushing out. In addition to the five hundred marks I'm obliged to pay the English Crown every Michaelmas, I've incurred heavy expenses trying to stave off Marcher forays, and the cost of garrisoning Dolforwyn is higher than we'd expected. The English King levies tallages upon his subjects anytime he needs funds, so why should we not take a leaf from his book?"

"But you're not the English King," Davydd said laconically, and Llewelyn laughed.

"You're right, lad. I suppose I should be thankful for small favors!"

Tudur laughed, too. Davydd did not, turned away abruptly. Intercepting one of the lay brothers, he grabbed a goblet from the man's tray. But he dared take no more than one swallow, dared not seek to steady his nerves with mead. Glancing at a candle notched to show the hours, he saw, disbelieving, that it was just past eight. More than five hours yet to go, for Owen had told him to await them between midnight and Matins, when all would be asleep. He'd not expected this, to feel so hollow, so edgy, for he'd fought his share of battles, had first bloodied his sword at sixteen. But the death that crept into a darkened bed-chamber was no kin to the death that claimed soldiers in the light of day. He'd not known that until this Friday eve, watching his brother laugh and drink and plan for the morrow. Like most men of his class, Davydd had a passion for the hunt, but he'd never before known what it was like to identify with the hunter's prey.

The door opened and Einion hastened inside, swathed from head to foot in a protective mantle, but soaking wet, nonetheless. Dripping his way toward the hearth, he joked to Davydd in passing that they'd best see if there were any local carpenters with experience in ark build-ing. Einion's arrival yesterday had jolted Davydd, for he was fond of his uncle. What was to happen seemed somehow uglier, less defensible, if viewed through Einion's eyes.

When Einion entered, Llewelyn's wolfhounds had begun to bark thunderously, but they quieted as Caitlin moved among them, bestow-ing pats and table scraps. Caitlin's presence at Llanfair Rhyd Castell had been the nastiest surprise of all; Davydd had assumed that Llewelyn would not bring her, for females were no more welcome at Aberconwy's granges than they were at the abbey itself. But here she was, and no matter how he tried, Davydd could think of no plausible excuse for sending her away, not without arousing dangerous suspicions. All he could do was to make sure she was not an actual eye-witness to Llewelyn's death, and in his heart he knew that was not enough, not nearly enough.

Never had Davydd been so restless. The windows were all tightly barred, but he could hear the rain thudding against the shutters. Men venturing outdoors told of broken branches strewn about like twigs, and one monk claimed that the normally placid Conwy was surging at such a flood-tide that it looked verily like a white-water cauldron. Not for the first time, it occurred to Davydd that Owen and his men might be held up by the storm. The way his luck was going so far, they were likely not to arrive till dawn—just in time for breakfast with Llewelyn.

Davydd laughed at that, but without humor. Einion had joined Llewelyn and Tudur, and Davydd was not surprised when his daughter drifted over, too. He soon followed, unable to help himself. Their con-versation was easy, random; one of the lay brothers brought them a plate of jam-filled wafers, mead for the men, cider for the child. They talked, naturally, of the storm, and then of a tragic fire that had recently claimed the lives of a valley herdsman, his family, and a passing stranger, who'd sought in vain to drag them to safety. His act was one of great gallantry, they all agreed, and the talk turned to other exploits of courage. Tudur related several stories of battlefield bravery. Einion paid a moving tribute to a priest he'd known, one who'd chosen to live amidst lepers, "so they'd not think God, too, had forsaken them." "What say you, Davydd?" he queried, once he was done. "What was the bravest act you ever saw?"

Davydd tilted his chair at a gravity-defying angle. "I was never sure if it was an act of bravery—or bravado. It occurred at the siege of Northampton, about a month ere Simon de Montfort won the battle of Lewes. Bran de Montfort had been taken prisoner by men-at-arms unable to believe their good fortune, for no ransom would be too high for Simon's son. But King Henry's whoreson half-brother rode up, William de Lusignan, the one who married into the earldom of Pembroke. De Lusignan told Bran that he'd spare his life—if he begged for it. We all knew he meant it, too, yet Bran never even blinked. 'Rot in Hell,' he said."

Caitlin's eyes had widened. "What happened to him?"

"Your father saw fit to spoil de Lusignan's fun," Llewelyn said with a faint smile, "reminding them that Edward did not want Bran harmed. They were cousins, you see, Caitlin, and still friends—then."

Davydd had not realized that Llewelyn had heard of the part he'd played at Northampton. "You know me, Llewelyn," he said with a shrug. "I never could resist a chance to meddle."

That earned him a laugh, from all but Tudur. Llewelyn now began to share his story of courage, one that hit home for Davydd, as it involved their father. Speaking to the child, Llewelyn explained how his grandfather had been forced to yield thirty highborn hostages to the English King, John of evil fame.

"One of them was my father, lass. The following year, John hanged the Welsh hostages at Nottingham Castle—all but Gruffydd. He was just sixteen, watched as his friends were dragged out to die, expecting his turn would be next. But John decided he'd be worth more alive. Do you remember, Caitlin, that John's daughter Joanna was my grandfather's wife? Well, John did love her in his way, and so he commanded Gruffydd to write to Llewelyn, to request that Joanna pay a visit to the English court. This was less than a year after the hangings at Nottingham. Yet Gruffydd dared to balk, refusing to write that letter. The Earl of Chester was present, and he told my grandfather years later that John had warned he could make Gruffydd write that letter if need be. But Gruffydd just said, 'You can try.' "

There was a moment of appreciative silence. Hostage taking was a fact of life on both sides of the border. Caitlin knew hostages could be held for years, as was the case with Tudur's son, Heilyn. But she'd not known they might be sacrificed. The hangings at Nottingham gave a new and sinister significance to the practice, and she turned troubled green eyes upon her father. "Were you not once a hostage of the English, too, Papa?"

Davydd nodded. "For seven years. My mother turned Rhodri and me over to the English King in return for his help in freeing my father."

There was much Caitlin did not know of her own House's history, for although Llewelyn enjoyed reminiscing about his grandfather, he rarely spoke of his childhood, the other members of their family. "What of you, Uncle?" she asked. "Why were you not offered as hostage, too?"

"That was my mother's intent. She'd brought Davydd, Rhodri, and me with her to Shrewsbury, where she hoped to come to terms with the English King. My father was being held at Cricieth Castle by his half-brother; war had broken out between them upon my grandfather's death. Henry promised her his aid. Of course he later reneged, sent my father and Owain to the Tower. But at the time, she believed him, agreed to surrender her sons. Davydd was only three, Rhodri even younger, but I was past thirteen, with a mind of my own. I overheard the English King talking in the abbey garden, and that same night, I ran away."

"You came first to our bedchamber," Davydd said suddenly, and Llewelyn gave him a surprised look.

"Yes, I did. You remember that?"

Davydd was surprised, too. "Yes . . . I do. You gave me something?"

Llewelyn nodded. "My crucifix. Also two of the angel's bread wafers I'd stolen from the abbey kitchen, one for you and one for Rhodri. Of course you ate them both!" Then his grin faded. "You asked to come with me, and for a mad moment, I truly considered it. I soon realized, though, that I'd not get far, a green, scared stripling with two bairns in tow. But it was hard, lad, leaving you behind." He smiled ruefully. "For the longest time afterward, I suffered the guilt pangs of the damned, fretted that—"

Davydd set his chair down with a crash. "That is ridiculous! Why should you feel guilty when it was none of your doing?" He'd spoken so sharply that they were all staring at him. Shoving his chair back, he pushed away from the table.

Snatching up his mantle, he strode toward the door. But as soon as he jerked it open, he reconsidered. The rain was gusting sideways, stung like sleet. He stood there for a time in the porch recess, watching the storm's fury, struggling with an anger no less intense and just as unforeseen. He'd often heard people speak of a "keening" wind, had dismissed it as poetic hyperbole—until tonight. As it whipped through the trees, his ears were filled with the sound, a high-pitched wailing that did evoke haunting echoes of grief.

"Davydd?" The wind had muffled Llewelyn's footsteps, and Davydd jerked violently at the sudden touch upon his arm. Swearing, he leaned back against the porch railing, away from the revealing glimmer of Llewelyn's lantern.

"Davydd, what is amiss? I've never seen your nerves on the raw like this. All night you've been shying at shadows." Davydd caught a flash of white, a fleeting smile. "I'd have wagered you were the one cock whose feathers could not be ruffled—had I not been watching you for these past hours. Is it trouble you can talk about?"

"Can you not guess? Whenever you see a man playing the fool, can you doubt that you're looking at a woman's handiwork?"

Llewelyn fought back a grin, tried to remember the name of Davydd's latest lady. "Tangwystl?"

"She wants us to wed, and I do not, was reckless enough to tell her so. Women do not fight fair. There are no formal declarations of war, no truces, and they take no prisoners. I won the battle. So why do I feel like the sort of lowborn knave who'd steal from a church alms box, seduce a nun, and for good measure, kick Caitlin's puppy?"

Llewelyn was laughing openly by now. "As you said, you won the battle. Just be sure to invite me to the wedding. Listen—did you hear that?"

Davydd had. He tensed as riders took form out of the wet blackness beyond the porch. They were heading for the stables when the lead rider recognized Llewelyn. "My lord, it's me—Cynan ab Ivor! We set out this morn from Llyn Tegid, did not think we'd make it this far. The roads to the south are all washed out, and we just missed a mudslide on the Powys border. I have never been so scared in all my born days, God's truth!"

"See to your mounts, Cynan, then go into the hall to dry off and get fed." The wind had shifted; the rain had begun to slant under the porch roof, and Llewelyn jogged Davydd's arm. "Let's go inside ere we drown."

Davydd did not hear him, had heard nothing after "The roads to the south are all washed out." He stared at his brother, and then began to laugh. So God, too, was on Llewelyn's side!

DOLBADARN rose up on a spur of high ground between two ice-blue lakes. Shadowed by the highest peaks of Eryri, the castle's vistas were among the most scenic in Gwynedd. Year after year, Owain ap Gruffydd had gazed out across the lake, watching as low-lying clouds drifted in from the southwest, spangling the valley with showers of silver rain, watching as December snows crowned the summit of Yr Wyddfa, as barren oaks budded anew and mountain ash embraced autumn gold. He watched wood sorrel bloom and die, watched as swallows arrived each April, fled before the first frost, watched as eagles soared above the crags of Eryri. The seasons blurred, his youth melted away with the spring thaws, and, ever so slowly, so did a lifetime's rage.

His hatred had sustained him during the early years of his captivity, his visions of vengeance. But time had proved to be as much his enemy as Llewelyn. It became harder and harder to cling to hope. Eventually he was forced to face a shattering truth, that the brother he'd so under-estimated was not going to free him. Llewelyn had won their war. The years that followed were the worst, for, without hope, he had only self-pity to hold on to. When it had begun to change, he could not say, so gradual had it been. He still hated Llewelyn, but it was a muted passion now, a banked fire when once it had been an inferno.

His confinement was not stringent. He was denied no comforts, treated with the deference due his bloodlines, and he was permitted an occasional visitor, was not cut off entirely from the world beyond Dolbadarn's walls. He had his good days, a bedmate when he had need of one, the satisfaction of knowing that he'd not been forgotten, that even among Llewelyn's staunchest supporters, he could find some sympathy for his plight. All he lacked was all that mattered—his freedom.

On this mild day in mid-March, he was dicing with Dolbadarn's castellan when the guards brought word of his brother's arrival. Owain was always delighted to have any visitors at all, but no one was more welcome than Davydd, the one person in Christendom to whom he still felt connected, his lifeline to memories of the man he used to be.

Davydd rushed through the usual courtesies, dismissed the castellan as soon as it was politely possible. As always, he felt a small shock at sight of his brother, found himself thinking: Jesú, he's an old man! Owain was fifty-five. In his youth, he'd been called Owain Goch—Owain the Red—a tribute as much to his fiery temper as to his fiery red hair. The hair had long since gone grey, and the temper was not much in evidence these days, either. Sometimes Davydd had the unsettling sense that he was visiting a ghost, tending a flame already quenched.

Once they were alone, Davydd shot the bolt into place, leaned back against the door. "Make yourself comfortable, Big Brother, for I have quite a tale to tell. Have you ever heard of a rebellion that was rained out?"

Owain was soon sitting bolt upright on the bed. But he did not interrrupt. Although it was obvious he was listening intently, his face was impassive. Usually his every emotion was flourished aloft like a battle banner, but now Davydd could read nothing of his thoughts.

When Davydd finally concluded with a deliberately dramatic account of the Candlemas storm, Owain waited a moment and then said crisply, "Go on."

"Go on? Is that not enough? What else would you like me to confess whilst I'm at it?"

For the first time, Owain showed surprise. "You did not make another attempt on Llewelyn's life?"

"No." Davydd's smile was sardonic. "Owen was nearly swept off a cliff by one of those mudslides. His night out in the rain seems to have dampened his zeal for our noble enterprise."

Owain did not share his smile, for as fond as he was of Davydd, he'd always been baffled by his brother's perverse brand of humor. "So it is Owen who is now loath to pursue this plot further?" he asked, with enough skepticism to shake Davydd's bravado.

"And me? Is that what you're asking, if I want to let it lie? What if I do?"

Owain had rarely heard him sound so defensive. "You know, lad," he said quietly, "there is no shame in balking at murder."

Davydd expelled a pent-up breath. "I had not expected it to be so hard, Owain. I had the right. It is Llewelyn who makes a mockery of Welsh law, not us. Why should I not try to take what was mine? But sitting across the table from him that night, knowing what I knew . . . Christ, Owain, I could not do that again. There has to be another way."

"I wish you'd known our father the way I did," Owain said unexpectedly, sounding so earnest that Davydd had to smile. "Papa used to say that each man's honor depended upon where he drew the line. Papa drew it too far out; it made him slow to suspect, easy to betray. I've wondered at times, lad, where you drew it."

"So did I," Davydd said slyly, and Owain smiled.

"Well, at least now you know. But why did it have to be murder? I'd have been more than willing to let Llewelyn have my chamber here at Dolbadarn."

Davydd gave him a look of amused affection, for that was as close as Owain ever came to humor. "Gruffydd and Owen were loath to take such a risk. They wanted him dead."

"I cannot blame them for that," Owain conceded. "Llewelyn makes a bad enemy. I should know!" Rising, he moved to the table, poured wine into two cups. Handing one to Davydd, he said, "But I shall miss you, lad. It's not likely, after all, that we'll meet again."

"Why not? Owain, are you ailing?"

"No, but you'll have to seek safety in England—" Owain broke off, staring at the younger man. "Mother of God, Davydd, you cannot mean to stay!"

"Why not?" Davydd repeated, quite coolly this time.

"Because it's bound to come out! Too many people are involved—the men Owen took with him, Gruffydd's retainers at Trallwng Castle, the monks at Tallerddig, your own escort. They do not even have to know all that much, just that you'd met secretly with the lords of Powys. How long ere someone confides in his wife, or begins to brag after a few tankards of ale? How long ere someone begins to wonder what his secret might be worth to Llewelyn?"

"I'll not deny that there is a danger, Owain. If I stay, I wager my lands, my freedom, mayhap my life. But if I flee, I lose all for certes."

Owain was appalled. "Davydd, the danger is too great. I know Llewelyn, better than you. Do not delude yourself that you could get him to forgive you. Have you learned nothing from my mistakes? I've lost nineteen years of my life because I held Llewelyn too cheaply, could not see the flint in his soul. It is true that there was ever ill will between us, and it is no less true that if he has a weakness, it is his fondness for you. But do you truly think that he'd overlook murder? You could not talk your way out of this, lad. God help you if you are foolish enough to try."

Davydd shrugged. "With so much at stake, Owain, God help me if I do not try."

DAVYDD and his men were having breakfast in the guest hall of Aberconwy Abbey. The other abbey guests had departed at first light, but Davydd was a late riser, and a hungry one. He'd never shared the common belief that breakfast was a shameless indulgence, liked to joke that he believed in indulging the flesh at every opportunity, a jest that shocked the brothers of this austere Cistercian order. He saw no reason this morn to hurry out into the rain, not with such a long ride ahead of him; his lands in Dyffryn Clwyd were a day's journey away, and the roads were mired in April mud. He was signaling for more cheese when new arrivals were ushered into the hall, but upon recognizing the man in the lead, he pushed the bench back, the food forgotten.

"What are you doing here, Rhys? This is an abbey, not a border bawdy-house!"

Rhys ap Gruffydd grinned, unoffended. He was Tudur's nephew, grandson of the great Ednyved, and like his celebrated kin, he had been long in Llewelyn's service. But Davydd knew what his brother did not, that Rhys's loyalties were not rooted deep. They'd struck up an easy friendship, "like recognizing like," Davydd joked, and to some degree, that was indeed true. Rhys did find Davydd's rowdy companionship more congenial than that of his aloof, intense elder brother.

"I thought you were with Llewelyn at Aber?"

"I was, rode out just this morn. I'm on my way to Creuddyn, but one of our horses threw a shoe. Davydd . . ." Lowering his voice. "Something right strange is going on at Aber. Yesterday a man high in Gruffydd ap Gwenwynwyn's favor was secretly taken to Llewelyn's chamber, and after he left, Llewelyn was as tautly drawn as my best longbow. My uncle Tudur was also in a vile mood, even more soured than usual. And soon after, Llewelyn announced abruptly that he would be leaving on the morrow for his castle at Dolforwyn. I know for certes that he'd planned to remain at Aber for another fortnight. Something is in the wind, but what? And why Powys?"

Rhys was disappointed that his news had such little impact; Davydd said nothing. "Are you heading east, too, Davydd? If so, we can ride together."

Davydd roused himself with an effort. "Where I go, you'd not want to follow."

Rhys couldn't tell if Davydd was joking or not. "And where is that, pray tell?"

"Into the lion's den," Davydd said, without a glimmer of a smile.

LLEWELYN's seacoast manor at Aber had long been a favorite residence of the princes of Gwynedd. One of its advantages was its location; it was but six miles from the see of the Bishop of Bangor, eight miles from the abbey of Aberconwy. Davydd rode through the gateway before noon. There he drew rein, looking upon a scene of utter confusion. Men were splashing through the mud, carrying saddles and bridles, leading pack horses from the stables. Others were lugging out small coffer chests and bedrolls and wooden crates. Dogs darted underfoot, barking furiously, dodging kicks from harried servants. The air was thick with sputtered oaths, with threats and counterthreats. Moving a princely household from one manor to another was a massive undertaking even under the most ideal circumstances. With but a day's warning, all was predictable chaos.

It was a sight that would normally have had Davydd roaring with laughter. As it was, the unintentionally comic antics of these pressured men barely registered with him. The impulse that had sent him galloping for Aber, that had compelled him to face trouble head on, rather than waiting and wondering, while fearing the worst, suddenly seemed an act of incredible folly. But it was too late to retreat. His uncle was emerging from the great hall, swerved abruptly in his direction.

"Davydd? What are you doing here, lad?"

Einion looked surprised, but not suspicious, and Davydd took heart from that. Surely Llewelyn would have confided in him? Or would he? Mustering a smile, he said, "Actually, Uncle, I was on my way into Llŷn to see you, was just stopping at Aber to pay my respects to Llewelyn. I had not known you were here, too . . . although not for long, it seems. Where does Llewelyn go in such a mad rush?"

"South . . . into Powys." Einion moved closer to Davydd's stallion. "There is trouble, lad. But I'd best let Llewelyn tell you."

As he followed Einion into Llewelyn's bedchamber, Davydd's nerves steadied; he'd always found the time before a battle to be more stressful than the action itself. "What has happened?" he asked, and then Llewelyn was turning toward him, and as their eyes met, he felt a surge of hot triumph. So Llewelyn did not know!

So intense was his relief that it took him a few moments to focus upon what his brother was saying. Gruffydd had been betrayed, but it was not as bad as he'd feared, as it could be. The informant knew nothing of the assassination plot, nothing of his own involvement. The details were sketchy, the tipster's account filled with life-saving blanks. But he'd learned—and revealed—enough to put Gruffydd in a very precarious position, under strong suspicion of scheming to annex the cantrefs of Ceri and Cydewain.

"Well?" Tudur said tersely. "Have you nothing to say?"

"I suppose I am still taking it in. I have to admit that I am surprised. I never thought Gruffydd ap Gwenwynwyn to be a fool—until now."

"He's not a fool, Davydd. He's Welsh," Llewelyn said, with such bitterness that Davydd caught his breath. It was not often that he saw his brother with his defenses down like this.

Llewelyn had begun to pace. "Our grandfather used to say that we Welsh were our own worst enemies. God Above, how right he was! How long are we going to play the game by English rules? They need not sow seeds of dissension amongst us; that is our most bountiful crop!"

Davydd was so elated by his reprieve that he'd cheerfully have agreed with virtually anything Llewelyn might have said at this point. "Too true," he said quickly. "A pity envy was not a cash crop, else Wales would be the most prosperous realm in Christendom."

"Why can we not make them understand, Davydd, how much is at stake? Why do they think the Scots have managed to keep the English from carving up their kingdom? Because the Scots have the sense to rally around their kings, to put their differences aside whenever they're threatened by the English Crown. But we Welsh . . . was ever a people so stiff-necked, so willfully blind? The Marcher lords have sunk their roots so deep into Welsh soil that we'll never be free of them. Why can our people not see the danger? Wales must be united, whole, with one prince to speak for us, as the Scots kings do. How can I hope to fend off the wolf at our door if I must constantly be on the alert for foxes under the window?"

Davydd said nothing, and Llewelyn gave him a sudden, searching look. "I know there are many who complain that I keep too heavy a hand on the reins. The Welsh are likely to balk at the first prick of the spurs—if not sooner. But do they truly think that Edward would be a more benevolent overlord?"

Davydd shrugged. "London is a lot farther away than Aber, Llewelyn."

"They think miles are all that matter?" Llewelyn sounded incredulous. "They honestly believe Edward would be content to reign, that he'd not want to rule, too? The English scorn us as a backward, primitive people, Godless and befouled with sin. Edward is a crusader King; he'd see it as his divine duty to bring us the dubious benefits of English custom and English law. And he'd open the floodgates to English settlers, charter English towns on Welsh soil, turn Gwynedd into an English shire. We'd become aliens in our own land, denied our own laws, our own language, even our yesterdays, for a conquered people are not allowed a prideful past. Worst of all, we'd be leaving our children and grandchildren a legacy of misery and loss, a future bereft of hope."

Llewelyn stopped abruptly, and for some moments, there was only silence, one haunted by his harrowing vision of a Welsh Apocalypse. "I would die ere I let that come to pass," he said at last. "Why is that not enough for the Gruffydd ap Gwenwynwyns? What more do they want of me?"

"If they could only have heard you just now, Llewelyn, you'd have converted half of Wales to your cause," Davydd said, and meant it. "For certes, you'd have gotten me to join your crusade," he added jauntily, and he meant that, too—almost—for his quarrel was with the messenger, not the message. "But your eloquence is wasted upon Gruffydd ap Gwenwynwyn. What happens now? Dolforwyn is conveniently close to his castle at Trallwng. I assume you've a siege in mind?"

Llewelyn slowly shook his head. "We shall summon Gruffydd before my council to answer these charges. If he can, well and good. If not, a forfeit will be levied against a portion of his lands."

Davydd's surprise was momentary. Almost at once, his skepticism reasserted itself. "I'd say that was most magnanimous of you, Llewelyn—if I did not know you so well. No prince forgives treason, not when such forbearance could prove fatal. What do you truly mean to do?"

Llewelyn's smile was sudden, approving. "You may have your faults, Davydd, but slowness of wit is not amongst them. The truth, then? There is more to this plot than we know. There has to be, for

Gruffydd is as wary as a treed cat, not one to jump till he is sure what lies below. If he'd moved into Ceri or Cydewain, I'd soon have followed, with an army at my back, and he would know that full well. So how did he hope to escape my vengeance? That is what I want to know, what I intend to find out."

No longer smiling, he said, "I shall give Gruffydd a chance to explain, and then . . . just enough rope with which to hang himself."

ON April 17, Gruffydd ap Gwenwynwyn was called before the council of his liege lord, Llewelyn ap Gruffydd. Gruffydd's son Owen blustered and ranted and denied—unconvincingly—all guilt. Gruffydd wisely chose to cut his losses, admitted that he had, indeed, been guilty of shameful disloyalty to his Prince. His was a public and harsh humiliation, followed by the seizure of the cantref of Arwystli and part of Cyfeiliog. He was compelled to yield his son Owen as a hostage for his future loyalty, and the remainder of his Powys lands were then restored to his control, with the significant, sinister proviso that, should further treachery come to light, he would forfeit all his estates in perpetuity.

But Owain's fears for Davydd had been well founded. The Welsh soil had always been a fertile breeding ground for rumors. Now, fed by speculation and watered by suspicion, a new crop was soon ripe for harvesting. Eventually, inevitably, these rumors implicated Llewelyn's younger brother, and in early October, Davydd was summoned to defend himself before Llewelyn's council at Rhuddlan Castle.

10

RHUDDLAN CASTLE, WALES

October 1274

DAVYDD was not surprised that Rhuddlan's great hall should be so full, every seat taken, every corner filled with jostling, craning spectators, every eye upon him. He knew how men flocked to bear-baitings, cheered themselves hoarse at cock fights, turned out in huge numbers for any public hanging.

He paused deliberately in the doorway, in part to make a suitably dramatic entrance, in part to give himself a chance to identify the enemy. Like patches of ice in a field of melting snow, the unbleached habits of the White Monks stood out prominently amidst so many tunics of russet and green. Davydd recognized the Abbots of the abbeys of Aberconwy, Cwm-hir, and Cymer. Not much hope there; the Cistercians were Llewelyn's, heart and soul. The Bishop of Bangor was a more promising prospect. He'd been feuding with Llewelyn for months, might balk out of sheer spite. Forget Tudur ab Ednyved; he'd want a front row seat at the gallows. Nor would he get any support from Goronwy ap Heilyn, Tudur's nephew; he could not begin to count the whores and wine flagons they'd shared over the years, but their friendship had not survived his alliance of expediency with the English Crown. Dai ab Einion, another one who'd prefer to reach a guilty verdict straightaway, without the bother of a trial first. Rhys ap Gruffydd? He'd be sympathetic for certes, but lacked the backbone to defy Tudur and Llewelyn. Their uncle Einion liked him well enough, liked Llewelyn better. Even Owen de la Pole was on hand, looking far less sleek and self-assured as a hostage than he had as a would-be assassin. He glanced furtively at Davydd, then away, and Davydd thought he deserved all of this grief, if only for his bad judgment in ever taking Owen as an ally. There were other familiar faces in the hall, but he paid them no heed, knowing they would follow wherever Llewelyn led.

And where would that be? Davydd's gaze focused at last upon his brother. Llewelyn was sitting in an oaken high-backed chair upon the dais. A spiked candle flared behind him, throwing his face into shadow; no accident, Davydd was sure. Never had there seemed so much distance between them. Davydd wondered briefly if this was how he'd feel come Judgment Day, and then he raised his head, swaggered into the hall, into the vortex.

The hall quieted. He walked toward the dais in the sort of funereal, respectful silence he'd always associated with the sickbed of a dying rich relative. The urge to shatter it, to shock, was overwhelming, but for once he resisted temptation. Halting before his brother, he made a very formal, elaborate gesture of obeisance, one that stopped just short of parody. "I am here, my lords. Ask of me what you will."

Tudur was quick to take up the challenge; as Llewelyn's Seneschal, it fell to him to act as Justiciar. "Serious accusations have been made against you, my lord Davydd. Witnesses have come forward, men of good repute, who swear that you met secretly with Gruffydd ap Gwenwynwyn, Lord of Powys, on at least two occasions, at Mathrafal in the spring of 1273 and then at Gruffydd's castle at Trallwng last November."

Davydd had long ago learned that scornful laughter was often the most effective weapon in his arsenal. But now he did not have to fake it; the laughter welled up on its own, so sweet and sweeping was his relief. If this was all they had, he could walk out of this trap blindfolded. "If I did not know you had no sense of humor whatsoever, my lord Tudur, I'd think you must be joking. You summoned me before your high tribunal for this? Because ale-house gossip says I may have met with Gruffydd ap Gwenwynwyn nigh on two years ago?"

Tudur was quite unmoved by his mockery. "The first meeting took place on the last Sunday in Lent, the second on All Soul's Day. Does that prick your memory any?"

"No . . . should it? If you're asking where I was on a March Sunday sometime last year, I'm damned if I know. I can tell you this, that I was not in Powys."

"There are men willing to swear that you were," Llewelyn said, and his voice, too, was shadowed, utterly unrevealing.

Davydd decided it was time for a flash of anger. "Well, if they do, they lie!"

"Can you produce witnesses able to attest to your whereabouts on the dates in question?"

Llewelyn sounded so cool, so detached, that Davydd no longer had to feign anger. Damn him, was this so easy for him? "Yes, I can provide witnesses," he snapped. Who, though? Tangwystl? No, a bedmate would be too obvious. He needed someone of unimpeachable authority; a pity the Pope was otherwise occupied. But a monk, yes, a monk would do. Rhys ap Gruffydd had a brother who was a Dominican friar, and he liked Llewelyn no more than Rhys did. If Llewelyn wanted witnesses, then by God, he'd get them, honorable and upright and ready to swear upon Llewelyn's fragment of the True Cross that he'd been on the moon if need be, anywhere but Powys.

Tudur made no attempt to conceal his skepticism. Instead, he flaunted it, so well armored in sarcasm that he put Davydd in mind of a human hedgehog, one abristle with poisonous barbs. "I shall await their testimony with bated breath," he gibed. "Will a fortnight be time enough for you to . . . find them?"

Davydd shook his head, was about to launch into an impassioned plea for delay when Llewelyn said, "I shall be at Llanfor in Penllyn for Martinmas. Bring your witnesses there and I'll hear them."

That was more than fair. As much as it galled Davydd to admit it, it was even generous, would give him the time he needed. "Penllyn at Martinmas. You may be sure I'll not forget." He moved forward then, up onto the dais. "And now what?" he asked, pitching his voice for Llewelyn's ear alone. "Do I ride off into the sunset? Or do we talk?"

He was close enough now to see the finely webbed lines around Llewelyn's eyes, the taut set of his mouth. No, not so easy, after all, he thought, with a queer sense of satisfaction, and then Llewelyn slowly nodded. "We talk," he said tersely.

CANDLES caught fire, dispelling some of the dark. Prodding the hearth with iron tongs, a servant stirred it back to life, rose, and discreetly disappeared. Einion and Tudur settled themselves inconspicuously in one of the window-seats, but Nia, Llewelyn's young greyhound, planted itself at his feet. So closely did it shadow his every move that he laughingly called it his "bodyguard," but tonight there was an added dimension to its vigilance; like many dogs, it was sensitive to its master's moods, and the tension in the chamber was stoking all of the animal's protective instincts.

The greyhound's watchful demeanor was not lost upon Davydd. "Your suspicions must be catching, Llewelyn. Even your bitch seems to have been infected with them. If I help myself to some wine, is she going to help herself to my forearm?"

Llewelyn's mouth quirked. "We'll not know till you try." But then he crossed to the table, reached for a flagon, and poured. "If you are as innocent as you claim, why did you demand a safe-conduct ere you'd come to Rhuddlan?"

Davydd took the cup. "That ought to be obvious. Because I am no longer sure that I can trust you."

"Trust me?" Llewelyn echoed, incredulous.

"That surprises you? It should not, for trust is a two-edged sword. Did it even occur to you that I might not be guilty? No, of course it did not. With you, suspicion and certainty are spokes on the same wheel."

At that, Tudur could keep silent no longer. "This man's gall never fails to amaze me, Llewelyn. That he should dare to profess such righteous indignation—"

"And why not?" Davydd ignored Tudur, kept his eyes upon his brother. "I'm not entitled to be angry? Brace yourself for another surprise, Llewelyn, for I happen to think I'm the one who was wronged! And with cause, by God. For the past seven years, we've been allies . . . or so I thought. I've been welcome at your court, a member of your council, privy to your secrets. You even led me to believe that you favored me as your heir. There was no breach between us, no falling out. And then this—an accusation without warning, without proof. How do you expect me to react?"

"I expect you to remember your own past. You're no stranger to conspiracy and rebellion. Can you truly blame me for my suspicions? Twice before you betrayed me, Davydd."

"And twice you forgave me, or have you forgotten that? More fool I, for I thought we'd made our peace, put the past behind us. But if I'm to be judged again and again for old sins, then we'd best talk about them. Let's begin with my first rebellion. I was but sixteen, seeking only to claim my fair share of Gwynedd. Now that may have been a mistake, but it hardly makes me another Judas. And if I erred, I paid for it— sixteen months confinement at Cricieth Castle. I argued then that it was not treason to seek what was mine. Do you remember what you said? 'It is if you lose.' And I did lose. But Christ Jesus, Llewelyn, that was nigh on twenty years ago!"

"Do you truly think I'd harbor a lifelong grudge for one act of youthful folly?" Llewelyn shook his head impatiently. "Davydd, I understood why you threw in with Owain. But that is more than I can say for your subsequent double-dealings with the English Crown. I'd forgiven you, restored you fully to favor, only to have you plot my overthrow with Edward. Since you saw fit to start this, finish it, then. Tell me how you justify an alliance with our greatest enemy."

"I cannot justify it—not to you. But I daresay Owain saw it in a kinder light."

"I see. So your only concern was freeing Owain. You should have spoken up sooner, lad. All this time we've been damning you as a rebel, instead of honoring you as a saint."

"Do not mock me, Llewelyn. For once in my life, I am serious. Of course I wanted Gwynedd, or a good portion of it. I was heartily sick of holding my lands at your pleasure, and why not? Lest you forget, Welsh law was on my side, not yours. But I also wanted to free Owain from your gaol."

"So you'd have me believe you rebelled to set Owain free. Why should I not believe, then, that you'd do so again? Owain is still my prisoner, still your brother. What has changed? If that was your motive once, why not a second time?"

Tudur sat up straight, already hearing the trap jaws snapping shut. But Davydd was smiling tightly. "What has changed? Good God, man, more than eleven years have passed! Mayhap time has not tarnished your good intentions, but my halo rusted away years ago. Lunatic gallantry came more easily to me at twenty-four. At thirty-six, I have too much to lose. I'll not deny that I'd free Owain tomorrow if the power were mine. But it is not, and I'm not willing to barter my freedom for his."

Davydd had forgotten his wine cup. He drained it now, too fast.

"I was not plotting with Gruffydd ap Gwenwynwyn. Jesú, Llewelyn, how do I convince you? What would you have me do, swear upon my honor, upon the soul of our—"

"No," Llewelyn said hastily. "Whenever you start talking of honor, Davydd, I always feel that I should start counting the spoons."

Einion sucked in his breath, and Tudur smiled faintly, expectantly. But Llewelyn knew his brother better than they did. He alone was not surprised when Davydd burst out laughing.

"I forget, at times, just how well you know me! But at least I nail my pirate's flag to the mast, never sail under false colors. Llewelyn, I've been honest with you tonight, at no small cost to my pride. Will you return the favor?"

"What do you want to know? The names of our witnesses?"

Davydd shook his head. "If someone had come to you, claiming that Tudur or Einion had met secretly with Gruffydd ap Gwenwynwyn, would you have asked either of them to verify their whereabouts? Would you even have given it a second thought?"

Llewelyn found that an unexpectedly difficult question to answer. Of Gruffydd's four sons, only Owain had gotten his flaming red hair. Llewelyn's was dark, Davydd's a sunstreaked chestnut, and Rhodri's a lackluster brown. But Davydd did have their father's eyes, a clear, compelling shade of green, eyes that held his own without wavering. "No," he said reluctantly, "I'd not have believed it of them."

Davydd felt a strange sort of letdown, almost as if he truly was the one wronged. "But for me, you believed it. You may not have wanted to, but you did. I can prove I was not in Powys conspiring with Gruffydd, but what of it? You said you'd forgiven my past betrayals. But tell me this, Llewelyn, and for God's sake, tell me the truth. When—if ever— do you start trusting me again?"

Llewelyn could not lie to him; the question held too much raw honesty. "Davydd, I thought I did."

Davydd's smile was bitter. "Until your faith was put to the test."

Llewelyn frowned, said nothing. Davydd's accusors were men of good fame, men whose testimony could not be easily dismissed. But he thought it only fair to deny himself that defense, for he could not make the obvious offer, the one Davydd had a right to expect, that his word alone was enough. "Bring your witnesses to me in Penllyn," he said at last, "and that will end it."

Davydd studied him intently for a long moment. "Fair enough." A shallow bowl lay on the table between them, filled with dried figs and dates and a large, fragrant orange. The latter was not often found on Welsh tables, for it had to be imported from Spain. Davydd knew it was one of Llewelyn's few indulgences, and it was the orange he took on his way to the door. There he paused, glanced back over his shoulder. "Till Martinmas, then. Llewelyn!" Sending the orange spiraling through the air. Llewelyn looked startled, but he caught it easily enough, and Davydd grinned. "You see?" he said. "I do not covet all that is yours!" The door closing on echoes of his laughter.

It was quiet after he'd gone. Llewelyn moved restlessly about the chamber, but he could feel their eyes following him. Turning abruptly, he said, "I'll not deny it. I want to believe him. Is that so hard to understand?"

Einion silently shook his head; he, too, wanted to believe Davydd. Tudur had rarely heard Llewelyn sound so defensive, but he felt obliged, nonetheless, to speak his mind. "No," he said, "it is only natural that you'd want to believe him. But Davydd might well be counting upon that, Llewelyn."

Llewelyn acknowledged the thrust with a twist of his mouth. "I know," he admitted. "It is just that I cannot forget what Davydd said, that I trusted him only until my faith was put to the test. If he is right, how can I ever make amends?" And this time, not even Tudur had an answer for him.

IT was sometime in October when the black boar emerged from the lower slopes of Yr Wyddfa, began roaming the wooded valley of the River Conwy. Those who saw it gave awesome accounts of its vast size, its bloodied tusks, its blinding speed, and people began to wager when their lord would arrive. That he would come, they never doubted. No huntsman alive could resist such a challenge, for there was no greater sport than matching wits with a Welsh wild boar. Indeed, Llewelyn was soon hastening south, reaching his Trefriw hunting lodge at noon on the eve of All Saints, more commonly known as Hallowmas.

Caitlin was delighted to have been included in the hunting party, although she would not be allowed to go on the hunt itself, of course. Like all princes, Llewelyn had a migratory court, and as he moved about his realm, so, too, did Caitlin, for her fall from the stable rafters had marked a turning point in her life, and nowadays her uncle rarely left her behind. But he'd not taken her to Rhuddlan Castle, and the waiting had been very hard, for she knew her father and uncle were somehow at odds. When her uncle said she'd be coming with him to meet Davydd in Penllyn, she'd been enormously relieved, for surely that must mean they'd made their peace. She was not absolutely sure of that, though, and she wished she had someone to confide in, to explain the often inexplicable adult world to her.

She had begun to hope that in time Eva might become such a

confidante, for Eva was the first one of her uncle's ladies to befriend her. It was because of Eva that they were now following the steep, winding path that led from Trefriw up to the ancient church of Rhychwyn. Soon after their arrival, Eva had coaxed Llewelyn into showing it to her, and as they set out, she'd looked back over her shoulder. "Do not dawdle, child. We're counting upon you to blaze a trail for us!"

Caitlin did, joyfully, racing Llewelyn's greyhound through a carpet of autumn leaves. Sun gilded the trees, setting every hawthorn bush afire, and the air was so clear and cool that it was like breathing cider; when she told that to Llewelyn and Eva, they both laughed. That was another reason why she liked Eva so much, because her uncle laughed so readily when Eva was with him.

Most reassuringly of all for Caitlin, Eva was no great beauty. Caitlin was familiar with the Welsh legends of the Mabinogion, with Chretien de Troyes's French fables of King Arthur, and their romantic heroines did not look like the cheerful, buxom Eva, who was neither fair-skinned nor flaxen haired, and not at all elegant or aloof. Caitlin already knew, at age ten, that she was not likely to grow into a great beauty, either, not with her flyaway straight hair, her pointed little chin, and a dusting of freckles across her nose. While she was not one to brood upon it, she'd begun to wish that she could have been prettier, and so her uncle's liaison with Eva seemed to bode well for her own future.

Ahead lay Llanrhychwyn, a small, rough-hewn chapel of weathered stone, shadowed by leafy clouds, surrounded by silence. Vast, ageless yew trees blotted out the sun, sentinels of a bygone time. Caitlin found it very easy to conjure up unseen ghosts in such a secluded setting, and Eva, too, hung back, for their first glimpse of this hillside church was not reassuring. It seemed to belong to a distant past, to the denizens of its dark woods, to those who slept under the high grass of its forlorn cemetery, not to the living, not to them.

To Llewelyn, though, the ancient church was enshrined in boyhood memory. "My grandfather and his wife often heard Mass here. The church down at Trefriw . . . that was his doing. He had it built for Joanna, to spare her the walk all the way up to Rhychwyn. He kept a fondness for the old church, though. I've not been up here for years, yet it is just as I remember." Like Caitlin, he, too, sensed the presence of spirits. But his ghosts were joy-giving. With a light step, he led them inside.

Within, the little church was far more welcoming. There was only one window, set in the east wall. But the interior was whitewashed with lime, gave off a mellow ivory glow. The floor rushes were freshly laid, and a clean linen cloth had been draped across the altar, proof that the elderly priest caretaker was still serving God and St Rhychwyn.

Llewelyn moved toward the alms box, ran his fingers along the wood until he found what he sought. "My initials," he said with a grin. "I carved them whilst waiting for my grandfather at Vespers. The Lady Joanna caught me at it, but never told on me. I was scared that she would, though, for my parents hated her enough to sicken upon it. You see, Caitlin, they believed that her son had usurped my father's rightful place. My grandfather could not let his realm be split in twain. Instead, it was his family that was rent asunder, for my father never forgave him . . ."

His face had shadowed. Eva joined him by the alms box, pretended to look for the initials, all the while wondering how to exorcise his darker memories. "The most amazing tales are told of the Lady Joanna. Did she truly set fire to your grandfather's bed?"

Her question was well chosen; Llewelyn's grin came back. "I heard that, too, as a lad; finally got up the nerve to ask my grandfather. How he laughed! Because Joanna had been just fourteen when they wed, they'd not shared a bed at first. But of course he had a concubine, and when Joanna discovered that, she had a heated row with the woman, ordered Llewelyn's bed dragged out to the bailey and burned. When my grandfather told me that story, Joanna had been dead for many months, yet he spoke of her as if she were waiting in the adjoining chamber, that jealous lass of fifteen who had dared to burn his bed."

Eva could not help herself, had to ask. "I know he founded a Franciscan friary in her memory. Few women are so honored, so loved. And yet . . . did she not betray him? From childhood, I heard the stories, that he found her with a lover. I even remember my cousin pointing out the man's grave to me, saying that Prince Llewelyn had hanged him. But Joanna, he forgave. How could he do that, Llewelyn? How could he ever forgive so great a sin?"

"I do not know, Eva. We never talked of it. I can tell you only that on his deathbed, it was her face he yearned to see."

Caitlin was fascinated by these tantalizing snatches of family scandal. "Uncle," she said shyly, "could you have forgiven such a betrayal?" And she was flattered when he considered her question as seriously as if it had been posed by an adult, thinking it over for some moments before finally shaking his head.

"No, lass," he said quietly, "I do not think I could. For me, it is not easy to trust. When I do, though, it is absolute, unconditional. Faith like that can be given but once, Caitlin. If it is betrayed, it can be patched, it can be mended. But it can never be made whole again."

Caitlin understood perfectly. "Me, too," she said, so solemnly that he struggled not to smile. "If I was betrayed, I'd not forgive, either . . . not ever." She had another worry upon her mind, though, a fear sparked by her first sight of her uncle's long boar spear, as ugly a weapon as she'd ever laid eyes upon. "Uncle . . . why must you fight that boar on foot? Would you not be safer on horseback?"

"You need not fret about me, lass. I've been hunting boars for more years than you can count. We'll take the alaunts with us, for they're the best boar dogs, and my greyhounds, too. Not Nia, though; she's too young and unseasoned—"

As if on cue, Nia began to bark, and Caitlin giggled. "I think she wants to come!" But Llewelyn had read the dog better than she; he was already turning toward the door.

"Llewelyn? Are you inside?" A moment later, Tudur materialized in the doorway, blinking at the sudden loss of sunlight. "I'm sorry to intrude like this, but after you left, a Cistercian monk arrived, bearing an urgent message for you. He says he'll speak to you and only to you, so I thought I'd best bring him along."

Llewelyn cocked a brow. "He could not wait till I got back? Why, Tudur?"

"Because," Tudur said, "this particular monk comes from the abbey of Ystrad Marchell . . . in Powys."

Llewelyn's face did not change, but Caitlin was close enough to see his hand tighten upon the edge of the alms box, and her heart began to race. Again, Powys! The word alone was enough to unnerve her these days, for it was somehow connected with her father, a connection as sinister as it was murky. But Llewelyn was already asking Eva to take her back to the lodge, and she had no choice except to obey, however reluctantly.

Tudur now ushered into the church a tall, gaunt monk of middle years, conspicuously clad in white. He was trailed by a younger man, this one bearded, wearing a habit of drab brown, the uniform of the conversi, the lay brothers who served God through manual labor. "Llewelyn, this is Brother Garmon, master of the lay brethren at Ystrad Marchell Abbey. That much I could get out of him!"

Brother Garmon cast Tudur an apologetic look. "What I have to say, my lord, is of a private nature. If you could—"

"He stays," Llewelyn said. "What have you come to tell me, Brother Garmon?"

"It is not me, my lord. It is Padrig. Go on, lad. Tell him what you told me." When the youth stayed mute, the monk sighed. "He is fearful, my lord. I ask you to be patient with him, for you must hear what he has to say. Padrig works at our grange at Tallerddig, in the mountains of western Powys. Tell him, Padrig. Tell him what happened at the grange in January."

Padrig swallowed. "My lord Gruffydd, his lady wife, and his son, Owen, came to the grange. Took us by surprise, they did, for we're at the back of beyond. They were waiting for someone, and he arrived at dusk, so muffled and hooded his own mother could not have recognized him."

The boy was beginning to relax, even to enjoy being the center of attention, a novelty in his young life. "We were all curious, my lord, and so I was right pleased when I was told to fetch them wine. When I entered, the other man was standing in the shadows, his back to me. It was just his bad luck, my lord, that I'd grown up in Gwynedd. I knew him at once, you see, had seen him so often . . . It was your brother, my lord. It was Davydd."

He paused, but Llewelyn did not react, continued to regard him impassively. Padrig swallowed again, felt color rising in his face, for it was hard to admit what came next. "As I said, my lord, I . . . I was curious. I wondered why they were meeting secretly like this, and so . . . when I left the chamber, I lingered at the door, put my ear to the keyhole." His blush deepened. "I ought not to have done it. But I—"

"What did you hear?" This from Tudur, impatiently.

"The talk was of a secret marriage. As far as I could tell, Lord Owen was going to wed one of Lord Davydd's daughters. I heard names: Angharad, Gwenllian, and a right odd one, Caitlin. They settled upon Angharad, and Lord Davydd made a joke, said that he'd given her Ceri or Cydewain for her marriage portion. I did not understand it, and he was the only one who laughed. That is all I heard, for I was called back to the kitchen by Brother Rhun. My lord, I know I ought to have come forward ere this, but . . . but I was afraid . . ."

Again Padrig paused, again got no response. Llewelyn's silence was beginning to frighten him. "My lord . . . I swear to you that I'm not lying. Upon the surety of my soul, I do swear it. It was Davydd, my lord. It was Davydd!"

"Yes," Llewelyn said softly. "Yes, lad, I know it was."

LLEWELYN stood before the altar, gazing up at the stark wooden cross that adorned the east wall of the church. He was alone, for Tudur had seen his need, escorted Brother Garmon and Padrig down to the lodge. But he'd be back. And then they must decide what to do with this poisoned gift.

Nia whimpered, pressed a cold nose against his hand. He stroked the dog's silky head absently. The numbness was fading. But there had never truly been surprise. Scriptures said that faith was the substance of things hoped for, the evidence of things not seen. That could well serve as the epitaph for the troubled brotherhood that bound him to Davydd. Hope blighted, faith blind to the facts. There in the empty, silent church, his anger was beginning to rise. He made no attempt to hold it back, even welcomed it. Of all the emotions surging toward the surface, rage was the safest, the easiest to acknowledge. Anger he could embrace, for a flood tide of fury swept all before it, engulfing more dangerous undercurrents. If anger could not heal, at least it could deflect.

It was the greyhound's growl that alerted him to his Seneschal's return. Opening the door, Tudur strode forward, saying briskly, "I got them headed down the path to the lodge."

Llewelyn turned away from the altar. "I believed him, Tudur."

"I know," Tudur conceded. "But let's give the Devil his due, Llewelyn. Davydd could lie his way to Hell and back, and never even work up a sweat. That is why we must lay our snare with caution. If only it were that dolt, Owen! But whatever his other failings, Davydd has never lacked for nerve. Even when we confront him with Padrig, I'll wager that he does not so much as blink."

"We could show Davydd a confession in his own handwriting, writ in his own blood, and he'd still try to talk his way out of it," Llewelyn said bitterly. "No, I want an end to this, Tudur. I want proof beyond denying, proof beyond excusing, beyond forgiving."

"What do you have in mind?"

"You said it yourself—Owen de la Pole. The weak link in their chain, the link in our hands. I want a confession from him, Tudur, a full confession."

Tudur nodded thoughtfully. "We do know enough now—the marriage—to try a bluff. But if the bluff fails? What then, Llewelyn? Do you care how I get the confession?"

Their eyes caught, held. "No," Llewelyn said, "just get it," and Tudur nodded again, turned, and walked swiftly toward the door.

Llewelyn moved back to the altar. Within moments, though, the door banged open again. The elderly priest was panting, had to catch the font for support. "Forgive me, my lord, for not being here to welcome you. I am Father Robat . . . do you remember me? So long it's been!" He came forward, with a smile that faltered as the window's light fell across Llewelyn's face. His eyes were rheumy, clouded by cataracts, but age had yet to dim his inner sight. "My lord . . . can I be of help?"

"Father Robat," Llewelyn said. "I do indeed remember you. But no . . . no, you cannot help."

OWEN was being held at Llewelyn's favorite castle of Dolwyddelan, only twelve miles south-west of Trefriw, and so Tudur was back within hours, just as the evening meal was about to begin. One look at Tudur's face and Llewelyn lost all appetite. Pushing away from the table, he in-

structed the startled servants to continue serving, strode across the hall
to intercept his Seneschal. As their eyes met, Tudur nodded, almost
imperceptibly, but that did not allay Llewelyn's edginess. Tudur should
be triumphant. Instead, he would not have looked out of place at a
funeral.

Beckoning for his mantle, Llewelyn took a horn lantern from one
of Tudur's men. "Come on," he said. "Let's go for a walk."

It was a mild, clear night, the Hallowmas sky a vast, boundless
black above their heads, afloat with hundreds of glimmering, bobbing
lights, ships sailing an uncharted sea. From boyhood, Llewelyn had
been intrigued by the study of astronomy, had long ago learned to use
the North Star as a reckoning point, just as sailors did. Tonight he never
even glanced at the starlit sky, kept his eyes upon Tudur. Leaning back
against an ancient oak, he said, "What happened?"

"You were right, Llewelyn. I've seen eggs harder to crack than
Owen de la Pole. When I told him that we knew about the marriage
plans, he lost color so fast I thought he was going to swoon like a lass.
Whilst he was still so shaken, I informed him that Davydd had fled to
England. There was a debt due, I said, a blood debt, one he'd have to
pay now that his conspirators were out of reach. And with that, it was
over. When I offered to spare his life, he snatched at my promise like
a drowning man, told me all I wanted to know. Their plot, where they
met, when they met—it gushed out so fast my scribe was hard put to
keep pace. He was truly a pitiful sight, as scared as I've ever seen a
man. If our bluff had failed, it would have taken but the blink of an eye
to force the truth from—"

"Tudur, enough! For a man usually as close-mouthed as an
Anchorite recluse, you're all but babbling. We already knew there was
a plot afoot. We needed only to learn the particulars. Now you have
them, yet you seem strangely loath to share them with me. Why? What
is it you do not want to tell me?"

Tudur did not answer at once. "In truth," he said slowly, "I got
more than I bargained for. We knew they had plotted your downfall.
But we assumed they had rebellion in mind. They did not, for they
lacked the courage to face you fairly . . . on the battlefield. It was not
the sword they meant to turn against you, Llewelyn, it was an assassin's
dagger."

"An assassin . . ." Llewelyn sounded stunned. "Davydd?"

Tudur suddenly felt absurdly relieved to be able to answer in the
negative. "No, Davydd was not to do the actual killing. Owen's men
were to do that. Davydd was to get them past your guards, into your
private chamber. But luck was not with them. Or rather, it was with
you. On the night they were to—"

"Candlemas," Llewelyn said, very low, and Tudur nodded.

"Yes," he admitted, "the killing was to happen that night. But the storm washed out the roads. Owen ended up stranded near the Powys border."

He waited for Llewelyn to ask the obvious question. When Llewelyn did not, he volunteered it on his own, while marveling that he, of all men, should be seeking now to paint Davydd's crime in less lurid colors. But Llewelyn's silence was filling his ears like a soundless scream. "I asked why they did not make a second attempt. For what it is worth, Llewelyn, it was Davydd who balked."

Llewelyn thrust the lantern at Tudur, moved farther into the shadows. "I want a writ issued for Davydd's arrest."

"It shall be done at once." Tudur hesitated. "Llewelyn, I am sorry . . ."

"No, Tudur. Save your pity for Gruffydd ap Gwenwynwyn. Save it for Davydd. My right beloved brother Davydd."

TANGWYSTL awoke slowly, languidly, as she always did. She'd been too tired to plait her hair into its customary night braid, and as she stirred, she discovered that she was unable to move, for her hip-length tresses had become entangled under Davydd's body. She tugged in vain, finally leaned over and shook his shoulder. "Davydd!"

Davydd's eyes opened, took in her predicament. "Well, look what I caught." When she made another attempt to free her hair, he slid his arm around her waist, drew her close against him. "What are you willing to offer up for your freedom, my love?"

Tangwystl had a husky laugh, a low-pitched sultry voice that Davydd found irresistibly erotic. Now she practically purred as she nuzzled his ear, began to make some intriguing ransom offers. But before he could decide which of them was the most promising, there was a sharp knock on the door.

"My lord, a man has just ridden in, claiming he has an urgent message for you. He says it is from the Lord of Cockayne. We've never heard of such a place, thought it might be in Ireland. But he is right persistent and—"

"I'll see him." Davydd was not surprised that none knew the Lord of Cockayne, for it was a fabled land, a mythical realm that existed only in the imagination. It was also a code concocted by Davydd and Rhys ap Gruffydd, used sometimes in jest, occasionally when either of them had news to impart, secrets he did not want attached to his own name or signet. As Davydd reached for the bedsheet, he was already sure that this would not be one of Rhys's jokes.

The messenger was young and disheveled, each mud smear, each sweat stain attesting to miles of hard riding. He showed no unease at finding himself in a Prince's bedchamber, instead was looking about with unabashed curiosity; the Welsh were less awed by authority than their English brethren. "Here it is," he said jauntily, holding out a folded parchment threaded through with cord, sealed with wax. "I ought to say straightaway that the man who gave it to me was a stranger. All I know is that he offered me the astonishing sum of two marks to get it to you, my lord Davydd. He told me not to spare my horse, said that if I reached you ere Morrow Mass, you'd owe me another two marks. Well, my lord, I did and you do!"

Davydd was already breaking the seal. "Pay him," he said, began to read.

The messenger was ushered out, with an appreciative over-the-shoulder appraisal of Tangwystl. She was accustomed to male approval, though, paid him no heed. Smothering a yawn, she poked Davydd playfully in the ribs. "If you are not going to collect your ransom, I am going to summon my maid. Davydd? Did you hear me?" He glanced up from the parchment, and she sat up suddenly, reached for his arm. "Jesú, you look ghastly! What is wrong?"

Davydd crumpled the message. Throwing the covers back, he rose from the bed, strode to the hearth, and thrust the parchment into the flames, then snatched the clothes hanging from a wall pole. Jerking up his braies, he knotted them about his hips. "Owen de la Pole has made a full confession. God rot him, the fool not only cut his own throat, he cut ours, too!"

"A confession— Oh, my God, Davydd! You swore to me that you were innocent!"

By now he had his chausses gartered, was pulling his tunic over his head, his voice muffled within the folds of wool. "What did you expect me to say, that I was as guilty as Cain?" Grabbing his surcote, he opened the door and shouted for Cadell, one of the few men he could trust. Turning back to the bed, he saw Tangwystl, still clutching the sheets, staring at him in disbelief.

There was an odd feeling of familiarity about the scene, as if he'd somehow lived through it before. And then he realized that he had, eleven years ago. Then, too, he'd been awakened at dawn with calamitous news: that his conspiracy had failed, Llewelyn knew all, and his only hope lay in flight.

TEMPERATURES plummeted suddenly during that first week in November. As Llewelyn dismounted, the leaves crunching under his boots were brown and brittle, and the tree branches above his head had been transformed, as if by evil alchemy, into stark woodland skeletons, stripped naked and barren by a relentless, alpine wind. The sky was clear and cloudless, but each breath that Llewelyn inhaled seemed glazed in ice, as if it were already deep winter.

He was close enough now to hear the rush of water. His people called it Rhaeadr Ewynnol, the Foaming Fall, and indeed, where the River Llugwy spilled over a jagged barricade of moss-green rocks, it did churn up as much froth and spume as a cresting wave. Wales had been blessed with cataracts beyond counting, but Rhaeadr Ewynnol was one of the most spectacular, a white-water surge that not even summer drought could long diminish. It had always been a special place for Llewelyn, and he stood for a time at the cliff's very edge, feeling the flying spray on his face, watching as the twilit sky slowly darkened.

He'd been sequestered with his council for hours, focusing upon the political and military consequences of his brother's betrayal. Retribution must be swift and sure, for no prince could allow treason to go unpunished. The conquest of Powys may have been inevitable; now it was urgent. A formal protest would have to be lodged with the English government, a demand made for Davydd's extradition. He and Edward were allies and his complaint was a just one. He did not hold much hope, though, that Edward would comply; the English Crown was far too fond of playing one Welsh prince off against another. But even if he did succeed in deposing Gruffydd ap Gwenwynwyn and bringing Davydd to trial, a shadow still lay across his land. No Welsh prince had ever scaled the heights that he had reached, had ever breathed such rarified air. Prince of Wales—not even his grandfather had soared so high. But he was forty-six years of age, had no son of his own, and now, no heir to inherit his hard-won crown.

He'd been attempting, with some success, to put distance between himself and this latest betrayal, to see Davydd as a traitor, a failed rebel, not as the brother he'd loved. But this woodland glen harbored ghosts, and the wind echoed with whispers. It was his mother's voice he heard most clearly, his mother who'd never forgiven him for the sin of loving his grandfather. He could not remember a time when there'd been a true peace between them. But he did remember their meeting at Aberconwy Abbey. He'd just won a resounding victory over his brothers, repelling their invasion with ease, taking them both prisoner. Owain had been his mother's ally, her favorite, and she'd confronted him at Aberconwy, demanded that Owain be released at once. When he refused, she'd made a prediction that had sounded, even then, like a curse. "You are going to pay a great price for Llewelyn Fawr's dream." The last words she'd ever spoken to him.

Picking up a rock, he flung it over the edge, watched it splash into the cauldron at the base of the cliff. Never had he felt so alone as he did at this moment, victorious, triumphant once again over his enemies.

At his stallion's sudden nicker, he whirled, hand on sword hilt. The mare, a delicate, small-boned grey, picked its way through the dead leaves, acorns, and exposed roots as daintily as a lady lifting a trailing skirt. Above the animal's tossing mane, the child's face was framed within a wide red hood. As she reined in before Llewelyn, the hood slipped down, revealing skin of winter white, so ashen it looked bloodless, and eyes glistening with blinked-back tears.

"How did you know I was here, Caitlin?"

"I remembered how much you love Rhaeadr Ewynnol, and since it was so close to Trefriw . . ." He could see Caitlin's frosted breath, lacing her words with faint wisps of smoke. He could see her pain. When she said, suddenly timid, "I'll go back if you want to be alone," he shook his head.

"No," he said, "we need to talk." Catching her as she slid from the saddle, he steered her toward a fallen tree. She settled herself upon the log almost primly, arranging her skirts in unconscious imitation of Eva, keeping those disturbing green eyes upon him all the while. Jesú, what could he say to her? How could he make this child understand what he could not fully understand himself?

"Men are saying that my father plotted to kill you. Is that true?"

He'd hoped to keep the worst from her, ought to have known it was bound to come out. How like her, though, to face it without flinching. Where in God's Name did she get her fearless, devil-be-damned honesty? For certes, not from Davydd.

"Yes," he said, "it is true," and heard her give a soft sound, almost like a whimper, quickly cut off. She'd ducked her head; he could see only a swirl of windblown hair. Her hands had knotted in her lap, fingers clenching until the knuckles whitened.

"Uncle Llewelyn . . . do you want me to go away?"

It was a moment before he realized what she was asking. "Ah, no, lass! None of Davydd's guilt attaches to you. You're my niece; nothing can change that."

She raised her chin and he could see a faint glimmer upon her cheek, a solitary tear track. "I would that I had comfort to offer, Caitlin. But I know there is none. Better than most men, I understand about conflicting loyalties."

"Your father and grandfather?" she whispered, and he nodded.

"I passed my early years at my grandfather's court . . . did you know that? He was a great man, Caitlin. As a lad, I was so proud to be his blood-kin, loved him enough to forgive him anything—even passing over my father in favor of his younger son, Joanna's son. And as I got older, I realized that he'd been right, for God never meant my father to rule. He was too hot-headed, acted on impulse without ever considering the consequences, and his hatred of the English verged upon madness. If I understood, though, the rest of my family did not. They blamed my grandfather . . . and me, for loving him. But you see, lass, I loved my father, too, and I oft-times felt as if I were being torn in two—"

"No!" Caitlin was shaking her head so vehemently that her hair flew about like swirling leaves, half-blinding her. "No . . . no, I do not love my father! I hate him, I hate him . . ."

She choked, and Llewelyn drew her to him, held her as she wept. Her sobs soon subsided, although an occasional tremor shook the frail little shoulders; once or twice, she hiccuped and swiped at her face with her sleeve. Llewelyn blotted her tears with the hem of her mantle, and then smoothed the hair back from her eyes.

"Come on, lass," he said. "Let's go home."

LLEWELYN led an army south, razing Gruffydd's castle at Trallwng to the ground. All of Powys was soon in his hands. But Gruffydd and his wife had fled to England, where they joined Davydd in exile at Shrewsbury. Edward not only gave them refuge, he provided for them generously, and with English backing, they began to launch forays across the Welsh border. Llewelyn raged in vain, and his suspicions of the English King's intentions grew apace with each rebel raid.

11

MONTARGIS, FRANCE

March 1275

NELL was starved for sleep. She dreaded the nights now, for she knew the horrors each one held. She'd fall into a fitful doze, only to awaken gasping for breath, sure that she was strangling. Propped up against pillows, she would lie alone in the dark, struggling to breathe. After endless hours, she'd finally get back to sleep. But by then, it would be dawn.

Just as she refused to sleep during daylight hours, so did she balk at lying abed. Each morning she would muster her dwindling strength, insist upon dressing, determined to face the day without flinching. With Juliana's help, she settled herself into a high-backed chair, began to sort through her correspondence, for this was one task she would not turn over to Ellen or Amaury.

Juliana hovered close at hand. All in the Countess's household treated her as if she were made of cobwebs and rose petals, fragile enough to be blown away by a breath, for by now all knew that she was dying. But Juliana was an incorrigible optimist; life's cruelties still took her by surprise. She alone held on to hope, taking solace in Nell's high color, the brightness of her eyes.

But when she offered such flawed comfort to Nell, the older woman said tersely, "It is the fever," although without the acerbic edge that foolishness usually provoked. It was a source of grim amusement to Nell that she should discover patience only now, as time ran out. Her throat was tightening and she made haste to request her potion of juniper, chamomile, and poppyseed. It headed off another coughing attack, but not, she knew, for long. She was about to summon her scribe when the Welsh messenger arrived.

Juliana was surprised by Nell's grimace, for letters from Llewelyn ap Gruffydd were welcome occurrences, evoking echoes of those days when de Montforts defied kings and prevailed upon popes. "Do you not want to see Prince Llewelyn's messenger, Madame?"

"No," Nell admitted, "for I know what message he brings. Ever since we learned of Davydd's treachery, I've been expecting it. Llewelyn lost more than a brother last November, he lost an heir. He will have to take a wife, try to sire a son. I think—I fear—that is what his man has come to tell us, for Llewelyn is too well-bred to let us hear of his marriage from others."

"But . . . Madame, surely you did not still harbor hopes that Prince Llewelyn and your daughter . . . ?"

"No, Juliana, of course not. Ellen lost all chance of a crown on Evesham field. She has had ten years to accept that. But she must have regrets for what might have been. When Llewelyn takes a bride, how can it not stir up memories, salt old wounds? For God and we know it should have been Ellen!"

Nell leaned back in her chair, for even this brief flare of passion was enough to exhaust her. For several moments she sat motionless, eyes closed. And then she said, "I'll see him now."

But her spirits lifted at sight of his grey cassock. The Grey Friars held a special place in her heart; her husband's most fervent supporters had come from the Franciscan ranks. And when Friar Gwilym revealed that he was a member of the Franciscan friary at Llanfaes, she favored him with the sort of smile she reserved for family and friends, for Llanfaes was very dear to Nell. The island friary had been founded in honor of her sister; Llanfaes was both Joanna's final resting place and a lasting tribute to her husband's love.

Friar Gwilym seemed in no hurry to reveal his mission, and they passed some moments in polite, casual conversation. Prince Llewelyn and the English King were still at odds, he reported. How could it be otherwise, though, as long as Edward continued to shelter those accursed traitors, Davydd and Gruffydd ap Gwenwynwyn? Little wonder his Prince had refused to attend Edward's coronation.

"Little wonder," Nell echoed, without conviction, for she knew Edward would never forgive such an affront to his royal dignity. But how could she fault Llewelyn for his recklessness? Her Simon would have done the very same thing. "Do you have a letter for me?"

He nodded and reached for the pouch at his belt, withdrawing a sealed parchment. But he made no move to hand it to her. "Prince Llewelyn has entrusted me to speak for him, to ask of you—"

Nell interrupted with an inadvertent, embittered laugh, for the days were forever gone when she might do favors for princes. "And what could your lord possibly want of me or mine?"

"Your daughter," Friar Gwilym said with a smile, and saw that he'd accomplished what her enemies swore to be impossible: he'd rendered the Countess of Leicester speechless. "Prince Llewelyn and the Lady Ellen would have wed years ago, if not for the tragedy of Evesham. It is his heartfelt wish to honor that broken vow, to take your daughter as his wife."

Nell was still struggling with her disbelief. Too stunned to dissemble, she could only blurt out the truth. "But I can no longer provide Ellen with the marriage portion that a Prince would expect!"

"My lord knows that, Madame. He does not seek to wed your daughter for gain."

It had been a long time since a dream had become reality for Nell; it had been ten years. "I know why he needs a wife. But why Ellen?"

Friar Gwilym's smile surfaced again. "My lord knows you well, my lady, for he foresaw just such blunt-spoken honesty, and he would answer you no less truthfully. Your daughter was an easy choice, indeed, the only choice. In disavowing the earlier plight troth, he acted in the interests of Wales, acted as a prince must. But he has long regretted forsaking the Lady Ellen in her time of need."

"What are you saying, that he seeks to satisfy a debt of honor?"

"Yes, Madame, he does." He saw her brows draw together and added hastily, "I do not mean to imply that wedding your daughter is in any sense a sacrifice. She is Plantagenet and de Montfort; if there is any better blood in Christendom, it is to be found only in Wales!" That won him a smile, and he relaxed. "Moreover, Madame, the Lady Ellen is said to be a beauty . . . and having seen her mother, I cannot doubt it."

"I had no idea that men of God were so gallant." If her words were wry, Nell's smile was dazzling. Her blinding, sunburst happiness did not deter her, though, from continuing her interrogation, not with so much at stake. "And what of Edward? My daughter is, as you say, beautiful and well-bred. She ought to have been wed years ago. But men fear the English King far too much to risk his wrath. If Llewelyn weds my daughter, Edward will be outraged."

Friar Gwilym grinned. "I'd wager, Madame, that Prince Llewelyn is counting upon that!"

Nell grinned, too; she had to, for she'd tweaked the lion's tail a time or two herself. "I thank you for your candor. I understand now why your lord seeks my daughter as his wife, and I approve." Holding up her hand before he could respond. "Wait, hear me out. When my husband and Prince Llewelyn agreed to the plight troth, it was only fitting that we should speak for Ellen; she was still a child, not yet thirteen. My daughter is now a woman grown, has the right to speak for herself. As I said, you have my approval. But you need her consent."

FRIAR GWILYM was impressed by Ellen de Montfort's beauty, but at the same time, he felt a sudden unease, for he found her to be impossible to read. Her initial, obvious shock had given way almost at once to an impenetrable, protective poise. She had murmured a conventional courtesy, that Prince Llewelyn did her great honor, then moved, as if by chance, toward the window. Studying her profile in vain for clues, it occurred to him for the first time that she might balk. He knew that, to many Englishwomen, not even the prospect of a crown would be enough to lure them into Wales. What if this girl shared that common bias, if she, too, thought that Wales was a backward, barren land, that the Welsh were as sinful and wild as the English claimed? He knew his Prince's heart was now set upon Ellen de Montfort. How could he face Llewelyn if he failed?

"I realize, my lady, that this is a decision of grave moment. I know my lord would not begrudge you the time you need. If you wish to think his offer over . . . ?"

Ellen turned from the window. "That will not be necessary. I am prepared to give you my answer now. It was my father's wish that I wed Prince Llewelyn. I need no more guidance than that, for I have utter faith in my father's judgment."

"You accept, then?" And when she nodded, he began to beam. "Ah, my lady, you have just made two men very happy, a Prince of Wales and a humble Franciscan friar!"

"Not to mention a papal chaplain," Amaury chimed in, and with that, they all were laughing.

Friar Gwilym hastened over to kiss Ellen's hand. "We have much to discuss. But I have a confession to make first. I am well nigh famished. Ere I pay my respects to the Prioress, might I have a meal?"

Amaury put his arm around the friar's shoulders, deftly steered him toward the door. "Gwilym, you are about to get the best meal of your life, that I promise you upon the honor of the entire de Montfort clan!"

As soon as they were alone again, Ellen flung her arms about her brother's neck. He laughed, whirled her around until they were both reeling and breathless. And as Nell watched, she felt tears pricking her lids, for Amaury's jubilant gesture was too familiar; it could have been Bran or Harry swinging Ellen in those giddy circles.

Reluctantly setting Ellen on her feet again, Amaury promised to be back "as soon as I get our good friar fed." Ellen at once sped across the chamber and dropped to her knees by Nell's chair.

"After Papa was killed and we had to leave England, I spun such romantic dreams, Mama. I was the damsel in distress and Llewelyn was my savior. In my darkest hour, he would ride up on his white horse and carry me away to his kingdom in Wales, having realized that we were fated to be together. Like Tristan and Iseult, Guinevere and Lancelot, my aunt Joanna and Llewelyn Fawr! Oh, I know they were foolish fantasies. I always knew that. Even though they did give me a measure of comfort, I never truly believed in them . . ."

"I know, love. But mayhap we should have!"

Ellen smiled, then confided, "I am not sure I believe it even now! I'll be back after I tell Juliana."

She was on her feet in an instant, dancing toward the door with a supple grace that Nell could not help envying, for her own body had once served her just as effortlessly. It was not death she despised, but that it had come to her in such an incapacitating, drawn-out guise. She would have preferred the sword to dropsy, would have chosen a bloody death over a lingering one. But nothing—not her chronic shortness of breath, not her heart palpitations, no amount of pain or weakness— could tarnish the triumph of this moment for her. As she watched her daughter glide across the chamber, her feet scarcely touching the floor, Nell had rarely been so happy, or so at peace.

Reaching the door, Ellen stopped suddenly, spun around to look at her mother. "It is almost like a miracle, Mama," she said in wonderment, and Nell nodded.

"Indeed, Ellen, it is," she agreed, no less gravely. And then she laughed, the husky, free-soaring laugh of the young girl she'd once been, the girl who had defied a King and a Pope to wed the man of her choice. "It would seem," she said, "that it pays to have a saint in the family!"

NELL's dreams were deeply rooted in her yesterdays. They were, for the most part, tranquil and reassuringly familiar. With the blurring of time's boundaries, her loved ones were restored to her, her family was once more intact, inviolate. She awakened from such dreams with regret, often with confusion. So it was now. The darkness was aswirl with floating lights; they swam before her dazzled eyes like phosphorescent fish in a black, black sea. For a moment she was lost, adrift on unknown currents. But as her eyes adjusted to the dark, the fish transformed themselves into the flickering flames of a servant's candelabra, and she returned to reality with a rueful smile. This was no alien world. She was in her chamber at Montargis, on an April eve in Holy Week, and although death waited in the shadows, she had nothing to fear, for she had made her peace with God.

There was a great comfort in knowing that all had been done. Her confessor had shriven her of her earthly sins, her will had been made, and she'd arranged for largesse to be distributed to members of her household, to the nuns and villagers who'd sought to make her exile easier. Nothing remained now except her farewells.

She was drifting back toward sleep when she heard familiar footsteps. "Mama, are you awake?" Bending over the bed, Ellen kissed her forehead. "Marguerite is here."

Nell welcomed the French Queen with a drowsy smile, thinking how lucky she was to have those she loved at her deathbed. Not all were so fortunate; her father, King John, had died alone and unmourned.

Marguerite could not conceal her shock; Nell had retained her good looks even as she aged, but dropsy had proven to be a more merciless foe than the advancing years. Nell gently squeezed the fingers clasped in hers, a wordless reassurance. "Marguerite . . ." The other woman begged her not to speak, to save her strength, but she knew better, knew how little time was left to her. "Dearest, I have a favor to ask of you. I made my will . . ." She could go no further, began to cough. Amaury hastened over with an herbal potion, and Ellen held the cup while Nell drank. But as soon as her breath came back, she reached again for Marguerite's hand.

"I want Ellen to have my jewels, Marguerite, except for my ruby pendant. That is for you. I've named Amaury as my heir, for Ellen will have Llewelyn to look after her, and the Church would not allow Guy to inherit. Dearest, will you and Philippe entreat Edward on my behalf, ask him to allow my will to be carried out? And . . . and urge him to be fair to my son. Amaury is innocent, should not have to pay for Guy's sins. Make Edward see that, Marguerite, make him see that he ought to let Amaury come home . . ."

"Of course we will, Nell." Marguerite tried to sound confident, as if she truly believed that Edward would heed them. But then, she doubted if Nell believed it, either. "Nell, you must not give up. I spoke to your doctor and he still has hope, thinks you might yet rally . . ."

"Simon does not think so," Nell said softly, and then smiled at the startled, dismayed looks on their faces. "My wits are not wandering. I always knew that Simon would come for me when my time was nigh. And now . . . now he is close at hand. I can feel his presence . . ."

"Truly, Mama?" Ellen whispered, sounding both awed and envious.

"Truly, love. And you know your father; he's never been one for waiting. He always swore that I'd be late for the Last Judgment . . ." Nell lay back weakly on the pillow, fighting for breath. "I will not let his first words to me be: 'I told you so!' " she said, summoning up one last smile, and her children discovered that it was possible to laugh while blinking back tears.

NELL DE MONTFORT died on Saturday, the 13th of April in God's Year, 1275, and was buried, in accordance with her wishes, in a quiet, simple ceremony at the priory church; her heart was taken to Paris, to be interred at the Abbey of St Antoine-des-Champs.

The following morning was mild and sun-splashed, an ideal day for travel. Friar Gwilym's escort was already mounted, but he still tarried, exchanging farewells with his lord's bride-to-be. Patting the breast of his tunic, he assured Ellen that he'd deliver her letter safely to Prince Llewelyn. "And what of you, my lady? Will you remain at Montargis?"

"No, it holds too many memories, too many ghosts. I think it best that I return to Paris with Amaury. Godspeed, Brother Gwilym. When we next meet, may it be in Wales."

He kissed her hand with somber gallantry. "Once your mourning time is done, my lord will send trusted men to bring you to him. My lady, may I caution you to keep our secret close? Were the English King to learn of your marriage plans, he would move Heaven and earth to thwart them."

After the friar's departure, Ellen walked across the courtyard to her mother's garden, where she filled a basket with violets and sunlit primroses. As she headed for the church, she was trailed at an unobtrusive distance by Hugh, and paused in the doorway to smile at him, touched by his silent, shadowy devotion. He would, she knew, willingly follow her to Wales, or anywhere else in Christendom, as would Juliana. A pity loyalty was not the coin of the realm; she'd have been a rich woman, indeed.

A hint of incense lingered in the air. Nell had been laid to rest before the High Altar; the funeral garlands of white and purple periwinkle blossoms had yet to wither, still exuded a light, flowery fragrance. Ellen scattered the violets and primroses about with a lavish hand, wishing that honeysuckle were in season, for her mother had always loved that sweet, heady scent.

"I am glad, Mama, that you are no longer in pain. But oh, how I shall miss you. I would that I could promise to name my first-born daughter after you. I am not sure, though, if 'Eleanor' can be translated into Welsh." It was strange and somewhat unsettling, the realization that her world would soon be so foreign, so mysterious and unknown; even her language would be alien. But it was exciting, too.

THE rain fell so relentlessly that September that even the Welsh, a people inured to wet weather, began to grumble. It was a very frustrating time for Llewelyn. He paced the confines of Ewloe Castle as if he were its prisoner, not its Prince, impatiently awaiting word from his emissaries, his uncle Einion and Maredudd, the Abbott of Aberconwy. They'd crossed the border days ago, and upon their success or failure might well depend the survival of his principality.

The summons had come as no surprise. As England's King, Edward had the right to demand that Llewelyn do homage to him, vassal to liege lord. He had commanded Llewelyn to meet him at Chester. Less than a dozen miles now separated the two men, but they might as well have been mired in quicksand. Llewelyn would not do homage as long as Edward harbored the brother and ally who'd betrayed him. And Edward would not redress his grievance as long as he refused to do homage.

It was to end this dangerous impasse that Llewelyn had sent his most eloquent envoys to Chester, in the hopes that a compromise might still be reached. But with each passing day, that seemed less and less likely. And so, when a shout from the castle battlements signaled incoming riders, Llewelyn crossed to the window with a leaden step, already braced for bad news.

The men ushered into the hall were shrouded in dripping, muddied mantles. As they jerked their hoods off, their tense, unhappy faces told all with no need of words. There were a few indrawn breaths, a few involuntary curses, and most drew back as they passed, as if failure, like plague, was catching.

Their uncle-nephew bond had always amused Einion and Llewelyn, for in age they were contemporaries; Einion was only seven years Llewelyn's senior. But he seemed to have added another decade in Chester; never had Llewelyn seen him look so haggard. "We tried," he said huskily. "As God is my witness, we did try."

Llewelyn asked no questions. There would be time for that later. The spectre of war was never far from Wales, but now it was right there in the hall with them. Edward was no man to defy with impunity. But to yield would be to abdicate in all but name. And how long would the Welsh follow a puppet Prince? Blood in the snow invariably attracted wolves.

Llewelyn could see his own thoughts reflected on the faces of his companions. It was Tudur who gave voice to their common concern. "If you balk, you'd best be ready to face Edward on the field, and we'd be fools to forget that he not only outfought Simon de Montfort at Evesham, he outwitted him, led him into a death trap as slick as you please. But if you do homage to Edward whilst he continues to shelter and befriend Davydd and Gruffydd ap Gwenwynwyn, what would your crown be worth? Your enemies would see it as weakness, Llewelyn, and I'd wager that Edward would, too. If you are going to risk all no matter what you do, then by God, follow your heart."

They were looking at him intently, expectantly, awaiting his decision. But there was no suspense in their silence, for all knew what he would do, what he had to do.

Llewelyn moved back to the window, stood gazing out upon the misted, sodden hills. His enemies often accused him of arrogance, and it was true that he could be imperious and arbitrary. But he was driven by demons bred of his own success, the dark side of his grandfather's legacy. Llewelyn Fawr had unified Wales, dictated peace terms to two English Kings, and by the time he died, even his foes called him Llewelyn the Great. Yet his triumphs had been as ephemeral, as fleeting as the good faith of the English Crown. His sons and grandsons lived to see the wreckage of his splendid, shining world; in seven short years, a lifetime's work lay in ruins. Llewelyn was to win back all that had been lost, but he would ever after be haunted by a fateful awareness, the memory of how easily a small, fractious land could be subdued by a powerful, predatory neighbor. Welsh victories were writ in sand, whilst English borders moved ever westward.

After a time, Llewelyn turned from the window. "We are done here," he said quietly. "Let's go home."

CHESTER CASTLE was filled to overflowing with the King's men. Cooped up indoors by the rain, they were edgy and bored, and the morning meal had been interrupted twice by sudden brawls, one involving the table cutlery. Edmund was beginning to understand how Cheshiremen had earned such a reputation for violence.

The rain stopped by noon, but all knew it would be a brief respite, and the hall was still crowded. Some of the men were throwing dice, but most were covertly enjoying the sight of two highborn lords snarling at each other like rival tomcats. Edmund even heard a few of the bolder ones making whispered wagers, trying to gauge how long it would be before the Earl of Gloucester's volcanic temper erupted.

Gloucester was sitting bolt upright in a window-seat, glowering at his tormentor. He had a redhead's fair, freckled skin, looked now as if he'd been sun-scorched, so deeply flushed were his face and throat. Men called him "Red Gilbert" and it was easy to see why. As unruly as it was bright, his hair stuck out in tousled, wayward tufts, bristling like the crimson quills of some unlikely paint-splattered hedgehog. Even at such solemn occasions as funerals, Gilbert's hair always looked as if he'd never owned a comb. Edmund, who cheerfully spent truly exorbitant sums on his own clothes, was puzzled by Gloucester's obvious indifference to fashion, for the man was, after all, one of the richest lords of the realm.

Because of his betrayal of his one-time ally, Simon de Montfort, Gloucester had gained a name for bad faith, for lightness of purpose, but Edmund thought that, in this, he'd been wronged. He'd readily agree that Gloucester was thin-skinned, irascible, obstinate enough to shame the balkiest mule, and so vengeful that men swore *forgiveness* was a word utterly alien to his vocabulary. Edmund did believe, though, that Gloucester was, in his own peculiar, prickly way, a man of some principles. And although he found Gloucester to be impossible to like, he could not help feeling a spark of sympathy for him now, the way he might briefly pity a raging, baffled bull, seeking to shake off a pack of wolves.

Edmund often thought of wolves in connection with the Marcher lords, for that was how he saw them, as tamed wolves who hunted for the English Crown, far more efficiently than any dog could have done. But a dog could be trusted, and Edmund trusted Roger de Mortimer about as much as he'd have trusted Sultan Baibars, who'd almost brought about Edward's death at Acre.

Roger de Mortimer was half Welsh; he was, in fact, a first cousin to Llewelyn ap Gruffydd, for his mother, Gwladys, had been one of Llewelyn Fawr's daughters. From his Marcher father, he'd gotten his height, his big-boned Norman-French body, from his Welsh mother, his snapping black eyes and straight dark hair. But Edmund was convinced that his knife-bladed tongue and utter lack of mercy could only have come from the Devil. He'd never met a man who took such perverse pleasure in muddying clear, calm waters—with the possible exception of Llewelyn's renegade brother Davydd. And just as he could not understand why Edward seemed to enjoy Davydd's contrary company, so was he perplexed by Edward's willingness to call de Mortimer "friend."

It was Edmund's conviction that asking the Marcher lords for advice in Welsh affairs was like asking those aforesaid wolves to guard a herd of sheep. He'd watched in disapproval as they did their best to hamstring the negotiations with Llewelyn's envoys. And in such a poisoned atmosphere, it was not surprising that the Welsh entreaties fell upon deaf ears. To Edmund, Llewelyn's presence in nearby Ewloe was proof that he did, indeed, want to resolve their differences. But to Edward, the only evidence that counted was that oath of homage, the oath Llewelyn had yet to swear.

It seemed to Edmund that his brother's eagle-eyed vision suddenly dimmed whenever he focused upon the rights and prerogatives of kingship. He had only to perceive a threat to his sovereignty, be it purported or real, and nothing else appeared to matter.

Edmund understood why this was so, for he, too, was a son of the hapless Henry III. He knew that Edward had loved the weak, well-meaning man who'd been their father, for in parenthood, Henry had excelled. In fact, he'd lavished such love upon his royal brood that many of his subjects saw his devotion as unseemly, even unmanly. When he and his Queen showed no shame, only pride, in their tiny deaf-mute daughter, that convinced many people that he was too sentimental to rule England's troubled realm. And Edward, growing up prideful and strong-willed and fearless, took each slur and insult to heart, swearing upon the surety of his soul that once he was King, no man would ever dare to defy him as they'd so often defied his father.

Yes, Edmund understood. The problem was that he also understood Llewelyn ap Gruffydd's position. The Welsh Prince did, in truth, have a legitimate grievance, for lordship was not like a river; the rights and obligations flowed both ways. In return for a vassal's homage and fealty, his liege lord owed protection. Giving refuge to a vassal's sworn enemies was, by even the most liberal interpretation, a breach of that duty.

Edward once claimed that Edmund had been cursed by a lamentable defect of vision, that he always saw both sides of every issue. He had meant it, possibly, as a jest, but not as a compliment, and like many of Edward's insights, it hit the target dead-center. Edmund sometimes envied men like his brother and his martyred de Montfort uncle, envied their absolute certainty, the distinctive blacks and whites of their world. He'd heard that some men were born color-blind, unable to distinguish reds and greens. He'd wager, though, that for Edward and Simon, the missing shade would be grey.

He had attempted to argue Llewelyn's case; perhaps not whole-heartedly, but he had tried. He felt, therefore, that he'd satisfied his sense of fairness, need feel no responsibility for whatever was to follow. The truth was that he had little interest in Wales or the Welsh. These days all of his thoughts were focused upon France. In just a few short months, he was to make the marriage of his dreams.

Blanche d'Artois was his kinswoman, for like him, she was a first cousin of Philippe, the French King. She was also the widow of Henry, King of Navarre and Count of Champagne. And she was beautiful. No man could ask for more, a wife who'd bring the riches of Champagne to his coffers and passion to his bed. She was fertile, too, having borne a healthy daughter for her late husband, and an infant son who'd died in a tragic accident. Edmund did not doubt that she'd soon give him a son and heir. He did hope, though, that she'd not be as fertile as Ned's Queen. Poor Eleanora seemed to conceive if she got within five feet of Ned; eight children in the past twelve years and another one due any day. But they were frail little bairns, five buried already, and their only surviving son, Alfonso, was a sickly lad. Alfonso, named after Eleanora's brother, the King of Castile. A queer name, though, for a future King of England! No, better that his Blanche was not quite so fecund, for more women died in childbirth than did men in battles. He'd lost one wife already, Aveline, dead of a fever at fifteen. He'd not loved Aveline, but he thought it would be very easy to love Blanche, Blanche with her great dark eyes, her smooth, soft skin and impish humor, her bountiful estates.

Edmund was so caught up in these pleasant reveries that the sudden burst of obscenity was particularly jarring. He blinked, found himself back in a congested hall that smelled of sweaty men, spilled ale, and muddy, dank hunting dogs, listening to a beet-red Earl of Gloucester call Roger de Mortimer a misbegotten son of a Welsh whore.

Whenever ale flowed freely, so did insults. But Gloucester had, in his blind rage, crossed the line. For a fleeting second, the faintest of smiles seemed to find de Mortimer's mouth; it was gone so quickly that Edmund might have imagined it—had he not known de Mortimer so well. But the bait having been taken, de Mortimer need only play the role of a man wronged. Rising slowly and dramatically to his feet, he demanded satisfaction.

Edward had been lounging on the dais, paying little heed to the escalating hostility. He saw at once that this confrontation was partly his fault, for he ought to have headed it off before it got so close to bloodshed. Both men now had hands on sword hilts. The trouble was that he liked de Mortimer, was amused by the man's lively malice, and he'd let him indulge that malice too long at Gloucester's expense.

"I'll not have us fighting amongst ourselves," he said coldly. "That benefits no one but Llewelyn ap Gruffydd."

Roger de Mortimer bowed to the royal will; he was always clever enough to know when to fish and when to cut bait. But Gloucester never made anything easy, for himself or anyone else. He continued to bluster, and Edmund hastily pushed his chair back, for he knew that Gloucester's complaints would drone on until Edward lost all patience. There was no question who would win; Gloucester would eventually subside, sulking. But Edmund saw no reason to subject himself to it. Rising, he headed for the door.

The hall porch led into the tower chapel. As Edmund started down the nave, a young chaplain stepped from the shadows, shyly offering his assistance, and Edmund explained that he wanted to light candles for his dead. For Aveline, his young wife. For his lord father. For his sisters, who'd both died that past spring. Edmund had not been close to either one; they'd long ago made brilliant marriages—Margaret to Alexander, the Scots King, Beatrice to the Duke of Brittany—and left England for foreign shores. But their deaths had come as a shock, for they were only in their thirties. Of their father's seven children, that left just him and Ned now, a sobering thought. He sighed, instructed the priest to pray, too, for Ned and Eleanora's dead babies, for his cousin Hal, martyred at Viterbo, and, as an afterthought, for his aunt Nell. It occurred to him that mayhap he ought to include Llewelyn ap Gruffydd in his prayers, for Ned was now talking about the man as if he were the enemy, and Ned's enemies did not prosper.

When Edmund returned to the hall, Gloucester was nowhere to be seen, although de Mortimer was still very much in evidence, trading affable insults with Reginald de Grey, the Justiciar of Chester. To Edmund's jaundiced eye, he looked verily like a king holding court. That must mean that Ned was elsewhere, for if he was present, there could be no confusion as to who was King. One glance confirmed this, and John de Arenwey, Chester's amiable Mayor, volunteered that the King's Grace had been called away for an urgent message. That was enough to send Edmund hastening to his brother's private chamber, for Eleanora had taken to her bed at Windsor Castle, awaiting the imminent birth of her ninth child.

Edward was alone, and there was something in his face that gave Edmund pause. "What is amiss?" he asked uneasily. "My God, Ned, Eleanora is not . . . ?"

Edward shook his head. "My news was not from Windsor, but from France."

The news was obviously unwelcome. It was not likely to come from the French court, for Philippe and Ned were allies, cousins, friends. Ned's only complaint against the French King was that he had not pressed the hunt for Guy de Montfort with sufficient vigor. De Montfort . . . of course! Guy de Montfort must have gotten the Pope to lift his sentence of excommunication. What else could make Ned look so grim?

"Did de Montfort—" He got no further; the mere mention of the de Montfort name was enough to unleash a torrent of profanity, some of it quite colorful. He listened admiringly as Edward damned the de Montforts to Hell Everlasting, but he was brought up short by a sudden "double-dealing Welsh whoreson."

"Ned?" With a quizzical smile. "You travel too fast for me. I thought we were in France with the de Montforts. How did we get back to Wales?"

Edward was not amused, was on the verge of rebuking him for his levity. But then he remembered; Edmund did not yet know. "Llewelyn ap Gruffydd was not content just to dally with treason. No, he must take it into his bed. You'll not believe what he has dared to do, Edmund. He has revived the plight troth, has sworn to take de Montfort's daughter as his wife."

Edmund was always astonished by men willing to defy his brother. He could never decide if such men were brave beyond belief or simply crazed. "Ned, are you sure? That would be so foolhardy, so . . ."

He fumbled for the right word, and Edward supplied a chilling one. "So fatal. Yes, I am sure. I have my share of French spies, people well paid to keep a close watch upon Amaury de Montfort. The best of them got herself a place in Marguerite's household. It has been a long wait, but it was worth it. Llewelyn and Ellen de Montfort plighted their troth last spring, and she is preparing to join him in Wales."

Edmund was suddenly glad that he had not argued more persuasively on Llewelyn's behalf. "Do you think it is true," he wondered, "that all the Welsh are born half-mad? I do not suppose it would do any good to forbid the marriage?"

Edward had begun to pace. "God rot his worthless soul, he is not going to get away with this!"

"Ned, I know you mean that. But what can you do to prevent the marriage?"

Edward did not answer at once. "I do not know—yet," he admitted. "But I will find a way." He swung around then, turned burning blue eyes upon his brother. "This I can tell you for certes, Edmund. That marriage will never come to pass."

12

THE ENGLISH CHANNEL, OFF THE COAST OF CORNWALL

January 1276

WHEN a sailor pointed out the distant Cornish cliffs, Amaury and Ellen hastened over to the rail to look, for it would be their last glimpse of land for a while. The master of the *Holy Cross* had warned them that once they headed north into the Atlantic, they'd no longer be shadowing the coast.

It had taken Amaury weeks to find the right ship. Because they would be sailing at the most dangerous time of year, he'd been determined to engage a cog. The cog was neither fast nor easy to maneuver. But it was almost impossible to capsize, and its high sides would make it difficult to be boarded at sea, a paramount concern in the pirate-infested waters of the Channel. Amaury might not be able to spare his sister the manifold miseries of a winter sea voyage, but he meant to do all that was humanly possible to see to her safety.

The *Holy Cross* was a French-owned merchant ship, based in Harfleur. Its master was French, too, but most of the eighteen-man crew were Bretons, for Brittany bred the world's best sailors. They'd not been thrilled to learn that their ship had been engaged by a highborn lady; they knew from sour experience that no passengers were more demanding or difficult than the gentry.

Nor were they pleased that the trip would be such a long and arduous one, for the de Montforts dared not put in at an English port. They'd have to sail through the Channel, around the Cornish Peninsula, and up the Welsh coast to the small port of Pwllheli. It was true that they could then make a quick run over to Ireland, unload their cargo of honey, almonds, and wine for a goodly profit. But they could have made several Channel crossings in the time it would take them to convey this pampered English bride and her princeling priest brother to the Welsh lord at Pwllheli. And so it only confirmed all their qualms when they were trapped in Harfleur for a fortnight, awaiting favorable winds. This was not going to be a voyage they'd remember fondly, no, by God!

It had taken them almost five days to reach the western tip of Cornwall, for the weather was raw and blustery, and for hours on end the cog seemed to make no headway at all, bobbing and tossing in the heavy swells like a child's spinning top. Most of Ellen's Welsh escort were soon violently ill, for they were a mountain race, deaf to the siren songs of the sea. The *Holy Cross* crew usually took malicious pleasure in the comic queasiness of landlubber passengers. But upon discovering that the stricken Welshmen spoke a language closely allied to their own Breton, they quickly thawed toward these Celtic kinsmen of theirs, and magnanimously forswore any rude gibes about feeding the fish.

If the crew was surprised by their unexpected camaraderie with Ellen's Welshmen, they were even more surprised by Ellen herself. The aloof, haughty, spoiled Princess turned out to be a blissfully happy young woman, and, as her excitement manifested itself in a cheerful indifference to hardship and a flattering, heartfelt curiosity about the *Holy Cross* and the men who'd chosen such a high-risk life, she soon had the crew vying with one another to answer her questions, to show off their sea-faring skills, to see her smile.

Amaury was amused that the sailors were so smitten by Ellen, but his amusement was not shared by the Welshman to whom Llewelyn had entrusted his bride. Morgan ap Madog was so concerned lest Ellen be subjected to improper advances that he insisted upon dragging himself from his sickbed whenever Ellen left her cabin.

Amaury had long ago observed that his sister had a remarkable talent for evoking protective urges in the most unlikely of men. He wasn't sure exactly how she did it, but he'd seen the results too often to doubt her witchery. Amaury could look upon his sister, see what others saw. He supposed that her delicate features, very fair skin, and slender, small-busted figure did convey a fragile image, conjuring up visions of Spanish lace and Venetian crystal, snowflakes and pasque-flowers. But Amaury knew what the others did not, that Ellen was much tougher, much more resilient than her would-be champions ever suspected.

He'd tried to enlighten the overly anxious Morgan, but the Welshman was very young and very conscientious and not immune himself to Ellen's appeal. It was no surprise to Amaury now to see him clinging to the rail, resolutely ignoring the surging waves and his own surging stomach, bleary eyes fixed intently upon Ellen and Brian, the Breton helmsman.

Brian was not as young as Morgan. Lean and weathered, he looked to be a man in his middle years, most of them spent at sea. He was the one indispensable member of the crew, for it was his navigational skills that would get the *Holy Cross* into a safe harbor. Taking advantage of his privileged status as helmsman, he'd appointed himself Ellen's personal paladin. Unfazed by Morgan's baleful stare, he was gallantly escorting Ellen toward the ship's stern. Whatever he meant to show her was apparently bolted to the deck near the tiller. As Ellen leaned over to take a closer look, Morgan squared his shoulders, prepared to abandon his death-grip on the rail.

Amaury grinned, thinking that he ought to commend the lad to Llewelyn; not many men would put duty above seasickness. But he was curious, too, as to what Brian was about. He'd taken a liking to the cocky little Breton, impressed in spite of himself by the helmsman's wizardry.

If it was true that most men had five senses, Brian had a sixth, a sea sense. If the wind felt moist, Brian knew at once that it was coming from the southwest, if it was cold, from the north. He tracked the flight of seabirds with a cat's hungry intensity, could tell when they were approaching an estuary by the changing flow and color of the water. He seemed to have memorized the entire coastline of Normandy and Brittany, a necessary skill for men who sailed from "view to view," but one that still struck his passengers as downright miraculous. To Amaury's amazement, Brian could even detect direction by the movement of the swells, and when he threw a sounding lead overboard, he was not only able to tell the depths of the ocean at that point, he could draw the most astonishing conclusions from the scooped-up contents. Just the day before, he'd explained that those grains of fine, pink-speckled sand meant that the Breton port of Ushant lay cloaked in clouds well off their larboard side.

Amaury knew that the Welsh claimed the legendary King Arthur as their own. After a few days at sea, though, he was ready to believe that the great sorceror, Merlin, must have been Breton-born, like Brian.

"Amaury, come and look!" Ellen whirled at sound of her brother's footsteps. "This is the most wondrous device!"

Amaury dutifully looked as directed into the pail of water, but all he saw was what appeared to be a floating sliver of cork, skewered by a needle. "Well?"

"Watch," Ellen said, and with a flick of her finger, sent the cork spinning. "There, do you see? The needle always points in the same direction. Brian says that if he rubs the needle against a lodestone, the needle will ever after seek out the polestar."

By now, Amaury was fascinated, too. "Yes, I've heard of such sailing needles whilst I lived in Padua. They've been known for years, but few ships make use of them. They truly do point to the north, Brian?"

"Indeed, my lord. Many helmsmen fear to use them, lest men think they practice the Black Arts. But our master and I care naught for wagging tongues, for the fear of fools," Brian said scornfully. "With yon sailing needle, we can find our way even in fog. By my lights, that is a godsend, not the Devil's work!"

"I would think that—" Whatever Amaury meant to say was lost, for at that moment, the deck seemed to fall away from them. Ellen gasped and grabbed for Amaury, who caught the windlass for support. But Brian merely braced himself, rolled on the balls of his feet, and rode the swell out.

"When she pitches like that, your heart ends up in your throat and your stomach in your feet," he said, sounding almost apologetic, as if he were somehow responsible for the vagaries of the winter weather. "But it is worth a bit of queasiness to keep the God-cursed pirates in port. They are not as likely to leave their lairs when the seas are this rough." He wanted very much to reassure Ellen, but being honest to a compulsive degree, he felt obligated to add, "Of course weather like this does please the wreckers right well."

Ellen's smile was quizzical. "I've heard that when a ship goes aground in Cornish waters, the local people can strip it bare in just the blink of an eye. But why call them 'wreckers'? That makes it sound so deliberate, as if they did more than take advantage of a ship's misfortune."

"They do, my lady. They've been known to walk a mule along the beach at night with a lantern tied to its saddle. Many a ship has mistaken that bobbing light for the lighthouse, followed it onto the rocks."

Ellen paled and made the sign of the cross. "How truly wicked," she said, and Brian nodded grimly, for he hated no men on earth as much as he did those who'd lure a ship to its doom.

"More wicked than you know, my lady. By the law of the sea, a ship that founders is not legally a wreck unless every man, woman, and child aboard perishes." Turning, Brian pointed to the ship's huge grey cat, comfortably curled up within a coil of rope. "If even Hotspur there survived, the ship and its cargo could not be plundered. So any poor soul who manages to make it ashore is as likely to get a dagger in the throat as he is to get a helping hand. No survivors; one way or another, the wreckers make bloody well sure of that."

Ellen shivered, drew her mantle more closely about her. "A sailor's lot is such a dangerous one, Brian. Do you never long for a life ashore, ground that does not move under your feet, your own hearth?"

"No," he said simply, "this is all I know. The men of my village have been going to sea since before Noah launched his ark."

The ship pitched again. As it sank down into a trough, a wall of water towered above their heads, and Amaury had to fight a sudden surge of queasiness. "Our father was one of the bravest men who ever drew breath. He spent a good portion of his life on the seas, for he sailed to the Holy Land, and as Governor of Gascony, he crossed the Channel as often as a Londoner might cross over the Thames to Southwark. But he often confessed that he never once set foot on shipboard without feeling his stomach lurch. After one voyage from Wissant to Dover, when his ship was blown back into the harbor three times by ill winds, he told me that sailors ought not to be allowed to testify in court, for any man who freely chose a life at sea could not have his full wits about him!"

"Amaury!" But Ellen's concern was needless. Far from being offended, Brian was vastly amused, laughing until he almost choked.

"Well, you need not fear for me," he said, still chuckling, "for I was baptized on Whitsunday, and all know a babe so blessed cannot drown!"

At that, Alain, the Breton boatswain, looked up from the halyard he was mending, held the rope aloft in a sinister, suggestive loop. "He is right, my lady. If he drowned, he'd be cheating the hangman!"

That triggered an exchange of friendly insults. At least Amaury and Ellen assumed they were friendly; even Hugh, who had a genuine gift for languages, had mastered only a few words of Breton. They watched now as Brian swaggered across the deck, no less sure-footed than Hotspur, joining his comrades hunched in the shelter of the spare boat. Neither Amaury nor Ellen took much comfort in the sight of that small, frail craft. Instead of reassuring them that they had an escape available, it merely served to remind them how often ships were lost at sea— swallowed by storms or sea monsters, sunk when their cargoes suddenly shifted, blown upon the rocks and split asunder, prey to pirates and the doldrums, to God's Wrath and the Devil's whims.

Brian had apparently related Simon's barbed jest, for the others had begun to laugh, too, casting glances their way. Ellen shook her head in exaggerated bemusement. "Men dare to chide women for our vanity, yet they take pride in the most peculiar things. If you want to flatter a man beyond all measure, just tell him that his courage borders upon craziness!"

"True," Amaury agreed, "men do value such praise most highly. I can think of only one other tribute that they prize more."

Ellen thought about that, then grinned. "Let me guess. It has to do with the male nether regions, and requires some woman to sigh, with a straight face yet, 'Oh, my, how huge!' "

Amaury let out a whoop of laughter. "For a maiden, you know entirely too much about the wages of sin!"

"And so do you, my dear brother the priest!"

Ellen leaned over, gave Amaury a sudden, quick embrace, smearing lip rouge across his cheek. As he hugged her back, he found himself thinking that he'd recovered a treasure he'd long thought lost, the Ellen of the old days, the playful, saucy minx of a sister who delighted in teasing and being teased, the Ellen who had not yet learned what evil could befall the innocent, the Ellen before Evesham.

"I've not seen you so joyful for far too long," he said. "But tell me the truth, kitten. Are you not at all nervous about living in an unknown land, wedding a man you've never even laid eyes upon?"

"Oh, mayhap once we drop anchor in Pwllheli's harbor. But not now, not yet. You see, Amaury, Wales is not unknown to me. As far back as I can remember, it was a place of magic and mystery. How Mama loved to talk about her sister and Llewelyn Fawr, and how I loved to listen! Other girls my age were bedazzled by tales of King Arthur and Guinevere, but I'd be begging Mama for bedtime stories about Aunt Joanna and her Welsh Prince. Wales became my Camelot, and when Mama told me I was to wed my Llewelyn, I could scarce believe my good fortune. I felt as if I already knew him, for Mama had been right fond of him, and we both know she was not easy to impress. But to hear her talk, he sounded almost as perfect as Papa! And then . . . after Evesham, it was as if I were drowning, and Llewelyn alone could keep me afloat."

Ellen paused, shot him a sideways look full of silent laughter. "I can confess to such foolishness now, for those childish dreams have somehow come to pass! But do you see what I'm saying? How could I be nervous about meeting Llewelyn when I've been half in love with him for most of my life?"

Amaury leaned back against the rail, studying his sister. She'd rarely looked prettier, for the wind had whipped high color into her cheeks and anticipation had given her a special sparkle. It amused him to discover that the folklore was true, that brides truly were radiant. But he was not so pleased to have his suspicions confirmed. Ellen's polished, poised shell was just that, a shell. She was at heart still a romantic, still his little sister who believed in happy endings, that good must prevail over evil, over Edward. He could wish—for her sake—that it was otherwise. Yet her innocence might serve her well in Wales. If Ellen was already so sure that Llewelyn ap Gruffydd would be to her liking, he thought it unlikely that she'd be disappointed; people usually found what they were looking for, harvested what they sowed. Or so he hoped; Jesú, how he hoped!

"Amaury, look!" Ellen pointed, and as the ship crested a wave, he saw it, too, several birds wheeling toward the horizon.

Brian had turned as she cried out. A quick glance was enough for him to identify the birds as herring gulls. "They were heading for the Isles of Scilly," he said matter-of-factly, as if recognition of flying, feathered specks was too commonplace to warrant comment. "The Isles lay to the west of us, but we'll not be putting in there." He had returned to the tiller, gave Ellen a jaunty grin. "I do not like the company the islanders keep. They've got more pirates lurking in their coves than we've got rats down in the hold!"

"That man is a marvel," Ellen murmured to Amaury. "Does nothing scare him?" She sighed when the birds vanished from sight; it had been comforting to watch them skim the waves, winged proof that land was just over the horizon. It made her feel less lonely somehow.

When she turned back to Amaury, her mood had changed. "Do you believe that gratitude begets love?" she asked, very seriously now. "If it is so, then I shall cherish Llewelyn ap Gruffydd till the day I die. I do owe him so much, Amaury. He gave Mama what we could not, a peaceful death. She was like a soldier who'd not abandon her post, holding on to life for my sake. I knew how much she feared for my future; I just did not know how to ease her mind. But Llewelyn did that for her, let her die without regrets, in God's Grace. I do not know how I can ever repay so great a gift, but I mean to try."

Smiling, she slipped her arm through his. "I only wish I could have convinced you that there was no need to accompany me. I could not have a more devoted bodyguard than Morgan, bless his seasick soul. As much as I enjoy your wicked tongue, Amaury, I'd rather you were not within a hundred miles of the English coast. And you'll be facing another long sea voyage back to France, still in the dead of winter. If any evil should ever befall you—"

"I'd come back to haunt you, never fear," he said, making Ellen laugh in spite of herself. As they talked, they'd moved along the rail toward the ship's bow, and as the prow cleaved through the waves, the spray it flung up was spangled by the sun, reflected shimmering arcs of iridescent color. When Amaury pointed this out to Ellen, she was delighted, exclaiming that they were riding a rainbow to Wales, and they both laughed, for rainbows were among the most auspicious omens.

After two days of fog and rain, it was good to see the sun again. It thawed the icy air, brightened the leaden sea to a more cheerful shade of blue, and raised all their spirits. Some of the Welshmen ventured out onto the deck, and Hugh started a dice game with Alain, the boatswain.

Hugh was the only one of the de Montfort party who had yet to suffer from seasickness. He endured the rolling, pitching waves with admirable aplomb, and shrugged off compliments about his fortitude by explaining that crossing the Channel was not as scary as crossing the Alps. Amaury was not surprised that by the second day out, the crew was treating Hugh as one of their own, for the affable young Englishman had an enviable knack for turning strangers into friends. In this Christmas season, he was even more obliging and good-humored than usual, for Ellen had arranged for him to be knighted before they left France, and he was still flying high. Like Ellen, he was drunk on dreams. Knighthood for a penniless orphan, Camelot for a dead rebel's daughter. Amaury smiled to himself at sound of Hugh's loud, ringing laugh. It was almost enough—almost—for him to start believing in happy-ever-after endings himself.

The wind was picking up again. As the sails began to billow, the cog heeled suddenly to the portside, hung there for a sickening stretch of eternity before finally righting itself. Even the sailors looked shaken, and two of the Welshmen and one of Amaury's knights dived for the rail.

"Good God," Ellen said faintly. "Will it discomfit you if I kiss the ground once we reach Pwllheli?"

"You say that now, but I'd wager you kiss Llewelyn first," Amaury said, and Ellen's smile came back.

"I ought to see how Juliana is faring. She had a dreadful night."

That, Amaury didn't doubt. Juliana's suffering had begun as soon as the command had been given to "unfurl the sails." So severe was her nausea that she'd eaten virtually nothing for days, and could not even keep down the syrup of ginger that Ellen tried to spoon into her mouth. She rarely left her bed, and they all were surprised now by her sudden appearance in the doorway of Ellen's cabin. She paused, blinking in the glare of sun, and Morgan hastened over to offer his arm.

So did one of Amaury's companions, Sir William Dulay. He'd been so solicitous of Juliana that Ellen suspected he was motivated by more than knightly courtesy. If he did have courtship in mind, it was a campaign most likely doomed to failure. Ellen had long ago realized a sad truth, that no man could compete with a ghost. She'd loved her brother Bran dearly, but she'd not deified him in death as Juliana had done. She could only hope that Juliana, too, would find a new life in Wales. Slipping her arm through Amaury's again, she started cautiously toward the aft-castle cabin.

Hugh had joined Juliana by the time Ellen and Amaury made their way down the foam-slick deck. Upon hearing Hugh announce that Alain had been telling him the most amazing stories, Ellen frowned. The last time that Alain had been spinning yarns, he'd terrified them all with lurid accounts of sea serpents and whirlpools vast enough to engulf ships and multi-armed remora monsters that attached themselves to a ship's hull, held it motionless in the water until the crew and passengers perished of famine and thirst.

"Hugh," Ellen said warningly, trying to catch his eye. She prided herself upon being less gullible than most people. She did not believe in fire-breathing, flying dragons. She did believe that the earth was round, just as scholars claimed. She understood that the child's fear of the dark was twin to the man's fear of demons. But as she gazed out upon that endless expanse of blue-grey ocean, rational thought was submerged in purely visceral dread. God alone knew what hid in those murky, dark depths.

She needn't have worried, though. Hugh had no horror stories to relate, was interested only in sharing his new-found knowledge of ships. He was sure they knew that King Edward's royal galleys were more dependent upon sails than oars. But Alain said the Mediterranean galleys still relied mainly upon oarsmen for power. The Italian city-states of Genoa and Venice manned fleets with infidel slaves and convicted felons.

"Alain says that the oarsmen are flogged whenever the galley needs a burst of speed. And they are chained to their oarlocks, go down with the ship if it sinks. They even have to bite upon wooden gags when a battle begins, so that if they are wounded, they will not be able to cry out!" Hugh was constantly being surprised by man's inhumanity to his fellow men. But even Amaury found himself agreeing with Hugh's indignant conclusion, that a galley slave need not fear Hell, for he was already there.

Catching sight of Juliana, Brian yielded the tiller to another crewman, came over to tell her how glad he was to see her up and about. The sickness truly was worse for those who stayed penned up in their cabins, he insisted. Juliana could only nod weakly, unconvinced.

A shout from the rigging drew all eyes. Diego, the Spanish lookout, came slithering down the mast at breakneck speed. "A sail," he panted, flinging up an arm toward the sun.

"Tell the master," Brian ordered. Amaury soon joined him at the larboard rail, and they watched the horizon intently, silently, until a sail rose above the swells, triangular, as bright as blood. Brian said softly, "A galley," no more than that, but Amaury felt a sudden chill.

"Brian? Are we in peril?"

"I'm not yet sure." Brian's eyes, sun-creased, were narrowed on that bobbing lateen sail. "It may come to nothing. But I'd say we have three reasons to worry. That it's a galley, for these days merchants favor cogs or nefs. That it's coming from those unholy isles. And that it's not flying any banners."

"I see." Amaury's voice did not betray him, revealed nothing of the fear churning his stomach, flooding his veins. He dared not look back at his sister. "I want the truth. If the worst comes, can we hope to fend them off?"

Brian's shoulders twitched, a half-shrug. "We might," he said slowly, "if those Welsh lads of yours are the bowmen they claim to be."

"They are." They'd not heard Morgan's approach. Aside from that laconic assurance, he asked no questions, offered no counsel. But Amaury had encountered such reticence before, recognized it for what it was, the single-minded absorption of the soldier, the focused intensity of a man about to do battle. He gave the Welshman an approving look, thankful that Llewelyn had chosen so well, and as their eyes met, Morgan said quietly, "We'll keep her safe, my lord, that I swear."

The ship's master had emerged from his fore-castle cabin, joining their vigil. Both of Llewelyn's Dominican friars were on deck now, too, jostling for space at the rail with the sailors and Welsh soldiers and French-born knights. Ellen had to push her way through to her brother's side, pulling Juliana along behind her.

"Can we keep them from boarding us?"

None but Amaury would know what that composed question cost her. Grateful that they'd not have to deal with womanly hysterics, the men hastened to assure her that she need not fear, that there was no danger to speak of, that even if it was a pirate galley, they'd be able to stave it off easily enough.

"God willing," Ellen said softly, never taking her eyes from her brother's face. He alone had not spoken, he alone had not lied. Reaching over, he caught her hand in his, squeezing her fingers so tightly that she had to suppress a gasp.

"I think," he said, "that you'd best wait in your cabin, Ellen."

"No," she said, "not yet."

Bran had once told her that when he'd been captured at the battle of Northampton, a prisoner who'd just heard his own death sentence passed upon him, it had all seemed very unreal, as if it were happening to someone else. Ellen felt like that now, as she watched the galley rise above the waves, sink down, rise again. It rode very low in the water. The hull was painted a garish red, the prow tipped in iron, like the battering rams her father had used in castle sieges. After a moment, she realized it served the same purpose, was meant to stave in the sides of its quarry. She had no doubts as to its evil intent, for its very appearance was predatory. Just as a rabbit froze instinctively when a falcon flew overhead, she knew that she was looking at a hawk of the seas, on the prowl for prey.

The galley was tacking, a navigational technique Brian had explained to Ellen in exhaustive if incomprehensible detail; she'd understood only that it somehow enabled a ship to sail against the wind. She would have expected it to plot a course to intercept them; when it did not, she felt a sudden flicker of hope. But Brian had begun to swear, in Breton and French.

"The whoresons are trying to get to windward of us!" Spinning away from the rail, he headed for the ship's stern. "Ivo, hard on the helm!"

With that, the deck erupted into chaotic activity. Amaury disappeared in search of a weapon. At Morgan's command, the Welsh bowmen clambered up into the fore- and aft-castles. Sir William Dulay took charge of the knights, who began to position themselves along the rail, while Alain emerged from the hold with an armful of long staves. They would, he explained to Ellen, be useful for fending off grappling hooks, or for breaking heads. Not that he thought it would come to that, God's blessed truth! Her ladyship must not fret. These pirate scum would rue the day they'd taken on the *Holy Cross*. Why, the Welsh lads would turn them into pin-cushions, see if they did not!

Ellen found herself agreeing with him, and not just because she so wanted to believe. Morgan's men had a superior vantage point from the heights of the fore- and aft-castles. Once the low-slung galley drew alongside and its crew sought to scramble up the cog's steep freeboard, they'd be facing a murderous fire, arrows raining down faster than the eye could follow. She knew about longbows, for her father had been most impressed with this Welsh weapon, even predicting it would eventually supplant the crossbow. How could the pirates overcome such formidable odds?

And then, Diego, the lookout, shouted down from his skyward perch, "Oh, Jesus, sail ho!"

As the second pirate galley hove into view, Ellen felt a hand upon her shoulder. "Madame." She turned, looked into the somber, ashen face of Friar Anian, the older of the two Dominicans. "I think we'd best go aft," he said.

Once they reached the cabin, Friar Teilo tried to barricade the door with the sturdy oaken table, forgetting, in his agitation, that it was bolted to the floor. No one knew what to say. It seemed to take forever before he realized his mistake. He flushed bright red, looked suddenly so young and vulnerable that Ellen's breath stopped. How many men would die ere this day was done? Blessed Lady, spare Amaury and Hugh and Morgan and Brian. Mary, ever Virgin, save our honor, keep us from sin. By thy goodness, deliver us from evil. Please do not let my brother die.

The cabin had but a single, small porthole; it was deep in shadow. Ellen sought to light a candle in one of the horn lanterns, but her hands were shaking too badly, and after she'd failed in several tries, Anian took the flint and tinder, struck a few, faint sparks.

Teilo was slumped down on a coffer, clenching and unclenching his hands, rubbing his palms repeatedly against his worn wool habit. He fidgeted, then blurted out, "Is it true that . . . that when a ship is taken at sea, those captured are thrown overboard?"

Anian frowned, jerked his head warningly toward the women. Juliana had perched precariously upon the very edge of the bed, like a bird about to take flight at any moment. She said nothing but flinched away from Teilo's words, and Ellen hastily shook her head.

"No, Brother Teilo. Whilst that might well happen during a sea battle, pirates care for naught but profit. They would much rather ransom their prisoners than drown them." She swallowed dryly, hoping that her voice sounded more convincing to them than it had to her own ears, then sat down beside Juliana. The waiting began.

Their cabin was located under the aft-castle; they could hear men moving about above their heads, hear occasional muffled shouts. Teilo climbed onto a coffer, peered out the porthole. Because of the cog's pitching, he could get only a glimpse of sea or sky. But then he tumbled backward, crying, "They have overtaken us, are manning their oars now!"

The noise on deck intensified. Occasionally they heard a scream, knew they were listening as men died. Juliana had closed her eyes, but tears were trickling through her lashes. Anian bowed his head, began to pray. The words made no sense to Ellen, sounded so garbled and slurred that she feared her wits were wandering. When she finally realized that Anian was entreating the Almighty in Welsh, she gave a sudden, shaken laugh. Their instant alarm was almost comical, but it was sobering, too. "Forgive me for interrupting, Brother Anian. Please . . . pray for us all."

The screams, shouts, and curses seemed much louder now. It was all too easy for Ellen to envision what was occurring beyond that bolted cabin door. The pirates were circling the cog, much like she'd seen mastiffs worrying a chained, baited bear, swinging their grappling hooks, awaiting the moment when the bear would drop its guard, allow them to leap for the jugular. The Welshmen's hail of arrows would keep them at bay for a time, just as the bear's claws held off the dogs. There were always bloodied bodies crumpled in the arena, savaged by those mighty jaws. But the dogs kept on the attack, and the outcome was not in doubt. Like Evesham, Papa riding out to die. Sooner or later, the bear would be overwhelmed by sheer numbers.

Rising inconspicuously, Ellen crossed to the coffer that held her silver-plate and cutlery. Selecting a slender-bladed eating knife, she tested its edge for sharpness. It traced a thin, white line across her finger. She felt no pain, but blood soon welled up, and she watched it drip down her hand. For so slight a wound, it took a surprisingly long time before the bleeding stopped.

Teilo had remained, frozen, at the porthole. "Christ pity us," he gasped, "for we are truly doomed! There are four galleys!"

They knew when the cog was taken, could tell by the changed, triumphant tone of the shouting. When the axe first thudded into the door, Ellen thought it was a demand for entry. So did Anian. He was reaching for the bolt when the wood splintered and a steel blade just missed his outstretched hand.

It took only three or four more blows to reduce the door to kindling. There was no sudden surge of sun, for the man filling the doorway blotted out the light, so huge was he. Towering above the friar, boasting shoulders as wide as planks and a wild black beard, he lacked only an eye patch to be the pirate of dark legend, the pirate of every seafarer's nightmare, a man able to terrify by his very appearance.

Anian, with commendable courage, stood his ground. "These women are under the protection of Holy Church. They must not be—"

The rest of his words were choked off. A mammoth fist twisted in the neck of his cowl. As if he were a child's rag doll, filled only with straw, he was lifted off his feet, flung across the cabin.

Ellen had concealed the knife in the folds of her skirt. With her free hand, she drew Juliana in behind her. "I must speak to your chieftain," she said, as evenly as she could. "It will be worth his while, I swear it."

He didn't reply, and she felt a new stab of fear. Jesú, what if he spoke no French? No man had ever dared to look at her with such blatant lust. Having stripped her with his eyes, he reached out, ran the back of his hand along her throat. She jerked free, retreated with Juliana to the far corner of the cabin, and when he followed, she brought up the dagger. He blinked, burst out laughing.

"Give me that ere you hurt yourself," he said in accented but understandable Norman-French. When she shook her head, he grinned, started to turn away, then grabbed for her wrist. But it had been a clumsy feint and he recoiled in surprise, staring at his slashed palm.

So intent was Ellen upon the black-bearded pirate that it was not until she heard the laughter that she became aware of the other man's presence. He was leaning against the shattered door, as if watching a play put on purely for his own amusement, and he laughed again when the giant said indignantly, "The bitch cut me!"

"Just be thankful she aimed at your hand and not your ballocks. I thought you had more sense than to snatch at a naked blade like that."

"So I was careless. But I've never yet known a wench who could tell a dagger from a serving spoon. These highborn milk-tit ladies, they're good only for—"

"You just never use your head, do you? The woman had five brothers. You think at least one of them would not have taught her how to defend herself?"

Their exchange meant nothing to Juliana, for it had been in English. But Ellen had once spoken the language. She'd lost a lot of it during her ten years in French exile, but she was still able to get the gist of what was said. Her first reaction was one of enormous relief, for if they knew her identity, it must mean Amaury had survived the battle. Unless . . . unless Morgan or Brian had spoken out, trying to protect her honor and her life. But at least they seemed to believe it. She'd been so frightened that they might mock her claims. Ransom now seemed within reach again.

Keeping the dagger close against her body, but tilted and at the ready, she transferred her attention to the second pirate. He was also uncommonly tall, but in all other respects, quite unlike his aggrieved companion. In appearance, he was very English, as fair as Hugh. The hair touching his tunic collar was a tawny yellow; it even looked clean. Surprisingly, so did his clothes. In fact, he had a hard-edged elegance about him that was utterly at odds with his chosen profession. She could not help thinking of all the times she'd teased Amaury about his vanity, so inappropriate in a priest. It would seem that pirates, too, could be fops. It should have reassured her that he was handsome and, judging from his speech, educated, possibly even a man of her own class; it was not unheard-of for knights to turn to piracy. But it did not. To the contrary, she found this man even more frightening than the first one. Never had she seen blue eyes so chilling, so devoid of warmth or pity.

"My lady de Montfort? I believe you were asking for me," he said, making a mockery of the courteous rituals that structured the upper reaches of their society, but confirming her suspicions that he was, indeed, born into her world. "I am Sir Thomas de . . . Well, no matter. We tend to be careless of surnames on the high seas. My men know me as Thomas the Archdeacon. Mayhap you've heard of me?"

She shook her head. Had he truly once taken holy orders? How could a man turn from God's Word, embrace the Devil so wholeheartedly? Could it be a profane jest? And yet she knew the most infamous pirate in her grandfather's reign had been a one-time cleric, Eustace the Monk.

"I think you ought to give me that dagger," he suggested, sounding polished and urbane and amused by her defiance. "You need have no fears for your safety or your honor. On that, you have my word."

And what was the word of a pirate worth? The words hovered on her lips. Her mother would have flung them out, scornful of consequence. Ellen bit them back. "What of my household? The priest . . . my chaplain, was he hurt?"

"I think he still lives. Your chaplain, is he? It had occurred to me that he just might be your brother."

"My brother? No, Amaury is in Rome."

Ellen met his eyes steadily, calmly, and rose slightly in his estimation. "Well, a natural mistake, you'll agree," he said and smiled. "A pity, though. You see, my men think it is bad luck to have a priest aboard. Conn," glancing back at the bearded giant, "that priest . . . throw him over the side."

"No!" Even as she screamed, Ellen knew she'd been outbluffed. But that was not a bluff she could ever have called. He grinned, and she saw that he'd been playing with her, cat to mouse, had known Amaury's identity all the while.

"Suppose we make a bargain," he said. "You give me that dagger and in turn, I'll let you go up on deck to tend to your brother."

He swaggered forward, as if deliberately daring her to strike, and her fingers tightened on the dagger's ivory handle. He had been quite right about her; under Bran and Harry's tutelage, she'd not only become familiar with knives, she'd learned to throw one at close range with some accuracy. Now she had a sudden, savage urge to thrust the blade into the pulse at his throat. Reversing the dagger, she handed it to him, hilt first.

He was still laughing at her, eyes agleam with such sardonic amusement that she wondered if he'd somehow read her mind. "Thank you," he said, and bowed mockingly. "Well, Lady Eleanor, shall we go?"

Sprawled in a far corner, Friar Anian had begun to stir, to mumble groggily. "See to him, Brother Teilo," Ellen said, and reached again for

Juliana's hand, for she was not about to leave Juliana with the brutal Conn. As they edged around him, Conn stepped in front of them, barring their way. Thomas said something shortly, sharply, in English. Ellen caught only "damaged goods," but it was enough. She understood, and so did Conn. After a long moment, he grudgingly yielded, cleared the path to the door.

Ellen paused briefly in the doorway, steeling herself for whatever lay ahead, not wanting them to know how much she dreaded what she might find on deck. Feeling Thomas's ironic gaze upon her, she said coolly, "I am ready."

It was even worse than she'd feared, for almost at once, she stumbled over a body, recognized Alain, the boatswain. The deck was always wet, drenched by spray and waves breaking over the bow. But now she glanced down, discovered that the hem of her gown was trailing in blood. She stopped, sickened, and Thomas put a supportive hand upon her elbow, steering her toward the rail. His touch made her quiver, so intense was her loathing, but she dared not pull away, dared not demean him in front of his crew. He was too dangerous a man to defy openly.

The surviving sailors and knights were under guard on the portside. She felt a surge of gratitude upon catching sight of Hugh's flaxen head. Blood matted his hair, streaked the side of his face, but when he saw Ellen, he struggled against his bonds, tried to regain his feet, only to be shoved back by one of the pirates. The man beside him sought to calm him, and Ellen thanked God for Brian's good sense, thanked God that Brian had not died in the assault upon the ship.

As they reached the rail, she had an unobstructed view of the fore- and aft-castles, and what she saw broke her heart. Bodies piled upon one another, some still clutching longbows, the Welshmen who'd died in her defense. The sailors had surrendered to save themselves, and for that she could not blame them. So had Amaury's knights, once all hope was gone. But the Welsh had held out until the last, offering up their lives for their lord's bride.

Tears stung Ellen's eyes. There was no surprise, then, when she found Morgan's body, sprawled by the tiller, close enough for her to see the gaping wounds, the dark, clotted blood. Pulling away from Thomas's grip, she knelt by the young Welshman, and slowly made the sign of the cross. Reaching down, she gently closed his eyes, then glanced up at the pirate chieftain.

"Where is my brother?"

NEITHER Ellen nor Juliana had ever been in the fore-castle cabin, and they hesitated in the doorway, unable to see into the gloom. "Amaury?"

Ellen's whisper went unanswered, and she was suddenly terrified that Thomas the Archdeacon had lied, that Amaury was dead and this a cruel pirate hoax.

"Ellen? Is he in there?" Juliana was whispering, too, her fingers clutching Ellen's arm in a grip that would leave bruises.

Ellen took a tentative step into the cabin. Her eyes were slowly adjusting to the dark. "Amaury? Juliana, over here!"

The man on the bed did not stir as she bent over him, and again she was tormented by the fear that he might be dead. "Amaury, can you hear me? Juliana, I've got to have light. See if there is a lamp on the table."

Amaury's skin felt cold and clammy. Searching for his pulse, Ellen discovered that his wrist was shackled to the bed. "Those whoring pirates have him in irons! Juliana, where is that lamp? Damn them, damn them all!"

Juliana was still fumbling with the oil lamp, trying to get it lit. Ellen could wait no longer. Jumping up, she ripped open the porthole shutters. "Oh, dear God! Amaury . . ." Her voice broke, but almost at once, she began ransacking the cabin.

Juliana was standing by the bed, staring down at Amaury. "Ellen, he must have been kicked in the face! What if . . . what if his jaw is broken?"

Ellen had finally located a water basin. Carrying it back to the bed, she started to clean the blood from her brother's face. "Do not say that," she hissed. "Do not even think that!" Amaury did not respond to her touch, not even to the cold water, and as she gently wiped his torn mouth, she found that he'd lost at least one tooth. "See if you can find a wine flask, Juliana." His breathing seemed shallow but steady, and she leaned over, pressed his free hand to her cheek.

The blaze of sunlight was blinding. She looked up, saw Thomas the Archdeacon framed in the doorway, and she felt so much hatred that it choked all utterance. She moved hastily back into the shadows lest he read her face.

"Has he come around yet?"

"No," Ellen said tersely, digging her nails into her palm until she could trust herself. Handing the basin to Juliana, she got slowly to her feet. "Set your ransom. Whatever it is, my husband will pay it."

He cocked a brow. "Husband?"

Ellen held out her hand so that the sun glinted off the jeweled wedding band. "We were wed in Paris by proxy more than six weeks ago, at Martinmas. My husband is Llewelyn ap Gruffydd, Prince of Wales, and he will pay well for my safe return, for my brother, and the rest of my companions."

When he didn't reply, she felt a throb of fear. Pirates always ransomed their captives, did they not? "Do you not believe me?" she demanded. "Llewelyn will pay your ransom, I swear it!"

"Oh, I do believe you." He let his eyes roam lazily over her body, watched with amusement as angry color rose in her face. "I do not doubt that your husband would pay any price to get you back. If you were my woman, I would. But unfortunately for you, and for him, the deal has already been struck. You, my prideful, pretty lady, are a very valuable commodity. As soon as we were told you were fitting a cog at Harfleur, we've been stopping every ship heading for Wales."

"What do you mean?"

"I think you know," he said, and she did. But she could not admit it, not yet, not even to herself.

"Listen to me," she said, in that moment more desperate than proud. "Whatever you've been offered, Llewelyn will match it and more. You need only name your price!"

But he was already shaking his head in mock remorse. "Alas, we both know better. No matter how much your Welshman wants you, sweetheart, he cannot hope to outbid the King of England."

13

THE COG *HOLY CROSS*, OFF THE ISLES OF SCILLY

January 1276

B y the time Thomas the Archdeacon responded to Ellen's urgent appeal, she was frantic with fear on her brother's behalf. As was customary for young women who'd one day be expected to manage vast households, she'd been given some medical training, was knowledgeable about herbs and ointments and the dangers of "proud flesh." She felt reasonably certain that Amaury's jaw was not broken, but she'd discovered a bloodied gash above his left temple, almost hidden by his hair, and when he did not regain consciousness, her anxiety was soon spiraling out of sight.

When the pirate chieftain finally came, he gave her no warning, suddenly thrust the door open, flashing the smile she was fast learning to hate. "I understand you crave my company, Lady Eleanor."

Snatching up the oil lamp, she held it above the bed. "I do not know much about head injuries. His skin is clammy, his pulse rapid, and he does not respond to my voice or my touch. I think that—"

"Why are you sharing his symptoms with me? Do I look like a doctor?"

The question itself was brusque enough to disconcert. Even more disturbing was his obvious indifference to Amaury's peril; he'd barely glanced at the bed. When Ellen had first begun to master the secrets of self-control, having learned how dangerous it was to let the world get too close, she'd resorted to a simple yet effective stratagem, combating raw emotion with deep, rhythmic breathing. It usually helped, and she tried it now, deliberately drawing breath into her lungs, willing herself into a state of camouflaged composure.

Setting the lamp down, she sought to sound matter-of-fact, eminently reasonable. "I thought you might have a crewman skilled in healing, for I know many ships do . . ." But he was already shaking his head. "There are herbs that can bring a dazed man to his senses. I know the *Holy Cross* master keeps a hoard of medicinal potions and ointments. Could you speak to him, find out if he has fennel juice or pennyroyal? Also betony, sage, and—"

"Is that all? Why not a feather bed, a tun of fine French wine, a servant to soothe his fevered brow?"

"I do not think you understand," Ellen said carefully, "just how dangerous head wounds can be. There is no way to know how serious it is. If my brother is denied care, he could die."

He shrugged. "So?"

She was shaken, but determined not to let him see it. "You told me you boarded and seized our ship at the English King's behest. He is not paying you to deliver a corpse!"

"He is paying me, sweetheart, to deliver a bride. And if it eases your mind, he gave express orders that we see to your safety. But from what I hear, he's not likely to grieve if Amaury de Montfort is buried at sea."

Ellen bit her lip, took another bracing breath. "Do you want me to beg, then? I will, if you'll but give me the herbs Amaury needs."

He grinned. "As entertaining as that would be, I cannot spare the time. Mayhap later?"

But as he turned toward the door, Ellen stepped in front of him, barring his way. "Edward is my cousin. You'd best remember that, for this I swear. If my brother dies because of you, I will tell Edward that you raped me."

"Is that an invitation?" They were close enough now for him to feel her fear, to see the involuntary flicker of her eyelids, the faint sheen of sweat on her upper lip. But she did not flinch away from him, nor did she back down. He was accustomed to intimidating women with ease. He was far from a fool, though, knew at once that this was no bluff, for she'd hit upon the only leverage she had—their society's insistence upon the virtue of highborn women.

Having made her threat, Ellen did not elaborate upon it, for they both knew there was no need. Even if Edward meant to cast her into the Tower for the rest of her days, he'd demand a truly terrible vengeance should she be dishonored. Thomas had already taken pains to warn his crew of that, making sure they understood that the King's kinswoman was not fair game. And then he'd posted guards outside her cabin, for until he handed her over to the constable at Bristol Castle, she was his responsibility, and he was not about to risk his neck and private parts on the good faith of his men, some of whom would have rutted with the Virgin Mary herself if given half a chance.

"That would not be very Christian of you, my lady," he said blandly. "An accusation like that could get a man strung up by his cock."

"I would hope so," she said, without blinking an eye, and he burst out laughing.

"I thought convent-bred blossoms like you were supposed to swoon dead away at the droop of a petal! Where did you learn to fight dirty, like a sailor in a whorehouse brawl?"

He was laughing again, but Ellen could not tell if he was truly amused by her effrontery or merely saving face. She said nothing, afraid to push her luck any further, and was very relieved when he drew back, put some space between them.

"I'll send a man to the cog's master." He paused, hand on the door latch. "In truth, I was going to give you the herbs all along. But by God, I'd not have missed your performance for the world!"

Ellen waited until he stopped laughing. "When I was out on deck, I saw that some of my men were wounded, some of the crew, too. I would like to share the herbs and ointments with them." Adding tonelessly, "If that meets with your approval."

"Why not?" He was still smiling. "You do have pluck, lass, damn me if you do not! I like that in a woman, have always fancied a cat with claws. But I cannot help wondering if Eleanor of Brittany had pluck, too—in the beginning."

Huddled in a far corner of the cabin, Juliana had been a mute and miserable witness, immobilized as much by her seasickness as by her fear. As soon as the door closed, though, she struggled weakly to her feet, for Ellen had gone ashen. She sat down abruptly upon the edge of the bed, and Juliana fought back her nausea, lurched unsteadily across the cabin. It seemed to her that, for all his talk about Ellen's claws, Thomas was the one who'd drawn blood, and she found herself fumbling for comfort when there was none.

"Your lady mother would have been so proud of you, Ellen. For certes, I was. But . . . but who is this Eleanor of Brittany?"

Ellen leaned over, reassured herself that Amaury's breathing was still steady. "She was our kinswoman, my grandfather's niece. She and her brother Arthur were his rivals for the English crown, and when they fell into his hands, Arthur disappeared into one of John's strongholds, never to be seen again. As for Eleanor . . . she was but seventeen or so, said to be very pretty. John sent her to Bristol Castle, kept her in comfortable confinement . . ."

Ellen's voice trailed off. After a long silence, she looked up at the other woman, her mask utterly gone. "They held her captive for the rest of her life, Juliana. For nigh on forty years . . ."

WITH Ellen's knights and crew locked up in the hold, Thomas manned the cog with his own sailors and headed back for the Isles of Scilly. When they dropped anchor in a sheltered cove at St Mary's Island, he'd planned to sail at dawn. But fog crept in during the darkness, ghostly grey sea-clouds that muffled sound and blotted out the sky, trapping them in a blind man's world of eerie, shadowed silence. The pirates did not share Brian's faith in his magnetic sailing needle, would not venture from port until the fog lifted, and the days dragged by. Ellen had never been claustrophobic—until now. The cabin walls seemed to be shrinking; at night she began to dream of sunless dungeon cells and open coffins. By the time they finally set sail, she was desperate to get under way again, even though Edward would be waiting at the end of her journey.

No one would tell her anything, but by observing sunsets from the porthole, she was able to determine that they were sailing north. There was no surprise, then, when the cog and its escort galleys turned east into the Bristol Channel, for she'd already guessed their destination, the English port of Bristol.

Ellen awakened at dawn. Beside her, Juliana still slept, and she rose as quietly as she could, making a half-hearted attempt to smooth some of the wrinkles from her gown. She'd always had her share of vanity, but it had not survived the first hours of her captivity. If she looked disheveled and haggard upon landing, so much the better. She wanted the world to see her just as she was, a woman abducted and imprisoned against her will by England's King.

Amaury was beginning to stir, and she crossed to the bed. "How do you feel this morn?"

"Well, I'm breathing," he said and gave her a lopsided smile, for his face was still badly bruised and swollen. "But I'd like to meet the fool who put about the fable that sea air is good for a man's health."

Ellen tried to smile back, although without much conviction. She knew he was still in pain. She had learned in this past week to recognize the subtle indications, for he would no more admit to his blinding headaches and aching jaw than he would to his fear. He had to be afraid; she herself was terrified for him and what he might face. But he'd chosen to confront that fate as his brothers would, and as much as she yearned for truth between them, she felt compelled to honor his choice. He was going to need whatever strength he could muster, from whatever source.

"How is your headache? I think there is some sage left . . ." She was turning to look when he reached up, caught her hand.

"Wait. I have something for you, kitten." Pulling a ring from his finger, he pressed it into her palm. "I want you to hold this for me."

The ring, a sapphire set into the shape of a cross, was far more than a family heirloom. For the de Montforts, it was an icon. Ellen closed her eyes, seeing it flash on her father's hand, seeing her mother clutch it to her heart as if it were a rosary. "I cannot take Papa's ring. Mama wanted you to have it, Amaury."

"And how long do you think I'd keep it?" he asked, quite evenly. "It will be safer with you."

She did not know what to say, for to deny it was to lie, and to agree was to abandon even the pretense of hope. Threading the ring through her crucifix chain, she concealed it in the bodice of her gown.

Just then a cresting wave slammed into the ship, and Ellen was sent careening across the cabin. She was clinging to the porthole as the cog righted itself, revealing the distant silhouette of snow-dusted hills. As she watched, they came into clearer focus, browned and stark, sloping down toward the sea, and she suddenly realized that she was looking upon Wales. It was her first glimpse of her husband's homeland, and it seemed likely it would be her last.

ELLEN had assumed that once they were no longer in the pirate chieftain's power, things were bound to get better. They did not. The constable of Bristol Castle, Sir Bartholomew de Joevene, treated her with impeccable courtesy, installed her and Juliana in a spacious bedchamber, even restored to her the personal belongings that had been seized on the ship. But she had been separated from Amaury soon after their arrival, and the constable politely refused to allow her to see him. He also rebuffed all her attempts to learn what Edward intended, and as the days passed, Ellen discovered that anxiety and isolation were as incendiary a combination as flint and tinder.

She'd not realized how much strength she'd drawn from Amaury's presence. While on the *Holy Cross*, at least they'd been facing danger together, and there had been comfort in that. Now, not knowing what was happening to him or how he was being treated, she was finding it harder and harder to keep her fears in check. Her imagination seemed set upon sabotaging her self-control, conjuring up lurid images of royal dungeons, of prisoners left to rot in bitter-cold blackness. She'd been at her bedchamber window when her household knights were herded into the bailey, and she'd been disturbed to see them all in fetters and gyves, even the Franciscan friars. Was Amaury, too, shackled in chains? And she began to be haunted by a harrowing daylight dream, seeing her brother lying alone in darkness, listening to the rustling as rats crept closer in the straw.

Ellen was worried, as well, about Hugh, for he had not been among the prisoners taken into custody by the Bristol constable. Where was he? Had he somehow managed to escape? Or had he died down in the cog's dank, fetid hold? Like so many of her questions, these, too, went unanswered.

By the time her first week's captivity finally drew to an end, Ellen had begun to fear that nothing was going to change, that her world was to be bounded forevermore by the stone walls of Bristol Castle, peopled only by regrets, solitude, and the sorrowful ghost of Eleanor of Brittany. But on January 29th, the ninth day of her confinement, a young knight was ushered into her chamber, diffidently identified himself as Sir Nicholas de Seyton, and after some hemming and hawing, revealed that he was here to deliver her into the custody of Sir Geoffrey de Pychford, constable of Windsor Castle.

De Seyton was so obviously embarrassed by his mission that Ellen took heart. Summoning up her most engaging smile, she assured him that she and Juliana would be ready to leave within the hour, "after I say farewell to my brother."

He looked, if possible, even more discomfited. "My lady, I am truly sorry. I would that—"

But Ellen had at last reached her breaking point. "I am not going to Windsor Castle until I see Amaury! You'll have to drag me kicking and screaming out to the bailey, gag me and tie me to my horse, and even then—"

"My lady, I would never do that! You do not understand. If it were up to me, I'd right gladly let you see your brother. But it is too late. He is gone."

"Gone? Where?"

De Seyton gave her a look of such unmistakable pity that Ellen's breath stopped. "According to the constable, Lord Amaury's escort left at first light . . . for Corfe Castle."

THEY passed the first night of their journey at a hospice in the village of Chippenham. But the next day winter took a nasty turn, and by the time they reached the royal castle at Marlborough, they were half-frozen, rain-soaked and mud-splattered. Saturday dawned just as raw and wet, and Juliana was grateful when Sir Nicholas de Seyton announced that they would be remaining at Marlborough until the weather cleared. It was not often, she'd confided to Ellen, that prisoners were blessed with such a gentle gaoler. Ellen had turned away wordlessly, and Juliana could have bitten her tongue in two, for she knew what Ellen was seeing—Amaury riding in shackles down a mud-mired West Country road.

February arrived in a frigid downpour. They'd been given one of the most comfortable tower chambers, boasting a wall fireplace and glazed windows. But not even a flaming hearth-log could dispel the chill. Jerking a blanket from the bed, Juliana came over and draped it about Ellen's shoulders.

"Ellen, we need to talk. When we were on that wretched cog, I was so greensick that I could be of no help at all. But now that I'm myself again, I can shoulder some of the burden, if you'll let me. At the least, I can listen. You've uttered nigh on a dozen words in the past three days, and I think I know why. It is Corfe Castle, is it not?"

Ellen glanced up sharply, and Juliana said apologetically, "I asked Sir Nicholas last night and he told me of its ugly history. He said it has long been a royal prison, that it is—"

"Infamous. The Crown sends to Corfe those prisoners they want to disappear, to be forgotten by the rest of the world."

"But well-guarded prisoners can be well-treated, too, Ellen. Remember what you told me about Prince Llewelyn's father? He was sent to the Tower! But you said he was kept in a large, comfortable chamber, even allowed visits from his wife. Why should you fear the worst for Amaury? He is Edward's cousin, after all."

"My father was Edward's uncle and godfather. That availed him naught at Evesham." Ellen jumped up, began to pace. "If only I'd insisted that Amaury remain in France! If not for me, he'd be—"

"Ellen, do not do this to yourself! I never met your lord father or Harry, but I loved Bran, and I know Amaury, and I've met Guy. The de Montfort men have always done just as they damned well pleased, and the Devil take the hindmost. How could you have stopped Amaury? Tied him to his bed whilst he slept? This is not your fault. Put the blame where it rightly belongs, squarely upon the head of your cousin the King!"

"I do," Ellen said, very low, "I do," and after that, there was not much more to be said.

Juliana wandered over to the window. It was set in glass, which, if no longer such a rarity, was still exorbitantly expensive, the best being imported from Normandy and Venice at great cost. But from what Juliana had heard of King Edward's father, he'd never been one to stint himself, not where his comfort was concerned. Although the glass was supposed to be white, it had an unmistakable green tinge, and it was so uneven, thick in places, thinner in others, that even on a sunlit day, it was like peering into a pond, viewing distorted images through a wavering wall of water. But a flash of color had drawn Juliana's eye and she rubbed her fist against the clouded pane until a clear spot appeared. "Just as I thought, riders in the bailey!"

She was pleased when Ellen came over to look, for this was the first flicker of curiosity to pierce Ellen's apathy in more than three days. "They look half-drowned, poor souls. How glad I am that we've passed the day at the hearth and not out on the road or in those fearful woods . . . what are they called again?"

"Savernake. A royal forest, if my memory—" Ellen broke off, leaned forward, and scrubbed furiously at the window moisture with the palm of her hand. "Dear God!"

She spun away from the window with such haste that she stumbled, had to grab the back of a chair for support. "It was not the rain that kept us here. We've been waiting for him!"

"Him?" Juliana looked again at the figures below, muffled and hooded and anonymous in muddied travel mantles. But as she strained to see, a gust of wind caught the sodden banner and it unfurled like a sail, revealing three golden lions on a field of crimson, the royal arms of the English Crown.

"I cannot face him, Juliana—not yet. I thought I'd have more time, I thought . . . What am I going to do?"

"Ellen, why are you so distraught of a sudden? You must not give way like this. Just remember how you dared to defy Thomas the Archdeacon. Surely you do not fear Edward more than that accursed pirate?"

"It is not Edward I fear, it is myself, my weakness."

"I do not understand."

"In this past week, you've sought to cheer me, to offer hope, even though I knew there was none. I've said nothing as you dwelled at length upon Llewelyn's anger, the indignation of His Holiness the Pope . . . as if they could set us free by the righteous fervor of their wrath."

"But surely—"

"No, Juliana, hear me out. Of course Llewelyn will be outraged. And the Pope will, indeed, protest, just as you say, for the Church tends to its own. But neither Llewelyn nor the Pope can prevail against Edward. God knows the Welsh do not lack for courage, but there are fully twenty Englishmen for every Welshman drawing breath. How could Llewelyn rescue me? He could only destroy himself in the attempt. As for the Church, if it comes to weighing a papal chaplain against a crusader-King, can you truly doubt how their scales will tip? And that would hold no less true for the French King; Edward is his cousin, a brother sovereign. You may be sure he'll not fight a war to right our wrong."

"Ellen, you must not despair like this, must not surrender all hope!"

"I cannot delude myself either, Juliana, not with so much at stake. Do you not see now why I am so frightened? Amaury and I are utterly at Edward's mercy, and I am not at all sure that he has any. We have just one chance, if I can somehow win him over, convince him that we pose no threat. But I am not ready for that, not yet. He is no fool. How can I make him believe . . ."

Too dispirited to continue, Ellen sank down in the chair, and Juliana dropped onto her knees beside her, caught Ellen's hand in her own. "Listen to me. You've never yet met a man you could not beguile. I know it will not be easy. But was it easy on the *Holy Cross?* You made yourself smile at that pirate, whilst wanting to spit in his face. You did what had to be done. You always do. I have faith, Ellen, faith in you."

"Faith," Ellen echoed, so bitterly that on her lips, it sounded almost like an obscenity. "I would to God I—" She stiffened, and Juliana heard it, too, footsteps drawing near their door.

De Seyton looked like a man doing gallows duty against his will. "My lady, forgive me for intruding upon your privacy. But the King's Grace has arrived, and he wishes to see you. I would be honored to escort you, if that meets with your approval?"

Ellen got slowly to her feet. "I am ready," she said, and then, "Thank you, Sir Nicholas."

His smile was pleased, but quizzical, too. "For what, Lady Eleanor?"

Ellen let her fingers slide along her crucifix chain until she found her father's ring. "For making it sound," she said, "as if I had a choice."

THE King's chamber was large and well-lit, wainscotted in Norway pine, strewn with fragrant floor rushes. All it lacked was Edward. De Seyton escorted Ellen to a cushioned window-seat, prepared to wait with her for Edward's return. She was heartened by his obvious protectiveness. If only Edward shared de Seyton's chivalry. Yes, and if wishes were horses, beggars would ride. Her father had been one for quoting that; he'd always liked to sound much more unsentimental than he truly was. Mayhap he had been as unforgiving and fiery-tempered as the rest of the world thought, but not to her, never to her. Thinking about Papa now would not help, though. She had to think about Edward, only Edward. Was he deliberately keeping her waiting? If so, he'd reckoned wrong, for she welcomed the reprieve.

Let him stay away until Lent and she'd thank God fasting. The more time she had to steady her nerves, to settle upon a stratagem, the more grateful she'd be. Edward Plantagenet. Her cousin Ned. Harry had called him Longshanks, for he'd not always been the enemy. There'd been a time when he and Harry and Bran had been inseparable. Would it help or hurt to remind him of that? It was said he had wept over Harry's body. Just hours after allowing her father to be butchered, hacked into so many pieces there'd been little left to bury. Jesú, no, she must not think of that now. Why did everything begin and end with Evesham?

"My Lady de Montfort." The man had come in a side door, which he was now holding open. Ellen rose, shadowed by the faithful de Seyton. Following him down a dark passage, she discovered it led into another large chamber, no less luxurious than Edward's. Servants were moving about, unpacking open coffers. They all turned to stare as Ellen entered. Raising her chin, she crossed the chamber and curtsied to her cousin's Queen.

The last time they'd met, Ellen had been a lively ten-year-old, Eleanora a young wife of nineteen, shyly stubborn, desperately in love with her handsome husband. She'd always been kind to Ellen, who remembered her fondly in consequence. But as they looked at each other now, it was uncomfortably obvious that there lay between them far more than the passage of thirteen years. Eleanora's dark gaze was coolly appraising; Ellen sensed at once that she'd been measured and found wanting. She'd had no illusions about Eleanora's influence. No matter how much Edward cherished his wife—and by all accounts he did— her sway did not extend beyond the boundaries of the marriage bed.

Yet even if Eleanora did not possess the key to her prison, Ellen had hoped for sympathy, woman to woman. It was not to be, though. Even before a word was uttered, she saw that she had no friend in Edward's elegant Spanish Queen.

"Well, you've grown up, for certes," Eleanora said at last.

"Yes, Madame, I suppose I have," was all Ellen could think to say, for she was beginning to understand. There were wives who disliked on instinct alone any woman who happened to be young and pretty. But there'd be little consolation in knowing that Eleanora's hostility was not personal, not when she had Edward's ear at night.

No sooner had Ellen drawn this dismal conclusion, though, than Eleanora seemed to thaw a bit. At the least, she remembered her manners, gesturing toward a chair. "You may sit whilst we wait for Eduardo."

Ellen sat as directed, and an awkward silence fell. Ellen would normally have felt obligated to keep the conversation going; she'd been taught that it was a woman's duty to smooth away rough edges, to put others at ease. Now, though, she rebelled, sat mutinous and still until Eleanora could stand the silence no longer, and began to talk grudgingly of that most innocuous and dependable of topics, the vile winter weather. Murmuring the appropriate replies, Ellen felt a perverse sense of pleasure. However petty her victory, it was a victory, nonetheless, the discovery that passive resistance could be a weapon in and of itself.

She had an instant or two of warning, alerted by the radiance of Eleanora's sudden smile, as if a candle had flared in the dark. Getting to her feet, she watched as her cousin strode into the chamber, and time seemed to fragment, all the way back to March of God's Year, 1265. Harry had brought Edward, a hostage for his father's good faith, to their castle at Odiham. A fortnight later, he'd ridden west with her father and brothers, but he'd soon contrived to escape, set out upon the road that was to lead them all to Evesham. Edward bore the intervening eleven years lightly, looked no different as England's King than he had as her father's prisoner of state, vibrant, lordly, a fire at full blaze. As he reached her, Ellen sank down in a deep curtsy. Almost at once, though, he caught her hand in his, drawing her to her feet.

"Glory be, lass, look at you!" The laugh, too, was just as she remembered, loud, cocky, dangerously disarming. "When I saw Aunt Nell at Melun, she said you'd blossomed, but I put it down to a mother's fond doting. What do you think, Eleanora? Has my little cousin not grown into quite a beauty?"

"Yes," Eleanora said, "she has," glazing the compliment in ice.

Edward was still holding Ellen's hand. "I am truly sorry you had to go through such an ordeal," he said, so sincerely that Ellen stared at him in amazement. What was her abduction—an act of God?

"I was terrified," she said simply, for it seemed safer to keep to the truth as much as possible.

His grip tightened. "I know, lass. I would to God there had been another way. But there was not, for Llewelyn ap Gruffydd and your brother Amaury saw to that."

"Ned, no! Amaury had nothing to do with it. This was my doing, not his. I wanted the marriage!"

In her agitation, she'd reverted without thinking to a childhood intimacy, to "Ned." But he seemed pleased rather than offended by the familiarity. "Of course you did," he said indulgently. "What lass would not be bedazzled by a crown? You could not be expected, though, to be aware of all the implications of such a union. I do not blame you, Cousin Ellen. There is a debt due, but you owe not a penny of it."

His well-intentioned attempt to reassure her fell far short of the mark, for he had just confirmed all her fears for Amaury. But he had given her the cue she needed. She knew now what role to play for him, and she could only wonder why she had not seen it sooner.

"I am sorry," she said softly, "that my marriage plans have stirred up so much trouble. It was never my intent to offend you, Cousin Ned. But it is already done. Llewelyn and I were wed in Paris by proxy last November."

She saw at once that Thomas the Archdeacon had already broken the news, for he showed no surprise. "Very foresighted of Llewelyn," he said caustically. "But sometimes a man can be too clever by half, as your husband is about to learn."

His smile was mockingly familiar, transporting Ellen back onto the *Holy Cross*, playing cat and mouse with her cousin's pirate. And she found that she could endure no more of it. No more suspense. No more cryptic threats. No more cruel games. "Your men would tell me nothing. I implore you to be more merciful. For God's sake, Ned, tell me the truth. If Windsor is to be my Bristol Castle, let me know and know now!"

"Bristol?" he echoed, genuinely puzzled. "You mean . . . Eleanor of Brittany? Jesus wept, is that what you feared, that I would imprison you for the rest of your days? Ah, Ellen, lass, no! You are my kinswoman and dear to me. Surely you must know that I never bore you or your mother any ill will. I argued against your mother's exile, did I not?"

That she knew to be true. He had spoken up on their behalf, had never understood that they could not forgive him.

Reaching out, Edward slid his fingers under her chin, tilted it up so that she had to meet his eyes. "I watched you grow up, teased you, brought you trinkets and sweets. And do you think I've forgotten your letters?"

He glanced then toward his wife. "When I was being held at Kenilworth Castle, Ellen wrote to me often, trying to cheer me with Harry's worst jests and daft rhymes, whatever foolishness she thought might take my mind off my troubles." Turning back to Ellen, he said quietly, compellingly, "I hated your father, I'll not deny it. But I loved Harry. Christ, we were companions from the cradle. I could never hurt his little sister."

But you could let his brother rot at Corfe Castle. Ellen swallowed with difficulty. "What do you mean to do with me, Ned?"

He smiled. "I mean," he said, "to restore you to your husband."

She did not believe him; she dared not. "When?"

"Well . . . that will be up to Llewelyn."

Beckoning a cup bearer into earshot, he ordered wine, waited until they'd all been served before continuing. "I will admit that I was set against this marriage. And I was wroth when I learned that you'd been wed in Paris. But once I thought about it, I began to see the advantages. Llewelyn has been a thorn in my side for some time. It has been eighteen months since I returned from the Holy Land, and he is still balking at doing homage to me. Such a brazen breach of a vassal's duty could not be tolerated, and a day of reckoning was coming. It was just a question of when—and how bloody. But now you've changed the equation, Ellen. Now I have something Llewelyn very much wants—you."

"I see," she said faintly, for she did, God help her, she saw all too well.

"Ah, lass, do not look so distressed. You'll have your happy ending, you'll see, for I'll hold no grudges. As soon as Llewelyn repents his past folly, formally recognizes me as his sovereign and liege lord, I'll hand you over to him with my blessings." Edward grinned suddenly. "Hellfire, sweetheart, I'll even give you a royal wedding, paid out of my own coffers!"

Ellen could not help herself. As much as it shamed her, she felt dizzy with the intensity of her relief, with the sudden resurgence of hope. He was offering her so much more than her freedom. He was offering to give her back her life with Llewelyn. But, Blessed Lady, at what cost?

Making an enormous effort, she smiled at them both, sought to look shy and submissive and grateful, while almost choking on the bile of her pent-up rage. But she would not make the mistakes her parents had. She would not give in to the compulsive Devil-be-damned candor that they'd so prided themselves upon, fuel for the fire that had eventually engulfed their world.

"Cousin Ned, what of Amaury?"

Edward's mouth hardened, almost imperceptibly, and she put a placating hand upon his arm. "I understand why you feel you must hold me as a hostage. But Amaury had naught to do with my marriage. He was simply acting as any brother would, seeing to my safety on a perilous journey. Ned, you would have done no less for your own sisters, I know you would! He's done nothing to deserve your hatred, bears no guilt for that killing at Viterbo. I swear it, Ned, swear—"

"Ellen, there is no need—"

"But he is innocent! If you would only talk to him, I know he could make you see that."

"We'll discuss this later," he said, giving her a smile that never reached his eyes, and her hand slid from his arm.

"Will you at least agree to that?" she pleaded, although she already knew the answer. "Will you talk to him?"

"We'll see, lass," he said. "We'll see."

JULIANA's nerves were shredded by the time Ellen was escorted back to their chamber. She managed to hold her tongue until de Seyton withdrew, but not a moment longer. "Sit here by the fire whilst I fetch some wine. You have no color in your face at all. Was it as bad as that? Were you able to hide your true feelings from him?"

"Yes."

"Ellen, you are frightening me, for you look so . . . My God, Ellen, what does he mean to do?"

"He means," Ellen said, "to set me free," and Juliana put the wine flagon down with a thud.

"I do not understand. Is it that . . . that you do not believe him, then?"

"Oh, I do believe him, Juliana. He intends, you see, to use me as bait, luring Llewelyn into a war he cannot hope to win. Is that not a marvelous marriage portion to bring to my husband?"

Juliana came hastily toward the hearth, thrust a dripping wine cup into Ellen's hand. "Mayhap it will not come to war. Mayhap they can settle their differences without bloodshed. Drink this, and move closer to the fire; you are trembling."

"I know. I feel so cold, Juliana, so very cold . . ."

"Ellen . . . did you talk to the King about Amaury?"

"Yes," Ellen said, her voice still sounding flat and far away. But her eyes had begun to brim with tears. "I pleaded with him. I begged, and Amaury would have hated that. He listened, my cousin the King. But he never heard me." Her tears had broken free, were streaking her face, but she made no attempt to wipe them away. When she finally spoke again, her voice was little more than a whisper.

"I do not think that he will ever let Amaury go."

14

BRISTOL, ENGLAND

January 1276

A<small>LTHOUGH</small> the crew of the cog *Holy Cross* had been dumped, penniless, on the Bristol docks, their plight was not as bleak as it might seem, for sailors the world over tended to their own. Many of the crewman had formed friendships on past voyages to this busy English port, and up and down the waterfront houses were opened to them. A few of the men took berths on out-going vessels, but so many ale-houses had extended credit that most of them elected to remain in Bristol until their cog could be ransomed.

Bristol was a thriving, brawling riverport, so prosperous that its citizens had been able to afford a remarkably ambitious and costly undertaking; they'd diverted the natural flow of the River Frome, dug a new channel to intersect with the River Avon. With so many seagoing ships anchoring at the new quays, ale-houses, inns, and brothels soon sprang up to accommodate them. To sailors like Brian, these river wharves and waterfront alleys were the heart and soul of Bristol, and most of them never even ventured as far as the marketplace, for their every need could be met within sight and sound and smell of the harbor.

At mid-morning on this last Wednesday in January, Brian was sitting down to an enormous dinner in his favorite riverside tavern, the Lusty Goat. His trencher was heaped with sausages and poached eggs and hot bread, for there were less than three weeks until Lent, and Brian was set upon indulging his appetite while he still could. Every now and then he tossed a scrap of sausage to the huge grey cat curled up at his feet. It would not deign to beg, but accepted his offerings as loftily as any lord, at the same time keeping a daunting eye upon the tavern keeper's shaggy mongrel dog.

"Brian!" A hand slammed into his shoulder in so boisterous a greeting that Brian nearly choked on a mouthful of sausage. But the face grinning down at him was a familiar one, and he swallowed his irritation with the sausage.

"Where did you come from, Abel? I heard you were in Spain!"

"I was. We dropped off a boatload of seasick pilgrims at Santiago de Compostela, then caught a fair wind for home. I got back yesterday, had heard the whole story by duskfall. Thomas the Archdeacon is a Bristol lad, so it's no surprise his latest outrage made such grist for our gossip mills. Hellfire, I'd not even kissed my own wife ere she was telling me about the *Holy Cross*!" Pulling a bench toward the table, he stopped at sight of the grey cat. "You even ransomed Hotspur?"

"Why not? He's the best mouser we've ever had!" Brian flipped a crust of bread into the floor rushes, laughing at the cat's disdainful disappointment. "In truth, Abel, there was no ransom at all for the crew. Your local lad, the Archdeacon, did not need to bother collecting crumbs, not when he'd come away with the whole blessed bake-house. Rumor has it that he'll get two hundred marks for de Montfort's daughter!"

Abel whistled soundlessly, and Brian nodded. "I suspect it is true, too, for I've seen him swaggering about the wharves with a whore on each arm, as bold as you please, looking like a man who could buy and sell sheriffs by the baker's dozen. And most likely he could, for in addition to his royal reward, he has the cargo we were going to unload in Ireland. Not to mention the ransom for the cog itself. The ship's master sailed last week for Rouen, bearing the bad tidings for the owner. He'll curse and fume and fret, but he'll come up with the money; what choice has he? I'd wager we'll be under sail again by Easter, and in the meantime, there are worse places to be stranded than Bristol."

"God's Bones, yes! Remember Tenby?" They both laughed, and Abel helped himself to one of the sausages. "Well, you'd best come home with me. We'll fix you a bed near the hearth, and my Agneta's cooking will taste like Heaven's own fare after all this ale-house slop!"

"I'd like that, Abel. But . . . well, there's a lad I've taken under my wing."

"Bring him along, then," Abel said expansively. "If you vouch for him, that is good enough for me."

"It is not that simple." Brian hesitated, then leaned across the table, lowering his voice. "This can go no further. Not even Agneta can know, for if word gets out, Hugh is likely to end up clapped in irons. The truth is, Abel, that Hugh is one of the Lady Eleanor's knights. But he is a good lad for all that, and so . . . when those whoreson pirates came down into the hold to get the knights and the Welsh, I heard myself claiming that Hugh was a member of our crew."

Abel grinned. "You've not changed a whit. As hard-baked on the outside as a rye tort, inside as soft as raw dough! So be it; we'll tell Agneta he's the *Holy Cross* boatswain. Now . . . where is this young lordling of yours?"

He was peering about at the men sitting in the shadows, and Brian shook his head. "He is not here. Likely as not, he's lurking outside the castle, for that is where he's been for the past week, keeping a hopeless vigil for his lady." Brian sighed, speared a sausage with his knife. "I tried to tell him he's but wasting his time, for all the good it did me. He even began to frequent one of the Wine Street taverns because he'd heard the castle grooms drink there. He had this idea, you see, that the stablemen would be the first to know if they meant to move the lady from the castle."

Brian paused to eat another sausage. "It sounded like a weak reed to me, but damned if he did not find a groom who pitied the Lady Eleanor's plight!"

"You Bretons think history begins and ends on your side of the Channel. As often as you've been in port here, you did not know that Bristol held fast for Simon de Montfort?"

Brian shook his head, and Abel snorted good-naturedly. "Hellfire, Brian, we took his reforms so to heart that we even rioted on his behalf, drove no less a lord than Edward himself to seek shelter within the castle! And when Edward burned the bridges across the Severn, trapping Earl Simon in Wales, we sent a fleet of flatboats to ferry his army across the Bristol Channel. But we were ambushed by Edward's galleys ere we could enter Newport harbor. Eleven ships we lost that day, and after Evesham, Edward bled us white, levied a thousand marks' fine upon our citizens. Memories like that do not fade, Brian, not in ten years' time. You were surprised Hugh found a friendly groom? I'd have been surprised if he had not. Half the men in this town would gladly turn a blind eye to help the Earl's lass."

"I'll confess, your English affairs always seem so murky to me that I never even try to make sense of— Ah, Hugh, there you are!"

From the outset, Brian had been impressed by Hugh's good manners, for experience had taught him that the wellborn rarely squandered courtesy upon people like him. Hugh had been different, though, and it was that difference that had prompted him to speak out on Hugh's behalf in that dark, foul-smelling hold. When Hugh now acknowledged the introductions with a distracted nod, Abel put it down to the usual high-handed rudeness of the gentry and began to regret offering his hospitality so readily. But Brian knew better.

"You can speak freely in front of Abel, lad. Tell us what is wrong. Has some evil befallen your lady?"

Hugh nodded, hesitated, then blurted out his bad news in one breathless wretched rush. "She is gone, Brian, they are both gone!"

"HUGH, you've not thought this through. Only a fool would try to cross those Welsh mountain passes in the dead of winter!"

"I did it once before—with Lord Bran—can do it again," Hugh said stubbornly, and Brian and Abel exchanged frustrated glances, for they'd been laboring in vain for nigh on an hour now to talk some sense into the lad. Catching that look, Hugh strove for patience. "I have to get to Wales, Brian. Prince Llewelyn is the only man who might be able to help my lady. He has to know!"

"I agree with you, just do not see why you must be the one to take such a risk. But if you're bound and determined to do this, we'd best start laying plans. Abel, know you any good-hearted samaritans willing to lend Hugh a horse?"

Abel looked as pained as if he'd been asked to produce an elephant. "Jesú, I do not know anyone who even owns a horse! I'm a sailor, Brian, have never so much as been astride one. There are two stables in town that rent mounts, but not for a winter trek into Wales. You'd have to buy the nag outright. How much does a horse cost, Hugh?"

"A decent one, good enough to get me into Wales and back . . . not likely less than ten marks," Hugh said reluctantly, knowing the sum would shock them. "And I'd need a saddle and bridle; also a sword. Supplies, too, for I doubt if there is an inn to be found in all of North Wales. So . . . somehow I have to come up with at least fifteen marks."

"Fifteen marks! You might as well ask for the keys to the King's Exchequer." Abel shook his head slowly. "Hugh, I'm sorry, I truly am, for I'd like to help you, and I'd like to help the Earl's daughter. But I do not know a soul who has that much money to spare."

"I know one," Hugh said grimly. "Thomas the Archdeacon."

"Do not talk crazy," Brian said hastily. "Your life is worth a lot more than fifteen marks, lad. Just give me a moment to think. . . . Do you not have Jews in Bristol, Abel? Mayhap Hugh could borrow from a money-lender?"

Hugh looked suddenly hopeful, as if a door had begun to open. Abel hated to slam it in his face, but he was loath to lie, too. "I cannot see it, Brian. Ever since the King forbade any more money-lending—"

"What?" Hugh and Brian were both staring at him, and Abel beamed; it was always gratifying to be the one to reveal events sure to startle. "You have not heard, then? Last November, the King issued an edict that Jews would no longer be permitted to charge interest on loans, usury being a mortal sin. Not," he added with a grin, "that such sinning ever kept our kings from claiming a fair measure of the profits! The Jews have fallen, though, on lean times. They might once have been the Crown's best milch cow, but their milk has dwindled down to a trickle, and who keeps a beast that's gone dry? When the Council of Lyons condemned usury so strongly last year, the King was stirred to action. Since his decree denied the Jews their only means of making a livelihood, he also proclaimed that they'd be allowed for the first time to become merchants or craftsmen. But that dog would not hunt, for what Christian would deal with a Jew if he did not have to?"

Brian knew little of the plight of the Jews, cared less. "So what are you saying?" he demanded impatiently. "That they no longer lend money?"

"Some were scared off, for certes. But others fear starving more than the King's wrath, and being a sly lot, they've sought to hide the interest charged on their loans, making the sum more than it was or calling it a 'courtesy' or a 'special fee.' But they've become as wary and skittish as any virgin lass, require much wooing ere they'll let you into their coffers!"

It was Hugh's turn now to interrupt. "But they will still make loans?"

Abel stopped laughing and scowled. "You'll never know if you are not willing to hear me out. The King's edict is but part of the problem. You see, we had some trouble here in Bristol a few months past. I do not know what set it off, but ere it was over, many of the Jews' houses had been looted and the Jewry was in flames. Since then, the Jews have been even more tight-fisted than usual. They're not about to make you a loan, Hugh, for you have nothing to pledge as security."

"Hugh . . . would you ask that little serving maid to bring us some ale?" Hugh looked surprised, but he rose without objection, far too fond of Brian to balk. As soon as he was out of earshot, Brian leaned across the table again. "Abel, listen. I know Hugh, know how desperate he is right now . . . mayhap even desperate enough to steal a horse. And if he did, he'd be honorable enough to bring it back afterward, and get hanged for his pains. If we let him sit around and brood, he just might go off to confront that whoreson pirate. Let's seek out a money-lender, even if it comes to naught. Mayhap we'll have been able to think of another idea by then."

Abel shrugged. "Hugh, come on back! My cousin Wat works for a vintner who borrows from money-lenders. Mayhap he might know one not as grasping as most of that accursed breed are. I'd not give you false hope, but if you want to try, I'm willing, lad."

Hugh's sudden smile was blinding. "What are we waiting for, then?"

ABEL's cousin Wat had once accompanied his employer into the Jewry, and he claimed he could find the house of the money-lender, Isaac ben Asher. But he soon had them wandering about the Jewish quarter in ever widening circles, all the while insisting that their destination was just around the corner. Hugh, usually so tolerant of other men's foibles, found himself fighting an urge to shove Wat into the path of the next passing cart.

It was not just his fear for Ellen that had rubbed his nerves so raw. As they backtracked along the narrow, twisting streets, he felt like an intruder, felt conspicuous and ill at ease in such alien territory. He had never had any personal contacts with Jews, for they were permitted to dwell in only twenty-seven English towns, and Evesham had not been one of them. Nor had there been any Jews in Montargis, for Jews throughout Christendom were barred from holding land and were, therefore, segregated by economic necessity in the cities. But if he'd never known any Jews, Hugh did know what was said of them. Servants of Satan. Disciples of the Devil. Infidels who dwelt in their very midst, crafty and false, enemies of the True Faith. Hugh frowned, and instinctively he groped for his crucifix chain, forgetting that his neck was bare; the pirates had taken everything of value.

They finally found the money-lender's house at the end of Small Street. It was an impressive stone structure with slate roof and walled courtyard, and Wat and Abel exchanged quips about the wages of sin, but their humor had a hard edge to it. They were admitted by a young maidservant, using the name of Master Bevis, the vintner, as their password, and were asked to wait in a hall of surpassing comfort.

Abel and Wat and Brian gaped at the spacious dimensions of the chamber, while conjuring up inevitable and embittered comparisons with their own cramped, sparse quarters. A decorated wooden screen closed off the door to the kitchen; a spiral stairway led up to additional chambers above. They wandered about the hall, examining the sturdy oaken tables, the cushioned chairs, the pewter plates stacked in a cup-board, and they thought of their own smoky hearths, the stale bread that served as mealtime trenchers, their backless stools. They counted the flaming wax candles that ringed this room in light, thinking of the reeking tallow candles that they hoarded till dark. And they felt the stirrings of a deep and resentful rage, that good Christians should have so little whilst this infidel unbeliever should have so much.

Hugh, too, was looking about with unabashed curiosity, but his was a soldier's eye. He noted the heavy wooden shutters, the iron door bolt. He studied the thickness of the stone walls, admiring how cleverly a door had been cut to fit into the stairway alcove, effectively sealing off the upper chambers. And he remembered what Abel had said about trouble, about the Jewry in flames.

Wat picked up a book, looked blankly at the Hebrew script, and set it down with a thud, as if he'd touched something unclean. "How long does he mean to make us wait?"

"We're being watched," Brian warned suddenly, making them all jump. They turned to stare suspiciously at the screen. It was a distinct letdown when a small boy toddled out.

"Look at him," Wat marveled, "hair like flax! I'd wager his mother found a bit of English seasoning to flavor her stew!"

"All Jews do not have dusky skin like Saracens," Hugh said curtly; he was fast losing patience with Abel's loud-mouthed cousin.

The unexpected testiness of his tone earned him speculative looks from Abel and Brian. "Hugh is right," Brian said mildly. "It is because the Jews do look like us that your King Edward ordered them to wear those yellow badges. Otherwise, they could pretend to be Christians, could take unfair advantage of our unwariness."

"I know one way they differ from us," Abel said mysteriously. "I've heard it said that when a male child is born, the Jews notch his cock, like we'd brand a horse, a secret way to know their own."

"Christ!" The exclamation was Wat's, but Brian looked no less hor-rified. Hugh, however, was grinning widely.

"You've got it half-right, Abel. They do not brand the babe, but they do cut off his foreskin. Lord Amaury says the Saracens do it, too. There is even a word for it, circum—something."

"Well, whatever you call it, the very thought of putting a knife to my privates makes my ballocks shrivel up like raisins," Brian declared with such heartfelt honesty that they all laughed, although only Hugh found any real humor in the subject.

"I wonder what it looks like," Wat mused, staring so intently at the child that Hugh found himself tensing, in case the man was stupid enough to try to satisfy his curiosity then and there. The little boy was just starting to walk; he wobbled toward a chair, caught a rung for support, and regarded them so solemnly that Hugh suddenly wanted to see him smile.

"Look, lad," he said, reaching for a bowl of nuts. "Shall I show you a trick I learned from a French jongleur? Watch carefully now." Deftly juggling a walnut back and forth, he added a second one to the arc, and the boy's eyes widened. After a few moments, Hugh had a third walnut airborne, too, but when he tried to introduce a fourth one, walnuts were suddenly raining everywhere. The child squealed with laughter as Hugh, laughing, too, knelt to retrieve them from the floor rushes. "You're not supposed to laugh when I fail," he chided, and pretended to find one in the tot's ear. The boy giggled again, but from the corner of his eye, Hugh caught a blurred movement. Turning his head, he saw Isaac ben Asher standing in the stairwell, watching impassively as he crawled about on hands and knees.

Hugh could feel his face getting hot. Scrambling hastily to his feet, he sought to recover his dignity as Isaac picked up the child, carried him behind the screen. He'd regained some of his poise by the time the man returned, but he could not hide his surprise, for Isaac ben Asher was not at all what he'd expected. He was young, not much past thirty; Hugh had assumed money-lending to be an old man's profession. His coloring was fair, and he seemed vaguely familiar. After a moment to reflect, Hugh realized why. As unlikely as it sounded, this Bristol Jew reminded him somehow of Amaury de Montfort. Isaac had Amaury's unaffected elegance, his air of quiet, watchful wariness. His eyes were blue, not greenish hazel like Amaury's, but they were startlingly similar, nonetheless, eyes that gave away no secrets, shuttered windows to a soul under siege.

"I am Isaac ben Asher. You wish to talk to me?"

Hugh nodded. "I am Sir Hugh de Whitton," he said, ignoring his companions' gasps of dismay. They had concocted an elaborate cover story to protect Hugh's identity, but he found now that he could not use it; it seemed dishonorable to lie to a man while asking that man for money.

It was not easy to reveal his need so nakedly; Isaac's cool, guarded gaze did not invite confidences. But Hugh forced himself to continue, and slowly the story emerged. "And now," he concluded bleakly, "the Lady Ellen has been taken to Windsor Castle. I must get to her husband, I must! You're my only hope."

"And how much hope do you want to borrow?"

"Fifteen marks," Hugh mumbled, as if garbling the sum would somehow make it sound less exorbitant. "I know it is a lot, but Prince

Llewelyn would never begrudge me the money. You'll be paid back, I promise!"

"Assuming you come back," Isaac said, and angry color flooded Hugh's face.

"When I give my word, I keep it!"

"I am not suggesting you would gainsay your promise," Isaac said calmly. "I was thinking of the dangers you'd be facing. Have you not thought that you might die on this quest of yours?"

In truth, Hugh had not. He opened his mouth to reassure Isaac, but the words caught in his throat. Why should this man risk so much upon the good intentions of a stranger? "I can indeed promise you that I'd hold to my word. But I cannot promise that no evil would befall me on the journey. I thank you for your time—"

"Will tonight be soon enough?"

Hugh blinked. "What?"

"If you return at dusk, I shall have the documents drawn up, the money waiting for you."

There was a moment of stunned silence. Hugh's companions were even more astonished than he was, for they'd harbored no hope at all. "You mean it?" Hugh gasped, and the corner of Isaac's mouth hinted at a smile.

But then Wat said aggressively, even angrily: "Ere this devil's deal is struck, Hugh, you'd best ask him how much interest he means to bleed from you. Master Bevis tells me he has paid as much as forty percent of the debt due!"

"And has your Master Bevis told you about all the times your King has seen fit to cancel Christian debts outright?" Isaac's voice revealed no overt anger, but his eyes had narrowed, belying his apparent sangfroid. "Did he happen to mention those occasions when Christian borrowers decide to discharge their debts by burning all records of them— and the Jewry, too?"

Wat had begun to sputter, but before he could give voice to his outrage, Hugh was at his side, his fingers clamping down like talons on Wat's arm. "The Evesham monks taught me," he said softly, "that it is the height of bad manners to insult a man in his own house."

Abel was looking resentful, too, and for a suspenseful moment, Hugh's hopes seemed to hang precariously in the balance. But then Brian took charge, ushering his friends hastily toward the door. "Hugh will be back by dusk," he flung over his shoulder, muttering when Hugh still hesitated, "Let's get out of here ere he changes his mind!"

At sound of the closing door, the maidservant emerged from behind the screen, leading Isaac's son by the hand. "May he play out here now?"

"Come to me, Elias," Isaac said, and the little boy tottered toward him. He was lifting Elias up onto a high-backed chair when he heard footsteps. Whirling, he saw Hugh standing just a few feet away.

"I came back," Hugh said, for when he was nervous, he tended to belabor the obvious. "I wanted to thank you. You have no idea how much it means to me, that you agreed to give me the money."

"I think I do," Isaac said dryly, "for you left without even asking what the interest would be."

Hugh's smile was sheepish. "I'm not good at business matters," he confessed. "I'd never borrowed money before. In fact, I . . . I'd never met a Jew before. You are not what I expected, not at all."

'No cloven hoof, you mean?"

Hugh flushed, but managed a game smile. "May I ask something? Why did you do it? Why did you agree to make the loan?"

"Does it truly matter?" Isaac parried, sounding cautious, but curious, too. "Let me put a question to you, instead. Why did you tell me your true identity? Did you not fear that I might betray you?"

Hugh shrugged. "It just did not seem right to lie, not when I was seeking a favor."

Isaac was silent for so long that Hugh decided the conversation was at an end. He was about to retreat when Isaac said abruptly, unexpectedly, "You must have been very young when you entered Lady Eleanor's service, for loyalty like yours takes years to forge. I assume then, that you've been dwelling in France?"

When Hugh gave a puzzled nod, Isaac hesitated, and there was another long pause. "It has never been easy to be a Jew in England," he said at last, speaking fast and very low. "But life is harder now than ever before, for King Edward despises us so. His father brought untold grief upon us by his attempts to convert us to your faith. He set up conversion houses throughout England, was truly disappointed when his nets caught so few fish. But Edward cares naught for our souls, cares only for the money he can wrest from us. And when a lemon is wrung dry, you throw it away . . . no?"

"I suppose so," Hugh said uncertainly.

"You are wondering what lemons have to do with this. But in the past year, the King's mother has banished all Jews from her dower towns, from Marlborough, Gloucester, Worcester, and Cambridge. The Gloucester Jews took refuge here in Bristol, so I saw for myself what misery the old Queen caused."

"You truly think King Edward might do that? Expel all the Jews from England?" Hugh's astonishment was genuine; he'd never even considered the possibility before. "But . . . but where would you all go?" he asked, and now it was Isaac who shrugged.

An awkward silence fell. Isaac was standing behind his son's chair and he reached down, ruffled Elias's bright hair, but it was obvious his thoughts were elsewhere; his was the taut, disquieted distraction of a man startled by his own candor. But then Hugh smiled.

"I think I understand. My lady tells me the Welsh have a saying, 'The enemy of my enemy is my friend.' "

"And was I right, Sir Hugh? Is Edward your enemy, too?" Isaac asked quietly, and saw Hugh's guileless blue eyes take on a sudden, hard sheen.

"With my lady on her way to a Windsor prison, need you even ask?"

They looked at each other, experiencing an odd sense of empathy, strong enough to take them both by surprise.

"Shall I tell you the second reason why I decided to lend you that money?"

"Because you were bedazzled by my juggling?" Hugh suggested with a grin.

"No . . . because my son was." And in those last fleeting moments before the barriers went back up, they exchanged smiles, as the child looked on, innocent, uncomprehending.

THE sky had been clear when Caitlin rode away from Cricieth Castle, but by noon, it was mottled with small, circular clouds. From time to time, she gazed upward uneasily, for those speckled wisps of white reminded her of the patterned splotches on a mackerel's back, and she was familiar with the folklore, "Mackerel sky, rain is nigh." Well, she'd have to risk it, for she did not know when she'd get another chance to seek out the soothsayer.

If the woman had a name, Caitlin had never heard it. People just called her the hag, for she was as ancient and gnarled as Llŷn's oldest oak trees. Sometimes they called her the witch. Caitlin was frightened of facing her alone, but she was determined to go through with it, for her uncle's sake. If it was true that the old woman could foretell the future, mayhap she could reveal what had happened to Uncle Llewelyn's English bride.

Men said the witch lived in a hut on the eastern slope of Y Garn, a stone's throw from the church at Dolbenmaen. Caitlin reckoned she could get there and back by dusk, for the trail was well marked, the snow packed down and solid. Glancing again at that dappled sky, she wondered if the hag could read minds, too. What if the witch could ferret out her own secret? If she could tell how much she'd dreaded the coming of the English bride?

Caitlin bit her lip, for it shamed her to think of another person knowing of her jealousy. It was not that she'd ever believed the taunting of her spiteful cousins; she'd never liked Tegwared's sons. Even if a new broom did sweep clean, even if the Lady de Montfort did not want Davydd's bastard waif, she knew her uncle would not abandon her, would not send her away to please a new wife. But life would never be the same. Sometimes it seemed to Caitlin as if she could already feel the new wife's disdain, see those elegant English eyebrows raising in the way ladies showed displeasure. And she'd begun to hope, even to pray, that her uncle's marriage to Eleanor de Montfort would never come to pass.

She'd often heard people joke that a man should watch what he prayed for, lest he get it. Like most adult humor, its point had escaped her—until now. Until the days dragged into weeks, January yielded to February, and her uncle's gaze strayed again and again to the grey winter seas, searching the horizon for a distant sail.

Caitlin looked skyward, but not this time to track clouds. "I did not mean it," she cried. "I did not want any harm to befall her. I just wanted her to stay in France!" She'd turned inland now, no longer heard the rumble of the surf or the screeching of gulls, heard only the echoes of her own words, long after the wind had carried them away.

So caught up was she in her own thoughts that she did not see the sudden dip in the trail until they were upon it. With another mount, it might not have mattered, but Caitlin's mare had an idiosyncrasy peculiarly its own; every time it came to the crest of a hill, even a slight incline, the horse felt compelled to run down it. Now, as the ground suddenly sloped away, it bolted, and Caitlin, caught off balance, went sailing right over the filly's head.

A snowdrift cushioned her fall, but by the time she'd gotten to her feet, the mare was vanishing into the distance. There was nothing for Caitlin to do except brush the snow from her mantle, while calling the mare all those names she'd heard her uncle call the English King.

There was no hope of catching the animal; she saw that at once. As furious with herself now as with her runaway filly, she turned, began the long, tiring trek back toward Cricieth. The horse might well find its way home on its own. But if the mare turned up, riderless, someone would surely recognize it, hasten to tell Llewelyn that his niece had suffered a mishap. She'd meant to ease his mind, not add to his troubles. Yet now it was likely all of Cricieth would be turned topsy-turvy, because of her. And once she was found, what in Heaven's Name could she tell them? Uncle Llewelyn would want to know why she'd been out on the road by herself. She could not lie, not to him. But how could she tell him about the soothsayer?

It seemed to her that the sky had darkened, and as she trudged along the winding trail, she thought she could hear the distant howling of wolves. People feared wolves more than any other predator, but her uncle had assured her that wolves were actually wary, cautious creatures, unlikely to attack men. If Llewelyn said it was so, that was enough for Caitlin; her faith was absolute. But she would rather not meet a wolf afoot and alone, would rather not put its character to such a tempting test, and she quickened her pace. When she stopped again to listen, the wind brought to her a far more familiar and reassuring sound, the jangle of a harness, the rhythmic thud of hooves upon hard, snow-encrusted ground.

Caitlin's spirits soared. But the horse now coming into view through the trees was not her fugitive mare, was a big-boned rangy bay. The gelding's rider looked as startled as Caitlin. His reflexes were good, though; he reined in beside her in a spray of snow.

While Caitlin would have preferred to find her mare, to keep her mishap between herself and the filly and the Almighty, she was grateful, nonetheless, for this stranger's providential appearance; Cricieth would have been a long walk. "How glad I am that you happened by! My mare threw me; you did not see her, did you? Can you give me a ride as far as Cricieth Castle?"

Puzzled by his silence, she moved closer, found herself looking up into eyes of a deep and uncomprehending blue. At the same time, she noted his beard, the blond hair shadowed by the wide-brimmed hat. "Blessed Lady, an Englishman!"

Hugh had yet to understand a word she'd said. "I speak no Welsh," he said apologetically, and Caitlin gave a vast sigh of relief.

"French, thank Heaven! Some of your countrymen speak only English, or so I've been told. Does it not get confusing for you sometimes, like the Tower of Babel in Scriptures?"

She stopped in surprise, for Hugh had begun to laugh. "If you are real, lad, and not conjured up by my lack of sleep, tell me what a Welsh imp speaking perfect French is doing all alone out here in this wilderness?"

"My uncle made me learn French because it is the court lan— A lad? I am a girl!" Caitlin exclaimed indignantly, and jerked back her mantle hood to reveal a long shining braid.

"Lord forgive me, so you are!" Hugh's demeanor changed dramatically, from friendly to protective in the blink of an eye. "It is dangerous for a lass to be wandering about on your own like this. I'd best see you home straightaway, no arguments now!"

"Who is arguing? No, there is no need to dismount; just give me your hand," Caitlin directed, and to Hugh's amusement, she scrambled up behind him, as nimbly as any boy. "Can you take me to Cricieth Castle?"

"If you tell me how to get there," Hugh said agreeably, and waited until her thin little arms were securely clasped about his waist before spurring his horse forward. "So . . . what is a little lass like you doing out here all by yourself?"

"I am not so little, will be twelve next month. Anyway, what is an Englishman doing all by himself so deep in Wales?"

Hugh grinned. "This uncle who taught you French must also have taught you military tactics. Whenever possible, carry the attack into the enemy's territory!"

Caitlin grinned, too. "I did not mean to pry, truly, but it is unusual to see an Englishman in this part of Gwynedd. Most of your countrymen keep to the south."

"I am on my way to Pwllheli, where I hope to find Prince Llewelyn."

Caitlin stiffened. "What makes you think he is there?"

Hugh hesitated from habit, before remembering that there was no longer reason for secrecy. "Because that is where he is awaiting his wife's arrival from France."

Caitlin's gasp was so audible that he turned in the saddle. "Prince Llewelyn is my uncle. Can you tell me, please, about the Lady Eleanor? We've been so worried. She is still coming?"

"No . . . no, lass, she is not."

LLEWELYN'S impressive self-control was acknowledged even by his enemies. But it had not come easily to him. He had learned wariness the hard way, only after years of youthful turmoil, scarred by irreconcilable family loyalties, by his unrelenting struggles with the English Crown, by his brother's betrayals. He had learned, too, to keep his own counsel. And so he did not confide his uneasiness, his growing fears for Ellen's safety.

For those who knew him well, though, there was no need for words. They watched him gazing out across Pwllheli's harbor, and they tried to help, each in his own way. His Seneschal, Tudur, sought to keep Llewelyn so busy, so preoccupied with statecraft and the affairs of Gwynedd that he'd have no time to worry. His cousin Tegwared tried to cheer him with jests and practical jokes, with surprise gifts and the songs of their best bards. And his uncle, Einion, confronted his fears head-on, brought them out into the open.

Llewelyn must remember that they did not know the Lady Ellen's exact departure date. Her last letter had expressed the hope that they'd be able to sail in mid-December, but it was just that, a "hope." It may be that bad weather or unexpected delays had kept the cog at Harfleur well into the new year. Even if they had sailed on time, storms could have forced her ship to seek shelter in any of a dozen coastal ports. If the wind was not with them, they'd make little headway in heavy seas. He himself could testify to that, having once endured a vile winter crossing from Ireland. Ill winds had driven them back into Drogheda's harbor so many times that he'd lost count, had become convinced he'd have to begin life anew as an Irishman.

Logically, Llewelyn knew that Einion was right, that his concern was premature. But instinct stronger than reason was communicating a message impossible to ignore, that something was very wrong. He spent so much time staring out at the harbor that he at last moved his household six miles up the coast to his castle at Cricieth. But he did not succeed in leaving his anxiety behind at Pwllheli. At Cricieth, too, he found himself gazing out to sea, and his dreams were troubled, as dark and murky as those surging, shoreward tides. For as he watched the waves splash over the rocks below the castle, he was slowly coming to the most appalling understanding of all, that he might never know what happened. If Ellen's ship had been lost at sea, there'd be no word of the disaster, only this endless, suffocating silence, a lifetime of silence.

And so when Hugh knelt and stammered out that Ellen had been taken by pirates off the coast of Cornwall, Llewelyn's reaction was one almost of relief. At least she was alive. As terrifying as her ordeal must have been, she was alive and could be rescued. Hugh's presence was proof of that, proof that she had been able to convince the pirates of her identity, not a woman to be raped and abused, one to be ransomed.

Hugh looked so distraught that he said reassuringly, "It will be all right, lad. We'll get her back, I promise. How much do they want for her release?"

Having to tell Nell and Ellen that Bran was dead was the most difficult task Hugh had ever faced—until now. "My lord . . . there is no ransom demand. It was not ill chance that put us in the pirates' path. They were waiting for your lady," he said, saw that Llewelyn was quick to comprehend.

"Christ Jesus . . . Edward?"

Hugh nodded miserably. "I do not know how he found out, my lord, for we took such care to keep the wedding secret. The man has unholy luck. How else explain it? If there had been fog that day, we would have gotten by them, or if the winds had shifted . . ." Hugh was talking too much, knew it, could not help himself.

Llewelyn was no longer listening. Moving to the window, he stared out at the churning sea, pressing his fist against the opaque glass pane, ordered for Ellen. He had never even met her, although she wore his ring, bore his name. But even before they'd taken those holy vows, there had been a bond between them, a connection he could not fully explain. Long after he'd disavowed their first plight troth, he'd found that he still cared about her safety, her welfare. A debt of honor, a memory made real—whatever the reason, when his need became urgent to take a wife, there was but one choice, one woman.

She was a stranger to him, but her presence in the room was almost tangible, for it had been furnished just for her. The walls had been wainscotted and then painted green and gold, in the English fashion. The bed was piled high with fur-lined coverlets, embroidered with the de Montfort arms. To please her, there were silver candelabras and February flowering Candlemas bells and delicate perfume vials. An ivory hairbrush and matching hand mirror had been laid out for her use. He had spared no expense to make her feel at home in an alien land, this young woman who'd gone from sheltered affluence to dishonored exile, from a Prince's betrothed to a dead rebel's daughter, all in the span of one bloodied sword thrust. He'd discovered that he wanted to give her back some of what she'd lost, and he'd begun here, at Cricieth.

This was to have been Ellen's bridal chamber. But she would never see it now. Her de Montfort blood and their marriage vows would condemn her to a lifetime's confinement in England. Edward would never let her go. Llewelyn had reached the table. Picking up the mirror, he turned it over; the back had been engraved with the letter *E*. When he flung it into the hearth, there was a splintering sound as the glass shattered, and Hugh flinched. With a sweep of his arm, Llewelyn sent the rest of the table's contents crashing into the floor rushes; a chair followed. Llewelyn's greyhound had begun to whimper softly, but all Hugh could hear was Llewelyn's ragged breathing. He was edging toward the door, stopped when Llewelyn looked toward him.

"Do you want me to go, my lord?"

Llewelyn shook his head, beckoned him back. It was very quiet after that; Llewelyn said nothing and Hugh was willing to wait until he did. Finally Llewelyn righted the over-turned chair, sat down, and gestured for Hugh to do the same.

There had been a flagon on the table; the floor rushes were soaking in mead. Hugh unfastened a travel flask from his belt, held it out with a shy smile. He was pleased when Llewelyn took it, drank, and passed it back.

Looking at the wreckage-strewn floor, Llewelyn said, very low, "It has been a long time since I lost control like that, more than twenty years. A woman very dear to me had miscarried of a baby, died of the resulting fever, and afterward, I tried to put my fist through a table. It did not help, and I damned near broke my hand, thought I'd learned a lesson . . ."

Hugh offered the flask again. "The woman . . . who was she, my lord?"

"My aunt. Passing strange, her name was also Elen, spelled in the Welsh way. She was Nell's kinswoman, too, her sister Joanna's daughter. Nell was there with me when Elen died. She was the one who bandaged my hand."

"At least the Lady Nell was spared this," Hugh ventured, so desperate was he to offer consolation of any kind, and Llewelyn's mouth twisted down.

"Yes, she died believing that I'd take care of her daughter," he said, so bitterly that Hugh's breath stopped. "What of Morgan? Is he dead?" He felt no surprise when Hugh nodded, and made a sign of the cross; he could do no more for his dead than he could for the living. "Tell me what happened," he said, and Hugh did, from their first glimpse of the pirate galley's crimson sail to the moment when he'd ridden away from Bristol on the horse purchased with Isaac ben Asher's money. Llewelyn listened in silence. Only once did he interrupt, when Hugh revealed that Ellen had been taken at first to Bristol Castle. "Bristol . . . I wonder if they gave her Eleanor of Brittany's old chamber."

Hugh had never heard of Eleanor of Brittany until he was stranded in Bristol. But since then, he'd been haunted by that unhappy lady's fate, and now he found himself pleading, as much for his own sake as for Llewelyn's, "You must not give up hope, my lord. We have to believe she'll be set free."

Llewelyn drank again. "How long have you been in my wife's service?"

"It will be five years come the summer."

"You must know her well then, Hugh. Tell me the truth. Do you think she is strong enough to survive this?"

"To look at her, you'd think not," Hugh said slowly. "When I was in Tuscany, I saw an ivory carving of the Madonna; that's what the Italians call our Blessed Lady. I tell you this, my lord, because your lady seems just like that Florentine church sculpture, delicate and finely made, breakable. But Brother Teilo told me that when the cog was seized, Lady Ellen held off one of the pirates with a knife."

He'd meant to reassure, saw how badly he'd miscalculated only as the blood left Llewelyn's face. "She has not been harmed, my lord! I am sure of it, for Thomas the Archdeacon would never be fool enough to rape the King's cousin."

Llewelyn rose abruptly, then bent down and picked up Ellen's hand mirror. The ivory case had been fashioned by a master craftsman, a thin sheet of clear glass fitted over a polished plate of copper. It had been a pretty piece of work, but now the glass was smashed and the metal dented and scratched, both beyond repair. "I believe you, Hugh," he said softly. "But she ought never to have faced a danger like that . . ." Letting the mirror drop into the floor rushes, he turned back to the young Englishman. "You are welcome at my court, welcome in Wales. I would be fortunate to have you in my service."

Hugh felt a surge of grateful admiration for the Welsh Prince's deft touch; rarely had an offer of refuge been tendered so gracefully, camouflaged as praise. "You do me honor, my lord. But I cannot accept, not yet. I would be beholden to you, though, if you could give me the money to repay Isaac ben Asher, and enough to get me, then, to Windsor."

"Windsor?" Llewelyn's voice was suddenly sharp. "You are following Ellen?"

"Of course," Hugh said simply. "But first I mean to go to Corfe Castle, to see if there is anything to be done on Lord Amaury's behalf."

Llewelyn had given no thought to Amaury's plight, no thought to anyone but Ellen. "Corfe Castle," he echoed somberly. "God pity him. Do you truly think you can even gain admittance? From what I've heard of Corfe, it would be easier to get into the Caliph of Baghdad's harem."

"I have to try, my lord. From Corfe, I shall go to Windsor, seek out my lady. After that, it is in God's Hands."

No, Llewelyn thought, in Edward's hands, God rot him. Strange, that hatred could burn with such a white-hot flame, yet be so utterly ice-cold at the core. But Hugh was still waiting patiently. "You'll not want for money, Hugh. Tell me . . . if I were to give you a letter, do you think you'd be able to get it to Ellen?"

"I'll find a way," Hugh vowed, "that I swear to you, my lord." He said no more, for there was no more to be said, quietly let himself out of the chamber.

Llewelyn crossed to a coffer, brought out writing materials, and took them back to the table. But he found himself staring at the parchment as his pen dripped ink onto the page. What was he to say to her? He'd sworn a holy oath to protect her, to cherish her, yet he could do neither. In truth, there was nothing he could do for her—only rage and grieve—and well he knew it. Looking blindly down at the blank parchment, he wondered if she knew it, too.

15

CORFE CASTLE, ENGLAND

March 1276

T HE whitewashed wall above Amaury's pallet was streaked with grime and yellowed by smoke, scarred by the scratched messages of men long dead. Upon his arrival, Amaury had begun to mark the days of his confinement, stirring the ashes in his charcoal brazier and drawing crosses on the wall above his head. But as February gave way to March and the crosses multiplied, he had a sudden harrowing vision of what his future held: row after row of those cinder-smeared symbols, filling the walls from floor to ceiling, crosses beyond counting. After that he drew no more crosses, counted no more days.

He'd been sleeping, awoke at sound of a key in the lock. He tensed, but the door did not open. He'd always been a realist, the only one of Simon de Montfort's sons capable of detached analysis, the only one not ruled by his passions, and he refused—even now—to console himself with false hope, at least during his waking hours. His dreams, though, were of midnight escapes and miracles.

Sitting up, he scratched a flea bite while trying to motivate himself to light a candle, for the daylight was fast fading. As barren and sparse as his prison was, he was thankful to be housed in the Butavant Tower's uppermost chamber. From his pallet, he could catch a grateful glimpse of sky, but the ground-floor dungeon was windowless. Below it, he'd been told, lay a chamber of even greater horrors, a pit deep in the earth, reached only through a trapdoor in the floor above. Amaury did not understand how a man could be buried alive like that and not go mad.

Lying back on the pallet, he sought in vain to get comfortable upon the thin straw mattress. He'd taken some of his holy vows more seriously than others, had never seen why poverty enhanced a priest's piety. Like many sons of noble families he'd found in the Church a career rather than a calling. Well, he'd be honoring all his vows now, he'd be living as austerely as any recluse, those holy men who shunned the world and all its pleasures, mortifying the flesh whilst devoting their every waking thought to the glories of God Eternal and Life Everlasting.

Here at Corfe, he had his anchorite's cell, and all the time he'd ever need for contemplative meditation upon his sins and hopes of salvation. He suspected, though, that he'd spare a thought or two for his royal benefactor, his right beloved cousin Ned.

Yielding the bed to the fleas, he got stiffly to his feet, moved restlessly to the unshuttered window. Dusk had begun to blur the edges of the Purbeck Hills, and slate-color clouds promised rain before morning. He wondered what view Ellen looked out upon from her Windsor chamber. He wondered, too, how he'd fill the day's dwindling hours. He'd always imagined that boredom must be a prisoner's greatest foe. But he'd not expected the solitude to be equally burdensome. Even as a boy, he'd been as independent as any cat, accustomed to going his own way. It came as a shock, therefore, to discover that loneliness could be so crippling.

So starved was he for companionship that he'd begun to look forward to those days when Bertram was on duty, for the genial, garrulous guard was always willing to linger and talk. A good-natured, unlettered man in his forties, Bertram had been untouched by the turmoil that had convulsed England during Simon de Montfort's struggle with King Henry. The boundaries of Bertram's world stretched no farther than the confines of his Dorsetshire village, and it mattered little to him that Amaury was a de Montfort. But that Amaury was a priest mattered greatly.

Bertram did not believe a man of God ought to be imprisoned like a common felon, and when he learned that Amaury was a papal chaplain, his indignation led him to perform small acts of kindness whenever possible, seeing that Amaury had extra candles, another blanket, even a wooden comb. And Amaury, who'd once dined with kings and consorted with popes, could only reflect, with rueful bitterness, that what Scriptures said was all too true. Pride indeed did goeth before destruction, a haughty spirit before a fall.

He stiffened suddenly, again thinking he'd heard the jangle of keys. This time, though, his senses had not played him false. As he turned from the window, the door swung open and Bertram entered with his supper tray. The food was the usual Lenten fare—salted herring, half a loaf of barley bread, a dollop of apple butter, and a tankard of tepid ale—edible, if not appetizing. But Bertram was beaming, looking as pleased as if he'd just brought Amaury a meal to grace a king's table.

"I've a joyful surprise for you, my lord," he declared, "a visitor!" And he stepped aside to reveal a grey-robed friar standing behind him in the shadows.

Amaury was delighted. But as he came forward to welcome the friar, the man pulled his cowled hood back, and his gasp was as audible as it was involuntary. "Friar—Hugh!"

It was a quick recovery, but needless; Hugh was grinning widely. "Bertram knows I'm no friar," he said breezily, and then found himself blinking back tears, for Amaury, the aloof, the proud, was embracing him like a brother.

Bertram deposited the tray, collected the chamber pot, and headed for the door, warning that they had only till the Vespers bells sounded. They squandered a few of those moments listening to the receding echoes of his footsteps on the stairs. Then Hugh said regretfully, "I'd hoped there might be some way to set you free—until I drew rein before the outer bailey walls. It would take a Merlin to contrive an escape from Corfe, my lord."

"I know, Hugh, indeed I know. I am astounded that you were even able to talk your way in to see me. That Franciscan disguise—very clever!"

Hugh grinned again. "Well, in truth, it was Prince Llewelyn's idea," he confided, fumbling under his robes.

"You've seen Llewelyn?" Amaury was incredulous. "By God, you truly are a marvel!"

Having untied the burlap sack knotted about his waist, Hugh now brought it out with a flourish. "Even if I cannot offer the keys to your prison, I do not come empty-handed, my lord." Reaching into the sack, he withdrew a small prayer book and a coral rosary. "I've a psalter and pater noster for you. Bertram balked at the razor, but he agreed to bring you a washing laver on the morrow. I have a hairbrush for you, and some soft Bristol soap, too. And there's a change of clothing, a tunic, chausses, a shirt, and several pairs of braies."

Amaury had resolutely refused to let himself think that far ahead, to the time when his clothes would become too ragged, threadbare, and dirty to be worn. "You've thought of everything, Hugh," he said, and when he looked into the sack, he saw that was, indeed, true. There were extra candles, monkshood root to kill rats and mice, and a larkspur seed powder for lice and fleas. An ink horn, several quill pens, and rolled sheets of parchment. Dried figs. Even a packet of needles and thread. "What prisoner could ask for more?" he said softly, and Hugh, missing the irony altogether, gave him a sunlit smile.

"There is more," he said, holding out a small, leather pouch;

Amaury heard the clinking of coins. "We thought this might come in handy, since most gaolers are more money-minded than Bertram. Ah, I almost forgot . . . there are some books, too, in the bottom of the bag."

Amaury was puzzled by his own emotions. He ought to be elated, for Hugh's bounty was a genuine godsend. And he was grateful. But at the same time, there was a curious sense of letdown, too, for the gift of these basic necessities, items he'd always taken utterly for granted, served to bring home to him his impotence, his outcast status as a prisoner, dependent upon others for even the most simple needs. But there was nothing in the least ambivalent about his reaction to the word *books*. "Ah, Hugh, bless you for that!"

"I wish I could say it was my doing, but alas, it was not," Hugh confessed cheerfully, for although he was proud of his literacy, reading for pure pleasure was an alien concept to him. "It was Prince Llewelyn who thought books might help to banish boredom. Shall I see what we've got for you?"

Drawing out a book bound with thin wooden boards, he held it up for Amaury's inspection. "Chretien de Troyes's *Yvain, the Knight of the Lion*. And here is Geoffrey of Monmouth's *History of the Kings of Britain*. *The Song of Roland*. I was fretting that you might have read some of these already, but Prince Llewelyn assured me that it is not unheard-of to read a book more than once!"

Amaury was watching so avidly as the books piled up on his bed that Hugh began to laugh. "I feel as if I'm pouring gold coins out for the counting! I know you are fluent in Latin, so we included the Roman poet Ovid's *Metamorphoses*, and Robert Grosseteste's *Dicta*."

Amaury reached out, picked up the last-named book. "My father had so many of Bishop Robert's books," he said, and only then did Hugh remember that Simon de Montfort and the Bishop of Lincoln had been more than friends; they had been political allies, spiritual soulmates who'd shared a vision of a new England, one in which the cleansing flames of a Christian chivalry could burn free and pure.

"Passing strange," Amaury said, "that there should be so many men who see both my father and Bishop Robert as saints. They pray to the Bishop, too; did you know that, Hugh?"

Hugh nodded. "The monks at Evesham used to tell us of a family who had brought their ailing child to pray at the Bishop's shrine. The lad swooned, and when he came to his senses, he said that the Bishop was not in his tomb, that he'd gone to be with his brother Simon, who was to die on the morrow at Evesham."

Amaury said nothing, but there was such an odd, distant look upon his face that, for the first time, Hugh found himself wondering what it was like to be the son of a legend. "Do you ever wish," he asked hesitantly, "that men did not see your lord father as . . . as St Simon of Evesham? It must be strange at times, sorting out your memories, making sense of it all . . ." He'd begun to stammer a bit, self-conscious, fearing he might inadvertently have offended.

No one had ever asked Amaury that before. "I think," he said slowly, "that sometimes I feel . . . cheated, as if I'd been robbed of something that was mine . . . my family's." Hearing his own words, he smiled thinly. "Does that sound utterly mad to you?"

"No, of course not," Hugh said, uncomprehending but invariably polite. "There is one more book in the bag. This one has a right interesting history. Your kinsman, the old Earl of Chester, bought it whilst on his way to the Holy Land, later gave it to his nephew, John the Scot, who was the husband of Llewelyn Fawr's daughter. John gave it to Llewelyn, and eventually it ended up in the hands of his grandson, our Lady Ellen's Llewelyn. He thought you might find it diverting, for it is all about alien lands, written by a Christian pilgrim. He relates some truly marvelous adventures, even includes a vocabulary of foreign words, mostly Arabic, I think."

"I suppose learning Arabic is as good a way to fill the hours as any. Have you ever heard of Robert, the Duke of Normandy? No? He was a distant kinsman of mine, a son of William the Bastard, first of the Norman Kings. He was the eldest, but his younger brother Henry ended up on England's throne and he ended up in an English prison. For a while, he was held here at Corfe. But then he was moved to Cardiff Castle in Wales, where he learned to speak Welsh. Of course he had all the time in the world for study. You see, he was caged until he died, nigh on thirty years, if my memory serves."

It occurred to Hugh that education could be a dubious blessing. For certes, it would have been better, he thought, if Prince Llewelyn had never heard of Eleanor of Brittany and Lord Amaury knew naught of this Robert of Normandy. He was determined, though, that their visit would not end on such a bleak note, and he said, as heartily as he could, "I've something else for you, my lord. Ale was never to your liking; I remember you saying you'd sooner swill goat's piss. Well, I have a full flask here of spiced red wine, and I thought we might celebrate my twentieth birthday together."

"Your birthday?" Amaury echoed, and Hugh nodded, although it was actually still a few days hence. "I'd wager this is the oddest setting for any birthday you'll ever have, Hugh!"

"No," Hugh said and grinned. "When I turned fifteen, your brother Bran took me to a whorehouse in Siena!"

"Did he for true?" Amaury almost laughed. "That does sound like Bran. He always was a lad for—"

He heard it before Hugh did, the sound of footsteps nearing the door. Bertram poked his head in, then tactfully withdrew, after alerting them to "say your farewells."

"Quick, my lord." Hugh shoved a parchment across the bed. "From here I am going to Windsor, and if you write to Lady Ellen, I may be able to get it to her."

As Amaury wrote, Hugh took this opportunity to inspect his prison. He'd not expected the chamber to be so bare, so stark, for he knew men of Amaury's rank were often confined in considerable comfort, even allowed their own servants to tend to their needs.

"I do not understand," he said suddenly, "why the English King is so set upon punishing you like this. Surely he cannot still believe you played a part in that killing at Viterbo. Jesú, the Bishop of Padua himself swore you'd never left the city!"

"Edward well knows that I am innocent," Amaury said, and signed his name with deliberation. "Have you never heard of a scapegoat, Hugh? According to Scriptures, it is an unfortunate animal that shoulders the sins of others ere being banished into the wilderness."

He saw that Hugh did not yet comprehend, and said quietly, "It is true that my cousin Hal betrayed our father, but he did not deserve to be hacked to death in a church. My brother Guy will never admit it, mayhap not even to himself, but he knows that to be true. God pity him, so did Bran. Hal died, not for his own sins, but for Edward's."

"You are saying, then, that King Edward is punishing you because he cannot punish Guy? But . . . but there is no justice in that!"

"Ah, but there is, Hugh," Amaury said trenchantly, "royal justice."

"And what exactly is royal justice?"

"Whatever the King says it is," Amaury said, with a cynicism that took Hugh's breath away. But when he opened his mouth to protest, he found himself unable to refute Amaury, for Edward was not his cousin and Corfe was not his gaol.

AFTER encountering so many obstacles in his attempts to breach the defenses of Corfe Castle, Hugh approached Windsor with some trepidation. But he was to discover that his qualms had been needless. Corfe was a state prison and, of necessity, virtually impregnable. Windsor Castle proved to be far more accessible, a royal palace that comprised no less than three baileys, two half-timbered King's Houses, several chapels, numerous stables, kitchens, a bake-house and buttery, a great hall, an almonry, kennels, and gardens, all of this in addition to the circular castle keep and fortified towers, spread out over thirteen full acres of ground, an area even larger than that of the Tower of London.

Just twenty miles from Westminster, Windsor had long been a favorite royal dwelling, and while Edward was not currently in residence, some of his children were, and the nurseries in the upper bailey resounded with their squeals, with the scolding of their harried nurses. Amidst the comings and goings of tradesmen and servants and guards and townsmen, no one looked twice at a lone Franciscan friar.

Unlike monks, who were not supposed to stray far from their monasteries, friars were expected, even obligated, to remain in the world, preaching God's Word in the streets and marketplaces. Hugh's presence, therefore, seemed not at all untoward, and he was able to wander at will about the castle grounds, prudently avoiding those buildings where security-minded sentries might be inclined to challenge him.

There was not a stable groom, not a kitchen scullion, who did not know that Simon de Montfort's daughter was the King's unwilling guest, and they were all quite willing to gossip about her. Hugh soon learned that Ellen was lodged in an upper chamber of the Round Tower, that she was being treated with the deference due the King's kinswoman, and that more than a few pitied her plight. But the most useful information came from old Emo, the royal gardener. Emo was vastly proud of the gardens and vineyards that lay beyond the castle walls; more than five flowering acres, he boasted, enclosed within hedges of blackthorn and alder. But the poor lass would not get to see his masterwork. She was only allowed to walk in the small garden plots safely set within the castle baileys, would miss the glory of his roses in full summer bloom.

King Henry had built a chapel in the northeast corner of the lower bailey, separated from the new royal apartments by a spacious cloistered garden. It was here that Hugh took up his post, safely hidden within the deep shadows of the silent chapel, watching the cloisters, waiting. His were virtues—a calm, steady nature, courage, and an enduring optimism—that were well suited for surveillance, and on the second day of his vigil, his patience was rewarded. Just before noon, a young knight escorted Ellen and Juliana into the garden.

Ellen was carrying the most exotic-looking dog Hugh had ever seen. The size of a small cat, with tufts of soft, milk-white fur, it put Hugh in mind of a walking powder-puff. As she bent down to put it on the grass, he slipped through the chapel doorway and drew back his hood from his face.

Juliana saw him first. She was the most spontaneous free spirit he'd ever known, yet now she did not even blink, turning casually and touching Ellen's arm. Ellen's response was equally circumspect; she gazed across at Hugh without a flicker of recognition. And then, in so smooth a maneuver it might have been choreographed between them, Juliana focused the full seductive power of her smile upon Sir Nicholas, drawing him aside, and Ellen tossed her dog's toy up into the air.

It landed almost at Hugh's feet, a small strand of braided rope, with the puppy in panting pursuit. Scooping them both up, he sauntered across the cloister garth. "Is this your dog, my lady?"

"Yes, thank you. She was a gift from my cousin, the King, comes from Bologna in Italy, he says . . ." Ellen sounded quite normal, even nochalant, but had no idea what she'd just said. From the corner of her eye, she saw that Juliana had lured Sir Nicholas out of earshot, and she expelled a shaken breath. "We thought you were dead!"

"Brian helped me to escape. Hold out your hand."

Puzzled, she did, not comprehending until she felt something smooth and metallic hidden under the rope. Cupping it cautiously, she found herself looking at a heart-shaped topaz pendant.

"Prince Llewelyn said to tell you that there are many who think topaz guards against grief. He does not know if he believes so himself, but he said that even if it is no talisman, it is a pledge, and that you can rely upon, my lady."

Ellen's fingers closed around the pendant, gripping it so tightly it would leave an imprint in the palm of her hand. "You've seen Llewelyn?" she whispered, once she was sure she could trust her voice, and Hugh nodded.

"Yes . . . and Lord Amaury, too. We were able to talk briefly at Corfe."

"Amaury? The truth, Hugh, please! How is he faring? How are they treating him?"

"His chamber is right Spartan, I'll not deny that. But it could be far worse, my lady. He has candles for the dark and blankets for the cold and two full meals a day. Fortunately, the King has agreed to pay for his keep—"

"Oh, has he?" Ellen all but hissed the words. "How very magnanimous of him!"

"Ah, no, my lady, you do not understand. We could not take that for granted. It is customary for the Exchequer to pay for the maintenance of hostages, and sometimes, but not always, for Crown prisoners like Lord Amaury. But for other prisoners, there are no provisions. When a man is arrested, his family must pay for his food, candles, all his needs. God pity the poor soul who is friendless. It is not unheard-of for men to starve in the King's gaols. If King Edward had not . . ."

But Ellen was no longer listening. Although standing in the glare of high noon, she still could not suppress a shiver. "Thank God I never knew that!" Reaching down, she cuddled the puppy in her arms, walked back and forth along the pathway, trying to regain her composure, to contain her rage.

"Ere my lord father rode out to face the King's army at the battle of Lewes, he told his men that he'd taken an oath to reform the realm, he told them that they were fighting for Christ's poor, for the weal of England, for the promises broken and the trust betrayed. He knew, you see, he always knew what he risked. He did not go blindly to his fate, knew what was at stake. And Guy and Bran . . . they must have understood the consequences of their killing. Just as I, too, understood. When I agreed to wed Llewelyn, I knew how enraged Edward would be. But I chose to risk it, I chose! Do you not see, Hugh? Each of us, in our own way, we chose . . . all but Amaury. He is not caged up at Corfe for anything he did, for any choice he made, and it is that which I find hardest to accept, to forgive."

Hugh nodded somberly; he would not insult her with facile, false comfort, would not offer platitudes. He'd kept a wary eye upon Sir Nicholas, knew that their time was running out, for the knight was beginning to cast curious glances their way. "Shall I fetch you some flowers, my lady?" And without waiting for Ellen's response, he moved into the grassy center mead.

Ellen watched, baffled and faintly irked that he should waste their last moments like this. It seemed to her that he took an eternity to pick a meagre bouquet of the first spring flowers, a handful of Lent lilies, a few yellow primroses. Holding it out to her, he smiled, said in a low voice, "There are two letters wrapped around the stems, from your brother and your husband."

"Oh, Hugh . . ." Ellen yearned to fling her arms around his neck, to cover his face with kisses. With Sir Nicholas's footsteps drawing near on the path, she dared not even touch his hand. "If I were not a married woman," she murmured, "I'd run away with you in a trice!"

He laughed soundlessly. "We may do just that," he promised recklessly, and saw her eyes widen as she took his meaning, filling with sunlight, with a sudden, desperate, dazzled hope.

THEY met again the following morning, and it went so well that they risked a third encounter two days later. By now they had worked out the basic elements of their escape. Their plan was a simple one, for there was less to go wrong that way. Ellen would lure Sir Nicholas into the empty chapel, where Hugh would be waiting. And while the knight lay, bound, gagged, and helpless, in the chapel sacristy, three Franciscan friars would be calmly making their way across the lower bailey, through the outer gate to freedom.

Ellen and Hugh both agreed that they must have allies. While Llewelyn was the natural choice, there were limits to what he could do, for a Welsh accent would betray them all. They needed invisible accomplices, English accomplices, and after some thought, Ellen came up with two names, John d'Eyvill and Baldwin Wake.

The first was a Yorkshire knight, the second a Lincolnshire baron. They'd been friends of her brothers, her father's most steadfast supporters, and not even Evesham had reconciled them to the Crown. Moreover, Baldwin Wake was wed to her cousin, Hawise de Quincy. Hawise was Llewelyn's kinswoman, too, for Elen, her mother, had been the daughter of Llewelyn Fawr and Joanna Plantagenet. Hawise and her sisters had been Ellen's own playmates in childhood, often in the de Montfort household, and she felt confident that Hawise and Baldwin Wake would shelter her at one of their Lincolnshire manors until Llewelyn could get her safely into Wales.

That made sense to Hugh, for he knew all the roads into Wales would be watched; it would not take a soothsayer, after all, to guess Ellen's destination. And so they agreed that on the morrow he would ride for the Wake manor of Bourne in Lincolnshire.

Now that action was imminent, Hugh's brain was racing. Walking toward the gatehouse, he could have been on the moon, so preoccupied was he, so oblivious of all but the plan taking shape so promisingly. It might be a good idea if Baldwin could arrange for three Franciscan friars to serve as bait, to lead the hunt astray. But if Baldwin did agree to help, they'd have to get word first to Llewelyn. Hugh did not doubt that the Welsh Prince would be outraged if his wife's safety was put at risk without his knowledge. He had struck Hugh as a man accustomed to command, and he'd want a say in this for certes.

At the very last moment, Hugh heard the sudden footsteps behind him and started to turn. But it was too late. There were three of them, and they hit him all at once, sending him sprawling onto the bailey ground. By the time he'd gotten his breath back, there was a sword poised at his throat.

THEY left Windsor Castle the next morning, in a driving rainstorm. Hugh's guards were understandably disgruntled by the weather, and irked, too, by the timing, not relishing a separation from their families in Holy Week. They took out their frustrations upon Hugh, isolating him within a surly silence, and by the end of the second rain-drenched day, knowing neither where he had been nor where he was going, Hugh had begun to despair.

That was a new and frightening feeling for him; even during those desperate, fever-stalked days out on the Maremma with Bran, he'd still clung to hope. But now he looked at what his future held, and it was like gazing down into an abyss.

He'd begun to wish fervently that he'd not been so stubborn. If he'd answered the Windsor constable's questions, he might have saved himself a great deal of grief. His bruises and scratches would heal. He didn't even blame the constable all that much; his obstinate silence might have provoked a less patient man than Geoffrey de Pychford. But had he openly admitted he was Ellen de Montfort's sworn man, he might well be on his way now to join her other household knights at Bristol Castle. If the Church was right and pride one of the Seven Deadly Sins, he could end up paying a terrible price for that presumptuous vice. Riding—wet, miserable, and manacled—along unknown roads toward an unknown fate, he found himself haunted by his own words. "God pity the poor soul who is friendless. It is not unheard-of for men to starve in the King's gaols."

On the third day of their journey, the third of April, the sun re-emerged, and the improvement in the weather brought a parallel up-swing in the mood of one of Hugh's guards. Unlike his comrades, he had no wife waiting back at Windsor, was young enough to look upon their escort duty as an adventure now that they no longer seemed in danger of drowning. He'd been impressed, moreover, by Hugh's stoical courage, for the fiery-tempered constable of Windsor was not a man he'd have dared to defy himself. And so, as the air warmed, hinted at spring, his reticence rapidly thawed.

Riding at Hugh's side, he was soon chatting companionably with his prisoner. Introducing himself as Henry of Dover, he volunteered that his friends called him Harry the Fleming, after the Flemish sailor who'd not hung around long enough to learn what a fine son he'd sired. Generously sharing his wine flask, he'd soon shared, as well, his entire history, at interminable length. But he'd also noticed that Hugh's wrists had been rubbed raw and bleeding by his manacles, and when they stopped to eat, he found rags to wrap around the irons. And he ended Hugh's suspense. They were heading north, he confided. They'd be halting that night at Leicester, again at Newark, with their final desti-nation the royal castle at Lincoln.

HUGH was awed by his first sight of Lincoln. The city was perched upon the summit of a hill so high that the cathedral's triple towers seemed to be scraping the clouds. As they passed through Stonebow Gate, they were nearly deafened by the sudden, pulsing sound. For the three days before Easter, church bells throughout the realm had been silenced.

Now, on Easter morn, they burst forth in joyful peals, in a musical epiphany meant to echo toward Heaven itself. Hugh's chains seemed to clink in mocking harmony as he made an awkward sign of the cross. Easter was one of the holy days upon which all Christians were expected to take Communion. This would be the first time that he would not receive the Blessed Sacrament, or be shriven of his sins. And it did not ease his conscience that his greatest regrets were not for those unconfessed sins, but that he had failed his lady by his lack of care.

The castle turrets loomed above them, crowning the crest of the hill. Hugh's stomach muscles tightened as he gazed up at the cloud-drifted sky, for within the hour, this mild spring sunlight might be only a memory. Mushrooms thrived in the dark and damp, but how could men? So caught up was he in these morbid musings that he was taken aback when they turned suddenly onto Danesgate, heading away from the castle.

Harry the Fleming was just as surprised by the detour, and urged his horse forward to catch up with the captain of the guards. He was back within moments, looking startled and excited. "I did not know, for our captain can be as close-mouthed as any clam. He's under orders to deliver you, not to the constable at Lincoln Castle, but to the Bishop of Lincoln's Palace. You must have stirred up more trouble than we thought, lad, for you're to be handed over to the King himself!"

As he followed his guards into the Bishop's great hall, Hugh could not help thinking of the many times Simon de Montfort must have crossed this same threshold, in the years when the Bishop of Lincoln had been the saintly Robert Grosseteste. But Grosseteste was long dead, and the current Bishop was the King's man. He repeated the words softly to himself, still unable to believe that he'd be facing the King within moments. He'd meant it when he told Isaac ben Asher that Edward was the enemy. But he was also God's anointed. He'd never bargained upon having to confront the King of England. Given a choice, he'd rather have braved those Welsh mountain passes again, mayhap even the Alps, the touchstone by which he measured all perils.

Leaning against one of the huge marble pillars, he tried to ignore the curious stares his shackles were attracting, and watched as the captain of his guards moved down the middle aisle. There was a spacious bay window at the upper end of the hall, and he knew without being told that the tall, dark-haired man sprawled within the recess was England's King. Beside him, Harry gave a low, wondering whistle. "I think half the peers of the realm are here! I know most of them on sight, what with the King coming so often to Windsor. But the court is rarely as gem-studded as this. I suppose they're here for the Easter festivities."

"Or to plan for war against the Welsh," Hugh said, and Harry shot him a surprised look.

"Well, I know naught of Wales," he admitted, conveying by his tone that he had no interest, either. "See that man in the red tunic? That is the Lord Edmund, the King's brother. Men say he's a good master, easy to serve. That must be his new French wife, the Lady Blanche. I had no idea she was such a little bit of a lass! And that tall, prideful lady in velvet is the Queen. See how her skirts are swelling? When they were at Windsor in December, there were rumors that she had another loaf in the oven. Let's hope," he added piously, "that this one will be a lad. A king ought always to have sons to spare, and they've already buried two of their three boys."

Harry was not in the least abashed by Hugh's lack of response, so intent was he upon showing off his familiarity with the King's court. "Now over there is the Earl of Gloucester, the one with the carrot-color hair. You might be right about war with Wales, for we do not often see so many Marcher lords this far from the border. They're a half-wild folk, the Marchers, doubtless from living so close to the Welsh. That kind of craziness can be catching!"

Laughing at his own joke, he nudged Hugh with his elbow. "That is Roger Lestrange, one of the few Marchers who does not count his grievances like pater noster beads. Not like Roger de Mortimer; he's the most dangerous of the lot. That's him, the one looking lean and hungry—like a Welsh wolf! He is half Welsh, you know. The talk at Windsor is that his nerves are very much on the raw these days, for he lost a son a few months ago, his firstborn. His second son was pledged to the Church, had to be snatched back just as he was about to take his vows. Fancy, one day you're to be a priest, the next you're supposed to step into your dead brother's shoes! You think he feels reprieved . . . or deprived?"

Hugh shrugged. He'd yet to take his eyes from the King. The captain had given Edward a letter, doubtless the Windsor constable's indictment. He swallowed with difficulty, watched as Edward began to read.

"See that lord hovering by the King?" Harry got his attention with another elbow jab. "You are looking at the most hated baron in all of England, God's truth. That is the Earl of Pembroke, the King's de Lusignan uncle. A right fine gentleman, if you judge by the flaxen hair and the elegant clothes. But if he died tomorrow, there would be so many men lining up to spit into his coffin that they would not be able to bury him till Candlemas!"

Never had Hugh felt so exposed, so vulnerable, for these men had been Simon de Montfort's most virulent enemies. They still were, for in some strange sense, they seemed to hate him even more since Evesham. Hugh raised his wrists, wincing as the shackles rubbed against his lacerated skin. What in God's Name was he doing in this den of vipers?

Harry poked him again. "Now him I do not know, that tall one with a mustache and no beard. An odd style, for certes. He must be a foreigner."

Hugh turned to look, and a dim memory flickered. "He is Welsh," he said tersely. "Prince Llewelyn's renegade brother." Never had he seen gathered in one place so many men deserving of damnation.

"You look greensick," Harry said suddenly, cocking his head in a belated appraisal that was not altogether lacking in sympathy. "Not that I blame you, but try not to let the King see you are scared. He hates it when men grovel. But for Christ's sake, do not swagger, either, for he hates that even more!"

Hugh had no chance to reply; the captain was beckoning to Harry. As they moved forward, people crowded in around them, straining to see. Hugh was not surprised, for he knew how impatient men were at the end of a hunt, how eager to be in on the kill. Kneeling before the King, he raised his head, forced himself to meet Edward's eyes.

"Sir Geoffrey tells me you have a liking for disguises, first a friar, then a deaf-mute. I trust you will be more forthcoming with me," Edward said, and Hugh marveled that he could invest so simple a sentence with such ominous overtones. "You may begin by telling me who you are and why you were seeking out Eleanor de Montfort."

"I am Sir Hugh de Whitton, and she is my liege lady."

Edward nodded, almost imperceptibly. "Well, that is a start. Go on."

Hugh did. The story he told was essentially true; his were lies of omission. He made no mention of Brian or Isaac ben Asher, said nothing of his detours to Wales and Corfe. What emerged was a straightforward account of a knight loyal to his lady. Could he be blamed for keeping faith? A frail reed in view of Amaury's fate, but the only defense he had.

"So you avoided confinement by claiming to be a crew member, then followed the Lady Eleanor to Windsor. What then? What were you planning?"

"I do not know, my liege. I did not have time to think that far ahead."

"The Lady Eleanor left Bristol for Windsor on January twenty-ninth. Yet you did not turn up at Windsor until late March. What were you doing in those two months, lad?"

The question was deceptively casual, all the more deadly for being so offhandedly posed. Hugh felt as if Edward's eyes were burning into his brain, smoking out his every secret. How could anyone dare lie to this man? "I was hurt, my liege, when the cog was taken." Fumbling with his irons, he brushed back the hair from his forehead, revealing a thin red scar. "My wound festered, and afterward, I was too weak to travel. God knows what would have befallen me if not for the *Holy Cross* sailors."

"Where did you get the money to buy a horse?"

This was the question Hugh had been most dreading, for he'd hidden Llewelyn's money in his room at a Windsor inn, and Sir Geoffrey had told him the room had been searched. But he'd not mentioned the money. Why not? If they knew about it, he'd have no choice but to reveal it had come from Llewelyn's coffers. He felt sure that the revelation would not matter in the least to Llewelyn. The Welsh Prince would move Heaven and earth to free his wife and cared not at all who knew it. But he felt sure, too, that the revelation would be disastrous for him. His one hope was that the money had been surreptitiously split up among the men sent to search his belongings. It was not a hope, though, that he'd ever wanted to test.

"I had a gold ring, my liege, bequeathed to me by my father. I hid it ere the pirates could steal it, and later . . . once I'd regained my strength, I sold it to a peddler in the Bristol market. I was loath to part with it, but I could think of no other way to raise the money, and I had to put my lady's need first . . ."

Edward leaned back against the window cushions, his face unreadable. Hugh held his breath, waiting. "Very sharp-witted of you, lad," he said at last, and Hugh felt almost dizzy with the intensity of his relief, for Edward was beginning to sound amused.

"Sharp-witted? I'd say gallant!"

Hugh turned his head, startled, and found himself looking up into a heart-shaped little face of piquant charm. As their eyes met, the Lady Blanche gave him a dimpled smile. "I think your devotion to your lady is wonderful," she said warmly. "You must love her very much!"

To Blanche's surprise, Hugh blushed beet red, and the other men guffawed. "My sister by marriage has yet to learn that the French courts of love never flourished in our fickle English climate," Edward said with a grin, with such friendliness that Hugh took sudden heart, began to hope in spite of himself.

"I think it was only natural that my wife should have assumed—" Edmund began, but he got no further, provoking another burst of male laughter.

"Ah, now there's a familiar sound," Edward gibed. "The besotted bridegroom, ever on the ready to be his lady's loyal echo, to swear white was black at her behest!"

Edmund took the raillery in stride. "I might swear Blanche was blanche," he said mildly, making a play upon his wife's name, and Blanche gave him a melting, seductive look that was only half in jest. Their marital harmony was so obvious that others deemed it either enviable or cloying, depending upon whether they were sentimentalists or skeptics.

Hugh now found himself another champion, this one even more unlikely than Blanche. "I think Sir Hugh is to be commended for his loyalty," Eleanora said gravely, sounding as if she'd just disclosed a verdict rather than offered an opinion; her low, throaty voice, her heavily accented French, and her precise, purposeful delivery inevitably gave her most casual comments the weight of a royal pronouncement.

"Thank you, Madame," Hugh stammered, taken aback at sight of so many approving faces. Even the Earl of Gloucester was regarding him with indulgence, for Hugh had unwittingly tapped into one of their society's most enduring myths, that of the vassal steadfast and loyal, true to his liege lord unto death. If such faithful, stalwart knights existed more often as legend than as flesh-and-blood men, that just made Hugh's fidelity seem all the more admirable. Only cynics like Davydd ap Gruffydd and Roger de Mortimer resisted the temptation to celebrate Hugh's story as the Second Coming of Camelot. The others smiled benevolently upon the young knight, ready to reward him as the fables demanded—until Edward shook his head, said regretfully:

"It seems a pity that a quest such as yours must end in gaol."

Edward saw surprise ripple through the audience, followed by disappointment. But when he spoke, he sounded matter-of-fact, not defensive, for Edward never felt the need to justify himself to others. "I bear you no ill will, lad, in truth I do not. But I cannot let you go free, cannot have you lurking under the Lady Eleanor's window with a ladder . . . now can I?"

Hugh did not know what to say. Before he could gather his wits, make an argument against imprisonment, a chaplain was approaching, leaning over with a message for the King's ear. Edward rose without haste, then gestured toward Hugh, permitting him to rise, too.

"I can spare you no more time, for the Easter Mass is about to begin." Beckoning to one of his household knights, Edward gave orders for Hugh to be lodged within the castle for the night, and on the morrow to be escorted back to Bristol. Glancing again at Hugh, he said, "I am indeed sorry it has to be this way. But you did know the risk you took.

When you chose to follow your lady to Windsor, you chose, too, to gamble with your own freedom. Unfortunately, you lost."

Hugh was mute, stunned by the swiftness of it all. Edward was already turning away. So were the others, for they might be sympathetic, but not to the point of quarreling with the King on his behalf. Just like that, he thought numbly. A snap of the royal fingers and it was over. As if to add insult to injury, he was jostled now by Davydd, with enough force to make him stumble. Davydd did not offer even the most perfunctory apology. Nor did he help Hugh regain his balance. What he did do, though, was so unexpected that Hugh could only stare after him in open-mouthed astonishment, wondering if he'd heard right. "Remind him," Davydd had murmured, "of Lewes."

There was no time to think it through, to think at all. Edward was nearing the door. "My lord King!" Hugh's voice was urgent, impossible to ignore. "You were right, I did choose to wager my freedom on my lady's behalf. But you made the very same choice I did!"

Edward had turned with his first words. "What are you talking about?"

Hugh was disconcerted by Edward's changed tone, flint-hard and imperious. But it was too late to reconsider. "My father fought at Lewes, and he . . . he told me that the Londoners, being green to battle, broke and ran. He said you pursued them from the field, and when you returned, the battle was over. Your lord father the King had taken refuge within the priory, and Simon de Montfort had won a great victory. The lords with you . . ."

Hugh could not help himself. Turning his head, he looked straight at Roger de Mortimer and the Earl of Pembroke. "The lords with you . . ." he repeated hoarsely, for never had his mouth been so dry, his throat so tight, "they chose to flee the field, but you scorned flight, my liege. Instead, you fought your way into the priory. You surrendered to Simon de Montfort rather than forsake your father."

There was utter silence when Hugh was done speaking. Edward had listened intently, eyes narrowed upon Hugh's face, an iced blue gaze that revealed nothing whatsoever of his thoughts. Hugh was only now beginning to realize the full extent of his audacity. When was the last time anyone had dared to challenge the King like this? Jesú, he must have been mad to heed Davydd ap Gruffydd, of all men!

"Your father was right," Edward said coolly. "It happened as you say. I did make the same choice that you did, and because of it, I lost a year's freedom." He paused then, very deliberately, for dramatic impact. "Since we both know so much about hard choices, I suppose it is only fair to offer you one now. You can go to Bristol on the morrow, join your companions in their confinement at the castle. Or . . . you can swear fealty to me, enter my service as one of the knights of the royal household."

Hearing a chorus of indrawn breaths, Edward could not help grinning. He liked nothing better than taking others by surprise, convinced that unpredictability was a virtue every king should cultivate. He had to laugh outright now at the stunned expression on Hugh's face; the lad looked like he'd been pole-axed, for certes. He thought that his solution—thwarting any threat Hugh might pose by keeping him close at hand—was as magnanimous as it was imaginative, and he'd fully expected Hugh to jump at the offer, as any sensible man would. When Hugh did not, Edward's smile chilled. "Well, what say you? Or do you need time to think it over?"

Hugh missed the sarcasm, took Edward's query at face value, and nodded gratefully. "Yes, my liege, I do. I was taught that a man ought never to give his word too lightly, for once given, he must stand by it," he said, with such disarming earnestness that Edward's mouth lost its hard edge. "My lord . . . Lady Ellen told me that you'd promised her she can join her husband in Wales once you and Prince Llewelyn resolve your differences. When that comes to pass, would I be free to go, too?"

Fortunately for Hugh, Edward had begun to see some perverse humor in it, that Hugh should need to weigh a prison term against a place in the royal household. "Yes," he said wryly, "God forbid that you should have to spend the rest of your life in the service of the King." Glancing about, he beckoned to one of his knights. "Get him shed of those shackles, fed, and cleaned up, then bring him back here after the Mass." Reaching out suddenly, he caught Hugh by the arm. "I'll have your sworn word, too, that you'll be planning no Welsh pilgrimages for your lady, and should you break that vow, even Lucifer himself might pity your fate. Understood?"

"I would not break my word—" But before Hugh could protest further, the Earl of Gloucester shouldered him aside, saying in a loud, shocked voice:

"What is this talk of sending de Montfort's daughter back to Llewelyn?"

"What choice has he?" Davydd's voice was very bland. "For whom God hath joined together, let no man put asunder."

That earned him a sharp, amused look from Edward. "My sentiments, exactly," he said, just as blandly, "provided that Llewelyn ap Gruffydd comes to his senses, of course."

Roger de Mortimer was no less pleased to hear this than Gloucester, and he was no less outspoken, either. "I thought you summoned us to

Lincoln to plan a campaign against that Welsh whoreson. Yet now we're talking of his marriage plans?"

"I'd not fret if I were you, Cousin," Davydd interjected, with a smile that could not have been more amiably insulting. "You are our kinsman, after all. If you ask him, Llewelyn might take pity and invite you to the wedding festivities."

The number of Marcher lords who'd have treated Davydd's hanging as a holiday was an impressive tribute to Davydd's trouble-making talents; his sardonic barbs often imbedded themselves deeper than even he realized. But few took their feuds quite as seriously as Roger de Mortimer, and Edward now thought it prudent to step between the two men.

"You'd all best heed what I am about to say. As disappointing as this will be for many of you, it is not my intent to grind Wales into the dust. The Welsh have their own identity, their own ways, their own language. I recognize our differences, am willing, too, to respect them, if I can, although I do think Wales would benefit greatly from further exposure to English custom and English law. Unfortunately for the Welsh, they are not a practical people. Even you would have to admit, my lord Davydd, that your countrymen get drunk as often on dreams as they do on mead."

"Would I?" Davydd said tonelessly, and Edmund, more intuitive than his brother, said hastily:

"Do you mean, my liege, the Welsh claim that their princes ought to have the same rights as the Scots kings?"

Edward nodded. "Precisely. It is dangerous enough for our island to be split in twain as it is now. To have it fragmented further could be fatal. A ship with more than one hand on the helm is likely to founder, to run aground on the rocks. But there'll be no shipwrecks during my reign, that I can swear upon the surety of my soul. Llewelyn ap Gruffydd can call himself Prince of Wales. He is still a vassal of the English Crown, no less than my other lords, but for certes, no more. That is a lesson he must learn. For my pretty cousin's sake, I hope he learns soon."

Edward's manifesto produced varying responses in those listening. Eleanora felt a surge of impassioned pride. Her life was not always easy. She'd come to dread her yearly pregnancies, so uncomfortable, confining, and dangerous. Nor did she understand why the Almighty had chosen to claim so many of her babies in the cradle. But her husband's smile could still light up her world, and it was a rare dark day when he could not convince her, as now, that she was blessed among wives.

Edmund was equally impressed by his brother's articulate and aggressive concept of kingship, but he was taken aback, too, for this was the first time that he'd realized Edward's ambitions extended beyond the Scots border.

Blanche, while giving every appearance of being the most rapt of listeners, was actually quite detached, for she was convinced that most men took themselves so very seriously that it behooved women to take them not seriously at all.

The Earl of Gloucester was struggling with his disappointment, for he'd long been coveting additional lands in South Wales, lands he dared not annex as long as Llewelyn ap Gruffydd ruled in Gwynedd. Edward's uncle Pembroke was no less disgruntled; he, too, had ambitions in Wales. Roger de Mortimer was genuinely fond of Edward, and truly admiring of the younger man's superior military skills. But he could not help thinking that his interests, England's interests, would be better served with a weaker king on the throne at Westminster. He had hoped to see Llewelyn's wings clipped for good this time, and if the opportunity arose to pluck Davydd's poisoned tongue out by the roots, so much the better. But there was no point in bringing Llewelyn down if his power would then be claimed by the Crown. Looking at his friend, the King, de Mortimer found himself unexpectedly nostalgic for the chaotic days under the foolish, feckless Henry.

But for Hugh, the most interesting reaction of all was Davydd's. As Edward was speaking, he'd glanced over, caught Davydd in a rare moment, one in which his defenses were down, and on his face, there blazed forth an intense, revealing rage.

WHEN Hugh was escorted back into the Bishop of Lincoln's great hall, servants were dismantling the trestle tables, removing the last traces of an elaborate noonday dinner. "Wait here," Sir Gervase instructed, "whilst I tell the King's Grace that you are ready to swear fealty to him."

Scrubbed clean of the grime of the road, freed of his manacles, Hugh felt much better physically upon his reentry into the hall. But emotionally, he was still shaken, still beset by doubts. He'd never actually accepted Edward's offer; that was just taken for granted. But even if he'd concluded that he could not be loyal to the King without being disloyal to his lady, he wondered whether he'd have dared to say Edward nay. The thought of finding himself day in, day out, in Edward's formidable presence was a daunting one. But then, so was the thought of that Bristol gaol. And at least now he'd be able to see Lady Ellen and Juliana whenever the King held court at Windsor. Had he been imprisoned at Bristol, she'd never even have known what had befallen him.

"You look like a man about to barter his soul to the Devil. Come to think of it, I suppose you are!"

Hugh turned, found himself looking into green eyes full of laughter and good-humored mockery. "I ought to thank you," he said reluctantly, and Davydd's brows shot upward.

"But it sticks in your craw. If and when you ever reach Wales, you and my sainted brother ought to get along right well. He is another one who's sure he's pure enough to cast the first stone."

There was nothing good-natured about the mockery now; it stung like a whip. Hugh flushed but stood his ground. "I am uncomfortable with you, I'll not deny it. But it's not because I am judging you. It's because I do not understand you."

"Well, you must know that Scriptures say the heart of kings is unsearchable. Mayhap that holds true, too, for rebel Welsh princes in English exile."

"You can laugh at me if you will, my lord. I still cannot make the puzzle pieces fit. You betrayed your brother, even plotted his murder." Davydd's smile disappeared, and Hugh said swiftly, "But you also saved Bran de Montfort's life after he was captured at the battle of Northampton. He told me you kept the Earl of Pembroke from killing him."

Davydd shrugged. "I saw a chance to do Pembroke an ill turn. I never could resist an opportunity to muddy the waters."

"The way you did this forenoon, when you came to my aid? If not for you, I'd still be in irons."

"I'd not make too much of that if I were you. I was just curious to see if a skilled puppeteer could pull the King's strings as easily as any other man's."

"If you say so, my lord. I find it strange, though, that you seemed indifferent to a charge of treason, yet felt compelled to defend yourself against two accusations of simple kindness."

Davydd snatched a wine cup from a passing servant's tray. "I am beginning to think I did you no favor. You'll be a lamb to the slaughter at Edward's court."

"I doubt that you belong here, either, my lord. I was watching you whilst the English King laid out his plans to humble the Welsh. Judging from what I saw, I'd say that you're on the wrong side in this coming war. What's more, I think you know it, too."

"For Christ's sake, Hugh, nothing is as simple as you make it out to be!"

"Some things are, my lord." Hugh insisted, with such infuriating, ingenuous certitude that Davydd drained his wine cup in several deep swallows.

"Ere I forget to ask, how did my brother take it when you told him his bride had been snatched on the high seas? Did his vaunted control slip—even a little?"

"I . . . I do not know what you mean. What makes you think I saw Prince Llewelyn?"

"Of course you saw him, lad. Where else would you go during those two 'missing months' of yours?" Davydd laughed, turning away before Hugh could muster up a more convincing denial. Hugh watched him saunter across the hall, more disquieted by Davydd's parting shot than he wanted to admit. Mayhap Davydd was right. How was he to cope at Edward's court, where nothing was as it seemed and men turned words into weapons? What if the King guessed the truth, just as Davydd had done?

"There you are," Sir Gervase said impatiently. "Why were you tarrying with that Welsh knave? Did you not see the King beckoning? You're not getting off to the best of starts, lad!"

Hugh said nothing, followed Sir Gervase toward the dais, where the King awaited him. It did not seem real to him, any of it, and as he knelt before Edward, he found himself thinking that, of all the unlikely turns his life had taken in the past five years, nothing could be more improbable than this, that he should be pledging his fealty to the King of England himself, and all because on a cold January eve, he'd offered to help Brother Damian carry candles into the sacristy at Evesham Abbey.

16

WORCESTER, ENGLAND

September 1276

THE citizens of Worcester turned out in a drenching rain-storm to welcome their King, escorting him through the mud-mired streets to the Bishop of Worcester's palace. But the weather was less hospitable; the rain persisted. It was three days before Eleanora was able to enjoy the celebrated splendors of the Bishop's lush riverside gardens. Coming in with an armful of autumn roses and Michaelmas daisies, she forgot all about the flowers at sight of the man sharing a wine flagon with Edward.

Davydd rose politely to greet her, but Eleanora was not mollified by his good manners, for Davydd's courtesy always seemed as suspect as his motives. It irritated her enormously now to find him in their private chamber, utterly at ease, laughing and jesting with her husband as if they were boon companions, equals. Why did Eduardo find his insolence so amusing?

"Davydd has brought me welcome tidings, sweetheart. Another of the lords of Upper Powys has agreed to forswear his allegiance to Llewelyn ap Gruffydd. Good work, Davydd! By the time we take the field against him, your brother will stand alone, bereft of allies and hope."

Edward smiled, but his eyes were focused intently upon Davydd's face, probing for a reaction. Davydd was not about to give him one, though. "Yes," he said evenly, "that is quite likely."

"I will authorize you to receive our new convert and his men into the King's Peace," Edward promised, and Davydd nodded, but his attention was straying from Edward to his Queen. Eleanora was bustling about the chamber, fetching a cushion for her husband's chair, then a bowl of shelled almonds, shifting the oil lamp so that he was closer to the light. Davydd was intrigued; was this the same woman who'd summon a servant to pour wine even if the flagon was right at her elbow? He'd occasionally wondered why their marriage was such an obvious success. Eleanora's ten pregnancies were irrefutable proof of the pleasure Edward found in his wife's bed, but Davydd had been blind to her appeal out of bed—until now. Good God, he thought, fighting back a grin, she dotes on him the way a mother might!

Davydd was so caught up in these unseemly speculations about Edward and Eleanora's bedsport that Edward was able to take him by surprise. "As it happens, Davydd, I have good news for you, too. I've found you a wife."

Davydd splashed wine onto his wrist. Setting the cup down, he said cautiously, "I was not aware that I'd lost one."

"I ought not to have said 'wife.' I ought to have said 'jewel,' for she is that, in truth. She is young, about eighteen, and very highborn. Not only is she an Earl's daughter, she is my own cousin."

"And you'd bestow this prize upon a Welsh rebel? Why . . . is she a leper, by chance? A half-wit?"

Eleanora stiffened indignantly; Edward just grinned. "Jesú, but you Welsh are a suspicious lot! All right, mayhap I did omit a few minor facts about your bride's background. There is a taint of treason in the family, but that ought not to bother you all that much, should it? Her father was ever one for hunting with the hounds and running with the hares, and eventually his double-dealing caught up with him. He—"

But he needed to say no more. "Derby," Davydd said, and Edward nodded.

"None other. Now I'll grant you that some men might balk at taking Judas as their kinsman. But do not forget that the girl is my kinswoman, too. Her mother was a de Lusignan, my father's niece."

Davydd was well acquainted with the Earl of Derby's chequered past. Robert de Ferrers had the dubious distinction of being the first English nobleman to have been imprisoned for a non-political offense. During the civil war between King Henry and his barons, Derby had taken advantage of the unrest to rob and plunder his Derbyshire neighbors, and Simon de Montfort had shattered tradition by casting him into the Tower of London. He'd been freed after Evesham, and had then been foolhardy enough to rebel again. Edward's response was swift, his anger understandable, but his justice less than scrupulous. Under the terms of the Dictum of Kenilworth, Derby's estates could not be confiscated outright. So Derby had been forced by buy his freedom for the exorbitant sum of fifty thousand pounds, a sum he could never hope to raise, and his lands and earldom were then forfeit to Edward's brother, Edmund. And there could be no better evidence of Derby's ability to make enemies that so blatant an extortion stirred up no sympathy among his fellow barons, who usually closed ranks against any abuse of royal power.

Davydd shared the prevailing view that Derby deserved the raw deal he'd gotten. His concern now was not with Derby's fall from grace, but rather with the consequences of that fall. Leaning back in his chair, he drawled, "My people have a saying, 'Diwedd y gân yw y geiniog.' Roughly translated, 'The end of every song is money.' And I doubt that Derby has any, not after you and Edmund plucked him cleaner than a Michaelmas goose."

"You ought to learn to be more forthright, Davydd, to speak your mind instead of hemming and hawing like this." Edward was still smiling, but his sarcasm had a sudden sting to it, for he had not been amused by the Michaelmas-goose gibe. "Derby is not destitute, still holds the manor of Chartley. I'll squeeze a marriage portion out of him. The lass has more to rely upon, though, than crumbs from Derby's table. She was wed as a child to William Marshal, a de Montfort supporter who died before Evesham, and she has dower rights in his manors at Cherleton, Norton, and Witlebury. So far she has not had much luck in asserting those rights, for Marshal had a son by an earlier marriage, and he has been resisting her claims. Of course, with a husband to support those claims . . ."

Davydd did a few mental calculations. "You left out something, I think. The little widow is still a virgin . . . no?"

Edward did some quick arithmetic of his own, then nodded. "You're right, by God. The marriage was never consummated for certes; she was only seven or eight when she was widowed. And I expect that Derby keeps her on a tight lead. So unless she's been creeping into the stables to meet one of her father's grooms, I think we can safely say that you'll be her first."

Edward and Eleanora were both looking at him expectantly. Davydd knew they were waiting for him to express his gratitude, his eagerness to wed Derby's daughter. Instead, he reached for his wine cup, saying, "Tell me what she is like."

"What else do you need to know?" Edward sounded bemused. "I've already told you what matters. In all honesty, I do not know her very well. The few times that she has been at court, she seemed a bit on the sullen side . . . though to be fair, living with Derby would be enough to sour a saint!"

"I very much doubt that she was ever a saint, Eduardo," Eleanora said, so sourly that Davydd gave her a speculative look, thinking that if Eleanora disapproved of his bride-to-be, the lass might have promise.

"Eleanora is right," Edward conceded. "She does have a temper. But then you'd tire right quickly of a docile, biddable bride. Now . . . what else? She is a tiny little lass, looks light enough to float on a feather." Edward at once regretted his candor; his own sexual tastes ran to statuesque, big-breasted women like his voluptuous wife. "She is pretty, though," he added hastily, lest Davydd be put off, "with fair coloring. You could do a lot worse, Davydd. Do you not realize how many men would leap at the very chance to wed the King's cousin?"

Davydd hid a smile. "Indeed," he agreed, "what Welsh prince would not consider himself blessed to be able to claim kinship to the King of England?" But he saw that Edward's patience was fast running out. "I am curious about one more thing," he said and grinned. "What is my bride's name?"

Edward grinned, too, good humor restored once he saw that he was to have his way. This marriage mattered to him, for he thought that offering Derby's daughter to Davydd was a master stroke, satisfying Davydd's demands for money at the girl's expense, whilst humiliating that whoreson Derby anew, denying him any say whatsoever in the marital negotiations. "Elizabeth. Her name is Elizabeth. Now if you want to satisfy your curiosity further, I suggest that you keep close to the priory, for she arrives tonight."

"I can see that you were awaiting my answer with bated breath!" But Edward had unwittingly planted a seed. Davydd began to look about the chamber with new interest. "As large as this room is, a man could sit over there in that window-seat and never be noticed—provided it was dark enough. What does Your matchmaking Grace think?"

Edward at once caught his drift, entered enthusiastically into the conspiracy. "We need only place a solitary candle here on the table, and everything beyond the flame will be utter blackness."

Eleanora looked from one man to the other in disbelief. "Surely you are not planning what I think you are? You'd actually spy on the lass?"

Edward looked a little sheepish, but Davydd nodded. "Yes," he confessed cheerfully, "that is exactly what we have in mind."

Eleanora had never liked Elizabeth de Ferrers. But now she felt a surge of sympathy for the girl. The poor child, was it not penance enough that she must share her life and her bed with this brazen Welsh rakehell? Men and their foolish games!

She did her best to dissuade them, but soon realized that she was wasting her time. Conceding defeat, she made a dignified departure from the chamber, marred somewhat by the slamming door.

Davydd pretended to flinch. "I do not think we are in your lady's good graces at this moment."

"Oh, you never are," Edward said with a grin. "I'm sure that comes as no surprise, though, for Eleanora's not one for hiding her feelings. She is a wonderful woman, but bless her, she is so very serious about everything! Not long ago, I ended up making this lunatic wager with my laundress. I told her that if she could ride my roan destrier, I'd give him to her. What could be a safer wager than that? But would you believe she did it? She hiked up her skirts, scrambled into the saddle, and away they went! I had to buy him back from her. It was worth it, though, for that is a sight I'll never forget. I laughed so hard I damned near ruptured myself. But Eleanora . . . she never so much as smiled, said it was not seemly to make wagers with servants. You know, Davydd, there are times when I wonder if the Almighty forgot to give women a sense of humor."

Davydd had begun to laugh. "That's passing strange, for the Welsh have long suspected the same about you English!"

ALTHOUGH nothing in her past justified it, Elizabeth de Ferrers was an optimist. She could think of only two reasons why her cousin the King should have summoned her so abruptly to Worcester. Either he had found her a husband or he had finally secured her dower rights in her late husband's lands. And because she so very much wanted to believe it, Elizabeth soon convinced herself that the latter was true.

It was not that she did not want to remarry. She did, for she well knew that a woman's only choice was between the marriage bed and the nunnery, and Elizabeth did not want to become a nun. What she wanted was to escape the life she presently led, trapped at Chartley with a father she feared and a stepmother she disliked, dependent upon their grudging charity, desperate for a home, a haven of her own.

But she was not so naive as to see marriage as her way out. A wife was too vulnerable—to her husband's will, his whims, his fists. Elizabeth had no marital memories of her own, but she'd too often seen her stepmother serve as the scapegoat for her father's erratic temper, had too often played that role herself. She did not want to wake up in bed with a stranger, a man handpicked by Edward for purely political purposes. She wanted a say in so momentous a decision, and although she knew women were rarely, if ever, permitted that privilege, she had spun out a fantasy in which it was so. Edward would intervene on her behalf, compel her hateful stepson to honor her claims. She would be given her own manor, her own household, and soon there would be a proposal from one of her neighbors, a man handsome and highborn and approving of her independent spirit. To Elizabeth, that did not seem so much to ask, and by the time she reached Worcester, she was already anticipating her liberation . . . at long last.

She was utterly unprepared, therefore, for what happened that evening in a darkened bedchamber at the Bishop of Worcester's palace. She'd been heartened by the warmth of Edward's welcome, and was further encouraged when he took her aside for this private audience. When Edward clinked their wine cups together in a playful salute, she could restrain herself no longer. "Have we something to celebrate?"

"Indeed, we have, sweetheart. I have made a brilliant marriage for you."

Elizabeth had wondered why the chamber was so poorly lit. Now she was grateful for it, pulling back into the shadows as she sought to get her emotions under control. "Who . . . who is he?"

"I've found you a Prince, Lisbet. Davydd ap Gruffydd, brother of—"

"No!"

Elizabeth was on her feet, looking so horrified that Edward was hard put not to laugh outright, although he could not resist glancing toward Davydd's hiding place in the recessed window-seat. "Sweetheart, you cannot believe half of what you've heard about Davydd. The man has enemies, I'll not deny it. But I can assure you that he—"

"No . . . please, you must listen to me. My father and husband were foolhardy enough to defy the Crown, and it cost them all they had. I'll not be yoked to another rebel. I'll not wed a Welsh malcontent whose only loyalty is to himself, for sooner or later, he'll fall . . . and drag me down with him!"

Elizabeth's first outburst had been involuntary, and she'd been encouraged to continue by Edward's unexpectedly mild reaction. But that indulgence, that odd amusement chilled with her first words of defiance. Getting slowly to his feet, Edward gave Elizabeth such a cold, forbidding look that she shrank back, the rest of her protest catching in her throat.

"You disappoint me, Elizabeth. I thought you had more confidence in my judgment. Do you truly think I'd have you wed a man who'd make you unhappy? Now . . . ere you say something you'll long regret, I would suggest that you think this over."

Edward paused for emphasis, but he was mollified somewhat by Elizabeth's submissive silence, and he said, more kindly. "I do have your best interests at heart, lass." Gazing over her shoulder toward the window-seat, he bit his lip, and again that unaccountable look of amusement crossed his face. "In fact, I think you ought to stay right here, have some time alone. I'll be back in a while. In the meantime, you make yourself comfortable, and give some very serious thought to what I've said."

Elizabeth stared at the closing door, fighting a mad urge to flee, for where could she go? She did not have the courage to defy Edward. Nor did her father; he feared Edward even more than he hated him. But . . . but what if she took holy vows? That would thwart Edward. At what cost, though? Bride of Christ or bride of Davydd ap Gruffydd. She'd heard that a trapped animal sometimes gnawed off its own leg in order to escape the snare. But most of them waited passively for their fate, defenseless, doomed.

All her life, Elizabeth had been drawn to drama. Even as a child, she'd been one for turning a scratched knee into a lethal wound, a playmate's rebuff into a blood feud, every joy, every slight, every dread magnified a hundredfold. She embroidered facts instead of threads, not because she was a liar, because she was a romantic. But now that she was facing a genuine calamity, she found herself unable to react, unable to scream or rebel or even to cry. She could only wait for Edward to return, listening for the sound of the hunter's footsteps in the snow.

It was this sense of her own helplessness that stung her into a sudden flare of futile rage. She looked at Edward's wine cup, the cup he'd used to toast her marriage, and then she was lashing out, sending it spinning off the table, down into the floor rushes.

Her burst of temper did not help. All she accomplished was to splatter her skirt and to lose the light, for some of the wine spilled into the oil lamp. Elizabeth muttered one of her father's favorite oaths, sank down into the nearest chair. What now? To whom could she turn? Her grandmother? No, she had disinherited Derby after his disgrace. Might the Queen . . . Elizabeth's head came up sharply. She was not frightened at first, for she knew that mice were no respecters of rank, as likely to be found in a palace as a peasant's hut. By now her eyes had adjusted to the darkness, and as she glanced toward the sound, she could make out a shadowy form within the window recess.

"Who is there? What do you want?"

Davydd had been hurling some very creative mental curses at Edward's absent head. But Elizabeth's quavering challenge brought him hastily to his feet. "Do not be afraid," he said soothingly. "I mean you no harm."

His words were wasted, though; she heard only the accent. She'd spoken instinctively in English, for that was her first tongue. If French was the language of the court, English reigned in the nursery; like most children of the Norman-French nobility, Elizabeth had been tended since birth by English wet-nurses and English maids. Davydd had answered her in English, too, but with a distinctive cadence, one that held echoes of his native Wales.

Elizabeth had jumped to her feet at sight of an intruder. Now, as she realized the identity of the man coming toward her from the shadows, she began to tremble. She was so obviously terrified that Davydd swore under his breath, half-expecting her to bolt at any moment.

"I startled you, I can see," he murmured, and before she could retreat, he grasped her arm, gently but firmly steered her back toward the chair. "I think you ought to sit down, catch your breath, whilst I get you something to drink."

Elizabeth sat on the very edge of the chair, watching as Davydd recovered the wine cup from the rushes, found a half-full flagon, favored her with a relaxed, reassuring smile. Gripping the cup with both hands, she drank until she'd gotten her courage back. "I know who you are," she said, very low, glancing swiftly up at him through her lashes and then away. "So . . . so why are you being so kind to me? After what I said . . ."

"Hellfire, sweetheart, I've been called far worse than a 'Welsh malcontent!' " But she did not return Davydd's smile. He could see that her breathing had steadied. In another moment or so, she'd be composed enough to comprehend the significance of his presence here, to realize what a shabby trick he and Edward had played upon her. To head off that moment of reckoning, he said quickly: "I'm glad you brought it out into the open, though. After all, when the body is lying right on the floor in front of us, still warm and twitching, we can hardly ignore it, might as well dissect it." But that earned him not even the glimmer of a smile. She looked at him so blankly that he sighed softly; this was not going to be easy. "The marriage," he said patiently. "I think we ought to talk about it. It is only fair that I begin by discussing the disadvantages of marriage to me. But in all honesty, I can think of nary a one!"

Again, he failed to get a smile. "Well, on to the advantages. Does a crown catch your interest? There is a very real possibility that I might one day be Prince of Wales."

That had not occurred to Elizabeth. But he might also end his days in English exile, dependent upon Edward's charity. She did not dare to say that, though, kept her gaze locked upon the hands clasped in her lap.

"Of course some people claim my future is more likely to hold a gallows than a coronation," Davydd joked, and she could not suppress a gasp, her eyes flying upward to his face; Jesú, had he read her mind?

He was laughing silently. "Be that as it may, there are other benefits to be found in marriage to me. Not the least of them is that I'd be able to secure your dower rights in the Marshal lands, to stop your stepson from cheating you. Then there is always the pleasure of my company. I'm easy to content, rarely riled, no small virtues in a husband, I would think. I'm not one for squabbling for its own sake, nor do I believe a man ought to take out his foul moods upon his wife. For certes, I'd never hit you, and—"

He'd thrown out that last reassurance almost as an afterthought. But her reaction stopped him in mid-sentence. Her head jerked up; a hand clenched on the arm of the chair. And he remembered stories he'd heard of the Earl of Derby's savage temper, felt for this unhappy girl a sudden flicker of pity.

"That . . . that is easy enough to say."

"Wales is not like England, Lady Elizabeth. Welsh law forbids a man to strike his wife except under extreme provocation, such as infidelity." But Davydd could never be serious for long; his mouth twitching, he added, "I might well give you headaches, lass, but not bruises."

That promise meant more to Elizabeth than the glimmer of a crown—if she could believe him. Reaching for her wine cup again, she was surprised to find she'd drained it dry. Davydd poured her another cupful; she drank gratefully, then remembered her manners and thanked him. "Does Welsh law truly protect women from beatings? Even the Church says a man has the right to discipline his wife . . ."

"Welshwomen have always been better off than their other sisters in Christendom. They can claim custody of their children, unlike English wives or widows. They have as much right as a man to end an unhappy marriage—although I ought not to be telling you that, should I? And unlike England, where a man can bring his concubine right into the castle keep if he so chooses, in Wales a man who did that would stir up a scandal of impressive proportions; he'd be answerable not only to his wronged wife, but to her outraged kinsmen, as well."

Elizabeth had never been alone with a man not her kinsman, and she could not quite believe she was really here now, sitting with Davydd ap Gruffydd in the tempting intimacy of a darkened bedchamber. He was very close, perched on the table edge, but his face was in shadow. Never had she been so physically aware of another person. His legs were long, booted to mid-calf in soft cowhide. One hand rested on his knee, and even in such subdued light, she could see a thin white scar snaking across his wrist; she wondered how the wound had occurred, wondered, too, if his body bore other scars. She drank again, and was then astonished to hear herself saying, "You said that . . . that you'd never bring a concubine under your wife's roof. But there would be concubines?'"

She'd caught Davydd off balance. "Yes," he said at last, "there probably would be from time to time. But I'd never shame you, would never flaunt them in public. That I can promise you."

In the silence that followed, he wondered whatever had possessed him to be so candid. But then Elizabeth startled him again. "Thank you," she said, "for being honest with me. My father . . . he treats me like a child, and a dull-witted one at that. And Cousin Edward is no better. 'I have your best interests at heart,' he says . . . in a pig's eye!" She paused for breath, no less surprised than Davydd by her outburst, and then glanced at him out of the corner of her eye. "I'd not have believed you had you sworn you'd always be faithful," she said, and Davydd finally saw her smile.

Davydd grinned and reached over, took the wine cup out of her hand. "Slow down with that wine, sweetheart. Wine works wonders for seductions, but I need you sober for a serious conversation about marriage."

"What is there to say? We both know that the King is giving me no choice in this."

Davydd slid his fingers under her chin, tilted her face up toward his. "Is it so strange that I'd want your consent? I've never enjoyed riding an unwilling horse."

To his amusement, Elizabeth blushed. "This is so odd," she said shyly, "this talking in the dark. I can tell that you're tall, but not much more. Do you . . . do you look like you sound?"

"How do I sound?" he asked, predictably, and before she could stop herself, she blurted out, "Dangerous!" He laughed, and she could feel her face getting hot again. "You sound," she said tartly, "like the sort of man my stepmother is always warning me about!"

He had drawn back into the shadows; she could hear him moving about the chamber. "That ought to be enough to send you racing into my arms, then. Do you not always do the very opposite of what Stepmother wants?"

Elizabeth did not know what to say to that; she'd never met anyone who talked like Davydd, saying outrageous things in the most matter-of-fact way. A sudden spark flared; Davydd had found flint and tinder. As the lamp's flame shot upward, she hastily averted her eyes. She could feel his gaze upon her, almost like a physical touching. Would he be pleased with her, find her pretty? When she mustered enough nerve to look up, she saw that he was smiling.

"Shall I give you your first Welsh lesson, cariad? 'Trech wyneb teg na gwaddol,' or, 'better a fair face than a dowry.' Fortunately for me, you have both, for I've always been a greedy sort!"

Elizabeth joined in his laughter; she was learning to like the sound of it. "My hair is a pale flaxen shade," she volunteered, for she was very proud of that; no hair color was more prized than hers. "See," she said, reaching up and unpinning the braid at the nape of her neck. Pulling it free of the wimple draping her throat, she triumphantly held up a plait of pure silver.

Davydd entwined the braid around his fingers, wondering if the hair between her legs was as blonde and silky. "How long do you mean to keep me in suspense, Elizabeth de Ferrers? Shall I have to drag you, kicking and clawing, down the church aisle?"

Elizabeth tried to look shocked and disapproving, but the corners of her mouth were curving up. Davydd brushed her cheek lightly with the tip of her braid. "Why are you still balking, cariad? Just what were you looking for in a husband? Not many mortal men have haloes."

"I was not seeking a . . . a saint," Elizabeth protested. "I just wanted what every woman wants, a man cheerful and good-natured, a devout Christian, a . . ." She was having unexpected difficulty concentrating upon the question. His mustache was lighter in color than his hair, held golden glints, and she found herself wondering if it would tickle when he kissed her.

"Then I am still in the race, for I'm good-natured even early in the morn, and I am for certes a Christian. Not even my worst enemies have ever accused me of being a heathen! Go on, what else?"

"He . . . he should be brave." Elizabeth faltered; he was stroking her cheek with her own braid again.

"Well, I agreed to marry you sight unseen. What could be braver than that?" She giggled and he moved closer. "What other virtues must your husband possess?"

Elizabeth tilted her head so she could look up into his eyes, green and glittering and surprisingly long-lashed. "He . . . he should be generous and good-hearted and . . ." She got no further; he'd begun to laugh again.

"Alas," he said, shaking his head in mock regret, "that I am not."

Elizabeth was flustered. "Not . . . not generous?"

"No . . . good," he said softly, and Elizabeth felt an odd shiver go up her spine, a physical chill that was both fear and excitement.

Davydd was very close now; his hand slid down her arm, propelling her forward until their bodies were touching. "Say yes, Elizabeth. I'll teach you to swear in Welsh and laugh in bed, and we'll have handsome children for certes!"

Elizabeth had the strangest sensation, almost of vertigo, as if she were teetering upon a cliff's edge. She hesitated a moment longer, and then let herself go, trusting in Davydd to catch her as she fell. "Yes," she breathed, "yes," raising her face for his kiss.

Davydd was too tall to embrace Elizabeth comfortably, a problem he solved by pulling her toward the chair, sitting down, and drawing her onto his lap. Edward had been right about her; she was featherlight and willow-slim, but he was discovering that her body was soft, with more curves than he'd first thought. He kept her kisses gentle, soon felt her lips part, her arms go up around his neck.

Elizabeth was lost, amazed by her own body, by feelings unfamiliar, erotic, and compelling; she never heard the door opening. But Davydd did, glancing up in time to see Edward come to an abrupt halt. And the startled look on Edward's face was sweeter even than Elizabeth's eager, virginal kisses.

ON November 12th of God's Year, 1276, the royal council of the English King judged Llewelyn ap Gruffydd to be in rebellion, and war was declared against Wales.

17

WINDSOR CASTLE, ENGLAND

May 1277

Upon his arrival at Windsor, Roger de Mortimer found Edward and Edmund in the sunlit upper bailey, watching a shooting match. Edward was in an expansive, relaxed mood; few would have suspected he was a man about to lead an army into Wales. "You're just in time, Roger. I want you to see this."

They'd already drawn a number of spectators, men as intrigued by the contest as by the King's presence, for the archers were not using the crossbow. The staves of these weapons were much longer than those of the more familiar bow, more than five feet in length, and they were firing fletched arrows with eye-blurring speed, evoking murmurs of awe from those watching.

Not from de Mortimer, though, for he was no stranger to the longbow; it was the weapon of choice in much of Wales, particularly in the South. Moreover, he was travel-stained and saddle-sore and irked by the nonchalance of Edward's greeting.

Although Edward did not expect to take the field himself until the summer, he had been waging war against the Welsh for months, having launched a three-pronged assault upon Llewelyn's lands from Carmarthen, Montgomery, and Chester. His battle commanders had won some impressive victories, but none had been as spectacularly successful as de Mortimer, for in April he had seized Llewelyn's castle at Dolforwyn and restored Gruffydd ap Gwenwynwyn to power in Powys. Having dealt Llewelyn ap Gruffydd such a crippling blow, de Mortimer felt that he deserved a more effusive welcome than he'd gotten, and he listened impatiently as Edward extolled the virtues of the Welsh longbow instead of his own exploits.

"Yes, yes, I know," he said testily, "the longbow has a greater range. And Your Grace is right; it is more easily mastered than the crossbow. But do you not want to hear my report?"

"Why? After all, you sent me word as soon as Dolforwyn and Buellt fell. What more is there to say?"

De Mortimer's fatigue had dulled his perception. His temper flared; not until Edward laughed did he realize he was being teased. Waving the others away, Edward clapped him playfully upon the back. "Tell us," he said, "and leave nothing out. If ever a man was entitled to boast a bit, you are for certes!"

Mollified, de Mortimer began, "Well, it was lack of water that forced the Dolforwyn garrison to surrender . . ." By the time he concluded, the sun was hovering over the horizon, reflecting the burnt orange of a summer dusk. "And ere I left Buellt, I gave orders to begin construction of a new castle on the site. The old one was razed to the ground by Llewelyn years ago, was beyond restoring. But once it is done, you'll command the entire Wye Valley."

"What of Llewelyn ap Gruffydd? Are his whereabouts known?"

"I heard that he was fighting along the Upper Severn. He's all but lived in the saddle for months now, trying to hold back the tide. But once you cross the River Dee, he'll disappear into the fastness of Snowdon, dare us to follow. This is what the Welsh always do. You can rarely draw them into a pitched battle. They prefer will-o'-the-wisp tactics, excel at ambush and night raids, and when you try to track them down, they disappear into blue smoke."

"They'd be fools to do otherwise," Edward said matter-of-factly. "No Welsh prince could ever hope to put as many men in the field as the English Crown can. So they rely upon that godforsaken, wild land of theirs to repel invaders. And often as not, it does. My great-grandfather, my grandfather, and my father—at one time or another, they all braved those Welsh mountain passes, and they all ended up fleeing back across the border, marking their trail with wooden crosses, shallow graves."

Edward, too, had sought conquest and glory in Wales, had suffered a humiliating defeat at Llewelyn's hands. But de Mortimer was not the fool who'd remind him of that youthful failure; he kept a prudent silence.

"No," Edward concluded, "whenever we did prevail, it was because we were able to turn their own weaknesses against them. Thank God they're such a jealous, quarrelsome people, more suspicious of one another than any enemy beyond their borders."

De Mortimer grinned. "Ah, we're talking now of Davydd, are we? I do owe you a debt, Ned, for not sending him to fight alongside me.

I hear he has driven poor Warwick well nigh mad with his griping and swaggering. Is it true he dared to demand that his men be paid wages, as if he were an English lord? That he even balked at sharing the booty from his raids into Wales?"

Edward nodded ruefully. "All true and a trial to my patience, I must admit. Having him with us, though, is like having a lance leveled at Llewelyn's throat, so it is worth the trouble to keep him content. Bear that in mind, Roger, for he's on his way to Windsor even as we speak. Warwick warned me that he's heard rumors about English lords laying claim to Welsh lands once the war is done, so we're going to be treated to yet another spectacle of Welsh indignation at full blaze. But now that you know, resist the temptation to bait him, if you please. He will be difficult enough to placate as it is."

De Mortimer made a gesture of exaggerated, extravagant submission. "As Your Grace wills it, so shall it be . . . even if it does spoil my fun! Now, if you have no further need of me, I am going to find myself a bath and a bed and a wench."

Edmund had so far taken no part in the conversation. But as de Mortimer started to turn away, he said, "Roger, wait. There is something I would say to you. As you know, our kinswoman, Eleanor de Montfort, is dwelling here within the castle. Upon his past visits to Windsor, my brother has made her welcome at his court, and I assume this visit will be no different. But I have no doubt that Ellen would find your presence painful—"

"Why?" De Mortimer's brows rose mockingly. "Because I adorned my gatehouse at Wigmore with her whoreson father's head? Surely the lass would not hold a grudge over a trifle like that?"

Edmund was not amused. "Stay away from her, Roger," he said bluntly.

De Mortimer's surprise was no longer feigned. "And if I do not?"

"You'll be giving grief to a girl who has had more than her share. And you'll be making an enemy, one you'll not want."

De Mortimer laughed. "I think I can bear the great burden of Ellen de Montfort's enmity!"

"Not Ellen . . . me," Edmund said, and Roger de Mortimer stopped laughing. To Edmund, it was like watching a house preparing for a siege, shutters slamming, bolts sliding into place; de Mortimer's face went blank, black eyes narrowing in sudden, wary appraisal. It was a look he'd never given Edmund before, one that took an adversary's measure and found reason for caution. It was a look Edmund liked. He rarely felt the need to wield his power as the King's brother in so blatant a fashion, but he never forgot that he had it. After today, he knew de Mortimer would not forget it, either.

Edward had been an interested, amused witness to this exchange. He genuinely enjoyed Roger de Mortimer's company, but he also enjoyed seeing the cocky Marcher lord discomfited, and he moved to Edmund's side, watching as de Mortimer strode away.

"Very deftly done, Little Brother," he said approvingly. "Roger needs to be thwarted from time to time, or else he tends to become utterly insufferable. But you need not have feared for Ellen. I care as much for her welfare as you do, would not stand idly by if she were being baited by Roger."

Edmund gave him a startled, searching look, but he could find no evidence of irony in his brother's last words; apparently Edward saw no conflict in being both Ellen's protector and her gaoler. "Ned . . . we're well into her second year of confinement. Surely you do not mean to hold her indefinitely?"

"Of course not! I truly do care for the lass, Edmund, and not just because she's Harry's sister. She has pluck and common sense, and the very sight of her is enough to please any man not stone-blind!" Edward grinned. "No, I wish her well, and if I can, I will see her wed to her willful Welsh Prince. If I cannot, I'll find her a more suitable husband. One way or another, we'll soon know what her future holds."

"And what do you think the future holds for Wales?" Edmund was very curious about his brother's ultimate aims in this war, felt he had a right to know, for he was to command Edward's army in South Wales. "I understand that you've ordered your Justiciar to introduce English law into Ireland, saying that Irish law is 'detestable to God.' I assume you are no less disapproving, then, of Welsh law and custom. And I know full well that you and Llewelyn ap Gruffydd were fated to clash, for you see him as just another of your vassals whilst he stubbornly insists upon seeing himself as an independent ally. So you have compelling reasons, both as a Christian and as a King, to seek the conquest of Wales. And I cannot help wondering if that is what you mean to do."

Edward looked thoughtfully at the younger man. "What you say is true enough. As England's King, I do believe Wales must be more securely yoked to the Crown. And as a Christian, I have a duty to wean the Welsh away from their more heathenish practices. But I am also a soldier, lad, am not about to snatch at any crown that comes within reach, the way our father would, never thinking to count the cost. Look at the needless trouble he brought upon himself by trying to make you King of Sicily! Yes, I want Wales. I am not sure, though, that it would be worth the price I'd have to pay. We'll have to see what happens,

Edmund, once we've brought Llewelyn to bay. Then . . . mayhap then we'll know what God wants me to do.''

WINDSOR had always been a favorite residence of the English kings, and Edward was no exception. This was his fourth visit since Ellen had been brought from Bristol Castle, and each time the royal entourage rode into the lower bailey, she was assailed by such a conflicting welter of emotions that she despaired of ever sorting them out. She'd been a prisoner now for seventeen months, and she was starved for news of the world beyond Windsor, desperate for any scrap of information about her husband or brother. She was also so lonely, so bored, and so restless that she welcomed the excitement of Edward's arrival, welcomed any escape from the deadly monotony of her days. One faded into the other, her life trickling away like the grains of sand in the hourglass by her bed, and if she found her comfortable confinement so onerous, what in God's Sweet Mercy must it be like for Amaury?

And yet the mere sight of Edward was enough to set Ellen's every nerve on edge; it was, she thought, the way a rabbit must feel when it caught the scent of fox. After an evening in her cousin's company, she was often too tense to sleep, for the pretense was taking its toll. She was finding it harder and harder to hide her true feelings, to play the role Edward expected, that of Harry's sweet little sister, an innocent pawn in need of male protection.

How could Edward be so blind? She and Juliana spent endless hours attempting to puzzle it out, for she was terrified that she might make a misstep, give herself away. They'd finally concluded that even the cleverest of men could have a flawed imagination, be utterly unable to put himself in another man's place, to see any point of view but his own.

That made sense of sorts to Ellen, for it also seemed to explain why Edward could not admit that Llewelyn had genuine grievances. She well knew that if Llewelyn had dared to harbor a man who'd plotted Edward's assassination, her cousin would have been outraged. Yet he'd not only sheltered Davydd and Gruffydd ap Gwenwynwyn, he shrugged off Llewelyn's complaints as if they were of no consequence.

Ellen suspected that most men shared Edward's affliction to some degree; her own brothers had, for certes. But whilst such singlemindedness had been vexing at times in Harry or Bran, it was truly frightening in a man who wielded the manifold and God-given powers of kingship.

Much to Ellen's disappointment, Hugh was not with Edward. He had been left behind at Westminster to nurse an infected tooth, would not be joining them until Edward departed for the west on June 10th. Questioning Edward at length, Ellen had been able to satisfy herself that Hugh's malady was not life-threatening. But Hugh was her only window to the world, and she felt his loss keenly, now more than ever, with war so close at hand.

She discovered, though, that even with Hugh gone, she would not have to face Edward alone and friendless, for Edmund and his wife were part of the royal entourage. Ellen and Blanche had known each other in France; in the years before her marriage to the King of Navarre, Blanche was often at the French court, a favorite with her aunt, Marguerite, and her cousin, Philippe. And with Edmund, Ellen did not have to feign affection. She did not even mind that he had been given her father's forfeited earldom, for he had played no part in her family's downfall, having been stranded in France until after Evesham.

But that nostalgic childhood fondness flared into intense, heartfelt gratitude once Blanche confided that Edmund had tried to persuade Edward to move Amaury from Corfe to Sherborne, a castle under his control. Ellen did not doubt that Edmund would be a far more generous gaoler than his brother, and she clung to the hope that he might yet sway Edward. It was a frail hope—she knew that—but the only one Amaury had.

WATCHING as Eleanora bade goodnight to her small son, Alfonso, Blanche observed, "That is a rare sight, indeed, England's Queen without a swelling belly. But it's been fully a twelvemonth since she was brought to bed of her last babe. So any day now I expect an announcement that yet another one is due."

Ellen nodded. "I cannot help wondering," she said, "if those constant pregnancies, one right after another, might be why her babies are so sickly. She never has a chance to regain her strength, does she? My mother raised six out of seven children, but Eleanora . . . My God, Blanche, she's lost five of her ten so far. How strong she must be, to have survived such sorrow . . ."

Blanche hesitated, on the verge of sharing a crucial confidence, that she suspected herself to be with child. But she did not, for she enjoyed keeping secrets; not even Edmund knew yet. "Edward has been very attentive to you tonight. Does he always show you such favor, Ellen?"

"Yes, we are very friendly, my cousin and I. He thinks it is quite natural that I should let bygones be bygones. I daresay he expects me to bid him a fond farewell on Thursday next, waving gaily from my prison window as he rides off to make war upon my husband."

"Ah, Ellen, be bitter if you will. God knows you're entitled. But self-pity serves for naught. Do not give in to it, not yet. I have a suggestion to make . . . if you're interested?"

"You know I am, Blanche. What do you have in mind?"

"Well . . . you'll not like it, not at first. Just do not dismiss it out of hand. I was watching as you and Edward were dancing earlier. He fancies you, girl. No—hear me out! If I'm right and he is partial to you, you'd be a fool not to use it against him. Flirt with him, flatter him, and—"

"I think you must be mad! Jesú, Blanche, how could you even suggest—"

"I'm not saying you should let him bed you! Just . . . just a bit of dalliance. It would cost you nothing and might gain you a great deal."

"You have an odd notion as to what comprises a risk. What happens when this little game of yours runs its course and he expects it to end in his bed?"

"Dearest, you say no, as simple as that! I'll grant you that a woman's no would not matter to some men. But I've never heard it said that Edward was one to force a woman against her will. I'm sure he strays from time to time, but he's most discreet about it. Why, he almost qualifies as a faithful husband! And for a king, that is truly remarkable, you must admit. Clearly this is a man who is ruled by his head, not his loins. And you have the perfect excuse, should it ever come to that. You're his first cousin, after all. To couple with him would be a mortal sin, no? So if need be, remind him of that. Or use that wedding ring on your finger. Men always expect women to take marriage vows more seriously than they do; if truth be told, they get downright uneasy when we do not!"

Ellen was laughing now in spite of herself. "Ah, Blanche, you have not changed a whit! But I cannot do what you suggest. I find it hard enough to be civil to Edward. Whenever I smile up at him, all I can see is Amaury, shackled to a bed in the cabin of that wretched cog."

Blanche frowned. "I do not like to hear you talk like this, Ellen. You sound as if you've given up all hope."

"I know," Ellen admitted, and smiled wryly. "If I were a rope, I'd be frayed to the breaking point. There are so many times when I truly think I cannot endure a moment more. But I must, and so I do."

Blanche reached out, gave Ellen's arm a sympathetic squeeze. "I would to God I had words of cheer. But all I have is a warning. The King is coming this way."

"WHENEVER you get that distant, distracted look, I can wager that you are contemplating some sort of mischief," Edmund murmured, slipping his arm around Blanche's waist. "Dare I hope it might take place in bed?"

"Oh, you can always hope." Blanche leaned back into his embrace. "Actually, I was plotting a crime."

He understood at once; he was far more attuned to the unspoken than most men. "Breaking out of Windsor Castle will not be easy, love. I hope you reconsider. Having lost one wife to fever, I'd rather not lose a second to the gallows." His attempt at humor falling flat, he nuzzled her cheek. "Sweetheart, you know I sympathize with Ellen's plight. But she'll not be held much longer. Ned assures me of that, says it will soon be over."

"Yes, but how? I'd not see Ellen a widow ere she had a chance to be a wife." Blanche sighed, but she let the subject drop. Why should she punish Edmund for his brother's misdeeds? She was about to ask him to dance when there was a sudden stir at the end of the hall. Turning to watch the man who'd paused, deliberately and dramatically, in the doorway, she wondered aloud, "Do you think Davydd ap Gruffydd ever enters a room the way other men do, just walks in without seeking to attract attention, to turn heads?"

"Only if he's trying to sneak into some absent husband's bed. Now, that surprises me; he's brought Elizabeth with him. I wonder why he did not leave her at Frodesham, that Cheshire manor he coaxed out of Ned. Davydd is the last man I'd expect to be playing the doting bridegroom."

"Edmund, use the eyes God gave you! It is obvious why he has her in tow, because she'd not be parted from him. You need only look at them to see it. That poor lass is daft about him. But then, she's too young yet to know no man deserves to be loved that much, least of all, hers."

"No man? Not even me?" Edmund laughed, and then swore. "Christ on the Cross—Ellen! I warned de Mortimer away from her, but I never gave a thought to Davydd!"

Edmund often thought he and Blanche made an excellent team; she proved it now. "I'll intercept Davydd and the little bride. You go find Ellen, ask her to dance, to run away with you, whatever it takes."

She was as good as her word, soon had Davydd and Elizabeth engaged in animated conversation. Edmund was not as successful, for the dancing had begun again, and by the time he spotted Ellen, the carol had swept her and Edward into Davydd's line of vision. Hastening across the hall, Edmund saw Davydd break away from his wife and Blanche. He could only shove his way toward them, knowing he'd be too late.

Ellen at once noticed Davydd's approach, and for a moment, she let herself hope that this Welshman might be one of Llewelyn's envoys, for Edward had permitted her to meet with the Bishop of St Asaph that

past year. But Davydd's obeisance was flavored with too much familiarity. Puzzled and curious, she moved closer. And then she drew a
sharp breath, for she realized who he was. The brother who'd plotted
Llewelyn's murder.

Edward knew that Davydd invariably trailed trouble in his wake,
knew, too, that it would be no easy task allaying Davydd's suspicions.
But he was pleased, nevertheless, to see Davydd, for whatever his other
failings, the Welshman was always amusing company. "I've been expecting you," he said affably, waving Davydd to his feet. "I understand
you've grown tired of bedeviling Warwick, think it is my turn. But not
tonight, so hoard your grievances till the morrow. Now . . . tell me how
my little cousin fares. Does she like Cheshire?"

"Your Grace can ask her yourself, for she is here with me. I was
loath to leave her," Davydd said blandly, "we being so recently wed.
And as I know just how much Elizabeth's happiness matters to you, I
daresay you'll be delighted to learn that she is so content."

Edward tried not to laugh, and failed. "You sound even more smug
than usual, which must mean that you've managed to do it again, to
bedazzle yet another innocent lass! In truth, I have never understood
your success. I've always found women to be cautious, timid creatures,
leery of taking risks, wanting comfort and security above all else. It
would go against the natural order of things to see a cat surrounded by
mice, begging to be eaten. So how, then, do you end up with mice
beyond counting?"

By now, Davydd was laughing, too; he enjoyed their jousting fully
as much as Edward. "Mayhap because I do not think women are cautious, timid creatures, leery of taking risks, wanting comfort and security
above all else. But then, why not let the mice speak for themselves? The
hall is full of lovely ladies. Why not ask them what they seek in a man?"

Davydd's borderline insolences usually irritated any English within
earshot; Eleanora was not alone in wondering why Edward indulged
him. But this was the sort of game all enjoyed, verbal sparring between
the sexes. Most of the women listening would have been quite willing
to take Davydd's side. Unfortunately for him, when he looked about
for allies, he chose the prettiest woman present—Ellen.

"What say you, my lady? Are Englishwomen truly timid and cautious? Or are Englishmen merely the most credulous in Christendom?"

Edward had forgotten Ellen was nearby. Swinging about, he saw
at once that she knew, that Davydd did not. He'd rarely had Davydd
at such a disadvantage; the temptation to stand aside and savor the
moment was considerable. But Ellen's silence was like sheeted ice, likely
to splinter with her next breath. "I think," he said, "that I ought to
introduce you, Davydd, to my cousin, the Lady Eleanor de Montfort."

Davydd's surprise was evident; there was an awkward silence. But he made a quick recovery, smiled as if nothing was amiss. "I'd heard you were here, Lady Eleanor," he murmured, with an oblique, glinting glance toward Edward. "But since I knew the King's Grace is holding you against your will, I assumed you'd be locked up somewhere. Welsh prisoners rarely get to dine with their captors."

Davydd saw, to his satisfaction, that he'd annoyed Edward, and he now took advantage of a servant's passing to snatch wine cups from the man's up-raised platter. "Just what we need," he said, and thrust dripping cups at Edward and Ellen. "Shall we drink to my brother's bride?"

Ellen would normally have been grateful to have Edward's court reminded that she was indeed a prisoner, being held very much against her will. But now she could think only that the man standing before her was the brother who'd betrayed Llewelyn, who'd played into Edward's hands at every turn. If not for Davydd, Llewelyn would have been able to do homage as Edward demanded, and mayhap then Edward would not have felt so threatened by her marriage, mayhap he'd not have sent Thomas the Archdeacon after the *Holy Cross*. Because of Davydd's treachery, Amaury was shut away from the sun, she had yet to look upon the man she'd married, and Llewelyn might well be dead ere this wretched war was done.

Wine sloshed from her cup, spilled over her fingers, so tightly was she gripping the stem. The urge to fling the contents into Davydd's face was overpowering, but she still clung to the shreds of her self-control. Instead, she held her cup out at arm's length, then tilted it, slowly and deliberately poured the wine into the floor rushes at Davydd's feet.

Edward had given up the hope of ever seeing Davydd thoroughly discomfited—until now. For an endless and—to Edward—enormously gratifying moment, Davydd was at a loss for words. Then he rallied his defenses and shrugged. "I suppose," he said, "that this means I shall not be invited to the wedding." He got what he'd aimed for—laughter— but the flippancy was belied by the angry color still staining his face and throat.

Ellen had already turned away; Edward was following. Davydd envied them their exit, for he would rather have been anywhere else in Christendom than the great hall of Windsor Castle. But he would not retreat, would never give his English audience that satisfaction. He looked down at his wine cup, then raised it to his lips, discovering— too late—that it was hippocras, a wine so heavily sugared and spiced that he almost gagged. Even the English taste in wines was noxious. Leave it to Llewelyn to find himself a woman just as self-righteous as he was. And she was beautiful, too, the de Montfort bitch. Llewelyn would likely be smitten at first sight—if ever he saw her. Davydd drank again, deeply; this time it went down more easily. He was about to drain the cup dry when he felt a hand tugging at his arm.

"Davydd? What has happened?" Elizabeth's blue eyes were anxious, for although Blanche had managed to keep her out of earshot, she knew at once that something was wrong; she was learning to read Davydd as monks read their prayer books.

Davydd lowered the wine cup. He'd deliberately set out to make her fall in love with him, in part because it made sense to have a fond wife, in part to see if he could. But it had not been much of a challenge, had been almost too easy. No one had ever shown Elizabeth tenderness before; it had taken no more than that. Once he realized the extent of his victory, Davydd had been assailed by qualms, fearing that he might drown in her devotion, find it cloying, a surfeit of sweets. Much to his surprise, he found that he liked it. Other women had loved him, of course, or so they'd claimed, but they'd not been his, and no one had ever loved him the way Elizabeth did, utterly and unconditionally and wholeheartedly. He'd thought himself to be familiar with love in all its erotic guises, had not known it could be soothing, too.

"Davydd? Can you not tell me what is amiss?"

"Later, cariad," he said, and found a passable smile for her. "I'll tell you later." And the odd thing, he thought, was that he probably would.

ELLEN wanted only to escape the hall, and she followed Edward like a sleepwalker, let him lead her out into the mild June night. "I think you need some time away from prying eyes," he said, and steered her across the bailey. Moments later, she found herself sitting upon a bench in the chapel gardens where she'd once plotted an escape with Hugh, watching Edward stride back and forth in the moonlight, filling the cloisters with echoes of his laughter.

"I nearly bit my tongue off, trying to keep from laughing aloud. Bless you, lass, for you've given me a memory to cherish into my dotage. I never thought it was possible to catch Davydd off balance; God knows, I've tried often enough!"

At last becoming aware of Ellen's silence, Edward moved toward the bench. "You still have not gotten your color back. Davydd truly did distress you; I can see that now. You're very loyal, Ellen. Llewelyn is luckier than he knows."

"I doubt that Llewelyn feels very lucky these days," Ellen said softly. Edward came closer. Straddling the bench, he reached over, tilted her face up toward his. Ellen went rigid at the touch of his fingers on her throat. *He fancies you, girl.* But after giving her a long, intent look, he leaned back, put space between them.

"An interesting evening, and a revealing one. I discovered that Davydd is not as imperturbable as he pretends to be, and that you do have a temper, after all, Little Cousin. I often wondered about that, for Aunt Nell could flare up faster than Greek fire, and Simon's temper was even quicker to kindle. I was beginning to suspect you must be a foundling."

Ellen managed a flickering smile, fidgeted with her wedding ring. She knew he must see how nervous she was, but she could not bring herself to meet his eyes; his gaze was coolly probing, speculative, daunting.

"I meant it when I commended you upon your loyalty, Ellen. That is an admirable trait. I daresay Llewelyn ap Gruffydd would be heartened to know that you've made his enemies your own. It does make me curious, though. When you tally up Llewelyn's grievances, why give so much more weight to Davydd's sins? I am his enemy, too, am I not?"

Ellen's mouth had gone dry. "Yes," she agreed, "you are his enemy." She swallowed, then raised her lashes, looked him full in the face. "But you are not his brother. You never betrayed him, or took advantage of his trust. You never sat across a table from him, smiled whilst knowing your hired killers were on the way!"

Her voice had risen, the rage spilling out at last. But it gave her outburst the ring of truth. Even before he nodded, she saw that he believed her. "I would that I could promise you a happy ending, Ellen," he said quietly. "But I cannot, and we both know that."

She nodded, too, thinking that she'd liked it better when he lied.

THE grass was littered with rose petals. Ellen had plucked them, one by one, until only the stem remained. It had taken her a while to convince Edward to return to the hall without her. He had balked at first, not agreeing until she confessed the truth, that she yearned, above all else, for time alone. He'd gone then, reluctantly, but he was likely to send someone out to check upon her if she did not soon return to the hall. She knew that he did not fear she might escape, for what was she to do, jump over the walls, tunnel under them? No, she was coming to believe that his concern for her well-being was genuine. But it mattered for naught; he'd not be swayed by sentiment. Amaury could rot at Corfe Castle for the rest of his days. Llewelyn could lose all in this coming war, even his life. And there was nothing she could do for either of them.

"My lady." She'd not heard the footsteps on the grassy inner garth, and she jumped hastily to her feet, resentful that her solitude had been cut so short. But her irritation vanished as soon as she recognized the man coming toward her. Nicholas de Waltham was a Gilbertine canon from Lincoln, a man whose loyalty to the de Montfort family had endured, both in good times and bad. Ellen had noticed his arrival that morning, but had been chary of seeking him out in public, for his de Montfort credentials were well-known; Nell had even named him as one of the executors of her will. What was not known, though, except to a select few, was that Master Nicholas was also a spy, Llewelyn's eyes and ears at the English King's court.

"When I saw you leave the hall with the King, I seized my chance," he said, and kissed her hand with a gallant flourish, for his manners had always been more evocative of the court than the priesthood. "But I'd best get right to the heart of the matter, for we ought not to be seen alone together." Reaching into the tunic of his cassock, he drew forth a small prayer book. "Reading this psalter will give you solace," he said sententiously, and then grinned. "But it will give you joy, too, especially the letter hidden within the binding—a message from your lord husband."

Nicholas de Waltham well knew the risks he took, but moments like this made it worthwhile, for Ellen was looking at him as if he were a candidate for canonization. He'd wager it was a long time since anyone had seen the Earl's lass smile the way she was now smiling at him, and as he smiled back, it was almost as if he were still serving Earl Simon.

"Lord Llewelyn is greatly concerned, my lady, that you do not despair. He worries lest you feel he has forsaken you, says—"

"No! Master Nicholas, that is not so! You must tell Llewelyn that for me, tell him that I know all he has done on my behalf. I know that he has appealed to the Pope. I know of the large ransom he offered for me. And I know that he even agreed to do homage as Edward demanded, offering to come to Montgomery or Oswestry under safe conduct—if only I were freed. Do you think I do not understand what it cost him to make that offer? He has nothing to reproach himself for, Master Nicholas, nothing!"

"So I told him, too. But it will mean more, I suspect, coming from you. Now . . . I have some news about your brother. His Holiness the Pope has instructed the Archbishop of Canterbury to speak out again on Amaury's behalf; they are seeking to have Amaury transferred into the custody of the Church. The Pope continues, too, to urge Edward to set you free. As does the King of France. So you see, my lady, you are not friendless, have not been forgotten."

"How glad I am," Ellen said, "that you sought me out tonight, for I was much in need of cheer. Master Nicholas . . . is there any way you could get a letter back to my husband?"

"I fear not. The roads have already become too dangerous, and once the King crosses into Wales . . ." He hesitated. "My lady . . . there is something else you must know, and I'd rather you hear it from me. The Archbishop of Canterbury has acted to excommunicate Prince Llewelyn and lay Wales under Interdict. It was done at the King's behest, of course. It is indeed sad, my lady, that political needs should carry such weight in spiritual matters, but that is the way of our world. The very threat of excommunication is enough to strike fear in any man's soul, and for that very reason, it is so effective—and so often abused. My lady, I know of a case where a Bishop excommunicated the men who dared trespass in his hunting park! Can you believe that the Almighty would deny a man salvation for so trivial a sin?"

"There is no need to convince me, Master Nicholas. I well know how meaningless—and how unjust—excommunication can be. I am Simon de Montfort's daughter, after all. No more devout Christian ever drew breath than my father, yet he died excommunicate, made an outcast amongst men of faith—because the Pope would curry favor with England's King."

Nicholas nodded. "I am glad you see that, my lady. Now I'd best get back to the hall ere I'm missed. But I do not want to leave you . . ."

"I think I'd like to be alone," Ellen said, mustering up one last smile for his benefit. But as soon as his footsteps faded away, she sank down on the bench. For all her brave talk about the dubious worth of a politically motivated damnation, it was not so easy to defy the teachings of a lifetime, and it chilled her to realize that Llewelyn must ride into battle with God's curse upon him.

Clutching the psalter to her breast, she made a hasty sign of the cross. "How can you ever forgive me, Llewelyn," she whispered, "for what I've brought upon you?"

18

ABERCONWY ABBEY, WALES

July 1277

Eₙɢʟɪsʜ invading armies rarely penetrated so far west. But whenever they did succeed in crossing the Conwy, they invariably fell upon the abbey spread out along the river's left bank, plundered and looted and burned. In these hot, humid July days, the White Monks of the Cistercian abbey of St Mary dreaded what might lie ahead for them.

Rumors traveled even faster than Llewelyn's hard-riding scouts in this summer of fear and foreboding. All knew that the English King had reached Chester, that he was poised for an assault into the very heartland of Llewelyn's realm. The monks knew, too, that he had assembled the largest army ever to threaten Gwynedd, four hundred archers and cross-bowmen, more than fifteen thousand foot-soldiers. After months of border raids, after months of turmoil along the Marches, after months of tension and reversals and retreats, the conflagration seemed almost upon them, and they could only search the horizon with anxious eyes, awaiting the first smudges of smoke.

The monks were much heartened, therefore, by the unexpected arrival of their Prince. They took an instinctive, elemental comfort in his presence, made excuses to neglect their chores and slipped into the guest hall, where they kept inconspicuously to the shadows, following Llewelyn with eyes full of faith, expectant in spite of themselves, willing him to find one more miracle for their abbey, for Wales.

Llewelyn's relations with the Welsh Church were not always harmonious; he'd had serious disputes with both the Bishop of Bangor and the Bishop of St Asaph. But with the White Monks of Wales, he had forged a bond beyond breaking. They scorned the Archbishop of Canterbury's English edict, scorned the perfidy of the Bishop of Bangor, the only Welsh prelate willing to publish the excommunication order, which he'd done with unseemly stealth, just before fleeing to England.

Cowardice seemed to be catching, the monks agreed. Most of their Prince's Welsh allies had bolted to the English camp. And the rumor sweeping the guest hall was that Prince Llewelyn was at Aberconwy to await a prisoner, one of his own bailiffs, seized ere he could flee to Edward. They speculated among themselves as to the identity of this latest traitor, damning him all the while in most un-monk-like language. Let others think only of saving their own skins. They'd hold fast, would not abandon their lord. And if they truly were facing Armageddon, then by the soul of St Davydd, they'd face it together, as Welshmen and Christians and free men.

As he moved among them, their Abbot heard these whispered pledges of fealty, heard, too, their murmured solicitude, and he had to smile, for these austere brothers of God sounded almost maternal in their worries for their lord's well-being, expressing concern that he was demanding too much of himself, that he was not sleeping or eating as he ought. Although he smiled, Maredudd was inclined to agree with them, for never had he seen Llewelyn so finely drawn, like a man fighting a fever, dark eyes hollowed and glittering, every line of his body communicating a taut, watchful wariness. Even now, sitting at ease in the window-seat, long legs entangled in the sprawled, sleeping wolfhounds at his feet, he put Maredudd in mind of an arrow nocked against a drawn bowstring, ready to fire. Appropriating the nearest man's mead cup, Maredudd carried it across the hall, handed it to his Prince.

Up close, Llewelyn's exhaustion was even more apparent, the sort of fatigue that burned into the bone, so familiar it was no longer noticed. "You look dreadful," the Abbot said, with the candor permitted of a long-time friend, and Llewelyn shrugged, then smiled.

"I know," he conceded. "I almost fell asleep in the saddle this forenoon. Luckily my stallion had no mischief in mind, else I might have gone head over arse into a blackthorn bush. I remember reading that Alexander the Great once stumbled whilst leaping from a boat, sprawled flat in front of his entire army. He saved face, though, by claiming he was embracing the terra firma of the Asian land he'd come to conquer. But the Welsh are a less credulous lot; they'd likely have laughed."

"I'd say that—" Maredudd got no further. Llewelyn was staring past him, toward the door. He turned, felt a jolt at sight of the man being escorted into the hall, shackled at the wrists. He'd thought he was beyond shock, but Rhys ap Gruffydd was a scion of one of the great families of Gwynedd, grandson of Llewelyn Fawr's legendary Seneschal, Ednyved ap Cynwrig. Maredudd liked to believe that breeding mattered, that good blood told in men as it did in horses. Remembering then that

Rhys had been a favorite carousing companion of Davydd ap Gruffydd, he felt some of his surprise begin to recede, for he also believed the Latin maxim, "Qui cum canibus concumbent cum pulicibus surgent." He who lies with dogs will rise with fleas.

Rhys ap Gruffydd was stiff from so many unwilling hours in the saddle. He was also angry and afraid. But after one quick glance about the hall, he decided he had as much to fear from his own kinsmen as he did from his betrayed lord. Llewelyn seemed to have his rage under control. His uncle Tudur, though, looked like a man contemplating a killing. His cousin, Goronwy ap Heilyn, gave him a burning stare, then spat deliberately into the floor rushes. Einion, a kinsman by marriage, wed to Rhys's elder sister, was standing by the door, yet he said not a word as Rhys passed, just slowly shook his head. Rhys swallowed with difficulty. He knew Llewelyn ap Gruffydd had never put a political foe to death. But he'd never been backed onto a cliff's edge before, either.

Rhys had often teased Davydd about his "forked tongue," but he'd have given virtually anything now for the merest measure of Davydd's glibness. Shoved to his knees, he struggled to regain his balance, sought to sound properly indignant as he cried, "My lord Llewelyn, what is this about? If this is the way you treat men of good faith, men loyal—"

"I know." Llewelyn did not raise his voice. Yet those two softly uttered words set the blood thudding in Rhys's ears. He'd always known Llewelyn ap Gruffydd was a dangerous man to cross. But the English King was just as dangerous, so what in Christ's pity was a man supposed to do?

"Did you hear me, Rhys? I said I knew." Llewelyn had not yet risen from the window-seat. Reaching out, he grasped the chain binding Rhys's wrists. "You've been in secret communication with my brother Davydd. He procured for you a royal safe-conduct. And then you waited, trying to judge the most opportune time to go over to Edward. Unfortunately for you, you waited too long."

Llewelyn's voice was still pitched low, but held so much scorn that Rhys flushed darkly. His uncle had moved to Llewelyn's side. "I am thankful," Tudur said roughly, "that your father is not alive to see how you've shamed us, Rhys."

Rhys could have dealt with their anger. But he found now that he could not endure their contempt. With a sudden yank, he sought to pull his shackles free, but Llewelyn had too firm a grip. He tightened the chain around his fist, jerked, and Rhys sprawled into the floor rushes. Hearing laughter, both from Llewelyn's men and the monks, he forgot all else but his own rage.

"I deny nothing," he snarled. "I was indeed going to make peace with the English King. And it would have been an easy trail to take, for I needed only to follow all who'd gone before me—including your own brothers! Yes, I said brothers! Rhodri is with Edward now, too. Ah, you did not know that? It ought not to surprise you. Why should men be willing to die with you? For you are going to die, you know. All of you fools are," he jeered, "unless you save yourselves whilst you still can!"

There was a silence, and then someone—Rhys never knew whether it was a monk or a soldier—shouted, "We'd rather die with our Prince than live as bondsmen under an alien, foreign-tongued King!" But Rhys paid that unknown voice no heed. Panting, he waited for the only verdict that mattered, and as Llewelyn leaned forward, he flinched from what he saw in the other man's eyes. For a moment, Llewelyn pulled the chain taut, then let it go.

"You are the one who is a fool, Rhys," he said scathingly. "We all die sooner or later, every mother's son. But there are far worse ways for a man to die than defending his homeland."

THE church was very still. The scent of incense lingered in the air, and wall torches bathed the choir in flickering red light. Llewelyn did not approach the candle-lit High Altar. God did not serve the King of England, would not deny salvation for the sin of loving Wales. By what right did they dare to appropriate the Almighty, seek to make of Him an accomplice in their plot to annex Wales for the English Crown? But no man was ever utterly deaf to whispers in the dark. When the priests banished an unrepentant soul from God's Grace, they cast flaming candles onto the ground, plunging the church—and the sinner—into darkness. Llewelyn gazed upward, his eyes probing the shadows until he found the carved crucifix high above his head. Only then did he turn back toward the tombs.

He had come to Aberconwy as much for this as for Rhys ap Gruffydd, for here were buried the dead of his House. His grandfather's sepulchre had been given the place of greatest honor, close to the High Altar. Nearby lay his sons, united in death as never they'd been in life. Davydd, the half-English son, Joanna's son, his heir, who'd died before his time. Llewelyn's own father, Gruffydd, the son fated to play Absalom to his sire's David, who'd died in a plunging fall from the uppermost chamber in the Tower of London's great keep. They were all many years dead. Llewelyn had been twelve when the grandfather he'd so loved had gone to God, sixteen when his father's escape attempt failed, and not yet eighteen when his uncle died suddenly at thirty-seven, bequeathing to Llewelyn and his elder brother Owain a land at war with England.

Footsteps sounded in the nave. As the Abbot paused by the rood screen, his gaze fell upon the impressive marble tomb of Llewelyn Fawr, and it occurred to him that history truly did repeat itself, just as men claimed, for these dead Welsh Princes had also been damned by compliant Popes. Thinking there might be comfort for Llewelyn in that, he said, "Your grandfather was excommunicated, too, was he not?"

"Indeed he was, fully three times." Llewelyn smiled as an old memory surfaced. "I remember him joking that he ought to have a turnstile installed in his private chapel. That was always his way; he found few troubles so great that they could not be laughed at. Never have I known a man so free of doubts. He truly could not conceive of defeat. Delays and setbacks, but not defeat. Even death did not daunt him. As he lay dying, he was joking that he must make haste about it, lest he keep his wife, Joanna, waiting. I did not understand, for I was just a lad, and loath to lose him. I demanded to know how he could jest even about death. I've never forgotten his answer. He said simply, 'What other way is there?' "

"Mayhap he could not conceive of defeat, but he knew it, nonetheless," Tudur said, moving into the torchlight. "It was right here at this abbey that he was forced to make an abject surrender to England's King John, forced to give up his own son, your father, as a hostage. Just as his son Davydd was compelled to yield to John's son thirty years later, almost to the very day."

"What are you saying, Tudur?" Llewelyn sounded amused. "That in losing to Edward, I would merely be upholding an old family tradition?"

Tudur gave a snort of abashed laughter. "I must be more tired than I thought. You do not usually read me so easily!"

Llewelyn grinned. "Yes, I do. I just do not always let you know it!"

Maredudd was bemused by their bantering. "How can the two of you be joking, now of all times?"

They both laughed at that. "Because," Tudur said wryly, "the Welsh are always at their best when things are at their worst."

"And," Llewelyn added, just as dryly, "things are so often at their worst that we get plenty of practice in staving off disaster." But he was not surprised when Maredudd still looked uncomprehending, for what could a monk know of soldiers' secrets, or battlefield bravado and gallows humor?

"It is an odd thing, Maredudd," he said, "but sometimes it is almost a relief to have the worst happen, to have the waiting done . . . at last. Can you understand that?"

Maredudd nodded. "Do you see no hope at all then?" he asked quietly, and was startled when Llewelyn responded with an explosive oath.

"Christ's Blood, Maredudd, of course I have hope! I'm still breathing, am I not? Rhys ap Gruffydd is a misbegotten malcontent, not a soothsayer. You need not instruct the bards to begin my eulogy because Rhys claims I am doomed! We still have a chance to stave off disaster again. Edward might be rash enough to follow me into the heights of Eryri. And even if he does keep to the coast, we may be able to wait him out. He will need vast amounts of food to feed that vast army of his. Hunger has sent more than one English king reeling back across the border. Then, too, the Almighty might send the autumn rains early this year, or even better, an early snow. Only a fool would dare attempt a winter campaign in Wales, and Edward Plantagenet is no man's fool."

Llewelyn had moved back to his grandfather's tomb, stood looking down at the red and gold enameled lions, a heraldic device he'd adopted as his own, just as he'd adopted Llewelyn Fawr's ambitious dream, that of a united, independent Wales. He'd never begrudged the cost, was not about to start now.

"So you see," he said, "the outcome of this war is still very much in God's Hands." He paused, then concluded with a gleam of very grim humor, "I only wish I could rid myself of an unsettling suspicion, one that comes too readily to mind whenever I think of our land's never-ending troubles—that God just might be English!"

19

BASINGWERK ABBEY, WALES

August 1277

Eᴅᴡᴀʀᴅ set up his headquarters at the abbey of the Blessed Virgin Mary in mid-July, at once began construction of a castle at the mouth of the River Dee. As soldiers stood guard, workmen began to dig a deep, defensive ditch. Others were dispatched to build a road along the Welsh coast. By month's end, more than two thousand axemen, carpenters, masons, blacksmiths, quarrymen, hod carriers, and charcoal burners were laboring on the King's behalf, and, as they hacked and burned their way through the ancient oak forests that had for so many centuries repelled foreign invaders, it was as if the very landscape of Wales was under assault.

The day was promising scorching heat, for already the sky had taken on a brittle blue-white glaze that put Edward in mind of the sun-bleached sky over Acre. He tilted his head, but could see nary a cloud. So dry had the summer been in this land of lingering mist and iridescent rain that it seemed to Edward's army that even the Almighty was on his side; Edward himself had no doubts whatsoever about that. He took one last approving look at that barren, cloud-free blue above his head, then moved into the shadows of the Chapter House.

The high stone ceiling deflected some of the heat, and as he stepped across the threshold, Edward felt a welcome rush of cooler air upon his face. He was late, his council already assembled. The men lounging on the uncomfortably austere monastery benches leapt to their feet at sight of him, but he waved them back. Striding toward the huge central pillar, he paused for a moment, looking out upon his audience.

They were all here, the premier lords of his realm. John Beauchamp, the Earl of Warwick, who'd had the unenviable task of keeping Davydd ap Gruffydd in good humor. Roger de Mortimer, just come up from Montgomery, and Edmund, his son, whose career in the Church had been aborted by his elder brother's untimely death. Gilbert de Clare, the temperamental Earl of Gloucester, and the unpopular William de Lusignan, King's uncle and Earl of Pembroke. Humphrey de Bohun, the young Earl of Hereford, and Edward's de Warenne cousin, the Earl of Surrey. Otto de Grandison, Burgundian nobleman and King's friend. The Marcher lords, Roger Lestrange and Roger Clifford. John Giffard, a de Montfort partisan who'd been one of the first to abandon the Earl and his doomed cause, ambitious, ruthless, and remarkably able. Bogo de Knovill, the tough, battle-tested sheriff of Shropshire. Reginald de Grey, one-time Justiciar of Chester, a man even more detested by the Welsh than Pembroke. And three men whose presence here gave Edward considerable satisfaction, for all three—Nicholas Segrave, Baldwin Wake, and John d'Eyvill—had been the sworn men of Simon de Montfort, unreconstructed rebels even after Evesham, now dutiful vassals, proving by their compliance that he was not a monarch to be defied with impunity, like his unhappy father, but one to be feared and respected and obeyed, for Edward had never made Henry's mistake, had never been so naive as to believe a king ought to be loved.

As his eyes swept their ranks, a frown began to form. "Where is Davydd ap Gruffydd?"

"Here, my liege, hanging upon your every word." Turning toward the sound of Davydd's voice, Edward saw that the Welsh Prince had ensconced himself in one of the recessed window-seats, lolling back upon cushions, a flagon at his elbow. Edward wondered idly where he'd found cushions in this monk's lair, wondered, too, if he'd bothered to rise with the other men; probably not. But he looked so lazily content that Edward smiled in spite of himself. As vexing as Davydd could be, the challenge of reining him in and breaking him to the royal will was one Edward relished.

"Try not to doze off," he said archly, "for I've a matter to discuss that will actively engage your self-interest. But first, I have news to share. A courier has arrived from my brother. Edmund's army has reached Aberystwyth, and he has begun construction of a new castle for the Crown."

There were pleased murmurs at that. Edward waited until they subsided. "I also have had word from Stephen de Penecestre, the Warden of the Cinque Ports. The fleet is under sail, will be at the mouth of the River Clwyd within a fortnight. Eighteen ships, with another seven to join us next month."

De Mortimer had arrived at Basingwerk Abbey only the day before, and was not conversant, therefore, with Edward's naval strategy. "Why so many ships? You could enforce your embargo with half that number."

"I mean to put them to better use than merely patrolling the Menai Straits, Roger. I mean to land an army upon Anglesey. What do you Welsh call that island, Davydd—Môn? For those of you who are not Marchers, Anglesey is the only fertile, flat land in all of Gwynedd, and harvest time draws nigh." Edward's smile was grim. "Llewelyn hopes to starve us out, the way Welsh princes have always done. But no English king ever had twenty-five ships at his command—until now, and the prideful Prince of Wales is about to learn that hunger can stalk Welsh encampments, too."

Turning back toward Davydd, Edward nodded to Anthony Bek, his clerk. The priest produced a parchment roll, carried it across the chamber, and handed it to Davydd. "A belated birthday gift for the new Lord of Snowdon," Edward said, with another smile, and Davydd sat up suddenly, for the title "Lord of Eryri" was one that belonged to the royal House of Gwynedd.

"Whilst my lord Davydd reads the grant, I shall tell the rest of you what it encompasses. I have promised to vest Davydd and his elder brother Owain in one-half of Gwynedd west of the River Conwy, the other half to remain in the control of the Crown. Should I decide, however, to retain the entire isle of Anglesey, Davydd and Owain shall then divide up all of Gwynedd beyond the Conwy. The four Welsh cantrefs east of the Conwy shall be Crown lands again, as they were in those years between the death of Llewelyn Fawr and the rise to power of Llewelyn ap Gruffydd."

Edward paused to see if anyone wished to comment; no man did. Theirs was the silence, though, of prudence, not approval. The Marcher lords in particular looked disgruntled, and with reason, for this grant would forever alter the balance of power in Wales, making the King of England the greatest Marcher lord of all. Edward was not surprised by their conspicuous lack of enthusiasm, for the Marchers defended their prerogatives with the passion that other men expended upon women, and were, indeed, no less suspicious of the Crown's intent than the Welsh themselves. But Edward had known they would acquiesce, however little they liked it, for they were slowly learning that a new day had dawned in their dealings with their King.

What did surprise Edward, though, was Davydd's continuing silence. He was still studying the document, his face hidden; Edward could see only a thick thatch of hair, reddish-brown where the sunlight struck it, dark in the shadows. "Well?" he demanded, only partly in jest. "I've just offered you half of a kingdom, for Christ's pity! Have you nothing to say? I should think a 'thank you' would be in order at the very least!"

Davydd's head came up at that, but his face revealed nothing. "Words fail me, Your Grace," he said, and in his voice, too, there was no emotion.

"Let it last, O Lord, let it last," Roger de Mortimer muttered, an aside meant to be heard, evoking laughter.

Davydd did not take the bait, did not even glance in the other man's direction. Looking down again at the parchment roll, it occurred to him that he was holding Llewelyn's death warrant, and, without warning, he found himself assailed by memory, so strong and so vivid that it seemed to blur time's boundaries. For a split-second, he was no longer in the Chapter House of the Cistercian abbey at Basingwerk. He was sixteen, riding again at Owain's side as they led their army into Llewelyn's lands, and the voice echoing in his ears was his own:

"Shall we leave nothing to Llewelyn, then?"

Owain's answer, coming back as if it were yesterday, as if those twenty-some intervening years had never been. "I'd leave him enough ground to be buried in."

His own cry, one of genuine shock, "I do not want Llewelyn killed!"

Owain reining in then, saying gravely, "I thought you wanted this, lad. I thought you wanted what was rightfully yours."

And his answer, "I do!"

He still did. And by God, why not? It was his birthright, a claim validated by Welsh law, the Welsh law Llewelyn flouted. Now Edward was promising to restore part of his lost patrimony. But not because it was his just due, as a son of Gruffydd ap Llewelyn. No . . . this was a bribe for betrayal, coming in the guise of royal largesse, as if the English King had a God-given right to apportion out Wales as he pleased. Half of Gwynedd . . . if and only if Edward claimed Môn, Gwynedd's granary. Could the Welsh survive such a loss? And what of the forfeit lands east of the Conwy? Welsh cantrefs to be transformed overnight into English shires, a feat worthy of Merlin. No, not half of Gwynedd, the bleeding scraps left over once the dismemberment was done. And yet still more than he had now, than Llewelyn had ever offered him. It was what he wanted, what he'd craved as long as he could remember, at last within reach. But on Edward's terms. He was to hold his Welsh lands at the English King's will. He and Owain were to come to the English parliaments when summoned, "as our other earls and barons come." English earls and barons. An English earldom with Welsh trappings, that was what he was truly being offered.

Davydd raised his eyes from the parchment, met Edward's gaze. "What of my brother Rhodri?"

"What of him?" Edward shrugged, then grinned. "What was it you said about him? Ah, yes . . . that men would not follow Rhodri out of a burning building!"

There was more laughter at that. Davydd did not join in, for once regretting his sharp tongue, his penchant for saying whatever came into his head, never counting the cost. He did not repent the cruel honesty of his gibe, only that it had been offered for English ears, English amusement.

But Edward was waiting for his response, looking expectant, pleased, and somewhat impatient. Davydd got to his feet, crossed the chamber, and thanked the English King for showing him such favor. He could be quite convincing when he chose, and Edward was not disposed to doubt him, for who would not be overjoyed at the offer of a crown? Only one man present sensed something discordant in Davydd's reaction. His quiet expression of gratitude just did not ring true to his de Mortimer cousin; that wasn't Davydd's style. But although suspicion came easily to Roger, in this case answers did not. For the life of him, he could not understand why Davydd was not triumphant.

DAVYDD could not understand it, either. He'd always known that Edward would demand a high price for his help; there were very real risks in taking the King of England as an ally. Edward's ally? Or his dupe? Davydd came to an abrupt halt on the cloister path. Christ, now he was beginning to sound like Llewelyn, even to himself

Those would have been Llewelyn's very words, though. Edward's dupe. He could well imagine the scornful sound of them, the disdainful tone, Almighty God talking down to mere mortals, to feckless younger brothers. Well, death stilled the most insistent voice, even Llewelyn's.

Cistercian abbeys were meant to be havens of calm, spiritual sanctuaries untouched by the turmoil and chaos of the real world. But such cloistered serenity could not withstand the arrival of a royal army; reality had intruded with a vengeance, penetrating into every quiet corner of their earthly refuge. As he stood in the sunlight of the inner garth, there came to Davydd a cacophony of sound, raucous, strident, assailing his ears, grating upon his nerves.

Many of Edward's workmen and men-at-arms were camped three miles away, at the site of the new castle, already christened "Flynt" by Edward. Others had pushed on toward Rhuddlan. For more than two hundred years, a castle had guarded the mouth of the River Clwyd, Welsh or English, depending upon the ebb and flow of border warfare. Llewelyn had held Rhuddlan since 1263, but now it was back in English hands. Edward's ambitions were not about to be satisfied, though, by such a simple motte and bailey structure; he'd begun to draw up plans for a new castle downstream.

Yet a third castle was to be erected farther upstream at Ruthin, but it was Rhuddlan that preyed upon Davydd's peace; he'd been astounded by the sheer magnitude of Edward's undertaking. Not only would the castle itself be the most formidable stronghold in all of North Wales, Edward even meant to divert the course of the River Clwyd, meandering and shallow as it neared the sea. Davydd had listened, stunned, as Edward explained how he would dig a two-mile channel, deep enough for English ships. The garrison could never be starved out then, he said, could outlast any Welsh siege, and Davydd, nodding numbed agreement, knew then and there that his brother was doomed. How could Llewelyn hope to repel an enemy able to impose his will upon the very rivers of their land?

He heard now the shouts that heralded the arrival of the expected supply carts, loaded with crossbow bolts, limestone, pickaxes and chisels and saws and hammers, thick sides of bacon and sacks of flour and salt, plus five barrels full of silver pennies, pay for the men aiding and abetting the English King's conquest of Wales.

A goodly portion of those men were Welsh, too. He ought not to forget that. He was not the only Welshman to side with the Crown against Llewelyn. Their numbers were legion, some motivated by the money, others aggrieved by Llewelyn's high-handed ways. But had any of them truly considered the consequences of an English victory? Had they thought what life might be like under Edward's rule? Llewelyn had, for certes. "Edward is a crusader King. He'd open the flood-gates to English settlers, charter English towns on Welsh soil, turn Gwynedd into an English shire." Davydd's mouth twisted down. One conscience was burden enough for any sensible man. Why was he of a sudden accursed with two, his own and his brother's?

"My lord Davydd!" Davydd turned, and then swore under his breath, for Hugh de Whitton was hastening toward him. "The camp is awash in rumors. Men are saying that the King told his council it is to be war to the utmost, with no quarter given. You were there. Is it true?"

"Well . . . they are about to carve up the pie." Hugh frowned, looking so earnest, so honorable, so steadfast, that Davydd wanted suddenly to see him shaken out of that righteous rectitude. "I can tell you this much, that you'd best hope your lady looks good in black." He got what he wanted; Hugh could not hide his dismay. But the satisfaction it gave him was spurious, the sort to leave a sour after-taste.

MONKS were pacing the walkways, paying no heed to Davydd and Hugh. But there was one very intent eye-witness. Sheltered within one of the shaded study carrels along the church's north wall, Rhodri ap Gruffydd had been watching his brother from the moment Davydd entered the cloister garth, waiting for Davydd to notice him.

Rhodri was better informed than Hugh, for Edward had spared him the indignity of finding out from camp gossip. He had not been surprised by Edward's disclosure, that once again Davydd had managed to land on his feet, with all nine lives intact. None knew better than he that sooner or later, Davydd always got what he wanted.

But he had been deeply shocked to learn that Owain was to be elevated from prisoner to reigning Prince. Why Owain? Why a soured, tired old man long past his prime? Why Owain and not him?

There may have been a time when he'd pitied Owain's plight—a little. No more than that, though, for Owain had always been a stranger. Twenty years Rhodri's senior, brusque and quick-tempered, Owain had played no role in Rhodri's life; he'd seemed as remote as the father who'd died when Rhodri was five. Llewelyn had been the elder brother who'd mattered—once. He, too, had seemed remote, beyond reach. But the eleven years between them had not been as formidable a barrier, and as Rhodri entered his teens, Llewelyn's star was already rising.

Rhodri had been proud of his brother's renown. He might even have been content with Llewelyn's casual kindness, Owain's benign indifference—had it not been for Davydd, Davydd whom they loved.

Rhodri had not begrudged Davydd that love, not at first, for he'd loved Davydd, too. Davydd had been all that Rhodri so desperately wanted to be himself, cocksure and droll and game for anything. Nothing ever daunted Davydd, not even a childhood as odd and unstable as theirs had been, seven years as hostages of the English Crown. Rhodri thought it only natural that Davydd should be the one favored, indulged, wanted. Even when the English King demanded a hostage again and he was sent back to England, at age eleven, even then he understood why it must be him and not Davydd. Or so he told himself.

And when Owain began a war with Llewelyn on Davydd's behalf, Rhodri sought to understand that, too. Owain had paid a high price, two decades at Dolbadarn Castle, but Davydd had been forgiven. Less than seven years later, he'd rebelled a second time, and when he fled to England, Rhodri waited, patiently, for Llewelyn to turn to him. It never happened. Instead, Davydd was forgiven yet again.

Rhodri was never sure when he'd begun to hate Llewelyn, but he knew exactly when he'd begun to hate Davydd—when he came back from English exile, jaunty, unrepentant, still able to take from Rhodri without even trying. Rhodri supposed it had always been that way. But he was no longer that bedazzled little brother, satisfied with their leavings. And so he'd tried to claim his fair share of Gwynedd, succeeded in attracting Llewelyn's attention at last; his brother cast him into prison. Owain's captivity was a source of some controversy. He had many sympathizers among those who held to the old ways, the old laws. Bards sang of Owain's lonely days at Dolbadarn, compared him to a caged eagle. When Rhodri was imprisoned, no one protested, and when he was freed, no one noticed.

Defecting to the English King had been Rhodri's vengeance. But that had not worked out, either—because of Davydd. Always Davydd. He seemed to have won over Edward as easily as he'd once beguiled Owain and Llewelyn. Rhodri was awed by the English King's generosity. He'd given Davydd his own kinswoman, an heiress who doted upon Davydd's every whim. He'd granted Davydd the use of a Cheshire manor. Just a fortnight ago, he'd even knighted Davydd. That might not be a Welsh custom, but it was a notable honor, one Rhodri would have cherished. Instead it had gone to Davydd, who cared naught for English accolades, joking that he'd rather be St Davydd than Sir Davydd. No, nothing had changed. Edward paid him two shillings a day, whilst Davydd was to be rewarded with a crown. Nothing had changed at all.

Rhodri stiffened suddenly, for Davydd had turned away from

Hugh, was striding rapidly up the pathway. But he did not glance in Rhodri's direction, passed the carrel without looking within. Rhodri said nothing, let him go by.

IN early September, an English army landed on the island of Môn. The soldiers were accompanied by more than two hundred reapers, and Welsh wheat soon fell to English scythes and sickles. At the same time, Edward moved west along the coast to the ruins of Deganwy Castle, razed to the ground by Llewelyn in more auspicious days. The River Conwy had always proved to be a formidable barrier for English invaders; only once in the past hundred years had it been crossed. But now Edward was in a position to strike from Môn, threatening Llewelyn's flank. The Welsh were masters at guerrilla warfare; despite the uneven odds, Llewelyn might have held his own had Edward attempted to follow him into the soaring, sky-high heartland of his realm. But Edward did not. He kept to the coast, and kept up the pressure. A deadly waiting game had developed. If the alpine citadel of Eryri was Llewelyn's most invincible fortress, it was now a citadel under siege.

DOLWYDDELAN was where Llewelyn stored his coffer chests, jewels, English money, for no Welsh prince minted his own coins. But Dolwyddelan held another treasure-trove, one made of memories. It had always been his favorite castle, the place where he felt most at peace. He'd walked by the river with his grandfather, hunted on the wooded slopes of Moel Siabod, taken more than one woman to see Rhaeadr Ewynnol by moonlight, and he'd once hoped to show Ellen de Montfort the view from the castle battlements—mountains and sky and a deep forest glen, festooned by a flowing ribbon of river, a haven to rival any earthly Eden.

The autumn was not a season he liked, winter's accomplice, slowly, inexorably stealing the daylight and icing the heights of Eryri. Llewelyn, a man who'd spent much of his life sleeping around campfires, living in the saddle, braving snow and drenching rains, harbored a secret loathing of the cold. But he knew that, even in springtime, the Lledr Valley would never look as beautiful as it did now, aflame with October golds and reds and burnished browns. There were hawthorn bushes by the river as bright and clear as claret, and mountain ash the shade of melted honey, rustling clouds of oak and alder, leaves swirling upon a deceptively mild breeze, the merest whisper of the winter winds to come.

"Uncle?" Caitlin burst through the doorway onto the battlements, disheveled and out of breath. She'd climbed the stairs so rapidly that she had to grab on to the closest merlon for support, waiting for the stitch in her side to ease. "I've been searching for you everywhere," she panted. "Is . . . is it true? Are you going to surrender to the English King?"

"Yes."

"But . . . but why?"

"Because," Llewelyn said tiredly, "this is a war I cannot hope to win."

Caitlin hastened along the parapet. "I do not understand. Why can you not stay here at Dolwyddelan, where you're safe, wait for the English King to lose heart and go home?"

"He is not going anywhere, lass, not until he has my seal upon a treaty of surrender . . . or my head upon a pike. England is so much larger than Wales, so much richer . . . and so many of our people do not fully comprehend the danger, even now. We dwell on the very brink of a cliff, and if we've managed so far to avoid plunging into the abyss, it is only because no English king was willing to commit all the resources of the Crown to a war with Wales—until now. That is the message Edward was sending me when he struck that devil's deal with Davydd. There'll be no winter respite for us, no English withdrawal till the spring thaw. Edward is the first of their kings able to sustain a winter campaign, and if need be, he will."

"Because of the grain he stole?"

Llewelyn nodded. "That was a two-edged theft, hurting us as much as it helped him. But his true power lies in his fleet. If he cannot be starved out, Caitlin, how can he lose? He is building castles to last until Judgment Day, putting down roots so deep he'll never be dislodged. If he can claim Eryri, too—or give it over to a puppet Welsh prince of his choosing—we will never be able to throw off the English yoke . . . never. Unless I can hold on to Eryri, the land west of the Conwy, we are well and truly doomed."

"But what can you gain by surrendering? Even if you are bound to lose, why make it easy for Edward? Why put the noose around your own neck?"

"My defeat may well be inevitable, lass, but it would also be pro-longed, costly, and bloody. I said Edward could fight a winter campaign; I did not say he'd want to do so. As long as I've not been defeated on the field, I do not come empty-handed to the bargaining table. By yield-ing now, I have a chance to save Gwynedd from utter destruction. I'd be sparing our people further suffering, a winter haunted by famine. And I'd be gaining Ellen her freedom. I'll not deny the danger involved, but with so much at stake, it is a risk worth taking."

Caitlin did not agree. "Uncle Llewelyn, please do not do this! The English King cannot be trusted. Did you not tell me that Edward's word would not bear a feather's weight? You said he'd left a trail of broken oaths across the length and breadth of England, that he'd made a truce with Harry de Montfort when he was trapped in Gloucester Castle, only to recant as soon as Harry rode away, and Harry was his friend!" She was running out of breath by now, but she plunged on, as if he might reconsider if only he'd hear her out. "You said he even dared to renege upon an oath given to the Bishop of Worcester, and . . . and when London's Mayor trusted to his safe-conduct after Evesham, he threw the poor man into a Windsor dungeon! Why should he not do the same to you? What is to keep him from casting you into a dungeon, too, once you're in his power?"

"Nothing," Llewelyn admitted reluctantly. "I'll not lie to you, lass. If I ride into Edward's camp, I may not ride out. Since I cannot trust in Edward's good faith, I shall have to put my trust in the Almighty."

"I am sure your father trusted in God, too. But he still spent his last days in an English prison! How can you hold your own life so cheaply? Are you not afraid?"

"Not being a fool, of course I am," Llewelyn snapped. But she was not quick enough; as she turned away, he saw how her mouth was trembling. Thirteen had been a troubled age for him; he'd never felt utterly at ease, even in his own body, no longer a child, not yet a man, buffeted by emotions and urges beyond his ken. Thirteen was an odd and unsettling time for lasses, too, he was discovering; in the past year, he'd learned to stand aside, to let his niece try her fledgling wings, flutter to earth, then try again. She was angrily blinking back tears now, Caitlin who never cried, and he reached out, grasped her shoulders, and drew her toward him.

"Listen to me, lass. I must do this. You'd not believe me if I said it was going to be easy for me. Even if Edward does keep faith, it will be the most difficult thing I've ever done, in this life or the next, I'd wager. Now I need you to accept what must be, just as I must. Can you do that for me, Caitlin?"

She bit her lip, nodded. "But . . . but what if Edward does not keep faith?" she whispered, and he hid a smile, marveling that such a fey little creature, as fine-boned and fragile as a bird in the hand, could be as stubbornly tenacious as a bear-baiting mastiff.

"Sufficient unto the day is the evil thereof," he said softly. "Do you know what that means, lass?"

"It . . . it is from Scriptures, I think," she ventured, "but . . ."

"It means that we'd do better to face our troubles as they come, one at a time. I want you to keep that in mind."

"I'll try," she agreed, quite unconvincingly. Belatedly recognizing the need for solitude that must have driven him up to the castle battlements, she offered, "Shall I leave you now?" and tried not to feel hurt when he nodded. But as she reached the stairwell, she came to an abrupt halt. "I hate my father," she said, her voice thickening. "I'll never forgive him, never!" The door slamming upon what might have been a sob.

Llewelyn started after her, then stopped, for what could he say? What comfort could he offer? Turning back to the battlements, he tracked a kestrel's flight, hovering high above the earth as it searched for prey. He was not as reconciled to what must be as he'd led Caitlin to believe. His head might be in control, but his heart was in rebellion, and he did not know how to silence the subversive inner voice still urging defiance, or how to steel himself for what lay ahead.

The sun was in retreat. As dusk muted the colors flaming in its wake, it disappeared beyond the distant hills. Daylight was fast ebbing away, and the landscape seemed to dim, taking on the soft, blurred contours of an autumn twilight. The wind had picked up, carried to him the faint chiming of church bells; Vespers was being rung. Still, Llewelyn did not move. He remained alone on the battlements, watching as the sky darkened and night descended upon the Lledr Valley.

IN response to Llewelyn's peace overtures, Edward dispatched his clerk, Anthony Bek, and Otto de Grandison to Aberconwy Abbey to meet with Llewelyn's Seneschal, Tudur ab Ednyved, and Tudur's cousin, Goronwy ap Heilyn. But although the English King was willing to accept a negotiated settlement, his terms for ending the war were harsh ones.

Llewelyn was compelled to yield to Edward the four cantrefs east of the River Conwy, and all land seized by Edward. He was to be allowed to retain control of the island of Môn, but he would hold it only as a vassal, paying one thousand marks a year for that privilege, and if he died without heirs of his body, Môn would revert to the English Crown. He must pay a staggering fine of fifty thousand pounds, a sum to cripple the Welsh economy for years, and to yield ten highborn hostages. He must free his brother Owain, and come to terms with both Owain and Rhodri. He must also free the would-be assassin, Owen de la Pole, and the would-be defector, Rhys ap Gruffydd. The lords of Upper and Lower Powys were to be restored to power. He was to swear homage and fealty to Edward, and to repeat his submission every year, with his own subjects required to stand surety for his continued loyalty. Lastly, he was to forfeit the homage of all but five lords of Gwynedd, all others to owe homage only to the English King.

Edward, on his part, agreed to allow Llewelyn to hold Davydd's share of Gwynedd for his lifetime, providing for Davydd out of his own conquests, granting him two of the four cantrefs claimed by the Crown. He agreed that when disputes developed between English and Welsh, the law to apply would be that of the land in which the conflict arose, excluding the four cantrefs. Llewelyn was absolved of the anathema of excommunication, restored to God's favor, the Interdict lifted from Wales. And he was permitted to retain the title that was now only a courtesy, Prince of Wales, a hollow mockery that seemed to Llewelyn the cruelest kindness of all.

On November 9th, Llewelyn came to Aberconwy Abbey to accept Edward's terms, feeling like a man asked to preside over his own execution. A remembered scrap of Scriptures kept echoing in his ears like a funeral dirge: Jerusalem is ruined and Judah is fallen. Gwynedd had been gutted by a pen, just as surely as by any sword thrust. He'd lost more than the lands listed upon parchment; he'd lost the last thirty years of his life, for Gwynedd had been reduced to the boundaries imposed upon the Welsh by the Treaty of Woodstock in 1247. Llewelyn had been just nineteen then, new to power and to defeat. That had been his first loss to England, and his last—until now, until the Treaty of Aberconwy, which destroyed a lifetime's labor in the time it took to affix his great seal to the accord. Never had he known such despair. And the worst was still to come, for on the morrow he must ride to Rhuddlan Castle, there make a formal and public surrender to the English King.

20

RHUDDLAN CASTLE, WALES

November 1277

THE sky was ashen, spattered with scudding clouds. The wind was churning the waters of the straits into a white-capped cauldron. By the time they reached the Clwyd estuary, sleet had begun to fall.

The fog was patchy, thicker to the north, blanketing the site of Edward's new castle; Llewelyn could only guess how far the construction had advanced. Downstream, Rhuddlan Castle was looming, rising from the mists lying low upon the river. Llewelyn drew rein, staring up at the banner flying above the keep. It flapped wildly in the wind, golden lions on a blood-red background, the royal arms of England.

After a time, Tudur nudged his stallion forward, joined Llewelyn at the water's edge. He was not the sort to offer counterfeit comfort, so he said nothing. They could detect movement now upon the castle's outer walls. Sentries had finally taken notice of them, and they soon saw curious faces peering over the battlements, soldiers jostling and elbowing for space at the embrasures.

"It seems that I'm to be the afternoon's entertainment," Llewelyn said bitterly. Tudur glanced sharply into his face, then away. They sat their mounts in silence, gazing across at the castle until Otto de Grandison broke ranks behind them. A soldier of some renown, he believed in a kinship born of the battlefield, a bond that transcended the barriers built up by national boundaries, be they English, Welsh, or the borders of his own Burgundy, for boundaries were subject to change, but manhood and pride and courage were enduring, immutable. And so, while Anthony Bek fidgeted at the sudden delay, he ignored the priest's impatience, waited until he thought Llewelyn was ready. Only then did he come forward, politely query if he should now summon the ferry from the castle.

Llewelyn and Tudur looked at him as blankly as if he'd suggested that they cross the river by walking upon the water. "That will not be necessary," Llewelyn said, with courtesy and just a hint of amusement. Raising his arm, he signaled to his men, then spurred his stallion forward into the river.

The English were taken aback, but followed once they saw how shallow the water was at that point. As they splashed toward the far bank, Otto kicked his mount to catch up with Tudur. "How did he know the river could be forded here?"

Tudur gave him another bemused look. "Why would he not know it? This is his country."

Not anymore, Otto thought, not anymore. But he refrained from saying so, and watched admiringly as Llewelyn sent his stallion galloping toward Rhuddlan's gatehouse, scattering the English soldiers loitering by the drawbridge, outdistancing his own men, so that when he rode into the castle bailey, he appeared, for the moment, quite alone and unafraid.

❦

ROGER DE MORTIMER was waiting for Llewelyn, leaning against the door-jamb, blocking the entrance to the great hall. "You're right on time, Cousin. I think you'll be pleased by the turnout, nigh on a hundred men eager to watch you surrender to the English King."

Llewelyn dismounted, dropped the reins to anchor his mount. "So many? That rivals the crowd likely to come out for your hanging."

To his credit, de Mortimer could take a jab as well as deliver one, and he grinned. "I see you've held on to your sense of humor. That is truly remarkable, considering the humbling ordeal ahead of you."

Llewelyn looked pensively at the other man, wondering how he could boast even a drop of Llewelyn Fawr's blood; it was almost enough to make him believe in those folk tales of babies switched at birth. "Make yourself useful, Roger. See to my horse whilst I meet with the King," he said, and, pushing past the Marcher lord, entered the hall.

De Mortimer had not exaggerated; the hall was thronged with spectators, many of whom had a very personal stake in his downfall. The Marchers were out in force, not surprisingly, for at one time or another, he'd crossed swords with virtually all of them. Roger Clifford and Roger Lestrange and the dangerous John Giffard, looking as smug as cream-fed cats. The Earl of Hereford, who'd clashed with him over Brycheiniog. The Earl of Pembroke, whose disdain for the Welsh was surpassed only by his lust for their lands. Reginald de Grey, a man capable of giving Lucifer himself lessons in vengeance. The tousled, redheaded Earl of Gloucester, looking truculent even in triumph.

They were watching him intently, expectantly. Llewelyn could feel their hostility; the very air was charged with it, with that odd, singed stillness just before a storm broke. But he did not care that he served as a lightning rod for the Marchers. It was inevitable that they should have clashed, for their interests were irreconcilable. It was the presence of the others, the Welsh lords, that he found hard to bear.

Llewelyn Fychan was standing several feet away. As his eyes met Llewelyn's, he raised his head defiantly. He was one of the lords of Upper Powys, and a kinsman, too, ought to have been an ally, not an English accomplice. Where had he gone wrong? Why had he not been able to hold the men like this, to keep them loyal when it counted?

Gruffydd ap Gwenwynwyn had aged in the three years since Llewelyn had seen him last, not long before his flight to England. He looked greyer, thinner than Llewelyn remembered. But his eyes were blazing with hatred. Stepping forward, he said loudly, "Fel y gwyneir y ceir."

As you do unto others, so it shall be done unto you. But for claiming

Powys, for ousting Gruffydd, Llewelyn had no regrets. Had the murder plot been Gruffydd's idea? Or Davydd's? He paused, looked the older man up and down, very slowly and deliberately, letting his silence speak for itself. Gruffydd's face contorted with rage, but after a moment, he moved aside.

Llewelyn had yet to spot Rhodri, but that did not surprise him, for his youngest brother was easily overlooked in a crowd. The only one of Gruffydd's four sons who'd not been blessed with his uncommon height, so unusual for a Welshman, Rhodri lacked presence, too, had never been able to command attention merely by entering a room.

Davydd could, though. Davydd never went unnoticed; he made sure of that. So where was he? Llewelyn's eyes swept the hall, cut toward the dais, where Edward awaited him. He ought to have been there, at Edward's side. But he was not.

Tudur and Einion had followed Llewelyn into the hall, hastening to overtake him before he reached the dais. He gave them both a glance of wordless gratitude, then murmured, "Have either of you seen Davydd?"

Tudur jerked his head toward the right. "Over there, against the far wall, looking strangely vexed for one of the victors."

Llewelyn followed his gaze. Davydd was standing in the shadows, arms folded over his chest, eyes narrowed and guarded, giving away nothing. For a moment, they looked at each other across the length of the hall, and then Llewelyn turned back to Tudur. "You're right, he does seem out of humor. You must remember, though, that he did not get all he wanted. I'm still alive, after all."

Tudur nodded grim agreement. Einion looked unhappy with Llewelyn's acerbic assessment of Davydd's aims, but he did not dispute it. Llewelyn glanced from one to the other, hoping they knew how much they were valued. "Wait for me here," he said quietly. "This I must do alone."

As he began walking toward the dais, men moved aside, clearing a path for him. Edward was sitting in a high-backed chair, much like a throne. He was enjoying this moment of triumph, made no attempt to hide his satisfaction. But there would be no unseemly gloating, no salting of open wounds. He'd won, as he'd known he would, was prepared now to staunch his defeated foe's bleeding, for he prided himself upon those very attributes his enemies swore he lacked, the generosity, forthrightness, and gallantry of the knight errant.

"My lord Llewelyn," he said, "you may approach the dais."

Llewelyn did, pausing just before he reached the dais steps to unsheathe his sword. Holding it out to Edward, hilt first, he knelt, saying

very evenly, in a voice meant to be heard throughout the hall, "I submit
myself unto the King's will."

LLEWELYN could not find fault with Roger de Mortimer's derisive de-
scription of his surrender—a humbling ordeal. The worst moment had
occurred upon his arrival, as he drew his sword from its scabbard,
handed it over to the English King. If this treaty was, indeed, bait for
a trap, that would have been the time to spring it. He would have chosen
death over captivity in England, for he was haunted by his father's fate,
shut up within the Tower of London, returning to Wales only for burial.
Surrendering his sword was surrendering, too, his ability to make such
a choice. Without its familiar weight at his hip, he felt vulnerable as
never before, naked and defenseless before his enemies, a new and
daunting sensation for him.

But if Edward did have treachery in mind, he was biding his time.
He had accepted Llewelyn's sword, symbol of his surrender, and then
handed it back once the ritual of submission was done. The following
morning, after a Martinmas High Mass in the castle chapel, attended
by English and Welsh, they assembled in the great hall, where Llewelyn
swore an oath of fealty to England's King.

LLEWELYN had brought Tudur, Einion, Goronwy ap Heilyn, and Dai ab
Einion, and Edward was attended by the Earls of Warwick and Gloucester, Otto de Grandison, Anthony Bek, and the ever-present de Mortimer.
Servants passed back and forth, pouring wine, serving honey-filled wafers, lighting candles. Llewelyn was slowly beginning to relax, the spectre
of an English betrayal no longer hovering at his shoulder, and in an
atmosphere of wary civility, agreement was reached for the surrender
of Llewelyn's ten hostages to the Crown.

THEY sat across a table, these men more accustomed to meeting across
a battlefield, waiting now for Edward's return. No one spoke; even the
irrepressible de Mortimer was taciturn, nursing a throbbing head, a
stomach queasy from a surfeit of wine.

The door banged suddenly; Edward entered, laughing. "I regret
the interruption," he said, reclaiming his seat. "But the news was worth
it, news too good to keep to myself. The courier came from my Queen,
but his tidings came from the Holy Land. The Sultan of Egypt, Rukn
ad-Din Baibars Bundukdari, is dead."

The death of Edward's Saracen foe meant little to the Welsh, but they politely chimed in when the English congratulated their King. Edward had begun to laugh again. "Nay, it is not his death that I find so pleasing, although it was right welcome, of course. He was an evil man; I still bear the scars from his Assassin's dagger. But he has reaped what he had sown, for God is not mocked."

Llewelyn felt a flicker of interest. "Was he murdered, then?"

"Better, far better! He'd prepared a poisoned goblet, one meant for a man he would murder. Instead, by mischance only the Almighty could have contrived, he drank from it himself!"

There was an astonished silence, and then a burst of awed laughter. It was, they all agreed, almost too perfect, a jest to amuse both God and the Devil, justice at once divine and diabolic.

"So shall all my enemies be vanquished," Edward said, reaching for a wafer. "Now then, my lord Llewelyn, shall we resume? I believe you had a question ere I was called away?"

"Yes, Your Grace, I do have a query," Llewelyn said, although he'd already guessed what the answer would be. "I wondered why you asked only that I swear fealty to you this forenoon, and not homage, as well."

"Ah, that is easily explained. I thought an act of homage deserved a greater audience, a better setting, if you will, than a shabby border castle. I think it more fitting that you come to my Christmas court, do homage to me there," Edward said and smiled.

Llewelyn had suspected as much. "Your Christmas court . . . it will be held in London?"

"Where else?" Edward asked blandly. "I thought you might enjoy a visit to my capital, for I understand you've not seen London since boyhood."

For Llewelyn, London would forever evoke thoughts of his father and the Tower. Edward's demand did far more than lacerate his pride; it drew blood, slashed through his defenses to the heart. He was grateful now that he'd been braced for just such a dagger thrust. "It sounds," he said, "as if you mean this to be a Christmas I'll long remember."

Edward's mouth curved. "I do, indeed. I'll make sure a safe-conduct reaches you by Advent." He signaled for a servant to pour more wine, all the while regarding Llewelyn thoughtfully. "Speaking of safe-conducts, I must confess that you gave me grievous offense last year."

"Only last year?" Llewelyn said dryly, but he had tensed. So had the other Welshmen, for they, too, were wary of entrapment.

"Mayhap I should have said you affronted me more than usual," Edward acknowledged good-humoredly. "It was when you offered to come to Montgomery or Oswestry to do homage, provided that I restore the Lady Eleanor de Montfort to you. You were insistent upon safe-conducts, too, requesting them from the Earls of Gloucester, Surrey, Norfolk, and Lincoln, my lord de Mortimer, the Archbishop of Canterbury, and the Bishop of Worcester—amongst others. Even taking into account the suspicious nature of the Welsh, that seemed rather excessive—and rather insulting, for you neglected to seek a safe-conduct from me. A man might well conclude that you thought a royal safe-conduct would be worthless. Tell me, my lord, was that indeed what you did think?"

Llewelyn reached for his wine cup and drank, seeking to gain time. Was this the moment when the trap was sprung? Was Edward daring him to admit the truth, that there was no coin of the realm as false as the King's sworn word? Or did Edward truly see himself as a man of honor? The de Montfort partisans had given him an insulting epithet—Pard—claiming that, like the leopard, he changed his spots at whim. But he had chosen "Keep troth" as his motto. Was it done in irony? Llewelyn thought not.

As his silence stretched out, suspense began to build. Tudur stirred uneasily, unable to see how Llewelyn could give an honest answer without offering the English King a deadly insult. He was contemplating a desperate gambit, distracting Edward by answering the question himself, in terms Edward would never forgive, when Llewelyn set his wine cup down, leaned across the table.

"I do find it difficult to trust the English Crown," he said, with a candor Edward had not expected. He stiffened, seemed about to interrupt. But Llewelyn gave him no chance. "When my father was being held at Cricieth Castle by his half-brother, my lady mother sought help from the English monarch. King Henry agreed, promised that he would be freed, and on the strength of that promise, many Welshmen joined in his war against Davydd ap Llewelyn. Davydd was defeated, but King Henry did not keep faith. Instead, he sent my father and my brother Owain to the Tower. I know you are aware of this history, my liege. But I lived it, and it left scars, like the dagger of Sultan Baibars's Assassin."

Edward did not respond immediately, nor was his face easy to read. But Tudur slumped back in his chair, too relieved to care about hiding it, sure that Llewelyn had managed the impossible, satisfying Edward while not being false to himself.

"Yes," Edward said at last, "we are all our fathers' sons." Another silence fell. Edward kept his gaze upon Llewelyn. "I think," he said, "that we do understand each other. It is my hope that this treaty will mark a turning point in the history of our two lands. Now . . . now I want to discuss payment of that fifty thousand pounds. I've been told that you would find it very difficult to satisfy this debt. Is that true?"

"It will bleed us dry," Llewelyn said tautly, for his outrage at that monstrous fine had yet to abate. Even in the most prosperous times, his annual income had never exceeded six thousand pounds.

"I want to be fair, do not want to impose upon you a burden you cannot hope to meet. I am willing, therefore, to remit payment of the fifty thousand pounds. And as proof of my good will, I will also waive the first annual rent due for the island of Anglesey."

He'd caught the Welsh off balance. As they exchanged startled looks, the same suspicion flashed silently among them, that Edward had deliberately demanded a sum they could not pay, so that he could then make this dramatic, magnanimous gesture. But whether his generosity was spontaneous or calculated, it was desperately needed. "Diolch yn fawr," Llewelyn said. "Thank you, my liege."

Edward glanced inquiringly around the table. "Well, I believe we have concluded all the matters of importance. I would suggest we return to the hall, make ready to dine."

"There is still one very important matter to settle," Llewelyn objected, "for we have not yet discussed my wife's release. I would like to arrange for her to be escorted to the Welsh border as soon as possible."

"Ah, yes, Ellen . . ." Edward had been about to rise, sat down again, and smiled across the table at Llewelyn. "We shall, indeed, have to discuss her future. But I think we ought to wait until you come to my Christmas court."

Llewelyn sucked in his breath. "What are you saying, that you do not intend to set her free? I was assured that you would not detain her once I yielded to you." He shot Otto de Grandison a burning look of accusation, before swinging back to confront Edward again. "Do you mean to renege upon your sworn word?"

"No, I do not. I did agree to release Ellen, and I will do so—as soon as I can be sure of your good faith."

"And when will that be?"

"That is up to you, my lord Llewelyn."

Llewelyn's fury was evident to them all, more intense and less controlled than Edward had anticipated. "I do not see why you are so surprised by my concern for Ellen's safety," he said brusquely. "She is my kinswoman, after all, and I want to do right by her."

"Ellen is not your ward," Llewelyn said, in a voice husky with rage. "She is my wife."

"I am not denying that," Edward snapped. "Prove to me that you mean to keep this peace and I will give her to you gladly, with my blessings! As I said, it is up to you."

The tension did not subside. One spark and the air itself might kindle, Otto de Grandison thought morosely, not at all happy with this unexpected turn of events. Had he so misread Edward, ignored the strings trailing from the offer to restore the Prince's lady? Had it truly been his mistake? He thought not, but it was now, for kings did not err. He gave Llewelyn an apologetic look, then turned at the sound of a muffled shout. Striding to the closest window, he unlatched the shutters. "My liege, the Welsh prisoners have just ridden into the bailey!"

RHYS AP GRUFFYDD had not been held long enough—four brief months—for it to have left its mark. He looked and acted like a man set upon savoring every moment of his triumph, shouting a bawdy greeting to Davydd, glancing up toward the open window and saluting Llewelyn with a mocking grin. But Owen de la Pole had been a prisoner for three years, and it showed. Utterly gone was the bluster, the swagger. Pale and nervous, he squinted suspiciously in the pallid winter sunlight, not seeming to trust in his changed fortunes until his father came forward and took the reins of his horse. Gruffydd ap Gwenwynwyn gazed up then, stared challengingly at the man standing at the window, just as Rhys had done.

Llewelyn would normally have been stung by their defiance, for he was not accustomed to it. But now it barely registered with him. His eyes were riveted upon the third prisoner, all others forgotten. Staring down at Owain, he was stunned by the realization that he'd not recognized his brother, not at first.

Owain Goch. Owain the Red. Stubborn, courageous, hot-tempered, proud, vengeful. Fettered memories now broke free, a lifetime of discord and strife, for Llewelyn could not remember a time when he and his elder brother had not been at odds. When last they'd met, in Llewelyn's command tent after the battle in the pass at Bwlch Mawr, Owain had been defiant even in defeat. "Post your guards," he'd said, with the bravado that came as naturally to him as breathing. "Your prison will not hold me for long." He'd been wrong about that, as he'd been wrong about so much. That was Owain, the brother who'd led an army onto his lands, the red-haired rebel who had learned every lesson in life the hard way, not this man below in the bailey, not this gaunt, aged stranger with silvered hair and hooded eyes.

"Jesú, is that Owain?" Tudur sounded shocked. "Do you think they released the wrong man?" he asked, not completely in jest.

Llewelyn said nothing. Owain was dismounting, having guided his stallion over to a horse block, Owain who had always jeered at men who could not leap, unaided, into the saddle. He seemed to favor his left leg, started toward the great hall at an unhurried, measured pace. He'd yet to look up, had not noticed Llewelyn, or given his surroundings

more than a cursory glance. He did not appear cowed like Owen de la
Pole, merely detached, and that, too, could not have been more unlike
the Owain Llewelyn remembered. But then Owain smiled, a smile from
his turbulent past, and quickened his step, moving forward into
Davydd's boisterous, exuberant embrace. As Llewelyn watched, they
stepped back, embraced again, then entered the hall together.

IT was dusk by the time Llewelyn returned to his chamber. Servants
had been there before him; the hearth had been stoked, a spiked candle
lit, a flagon and cups put out upon the table. It was a welcome sight;
never had Llewelyn been so exhausted, body and soul. But as he crossed
the threshold, he was suddenly sure that he was not alone. It was an
instinctive awareness, a sixth sense, a soldier's sense, one he'd learned
to trust. He froze, hand on the door latch, eyes probing the darkened
corners of the room. "Who is there?" he challenged, dropping his other
hand to his dagger hilt.

He heard the sound of a chair being shoved back. And then Davydd
stepped out of the shadows. "I've been waiting for you."

"Why?"

"For nigh on two days now, you've been looking right through me.
I was beginning to think I'd become invisible, like poor Rhodri. Since
we need to talk, I thought I'd best seek you out ere you go deaf as well
as blind."

Llewelyn had yet to move from the door. Nor had he closed it.
Opening it still farther now, he stepped aside, clearing the way for
Davydd's departure. "I have nothing to say to you."

"Oh, but you do! You've had three years to think about what you
wanted to say to me, and most of it would likely blister the paint off
these walls. Well, this is your chance. Here I am, so go ahead, say it!"

Earlier that day, Owain had seemed like a stranger; so now did
Davydd. Llewelyn had never heard him sound so angry, a raw, exposed
rage that could not be faked, even by as accomplished an actor as
Davydd. He moved closer, curious in spite of himself. "You're oddly
out of sorts for a man on the winning side in this war."

"On the winning side?" Davydd echoed. "Is that a joke?"

"You can be sure I do not see the Treaty of Aberconwy as a joke."
Their eyes caught, held; Davydd was the first to look away. As he drew
back, out of the range of the light, Llewelyn followed.

"So you do not think you won? I do not see that you have much
to complain of, in truth. You did not come away empty-handed, profited
almost as much as Edward from this English peace—the cantrefs of

Rhufoniog and Dyffryn Clwyd, the lordships of Dinbych and Caergwrle. That would content most men. Ah, but then I am forgetting that you expected so much more. It must have been a great disappointment to you when I came to terms with Edward. You were counting upon him to do your killing for you."

"If I wanted you dead, Llewelyn, you'd have died three years ago!"

"I damned near did die three years ago, and likely would have, if not for the one thing you could not foresee—that Candlemas storm!"

"Storms pass, floods abate. We had other chances, had we wanted to take them."

"Jesus God!" Llewelyn gave an incredulous, angry laugh. "Only you could botch a murder attempt, then expect to get credit because you lacked the nerve to try again!"

Davydd spat out an extremely obscene oath. "The one thing I've never lacked was nerve, and you, of all men, know it!"

"What are you telling me, Davydd? That I should be grateful to you for confining yourself to just one assassination attempt? Or am I supposed to believe this is some sort of oblique apology?"

"No, damn you!"

"So what you're saying, then, is that you did plot my murder, but you did not really want me dead, and you're not sorry, but you'll not do it again. Do I have it right?"

Davydd flushed; he was not accustomed to being the one mocked. "You have not changed at all! Still so self-righteous, so sure God is on your side, even with an English dagger pricked at your throat. Whatever I did or did not do, you're not blameless in this. For all your fine talk about Wales, about the need to defend Welsh sovereignty, Welsh borders, and Welsh tradition, you are the one who was defying Welsh law!"

"You still do not see, do you? We're well past arguing about Gwynedd's succession. It has now become a question of Gwynedd's survival. How can you not understand that?"

Davydd did; that was the trouble. He said nothing, and Llewelyn strode to the window, jerked the shutters open. "That castle they are building out there will control the vale of Clwyd, and that is only one of Edward's planned strongholds. He told me today that he intends to charter a town here, too. I suppose you knew that already. Did you also know that no Welsh will be allowed to live in that town? Or in the other towns he means to establish on Welsh soil—"

"Oh, no, by God, no! You're not going to blame me for Edward's victory. I'll be damned if I'll take the responsibility for your mistakes!"

"Or your own mistakes, either! You've gone through your whole life like that, never once taking responsibility for what you've done!"

"Damn your—" Davydd began, then started visibly as the door slammed behind him. Llewelyn flinched, too, spun around even faster than Davydd.

Owain was standing by the door, regarding them both indignantly. "Do the two of you know how long I've been here, listening to you?" he demanded. "It's not enough that you were shouting to be heard across the English border, no, you had to leave the door open, too! What if I'd been Gruffydd ap Gwenwynwyn, or one of the Marchers who speak Welsh, like de Mortimer?"

"Bugger de Mortimer!" Davydd said savagely. "Let him hear, let all of England hear!" He drew a deep, constricted breath, then looked back at Llewelyn. "My lord Prince of Wales, rot in Hell!" Wheeling toward the door, he roughly shouldered Owain out of the way when he did not move aside quickly enough, banging it behind him with such force that the candle guttered out.

Llewelyn stood very still for a moment, then startled Owain by slamming the shutter back, hammering it into place with his fist when it recoiled. The wood was aged, warped by years of exposure to Welsh rain and wind, and it splintered near a hinge when he hit it again. He swore then, long and hard; it didn't help.

"If you mean to break anything else, give me fair warning," Owain said calmly. "My nerves are not as steady as they once were." He was moving about the chamber, relighting the candle with a spark from the hearth. Returning to the table, he poured wine into two cups. "It's odd," he said, "but watching the two of you together tonight, I finally understood what the bards meant when they claimed that love and hate were two sides of the same coin."

Llewelyn moved away from the window. "What do you want, Owain?"

"Edward told me that I have a choice. I can stand trial in your high court for my past offenses, or I can make peace with you. I am here to make peace. Settle some of my old lands in Llŷn upon me, Llewelyn, so I can go home."

"Just like that?" Llewelyn circled around the table. "I'm supposed to believe it is that simple for you? That you bear me no grudge for the last twenty years? What kind of a fool do you take me for, Owain? You never forgave a wrong in your life, not until you'd repaid it twice-over!"

"Twenty-two years, four months—if we're counting. And yes, you're right. I did take 'an eye for an eye' as my own verse of Scriptures. But where did it get me? Nigh on half my life as someone's prisoner, first our uncle Davydd's, then the English King's, then yours. You'd think I'd have figured out that I was doing something wrong, but I was ever a slow learner."

"Until now?" Llewelyn sounded quite skeptical, and Owain nodded.

"You do not believe me. But is it truly so surprising? Do I look like a man in his prime? Why should I squander my last years seeking vengeance against a man I could not hope to defeat on the field—and for what? You only did to me what I would have done to you, had fortune favored me that day."

"That sounds very logical, very rational, very unlike you, Owain."

Owain almost smiled. "Do not mistake me. I'd never be one to weep at your funeral. But I do not seek revenge, not anymore. The Owain you remember may have hoarded his grievances as if they were gold, but would he lie about them?"

Llewelyn gave the older man a long, searching look. "No," he said slowly, "you were never a liar, Owain. If you truly do want peace, we can reach an agreement about the lands in Llŷn. I think it only fair to warn you, though, that if you play false with me, you will have reason to regret it."

"You still find it hard to believe me. Does it truly seem so incomprehensible to you, that a man might grow weary of the strife, the endless struggle? Yes . . . I see it does."

Owain drained one of the wine cups. "It is passing strange. I never liked you, Llewelyn, never, and, for a goodly number of years, I can say that I hated you, as I've never hated another living soul. You knew that, of course. Did you also know how envious I was of you?"

Llewelyn was startled; that was the last thing he'd have expected to hear from Owain. "Envious of me? Why?"

"You were my younger brother. You ought to have followed my lead, my advice. But you blazed your own trail, and soon it seemed to me that you'd left me far behind. Men paid heed to you, as young as you were, trusted in your judgment, in your damnable, dazzling vision for Wales. You had a way of making a border raid sound like a holy crusade, for you knew how to take words and send them soaring as high as hawks. Me . . . hellfire, I could count myself lucky if I'd not trip over my own tongue. I was fully nine years older than you, and I had to stand by whilst you proved yourself to be a better rider than me, a better hunter than me, and then—at Bwlch Mawr—a better battle commander. Not being a bleeding saint, of course I was envious of you, enough to choke on it!"

"Why are you telling me this now?"

"Because I realized tonight that, after dwelling so many years in your shadow, I might be the lucky one, after all. You see, I can do something you cannot. I can just walk away."

Setting the cup down, Owain turned toward the door. But there he paused. "There is one more thing—about Davydd."

"Let it be, Owain," Llewelyn said sharply. "There is nothing you can say about Davydd that I'd want to hear."

"Do you remember the first time he saw a pond? He was just a tadpole, two at most. He took one look, dived in, and sank like a stone, would have drowned for certes if you had not fished him out. I cannot believe you've forgotten?"

"I remember. What of it?"

"He's gone through his whole life doing that, never looking ere he leaps. Inevitably, he sometimes dives into water over his head. He told me about that murder plot, had no reason to lie, not to me. I'm telling you this, not for your sake, but for his. He truly did regret it, Llewelyn."

Llewelyn's mouth tightened. "He could have more regrets than Rome has priests, and I'd not care . . . not now, not ever again."

Owain smiled thinly. "You care," he said, and moved into the stairwell, closing the door firmly behind him.

THE flagon was almost empty and the candle had burned down to its wick. Llewelyn had moved a chair closer to the hearth. Gazing into the flames, slowly drinking the last of the wine, he traveled again the road that led to Rhuddlan Castle, reliving the past, reviewing his choices, his decisions, his mistakes. What should he have done differently? Where had he gone astray? Must he believe that this was fated to be, God's Will? No, not God's Will—Edward's.

Poor Wales, so far from Heaven, so close to England. His grandfather's jest, humor that twisted like a knife. The hearth was sputtering; he leaned over, prodded it with the tongs, and the flames shot upward in a sizzle of white-gold sparks. A pity hope could not be so easily rekindled. Would Edward ever let Ellen go? He could sense her presence at times, marveled that he could feel so close to a woman he'd never met, a woman who might never look upon his homeland, yet bound to him by more than a Sacrament, by thwarted hopes and bitter regrets, by all that might have been.

A sudden, loud knock pulled him away from Windsor, back to the realities of Rhuddlan Castle. Glancing over his shoulder at the door, he said, "Come in, Rhodri."

After a moment, the door swung open. "It is not Rhodri, my lord; it is me." Goronwy ap Heilyn hesitated on the threshold. "Jesú, it is dark in here! Are you expecting Rhodri? I think I saw him in the hall . . ."

"I was just waiting for the circle to close. Never mind, Goronwy, it is a private jest . . . of sorts. Find yourself a seat."

Goronwy was a nephew of Llewelyn Fawr's celebrated Seneschal,

Ednyved ap Cynwrig. Ednyved had briefly served as Llewelyn's Seneschal, too, and after him, his sons. They'd been all stamped from the same mold, sardonic, brusque, and dispassionate. Goronwy was an anomaly, therefore, for he was by nature impulsive, voluble, and given to hell-raising. But he did share certain attributes with his more cynical kinsmen—a quick wit, courage, and loyalty to last until his final breath—traits that had guaranteed his rapid rise in Llewelyn's service.

Dragging a chair over to the hearth, Goronwy glanced at Llewelyn's empty flagon, then unfastened a wineskin from his belt. "It looks like the well ran dry. But I come prepared for every crisis, have a flask full of mead I'm right happy to share, much better than the sugared swill the English like to guzzle."

Passing the flask to Llewelyn, Goronwy dropped down into the chair, stretching his legs toward the fire. "I have something to tell you, my lord, for I thought you'd best hear it from me. I know you like it not when your orders are disobeyed. You warned us not to let the English bait us into doing anything foolish, and I did not . . . well, not exactly . . ."

"It is amazing," Llewelyn muttered, "how consistent this day has been. Spare me any more suspense, Goronwy. What did you do?"

"It was not all my fault, my lord. That whoreson cousin of mine was the one to seek me out, and I did try to hold on to my temper, but I swear Rhys could provoke the Pope. I could stomach just so much of his boastful crowing. When I reached my limit, I hit him in the mouth, and that caused a . . . a bit of commotion."

" 'A bit of commotion.' That would not be your quaint way of describing a riot?"

"Oh, it was not as bad as that," Goronwy said reassuringly, "some bruises and broken furniture, some spilled ale, mayhap a few blackened eyes. In truth, it could have been far worse!"

"I daresay," Llewelyn said laconically. "Tell me, did you, by chance, break Rhys's jaw?"

Goronwy's relief found expression now in laughter. "No such luck! But I did chip a tooth—if that counts?"

"It will have to do." Llewelyn drank deeply of Goronwy's flask, then handed it back, and Goronwy drank, too, delighted to be sharing so private a moment with his Prince.

"You said Rhodri was below in the hall. What of Owain and Davydd? Were they there, too?"

"Owain has gone to bed. I overheard the castellan offering him one of the English whores who'd followed Edward's army, but he said he wanted only to sleep. I do not know where Davydd is." Goronwy, who'd

once considered Davydd a friend, could not help frowning. "I expect
he's off licking his wounds. I do not know what ails him, but I've never
seen him in such a brooding, black mood, almost as bad—" He caught
himself, not in time.

"As bad as mine," Llewelyn said, finishing the thought for him,
and he nodded, unperturbed.

"You have reason, my lord," he said, with such unaffected, heartfelt
empathy that Llewelyn allowed himself a rare indulgence; he dropped
his defenses.

Goronwy was watching him, wondering if there were words to ease
so great a hurt. "You did your best, my lord."

Llewelyn's dark eyes flicked toward him, then away. "Yes," he
said, "but it was not good enough."

There was an odd intimacy about the moment; the firelit darkness
seemed to invite confidences. "You're too hard on yourself," Goronwy
said softly, not surprised when Llewelyn merely shrugged. "What will
you do now, my lord?"

Llewelyn was quiet for a time, keeping his eyes upon the smoldering
hearth. The log was charred and blackened, but the fire was not yet
spent; as he watched, dancing flickers of flame sprang up again, flared
into fitful life. Reaching for the flask, he gave the younger man a crooked
smile.

"Tonight," he said, "we shall get quietly and thoroughly drunk,
Goronwy, in memory of all that was lost. And on the morrow, I begin
the struggle to win it back."

21

WESTMINSTER, ENGLAND

December 1277

Edward provided Llewelyn with an impressive
escort for his journey to London, a delegation headed by his Chancellor,
the Bishop of Bath and Wells, and the Marcher lords, Roger de Mortimer

and Roger Clifford. Llewelyn had been given a royal safe-conduct, which he thought to be worth as much as Davydd's sworn word. But he no longer had the right of refusal, could only hope that the English King had nothing more sinister in mind than a public humiliation.

They reached Westminster by mid-afternoon on the eve of Christmas, just ahead of gathering snow clouds. Arrangements had been made to billet Llewelyn's men in the village of Islington, north of the city walls, and Roger de Mortimer elected to take them on to their lodgings, while Llewelyn and the Chancellor stopped at Westminster to advise Edward of their arrival.

Upon his entry into the great hall, Llewelyn was welcomed so cordially by Edward that some of his suspicions began to abate. While he knew Edward was quite capable of violating a safe-conduct, he did not think the English King would publicly befriend a man he was about to imprison. Exchanging courtesies with Edward and his very pregnant Queen, Llewelyn took this opportunity to study his surroundings. Here on the morrow he would do homage to Edward, before the largest audience of his life. He'd never seen a hall the size of this one, well over two hundred feet long, more than fifty feet wide, and nearly twice as high. He'd heard tales of English feasts in which thousands of highborn guests were feted, had never believed such boasting—until now.

As he watched the men gathering at the huge open hearth, mingling in the three vast aisles, Llewelyn was not surprised to see so many of the Marcher lords. But amidst the familiar faces was one he'd not expected to find, and as soon as he could politely take his leave of Edward, he crossed the hall to confront his brother.

"Rhodri?"

The younger man jutted out his chin. "You mean you actually recognized me?"

"What are you doing here, Rhodri?"

The peremptory tone brought a flush to Rhodri's cheeks. "What do you think? Tomorrow is your day to eat humble pie, a meal I'd not have missed for the world!"

Rhodri glared at his brother, but his triumph soured when Llewelyn gave him a scornful look, then turned away. It was as if they did not even think he was worth arguing with, for he'd gotten an identical response from Davydd earlier that day. "I'll be here on the morrow," he vowed bitterly. "You can count upon that!" But his threats served only to amuse some of the bystanders; Llewelyn did not look back.

LLEWELYN had been in London once before, visiting his father in the Tower soon after Gruffydd's imprisonment began. He'd been just thirteen, but his memories of London had not faded much over the years, perhaps because they were not pleasant ones. He'd taken a great dislike to the English city, so noisy and crowded and dirty to a lad country-born and bred, had promised himself he'd never be back, and the man had kept faith with the boy's vow—until now.

But Westminster was utterly unknown to him, and he was admittedly curious about this palace of English kings. And so, when he and his companions exited the hall, he saw no reason to call at once for their horses. After admiring the cloistered quiet of St Stephen's Chapel, they eventually found themselves walking by the river wall, through gardens dormant and bare, a lifetime away from spring's rebirth.

Ahead lay another expanse of gardens, sheltered within a courtyard formed by the King's Painted Chamber, the Lesser Hall, and the chapel. As they approached, Tudur came to a halt. "I've got a cramp." Limping over to one of the garden benches, he began to massage his leg. "I never realized," he said, "that Rhodri hated you so much."

Llewelyn gave him an intent, sideways glance before admitting, "Neither did I." He was amused now to see that the other men were taking a sudden interest in the frozen December landscape, dropping back upon the pathway so that he and Tudur might have some moments of privacy. "I could come to like the sort of service I've been getting lately," he said. "I'm given what I want even before I know I want it! Unfortunately, theirs is the solicitude people usually save for those suffering a mortal illness."

Tudur smiled, momentarily forgetting his fatigue, for it had been days since he'd heard Llewelyn joke about anything, least of all his impending act of submission. In the ten years that he'd served as Llewelyn's Seneschal, he'd gotten to know his Prince as few men had, and he continued to rub his calf muscles, waiting until Llewelyn was ready to talk about his brother.

"I do not know him, Tudur, doubt that I ever did. Not so surprising, I suppose. He grew up at the English court, eleven years as a hostage. How could we not be strangers? He was always so quiet, so secretive; in truth, I never had a clue as to what he was thinking. I probably ought to have tried harder to find out. But I did not, and I have enough regrets on my plate right now, without fretting over one that's twenty years too late."

"Most regrets serve for naught, and that one for certes, Llewelyn. You could not have agreed to cut up Gwynedd like a Christmas pie, and what else would have satisfied him?" Tudur rose stiffly from the bench, stamping his feet to get the blood flowing again. "I can see why Rhodri is so jealous of you, but what puzzles me is that he's turned against Davydd, too. They were close as lads, were they not?"

Llewelyn was quiet, looking beyond the desolate gardens toward the frigid grey gleam of the river. "When Owain and I came to Woodstock to surrender to the English King, we found our mother there, with the lads. Another of Henry's misguided kindnesses. He meant well, but it never occurred to him that we'd not want them to witness our shame, no more than I'd have wanted Caitlin at Westminster Hall on the morrow. I can still see Davydd standing on the stairs; he was only eight or so, but if he was afraid, he was hiding it well. Rhodri was there, too, and yet I have no memory of him, Tudur, none at all."

Tudur nodded slowly. "I see what you mean. Davydd, damn his soul, always did cast a long shadow, even as a lad."

"You asked why Rhodri was jealous of Davydd. A harder question is why he was so often overlooked, and for that, I have no answer. It seems too simple to say he had the bad luck to be the lastborn. Mayhap if we'd all been closer in age . . . There was Owain, and nine years later, there was me, and then, when I was ten, my mother gave birth again, long after they must have given up hope. I remember how joyful we all were. To my parents, Davydd must have seemed like a gift from God, and to me, he was a blessing, too, special if only because he was not Owain!" Llewelyn smiled, without mirth. "So our family doted upon Davydd, right from the first breath he drew, and then, fifteen months later, there was Rhodri. But a second miracle baby is somehow not quite as wondrous, is it? Davydd was the marvel, Rhodri the afterthought, and I suspect that's how they saw it, too."

They'd begun to walk again, and as they drew nearer the Painted Chamber, a group of women came out. Eleanora had withdrawn from the great hall soon after greeting Llewelyn, and he assumed now that these were ladies in attendance upon her. One of the women stopped abruptly at sight of him, then hastened down the stairs.

"My lord Llewelyn? I am right, am I not? You are the Prince of Wales?" She was close enough now for him to appreciate how pretty she was, enveloped in a bright wool mantle, her face framed by a graceful hood lined with silver fox fur. As he confirmed his identity, he found himself looking down into dancing dark eyes, eyes that were studying him quite openly and unabashedly. "Oh, my, yes," she murmured, "you will definitely do!"

Llewelyn laughed. "Dare I ask for what?"

She laughed, too. "Lord, how that must have sounded! I was just so gladdened at the sight of you— Damnation, I did it again! I was speaking on behalf of a friend, but I suppose that sounds odd, too?"

"Yes" he said, grinning, "but I am not complaining."

"I think," she said, matching his grin with one of her own, "that we'd best start over." Holding out a soft hand for him to kiss, ablaze with jewels. "I'm afraid I dare not curtsy," she confessed, "for I might not get up again. Beneath this mantle is one very expectant mother-to-be. I hear the court is laying wagers as to who begins her confinement first, the Queen or me!"

"I'm learning more about you by the moment. I know now that you are a wife, soon to be a mother, and I'd venture that you are French," Llewelyn said, for he had a good ear for languages, and her pronunciation was more precise than that of most speakers of Norman-French, whose speech reflected more than two centuries of English influence. "I can also say with certainty that you are highborn and very lovely, that you have a sense of humor and a lively sense of mischief, too, I suspect. So far all I'm lacking is a name."

"I knew I'd forgotten something! I am the Lady Blanche Capet, Countess of Lancaster and Champagne, Queen of Navarre."

"I am honored, Madame," Llewelyn said, and kissed her hand again, with flawless courtesy.

But Blanche suddenly felt as if they were on opposite sides of a yawning chasm, one that was widening with every breath she took. "Wait, my lord," she said hastily. "Do not haul up the drawbridge just yet. I am indeed the King's sister-in-law. But I am also your wife's friend."

"You know Ellen?" Llewelyn's fingers tightened on hers; only when she winced did he realize he'd inadvertently hurt her, and swiftly eased his grip. "Can you tell me how she does—truly?"

"Yes, I can. She has not been maltreated. You may set your mind at rest on that. I think Edward has become genuinely fond of her, and he has seen to it that her confinement is comfortable. But she is heartsick, my lord, and her hurt will not heal, not until the day she can join you in Wales."

IT had begun to snow by the time Llewelyn returned to his companions. They were waiting patiently, all but Tudur, who was feeling the cold keenly this winter, feeling his age as never before. He was restlessly pacing up and down by the river wall, but his scowl faded as Llewelyn came closer. "You must have gotten good news," he said, and Llewelyn nodded.

"I did. I learned that Ellen is not as friendless as I feared." Now Llewelyn was the one to frown, taking notice of the older man's sallow color. "Tudur? Are you ailing?"

Tudur shook his head, and Llewelyn did not press it; he knew Tudur too well for that. "Come on," he said, "let's get our horses, see if we can find this English hamlet. What was it called again, Islington?"

The snow was coming down more heavily now, and the afternoon light was fast fading. They'd almost reached the great hall when they saw familiar figures hastening toward them. "My lord, we've been searching everywhere for you!" Goronwy quickened his pace, with Dai ab Einion on his heels.

"What are you doing here, Goronwy? Why are you not with our men?"

"Our men are back at Islington. But I could wait no longer, had to find you, to tell you what happened in London."

Goronwy's agitation was not that unusual, for his emotions always lay close to the surface. But Dai ab Einion was older, cooler, so dignified that he occasionally seemed somewhat pompous, and yet he was as flushed now as Goronwy, as obviously angry; for once, the two men seemed in rare accord. Llewelyn looked from one to the other. "Tell me," he said.

"You warned me that we'd be stared at, my lord, and you were so right. The Londoners gaped at us as if we were circus freaks, pointing and smirking. I swear I've never been so wroth in all my born days. But I remembered what you said, that we were not to let them provoke us, though by Christ, it was not easy!"

Dai and Goronwy had never been friendly; they were too unlike for a genuine rapport to develop. But now Dai gave the younger man an approving look. "Goronwy speaks true, my lord. His conduct was admirable. He refused to be goaded by those lowborn knaves and malcontents, and between us, we kept our men under control—until we got to that accursed ale-house."

"Ale-house? What were you doing at an ale-house?" Llewelyn demanded, for he could imagine no more dangerous a combination than English, Welsh, and wine.

"Ah, no, my lord, we were not drinking! De Mortimer said Aldersgate would be the quickest way out of the city, but St Martin's Lane was blocked by a huge cart; it had broken a wheel, spilled its load into the street. De Mortimer rode over to harry the driver, and a crowd gathered. There was an ale-house nearby, and the customers came out to watch. Those besotted hellspawn began to laugh at us, my lord! They started to yell out insults, wanting to know if we had tails, if we were heathens like the Jews and Saracens, if it was true that we bedded down in the stables with our cattle!"

Llewelyn's men began to swear, to mutter among themselves. But he made no attempt to mute their outrage; he shared it. "Go on," he said tersely. "What happened then?"

"It was God's mercy, my lord, that most of our men speak no

English." Dai shook his head slowly. "It was bad enough as it was, but had they known how foul, how offensive were the insults—"

"We could take just so much, my lord! Surely you see that?" Goronwy's dark eyes glittered like polished jet. "The worst of the lot was a loud-mouthed lout with a laugh like a mule's bray. He kept egging the others on, and as I tried to calm our lads down, he turned his taunts upon me, shouted out that he had a riddle for us. How could we tell the difference between a whore and a Welshwoman? His answer, my lord, was that there was no difference!"

Tudur said, "Oh, Christ," very softly, and he and Llewelyn exchanged grim glances, bracing themselves for the worst.

"What did you do, Goronwy? You did not kill him?"

"No, my lord," Goronwy said, but he was too honest to claim credit he did not deserve. "I might have, though. I'll never know for sure, as I did not get the chance. Roger de Mortimer came back then, just in time to hear. He reined in his stallion beside the man, smiled, and said, 'My lady mother was Welsh.' He'd sounded almost pleasant, and so it took us all by surprise, what happened next. Ere anyone realized what he was about, he swung his boot free of the stirrup, kicked the man in the face. He went down like a felled tree, spitting blood and teeth," Goronwy said, with savage satisfaction. "The others sobered up right fast after that, retreated back into the ale-house in the blink of an eye, leaving their comrade bleeding and retching into the gutter. So there you have it, my lord. If you want to chastise me . . ."

"For what, Goronwy? You did not act upon your anger," Llewelyn said, and turned away.

They watched him go, held by Tudur's upraised hand. After a moment, Dai said, "I must admit that de Mortimer rose somewhat in my estimation. I never had much use for the man—until today."

"I'm not surprised by what he did," Tudur said, rather absently, for his eyes were following Llewelyn. "For all that he chose his father's people, he never scorned his Welsh blood. Though no man could have been ashamed of a mother like the Lady Gwladys. She was a remarkable woman, and de Mortimer was devoted to her—Goronwy, wait!"

But Goronwy paid him no heed. Llewelyn had stopped by the river wall, and turned with reluctance, for he was not sure he had his emotions under control yet. Fury, frustration, an almost intolerable sense of helplessness—it all showed briefly upon his face as Goronwy drew near. It came as a surprise to Goronwy, the realization that his Prince's passions were no less intense or heartfelt than his own, just ridden with a curb bit. He looked at the other man, feeling such a surge of desperate, despairing loyalty that it momentarily robbed him of speech.

"It is very clear," Llewelyn said, "that we must confine our men to our camp at Islington. Only the most trustworthy can be allowed into London. Now . . . what of you, Goronwy? Will you be able to keep your temper in check on the morrow?" .

"If you ask it of me, yes," Goronwy promised solemnly, and after a moment, Llewelyn nodded.

"Good lad, for I confess that I do want you with me." He paused, his eyes searching the younger man's face. "I understand your rage, Goronwy, more than you know. Having to tell our men that they must endure English insults and abuse was as difficult a command as I've ever given. But I had no choice." He paused again, then said bleakly, "That is what happens when we lose a war."

CHRISTMAS DAY in the great hall of Westminster was a scene of splendor. A yule log burned in the open hearth, and evergreen festooned the window recesses, holly decorated the dais, mistletoe adorned the doorways. Candles and torches and cresset lamps blazed from all corners of the hall. Fresh, sweet-smelling rushes had been laid down, and the air was fragrant with costly incenses from the Holy Land.

Soon there would be an elaborate feast in which the traditional fare, a roasted boar's head, would be served with great pomp and ceremony. There would be venison and swans and oysters and feathered peacocks, and such seasonal favorites as frumenty porridge and minced pies. To drink, there would be sweet milk possets and free-flowing wine, and the spiced ale of the wassail cup.

Afterward, there would be dancing and a mumming and a shepherd's play, and the night would end with the chiming of church bells throughout all Christendom, with each joyful peal heralding the blessed birth of the Holy Child. And the revelries would continue from Christmas until Epiphany, twelve precious days in which to defy winter and cold and dark, to embrace the light one last time before the season of deprivation and want, the coming of Lent.

Llewelyn had already removed his spurs and his mantle, bared his head. Slowly he unbuckled his scabbard. But as he handed his sword to Tudur, he drew a sudden, sharp breath. At Tudur's questioning look, he said, very low, "I just saw my brother."

"Well, Rhodri did say he'd be here, God rot him—"

"No . . . Davydd."

Tudur gave a startled oath, calling Davydd a highly unflattering name. More than that, he could not do, and he watched helplessly now with the other Welshmen as Llewelyn strode into the center of the hall, waited until all eyes were upon him, and then began his walk toward the dais.

Edward's dark head was graced by a royal crown, worn only upon occasions of state. He looked quite regal in red velvet, blue eyes intent upon the Welsh Prince. Kneeling before Edward, Llewelyn placed his hands together in the prescribed gesture of submission, for the ceremony of homage was choreographed down to the last detail. Edward rose to his feet, took Llewelyn's hands in his own, and Llewelyn began to speak.

"My lord King and liege lord, I, Llewelyn ap Gruffydd, Prince of Wales and Lord of Eryri, do willingly enter into your homage and faith and become your sworn man, and to you faithfully will I bear body, chattels, and earthly worship, and I will keep faith and loyalty to you against all others."

The act of homage was not a humbling experience for English vassals; they saw it as a natural expression of the obedience owed to one's liege lord, for theirs was an ordered, hierarchical society structured upon military tenure of land. But it was an alien concept to the Welsh, imposed upon them by force of arms. Llewelyn had been the first Welsh prince able to turn this English weapon against them, to use homage as a means of unifying Wales. He would have found it easier to do homage himself if he could have believed that the English King recognized and respected the very real differences that existed between the English and the Welsh. He was convinced, though, that Edward saw no distinction between Wales and any English earldom, and that made his act of homage an act of self-betrayal.

But he'd done it, and he waited now for Edward to perform his part, to make an utter mockery of these solemn oaths sworn before God and witnessed by men. For homage was a reciprocal obligation, bound both men to each other in a relationship of dependence and protection. Just as the vassal must obey his liege lord, so must the liege lord make the vassal's enemies his own.

Edward looked out upon their audience, back toward Llewelyn. "We do promise to you, as my vassal and liegeman," he said gravely, "that we and our heirs will guarantee to you and your heirs the Welsh lands you hold of us, against all others, that you may hold said lands in peace."

And then, Llewelyn having sworn allegiance to the man who'd sheltered his would-be assassins and abducted his wife, Edward raised him to his feet and gave him the ritual kiss of peace.

LIFTING his wine cup, Edward suggested, "Shall we drink to new beginnings?" Llewelyn clinked his cup against the King's, and the hall erupted in applause.

Edmund and Blanche were approaching, and Edward beckoned

them up onto the dais. "You know my brother, of course, but you have not yet had the pleasure of meeting his wife . . . or have you?" Edward amended, for Blanche and Llewelyn were smiling at each other like old and familiar friends.

"Oh, the Prince of Wales and I have known each other forever," Blanche said blithely, amusing Llewelyn and baffling everyone else within hearing, except Edmund, who was no longer surprised by anything his wife said or did.

Eleanora was frowning, and knowing that his sister-in-law was nothing if not literal-minded, Edmund said hastily, "Eleanora, trust me. Do not even ask."

"Sometimes I suspect that if we traveled to Persia, Blanche would still encounter old friends," Edward said, with a smile and just a suggestion of sarcasm, for he found his sister-in-law to be very entertaining company, but a bit too flippant for his taste; the irreverent humor that amused him coming from a Davydd or a Roger de Mortimer seemed inappropriate in a woman's mouth. "But I see someone whom I know for certes that you have not yet met, my lord Llewelyn, even though she is your kinswoman twice-over. Fortunately we can remedy that right now. Davydd, bring Lisbet up onto the dais."

Clinging to Davydd's arm, Elizabeth mounted the steps of the dais, where she curtsied first to Edward and then to Llewelyn. "Lady Elizabeth," Llewelyn said, and kissed her hand. "You'd be a welcome addition to any family." And because he was not about to expose Welsh wounds to English eyes, he looked then at his brother, said coolly, "Davydd, what a surprise."

"A happy one, I trust." But Davydd's riposte lacked his usual verve; to Llewelyn, who knew him so well, he looked tired and tense.

"Marital alliances entangle us in the most remarkable webs," Edward said, his eyes shifting curiously between Llewelyn and his brother. "Who could have guessed that one day I would be kinsman to you both, compliments of my lovely cousins, Elizabeth and Ellen." He smiled at Elizabeth, before turning his attention back to Llewelyn.

"Ellen is our phantom guest," he said wryly, "unseen but not forgotten. I know she is foremost in your thoughts. I can tell you, too, what those thoughts are. You've come to Westminster, done homage at my Christmas court. Now you want me to hold to our bargain. Fair enough, and I have every intention of honoring my word. We obviously cannot talk here and now, with the trestle tables about to be set up at any moment. But I doubt that you'll want to wait, for in truth, I've never met a more restive people than you Welsh! Will tomorrow be soon enough?"

"No," Llewelyn said, and smiled, "but it will have to do."

"Good, it is settled then. I'll be at the Tower in the morning. Meet me there at noon, and we'll see if we cannot reach an agreement about Ellen's release."

"At the Tower?" For a moment, Llewelyn could not believe what he'd heard, for Edward was still smiling, and the others showed no signs that anything out of the ordinary had just been said. It was only when he glanced over at Davydd, saw his brother's face mirroring his own shock, that he knew he had not misunderstood. The English King had indeed ordered him to come to the royal fortress that was England's most notorious prison, where his father had been confined and where he had died.

LLEWELYN shivered as the wind gusted through the cloisters, for he had seized his first chance to leave the hall, and he'd not bothered to retrieve his mantle. Snow glazed the ground of the inner garth, but he could catch glimpses of sun amidst the circling clouds. Hungry birds wheeled overhead, and he heard an occasional muffled shout as boatmen hailed one another; even Christmas was not a day of rest on the River Thames. He knew he had to go back inside soon, before he was missed. But he was not yet ready, still seething with rebellious, impotent rage.

"There you are!" Llewelyn whirled at the sound of Welsh, saw Davydd hurrying toward him along the path. Flushed and out of breath, he stopped a few feet away. "Jesú, but it's cold out here! You were too quick, I did not see you leave. Llewelyn, listen. Edward did not mean that as it sounded. I know him better than you. Granted, he can be mean-spirited, but not like this. I do not think he even realized that he'd given mortal offense. Most likely he just did not remember that our father— What? Why do you look at me like that?"

"What sort of twisted game are you playing now, Davydd? You make a two-hundred-mile journey on winter roads, just so you can watch me bleed before the English court, and then you dare to pretend concern over my peace of mind? Do you truly think I'm that big a fool?"

"That is not so! I did not come here to gloat!"

"No? Then why did you come? I believed your lies often enough in the past, God knows, but I'm no longer as easily duped. So you'd best make this tale a memorable one!"

Davydd's eyes narrowed. "As it happens, it has naught to do with you. My wife wanted to come to her cousin's Christmas court, and since she's breeding, I thought it best to humor her whims. Does that satisfy you? And now I am going back into the hall, and you . . . you can go to Hell!"

Davydd spun around, stalked back up the pathway. Llewelyn

watched him go. He'd begun to shiver again, for the wind was coming off the river now. But he was too angry to risk returning to the hall. He glanced around, then crossed to the south walkway, entered the chapel of St Stephen.

Within, all was quiet, so still that he could hear the sound of his own breathing, rapid, uneven. His inner turmoil seemed to make a mockery of God's peace. Moving down the nave, he paused before the High Altar, ringed with flaming white candles. His father's temper had been the stuff of which legends are made. His rages had been as spontaneous as they were spectacular, for he'd remained as ignorant and as innocent as a child about the consequences of those firestorms of fury. And he'd passed on the lion's share of that fabled temper to his son Owain, who'd followed all too closely in Gruffydd's scorched footsteps. Llewelyn, too, had been bequeathed a portion of that dubious and dangerous legacy. But he'd long ago learned what Gruffydd never had, hard lessons in self-control. That was why he was so shaken now by his confrontation with Davydd. Why had he let his temper catch fire like that? How was it that Davydd always managed to get past the moat and the outer walls, to assault the keep itself? Why could he not master the one defense that could never be overcome—indifference?

Hearing footsteps in the nave, he turned, expecting to see a priest. But it was his young sister-in-law. Elizabeth stopped by the rood screen. "Forgive me for intruding like this," she said hesitantly, "but I needed to talk to you alone, and I did not know when another opportunity might arise."

"You are a welcome diversion, not an intrusion," Llewelyn said, not altogether truthfully, and smiled at her. As Elizabeth stepped forward, he saw that she'd been more sensible than he or Davydd, for she was wrapped in a warm wool mantle. "I understand that congratulations are in order. Davydd tells me that you are with child."

"It is still too early yet to be utterly sure, but I have hopes." She smiled suddenly. "God willing, I will give Davydd a son in the new year," she said, and Llewelyn felt an unwonted prick of envy.

Moving toward her, he shook his head when she called him "my lord," saying, "We have no need for formality between us, for not only are you my sister by marriage, you are my wife's cousin. What can I do for you, Elizabeth?"

"Davydd and I are staying at the Swan Inn on Thames Street. It is very comfortable and conveniently located, just above the bridge. I . . . I was wondering if you might come there and dine with us."

She looked like an eager child to Llewelyn, squeezing her hands together as she spoke, biting her lip as she waited now for his answer. Edward had told him her age—nineteen—but she seemed much younger to him at that moment, and he found it unexpectedly difficult to turn her down.

"I am sorry, lass," he said, as kindly as he could. "I cannot do that."

Elizabeth was quiet for a moment, struggling with her disappointment. "I suppose I knew all along that you would not," she admitted. "But I had to try."

"Davydd does not know about this planned dinner of yours, does he?" Her silence confirmed his suspicions, and he said, very seriously, "Elizabeth, I am sure you meant well. But you'd do better not to involve yourself in our conflict. I am afraid, lass, that Davydd would be very wroth with you should he find out what you tried to do."

"Do you think I fear Davydd's anger?" She sounded surprised, and then indignant. "You know Davydd, so you should know better! I get so heartily sick of it, the way people always think the worst of him. This is why I hate coming to Edward's court. They all act as if I were a . . . a sacrificial lamb. And the older women, they are the worst. Giving me motherly pats and covert looks of pity. The fat cows, if they only knew!"

Llewelyn glanced away so she'd not see his grin. The change in her was startling; he tended to forget that even a kitten had claws. "So you do not like visits to the English court?" he asked, and she responded with an emphatic shake of her head, a forceful "Jesú forfend," one of Davydd's favorite oaths. "That is odd," he said, "for Davydd told me that he'd come to Westminster merely to please you."

The blue eyes flickered, but she never hesitated. "Yes," she said, "I did coax him into coming. The Christmas court, after all, is different, is not to be missed."

Llewelyn looked into her upturned face. "You are very loyal," he said quietly, "and Davydd is very lucky."

"No," Elizabeth said, "I am the lucky one!" She turned to go, then gave him one last hopeful look over her shoulder. "If you should change your mind . . ." He said nothing, but there was something implacable in his silence, and she sighed, mouthing under her breath another of the oaths she'd learned from Davydd. At the rood screen, she paused again. "I never knew what it was like to be happy," she said softly, and without waiting for his response, she moved toward the door, leaving behind echoes of her quick, light steps, faint traces of her perfume, and a few puddles of melting ice upon the floor of the chancel, where her skirts had swept the snow-laden ground of the cloisters.

Llewelyn followed her to the door. He did not think it was easy to be a woman in their world, but he had known a number of women who could match any man in daring, determination, and common sense. Joanna, his grandfather's wife, had often acted as his envoy to the English court, had once averted a war. His aunt, Elen de Quincy, had braved public scandal to wed the man she loved. His own mother had made a devil's deal with the English King in a vain attempt to gain her husband's freedom. Nell de Montfort had ridden the whirlwind with Simon for nigh on thirty years, his partner, his confidante, his consort. But now, as he stood, watching as Elizabeth headed back toward the hall, Llewelyn thought he had never known any woman so in need of protection as his brother's young, pregnant wife.

IT snowed again that night, and by the next morning London's streets were shrouded in white. The sky was still overcast, and wind-blown drifts covered the usual refuse and debris littering the city's center gutters. The streets were almost deserted, for Sunday was God's day, and most Londoners were home before their hearths. Llewelyn's escort had been handpicked for their equanimity, all but Goronwy, who was pledged to be on his best behavior, but Llewelyn was glad, nonetheless, that his men's sangfroid would not be put to the test. They crossed the city without incident, and shortly before noon they rode through the landgate into the outer bailey of the vast, formidable stronghold known, with sinister simplicity, as the Tower.

The White Tower, the fortress's great keep, soared ninety feet into the somber winter sky. Llewelyn reined in his stallion, gazing up at those grey stone battlements. Gruffydd had knotted sheets together, climbed out of one of the chapel windows, and begun a slow, laborious descent toward the ground so far below. But courage was not always its own reward, and his makeshift rope had given way. They'd found him crumpled at the base of the forebuilding, and Llewelyn had heard that men sickened at sight of the body, for Gruffydd's head had been driven into his chest upon impact. The ground had been snow-covered that night, too, and for days afterward, people had come to stare at the blood-soaked snow, at the dried blood splattering the roof and wall of the forebuilding, until the Tower constable obliterated the evidence with shovels and whitewash.

Llewelyn had demanded all the gory details, for he'd been only sixteen, too young to realize that sometimes it was better not to know. A muscle twitched in his cheek. More time passed, and then he looked over at his men, watching in a hushed, respectful silence; some had even doffed their hats, as they would in a church or cemetery. "Let's go," he said. "The English King is waiting."

The great hall was packed with jostling, shoving men, echoing with boisterous laughter, catcalls, and curses. Edward broke away from the others, strode over to greet Llewelyn with cheerful, disarming informality.

"If the Archbishop of Canterbury hears about his, he'll pitch a fit

for certes. Cockfighting on a Sunday is bound to be a sin of some sort!"
He grinned, and Llewelyn wondered if Davydd had been right, after
all. Was he here at the Tower as a spiteful exercise of royal power? Or
merely as a matter of royal convenience?

"My private chamber in the Blundeville Tower adjoins the hall. We
can talk there whilst your men lose their money on the fight," Edward
said, to Goronwy's obvious dismay. He looked so alarmed that Llewelyn
drew him aside, quietly assured him that if Edward had planned treachery, it would have occurred before he'd done homage, not afterward.
Goronwy did not look completely convinced, but the rest of their men
had already joined the circle of spectators, and as Llewelyn and Edward
exited the hall, they looked back upon a scene of rare English-Welsh
harmony.

"I thought we'd do better on our own," Edward explained. "It is
not as if we need an interpreter, after all. I want you to know, Llewelyn,
that I'll not keep Ellen in England a day longer than necessary. But I
have to be sure that she'll not find herself wed to a rebel, trapped in an
alien land at war with the Crown."

"It seems then, that we are in agreement," Llewelyn said, hoping
he'd managed to keep all traces of sarcasm from his voice. "We both
want Ellen in Wales, not Windsor. So it is just a question of when. I
suggest we begin by discussing something we can agree upon here and
now. I've been hearing about the efficiency of the English Chancery.
Why not put it to a test, see if they can get a safe-conduct issued for
me by the morrow?"

By now they'd reached the end of the passageway, were at the door
of Edward's chamber in the Blundeville Tower. "A safe-conduct? For
where?"

"Scotland," Llewelyn said, a little too sharply. "Windsor, where
else? It is only twenty miles from here, is it not?"

Edward nodded, and then stunned Llewelyn by saying, "Well . . . I
do not really see a need for that."

As difficult as Llewelyn found it to give Edward the benefit of the
doubt in anything, it still had not occurred to him that Edward might
refuse him the right to visit Ellen at Windsor. Edward had already
opened the door, and he followed the English King into the chamber,
too outraged to keep up the pretense.

"So you do not think I need to meet my wife? You'd best explain
yourself!"

"That was not what I said," Edward protested, with surprising
mildness. "What I said was that there was no need for you to go to
Windsor." And then he grinned, and Llewelyn realized, belatedly, that
they were not alone in the chamber.

A woman was standing on the far side of the room, holding what looked like a white fur muff. But as Llewelyn turned toward her, she set the muff in one of the window-seats, revealing it to be a very small dog, and sank down in a deep curtsy.

"My lord Prince of Wales," Edward said, "I have the pleasure to present to you my kinswoman and your wife, the Lady Eleanor de Montfort."

Llewelyn crossed swiftly to Ellen, reached down, and raised her to her feet, then brought her hand up and kissed it. Ellen gave him a dazzling smile, then turned it upon Edward. "Ned," she said, "do you not have an invasion to plan or a castle to besiege?"

Edward's grin widened. "No, sweetheart," he said innocently, "I have the entire afternoon free to spend with you and Llewelyn."

"Ned. Dearest Cousin. Go away," Ellen said, giving him a playful push toward the door. He leaned down then, whispered something in her ear, and at last made a jaunty departure, leaving behind a trail of laughter.

Llewelyn was not often disconcerted, but he was now, caught off balance first by Edward's surprise, and then by the surge of emotions it set free. The pendulum had swung too far, too fast, from fury to astonishment to joy to wariness. When he'd envisioned his first meeting with Ellen, he'd never imagined for a moment that she might not be to his liking. But that was indeed his first, instinctive reaction. Watching as she exchanged quips with Edward, he found himself wondering suddenly if he'd not made a great mistake.

She was beautiful, one of the most beautiful women he'd ever seen. But her nonchalance, her perfect poise in an admittedly awkward situation struck uneasy echoes deep within his memory, bringing to mind another woman from his past, one he'd bedded briefly and long since forgotten, or so he'd thought. The name came back now—Arwenna— and so did the memories. She'd been just as lovely as Ellen, just as worldly, as sure of her power to enchant. And she'd also been shallow, selfish, and frivolous. That did not sound, he knew, like the Ellen de Montfort he'd been led to expect. But then, he'd not expected, either, to find her on such intimate, affectionate terms with her cousin and captor, the English King.

Ellen shut the door, and when she turned back to face Llewelyn, he found himself looking at a different woman altogether. The bright, brittle pose fell away; even her voice changed timbre. "Can you ever forgive me," she said, almost in a whisper, "for all the trouble and grief I've brought upon you?"

"Ah, no, lass, there is nothing to forgive!" In three strides, Llewelyn was at her side, taking her hand in his. "I'll not deny that this war wreaked havoc upon my homeland. But you were one of its victims, Ellen, not its cause. This I can tell you for an utter certainty, that all my regrets were for your abduction, your suffering, and our separation. Never for our marriage."

Ellen's eyes never left his face; her fingers had entwined with his. "I so needed to hear you say that. This has been one of the worst mornings of my life, and it should have been one of the best. But the longer I had to wait, the more nervous I became. No woman ever had more reason to be grateful to the man she married, and whilst on that cog, I vowed that you would never be sorry. By now I ought to have borne you our first son. Instead, you had two years in Hell. I kept telling myself that I could not blame you if you did regret our marriage, but I think it would have broken my heart."

Llewelyn's hand tightened upon hers. "You could as easily have blamed me, for a wife has the right to expect her husband to keep her safe. But I failed you twice-over, in letting you be taken, and then in not being able to win your release."

She shook her head. "I am Simon de Montfort's daughter," she said, with a sad smile. "Who would know better than I the might of the English Crown?"

After that, a silence fell, but not an uncomfortable one, for they were rapt in their discovery of each other. They were standing close enough for Llewelyn to catch a faint hint of violets. It was a fragrance that he had never fancied—until now—breathing in Ellen's perfume, a scent of spring twilight on a day of drifting December snow.

Ellen had the advantage of Llewelyn, for she'd not been taken by surprise. But now she found herself doubting the evidence of her own senses. "For nigh on half my life," she said, "I've been holding fast to a memory of you. It was not my memory, of course, although it came in time to seem as if it were, as if my mother's recollections had somehow become mine, so vivid was your image to me, so real. I saw you through her eyes, tall and dark, with a smile that she called 'sudden.' When you walked in that door, it was as if you'd walked out of my own past, for you were just as I'd envisioned you. I suppose that is not so surprising, but . . . but you also sound exactly as I imagined you would, your voice low-pitched and husky, with a wonderful Welsh lilt. How did I know that? Have I been stealing into your dreams? Or have you been invading mine?"

Llewelyn was intrigued by her candor, and by gold-flecked cat eyes, long-lashed, as clear as crystal. "I might be what you expected," he confided, "but you, my lady, are a surprise for certes!"

"In what way?"

She was flirting with him so obviously now that he grinned, tilted his head to the side in a very approving appraisal. "Well . . . you are more beautiful than I expected, more worldly, more assured, and best of all, you are not still thirteen!"

She looked so puzzled then, that Llewelyn could not help laughing. "We have an odd history, you and I, twelve years in the making. I cannot say that you haunted my dreams, as you aver, but you did claim a corner of my brain and took up residence. You were so young then, and you'd been hurt so much. I did what I must, I disavowed our plight troth, but I was troubled by that lost little girl, more than I realized. If someone had asked me today how old you are, I would have answered without hesitation: that you are twenty and five. But that little lass of thirteen was a most persistent ghost, always hovering close at hand, in need of all the protection I'd denied her after Evesham, and in some strange sense, it was she I expected to find." He laughed again, this time at himself. "Does that sound as mad to you as it does to me?"

Ellen was touched by his admission. But she was not surprised that he should have felt so responsible for that "lost little girl," even after severing their betrothal bond, for it seemed to bear out her own secret, heartfelt hope, that their marriage was fated to be, that just as they'd defied the odds and somehow survived the ruination of Evesham, so, too, would they be able to prevail over Edward.

"It does not sound mad at all," she said softly. "I do not mind in the least being a surprise, as long as I am not a disappointment?"

Llewelyn grinned again. "A woman surpassingly fair instead of a timid child bride? What man would not be disappointed?"

Ellen was quite unrepentant and not at all abashed at being caught out. "Mea culpa," she said, "I was indeed fishing for a compliment. But I had no courtship; would you begrudge me a bit of flattery?"

"I think," Llewelyn said, "that I would begrudge you very little in this life." He still held her hand, and drew her now toward the window-seat nearest the hearth. They settled themselves side by side on the cushions, joined at once by Ellen's little dog. Llewelyn watched as she sought in vain to push the animal away, for he was unable to take his eyes off her. "I cannot begin to count the people who told me you were a beauty, starting with Simon. I assumed, though, that you'd resemble Nell, and you do not. You have the most astonishing eyes; they catch the light like gemstones. That color is rare in my homeland. I've seen it but once that I can remember, and she was a kinswoman of yours— my grandfather's wife."

Ellen was delighted. "My aunt Joanna! It is one of the great regrets of my life that I never knew her. Are my eyes truly like hers?"

"The color is the same, water over mossy rocks. But I doubt that her eyes could change as quick as yours do. What of your hair color? Is it as dark as Joanna's was?"

"See for yourself," she said, and reaching up, she removed her veil. She began to unfasten her wimple next, and Llewelyn found himself staring at the slender white throat she'd just bared, wanting suddenly to touch her, to see if her skin was as soft, as smooth as it looked. But she was an innocent, he must not forget that, must go slowly for her sake. She'd withdrawn the last of the wimple's pins, revealing a crown of bright hair, a shade Llewelyn had not seen before, a deep copper-gold midway between blonde and red.

"Your hair is like your eyes," he marveled, "a color all your own," and she smiled at him, then unpinned her fret, the fashionable net of gold mesh binding her hair. She smiled again, then shook her head, and Llewelyn caught his breath, for as her hair swirled about her shoulders and cascaded down her back, framing her face in provocative disarray, she looked suddenly and wonderfully wanton, looked like a woman just risen from a lover's bed.

"Good Lord, girl," he said, with a shaken laugh, "do you have any idea what you just did to me?" To his surprise, she flushed deeply. "Ellen? I did not mean to discomfit you. But in truth, you did not seem shy."

"Shy—me?" Ellen's smile was wry. "That very suggestion would have sent my brothers rolling onto the floor with laughter."

"You may not be shy, but you are flustered," Llewelyn said, and when she did not deny it, he reached for her hand again. "Can you tell me why?"

She hesitated, but she had to be honest; with him, there could be no other way. "I am not sure I can make sense of what I am feeling, for I've never felt like this before, so . . . so anxious. You said I was assured, and you were right; usually I am. That is what being pretty does for a woman, for I learned early on that I could turn male heads without even trying. What I did not learn was how to play the role of the proper modest maiden, to keep my eyes downcast and my speech demure. I always spoke my mind."

"That is hardly surprising for the daughter of Nell de Montfort," he said, and made her pulse jump by turning her hand over, pressing a kiss into her palm.

She focused her thoughts with an effort. "Moreover, I had five doting brothers, in whose eyes I could do no wrong; it amused them enormously that their little sister could swear like a soldier, that I could tell a bawdy joke and keep their guilty secrets. And so, when I began to attract men in earnest, at the French court, I saw no reason to guard my speech, to pretend to be what I was not. In truth, the hypocrisy of it all seemed ridiculous. Women are supposed to be daughters of Eve, born temptresses, or so the Church would have us believe. But virgins are expected to act as timid and skittish as newborn fawns."

He laughed at that, and she said reproachfully, "You know I am speaking true. Men want their wives to be nuns before marriage and concubines afterward. At least the men at the French court did. I never fretted, though, that I might be giving the wrong impression, for none of those men mattered to me. They would flirt, try to get me into bed, fail, and I'd forget them. I never truly cared about pleasing a man . . . until now. When I let down my hair for you, I knew full well what I was doing. I wanted you to want me. But when you jested about it, I was of a sudden assailed by doubts, by the fear that I might have seemed too . . . too brazen."

Llewelyn was awed by her utter honesty. Just as she'd bared her throat, now she was baring her soul, and he knew better than most men the courage that took. "Ah, lass," he said, "you do not realize just how dangerous you are." When he lifted her hand, she thought he meant to kiss it again. Instead, he held it against his cheek, a gentle gesture at variance with what she read in his eyes. "I do not think you are brazen, cariad, only that I am luckier than I deserve."

He smiled, then leaned toward her, and she closed her eyes, raised her face for his kiss. But they'd forgotten they were being watched by jealous eyes, and as Llewelyn took Ellen in his arms, the dog went into action, squirming between its mistress and the intruder with ferret-like speed, so that their first kiss proved to be memorable in a most unexpected manner; they found themselves sputtering, inhaling mouthfuls of fluffy white fur.

"Blessed Lady Mary!" Ellen gasped, at the same time that Llewelyn said something in Welsh, which by the tone of it, sounded suspiciously like an oath. Rubbing the back of her hand against her mouth, she glared at the dog, then looked apologetically at her husband. No sooner did their eyes meet, though, than they began to laugh.

The dog had staked out possession of Ellen's lap, daring Llewelyn to trespass again. But there was a leather lead on the table, and before the little creature could rally its defenses, it found itself tucked under the enemy's arm, being carried across the room. Looping the leash over a chair, Llewelyn said, "This dog has got to be an agent of the English Crown," sending Ellen into a fresh fit of giggles.

"My God, how did you guess? Ned gave her to me!"

Again it jarred, the easy familiarity of "Ned." But this time Llewelyn shoved it aside, back into the shadows where it could be ignored. A handsome pair of deerskin gloves lay on the table, and picking up one, he handed it to the disgruntled dog as a consolation prize. "I'm sure," he said, "that Edward would not begrudge a glove or two in the interest of marital harmony," making Ellen laugh again. But as he reached for the wine flagon, she said something so unexpected that he spun around to stare at her, the wine forgotten. "Say that again," he demanded.

"I said that I'd given her a Welsh name, that I'd called her 'Hiraeth.' "

Llewelyn came back to the window-seat, pulled Ellen to her feet, and into his arms. "How in the world did you know about that?"

"My aunt Joanna. She once tried to explain to my mother why it was that the Welsh sickened when they were uprooted, banished from Wales. She said the Welsh had a special name for it—hiraeth—that it meant a love of their homeland, a sadness for what had been lost, a yearning for what could be—"

She got no further, for it was then that Llewelyn kissed her. Their second effort was much more satisfactory than their first, and Ellen felt bereft when he let her go, not wanting the embrace to end. He smiled at her, then retrieved the wine from the table, and brought it back to the window-seat, where he kissed her again. She knew she was being foolish, but it bothered her to see how deftly he'd tilted their wine cup as he embraced her; it was too smoothly done, the sort of trick a man learned only by experience. How could she be jealous of his past? That would be madness, for he'd lived almost half of it ere she was even born. But she wanted him to feel what she felt now, the wonder and newness of it, and that was impossible, for there were twenty-four years between them, and God only knows how many women. She accepted the wine cup, watching him as she drank. Well, she could never be his first love, but by all that was holy, she'd be his last.

"How long do we have ere Edward sends you back to Windsor?"

She'd been worried that he might think her presence here meant Edward had relented, and she was glad that he seemed to read her cousin so well. "Only a few days," she said, wondering how she could endure being parted from him now. He'd begun to kiss her throat, and she shivered, for he was evoking the most amazing sensations. How wonderful that their lust was sanctioned by Holy Church, so she could give in to it without guilt! He was stroking her hair, brushing it aside to kiss her throat again, and she pressed closer, sliding her hands up his back, thinking that if only she held him tightly enough, mayhap the world would go away.

Llewelyn was the one to break free first. "Ellen . . ." No more than that, just her name, but it was enough. Ellen felt a surge of triumph, sure now that he wanted her, too, just as much as she wanted him.

"Llewelyn . . . is it always like this between men and women?"

"No," he said, discovering that she liked being kissed on her ear lobe. "The flame burns hotter at some times than others, cariad."

"And with us? Is this one of those times?"

He seemed to be considering. "Well," he said at last, "I think we're kindling a fair amount of heat."

She knew she was being teased, did not mind at all. "How much heat? Enough to melt a candle? To start a bonfire? Could you be more precise, please?"

By now they both were laughing. "Enough heat to set half of Wales ablaze," he said, drawing her across his lap so that her head nestled into the crook of his arm and her long hair swept the floor. "I think you're right. It is a pity we had no courtship. Then I could have told you how very fair you are. I could have compared your hair to autumn bracken and your skin to silk, said all the foolish and fanciful things smitten lovers have said down through the ages."

"Why can you not say them now?"

"Alas, it is too late, two years too late. No man ever says things like that to his wife."

"No? We shall see about that," Ellen promised, and entwined her arms around his neck, pulling his head down so she could kiss him. This time it was different; the passion flared up between them so fast that Llewelyn was caught by surprise, and he stopped thinking, yielded to it. So did Ellen, shifting so he could unpin the brooch closing the neckline of her bodice, stroking his face, his hair, gasping as he licked the soft hollow between her breasts. He was murmuring Welsh endearments she could not understand, but the sound of his voice stirred her senses almost as much as his breath on her throat, his hands on her body. "Oh, love," she whispered, "love, yes," not even knowing what she said, wanting only to taste his mouth on hers, to feel the weight of his body pressing down upon hers, and when he lowered her back onto the cushions, she looked up at him with starlit eyes and a smile to make him forget everything but the here and now, the woman under him in the window-seat.

He was never to know what stopped him, whether it was simply a lifetime's habit of control, or a protective urge stirred by her utter trust, or even the insistent whimpering of the dog. It took an intense effort of will to pull away from the soft body straining against his, but as he sat up, he became aware that the dog was no longer whining; it had begun to growl. His reaction came without thought, came from instinct honed sharp as any sword. Grasping Ellen's wrist, he jerked her upright on the seat, just as the door opened and Edward entered.

Edwards smile froze, and for one of the few times in his life, his sense of humor failed him; instead, he experienced something oddly like embarrassment. Ellen's hair streamed down her back in tangled disorder. Clinging to Llewelyn as if she needed support, she gazed up at him with glazed, unfocused eyes; it was a look he'd often seen upon his own wife's face, but only in the privacy of their marriage bed. Edward knew that he was staring. He couldn't seem to help himself, though, unable to believe that this disheveled, desirable wanton was his proper, staid little cousin, Ellen the untouchable, the ice maiden. But whatever had been happening in here, it was for certes not rape.

It was their silence that brought him back to his senses, to the reluctant realization that he was somehow in the wrong. "I am sorry," he said, not very convincingly, for he'd not had much practice at apologies. "I should have knocked."

"Yes," Llewelyn said, "you should have."

Edward was so astonished that anyone would dare to criticize the manners of the King that he forbore to take offense. He supposed he could not fairly blame the Welshman for being a bit churlish; in truth, he'd not have taken it with good grace either, had he been in Llewelyn's place.

By now, Ellen had managed to reorient herself, had adjusted her gown to make sure she was not showing Edward what was for Llewelyn's eyes only. But she had not drawn away from Llewelyn, had deliberately moved closer, in fact, and when he put his arm around her shoulders, she leaned back against him, then smiled at Edward. "You wanted something, Ned?"

"Edmund and Blanche are down in the great hall. I thought you might like to surprise them." Edward was slowly beginning to see some humor in the situation, and he added, "It seems to be a day for surprises. Shall I send up your maid to you, Ellen?"

"Oh, you mean this?" she said, running her hand through that wild, coppery mane. "Thank you, but that will not be necessary. I'm sure my husband can help make me presentable."

"As you wish," Edward agreed, torn between amusement and annoyance at the emergence of this new Ellen. "When will you be ready?"

"Thursday," Llewelyn suggested, so laconically that Edward took it as a joke and laughed.

"We will await you then, down in the hall." As he moved toward the door, Edward began to laugh again. "I am going to have to learn the Welsh art of seduction, for certes. And to think I once thought that when it came to courting, Davydd was the quick one!"

Ellen could feel the muscles of Llewelyn's arm contract under her hand, and she was relieved when he kept silent. As soon as they were alone, she reached up, touched his cheek. "You need not be angry on my behalf, love. Ned can tell the entire court, and I'd not care. You are my husband, and what happens between us is not cause for shame."

Llewelyn tightened his arm around her, drawing her in against his chest. It was clear to him that she did not understand the significance of what had just occurred, or the probable consequences, but he could not bring himself to burden her with more cares. Smoothing her hair back over her shoulders, he kissed the corner of her mouth. "In truth, cariad, I am angry with myself, too, for it is folly to keep stoking a fire when there is no means at hand of quenching it. I may have cheated you of a courtship and a lavish wedding, but at the very least, I ought to provide a marriage bed."

She laughed softly. "It is rather like being drunk, is it not?"

He grinned, thinking she spoke truer than she knew, and got reluctantly to his feet, got them both away from the tempting proximity of that cushioned window-seat. "You go to my head, Ellen, not to mention those body parts farther south. Being alone with you is going to put severe demands upon my self-control." And although he said it as a joke, he knew it was not.

Ellen gave him a look of such yearning that he could feel his treacherous body already rebelling. "There is an easy answer to that," she said. "Tomorrow we bolt the door."

Llewelyn could only marvel at the mysterious ways of the Almighty. His world in charred ruins about him, a lifetime's efforts set at naught, and suddenly this remarkable woman, this bond that went beyond a fever of the flesh. "No, cariad," he said gently, "we cannot."

"Why not? Why should we wait for Edward's court wedding? That is a misguided generosity on his part, for we are man and wife in the eyes of God and Christendom. I have been your bride for two years, Llewelyn, but I want to be your wife. How can that be wrong?"

"It is not wrong, Ellen, but it is dangerous." He saw she still did not comprehend. "We cannot risk laying together until you are free, for we cannot risk giving the English Crown two hostages for the price of one. What if you got with child?"

"Oh, God . . . " Ellen was shaken. "What a fool I am!" The thought of delivering her child, Llewelyn's heir, into Edward's power was so horrifying to her that she shuddered, and Llewelyn pulled her into a close embrace. Looking up into his face, she said, "I thought that if only we could meet, the separation would be more bearable. But it is not going to be easier at all, is it? It is going to be even harder now to abide being apart, to keep faith."

She sounded desperately unhappy, she who'd been joyous but moments before. "I know," he said. "In the past, I was counting the days till you were freed. Now I'll be counting the nights, too."

As he'd hoped, that coaxed a smile. "So will I," she said, with a fervency that was only partially exaggerated for comic effect, "oh, indeed, so will I." But she had an idea then, and fumbling in the bodice of her gown, she drew out a man's ring looped upon a beaten gold chain.

"So that is what I felt," Llewelyn said, and she gave him another smile, this one bright and bewitching and hot enough to singe his good intentions.

"This is my father's ring, never off his finger until he rode out to die on Evesham's bloody field. It became my mother's most cherished keepsake, and on her deathbed, she bequeathed it to my brother Amaury. I in turn promised that I'd hold it for him, keep it safe until he regains his freedom. I want you to wear it, Llewelyn, and each time you look at it, think of me and know that we'll soon be together in Wales."

"I shall guard it well, cariad," he said, "and return it to you upon our wedding night." He kissed her then, long and hard, for never had their wedding night, their life together, seemed so far out of reach. It was no longer a matter of honor, of marital vows and injured pride. There was just one woman now in all of Christendom whom he wanted, whom he had to have, no matter the cost. But God help them both, for Edward now knew that, too.

22

WINDSOR CASTLE, ENGLAND

January 1278

THE sky was still shrouded at noon, for the rain had yet to slacken, a stinging, icy rain that spilled steadily from clouds thick enough to smother the sun, threatening to blot out the light for days to come. As she stared down into the dismal, deserted quagmire of the middle bailey, Ellen found it easy to believe that the rain could go on like this till spring.

She had been sitting in the window-seat for hours, heedless of the chill and damp and Juliana's futile attempts at cheer. Juliana had never seen her moods swing so wildly as in these days after her return to Windsor; she was either in euphoria or despair, sometimes within the span of the same hour. Juliana was still adjusting to the change; it was a revelation that the even-tempered Ellen could be just as volatile as her high-strung mother. But Juliana needed no doctor to diagnose Ellen's ailment, for it was evident to her that Ellen was smitten with her own husband. And remembering her sweet, stolen moments with Bran, Juliana was both thankful and envious that Ellen was to have so much more, a lifetime more—if Edward could be trusted to keep faith.

Juliana was about to propose a chess game in another effort to raise Ellen's spirits. But Sir Nicholas de Seyton spared her the trouble. Drenched to the skin by his dash across the bailey, he dripped his way toward the hearth, and between sneezes, announced that the Lady Ellen had a visitor, one sanctioned by the King.

The unexpected guest was just as rain-soaked as Sir Nicholas, but he did not seem to mind it as much. He looked surprisingly cheerful for a man so mud-splattered, and immediately made a favorable impression upon Juliana, who liked his slanting dark eyes and cleft chin, and could not help noticing, too, his compact, sturdy build. All that Ellen saw, though, was that he was clean-shaven. "You are Welsh!"

"Indeed I am," he confirmed, stroking his telltale mustache. Striding over to kiss her hand, he gave her an appraising look, and then, a boyish, summertime smile. "I am Goronwy ap Heilyn, my lady, and I have been sent by my lord Prince to speak with you—in private," he added pointedly.

"That was deftly done," Ellen said approvingly as soon as Sir Nicholas withdrew. "You do know how to get your own way, I can see that. But come over by the fire ere you catch a chill. Juliana, do we have any wine?"

Goronwy was amused. "I came only from London, my lady, not the Holy Land, and if there are any folk in Christendom inured to rain, for certes it is the Welsh. My lord has good news for you. On the Friday eve after Christmas, the Countess of Lancaster gave birth to a son."

"That is indeed good news. Blanche and the babe are both well?"

He nodded. "They christened him Thomas, after the holy martyr, Becket. Nor is that all. What I have to tell you now, my lady, will be even more welcome. The English King has agreed to turn your brother over to the Archbishop of Canterbury and the Bishops of Worcester and Exeter— Ah, no, my lady, Lord Amaury has not been set free! But he will now be held in the more merciful custody of the Church, and will soon be transferred from Corfe to the Lord Edmund's castle at Sherborne—"

He got no further. Ellen had whirled and flung her arms around Juliana. To Goronwy's delight, she embraced him next, laughing and smearing lip rouge across his cheek, and Goronwy, who'd doubted that any mortal woman was truly good enough for his Prince, decided that mayhap this one would do well enough.

"Thank God Almighty, thank the Lord Jesus and the Blessed Mary and all the saints! You do not know, Lord Goronwy, two years at Corfe Castle, two years penned up in that hellhole . . ."

"I do know, my lady," he said softly. "You see, I was once a hostage of the English Crown, too. No one can give your brother back those two years, but at least he'll have some comfort at Sherborne. Now . . . I have something else likely to be of interest to you." Smiling, he drew forth from under his sodden mantle a parchment threaded through with braided red cord and sealed with green wax.

Ellen could not hide her eagerness, all but snatched the letter from his hand. "Would you think me very rude if I read it now?"

He shook his head and grinned, for she was already retreating toward the window-seat, pausing only long enough to grab a wick lamp. Accepting a wine cup from Juliana, Goronwy watched with alert interest as Ellen read her husband's love letter. That it was a love letter, he did not doubt, for the soft curve of Ellen's mouth and the color in her cheeks testified to its contents without need of words. It intrigued Goronwy to discover that the man he'd fought beside and drunk with and would, if need be, die for was not so different, after all, from other men, not when it came to love and lust and those secrets to be shared only with women, only in bed.

Ellen read Llewelyn's letter twice, knowing she would soon have every word committed to memory. "He wanted to bid me farewell," she said at last, more for Juliana's benefit than Goronwy's, for he already knew they were soon to depart for Wales. She'd found it almost intolerable this past week, knowing Llewelyn was just twenty miles from Windsor. But Wales was so far away, a world away. "He says that Edward is sending agents of the Crown into Wales, so they may inspect and approve those lands Llewelyn means to assign to me in dower." She could well imagine how much Llewelyn must have resented that. For herself, she was infuriated that Edward dared to play the role of benevolent guardian while holding her against her will. But soon none of that would matter, very soon now.

"One thing does perplex me, Lord Goronwy," she confided. "Llewelyn says that Edward is insistent upon giving us a court wedding. But he says nothing of when that wedding is to be. We have less than two months, for there can be no marriages during Lent . . ." She paused, for the Welshman's face was an easy one to read. "What is it? What have you kept from me?"

"Lord Llewelyn told me that I was to say nothing—unless you asked. He has no proof, my lady, just suspicions, and he did not want to burden you with them. But he fears that there will be no wedding by Lent, mayhap not for many months."

"No!" The cry was Juliana's. Ellen said nothing, just stared at Goronwy with eyes that would haunt him in days to come. "But why?" Again the protest came from Juliana. "It is all settled. Llewelyn has done homage as Edward demanded. What more does he want? Why should he continue to hold Ellen prisoner?"

To Goronwy, the answer was obvious. "To prove that he can," he said bitterly. Ellen had turned away. Moving back to the window-seat, she stared unseeingly at the clouded window pane. The rain was still coming down in torrents, streaking the glass like tears. But her eyes were dry, for she would not weep. That she had sworn to herself, that Edward would never again make her cry.

"A PROPHET is not without honor, save in his own country." There were times that spring when Llewelyn felt tempted to amend Scriptures, to add: "not until it is too late." After failing to rally his countrymen in the defense of their homeland, he now found himself forced to listen to their complaints about the English Crown. Men who had seen Edward as the lesser of evils, reasoning that Westminster was much farther away than Aber, were now reaping what they'd sown, having to argue Welsh ways and Welsh customs with haughty English castellans and bailiffs. Men who'd chafed under Llewelyn's demands now began to make their way to Aber and Dolwyddelan, to pour out their grievances to the man who, for all his willfulness and inflexibility and impatience with dissent, was one of their own.

Llewelyn might have taken a certain ironic amusement in the turn-around, had so much not been at stake. What did it matter if he was proved right, if the forfeit demanded was the loss of Welsh autonomy? He had his own grievances, too. Some of them were wounds to his pride. They were painful, but would heal. Others were likely to fester.

Two of his men had been hanged in the town of Oswestry, in defiance of the King's safe-conduct, and so far his complaints had gained him no more than a promise to investigate. Edward had appointed seven English and Welsh justices to hear and determine all lawsuits and pleas in the Marches and Wales. To Llewelyn, this was an outrageous encroachment upon Welsh law, upon his own courts. He had no choice, though, but to acquiesce in this further erosion of Welsh sovereignty, even to plead before this alien court himself, for he was involved in a bitter dispute with his old enemy, Gruffydd ap Gwenwynwyn, over the lordship of Arwystli.

Arwystli had long been a source of contention between Powys and Gwynedd, its possession shifting with the fortunes of war. Llewelyn had ousted Gruffydd ap Gwenwynwyn from Arwystli as punishment for his aborted assassination plot, and he was determined to hold on to it, for the upland cantref was strategically vital to the defense of his southern borders. Gruffydd was just as set upon regaining it. Llewelyn was not worried by his challenge, though, for he thought Gruffydd's argument to be ludicrous in the extreme; Gruffydd contended that he was a baron of the March, a vassal of the English King, and therefore the case ought to be tried in the King's court under English common law. Since Arwystli was undeniably in Wales, both claimants were Welsh, and the Treaty of Aberconwy itself provided that Welsh law should apply to disputes arising in Wales, Llewelyn did not see how he could not prevail, even in Edward's court. Yet he did not. Instead, the suit dragged on, and when he protested, he received a brusque reply from the English King, that he was to come before the King's justices whenever and wherever he was summoned, to receive "what justice shall dictate." To Llewelyn, that was a barb that lodged near the heart, dripped daily poison into suspicions already raw and inflamed. If Edward was not willing to abide by his own treaty, what would keep him from meddling further in Welsh matters, taking more and more until all the meat was stripped from the bone?

As he tallied up his losses in that summer of God's Year, 1278, Llewelyn could see naught but troubles ahead. His griefs were not all to be laid at Edward's door, though. Death claimed the man who'd been his mainstay, his Seneschal, and his friend for ten turbulent years. Tudur had died slowly, in great pain, and Llewelyn could do nothing for him. His passing was, for Tudur, a mercy, for Llewelyn, an amputation. Like a man who still felt phantom pain for a lost limb, he ached for his other self, for that rarest of God's blessings, a soulmate.

And then there was Ellen. There was always Ellen. He had braced himself for the worst, or so he'd thought. But even in his most despairing moments, he'd not truly believed that Edward would hold her indefinitely. Yet now it was eight months since he'd done homage at Westminster, and still she languished at Windsor, his wife, Edward's prisoner.

When Edward wrote that he would be at Rhuddlan Castle in September, Llewelyn's first reaction was one of relief. He and Gruffydd ap Gwenwynwyn could plead their cases before the King's court, resolve it once and for all. And he could confront Edward in person, demand that Ellen be released.

But within a fortnight of his summons to Rhuddlan Castle, Llewelyn received a second communication from Edward, this one far more ominous. He'd been half-expecting Davydd to start muddying the waters, to take advantage of his weakened position. When trouble came, though, it came from another quarter, from Rhodri. He had brought suit in Edward's court for his share of Gwynedd, and Edward was giving formal notice that Llewelyn should be prepared to answer Rhodri's claim at Rhuddlan in September. He also warned Llewelyn that if he defaulted to Rhodri, royal officers would be sent into Wales to distrain his lands and chattels. Llewelyn could only marvel that he'd been so blind, for what ploy could be more obvious—or more dangerous? He would never agree to rend Gwynedd further, and surely Edward knew that. But when he refused, he would be giving Edward the perfect excuse to keep Ellen in England, mayhap even to renew the war.

IN the ten months since the Treaty of Aberconwy, Edward had effected dramatic changes in the Welsh landscape. His castles had taken root like the dragons' teeth of folklore, formidable strongholds silhouetted against the blue September sky, testifying to the might of England and the indomitable will of its King. Llewelyn had long known of Edward's plan to divert the flow of the River Clwyd. It still came as a shock, though, to see for himself just how fast the work had progressed; eighteen hundred ditches had been dug, channeling the river into a canal that would wash the walls of Edward's new castle. But for Llewelyn, the most troubling sight of all was the earthen banks and deep trenches encircling Edward's new borough, a town on Welsh soil in which no Welsh would be permitted to dwell.

Never had Llewelyn missed Tudur so much as when he rode through the gateway of Rhuddlan Castle. His men shared his tension, and they were unusually silent, uncommonly subdued as they dismounted in the bailey, hands never straying far from sword hilts, eyes never straying far from their Prince. They were all anticipating trouble, were just not sure what form it would take.

But right from the outset, nothing went as expected. The first surprise was the relaxed mood of the castle garrison; if Edward and Llewelyn were indeed on a collision course, no one had bothered to warn them of that fact. The second surprise was the identity of the man emerging from the hall to bid Llewelyn welcome; Edmund had passed most of the year in France, and word had not gotten out yet of his return. His cordial greeting was not in itself a surprise, for he'd always been on friendly terms with Llewelyn. But his message was most surprising: Edward wanted Llewelyn to join him in the stables.

Powys was celebrated for its fast, spirited horses, and Llewelyn knew at once that the stallion was one of the best of the Powys breed, for it had the broad chest, the long fetlocks, and lengthy flanks that a knowledgeable horseman looked for and did not often find. Its coat was a deep, dappled grey, its tail a swirl of purest silver; it would have been an extremely handsome animal were it not in such obvious discomfort. The silver tail was switching ceaselessly, its withers were streaked with sweat, and it kept striking upward with a hind foot, as if trying to reach its belly.

As Llewelyn drew near, Edward emerged from the stall. "Good, you're here," he said, with the disdainful disregard for protocol that only the very powerful could afford. "This is my new Welsh palfrey. I dare not tell you what he cost me, for you'd think me an utter fool, since it now seems that I might lose him. Will you take a look?"

"Did this come upon him suddenly?" As Edward nodded, Llewelyn moved into the stall, speaking softly and soothingly until the stallion accepted his presence. After gently palpitating the animal's belly, he ran his hand along each of its legs, and then felt the twitching ears. Straightening up, he said succinctly, "Colic."

"I thought so, too, but my head groom fears it could be an inflammation of the bowels. And I need not tell you that if he's right, we might as well start digging the grave."

"He's not. If he were, the belly would be tender, and the ears and legs would be cold. What have you been doing for him so far?"

"We gave him a drench of hot water mixed with ginger, and then linseed oil. They insist I ought to bleed him, but to tell you true, I've never thought that does as much good as men claim."

Edward's views on bleeding verged on the heretical, but Llewelyn happened to be another such heretic, and as their eyes met over the stallion's back, they shared an unexpected flash of empathy, one that had nothing whatsoever to do with crowns or conquest, a moment in which they were just two men in a stable, united in a common concern for a suffering stallion. When Llewelyn suggested they try a hot bran poultice, Edward said he'd already ordered it, and Llewelyn nodded approvingly, one horseman to another.

After giving the groom strict instructions to bring him hourly reports on the stallion's progress and to fetch him straightaway if the palfrey took a turn for the worse, Edward swung the stall door open, and they walked back out into the sunlit bailey.

"I have to admit," Edward said, "that I feel more easy in my own mind now, knowing that you agree it's colic." Reaching out, he brushed straw from Llewelyn's sleeve, surprising the Welshman not so much by the gesture itself as by the casual way he did it, as if they were intimates, not enemies. "I want to thank you," Edward said, "for your letter of condolence when our baby died. At least she lived long enough to be baptized . . ."

"And your Queen . . . she is well?" Llewelyn felt a genuine sympathy for Eleanora, who'd now borne Edward eleven children, and buried seven.

"Eleanora is a very strong woman, as is her faith. She knows the ways of the Almighty are mysterious and not for us to question." After a moment, Edward smiled. "It was a comfort, too, that she conceived again so soon. The babe will be born early next spring, a lucky time for a birthing, I'm told."

Even as Llewelyn offered his congratulations, he was puzzling over Edward's behavior. Why would Edward reveal to him something so very personal?

"I heard about the death of your Seneschal. He struck me as a man with a keen eye for the truth and no patience with pretense. I'm sure he'll be missed."

Llewelyn agreed. For the life of him, he could not figure what Edward was up to. It made no sense that he should be so friendly, not with Rhodri's claim leveled at the heart of Gwynedd, a weapon sharp as any sword.

Edward continued to make easy, offhand conversation as they crossed the bailey, offering to show Llewelyn the downstream site of his new castle, pausing to dispatch a servant to fetch the Queen from the Dominican friary, explaining to Llewelyn that was where he and Eleanora were lodging, expressing the hope that Llewelyn had included a few attorneys in his entourage. "I'd have wagered that Wales had more sheep than lawyers," he said with a grin, "and I'd have been wrong, for Gruffydd ap Gwenwynwyn rode in yesterday with enough lawyers to sue half the souls in Christendom."

By now they'd reached the steps of the great hall, and Edward stopped suddenly, put his hand on the other man's arm. "Llewelyn, there is something I would say to you ere we go inside . . . about Rhodri. He had the right to plead his case before my court, and the session is set for the morrow. But I think we'd do better to try to settle this amongst ourselves. Rhodri awaits us above-stairs in the solar. Let's go up and talk to him. We ought to be able to come to terms, I should think, as long as we are reasonable, willing to compromise."

Llewelyn shrugged, said with equal nonchalance, "It is a bad bow that will not bend," words just as empty and hollow as he knew Edward's to be. At least he was not to be kept in suspense. Whatever game the English King was playing, it was about to begin.

RHODRI was pacing restlessly back and forth. At sound of the opening door, he spun around to confront his brother, shoulders squared defiantly, eyes narrowed to suspicious slits, for although he was sure that he at last had the upper hand, he could not stifle an irrational fear that victory might still be snatched away at any moment.

Llewelyn noted Rhodri's nervousness, but it was the other man in the solar who drew his attention. Davydd was perched on the edge of a table, looking very much at ease, in decided contrast to their last two meetings. "Let the games begin," he said breezily. "That is what the Roman emperors said, was it not? Just before they sent the Christians out to convert the lions?"

"Now why," Llewelyn said, "am I not surprised to find you here, Davydd?"

Davydd grinned. "You know me, Llewelyn. I would never miss one of our fond family reunions."

"Or a chance to meddle," Rhodri snapped, and Llewelyn dismissed any lingering suspicions that the two of them might be in collusion.

A servant had followed them up to the solar, and began now to pour wine. Edward waited until he was done before saying pointedly, "It is going to be difficult to mediate if I cannot understand what is being said. I would suggest that you leave Welsh by the wayside for the rest of the conversation, confine yourself to French or English. Edmund, can you get the door? My lord Rhodri, let's hear your grievance."

"My claim is a simple one, my lord King, and impossible to refute. Welsh law provides for the equal inheritance of all sons. I want my fair share of Gwynedd, want what is mine."

"That claim is no longer valid," Llewelyn said coolly. Drawing a parchment from the pouch at his belt, he unrolled it and handed it to Edward. "I have here a deed in which Rhodri renounced all rights to Gwynedd in return for payment of one thousand marks. As you can see, it is dated at Caer yn Arfon more than six years ago, and that is Rhodri's signature, Rhodri's seal."

"It is in Latin? Ah, good." Edward scanned the deed rapidly, but the contents came as no surprise, for although Rhodri had omitted any mention of it, Davydd had been more forthcoming. Edward wondered just how freely Rhodri had entered into this pact, but he was much more interested in Llewelyn's motivation. It would seem he had an unease of conscience where his brothers were concerned, else why would he have bothered to redeem Rhodri's claim? God knows, it was not to eliminate a threat. Glancing up from the deed, Edward gave Rhodri a look of amiable contempt, and then turned his gaze upon Llewelyn. "This does seem to be in order. Lord Rhodri?"

"I agreed to it because I hoped to wed an Irish heiress, the daughter of John Botillier. But the marriage plans came to naught, and I never received the money." Rhodri swung back toward Llewelyn, said challengingly, "Why not tell the King how you defaulted on the deal? Tell him how you refused to pay me my thousand marks!"

"I stopped payment because you rebelled."

"I rebelled because you stopped payment!" Rhodri was flushed with rage. "Only God can disinherit a man, and you, for all your accursed ambition and high-flying ways, are not God! You, my lord Prince of Wales, are a vassal of the English King, no more, no less—just as I am!"

"I owe you nothing, Rhodri. You were not turned out to starve. But what have you ever done to deserve Gwynedd? Do you think it was given to me? I earned whatever I hold, and I have the scars to prove it. I was willing to put Wales first, to fight and bleed for it." Llewelyn was not even aware that he'd lapsed back into Welsh; in his fury, it came naturally to his tongue, for only Welsh could convey his outrage. "Where were you when I was struggling to keep the English at bay? We both know the answer to that—you were in their camp, on their side. And now you expect me to gut Gwynedd further for you? For you—the English King's lapdog? I will never agree to that, never!"

"A very pretty speech, but that is all it is—just words! You seem to have forgotten that you are no longer the king of your own little dunghill. You'll give me what I want, for the English King will give you no choice!"

Edward and Edmund had been riveted by the intensity of the exchange, even without understanding a word of it. But now Edward said impatiently, "Enough!" Glancing toward Davydd, he demanded, "What did they say?"

Davydd had yet to take his eyes from his brothers. "Llewelyn expressed his reluctance to partition Gwynedd any further. And Rhodri declared his faith in English justice."

There was a moment's silence, and then Llewelyn gave an abrupt, involuntary laugh, turned aside to pick up his wine cup. Edward looked at him, then back at Davydd, beginning to think that nothing was as it seemed in Wales. What could have been more simple than a blood-feud between brothers? Davydd, the aggrieved, the resentful one, an ideal ally for the English Crown. And Llewelyn, the ruthless one, the victor. So simple . . . or was it?

"For all I care, you can shout at each other from now till Judgment

Day. But not in Welsh! Actually, I think I can resolve this right quickly, if given half a chance."

"Do you?" Llewelyn said softly. "Do you, indeed?"

"Yes, I do. It is rather simple, in truth. We have the answer at hand—here," Edward said, holding up the deed. "What say you, Llewelyn? Are you willing to abide by its terms, to pay Rhodri the thousand marks?"

Llewelyn was trying to master his shock. "Yes," he said warily, unable to believe Edward was taking his side, "I am willing."

Rhodri was even more stunned. "Well, I am not! I do not want the money, I want the lands!"

"You may, of course, make that argument tomorrow before my court." Edward leaned back in his chair, watching Rhodri over the rim of his wine cup. "But I would offer you some advice. When you cannot get what you want, it is wiser sometimes to want what you can get."

Rhodri was mute, so enraged and dumfounded and disappointed that he feared he might choke upon it. His throat had closed up; each breath he drew hurt. "What proof would I have that I'd get so much as a farthing? What reason do I have to trust his word?"

Edward glanced toward Llewelyn. "Can you provide sureties for payment?"

"Yes," Llewelyn said grudgingly, giving Rhodri a look that all but seared the air between them, "I will provide sureties." But then, prompted by an impulse he could not explain even to himself, he said, "What about you, Davydd? Do you want to act as a pledge for my good faith?"

If he'd meant to startle Davydd, he'd succeeded. But if his intention was to discomfit his brother, he'd failed. As their eyes met, Davydd grinned. "Why not? We might as well keep it in the family."

"A right fine pairing," Rhodri said acidly, "for your word is as worthless as his!"

"Did you always whine so much back when we were lads?" Davydd asked, still with a smile. "If so, little wonder my memories of you are so dim. I must have blotted them out in sheer self-defense."

Llewelyn had long known that Davydd had an uncanny knack for hitting where it would hurt the most; he bore enough scars of his own to testify to that. But he doubted that Davydd had meant to draw this much blood, for Rhodri lost color so fast that he looked suddenly ill, and then, murderous. The Welsh came tumbling out as if escaping, engulfing them in an outpouring of embittered, venomous invective that needed no translation, that seemed to echo in the air even after Rhodri whirled toward the door, slammed it resoundingly behind him.

Davydd slid off the table, setting down his wine cup. "Ere you ask,"

he said to Edward, "Rhodri urged the Almighty to smite me with leprosy, to shrivel my crops in the fields and bedchamber, to curse my
name down through the ages, and I might be mistaken, but he may
have thrown in something about Llewelyn and snakes. Now . . . if the
afternoon's entertainment is done up here, I think I'll go back to the
hall. I'm sure I can find some way to amuse myself: see how long it
takes to bait Gloucester into a foaming frenzy, tell Clifford what I heard
de Mortimer say about that haughty French wife of his . . . The pos-
sibilities are endless."

Davydd was talking too fast, trying a little too hard to be clever,
and Llewelyn caught it, saw that Edward had not. But then, he had a
distinct advantage over Edward, had a lifetime's experience in trying to
read Davydd's mercurial moods—for all the good it had ever done him.
He looked at his brother, and, against his will, he found himself remembering the night that forever changed things between them, the
night when Davydd had laughed and joked and lied, all the while expecting him to be dead before dawn.

Davydd was half-way to the door when Edward stopped him. "Do
not go just yet, Davydd. First let's drink to your good fortune. Did he
tell you, Llewelyn? My cousin Elizabeth has borne him a son."

Llewelyn had never known before how powerful an emotion envy
could be. The impact was physical, a blow that he'd not been braced to
withstand, for he'd not expected to feel like this—cheated. He did not
like the feeling; envy was a petty emotion, a sin too shameful to admit.
With an effort, he shook it off, retreating behind the impenetrable shield
of courtesy, and offered Davydd his congratulations. "You both must
be very thankful," he said evenly, "for a man's first son is indeed a
blessing from God. Tell Elizabeth how pleased I am for her. What did
you name the lad? Gruffydd, after our father?"

Davydd hesitated, and an enigmatic, guarded look crossed his face.
He smiled then, but the smile, too, had an odd edge to it, was both
defensive and defiant, with a hint of his familiar mockery. "No," he
said, "as it happens, I named him Llewelyn," and watched, still with
that twisted smile, as his brother choked on his drink.

IT was quiet after Davydd departed the solar. Edward finished the last
of his wine, watching Llewelyn intently all the while. "You expected
me to back Rhodri's claim," he said abruptly, almost accusingly. "You
could have spared yourself a great deal of anxiety had you only remembered that I swore to defend your possession of Gwynedd against all
others. Why would that not include Rhodri? Sooner or later, you are
going to have to learn to trust me, Llewelyn."

Llewelyn looked at the younger man for a long moment. "I would find it easier to rely upon your good faith," he said, "if you were not still holding my wife at Windsor."

Edmund drew an audible breath, swiveling toward his brother. But Edward seemed unperturbed. "You need not fret, Edmund," he said. "I did not take offense. We cannot in fairness blame the man for wanting his wife." Edward then looked again at Llewelyn. "I understand your impatience. But you have to understand that I promised Ellen I'd give her a court wedding, and that takes time."

Llewelyn surprised himself; he somehow refrained from pointing out that in the eight months since he'd done homage, they could have married off half of Wales. "I have a suggestion to make. I never knew any bowman who did not need a target to aim for. Let's aim for one then, give your wedding planners the proper incentive. Since Ellen and I are already wed, we need not wait to post the banns. So . . . why not a fortnight from now, in Michaelmas week?"

"Well . . . I am not adverse to picking a date. But I have a better one in mind than that. What could be a more propitious day for a wedding than St Edward's Day?"

"October thirteenth? This October thirteenth?"

Edward grinned. "Yes, this October thirteenth! There may be a more suspicious soul than you walking God's green earth, but if so, I hope to Christ I never meet him! I'm making all the arrangements, assuming all the costs, taking care of everything. All I ask is that you be at the church on time, that you do not leave my little cousin stranded at the altar."

Edward laughed; Llewelyn did not. To Edmund, it was very evident that his brother was expecting to be thanked profusely, but it was equally obvious to him that, whatever emotions Llewelyn was experiencing just then, gratitude was not among them. Edmund sighed, wondering how he so often found himself playing the role of peacemaker, instead of being able to stand back and enjoy the turmoil the way the Davydds and the de Mortimers seemed to do. But the habit was too deeply ingrained, and he was trying to think of a distraction when a glance out the window provided him with one.

"Ned, Eleanora and Blanche have just ridden in from the friary." Making up his mind then, he said, "Llewelyn, I think you'll want to go down to the bailey. Ellen is with them."

THE door was ajar, and they could hear the clinking of Llewelyn's spurs in the stone stairwell, and then silence . . . until Edward said, "Are you going to tell me why you did that? You know Ellen's arrival was meant to be a surprise."

"Too many surprises can leave a bad taste in a man's mouth, especially a man as prideful as that one, Ned. I just wanted to make sure that Llewelyn did not take offense when none was intended."

Edward responded with a Welsh oath he'd learned from Davydd. "That is absurd. It is lucky that you have so many worthy qualities, for I'm sorry to say that you have no more humor than . . ." He paused, groping for a comparison, and Edmund supplied one.

"Than the Earl of Gloucester?" he suggested, with a straight face, and Edward struggled in vain to keep a straight face of his own.

"Jesú, no," he said, "I am not that irked with you, lad!" A sudden clamor drew him then, to the open window, just in time to see Llewelyn reach up, lift Ellen from her saddle. She slid down into his arms, into an embrace ardent enough to stir enthusiastic cheers from the soldiers thronging the bailey.

Watching, Edward said wryly, "Are they ever coming up for air? You are right, Edmund, about his overweening pride. But to give the Devil his due, he does not lack for nerve. Not many men would have dared to challenge me the way he just did. No, the man has cojones," Edward said approvingly, whetting Edmund's interest, for he knew that slang Spanish expression, picked up from Eleanora's brother, was Edward's ultimate accolade; Edward's creed was simplicity itself, that a man without courage was no man at all.

"Is that why you agreed to Llewelyn's surrender last year? You think we're better off with him than with Davydd?"

"By the Rood, no!" Edward said, and laughed. "Nothing could be further from the truth. Llewelyn poses a greater danger to England than Davydd ever could, for he is the one man the Welsh might rally around. They'd never trust Davydd. Why should they, when his loyalty is for sale to the highest bidder, for who can outbid the King? No, England would have been better served with Davydd at the helm, for he'd be far more likely than Llewelyn to run their ship up onto the rocks. But Llewelyn was not about to turn the helm over of his own free will. I told you once that I wanted Wales, but it would have cost more than I was willing to pay to see Davydd enthroned at Aber."

"Was that why you turned a deaf ear to Rhodri's plea?"

"Of course. Why would I risk pushing Llewelyn into rebellion again? To please a meagre whelp like Rhodri? Not bloody likely! Nor am I displeased with my new vassal so far."

The noise from the bailey was intensifying, for the Welsh had emptied the hall, eager to get a first glimpse of their lord's lady. Ellen and

Llewelyn were encircled by jostling, jesting men, and to judge by all
the smiles, Ellen was winning them over with ridiculous ease. Edward
was not surprised, for it would have been hard to resist her at that
moment. She was so radiant that not even the most cynical Welshman
could doubt her joy at being reunited with her husband, and when,
under Llewelyn's coaching, she gamely attempted a few halting words
in Welsh, Llewelyn's men would willingly have forgiven her any sin
under God's sky, even the sin of being English. Edward watched for a
few moments, then turned back to his brother.

"No," he repeated, "I am not displeased. It was not easy to snare
our Welsh hawk, and it took patience, but we've been able to bell him,
to break him to the creance, and to teach him to fly to the lure. A pity
we have to lose her now. But I suppose it is time to test his tameness,
to see if he can be trusted to fly free."

23

WORCESTER, ENGLAND

October 1278

Aʟʟ the towns in the Marches were eager to host
a royal wedding, but it was Worcester that won the coveted prize. Its
citizens were delighted at the prospect of such a splendid spectacle
taking place in their midst, although the town was hard put to accommodate so many highborn visitors. The Bishop of Worcester had the
honor of providing hospitality for the King, his Queen, and the bride.
The Prior of St Mary's turned his own residence over to Edward's
brother-in-law, the King of Scotland, and the Franciscan friary was chosen to lodge Llewelyn and his entourage. The other wedding guests had
to find beds as best they could: in the priory guest hall, in the old castle,
in the few inns, with local gentry. To the awed townspeople, it began
to seem as if Worcester had suddenly become the center of the world.

UNLATCHING the shutters of his chamber, Llewelyn looked out upon a day of surpassing fairness, upon colors vivid enough to delight the most exacting artist's eye: gold-tinted sunlight, autumn-splashed trees vying for attention with the last lingering flowers of summer, under a sky so bright it could not long take unshaded stares. Joining him at the window, Einion breathed in the clear, crisp air, saying, "I know this day has been long in coming, but now that it's here, it's well nigh perfect. I have to admit, Llewelyn, that Edward has surprised me. I had no idea this wedding would be so lavish, that Edward could be so generous."

"Generous? I suppose so," Llewelyn said, but he sounded skeptical. "It is just that I cannot help thinking how unnecessary this wedding is, Einion. In the eyes of the Almighty and all of Christendom, Ellen and I have been husband and wife for nigh on three years. But Edward would insist that we marry again, almost as if we are not well and truly wed without his approval, his blessing."

He glanced sideways at his uncle, then smiled. "I'm not exactly overflowing with gratitude, am I? Mayhap I ought to make a vow, that I'll give Edward the benefit of every doubt—just for today! It is true that he has been open-handed, and I'll not deny that he gave me a right welcome wedding gift when he agreed to free my hostages. I only wish he'd thought to consult Ellen and me about what we might have wanted for this wedding."

"You mean the guests," Einion said shrewdly, and Llewelyn nodded.

"Indeed. Pembroke, Clifford, Hereford—those are men who'd rather be attending my wake than my wedding!" Llewelyn laughed shortly. "At least I was able to prevail upon Edward about de Mortimer; Edward agreed that his presence would be distressing to Ellen. But he insisted upon inviting Gloucester. He said de Mortimer might not like being omitted, but he'd understand, whereas Gloucester would have nursed a grievance to his grave, and I have to admit he is likely right about that. We'll just have to see that he stays away from Ellen."

"Is it true that Davydd will be here?"

"Yes, I regret to say he will. He told Edward that Elizabeth wanted to come." Llewelyn said no more, and Einion tactfully changed the subject, asked if it was true Llewelyn had postponed sessions of his high court for the next fortnight.

"Yes, I wanted to have enough free time to show Wales to Ellen—and vice versa. We'll pass a few days at Dolwyddelan, and then move up the Conwy valley to the abbey and on to Aber. Then we'll cross over to Môn, for Ellen wants to visit the friary at Llanfaes where Joanna is buried." Turning from the window, Llewelyn moved to the table, reaching for a small casket. "Let me show you Ellen's bride's gift."

"I thought you gave her that white mare?"

"I did. When I found out that my grandfather had given Joanna a mare on their wedding day, I knew nothing would please Ellen more. Whilst we were at Rhuddlan, I asked her if she wanted a new wedding ring, too, but she said no, that the one she'd been given in France had been a talisman for her during these past months. So we'll have it blessed anew by the Bishop during the ceremony. But I got the idea then, to give her this." Llewelyn held up a circular silver brooch for Einion's inspection. "The inside of her ring is engraved in French with 'You are my heart's joy.' I had this brooch engraved with the same words, in Welsh!"

The expression was a conventional motto, to be found in many wedding bands and lover's rings, in itself meant little. But Llewelyn's smile gave it an echo of truth. He seemed to sense that himself, for he laughed suddenly. "Do I sound like one of those lovesick fools the bards like to sing about? Jesú, I hope not! But in truth, Einion, Ellen is indeed special."

Einion agreed that she was, with such evident sincerity that Llewelyn felt a surprising surge of pleasure; he was only now discovering how much it pleased him to hear Ellen praised. "You and I can see her virtues easily enough, but will our people? Joanna was never popular with the Welsh. Tell me the truth, Einion. Do you think Ellen will fare better?"

Einion did not give a snap reply, for that was a serious query, deserving of serious consideration; a ruler's troubles could be compounded by an unpopular consort. Henry III's subjects had detested his French Queen, blaming Henry both for his own flaws and hers, too. But Einion knew that if the man was securely in power, the impact would be negligible, as was the case with Llewelyn's grandfather. Or Edward, for Eleanora was not beloved by the English, who suspected her of being grasping, and convicted her of being foreign. Edward was too well entrenched, though, for whispers and gossip to matter. Whether that was still true or not for Llewelyn, Einion did not know.

"You were too young to remember much about Joanna," he said slowly. "I do, though. She was shy in public, and people oft-times thought her aloof, even arrogant, when nothing could be further from the truth. Then, too, she squandered whatever good will she'd earned over the years with that one mad act, taking a lover, and an English lover at that. Even from the first, though, our people viewed her askance, for there were those who could not forgive her for a sin of birth, for being King John's daughter. But I think Ellen has already won Welsh sympathy; who'd not pity her plight these three years past? Nor is she shy, your lady, will find it easier than Joanna to woo Welsh hearts. And our people are not likely to blame her for her kinship to the English King, for who does not know about Evesham?"

Llewelyn gave him a sharp, probing look, for between them, there was not always a need of words. "You see it, too," he said, and Einion nodded.

"Yes," he admitted. "I'll not deny it did surprise me, that she seems so at ease with Edward. I did not expect that."

"Nor did I."

"Have you talked to her about it, Llewelyn?"

"No, not yet. We've had so little time together. And . . . I thought it would be fairer to Ellen if I wait until she feels at home in Wales, until we know each other better."

"And if she is as fond of him as she seems to be?"

"I doubt that I could ever understand it. But I suppose I'd have to try to accept it." That was a prospect that troubled Llewelyn more than he was willing to admit, even to himself. Today was not the time to dwell upon it, though, and he began to tell Einion about the remarkably vivid names the English gave to the streets of their towns and cities, about London's Cheapside, Fish Street, Cock's Lane, and Stinking Lane, about Shrewsbury's Dogpole, the Shambles, and Grope Lane, where, as a lad of thirteen, he'd seen his first harlot. He was trying to convince Einion that Worcester really did have a Cut-throat Lane when Goronwy and Dai sought entry.

"Ere we depart for the church, I want to give you these, my lord." Goronwy produced a woven sack, and launched into a perfect mimicry of those glib-tongued, itinerant peddlers who could make wooden beads seem like pearls beyond price. "Well, what do we have here? It looks like—indeed it is—a shard of unicorn horn. Very useful for a man about to dine with the English, for you need only drop it into your wine cup, and lo, it will protect you from poison."

"Whilst mortally offending the English King," Llewelyn said, and they all laughed, envisioning for a moment Edward's incredulous rage at such an insult.

"What?" Goronwy feigned a peddler's dismay. "You'd turn down so rare a relic? Indeed, my lord, you are a hard man to please. Mayhap this will be more to your liking?"

"What is that?" Llewelyn reached for the root. "A turnip?"

" A turnip? My lord, this is mandragora! Coax your lady into taking but one bite, and she will ever after be bedazzled by you, loving, docile, obedient to your every whim."

"I'd rather bedazzle her myself." Llewelyn dropped the ugly, twisted root back into the sack. "What else have you in your bag of tricks?"

"You are indeed in luck, my lord, for I have here a patch of wolf's hair, plucked from the rump of a live wolf." With a flourish, Goronwy held it up, scowling at sight of their grins. "Do not scoff, my lords," he said loftily, "for all know wolf's hair plucked from a live animal will give a man great vigor, enable him to perform truly miraculous feats, all night long." Goronwy abandoned the game then, grinned at Llewelyn. "In truth, I was tempted to keep this for myself. I doubt that you'll have need of it, for I've seen your lady."

Llewelyn laughed. "I'd wager a beautiful woman will always embolden a man more than a clump of fur! What does a man do with this, anyway? Stick it under his pillow? God forbid, swallow it?" They were all laughing now, able to imagine any number of indelicate uses for the wolf charm, and were still laughing when the friary warden ushered in two unexpected guests, the King and his brother.

They both were magnificently attired, Edward in a purple silk tunic under a bright green surcote, and Edmund less colorfully but no less richly dressed in contrasting shades of blue. They were well matched in high spirits, too, for few occasions offered more opportunities for revelry than a wedding.

"The women chased us out," Edward complained cheerfully. "They said they needed time to dress and then to make Ellen ready, and we'd just get underfoot. So we're here to wish you well, and to give you this." He held out a small leather pouch. "The gold and silver to put on the Bishop's plate ere he blesses Ellen's ring."

The coins in question were of no great value, but the gesture was a symbolic one, a sign of royal favor. Brushing aside Llewelyn's thanks, Edward said, with a smile, "I daresay you are still set upon departing for Wales on the morrow. I daresay, too, that you have no idea how much baggage your bride is bringing. You've not yet learned about wives and their chattels, or that after today, you'll not have a coffer chest to call your own. But as one burdened husband to another, I want to pay the costs of transporting Ellen's belongings and the wedding gifts into Wales, as far as . . . shall we say Oswestry?"

"That is very generous," Llewelyn said, and got from Edward another smile, a shrug.

"I am very fond of Ellen, want to get her marriage off to a good start. Now, we'd best ride back to the Bishop's Palace, for Eleanora made me swear a blood oath that we'd not be late for the ceremony. Ere we go, there is one minor matter to be dealt with, so if I may have a few moments of the Prince's time, I promise that you'll have the rest of the day—and night—for the bridegroom."

Llewelyn's smile was quizzical and slightly wary, but he took the parchment Edward was holding out, moved to the window, and began to read. Edward leaned back against the door to wait. Edmund's attention, though, was drawn to an object on the table. "Is that what I think it is? Wolf's hair, right? I hear that it works wonders in bestirring a man's lust," he said with a grin. "Is it for sale?" Recognizing a kindred spirit, Goronwy grinned back, and they began a bawdy, enthusiastic discussion about the various aids and potions and herbs that were thought to be aphrodisiacs. But then Goronwy happened to glance toward the window, toward his Prince.

"My lord, what is it?" He'd spoken instinctively in Welsh, but Edmund caught the undertones of concern, and turned, too. Llewelyn was staring at Edward; if he'd heard Goronwy, he gave no sign of it.

"Is this some sort of jest?" he said, and there was disbelief in his voice, but also the first flames of a white-hot rage.

"It is," Edward said calmly, "just what it appears to be."

The Welsh were now clustered around Llewelyn, and as they read the document he held, they, too, looked first incredulous, and then, enraged.

"What is happening here?" Getting no answer from Llewelyn, Edmund swung back toward his brother. "Ned, what is this about? What does that charter say?"

"It states that Llewelyn agrees he no longer has the right to offer sanctuary or refuge to men who are the King's enemies. It is not an unreasonable demand," Edward said coolly, "and I do not see why it should stir up such a commotion. It is, after all, merely an admission of the sovereignty of the English Crown in Wales."

EDMUND had loved his father, but Henry was not a parent a son could take pride in; he was too weak, too ineffectual. As far back as Edmund could remember, though, Edward had filled that void, for who would not have been proud of such a brother? He'd given his admiration as unstintingly as he did his love, and he was shaken now by what he was feeling as they rode back to the Bishop of Worcester's Palace, for he would not have believed it possible that he could ever be ashamed of Edward.

He was unwilling to speak out in front of their men, but as soon as they dismounted before the Bishop's great hall, he drew Edward aside. Edward did not object, and followed him into the Bishop's riverside garden. Coming to a halt by a trellised arbor, Edmund said abruptly, "Whatever possessed you, Ned? I'd not have believed it had I not seen it with my own eyes!"

"I do not see why you are so wrought up about this. Does it truly surprise you that I should want to abolish a dangerous custom, to prevent Llewelyn from giving shelter to my enemies?"

"I am not objecting to what you demanded of him, but to the way you did it. Christ in Heaven, Ned, how could you go to the man on the very day of his wedding?"

"What better time than today? When would he be most likely to yield?" Edward looked challengingly at his brother. "And he did yield, did he not? Do not make too much of this, Edmund. I did what I had to do; so did he. What else matters? Now I would . . . Good God, Edmund, will you look at that? Did you ever see a prettier sight in all your born days?"

Eleanora and Blanche were laughing at Edward's playful chivalry, but Edmund agreed with his brother, for they both did look lovely, each in her own way. Tall and stately, Eleanora was exceedingly elegant in a deep purple gown that matched Edward's tunic, set off by a surcote of lavender fretted with seed pearls. She had the right to wear her hair loose, a privilege permitted only to queens and virgin brides, but she had chosen to conceal her dark hair under a linen barbette and fashionable fillet, so as not to draw attention away from Ellen on her wedding day. Quite a few people had noticed how much Eleanora had thawed toward Ellen as the date drew near for her departure into Wales. Blanche did not have Eleanora's advantage of height, but she was still likely to turn heads, too, for her tastes were less traditional, more flamboyant, than Eleanora's, and she was clad in a daring new Italian style. Her gown was cut conventionally, a royal shade of blue belted at the waist, but her surcote of burnt-orange velvet reached only to her knees, flaunted an exotic, uneven hem.

"If you think we look alluring," she said, "wait till you behold the bride!"

Ellen paused in the doorway of the hall, then stepped out into the bright, blinding light. She wore an emerald-colored surcote over a gown of sunlit silk, a shade sure to startle, for yellow was no longer fashionable in England, that being the color of the badges worn by the Jews. But Ellen had been stubbornly set upon it, having learned that yellow was greatly favored by the Welsh. And though her choice might be controversial, none could deny that it was extremely becoming. Her most striking adornment, however, was her long, free-flowing hair, a coppery cascade that reached her hips, that stirred Edward to murmur admiringly, "If a woman hath long hair, it is a glory to her."

"Tell me the truth," Ellen entreated. "How do I look? I decided not to wear a veil, after all; does it matter?" Laughing, then, at herself, she confided, "I cannot believe I am so nervous! It is just that I want today to be perfect, perfect in every way."

They assured her that she need not fret, that she looked lovely, that the day would be all she hoped and more. Only Edmund said nothing, for as he looked at Ellen, he was seeing again Llewelyn's white, tense face, his blazing dark eyes, and he knew that Edward had done more than ruin the wedding for Llewelyn, he had ruined it for Ellen, too.

THE townspeople were eager to catch a glimpse of the wedding party, and Bishop's Street, south Frerenstrete, and St Mary's Knoll were lined with spectators. While the presence of their King was always exciting, on this sunlit October Thursday, they saved their loudest cheers for the bride. Ellen enjoyed herself immensely, reining in her new white mare before the priory's great gate to accept a bouquet of daisies, to scatter coins to cocky street urchins, and to acknowledge the heady acclaim with smiles and waves. She had argued in vain against this wedding, had not found it easy to be parted from Llewelyn at Rhuddlan Castle, wanting only to ride pillion behind him into the heartland of his realm, far beyond Edward's reach. But she could not deny that so much attention was flattering, and she was delighted to be reunited with her de Quincy cousins, to see again some of her father's friends. Sometime in the past few days, this wedding had stopped being Edward's, and become hers, and she had begun to feel the way a bride ought, she'd begun to have fun.

Upon their arrival at the cathedral church, they found that Llewelyn was not yet there, and it was decided to await him in the priory Chapter House. As time passed and he still did not come, men began to make the usual trite jokes about reluctant husbands and absconding bridegrooms. Ellen bore it with good grace, and remained serenely self-possessed even as the delay lengthened, as the Bishop of Worcester and other guests grew increasingly impatient. She deflected the jests with a smile, and laughed outright when someone seriously suggested that Llewelyn truly might not be coming.

"My husband is worth waiting for," she was assuring them when a sudden burst of cheering wafted through the doorway. Lifting her skirts, Ellen hastened out into the cloisters just as Llewelyn came through the south passage, emerged into the sun. Belatedly remembering Eleanora's lectures about maidenly decorum, Ellen did not fling herself into his arms, instead sank down on the pathway in a deep curtsy. As Llewelyn raised her to her feet, she whispered, "You look so handsome," for she thought his red wool tunic and gold sleeveless surcote were admirably suited to his dark coloring. But as she smiled up at him, she saw that he was looking past her toward the Chapter House, where Edward stood framed in the doorway.

SINCE Edward was giving Ellen in marriage, he was the one who led her through the church and out onto the steps by the west door. Weddings were always performed outdoors to accommodate as many eyewitnesses as possible, and a sea of faces looked up at them; people had even gathered in the cemetery by the charnel chapel. But the crowd was well behaved, quieted at the command of the Bishop of Worcester, so that Llewelyn could announce what lands he would be giving to Ellen to hold in dower. He then placed Ellen's ring upon the Bishop's plate for the blessing, and the Bishop joined their hands, began the ceremony.

By then, Ellen was aware that something was wrong. Studying Llewelyn through her lashes, she had the eerie, unsettling sensation that she was holding hands with a stranger. In the bright glare of sunlight, she could detect in his face the evidence of stress; there were sharp grooves shadowing the corners of his mouth, and finely drawn lines around his eyes, the sort that crinkled when he laughed. But laughter seemed very alien to him at that moment, there on the church steps. Ellen had never given any thought to their age difference, for it was very common for a man to wed a much younger wife. This was the first time that he'd looked his age to her, looked drawn and tired and so remote that it alarmed her.

She barely heard Llewelyn's vows, and only a titter from the crowd jarred her from her troubled reverie in time to say her own vows. "I, Eleanor," she said hastily, "do take thee, Llewelyn, to be my wedded husband, to have and to hold from this day forth, for better or worse, for richer or poorer, in sickness and in health, till death us do part, if Holy Church it will ordain, and thereto I plight thee my troth."

The Bishop then handed Llewelyn the ring, and he slid it upon each of her fingers in turn, saying, "With this ring I thee wed, and this gold and silver I thee give, and with my body I thee worship, and with all my wordly chattels I thee endow, in the Name of the Father and of the Son and of the Holy Spirit, Amen."

And then it was over, and they were throwing alms to the crowd before entering the church for the nuptial Mass, and Ellen could only look at her husband in uncomprehending dismay, for never in these past three years had he seemed so far from her as he had just then, while making that beautiful pledge of marital faith and fidelity.

WORCESTER Castle had once been a royal stronghold, but upon the death of King John, the bailey and the King's houses within it were deeded to St Mary's Priory. Here would be held the wedding feast, for although the castle keep, now held in fee by the Earl of Warwick, was in shabby condition, the monks had kept up repairs on the great hall, and it could accommodate more guests than even the Bishop's spacious lodgings. Richard de Feckenham, the Prior, found himself cast in the role of host, and he'd hastened from the church in order to bid his highborn guests welcome, thankful all the while that the banquet costs would be billed to Edward's Exchequer.

The monks had done an admirable job of transforming the ancient hall for this festive occasion; fresh rushes were spread about, the walls newly decorated with depictions of the Wheel of Fortune, the trestle tables draped in white linen, the table on the dais adorned with silver candlesticks. The musicians and minstrels were already on hand, and as Ellen and Llewelyn were ushered into the hall, they struck up a trumpet fanfare, focusing all eyes upon the bridal couple.

Ellen had tried to talk to Llewelyn as they left the priory, but then the church bells had begun their pealing, drowning out all conversation, and now it was too late. She knew what lay ahead. The feast would last until dark and then the entertainment and dancing would begin, the festivities eventually culminating in the bedding-down revelries. It would be at least eight, possible ten hours before she and Llewelyn were finally alone in their bridal bedchamber, and until then they would have no chance to talk in private. Eight or ten hours in which she must play yet another role, that of the carefree, blushing bride, smiling and laughing and dancing as if nothing were amiss. And she knew suddenly that she could not do it.

They were being congratulated now by Alexander, the Scots King, who offered graceful good wishes for their future happiness, hoping that they would find in their marriage the contentment that he had once enjoyed with Margaret, Edward's deceased sister. Under other circumstances, it was a conversation Ellen might have enjoyed, for she had a genuine respect for Alexander, who'd been happily wed to an English Princess, maintained affable ties with his English brother-in-law, and yet never forgot for a moment that Scotland's sovereignty was as safe with Edward as a chicken with a hawk. Now though, Ellen was hard put even to make a pretense of polite interest, to murmur the proper responses, to keep her eyes from her husband's face.

As soon as Alexander paused, she plunged into the breach, begged to be excused so that she might thank her cousin Edward for such a splendid wedding. And then she fled across the hall, not daring to look back at Llewelyn, to see a stranger again.

She had a stroke of luck now, though, was able to catch Edward between conversations, to draw him toward the comparative privacy of the dais. "Ned, I need your help. I must have a few moments alone with Llewelyn, for I . . . I have something to give him."

"I'm sure you do, sweetheart, but if you've waited this long, you ought to be able to wait until tonight."

He smiled at her, and Ellen longed to slap him. "Ned, I am not jesting. This is very important to me, and you well know we cannot just leave the hall. Will you help me . . . please?" she added, for if she could not afford anger, neither could she afford pride. But at that moment, she found an unexpected ally. Eleanora had come up just in time to hear, and said:

"Eduardo, do not tease her. Of course he will help you, Ellen."

"Women," he said, with a comic grimace. "What other English King ever suffered the indignity of having to play Cupid? Just what do you want me to do, Little Cousin?"

"I want you to wait till I slip from the hall, then seek Llewelyn out, tell him you need to speak with him in private."

"I daresay he'll be thrilled to hear that," Edward said, very dryly, and Ellen was suddenly sure he already knew the answers she hoped to get from Llewelyn. "But I never could resist a maiden in distress, at least not when she has my own wife acting as her champion. Very well, I'll do it. Here, first give me my bridal kiss," he said, sliding his fingers under Ellen's chin and lowering his head. She stiffened in spite of herself, but his mouth barely grazed hers, and then he stepped back, laughing. "Go now, make your escape."

Ellen remembered just in time to thank them both. As she turned, she already knew that Llewelyn would be watching them, his face stonily impassive, dark gaze opaque and impossible to read. Damn you, Ned, what have you done? Ellen drew several bracing breaths, and then saw the man she wanted.

"Hugh, I need you." Pulling him away from a pretty girl with a rudeness she hoped her desperation would excuse, she said softly and urgently, "I want you to wait till I make my way across the hall to the screen. Then create a diversion, the noisier the better." She never had more reason to bless the day Bran had found him at Evesham Abbey, for Hugh never even blinked, even more remarkably, asked no questions, and once she'd drifted casually over to the screened entrance, he came through for her as always, crashing into a servant laden with a tray full of brimming wine cups. Ellen felt unexpected tears prick her eyes, knowing that there was not another man in Christendom who'd have been so willing to make a fool of himself for her sake, without even knowing why. And then she seized the chance Hugh had gallantly given her, ducked behind the screen.

The solars and bedchambers of Edward's reign were now being built above the great hall, but the castle dwellings dated from the time of Edward's grandfather, when the king's bedchamber adjoined the hall, so Ellen had only to go through one doorway, into another, and she was in her bridal chamber.

It was like walking into a garden, so fragrant was it, for the floor was strewn with basil, marjoram, sweet woodruff, and costmary; cinnamon and cloves had been burned to perfume the air; and the chamber was filled with late-blooming flowers, daisies, honeysuckle, lavender. The walls had been painted green, starred in gold, and a beech log was stacked in the hearth, ready to be fired. The bed hangings were drawn back to reveal turned-down linen sheets, swansdown pillows, and coverlets garnished with a scattering of rose petals. The windows lacked glass, for it had been many years since this chamber had housed a royal guest, and the shutters were opened to the streaming afternoon sun. There was even a caged nightingale on the table, an imaginative touch that could only have come from Blanche. The bedchamber was perfect, Ellen thought, perfect, and she stifled a mirthless laugh.

Edward acted with a swiftness she'd not expected. She'd been in the chamber only a few moments when the door swung open. She heard Llewelyn's voice first, barely recognizing it as his. "After this morning, what else is there to say . . . or surrender?" He saw Ellen then, came to an abrupt halt.

"Here you are, lass," Edward said. "I always deliver what I promise. But bear this in mind, that the longer you are gone from the hall, the greater the scandal." For once he did not make a grand exit, closed the door quietly behind him.

Ellen took several steps toward her husband. "I realized today that I do not know you as well as I thought I did," she said, "but I do know that something is very wrong. I could not wait until tonight, had to talk to you now."

"And so you turned to Edward for help." The fury that had slurred his voice just moments ago was gone, but he sounded very distant to Ellen, as if he felt the need to weigh his every word, and that frightened her.

"I can see you do not want to talk about it, and I know this is not the time. But can you at least tell me if it is something I have done?"

He knew then that he had to tell her, and he resented her for it, for making him lay bare his shame whilst it was still so inflamed and raw. "This morning . . . Edward came to the friary, and demanded that I agree to relinquish the right of sanctuary in Gwynedd."

Ellen stared at him, rendered mute at the very moment she had the most need of words. It all made sense now, dreadful sense: his pent-up rage, his lacerated pride, even his coolness toward her. She had only to envision her father or one of her brothers confronted with Edward's treachery and she understood Llewelyn's emotions as if they were her own. And she knew without being told that his wounds were two-fold, one that was Edward's doing, one that was self-inflicted. He confirmed that now by saying tautly, "You have not asked whether or not I agreed."

"Of course you did. What choice did you have? Llewelyn, you must not blame yourself for yielding. Better that you should blame me, for you did it for me. No wonder you look at me as if . . ." She turned away, leaned for a moment against the edge of the table.

"Ellen, I do not blame you for this."

"How could you not blame me? When I think of all the griefs I've brought upon you, all the troubles that have haunted you since the day I became your wife . . . Oh, God, Llewelyn, I am so sorry! I never—"

"Ellen, listen to me. I do not blame you. I swear that to you upon the surety of my soul, upon the souls of our unborn sons. I do not blame you."

She had to steel herself to look up, so afraid was she that he was offering a lie born of kindness. But as she met his eyes, she found in them only an anguished honesty, and her despair gave way to bewilderment. "I believe you," she said, "and I thank God for it. But . . . but if you truly do not blame me, why is there suddenly so much distance between us? What is it, then, Llewelyn? Please, you must tell me . . ."

How could he, though? How could he tell her what had been in his heart as he'd watched her laughing and jesting and even flirting a little with Edward, her cousin Ned. Later, yes, but not now, not until he could trust himself not to lash out at her, not to blame her for being so susceptible to the claims of kinship.

Watching as he moved to the window, Ellen saw that her pleading was in vain, that he would not or could not reveal the rest. But how could they leave it like this? Only a man could think it was possible to store grievances away like coins, bring them out to spend at a more convenient time. Through the haze of hurt and confusion, anger was slowly beginning to stir. He was still standing by the window, and on his face was that same shuttered look that she'd seen in the hall, just after Edward had kissed her. And then she knew. "It is Edward," she said. "It is Edward and me."

His head jerked up, so fast that she knew she'd guessed right. She seemed dazed to him; even as he watched, she lost color, and he swore under his breath. Why could she not have let it lie?

"Yes," he said, "it is you and Edward. I told myself that he was your kinsman, that he had been kind to your mother after Evesham, that the heart cannot always be trusted." And for a moment, he thought of Davydd. "I told myself, too, that I could learn to live with it. But not today, Christ, not today! And when I saw . . ."

He got no further, for Ellen had begun to laugh. It held no humor, had an odd brittle ring to it, echoes of shattering glass, and he crossed the chamber in three strides, caught her by the shoulders. "Ellen!" He repeated her name, tightening his grip, and her laughter stopped as suddenly as it began. Her eyes looked enormous to him, almost black, the pupils so dilated that they swallowed all the light, all the green.

"When my father lay dying in the rain and the mud," she said, "his enemies were not content with that, with his death. So they cut off his head, chopped off his arms and legs, and gelded him. But even that was not enough for them, so they threw his mangled body to the dogs. And Roger de Mortimer claimed his head, a keepsake for his wife, I've been told. They impaled his head upon a pike, and then . . . then they took his severed privy member, stuffed it into his bloodied mouth. They did that to my father."

She stared up at him, eyes wide and glazed, but dry; she'd shed not a tear in the telling, although he could feel the tremors shaking her body. There were no words, and he knew that, did the only thing he could, pulled her against his chest, held her close. She was rigid in his arms, but after a few moments, she shuddered convulsively, and then she clung. He continued to hold her, gently stroking her hair, and after a time, she said, in a muffled voice, "I never told anyone that I knew. My mother and brother tried to keep it from me, and for a long time, they did. But one day I overheard some of our men talking . . ."

She looked up then, into his face, still tearless, but with a chalk-white pallor that caught at his heart. "Edward did that," she said. "He may not have wielded the knife himself, but he let it happen. He was there, he had the command, and Roger de Mortimer was his friend, his boon companion. He dared to tell me that he'd wept for Harry, after letting my father be butchered, and when the monks crept out onto the field to bury my father's body, Edward ordered him dug up, as if he were a dog, denied him Christian burial. He would lie today in unconsecrated ground if not for Amaury. Edward's generosity to a fallen foe, and who knows, mayhap that is the real reason Amaury has passed nigh on three years in English prisons. Even if Edward could somehow convince me that he was not to blame for what they did to my father's body, even if I could somehow forgive him for that, how could I ever forgive him for Amaury?"

"That," he confessed quietly, "was what I could not understand."

"I had to make him believe I bore him no grudge. If I could have bought Amaury's freedom with my smiles, I'd have given him every one I had. If we had not been wed I might even have offered more than smiles. But I could not bring dishonor to your name, even for Amaury's sake."

She at once worried that she'd been too honest, but he did not seem shocked. "You are very loyal to your brother," he said, and she nodded somberly.

"Loyalty is all that was left to us after Evesham. But I will be just as loyal to you, Llewelyn. I'll never give you reason to doubt me, that I swear to you."

He looked for a long moment into her upturned face, then kissed her, very gently. "This ought to have been a day you'd take joy in remembering. But between us, Edward and I have turned it into one you'll want only to forget."

"It does not matter," she said, and discovered, to her surprise, that she meant it. "All that matters is this . . ." Sliding her hand up his chest and over his heart. "When I touch you now, our souls touch, too. That may sound foolish, but I truly did feel as if you'd gone where I could not follow, and it frightened me. Llewelyn . . . I realize you are not a man accustomed to sharing secrets of the heart. And I will try not to ask of you more than you are able to give. But do you think you can learn to be more forthcoming, to treat me not just as a wife, but also as a confidante?"

"You are right," he said, "I've never been one for confiding your 'secrets of the heart.' But then, I've never had a wife before. I cannot promise you that I can change overnight. But I can promise you that I'll try. That is the least I can do for you, my love."

She smiled, almost as pleased by the endearment as by the promise. But what could she do for him? She seemed to have been able to staunch the bleeding, but the wound was a deep one, would take a long time to heal. She could think now of only one offer to make, and she said softly, "We do not have to return to the hall, Llewelyn. We can bolt the door, stay right here in our bridal chamber. I do not imagine you are much in the mood for wedding revelries."

She was right, he wasn't. "That is a very tempting offer. But we'd be creating a great scandal."

"I do not care about that."

"No," he said, "this is your wedding day. I'll not cheat you of it,

Ellen. Every bride deserves that much, her time in the sun, and this is yours, cariad. Kiss me now to seal our bargain, to remind me what I have to look forward to, and then we'll return to the hall and enjoy our wedding."

"Are you sure?" she asked, and he nodded.

"Very sure. If we do not, Edward will have won. And I think he has already won enough today."

THE wedding guests were not long in noticing their absence, and when they returned to the hall, they were subjected to merciless teasing, to a bawdy bombardment that gave them a foretaste of the bedding-down revelries still to come. But Llewelyn and Ellen did not seem unduly perturbed. Although some of the jokes caused Ellen to blush, they met all queries about their disappearance with shrugs and enigmatic smiles. Blanche, watching intently, heaved a heartfelt sigh of relief. The dinner was about to begin, and she took advantage of the accompanying confusion to pull Ellen aside.

"All is well now between you?" she asked quietly, and Ellen nodded.

"I think so. You know then, Blanche?"

"Edmund told me. He was truly taken aback, thinks that Edward's timing is lamentable. I'd say it was well nigh perfect."

"Yes," Ellen said grimly, "so would I." She felt very thankful at that moment for Blanche's friendship, started to tell her so. But a young woman was bearing down upon them. Reaching the dais, she made a deep curtsy, as Ellen looked at her in dismay, having seen her earlier with Davydd.

"Cousin Eleanor, I am Elizabeth de Ferrers, Davydd's wife. I . . . I want to ask your pardon. A bride should be able to choose her own wedding guests, and I know you would not have invited Davydd and me of your own free will."

Ellen was startled by the girl's stark honesty, was silent for a moment as she decided how to respond to it. "Elizabeth, I'll not insult you by pretending I do not know what you mean. Nor will I tell you that you are welcome here, for although it is true, I do not think you would want to be welcome if Davydd were not. Ah, Elizabeth, I truly do not want you to be uncomfortable. Today I want only to enjoy my wedding. As for Davydd . . . well, he is Llewelyn's brother, so he probably has more right to be here than many of the others. You need only look over there, at the Earl of Gloucester. I want him at my wedding for certes—when pigs roost in trees!"

Blanche grinned, amused by how deftly Ellen had managed to steer the conversation into smoother waters. "Ellen is right," she said, entering into the game with zest. "And let's not forget the Earl of Pembroke. If that one got his dinner invitations only from those who fancied his company, he'd soon starve to death!"

"That holds true, as well, for the man by the hearth, John Giffard. Wherever he belongs, it is not at my wedding," Ellen said, with a grimace of distaste, eliciting an unexpected response from Elizabeth.

"John Giffard belongs by rights in the deepest pits of Hellfire Everlasting," she said, so venomously that Blanche and Ellen looked at her in surprise.

"I have good reason to scorn that man," Ellen said curiously, "for he betrayed my father. But why do you detest him so, Elizabeth? Did he ever harm you?"

"No," Elizabeth said, "but that is more than his wife can say. That is her over there, standing behind him. I think you know her, Cousin Ellen—Maude Clifford?"

"Good Heavens, yes," Ellen exclaimed. "Is that Maude? I'd never have recognized her! She was wed to my cousin, the Earl of Salisbury's son, widowed young, at seventeen or so, left with a little girl. We were never close, for she was at least twelve years older than I, but Salisbury was one of my father's most steadfast friends, and so I did see her from time to time. In fact, we are now kinswomen," Ellen said, explaining for Blanche's benefit that Maude Clifford was a granddaughter of Llewelyn Fawr, and thus a first cousin to Llewelyn. "I had not heard that she'd wed John Giffard. Jesú, what a choice!"

"Believe me," Elizabeth said, "choice did not enter into it. He abducted her from her Dorsetshire manor, took her by force to his stronghold at Brimpsfield, where he raped her and then found a biddable priest to marry them."

There was a silence then, as Blanche and Ellen gazed across the hall at Maude Clifford, their pity heightened by the understanding that Maude's unhappy fate could have been theirs, too, for there was no shortage of men willing to gain a rich wife by John Giffard's methods. Ellen slowly shook her head, thinking of her own great-grandmother, the legendary Eleanor of Aquitaine, who'd barely escaped two such abduction attempts herself. "And I suppose Maude felt too shamed to make a public protest," she said sadly, knowing how often that was the case, but knowing, too, that she would have denounced Giffard as long as she had breath in her body, and so, she suspected, would Blanche.

"No," Elizabeth said, "he'd not yet broken her spirit, and she found a way to complain to the King—for all the good it did her. Our uncle Henry was in his dotage, Edward was on crusade, and Maude's plea came to naught. Giffard denied taking her by force, claimed she was too ill to come to court, and offered to pay a fine of three hundred marks for having wed her without the King's permission. By then she was already pregnant, and so that was that," Elizabeth concluded, with a very cynical shrug.

"No wonder we heard nothing of this, Ellen." Blanche had been doing some rapid mental arithmetic. "If Henry was still King and Edward in the Holy Land, we're going back seven or eight years, and you and I were both living then in France. I can see why Llewelyn could not help her, for his influence has never extended into England. But the Cliffords are a power in the Marches. What of her cousin, Roger Clifford? Could he do naught for her?"

"Roger was too busy stealing Culmington Manor from Maude's widowed mother, his own aunt. In fairness, there might have been some who'd have tried to help her, had they but known of her plight. But it was hushed up. My father just happened to hear about it because he was in Gloucestershire at that time."

"You must have been very young, Elizabeth. Yet you seem to remember it so well?"

"I was thirteen," Elizabeth said, "and oh, yes, I remember. You see, I was not happy living under my father's roof, and I was eager to wed, to have a husband and household of my own. Then I learned about Maude Clifford, and I learned, too, that marriage was not always the escape I'd fancied it to be. After that, I was not quite so eager to be a wife again."

Elizabeth paused, looked Ellen full in the face, and said, without the flicker of a smile, "But then, you and I are more fortunate than Maude Clifford. After all, we are the King's cousins, and we both know Edward would always act only in our best interests."

Ellen's mouth dropped open; so did Blanche's. They both stared at the younger woman, as astonished as if a butterfly had suddenly drawn blood. After a moment, Ellen smiled. "I think," she said, "that you and I are going to get along very well, Cousin Elizabeth."

THE wedding guests would be talking for weeks to come about the delectable repast they were served that afternoon in Worcester Castle's great hall. For those lucky enough to be seated at the high table, the service was as excellent as the food. Dinner guests were expected to provide their own knives, and to hack out their own plates from stale bread. But for the favored guests upon the dais, an ivory-handled knife was laid out for each diner, and the panter carefully cut their trenchers from round loaves marked with holy crosses. The saltcellar, an intricately sculptured silver nef, sails billowing, was carried with great ceremony to the high table, placed before Edward, and at every trencher there was a wine cup of silver gilt. They enjoyed other privileges as well. To them first came the ewers, carrying warm, scented water and linen hand towels, and when the meal began, they would receive the dishes first, too, still hot and steaming. And from their vantage point, at the head of the hall, they had an unobstructed view of the musicians, the minstrels, and the other guests.

A trumpet fanfare ushered in the first dish of the first course, roast venison, a great favorite. It was later followed by quails in aspic, and then, fried apple fritters. Another trumpet flourish called attention to the subtlety that ended the course, a marvelous marzipan sculpture of a young maiden, her long hair colored with saffron dye, her gown tinted green with parsley juice; at her feet knelt the noblest of beasts, the elusive unicorn that could be caught only by an innocent virgin. The cooks had taken some artistic license with the unicorn, for all knew it should have been snowy white, but that was not an easy shade to reproduce, and so this particular unicorn was a vivid saffron gold, a safe choice, though, for the brighter a color, the more likely people were to appreciate it.

The second course began with a dish so spectacular it drew applause: roast peacock, bones painstakingly strutted and skin and feathers refitted to give the illusion of life. After it, pike stuffed with chestnuts was served, and then beef and marrow fritters, and spiced pears. The subtlety for the second course was a culinary triumph, a marzipan dragon that owed its rich red color to sandalwood, its fiery breath to a cleverly concealed bellows. It was, all agreed, an inspired choice, for the dragon had long been linked in the popular imagination with Wales.

As the guests dined, the musicians strolled about, filling the hall with the music of harp and gittern, flute and viol, and the unique bagpipes brought by the Scots. There were numerous minstrels, too, eager to perform, hoping to find positions in the households of the highborn guests. The minstrel who was to have the greatest success, though, was already securely tenured, standing high in Alexander's favor. He was French by birth, spoke half a dozen languages or more, and had seen, or so he claimed, most of the great courts of Europe, picking up in his travels a remarkably varied repertoire of songs and ballads and lays.

After taking several requests for jaunty, sprightly songs, he announced that he would now sing for the bridal couple.

> Now is the time for pleasure,
>   Lads and lasses,
> Take your joy together,
>   Ere it passes.
> With the love of a maid

Aflower,
With the love of a maid
Afire,
New love, new love,
Dying of desire.

The audience joined in after each new stanza, zestfully echoing the chorus, and he finally concluded with a lover's plea to:

Come, mistress mine,
Joy with thee,
Come, fairest, come,
Love, to me.

Ellen was delighted with the song, and the minstrel cheerfully obliged her request for more, sang to her of a lover's vow, a faith unbroken, but then, with an impish grin, he launched into a hunter's boast, that "Woman and falcon are easily made tame. Both will come flying to a man's lure the same." The women all hissed, the men laughed and cheered, and he reaped another windfall, coins sailing his way from all corners of the hall.

Trumpets now heralded the beginning of the third and final course. As stewed lampreys were ladled onto their trencher, Llewelyn wielded his knife on Ellen's behalf, cutting the eel into pieces she could pick up with her fingers. It was the common practice for a couple to share the same trencher and wine cup, but Ellen had not known until now that such sharing could be so erotic. As Llewelyn fed her choice tidbits, washed down with spiced red wine, she realized they were indulging in a leisurely three-course seduction. It was wonderful to whisper that in his ear, to see him smile. When she thought how different this meal could have been, she shivered, and when Edward made a courtly toast, wishing them all the happiness he had found with his Eleanora, she was able to smile without strain, to act as if she believed him.

Llewelyn was discovering, as the meal progressed, that some of his tension was subsiding. His fury had congealed; it was still there, just beneath the surface, but safely sheeted in ice. And if he could not truly enjoy the wedding festivities, it was enough for him that Ellen was enjoying herself. She was flirting outrageously with him, even surprised him with a Welsh toast, "Tangnevedd," asking later if it truly did mean "Peace be with you," confessing that she was not sure Goronwy's translation could be trusted. He listened now in amusement as she described for Alexander an exotic eating utensil that Amaury had supposedly seen at an Italian banquet. It was meant to replace fingers, she explained, a notion so ludicrous that she soon had all within earshot laughing, but she kept a straight face, even when she claimed it looked just like a shrunken pitchfork. Afterward, she winked at Llewelyn, and he realized he still did not know if she'd been serious or not about Amaury's Italian forks. She was full of surprises, this wife of his, and getting to know her better was going to be a very interesting experience.

It was dusk before the sugared nebula wafers and Lombardy custard were served, and torches were flaring, shadows advancing, as the final subtlety was brought into the hall. Another fair marzipan maiden, but this time the tamed beast at her feet was not a unicorn, but a blood-red Welsh dragon. The guests roared their approval, applauding enthusiastically. Ellen, blushing and laughing both, glanced quickly toward Llewelyn, and her spirits soared when she saw he was laughing, too, for she knew that even a few short hours ago, he'd not have been amused. We won, Ned, she thought, smiling down the table at her royal cousin, damn your swaggering, deceitful soul to Hell, this time we won.

AFTER the trestle tables were cleared away, Alexander's minstrel was called upon to entertain again, and he made ready to perform a lay written, he claimed, by a highborn lady.

> I dwell in deep anxiety,
> For a knight who gave himself to me.
> I wish my knight might share my bed,
> And hold me naked in his arms,
> That now he might win joys for hours,
> With me the pillow for his head.

The song was a great success with the audience, although not with the Bishop of Worcester, who'd been to enough weddings to know the bawdiness was just beginning. And as he feared, the minstrel's next song was a rollicking account of a woman crusader, Maria Perez, who'd returned from the Holy Land laden with indulgences. Some were lost, some were stolen, but that, he explained, was because:

> Maria's treasure chest was not too safe
>   a place for that—indeed it could not be,
> For since the time the padlock was first broken,
>   Her treasure chest has always been wide open.

After that, it was all downhill, at least in the Bishop's eyes. At times like this, his Church's teachings about the wages of sin seemed to fall on deaf ears. How else explain the laughter and lewd jokes, the cheers when the minstrel announced he'd now sing everyone's favorite, "Under The Sun I Ride Along."

The Bishop was all too familiar with the song, which had been written, God forgive him, by a highborn lord, a Count of Poitou, kinsman both to Edward and Ellen through his granddaughter, Eleanor of Aquitaine, but a man burning in Hell lo these many years past; of that, the Bishop was sure, for the Count's life had been as lascivious as his music. But the minstrel was already into the song, a ribald tale of a knight who'd pretended to be mute, thus duping two lust-filled ladies into thinking it was safe to dally with him, for "Such sport as we'll devise with him will ne'er be known." They tested him first, set a savage tomcat to raking its claws along his back, but he made no sound, although "keen could I feel its talons ripping down my flank." Convinced, they then took him off to bed, where for more than a week, he sinned lustily and often, "a hundred four score times and eight," until "a woeful state they left me in, with harness torn and broken blade." When he recovered, he sent his squire back to the women, "And tit for tat, ask them in memory of me, to kill that cat!"

For reasons that eluded the Bishop altogether, people never failed to find that last verse hilarious, and he knew that for the rest of the night, men would be crying out at odd intervals, "Kill that cat!" convulsing themselves by their own drunken wit.

Never did his sheep stray so far from the fold as when they flocked to weddings. Marriage was a Sacrament, yet these festivities more often resembled pagan rites than Christian nuptials. The Church frowned upon dancing, and yet they whirled from one carol to another until they reeled. The Church exhorted newly wed couples to refrain from consummating their marriage for the first few days, yet he'd never known a single case in which they did. And the Church's attempts to discourage the bedding-down revelries met with obstinate resistance. No state was as exalted as virginity; when a woman lost it, even in wedlock, she was diminished, and to turn that loss into an excuse for drunken, shameful debauchery was truly deplorable. But the worst of it was that he'd have a part in it, for he'd have to bless the bed ere they could sin.

EINION had been watching Llewelyn closely throughout dinner, and he'd been heartened by what he saw. He still wanted, though, to be sure he was right, and he seized the first opportunity after the meal to have a few private moments with Llewelyn. But they were interrupted almost at once by Hugh de Whitton.

"My lord Llewelyn, may I have a word with you? I just heard a disturbing rumor, that King Edward plans to arrest all the Jews in England, charge them with coin clipping. I was wondering if you knew anything about it?"

"No, Hugh, I do not. I am not the best one to ask about this, for there are no Jews in Wales. But I do know that Edward loathes them. When he forbade them to act as money-lenders, it was inevitable that some of them would start clipping coins, for how else could they live? So it does not bode well for them, the innocent or the guilty. You're thinking of the Bristol money-lender, the one who helped you?"

Hugh nodded unhappily. "My lord, do you think you might . . . ?"

"All right," Llewelyn said indulgently, "I'll see what I can find out for you. But for now, look about you, Hugh. What do you see? People enjoying themselves. That is what you are supposed to do at a wedding, lad. Your cares will not go away; you'll find they're more loyal than greyhounds. So put them aside just for the night, go forth and have fun."

Hugh grinned. "Diolch yn fawr," he said, in very passable Welsh, and hied off to join the circle forming for the carol.

"What about you, Llewelyn? I hope you mean to follow your own advice?"

"As it happens, Einion, I do." Llewelyn smiled unexpectedly. "What better way to vex our royal host?"

THERE was at least one guest at the wedding, though, who was not following Llewelyn's advice. Caitlin was not having any fun at all. Never had she felt so out of place. A fourteen-year-old girl was not likely to attract much notice in a gathering of adults, and Caitlin had the additional misfortune to look even younger than she was. Moreover, all her anxieties had come flooding back with her first glimpse of Llewelyn's wife. Ellen was so fair; what man would not be bedazzled by her? And she could not help wondering if there would still be room for her in her uncle's new life.

But these misgivings paled in comparison with the jolt of panic she experienced now, watching in dismay as the man she'd sought so desperately to avoid strode purposefully toward her, cutting off escape.

"Caitlin? Do you not think," Davydd said, "that it is time we talked?"

IT had been a long time since Maude Clifford had enjoyed herself so much. It had been a long time since anyone had treated her as if she truly mattered. She'd been shy at first, not sure why the Princess of

Wales and the Countess of Lancaster should be showing such interest in her. But Ellen and Blanche were skilled practitioners of their society's social graces, and they soon put Maude at ease. She blossomed under the attention, reminiscing with Ellen about mutual friends, telling them proudly about her young daughters. There was only one awkward moment, when Ellen impulsively extended an invitation to Llewelyn's Christmas court. Maude's smile seemed lit by a hundred candles as she accepted, but almost at once they dimmed, and she said in a voice suddenly dulled and flat that her husband would want her at Brimpsfield for Christmas. Ellen looked into the older woman's face, and then heard herself saying that he would be welcome, too, for as she would later tell a bemused Blanche, at that moment she'd wanted only to see Maude's smile come back, even if it meant—as it did—dining with the Devil.

"But ought you not to ask your lord husband first?" Maude asked anxiously. "Your offer was most generous, but I would understand if—"

"There is no need to fret about that, Cousin Maude. You are most welcome at my husband's court, for I am sure Llewelyn would not mind if I speak for him in this," Ellen said, with such blithe certainty that Maude could not help wincing, envious of Ellen's innocence, but knowing, too, how dangerous it could be. As she started to speak, though, she saw that Ellen's attention was wandering; she was staring across the hall. "I'll be right back," she said abruptly. "I think my husband's little niece is in need of rescue."

DAVYDD was surprised that he was encountering such resistance. "Do you not even want to hear my side of it, lass?"

"No," Caitlin muttered, refusing to meet his eyes. All her life she'd been taught that she owed respect to her elders, and those lessons came back to haunt her now, so that her anger and confusion were compounded by guilt, too. But when Davydd touched her arm, she stiffened, spat out in shaken defiance, "I love Uncle Llewelyn, more than anyone!"

"Well and good. I do not begrudge him your love. But he is not your father, Caitlin, I am."

She felt the tears coming then, hot enough to burn. Her mouth contorted, but the voice that filled her ears was not her own. "There you are, Lady Caitlin!" And the next thing she knew, there was a hand upon her elbow and a stranger was sweeping her out onto the dance floor, smiling over his shoulder at Davydd. "You do not mind, do you, my lord, if I borrow her? She did promise me this next dance!"

The hall was still blurring for Caitlin; she blinked until the young

Englishman came into focus, tall and flaxen haired and faintly familiar. "I am sorry," she said, surrepititiously brushing the wetness from her cheeks. "Do I know you?"

"Of course you do," Hugh said, thinking that she looked like a bedraggled kitten. Poor little lass. "Do you not remember? We met on a Welsh mountain road, and after you begged a ride back to Cricieth, we agreed to dance at your uncle's wedding. No? You are sure? Well then, if I may ask now . . . Lady Caitlin, will you dance this carol with me?"

"I do remember you now," she said, but she was thinking that she'd never seen eyes so blue. "I would indeed like to dance with you."

DAVYDD's edgy mood was not improved by Hugh's meddlesome chivalry. He felt no real surprise when he later spotted Hugh and Caitlin on the dais with Ellen, for he well knew whose lapdog Hugh was. So his new sister-in-law was already throwing down the gauntlet. Had Llewelyn confided in her? Yes, he'd wager she knew. He alone did not.

By now Davydd was thoroughly frustrated, for he'd had no luck whatsoever in finding out what sort of wedding surprise Edward had sprung upon his brother. He'd known something was amiss for hours, ever since his first look at Llewelyn's face in the priory cloisters. And once he concluded that Llewelyn had been stabbed in the back, it was easy enough to identify the suspect. But so far he'd been thwarted at every turn. He'd had no chance at all to confront Llewelyn directly, for his brother was doing a masterful job of keeping him at a distance, never so obvious as to be conspicuous, but always just out of reach. So he'd tackled their uncle Einion, only to be met with a blank stare, a shrug. He'd tried Goronwy next, and had finally approached Dai ab Einion, Llewelyn's new Seneschal, who distrusted him even more than Tudur had, if that was possible. But they'd closed ranks against him, treating him like an outsider, like an Englishman.

Looking about for Elizabeth, he at last located her by the open hearth, and as he drew near, he saw that the man engaging her in animated conversation was Goronwy. Coming up quietly behind them, he said coldly, "Stop flirting with my wife."

Elizabeth looked startled, for he had never shown a possessive streak before. But Goronwy did not seem flustered, and as Davydd slipped his arm about her waist, she realized that he was jesting. "Take care, Elizabeth," he said, "for this man could not be trusted with a novice nun, much less a tempting morsel like you. And I know whereof I speak, for I was an eye-witness to many of his unseemly escapades."

"What he neglects to tell you, Lady Elizabeth," Goronwy parried, "is that I was merely following in his footsteps. Indeed, some of his exploits have since passed into folklore, amongst those too depraved to know any better."

To a casual ear, it might have sounded like the usual barbed male banter, but Elizabeth sensed undercurrents just beneath the surface, and remembered that Davydd and Goronwy had once been friends.

"Goronwy was once a veritable patron saint for sinners, Elizabeth. But these days he has moved on to greater things, showing off a sleight of hand that even Merlin might envy. Not only has he been appointed to act as a justice in Edward's new commission, he has agreed to serve as bailiff in one of the cantrefs Edward took from Llewelyn."

"Why is that so surprising?" Goronwy said coolly. "Where can I do more good? Whom do you think the Welsh would rather turn to for help? Me—or someone like your renegade friend, Rhys ap Gruffydd?"

"We're not talking about Rhys; we're talking about you. The truly amazing aspect of all this, Elizabeth, is that he has somehow managed to stay in Llewelyn's favor. Other men get fevers; my brother, bless him, gets suspicions. So suppose you tell us how you do it, Goronwy? How is it that Llewelyn is of a sudden willing to trust a servant of the English Crown?"

"That is very easy to answer. You see, Llewelyn well knows that my loyalties are pledged to Wales, only to Wales."

Davydd's eyes narrowed. "You think mine are not?"

Goronwy gave him an intent look. "If they are," he said, "then I am indeed sorry for you, Davydd," and to Davydd's fury, he sounded quite sincere.

ELLEN was surrounded by friends. Her de Quincy cousins, who bore the blood of Joanna and Llewelyn Fawr: Hawise, wed to Baldwin Wake, and Joanna, who'd been widowed at Evesham. John d'Eyvill and his wife, Matilda. Nicholas Segrave. These men had been loyal unto death to her father; Nicholas Segrave was one of the few who'd survived the carnage of Evesham, and Baldwin Wake and John d'Eyville had been with Bran during his last doomed campaign. For them, there was a special poignancy in this reunion with their dead lord's daughter, a brief escape from Edward's England to what might have been, and they laughed and jested and remembered, even if they dared not share those memories aloud.

There'd been a break in the dancing, and Ellen gave a theatrical moan when the musicians moved back onto the dance floor. She'd always loved dancing, but a bride was expected to dance with any man who asked her, and she'd already spun through so many carols that night that she felt like a child's whirling top. They commiserated play-fully with her plight, and John d'Eyvill suggested that the men link arms, refuse to let any of her would-be partners up onto the dais.

Ellen laughed, shook her head. "That is a most chivalrous offer, but I mean to do something even more scandalous. For the rest of the night, I shall dance only with my husband. So I'd best seek him out, ere the music begins again."

Rising, she experienced a moment of light-headedness, not her first warning that she was fast approaching the limits of her wine intake. Normally she was a moderate drinker, but they'd begun the festivities with hippocras, followed by a hearty red wine, then claret, and for the past hour, an adoring-eyed young page had shadowed her every move, keeping her cup brimming with vernage, her favorite white wine. Hold-ing the cup carefully now, she lifted her skirts so she could descend the shallow steps of the dais. But she was concentrating so intently upon her long, trailing train that she did not even notice the man in her path, not until it was too late.

She stumbled, but managed to regain her balance and even to direct her spilled wine away from him; only a few drops splattered onto his surcote sleeve, the rest splashing into the floor rushes. "I am indeed sorry," she began, but her smile froze as she realized that the man she'd almost drenched was Davydd.

"I have never met a woman so set upon wasting good wine. Are you always like this, or is it only around me that you get the urge to water the floor rushes?"

She supposed she had to give him credit for daring to remind her of the way she'd discomfited him at Windsor, but then, he'd never lacked for gall. "If you will excuse me . . .?"

But he did not move aside. "There is no need to run away," he said, "for have you not noticed that I'm on my best behavior? I've not gotten into a single brawl today, I've gallantly refrained from claiming the traditional dance with the bride, much less a bridal kiss. And," he added, with a smile that mixed both mischief and malice, "I have not reminded Edward about your quaint English custom, the one that sup-posedly gives a lord the right to spend the first night with his vassal's bride."

He was intrigued to see how green her eyes suddenly shone; just like, he thought, a cat on the prowl.

"You remind me," she said, "of my brothers. You see, in their youth, they, too, took a perverse pleasure in saying things they hoped would astound or dismay. But they outgrew it."

"This is just conjecture, of course, but I am beginning to suspect you do not like me very much, Lady Ellen."

She smiled. "I do not like you at all, and you well know it. Moreover, I doubt that I'm one of your favorite people, either. So I cannot help wondering why you took the trouble to seek me out." She paused expectantly. "Well? Do not tell me that you, of all men, are at a loss for an answer?"

"Oh, I have any number of answers. I was just deciding which one you'd be most likely to believe."

"Why not be truly daring and try the truth?"

"We Welsh have a saying, 'cynghor y gobenydd,' which translates as, 'the advice of the pillow.' It occurred to me that your pillow talk might be more dangerous than most, since my brother is obviously smitten. So I thought I'd best find out if hostilities are about to begin. Being a de Montfort, I assume that you would at least issue a declaration of war first?"

Ellen was surprised, for she'd never expected that he really would be honest with her. "You may set your mind at rest, my lord Davydd. I'll not try to turn Llewelyn against you," she said, thinking that he'd already done that all on his own.

Davydd seemed to read her thoughts, saying, "You'll leave that up to me, then? Fair enough, I— Oh, Christ Jesus, Hugh, not again! Believe me, your lady is no maiden in distress. In fact, I'd back her against the dragon any day." He smiled, bowed mockingly, and was gone before either Ellen or Hugh could respond.

"Thank you, Hugh." Ellen raised up, kissed him on the cheek. "But Davydd was right for once; I was not in need of rescue." Shaking her head, she said wonderingly, "How can two brothers be so different, like chalk and cheese?"

"In truth, my lady, Lord Davydd is not as much the black sheep as he would have people think." Hugh saw her eyes widen, and said hastily, before her indignation could take fire, "I have not forgotten how he plotted against Lord Llewelyn's life, and indeed, that is a betrayal only God could forgive. But he can be kind, too, at times, for whatever reasons. He did intercede, after all, for Lord Bran at the battle of Northampton. And I never got the chance to tell you this, but he came to my aid when I was dragged before the King at Lincoln. If not for him, Lady Ellen, I'd have been banished to a Bristol gaol."

Ellen was still puzzling over that a few moments later as she resumed her search for Llewelyn. But he found her first. "What did Davydd want?" he asked. "He did not vex you, did he?"

"No, he assured me he was on his best behavior, and I think he may even have meant it. I have a confession, though, Llewelyn. I do not understand your brother at all!"

"You think I do?" He gave a bemused laugh. "Who else in

Christendom would name his firstborn son after the man he'd tried to murder?''

Ellen reached for his hand. "When Davydd ambushed me," she said, "I was coming to ask you if you'd like to dance with me, and only with me, for the rest of the evening?"

"Actually," he said, "I had a more intimate activity in mind. I think it is time, cariad, that we begin our private celebrating."

"Now? Oh, Llewelyn, you want me to leave the dancing?" But Ellen could not carry if off; even as she pretended to pout, she began to giggle. "After waiting nigh on three years to celebrate with you, I do not think you have to talk me into it. But love, you know you cannot be the one to suggest it is time for the bedding revelries. I've never understood why people think it is so much fun to torment the poor bridegroom, but if you even hint that you're eager to be alone with me, we'll be lucky to get to bed by dawn. And if I suggest it, imagine the scandal! After all, I am an innocent maiden, and not supposed to think about what I've been thinking about all evening."

He grinned. "You're showing great promise as a wife, lass. But you need not worry, for I have a battle plan. I will need your help, though. I want you to look at me with heartfelt yearning, and the more attention we attract, the better. Can you do that?"

She nodded, but after one attempt at soulful passion, she started to giggle again. "I'm sorry, Llewelyn, I just cannot do it!"

By now he was laughing, too. "I can tell the wine has been flowing freely tonight! Let's try it again . . ." Turning her hand over, he pressed a kiss into her palm. "Do you remember that song you fancied? 'Come, mistress, mine, joy with thee, come, fairest, come, love, to me,' " he quoted softly, and by the time he was done, she looked utterly bewitched, and so bewitching herself that he lowered his mouth to hers. She came into his arms as if she belonged there, her lips parting under his as he prolonged the embrace, thinking he could get as tipsy on her perfume as she'd gotten on her wedding wine. But it was a private kiss in a public setting, ended by raucous cheering.

Llewelyn's allies now did their part, though, as promised, Blanche and Edmund declaring loudly that it was clearly time to get these poor, lovesick souls bedded down for the night, and others at once took up the cry.

Ellen had been to many weddings, had known full well what to expect. But it was still somewhat startling to find herself suddenly encircled by laughing, clapping spectators, many of them drunk, some of them strangers, all clamoring in unison, "To the marriage bed!" She was grateful when Llewelyn slid his arm around her waist, and when he whispered against her ear, "Do you think there is something to be said for elopements?" she laughed, but she still kept close to his side as the wedding party trooped from the hall.

As Llewelyn and Ellen knelt by the bed, the Bishop of Worcester offered the traditional blessing, prayed that their marriage would be fruitful and that they would find favor in the eyes of the Lord. He then sprinkled holy water about, and gave a brief homily in which he reminded them that the Church expected its sons and daughters to refrain from consummating a marriage until they had allotted a proper time for prayer and meditation, trying to ignore the snickers and nudges from the audience as he did so. He made a speedy departure then, more from disapproval than discretion, but the end result was the same; freed of any lingering constraints, the wedding guests, all who'd been able to squeeze into the bedchamber, now crowded around the bridal pair.

Llewelyn surprised Ellen then, for when someone asked who was going to undress the bride, he cut off the predictable spate of offers by saying that he might be persuaded to give her a hand, and that did not seem like his sort of humor to her, not in public. He was naturally hooted down, and only then did she see what he'd had in mind. "A man cannot be blamed for trying," he said, "but it is probably best that she gets to choose those who'll attend her."

"Yes, I shall choose straightaway," Ellen said hastily, before anyone could object, for many of these women were total strangers to her, and some she knew but did not like. This was an intimate ritual, making a bride ready for her husband. It ought to be done amidst friends, and now, thanks to Llewelyn, it would be, for there were a few dissenting murmurs, but no outright opposition. People expected a certain amount of modesty in a virgin bride, and were usually willing to indulge it.

"I would be honored by the presence of the Queen," Ellen said, and as Eleanora smiled and nodded, she shot Llewelyn a triumphant "Who says I am not a diplomat?" look. "The Countess of Lancaster. Dame Juliana. My kinswomen, Hawise Wake and Joanna de Bohun. Matilda d'Eyvill." For a moment, her eyes met Elizabeth's eager ones, and she hesitated, but not long enough for anyone to notice, before saying, "My cousin Elizabeth." She had an inspiration then, added Maude Clifford's name to the list, and was rewarded by a look of incredulous delight. "And last, but for certes not least, my new niece, the Lady Caitlin."

It was left to Blanche to clear the chamber, which she accomplished with her usual verve. Servants had already lit a fire in the hearth, ringed the room in flaring white candles, and laid out sugared wafers and a flagon of mead, in deference to Welsh tastes. As the chamber had been made ready, the women now turned their attention to Ellen. Blanche and Juliana helped her out of her surcote and gown, and then the soft saffron hose, Blanche advising her that in future nights, she might want to leave the stockings for Llewelyn to remove, as men seemed to take particular pleasure in garters and silken wisps and the like. Sitting Ellen down by the fire then, clad only in her chemise, they began to brush her hair, to polish it with lemon-scented silk, while counseling her that men were, without exception, stirred by long, loose hair, doubtless because it was only seen like that in bed; so if she should be in the mood for lovemaking, she need only let her hair down and her husband would, as likely as not, suddenly discover that he was in the mood, too, without even being aware that he'd been prompted. Laughing, Ellen declared this was indeed an education for her, and far more interesting than any lesson learned in books.

It was proving to be an education for Caitlin, too. She'd been enormously honored to be included, for she'd not had much contact with her own sex; she'd never known her mother, and there was no mistress of her uncle's household, only concubines who came and went and rarely paid her any mind. It was a revelation now to discover that women could be as fascinated by carnal matters as men, but as she carefully folded each of Ellen's bridal garments in turn, her bewilderment was increasing.

"May I ask you something, Lady Ellen?" she blurted out at last. "The Bishop said you ought not to lay together this night. But you and my uncle . . . it does not sound as if you mean to abstain?"

As the laughter subsided, Ellen said hastily, "Ah, no, Caitlin, we were not laughing at you, truly we were not. It is rather complicated, lass, for the Church sees lust as a grave sin. We are taught that its pleasures are suspect, that chastity is the ideal state, and Christians ought to lay together only to beget children. That is why the Church places so many restrictions upon the carnal act, declaring it sinful during Lent or Advent or on Sundays or holy days, whilst a woman is pregnant, or when she has her flux."

"And why," Blanche chimed in, "the Church warns that husbands and wives must always guard against finding too much joy in each other, admonishing us that lovemaking ought to be done in the dark, not in daylight, and only in one position, with the man on top."

"And do people obey these prohibitions?" Answering her own question then, Caitlin said thoughtfully, "If they did, would they not have far fewer babies?"

"Yes, lass, they would indeed. The problem is that people find it hard to resist their carnal urges, and for the very reason that the Church seeks to suppress them, because of the great pleasure they give. Or so," Ellen added with a grin, "I've been told! I am not saying that Christians do not try to heed the Church's strictures, but I suspect that they often fall from grace. My brother Amaury told me that when he was studying to be a priest, they were taught not to be too specific when preaching against sins of the flesh, lest they give their parishioners ideas!''

That provoked another burst of laughter. Caitlin was finding that it was possible to tell which of the women were more knowing about these pleasures of the flesh, just by the way they responded to these bawdy jokes. The Queen, the Lady Blanche, Dame Juliana, and her young stepmother Elizabeth had found the most joy in a man's bed, she decided, and the Lady Maude none at all, for her laughter was forced, her face flushed. Caitlin wondered how it would be for her when it was her turn to be a bride; would she be as eager as Ellen? And she blushed then, astonished at her own thoughts, for there suddenly came into her mind an image of the young blue-eyed Englishman, the one called Hugh.

Now that Ellen's hair had been brushed to a burnished gold and her lip rouge carefully blotted, she shed her chemise so she could be dusted with a fragrant powder. She allowed herself to be perfumed in some very provocative places, but balked at agreeing to rouge the tips of her nipples, blushing in spite of herself, shocked as much by the source as by the suggestion, for it came from the dignified, ever so proper Eleanora.

Seeing her discomfort, Blanche said swiftly, ''No woman need worry about stirring male ardor on her wedding night. But I thank you, Eleanora, for the idea, and I daresay that so will Edmund! You cannot make me believe, though, that you, of all women, must strive to attract your husband's attention. After eleven children? My heavens, dearest, if he paid you any more attention, the two of you would never get out of bed!''

Eleanora was unfazed by her sister-in-law's teasing. She well knew how lucky was her lot when compared to that of most queens, for her husband not only found her desirable, he loved her. ''I could not admit this to my confessor,'' she said serenely, ''but I do not see why it is a sin to want to please the man you love. And it is eleven and a half. With a surcote so fully cut, I could be about to drop twins and no one could tell. But I am indeed with child again, due in early spring.''

Eleanora's intimates knew that she was pregnant, but there'd been no formal announcement as yet, and her news came as a surprise, therefore, to most of the women. There followed a flurry of congratulations, while Ellen calculated rapidly, realizing that if she conceived at once, she could give Llewelyn a son by summer's end, a thought that— after nearly three years in limbo—seemed almost miraculous to her.

They were almost done now, performed the few remaining tasks with dispatch, tucking Ellen into bed, arranging her long tresses in tempting disarray upon the pillows, lighting a candle and placing it in one of the headboard niches, for—Blanche explained—there was something to be said for looking ere you leaped. They then poured Ellen some mead, one by one kissed her, and finally pulled the bed hangings together, enclosing her within a private cocoon of glazed Holland cloth.

Forgetting her resolve to forgo any more wine, Ellen sipped the mead, sought to banish her tension with deep breaths. If only she could close her eyes, then open them to find the bedding-down revelries were over, the men were gone, and she was alone in bed with Llewelyn. If only there would be no trouble. She'd heard too many tales of brawling and drunken rowdiness and crude practical jokes to be at ease, though. Guy had once told her of a particularly nasty wedding prank in which the bridegroom's drink had been heavily laced with a strong purgative, and there were always stories circulating, usually unverified, of sleeping draughts being given to unwary bridegrooms, of wedding guests bursting in upon couples who'd neglected to bolt the bedchamber door. And always there was the risk of violence, for wine could be the most combustible fuel of all.

She'd just put the mead cup down on the floor by the bed when the men entered, making so much racket that it seemed as if half of Worcester had invaded her bedchamber. There was only a faint break in the bed hangings, not wide enough for her to see more than a blurred motion, a flash of color. And it was difficult, she was discovering, to hear all that was being said, for they kept interrupting one another, the words wine-slurred, the voices not always easy to recognize.

It sounded as if they were drinking a toast to Llewelyn, and she frowned, for if they'd brought wine in with them, it might be difficult to get them out; for reasons she did not fully comprehend, men seemed to think it was very funny to prolong the bridegroom's suspense as long as possible. She'd always heard people jesting about being a fly upon the wall whenever some great drama had taken place; she felt like that now, an invisible spy in a foreign kingdom, one usually barred to women. Just within the first few moments, she learned some new slang terms for the male sexual organs, not as easily explainable as the more familiar cock, shaft, and lance—yard, stalk, baubles. And what she'd always suspected was confirmed within those same few moments, that drinking did not make men more amusing, it only made them think it did.

The jokes were predictable and banal, most of them couched as helpful tips for the bridegroom. There was much talk about how best to ride a skittish, unbroken filly: without spurs, bareback, and with a bridal bit. Ellen wished she'd recognized the author of that last pun, for she thought "bridal bit" was a clever play upon words. But they were not making it easy for eavesdroppers; sometimes it sounded as if they were all talking at once.

"I want to say a few words, so cease your caterwauling!" She recognized that imperious voice at once, for it was Edward's. "I know the Welsh are huntsmen, not farmers. But tonight I hope that the Prince of Wales plants his seed in fertile soil!"

There was laughter, and then Alexander took his turn, saying that a maiden without a man was like a ship without a rudder. Ellen was amused by that, but not by what followed, for he'd opened the floodgates to a wave of nautical jokes about sailing into friendly ports and dropping anchor in deep waters and keeping hard on the helm. Ellen sighed, wondering what the reaction would be if she entered into the spirit of things and called out that their jests were very unseaworthy. Blessed Lady, were they going to be here all night?

Someone had started to sing a lewd ditty about a tavern wench named Delilah, but fortunately he was too well lubricated to remember the words. That reminded the others, though, of the minstrel's bawdier songs, and Llewelyn found himself fending off warnings about "broken blades" and offers to help if he discovered a treasure chest that could not be opened. His blade, he assured them, was in perfect working order, right easy to sheathe, and he had no need for locksmiths, already having the key. He sounded good-natured, but impatient, too, like a man who'd been talked into something against his better judgment and was trying to be a good sport about it, at least for a while.

Ellen had raised up at sound of his voice, now sank back against the pillows. Did any bride and groom truly enjoy being in the center ring of this circus? For a young girl like Caitlin or a woman about to share a bed with a man not of her choosing, it could be a very unpleasant experience. She did not think she was unduly modest, but she would have much preferred a quiet seduction for two. And she suspected that most bridegrooms did not really find it much fun, either. In some ways it was more trying for them, she decided, for male humor, as any woman with five brothers well knew, could be raw. God help the poor groom who could not flaunt an erection as he was being put to bed with his bride.

No, Llewelyn was right, there was something to be said for an elopement. Or a clandestine wedding. Her parents had been wiser than she knew, a secret ceremony with only the King as witness—much more pleasurable. And safer, for certes. She tried to imagine her fiery-tempered father submitting to gibes about his manhood and lewd jests about his bride, could not even begin to envision such a scene without it ending in bloodshed. For that was the real danger of these bedding-down revelries, that a man was expected to smile whilst drunken strangers discussed his wife in terms that might lead to a killing if said outside the bridal chamber. It was true that some decorum was supposed to prevail; there was an unspoken agreement about what was permissible and what was not. But all it took was one fool who fancied himself a wit.

Much later, she would look back upon that moment and marvel at her own prescience. The jokes were getting raunchier, but sillier, too. Someone expressed the hope that Llewelyn's plough would never furrow, and she had no idea what that meant. A voice that sounded like John d'Eyvill's declared that a bell was useless without a hard clapper, and there was a jest she only half-heard about cocks and capons. And then the competing voices were drowned out by a sudden clanging, the sound a dagger hilt might make when banged against a wine cup. "Silence! Raise your cups high, for it is time to drink to the fall of the Castle de Montfort. May her defenses be breached, her drawbridge rammed, and her portals filled to bursting ere this night is done!"

Ellen could feel her face getting hot, as much with anger as with embarrassment. There was laughter, but not a lot, and then she heard her husband's voice, a whip-lash of tautly coiled fury. "I have some advice for you, Clifford. Better that people merely suspect you of being a witless, illbred lout, than that you open your mouth and prove it!"

Ellen gasped, sitting up in alarm. There was sudden movement beyond the bed curtains, as if men were getting hastily out of the way. But Clifford's enraged reply was cut off in mid-oath. "Let it lie, Roger." Edward's voice was very cold, iced with authority. "You asked for that and well deserved it. Who can blame the man for taking offense? If you said that about my wife, by Christ, I would!"

Ellen could not have imagined she'd ever feel grateful to Edward, not in this life or the next. But she did now, was very thankful that he'd averted bloodshed. She got some additional help then from another surprising source—Davydd.

"Are we planning to spend the rest of the winter in here?" he demanded impatiently. "The bridegroom is not the only one with an eager wife waiting in his bed. Let's drink to his health or prowess or whatever whilst he sheds the rest of his clothes, show him where the bed is, and get back to our own women, ere I start thinking that sinning is merely a spectator sport with you English."

That speech won Davydd few friends; there was some murmuring among the English. But he seemed to have prodded them into action, and Ellen listened with relief as they clinked their wine cups together, drank to "Night-time sins and morning-after regrets." Ellen breathed a quick prayer of thanksgiving, first to the Queen of Heaven, who was said to smile upon young wives, and then to St Edward, whose day it was, for she could tell that the men were no longer roused and ready to raise hell, would soon be gone. So when trouble came, it took everyone, but especially Ellen, by surprise.

It was all the more disturbing because she could not see what was happening. But suddenly the Earl of Gloucester was shouting. "You clumsy dolt! I'm soaked clean-through!" A scuffle seemed to have broken out. There was a muffled curse, a grunt, and then a body came hurtling through the bed curtains, sprawled across her legs. Ellen screamed, grabbing for the sheets, and found herself gazing into the face of a total stranger, one who looked just as shocked as she did. He essayed a weak, sheepish smile, started to push himself up, realized he had his hand on her thigh, and jerked it away as if he'd been burned, which caused him to topple backward onto the bed coverlets again, just as the curtains were ripped aside. Grasping the intruder's arm, Llewelyn pulled him roughly off the bed. His coordination seemed rather the worse for wine; as boneless and limp as one of Ellen's childhood rag dolls, he flopped over into the floor rushes, where he blinked up at them, mouth ajar, in utter, innocent bewilderment.

Ellen looked down at her surprise bedmate, back up at her audience. They did not seem to know how to react, not yet sure whether they should be amused or abashed, but they were quick to crowd closer to the bed, to get a glimpse of the bride. Clapping her hand to her mouth, Ellen rolled over and buried her face in the pillow. Llewelyn swiftly leaned over the bed, seeking to comfort his distraught wife, and then glanced over his shoulder at the suddenly silent men. "Out," he snarled, "all of you, out!"

They shuffled their feet, looking oddly ill at ease, for these men, who faced without flinching the dangers of the battlefield, could be strangely daunted by a woman's tears. Even if there had been some among them unwilling to take orders from a Welshman, Prince or no, they had no chance to balk, for Edward was quick to echo Llewelyn's command.

"Damned fool drunken sots! You do not behave in a maiden's bridal chamber the way you do in a Southwark whorehouse!" And there was enough disgust in his voice to propel them all toward the door, arrows shot from one bow, eager now only to escape out into the night.

"You've just lost your audience, cariad," Llewelyn said, and as Ellen turned over, it was as he'd suspected. Her eyes were very bright, reflecting the gold of the candle flame above her head, but without even the glimmer of a tear, for it was laughter she'd been trying to muffle, not sobs.

"How did you know?"

"A woman who prevailed against pirates, Edward, and my dark demons was not likely to fall into a swoon over a drunkard's tomfoolery," he pointed out reasonably, and then laughed, for she'd flung herself into his arms, so exuberantly that he came close to tumbling off the edge of the bed, dragging them both down into the floor rushes.

"I truly could not help myself, Llewelyn. He looked so silly, sitting there on the floor with his mouth open, like a poor fish that did not understand how it had gotten hooked!"

"Little wonder he looked dazed, for none of it was his doing. It was one of the other men who jostled Gloucester, dousing him with wine. But when Gloucester shoved him, he fell against your poor fish, who went shooting into the bed like a salmon looking to spawn!"

That set Ellen off again. When she finally got her breath back, she confided, "I could feel the laughter about to spill out, and I knew if I gave them any encouragement, we'd not get rid of them till dawn! So it seemed as good a time as any to develop some maidenly modesty, and you, my darling, were so quick to seize the moment!"

"Let's just say I had a powerful inducement." They were entangled together in the bed covers, and as they sat up, she lost even more of the sheet. But when she started to tuck it back around her, he caught the corner, pulled it down about her waist, and then took her in his arms, wanting to feel her breasts against his chest as he kissed her. Almost at once, though, he ended the embrace. "Jesú, the door!"

Once the bolt had been safely shot into place, he came swiftly back to the bed. To his delight, she sat as he'd left her, having made no attempt to draw the sheet up again. He was clad only in chausses and braies, the rest of his clothes scattered about the chamber. Ellen watched with flattering interest as he tugged at the cords binding hose to braies, jerking impatiently when they did not at once come loose. "You seem like a man in a tearing hurry," she teased, and he grinned.

"Yes and no." Stripping off the braies, he quickly joined her in bed. "I am eager, I'll admit, to begin this quest of ours, but I do not want to find the Grail too soon, not until we've searched high and low, long and hard. There are many sorts of pleasures in this world, cariad, but tonight the only pleasure I'm seeking is prolonged."

She laughed, and when he reached for her, she rolled over into his arms. Almost at once, she discovered that their time together at the Tower and Rhuddlan Castle had not prepared her for the intensity of what she was experiencing now, in the intimate embraces of their marriage bed. As he began a leisurely exploration of her body, it seemed to her as if a fire was being kindled, slowly and deliberately, but hotter than she could ever have imagined. She soon found even the light weight of the sheet was stifling, and each time he claimed her mouth with his, she could not help thinking that this must be what Scriptures meant by cloven tongues of fire. Only when he parted her thighs was she hesitant, at first. As she shuddered suddenly, biting back a cry, he gently brushed her hair away from her face.

"Do you want me to stop?" he asked, and as her arms tightened around his neck, he barely heard the whispered "eventually" she breathed into his ear. "Ah, love," he laughed, "that is a very old joke, probably going back to Adam and Eve," and as her lashes swept upward, he found himself looking into eyes wide and wondering and suddenly hurt.

"Not to me," she protested. "This is all new to me, this is . . . Do you not see, Llewelyn? I am Eve, at least for tonight."

"You're right, love," he conceded. "I might as well confess that I have not bedded that many virgins, for with one long-ago exception, I never fully understood why men put so much importance upon being first—until now."

"Would you be jealous, then, of me?" she asked hopefully, and as he assured her with a grin that if another man touched her, he'd merely kill him, he realized in surprise that he might well mean it.

"I want you to be jealous," she confided. "I am, for certes. Were you jealous of her, too? You know which 'her,' that long-ago exception of yours. Surely you've not forgotten her name?"

"Do you really want to talk about her now?" he laughed, but when she persisted, he admitted that he did remember, that her name was Melangell.

He'd begun to kiss her throat again, and she gave a soft sigh, putting him in mind of a cat's purring. "I love it when you do that," she murmured. "But I suppose your Melangell did, too. Your first time together, was it all you'd hoped it would be? Did— Llewelyn, you are laughing at me!"

"Of course I am! Cariad, would you have me believe you're truly jealous of a woman I bedded ere you were even born?" He laughed again, at the sheer, sweet absurdity of that, and then said, "But to satisfy your unseemly curiosity, our first time was not all it ought to have been, at least not for her, as I was a green lad of seventeen, more keen on my own pleasures than hers."

"That is a fine recommendation, indeed! Why did you not tell me this sooner?" she chided, breathing again into his ear, nipping unexpectedly. "I see I ought to have examined your credentials much more thoroughly, my lord husband—" She gave a sudden squeal then, for he'd rolled over on top of her, pinning her easily under the weight of his body.

"You can examine my credentials anytime you like," he offered gravely, "and as often as you like. My love, you're flying much higher than I first thought. Just how much wine did you have tonight?"

She smiled up at him. "Oh, a lot! But it was not the wine. It is the mead that has suddenly gone to my head. I ought to have taken more care, but I did not yet know that things Welsh are so potent."

"Jesú," he said, very softly, "when I think of the three years that English whoreson kept us apart . . ." Kissing her before she could reply, regretting the words as soon as they were uttered, for there was no room for three in a bed, and he'd not let Edward poison their pleasure again, not tonight. "I must be squashing you as flat as a water reed." Rolling over, he drew her down on top of him, marveling how soft her skin was. "You need not worry, cariad, for I'll do better by you than I did by little Melangell. There are some distinct advantages, you see, in wedding a man past his youth. A seasoned archer knows an arrow must be well aimed, slow and steady, taking his time, whilst a raw lad is so eager to shoot the arrow that he oft-times misfires, thinking speed is all that counts, when accuracy and endurance matter even more."

She didn't laugh, though. Reaching out, she caressed his face with her fingers. "Do not," she pleaded, "do not talk of all the time we've lost, for we can never get it back, never . . ."

After that, it was quiet for a time, and as he stoked the fire higher between them, he realized that their pleasures were not going to be as prolonged as he'd hoped, for he was finding her to be too apt a pupil, eager to learn, able to excite him by her very innocence, her utter trust. "It is going to have to be soon, my love. I want you too much to hold back . . ."

"Llewelyn . . ." As he raised his head from her breasts, she ensnared him with a long strand of her hair, trailing it across his chest and twining it about his throat. He thought it looked as if they were bound by a rope of flame, for wherever the candle's light touched her hair, it gleamed like gold, dark and lustrous. "Did you love her? Melangell?" she asked, very low, and he nodded.

"Yes," he said, "I did."

"Do you think you could love me?"

Her face was very still; she seemed utterly intent upon his answer. He gave the only one possible. "Yes," he said, "oh, yes," and she slid her arms up his back, keeping her eyes upon his face.

"Love me, then," she whispered. "Love me now."

LLEWELYN awoke sometime before dawn. The hearth fire still smoldered and a few candles still flickered, and through a crack in one of the shutters, he could see no trace yet of light. It took him several moments before he could slide out of bed, for they'd fallen asleep in each other's arms, and it was not easy to disengage himself, to avoid tugging upon the long hair that had mantled them both in the night. After using the corner privy chamber, he poured a cup of mead and brought it back to the bed. It was not his choice for early morning, but it was all the chamber held, and he knew that if he felt so thirsty, Ellen's craving upon awakening would be far worse.

After drinking his fill, he set the cup down in the floor rushes, got back into bed. As he did, Ellen stirred and her eyes opened. "I was trying not to wake you," he said, and leaned over to give her a quick kiss.

"I do not mind." She smiled sleepily at him, looking so content, so appealingly disheveled, that he put his arm around her shoulders, drew her in against his chest as he asked about any wine-induced after-effects.

"I feel fine," she assured him, stifling a yawn. "But my mouth . . . it's so dry!"

"Here." Reaching down for the mead cup, he passed it to her, watched as she drank, grimaced, and drank again, sparingly this time. "Not exactly a breakfast beverage, I know, but the best I can offer. You truly do feel well, Ellen? No throbbing head, no queasiness, no alarming gaps in your memory? You do remember last night?" he said, with a sudden grin.

"Why?" She yawned again, delicately, behind her hand. "Did something happen that I ought to remember?" she asked, and then smiled, a smile that left no doubts whatsoever as to the accurate functioning of her memory.

"It is still early yet," he said, "so we can have a few more hours to sleep . . ." It was very pleasant to lie there in companionable quiet, her body cuddled against his, her head pillowed in the crook of his shoulder. But as he watched, he saw a frown begin to furrow her brow.

"Llewelyn . . . there is something I do not remember," she said, speaking with hesitancy at first, and then, with growing certainty. "I do not remember feeling any pain! Llewelyn, were you not supposed to hurt me?"

"Jesú, lass, it is too early for you to make me laugh," he protested, but laughing, nonetheless. "Of all the complaints a man could get about his lovemaking, for certes, that has to be the most peculiar!"

"I am serious," she insisted, and as he looked into her face, he saw that she really was. "I was always taught that a woman experiences pain when she loses her maidenhead. But I honestly do not remember it."

She was gazing at him expectantly, as if he could provide answers, and so he did his best to oblige. "Well," he said, "a female friend of mine—not Melangell—once told me that a woman's discomfort is much greater if she is tense or fearful. So why would not the reverse also be true? The more relaxed a woman is, the less pain. And this I can assure you, cariad, that there has probably never been a more relaxed bride since Eve woke up in Eden. Then, too, I made sure you were ready for me. My guess is there was probably a small amount of discomfort, but it was soon over, sooner forgotten."

She nodded slowly, agreed that seemed likely, but he could see she was still pondering the puzzle, trying to recapture any elusive memory of that fleeting lost moment. "I just thought of something else," he said. "That same confidante also told me that there are many misconceptions about a breached maidenhead. Most men think there ought to be a lot of blood, but she said that was not always so. It seems to me that if bleeding can vary, why cannot pain, too?" He hid a smile then, for it was dawning upon him what an incongruous conversation this was, about as unlikely a topic as he could have envisioned to start off the first day of their married life together.

"I suppose you are right," she said, "but I— Oh, dear God, blood!" And with that, she dived under the covers.

"Dare I ask what you're seeking?" he queried, trying not to sound too amused. "I can see right off that life with you is not going to be dull!"

The covers were rippling and undulating as if the bed was being struck by an earthquake. After another moment or so, she came up for air, looking flushed and dismayed. "I cannot find any blood," she blurted out. "Llewelyn, I did not bleed!"

"So? Ellen, why does it matter? I need no proof—"

"Not for you," she said impatiently. "I know you'd not doubt me. But what of the others, Edward's court? In a few hours, the wedding party will be bursting in here to inspect the sheets, and I am not going to be shamed before them! That I swear, even if I—"

"Easy, lass, easy. We'll deal with it. I'd forgotten about the sheets," he admitted, "but I'm sure there must be some blood." With that, he flung the covers back. "There," he said, "a small stain of purity, enough to satisfy the most suspicious witness."

"You can afford to laugh," she said wryly, "for you men never have to offer proof of your honor, and a lucky thing it is, too." Reaching out tenatively, she touched the blood-stain with her finger. "It is not very much," she said, sounding faintly disappointed, "and how did it get all the way down there? Little wonder I could not find it!"

"I thought you said you remembered everything about last night," he said, and she looked at him, then grinned.

"We were . . . active," she conceded. "Llewelyn . . . I'd wager I know a story about your grandfather that you do not, about his wedding night with Joanna."

"A wager? What are the stakes?"

Ellen was well aware of the direction his thoughts had suddenly taken; for several moments now, his eyes had been straying to those parts of her anatomy revealed when he'd thrown back the sheets. "Well . . . if you win, we make love, and if I win, we make love. Does that sound fair?"

"Very fair," he agreed, wondering how he could have gotten so lucky so late in life. He really was curious, though, about her story, so he settled back against the pillows, willing to wait.

"You know that Joanna was very young, just fourteen, and not a willing bride. You can imagine how scared she was then, on their wedding night. But your grandfather was a remarkable man; I see where you get your gallantry from! He assured her that they need not consummate their marriage that night, that there was no reason why they could not wait till she was more at ease with him. As you'd expect, she was relieved and grateful, but just as she was falling asleep, she remembered that the wedding guests would come in on the morrow to check the sheets for blood. They found it, too, courtesy of your grandfather!"

Llewelyn liked the story immensely. "Did he truly do that for her?"

"Indeed he did, cut his arm and said that of all the wounds he'd ever gotten, that had to be the strangest one of all!" Ellen laughed, moved over beside him. "Joanna told my mother about it years later, no surprise that, for it does put him in a very favorable light! And eventually Mama told me. I take it, then, that I win the wager?"

He nodded. "It is passing strange, the odd twists life takes. Imagine their reaction on that long-ago wedding night if a soothsayer had told them that seventy-some years later, his grandson would be wed to her niece." He reached over then, pulled her closer. "Now, about that wager . . ."

She smiled. "I am so glad," she said, "that you are a man who pays his debts!" Which he proceeded to do, to their very mutual satisfaction.

LLEWELYN awoke reluctantly several hours later, exhaustion warring with an enormous sense of well-being. The last of the candles had guttered out; so had the fire. Reaching for Ellen, he discovered that he was alone in the bed. He was starting to sit up when he saw the slender blanket-clad figure huddled in the window-seat.

"Ellen?" She jerked at sound of his voice, turning toward him a face white and streaked with tears. "What is wrong?" There was so much shock in his voice that she flinched, came hurriedly back to the bed.

"Ah, no," she cried, "it is nothing you've done, I swear it!"

Sliding over, he made room for her in the bed, keeping his eyes upon her all the while. Dropping the blanket, she climbed in, reassuring him by how readily she now sought his embrace.

"Will you hold me?" she asked, blotting away the last of her tears with the corner of the sheet. "I am so sorry, Llewelyn. I did not want to ruin our first day together . . ."

"Can you tell me?"

"I woke up first, watched you whilst you slept, and I was so happy, Llewelyn, that it actually scared me a little. How often do we get in this life all that we ever wanted? Today, I told myself, today we will ride into Wales, into Llewelyn's world—my world now, too—and I thought about the life we'd have together. I thought of the pleasures of your bed, and how easily you make me laugh, and I thought of the children we'll have. And then I thought of Amaury, and what this day would bring for him."

She drew an uneven breath, said more calmly. "I know he is better off now that he is at Sherborne, not Corfe. But it is nigh on three years, Llewelyn. What if Edward never lets him go?"

"I think Edward will eventually have to free him, for it is becoming obvious that the Church is not going to forsake Amaury. Sooner or later, Edward must conclude that whatever pleasure he is getting from Amaury's captivity is not worth the trouble he is getting from the Pope." Llewelyn smoothed her tumbled hair over her shoulders, held her quietly for a few moments. "I realize," he said, "that it is hard to derive much comfort from a hope so far in the future. But at least now you can help."

She looked so bewildered that he saw she'd not comprehended yet that she was no longer powerless. "You are not a prisoner of the English Crown anymore," he said, "you are the Princess of Wales. You can petition the Pope every day on Amaury's behalf, appeal to the Kings of France and Scotland, to every prince in Christendom. And you can make Amaury's life easier, more comfortable, until that day when he is freed. My love, you can send him anything your heart desires—books, clothes, food, games of chance, whatever you think he'd want—every hour on the hour if you wish."

"But what if Edward refuses to let me do that?"

"He'll not dare refuse, for you will ask him today, before the King of Scotland and his brother, Edmund, and the Bishop, and the entire English court. All know that Amaury has done nothing to deserve his fate. We are talking not of Guy, but of a priest who never took up arms against the English Crown, a papal chaplain still in favor with the Pope. And now his sister asks only to be able to send him a few comforts in his wretched confinement. To turn down your plea—before so many witnesses—would be an act so mean-spirited, so petty, so impossible to justify that he'll have no choice but to agree."

The look Ellen gave him now was even more ardent than the looks he'd gotten from her during their lovemaking. "I think," she said softly, "that I must give you fair warning, for I am afraid that I am going to fall hopelessly in love with you."

"Why a warning?"

"Oh, an overly fond wife is a mixed blessing. There are disadvantages, too. I would be harder to neglect, I'd want to be with you all the time, I'd probably discomfit you before your friends by hanging on your every word and praising you to the heavens, and you may be sure I'd be jealous. Now I well know you did not live like a monk these three years past, and I did not begrudge you those bedmates, truly I did not. But if infidelity at a distance is understandable, infidelity at close quarters is grounds for murder, my love."

She smiled so sweetly then, that he began to laugh. "Let me guess," he said. "Joanna just happened to tell your mother, too, that Welsh law condemns adultery for husbands as well as wives!"

"She may have mentioned it." Ellen reached out, ran her fingers gently along his arm, tracking the path of an old wound, not the first one she'd found, for he'd passed most of his life in the saddle and on the battlefield, and although that life had made his body hard and lean, that body bore the scars of sword-thrusts he'd failed to deflect, old injuries that now took on a frightening immediacy to her. "Llewelyn, I have a question to put to you. Do you think you could learn to love me?"

"You asked me that last night, cariad."

"I remember," she said. "But I wanted to hear your answer when we both were sober."

Laughing, he leaned over, kissed the curve of her smile. "I think," he said, "that it would be very easy to love you."

FROM the English Chronicle of Osney: Thus did Llewelyn win, "with a heart that leapt for joy, his beloved spouse, for whose loving embraces he had so long yearned."

From the Welsh Chronicle of the Princes: "King Edward and Edmund, his brother, gave Eleanor, their first cousin, daughter of Simon de Montfort, to Llewelyn at the door of the great church at Worcester. And there he married her. And that night their wedding banquet was held. And on the following day, Llewelyn and Eleanor returned joyfully to Wales."

24

ABBEY OF ABERCONWY, WALES

September 1279

O<small>N</small> November 12, 1278, the Jews throughout England were arrested, and a house-to-house search was made in all the Jewrys of the country. Six hundred and eighty men and women were sent to the Tower of London for trial on a charge of coin clipping. The number of Jews hanged was given as nineteen in the official records, as two hundred and ninety-three by the chroniclers of the time.

T<small>HE</small> Bishop of Bangor departed the abbey in a soft September mist, but even as the Abbot bade farewell to his distinguished guest, thunder was echoing down the Conwy Valley. As lightning blazed through the clouds, showering the abbey garth in sparks, Maredudd flinched, made a hasty sign of the cross. By the time he reached the shelter of the cloisters, he was soaked.

As he plunged into the parlor, a gust of wind caught the door, slammed it resoundingly behind him. The two men seated by the hearth turned startled faces toward the sound. "You look half-drowned, Maredudd. Get over here by the fire." Maredudd did, quite gladly, pulling up a chair beside Llewelyn, accepting a wine cúp from Goronwy. Watching as the Abbot stripped off his muddied sandals, wrung out the sodden folds of his habit, Llewelyn said, "I hope the Bishop knows how to swim."

He sounded, though, as if he hoped just the opposite, a sentiment that Maredudd not only understood but shared; he had no more liking for Bishop Anian than Llewelyn did. He was not surprised that the Bishop and his Prince had failed once again to reconcile their differences; they were both proud men. Nor had Edward helped any by siding with the Bishop. To the contrary, he'd flung a few more boulders onto an already rock-strewn road by ordering Llewelyn to be more conciliatory, more accommodating to Anian's demands. Maredudd could not recall a time when the English Crown was not eager to meddle in Welsh matters, but never before had the meddling been so blatant or so pervasive. He'd often heard men laud Edward as a superb rider; so why then, did the English King have such a heavy hand on the reins?

"If the storm does not abate by the morrow, I'll inform our hospitaller that you will be delaying your departure until Wednesday." To Maredudd's surprise, though, Llewelyn was shaking his head. "Why not, my lord? I should think you've had more than your share of wretched rides in vile weather. Why get wet when there is no need for it?"

Llewelyn hid a smile, for he knew that if he admitted the real reason for his haste, Maredudd would be even more baffled; the aging, celibate monk was not a man to understand the lure of a loving young wife. But Goronwy did, without a doubt; he was grinning widely.

"I thank you for your hospitality, Maredudd. As always, I have enjoyed my stay at the abbey. But I do need to depart at dawn, rain or not. I am expecting a courier from the English King," Llewelyn said, avoiding Goronwy's amused eyes.

Maredudd nodded sympathetically; duty he understood, for it had long been his own taskmaster. "May I ask if the King's letter concerns Arwystli? I must confess, my lord, that I do not see why your case has not yet been heard. It has been dragging on now for . . ." He paused to calculate and Llewelyn supplied the answer for him.

"Nigh on eighteen months," he said, and though his voice was even, his mouth had a bitter twist to it. "We have not even resolved the issue as to which law should apply, Welsh or English. Edward's court keeps adjourning on one pretext after another. The latest was the claim that my lawyers had not been properly empowered to act on my behalf. The truth is that Edward fears my claim will prevail if ever it is heard, and he owes Gruffydd ap Gwenwynwyn too much to let that happen."

There was a moment of silence, and then Goronwy said, "To English justice," and raised his wine cup high, a salute meant in jest, but the mockery was hollow.

There was another silence. "No," Llewelyn said, "not English justice. Edward's justice."

It was quiet after that, a pensive, brooding quiet that lasted too long for Goronwy's liking. The sooner they exorcised Edward's intrusive ghost the better, he decided, and set about doing just that. "Have you heard yet, my lord, about what your brother did in Cheshire?"

"Davydd? The last I heard, his time was taken up building new

castles in the lands Edward gave him, at Caergwrle and Dinbych."
Although Llewelyn sought to sound casual, he was not entirely successful; despite their estrangement, Davydd could still kindle his interest
as easily as ever. "What trouble has he been stirring up now?"

"For once it is not trouble of his making. An English knight named
de Vanabeles brought suit against him in shire court, seeking a writ of
entry."

Llewelyn's eyes narrowed. Davydd was not the first Welshman to
have to defend himself in an English court, and he would for certes not
be the last. "Did Davydd come as summoned?"

"Indeed he did, and they're likely still talking about it! He strode
into the court, declared that he was not answerable to English law, for
the lands in question were located in Wales, not Cheshire. Suit could
be brought in Wales, he said, or by God, not at all. And then he turned
around and stalked out, without so much as a by-your-leave."

Goronwy paused, ostensibly to take a swallow of wine, actually
to gauge Llewelyn's reaction. He need not have worried, though.
Llewelyn's dark eyes were aglint with amusement. "I often thought
Davydd would have made a marvelous actor," he said wryly, "for he
has always had a remarkable talent for staging dramatic entrances and
departures." But there was no malice in his observation; both Goronwy
and Maredudd caught the echoes of approval.

When the hospitaller entered a few moments later with word of
new arrivals, the Abbot was not surprised; there'd be many travelers
seeking shelter from the storm, for Wales had no inns. But he could not
suppress a gasp at sight of the man who now appeared in the doorway.
Llewelyn noticed the look of fleeting dismay on his face, and turned to
see who was so unwelcome, just as Davydd sauntered into the parlor,
almost as if he'd been lurking in the wings, awaiting Goronwy's cue to
take center stage.

"A clever conjuring trick, Goronwy," Llewelyn muttered, but his
humor was forced, and he watched warily as his brother moved toward
them, offering jaunty greetings that belied his rain-soaked, mud-
splattered appearance. The responses Davydd garnered were notably
lacking in enthusiasm, for none of the men were in the mood for the
verbal jousting that passed for conversation whenever Davydd was present. If he noted the coolness, Davydd gave no indication of it, and as
Maredudd excused himself to confer with the hospitaller and their cooks
about that evening's dinner menu, Davydd appropriated the Abbot's
chair, helping himself, as well, to the Abbot's wine cup.

"Did you know," he queried, "that if you get an English invitation
to dine, they actually expect you to show up well before noon? And

then they have the gall to mock us for dining at dusk! I can never make up my mind whether they are mere philistines or true barbarians—except for their women, of course," he added, with a sideways smile aimed in Llewelyn's direction. "Speaking of which, where is your bride? I've heard you've been keeping her even closer than your own shadow."

"Ellen is at Dolwyddelan. Strange, is it not, how often our paths seem to cross? What are the odds that we'd both be at St Mary's Abbey today?"

"Marriage has not mellowed you much, has it? Save your sarcasm, Llewelyn. I am not going to claim this was a chance encounter. I heard you were at the abbey, and I needed to talk to you."

Llewelyn was not disarmed by Davydd's candor; he knew from painful experience that honesty was just one more weapon in his brother's armory. "Talk to me about what?"

"About the corn crop and chess and mayhap the weather . . . what else would we have to discuss? Hellfire, Llewelyn, you know what I want to talk about, a conversation that begins and ends with Edward. I daresay Goronwy told you that I was summoned to defend my possession of Welsh lands in an English shire court? But you do not yet know the worst of it. When I complained to Edward, I told him that the laws of Wales ought to be honored no less than the laws of other lands. And Edward's response? He said he would uphold only such Welsh laws as he deemed 'just and reasonable.' "

Both Llewelyn and Goronwy well knew that Davydd could summon up anger purely for effect, and quite convincingly, too. They exchanged speculative looks now, trying to decide if his outrage was sincere or not. Davydd waited with obvious impatience, then demanded, "Well? Have you nothing to say to that, Llewelyn?"

"I do not know what you want of me, Davydd. What you say hardly comes as a surprise to me. I find it difficult to understand how it could be a surprise to you, either. You were Edward's ally, ought to know the workings of his brain if any man does—"

"Christ on the Cross! I cannot believe we're still bogged down in the same swamp. Whilst you dwell on old grievances, the English King is laying snares all over Wales!"

" 'Old grievances'?" Goronwy sputtered, sounding so incredulous that Llewelyn almost laughed. He was more amused than angry himself, amazed by the sheer sweep of his brother's presumption.

"You are right," he said and grinned. "How could I be so petty as to still hold a grudge? It is not as if you've ever given me reason!"

Davydd could and did shrug off mockery—from any man but

Llewelyn. "And of course you have nothing to reproach yourself for," he snapped. "No, you were the aggrieved innocent, as always. After all, we both know you never make mistakes, not like the rest of us mere mortals!"

Llewelyn frowned. Did Davydd mean that he'd come to see his betrayal as a mistake? He started to ask that, but Davydd gave him no chance. Getting abruptly to his feet, he slammed his wine cup down with such force that the clay cracked wide open. Davydd did not even notice, never taking his eyes from Llewelyn. "What I could never understand," he said, "was why you bothered with a crown. What need did you have of it, when you had your very own halo? Tell the Abbot that my men and I will not be staying."

Davydd turned away, then looked back at his brother. "I do have other news for you. My Elizabeth is with child again. I suppose I should ask if your wife is pregnant yet. Wales is about due for a miracle, after all."

That was a thrust Llewelyn had not been expecting. His hand jerked, wine splashing into the floor rushes. Davydd whirled, in three strides was at the door. But there he halted, his fingers clenching upon the latch. Without turning around, he said, very low and very fast, "More fool I, for I somehow keep forgetting that words are verily like arrows, and once fired, cannot be called back. You are not likely to believe me, and so be it. But the truth is that I know as much about regrets as any other man." He did not wait for Llewelyn's response, disappeared into the rain-drenched dusk beyond the door.

Goronwy glanced at the door, then at Llewelyn. "I've known Davydd for many years," he said, "and that was as close as I've ever heard him come to offering an apology. I think he had more in mind, my lord, than one heedless taunt."

"Yes," Llewelyn agreed, "I think he did, too."

Goronwy was, for once, displaying uncharacteristic discretion. "Tell me, my lord, if I am treading too close to that swamp Davydd mentioned . . .?"

That earned him a quick smile. "Ask your question, Goronwy," Llewelyn said, for Goronwy might be the one person able to understand, as even Ellen could not, that some bridges could not be burned.

"Are you coming to believe then, that Davydd wants to make his peace with you? As for myself, I truly think he does. Why else would he have named his son . . ." Goronwy stopped, looking quizzical, as Llewelyn held up his hand.

"Let's just say I find it more believable than I once did. His behavior makes more sense, I'll admit, if viewed in that light. He'd never be able to say it straight out, of course, not Davydd. I think I can even understand—a little—his anger. Forgiveness always came so easily to him, Goronwy, too easily . . ."

Goronwy nodded. "But I do believe, my lord, that his regrets are real enough."

"Mayhap they are," Llewelyn conceded. "I suppose I'd like to think so . . ."

"But you cannot forgive him?"

Llewelyn took his time in answering. "When I was warned that Davydd had been implicated in Gruffydd ap Gwenwynwyn's treachery, I summoned him to Rhuddlan Castle to defend himself. You were there, were you not, Goronwy? Davydd denied all, rather persuasively, too, although we did not yet know even half of the plot. And once we were alone, he made an accusation that I found very troubling. He wanted to know if I'd have suspected Tudur or Einion. I had to say no, and I realized only then how I'd wronged him, how quick I'd been to believe the worst of him . . ."

Goronwy sucked in his breath. "And all the while, he was lying to you, all the while he was Cain," he said, and Llewelyn's eyes met his own.

"Just so," he said softly. "So you see, Goronwy, I cannot give Davydd what he wants, what I even want myself sometimes. For what is forgiveness worth without trust?"

THE Abbot's concern about the rain proved unwarranted. After a spectacular dawn, one that too briefly gilded the sea and estuary in rich shades of red, copper, and then a shimmering, spangled gold, Llewelyn and his men rode south under a summer-blue sky. The sun soon dried the road, and as Llewelyn traveled fast even in inclement weather, they reached the Lledr Valley well before dusk.

They were not yet in sight of Dolwyddelan when they saw riders up ahead. As they drew nearer, Llewelyn recognized his niece and Hugh de Whitton. He was not surprised to see them together, for they'd developed a fast friendship in the months since he'd wed Ellen at Worcester. Llewelyn had been rather dubious at first of Caitlin's attachment to the young Englishman. He still thought of her as a child more often than not, and he'd been very willing to indulge her when she entreated him to put off finding her a husband; he saw no reason not to wait until she was ready, had no intention of forcing her to wed against her will. But nonetheless, she was fifteen now, of marriageable age, and it was only after he'd had a long and candid talk with Hugh that he'd felt reassured, having satisfied himself that Hugh's devotion to Caitlin was honorable, protective, and quite brotherly.

Caitlin and Hugh were in high spirits, and greeted Llewelyn with exuberance, eager to confide their mission. They were both talking at once, and there was some confusion before Llewelyn learned that one of his huntsmen had found a remarkable fawn, white as snow with eyes as red as garnets. "I know it sounds fanciful, Uncle Llewelyn, but Phylip swears it is so. We are on our way now to his house, for Phylip says he means to keep it as a pet, that people will likely pay to see it!"

"Tell Phylip I'd be interested in seeing this wondrous beast myself." Llewelyn waved them on, and within moments they were out of sight, disappearing around a sharp bend in the road. Llewelyn laughed and urged his stallion forward, on toward the castle where his wife awaited him.

As always, Llewelyn's arrival created considerable excitement, people hastening out of the hall, kitchen, and stables to welcome their Prince home. But Ellen was not among them, and that surprised Llewelyn somewhat, for he and Ellen had been playing a newlyweds' game, in which he sought to reach their bedchamber and catch her unawares, a game he rarely won, for she was almost always alerted by the inevitable commotion heralding his return. This time, though, she did not appear, and he mounted the steps, crossed the drawbridge linking the fore-building to the keep, and entered his bedchamber, where he discovered that he'd won by default, for Ellen was nowhere in sight.

Juliana jumped to her feet, looking oddly flustered. "My lord! We did not expect you back for another day or two!"

Llewelyn was fending off the enthused welcome of his favorite greyhound. "Nia, down! I missed Ellen," he said with a smile. "Where is she?"

Seeing him glance toward the corner privy, Juliana reluctantly shook her head. "She . . . she is not here, my lord. She took Ivory out for a ride."

"Not by herself?" Llewelyn frowned, for this had been a source of contention between them. While he understood that a woman imprisoned for nigh on three years would revel in her newfound freedom, he did not want Ellen wandering about on her own, for he was finding that he worried more about her safety in a mountain meadow than ever he had about his own safety in the midst of a battle.

"I know she promised you not to venture out without an escort," Juliana said hastily. "But she was very distraught, needed to be alone for a time."

"Distraught?" But there was no need to ask why; he knew. "Her flux came, after all," he said, and felt a dulled throb of disappointment when Juliana nodded. He'd refused to let himself hope too much, for he'd known that a week's delay was not proof of pregnancy. But Ellen had not been as realistic, and he could imagine all too well the depths now of her despair.

"She was so sure," Juliana said miserably. "I could not convince her that it was much too early to hope. She said she'd never been overdue this long, a fortnight yesterday, that it had to mean she was pregnant. And then this morn, when her flux came . . ." Her voice trailed off. "She so wants to give you a son, my lord."

"Yes," he said, "I know . . ."

IT was easy enough for Llewelyn to guess where Ellen had gone. It was not just the sylvan setting of Rhaeadr Ewynnol that drew her so often to the white-water cauldron; the waterfall had become a romantic shrine from the moment she learned it had been a favorite trysting place for Joanna and her Llewelyn. Reining in his stallion beside Ellen's tethered white mare, Llewelyn dismounted swiftly. Crossing the clearing, he found his wife standing at the cliff's edge. She was wrapped in a wool mantle of bright scarlet, and patches of crimson burned into her cheeks, too, as she turned, saw him step from the forest shadows into the sunlight.

"Llewelyn!" But there was no gladness in her voice. Nor did she move toward him. "How did you find me?"

"Does it matter?"

"No," she said, sounding as if nothing mattered, not anymore. "I am sorry you came back early, for I needed more time ere I'd be ready to face you. I've failed you, Llewelyn. Once again I've failed you."

"No, Ellen, that is not so."

"But I did! You do not know—"

"I do. I spoke to Juliana, cariad."

"Then . . . then how can you say I've not failed you? You need a son, a son I may not be able to give you. That is why you married me, to get an heir. Can you deny it?"

"No," he said slowly, "I'll not deny it. When Davydd betrayed me, I lost more than my brother, I lost my heir. I had no choice but to wed as quickly as I could, to try to sire a son. But that was nigh on five years and three unforeseen happenings ago. My life has changed since then, in ways I'd not anticipated."

" 'Three unforeseen happenings,' " she echoed. "I do not understand."

He closed the space between them, took her hand, and drew her toward the shelter of a vast and ancient oak. "When Davydd fled to England, I did not expect to look upon him again in this life. Still less did I expect that the pull of the past would prove so strong for us both. I am not saying we have now reconciled, but we seem to have contrived an uneasy truce, and that unlikely development is what gives such significance to the second occurrence—the birth of Davydd's son, my nephew and namesake, and if need be, my heir." He smiled faintly. "I daresay Davydd would be sorely vexed if he was passed over in favor of his little lad, but that would be his problem, not mine."

"I'd not thought of your nephew as a potential heir," Ellen admitted, "just as painful proof that Elizabeth could give Davydd what I could not give you. I truly thought I would conceive at once, Llewelyn. I never doubted . . ."

"And each month you await the coming of your flux like a condemned prisoner awaiting the axe, and when it does come . . . Ellen, you cannot keep tormenting yourself like this. It serves for naught, cariad. You have to accept whatever happens, whatever the Almighty wills, for both our sakes."

"Can you accept that, Llewelyn? Can you honestly tell me that you'd not barter your very soul to have a son of your own?"

"Of course I want a son, Ellen, and if it is not to be, there will be a great emptiness in my life. But I've had years to come to terms with it. As you yourself said, my love, I've not lived as a monk. I've had my share of bedmates, yet not one of them ever quickened with my seed. How likely is it that every one of those women was barren? It may not be God's Will that I have a son."

"I do not believe that. You deserve sons if any man does. I was so sure this time," she said, in a voice barely audible above the surging rush of the falls, "so sure I was with child . . ." She gave him one swift, heart-wrenching glance, then looked away. "Llewelyn, what if I am barren? Another woman might . . ."

He marveled at her courage, for he knew what it had cost her to say that. He ran his fingers lightly along the curve of her cheek, and found her skin wet to his touch. "I cannot answer that, lass, no more than you can. Mayhap another woman could give me a son, mayhap not. But that brings us to the third unforeseen turn of events. When I sent Brother Gwilym to Montargis, I got more than I bargained for, Ellen. I did not expect to fall in love with my own wife."

"I know you love me, Llewelyn. But is that enough? What if I cannot ever give you a son?"

"You give me joy, cariad, more joy than I've ever had in this life, or expect to find in the next." He smiled, for he still found it easier to jest than to reveal secrets of the soul. "If it is true, as the Church claims, that a man who loves his wife with excessive passion is guilty of adultery, then I am sinning on such a scale that I'll likely be atoning for all eternity."

Ellen found herself smiling even as she blinked back tears. She could think of no promise extravagant enough, no vow sweeping enough to convey what she felt at that moment. She tried, though. "I may not be able to promise you a son, but this I can and do swear, that I shall devote my every waking hour to making you happy. You'll have no regrets, beloved, not as long as I have breath in my body . . ."

And then she was laughing, laughing as she'd not have believed possible even a quarter hour ago, for he'd murmured, "Could I persuade you to pledge that upon a holy relic?"

Kissing her upturned face, tasting the laughter of her lips, breathing in the violet scent she'd long since tired of, but kept using because she knew he liked it, Llewelyn felt as if a burden had been lifted from them both. Mayhap now she'd no longer be haunted by dreams of empty cradles, mayhap she'd no longer flinch at sound of a baby's wail. Mayhap now he could tell her of Elizabeth's pregnancy.

"But I do not want you to give up all hope, my love," he said quietly. "For all that we'll be wed four years at Martinmas, we've only been sharing a bed for less than a twelvemonth. If we keep planting enough seeds, who knows what crop we might eventually harvest?"

Ellen wrapped her arms around his neck. She was taller than most women and they fit together well; he slid his hands under her mantle, almost able to span her waist with his fingers. She surprised him then, said in perfect Welsh, "Rydw i eisau cusan."

Laughing, he did as she bade, gave her a probing, passionate kiss that lasted until they both were breathless. "Promise me," he said, "that no matter what lies ahead for us, you'll remember what I am about to say now. You hold my heart and I could not envision my world without you. I want a son, yes, but it is you I need, and that is something I've never said to any woman."

"I promise," she said softly, and he looked for a long moment into her face, until he was satisfied that she meant it.

"Come, cariad," he said. "Let's go home."

25

ABEREIDDON, WALES

July 1280

HUGH returned to North Wales in mid-July, reaching Abereiddon soon after the turquoise twilight had begun to shade into the star-scattered dark of a summer night. The conversi— the lay brothers who worked the mountain granges of the Welsh Cistercian abbeys—were already abed. But light and laughter drifted from the open window of the guest hospice, and Hugh headed in that direction.

The door was ajar, and Hugh paused on the threshold to savor the sight before him, to savor his homecoming. The scene—so pleasing to Hugh—was not one to please their austere hosts, though, the somber Cistercians who sought rustic solitude, spiritual peace, and a Spartan life far from urban enticements and feminine wiles. The White Monks scorned cities as cesspools of corruption and sin. Nor did they welcome women—daughters of Eve—into their pristine domains, not even their Prince's lady. Yet here in their own guest hospice were gathered those worldly temptations they'd chosen to shun, boisterous banter and clinking mead cups and soft female laughter.

A noisy dice game was in progress, to the inevitable accompaniment of rowdy jesting and good-natured squabbling; Hugh made a mental note to join in the fun after he'd reported to Lady Ellen. Not all the men in the hall were focusing upon the dice game. Nearby, Juliana was being besieged by the most persistent of her suitors, brothers who seemed vastly amused that they should be rivals for the same woman. Juliana appeared to be enjoying their joint courtship, laughing as they took turns whispering sweet nothings in her ear. But she was not likely to accept either one as a serious swain, although Hugh and Ellen wished she would, for Rhun and Rhys were both good lads, and Bran was nine years dead.

Shifting his gaze from Juliana, Hugh began to look for his lady, soon found her ensconced in a window-seat. She'd not yet noticed him, utterly intent upon the harp balanced on her knee and the man seated at her side. At Montargis, Hugh had often seen Ellen in just that pose, frowning over the harp that had been her betrothal gift from her Welsh Prince, a bittersweet keepsake of all she'd lost. It seemed miraculous to Hugh—even now—that those girlhood hopes should have been resurrected from the ashes of Evesham, that she should be sharing the window-seat and harp on this summer's eve with Llewelyn ap Gruffydd. Llewelyn had his arm around her waist, and as he showed her a new chord, their fingers brushed and then entwined upon the harp strings. Hugh stayed where he was, reluctant to intrude, for he knew such tranquil moments were hard to come by. It seemed to him that in Wales, trouble was always lurking in ambush, just down the road.

Mountain nights were often chill, even in July, and fire burned in the center hearth; smoke smudged the whitewashed walls, clung to clothes, watered eyes, and occasionally a puff or two would escape through the roof louvre out into the starlit sky. Caitlin had pulled a stool as close to the light as she could get without being singed. She was scowling down at the cloth draped across her lap, wielding her needle with such obvious distaste that Hugh could not help grinning. Caitlin's aversion to the needlework at which even queens were expected to excel was almost as notorious as her unseemly penchant for solitude and cats and secrets. But the very idiosyncrasies that made her so suspect in other eyes were what endeared her to Hugh; he who valued integrity above all else could recognize it in any guise. Moreover, he took pleasure in Caitlin's utter unpredictability; he never had a clue as to what was going on behind those leaf-green eyes of hers, never knew what to expect from her.

As he stepped into the hall, Hugh was met with a crescendo of barking. Ellen's pampered pet led the charge, sprinting toward him, low-slung white belly scraping the floor rushes, for Hugh had managed to win what still eluded Llewelyn, the jealous little dog's good will. The other dogs were in full tongue now, too: Llewelyn's elegant greyhounds, and Sampson, his huge, stately wolfhound, and the stable dogs that sneaked into the hall every chance they got.

"Hugh!" Caitlin's sewing had fallen, forgotten, into the rushes. Her smile, all too rare, flashed. "I've missed you," she confided, for with Hugh, she was never wary. "You were gone so long! Did you see Ellen's—" She stopped, laughing. "Why are the dogs slavering over you like that?"

Hugh was under siege, backed up against the door, unable to break through the canine circle until Juliana sent Rhys and Rhun to his rescue.

As they chased the stable curs outside, Llewelyn summoned his own well-trained dogs with a whistle, and Hugh joined Caitlin by the hearth, reaching into his mantle to reveal the real attraction, a kitten tucked into a woven pouch.

Caitlin gave a delighted cry. "It is as white as Phylip's deer! Wherever did you find it?"

"At an inn in Dorsetshire. The innkeeper was going to drown her, and so I offered to take her." Hugh smiled sheepishly, a little embarrassed by his own soft-heartedness. "She's stone-deaf, but I figured you'd just see that as a challenge," he said, depositing the tiny, spitting creature into Caitlin's outstretched palms. With Ellen's Hiraeth at his heels, he then crossed the hall, knelt by the window-seat.

Llewelyn at once waved him up, and he reached again into his mantle, this time drawing out several rolled sheets of parchment. "This is for you, my lady. Lord Amaury asked me to thank you both for your generosity. He was especially pleased by the books, marveled that you had been able to find so many, for he said he well knows books are scarcer than hen's teeth, and as costly a luxury as sugar."

Ellen was running her fingers over her brother's letter, but she seemed hesitant to untie the cord. "Tell me how he fares, Hugh—the truth," she added, needlessly, for Hugh could not lie to her.

"There must be days when he despairs," he said, feeling his way with care. "But he is not a man to admit to them."

"No," Ellen agreed, "he would not do that . . ."

Hugh felt very thankful then, that he did have some comfort to offer. "This I can say for certes, my lady, that Lord Amaury finds life far easier at Sherborne than ever he did at Corfe. His chamber is not as barren, or as cheerless, and he does not lack for blankets or candles or food to his liking. The castellan is quite friendly, too, comes and plays chess with Lord Amaury when his duties allow."

Hugh paused to smile at Juliana, who'd just joined them; Caitlin and her kitten had long since sauntered over. "Lord Amaury even has a pet popinjay now, a gift from his friends at the papal court. He says it comes from the Holy Land, and it is a rare sight to see, screeching like a Paris fish peddler, preening feathers green as emeralds. Lord Amaury keeps it in a wicker cage, and amuses himself by teaching it to swear in Latin!"

As Hugh hoped, that evoked laughter. "He did bid me, my lady, to ask you to procure for him a lute or gittern. I assured him you—" Hugh seemed to swallow his own words, so abruptly did he cut himself off. "Who is she?"

Even before they followed Hugh's awestruck gaze, they knew who they'd see entering the hall, for in the fortnight since she'd joined Ellen's household, Eluned ferch Iago had been turning male heads like spinning tops.

"Who? That plain, drab little sparrow in the green gown?" Llewelyn queried, and Hugh looked at him as if he'd lost his mind before realizing that he was being teased.

"For a moment there, my lord, I thought you'd either gone blind or daft! She is . . ." Words failing him, Hugh could only shake his head in wonderment. They were all laughing at him now, but he was too bewitched to care, unable to take his eyes from the vision across the hall. "What is her name? Does she have a husband? Do you think she—"

"Give me time to answer, Hugh." Ellen was delighted, for she was a born matchmaker. "Eluned is a widow, and my newest lady of the chamber. I had suggested to my lord husband that if I had one of his countrywomen as a handmaiden, I would have more opportunities to practice my Welsh. So what does he do? He finds me the most bedazzling creature to draw breath since Helen first looked upon Troy!"

"Really?" Llewelyn sounded surprised. "I cannot say I noticed."

"Of course not, darling," Ellen said. "Why, it was by pure chance that you nearly walked into that wall yesterday just as Eluned was passing by."

Llewelyn bit his lip, struggled manfully to keep from laughing, a battle he lost as soon as his eyes met Ellen's. Hugh was normally amused by their bantering, but now he shifted impatiently and cleared his throat, hoping they'd take the hint. Mercifully, Llewelyn did. Rising to his feet, he winked at his wife. "I'll be back, cariad, once I've had a few words with the Lady Eluned. Hugh . . . is there any chance you'd like to come with me?"

Watching as the men crossed the hall, Juliana nudged Ellen playfully. "You have that look again," she chided, "that melting, dewy-eyed, adoring-wife look!"

"I do not!" Ellen protested, and then, "How can I help myself? He is so generous, Juliana. Once Eluned sees how high Hugh stands in her Prince's favor, she is bound to be impressed. Yet if I try to thank Llewelyn, he'll act as if he'd done nothing at all."

"I'm sure you will find a way to show your gratitude," Juliana murmured, slyly enough to make Ellen laugh and blush at the same time. "It appears," she said cheerfully, "as if our Hugh is well and truly smitten—at long last!"

"And to judge by the way she is smiling at Hugh now, I'd venture his chances are—" Ellen stopped suddenly in mid-sentence, having belatedly become aware of Caitlin's utter stillness, her frozen silence. One glance at the girl's white, stunned face was enough. She caught her breath, reached out. But her fingers just brushed the sleeve of Caitlin's gown, for her indrawn breath had broken the spell. Still clutching the kitten to her breast, Caitlin turned, began to walk rapidly away. Her name hovered on Ellen's lips; she bit it back, let the girl go.

Juliana was watching, too, at first quizzical, and then, as comprehension dawned, pitying. "Ah, no, that poor lass . . ."

Ellen nodded. "We've all been so blind," she said sadly, "Hugh most of all."

LLEWELYN's favorite castle was Dolwyddelan, but his wife was more partial to Castell y Bere, deep in the mountains of Meirionydd. From the solar window in the upper chamber of the keep, Ellen looked out upon a vista of truly dramatic dimensions, for Castell y Bere was situated upon a rocky ridge above the Dysynni Valley, almost in the shadow of the lofty range, Cader Idris. But she valued Castell y Bere as much for its isolation as for its scenic panoramas; the castle was one of the most inaccessible of all Llewelyn's mountain citadels, and it gave Ellen an illusory sense of security, being so far off the beaten track, so far from England.

She lingered a while longer at the window, enjoying the warmth of the August sun upon her face. She thought she heard the distant, muffled echoes of a hunting horn, wondered if it could be Llewelyn's; it was difficult to tell, for she knew sounds could carry for miles on the quiet country air. Turning back toward the man waiting patiently at the table, she said, "How many letters have we completed so far, Adda?"

Her scribe riffled through the parchments piled before him. "There is a letter to your brother, the Lord Amaury. And one to your kinswomen, the Lady Hawise Wake. A brief letter to our lord's cousin, Mallt Clifford. Giffard, that is," he amended, grimacing as if the very name tasted foul, for John Giffard was proving to be one of the most rapacious and predatory of the King's officials. "There is a letter to the Abbot of Cymer, thanking him for offering the hospitality of his grange at Abereiddon. And a letter to the vintner at Shrewsbury, ordering a cask of vernage. A promise to send honey to the priory at Beddgelert. Accounts paid: to the silversmith at Bangor who crafted the saltcellar for Sir Huw and the Lady Eluned, to Ithel ap Maelgwn for the fox pelts, to the peddler who brought the salt and needles and velvet from Cheshire. And lastly, a letter to Marged, the French Queen."

Ellen smiled, amused by Adda's persistent habit of translating names into Welsh whenever possible, so that Hugh became Huw, Maude was transformed into Mallt, and the Gallic Marguerite emerged as the Celtic Marged. "I have one more letter to write, Adda, but I'll take care of it myself. I would like you to seal these letters now and arrange for couriers."

Once she was alone, she sat down in the seat Adda had just vacated, reaching for a newly scraped sheet of parchment. "To the Lady Blanche, Countess of Lancaster, greetings. I was gladdened by your good news, and went at once to the chapel to light a candle for your safe confinement and an easy delivery. This past spring my cousin Elizabeth was brought to bed of a second, healthy son. I am sure you will be just as blessed, dearest."

She paused then, for so long that the ink dripped from the quill point, dribbled onto the sheepskin. Taking up the pen again, she wrote: "We had a most illustrious guest this summer, none other than John Peckham, the new Archbishop of Canterbury. He came into Wales in June, seeking to mediate between Llewelyn and the Bishop of Bangor."

Her pen hovered, not quite making contact with the parchment. The Archbishop's visit had been an amiable one—on the surface. Peckham was surprisingly tactless for a man who'd risen so high in the Church hierarchy. It had been Ellen's experience that papal princes were subtle, urbane, even devious men, shrewd practitioners of the arts of persuasion and politics. Yet for all that Peckham appeared to be lacking in even the rudimentary skills of diplomacy, he did strike Ellen as well-intentioned; it spoke well for him that he had been willing to undertake an arduous fifteen-day journey into Llewelyn's domains. Nor was she unduly troubled by Peckham's imprudence, for no man had valued plain speaking more than her own father. Brashness she could overlook, but bias she could not, and Peckham's bias was too inbred, too heartfelt, to be camouflaged in courtesy. It had soon become appallingly obvious that England's premier prelate had a deep and abiding contempt for Wales and the Welsh.

Ellen frowned down at the parchment. Should the Archbishop ever be called upon to mediate between her husband and the English Crown, what sort of peacemaker would he be? She thought she knew the answer to that, all too well. Peckham would see the conquest of Wales as Edward's divine duty, just as popes had exhorted Christian kings and knights to take the cross, take back the Holy Land. She was far too circumspect, though, ever to commit such dangerous thoughts to print, for letters might always fall into unfriendly hands, and she had bitter, personal knowledge of the efficiency of her royal cousin's surveillance system.

"We sent Hugh de Whitton—you remember Hugh—to Amaury at Sherborne Castle, and upon his return last month, Hugh stirred up quite a hornet's nest by falling head over heels for a young Welsh widow. Whether it was love at first sight or—as Llewelyn claims—lust at first sight, nothing would do but that he must marry her, and since she was no less smitten with him, marry they did, without even waiting for the banns to be posted."

Ellen could not help smiling at that, for although she did not approve of their haste, she understood it. A man of honor like Hugh would accept as a tenet of faith their society's dichotomy, that there were women to be bedded and women to be wedded. The Lady Eluned was a woman of good birth, of good name, and therefore a bride, not a bedmate; Ellen knew that, for Hugh, it was as simple as that.

"Eluned's family was not that keen on the match. The Welsh do not object to an alltud woman—a foreigner—wedding one of their own, for the woman takes her husband's nationality. It is different, though, when a Welshwoman weds an alien, a Sais like Hugh. In England, her family's opposition would have ended their courtship then and there. But Welshwomen enjoy freedoms that their sisters in Christendom would not dare to dream about, Blanche. Welsh law says that 'a woman is to go the way that she willeth.' Whilst a virgin maid must consult her kin ere she weds, a Welsh widow may wed whom she pleases, and it pleased Eluned to wed our Hugh. I would rather they had waited, that they slowed their headlong race to the altar, but they were deaf to my pleas, and I could not very well insist. Hugh is a man grown of four and twenty, old enough to know his own mind, and I owe him more than I can ever repay. I could only wish him well, wish them luck."

Rereading her last words, she found herself hoping that Hugh and Eluned would not need as much luck as she feared. Dipping the pen into her ink-horn, she confessed to Blanche her concern for the Pope's health; the Archbishop had heard he'd been ailing. Left unsaid was her fear that a new pope might not be as willing to champion Amaury's cause as Nicholas IV had been.

"I always dread the coming of August, Blanche. It was even more troubling than usual this year, for this was the fifteenth anniversary of Evesham. Llewelyn knows it is ever a difficult time for me, does whatever he can to raise my spirits. And so last week he gave me the most amazing present. It is a mirror, but utterly unlike any I'd ever seen, for it is neither polished brass not a sheet of glass over metal. This mirror's glass has a silvered back, and reflects images with uncanny accuracy. Llewelyn said they are crafted in Germany, and he'd been trying for months to obtain one for me. Once he did, he saved it for when he knew I'd need it the most, in Evesham week. For days afterward, people were coming to my chamber, shyly asking if they might see it. I began to feel as if I had a holy relic, like Llewelyn's fragment of the True Cross!"

When the knock on the door sounded, Ellen's hand jerked, smearing the ink. "Enter," she said absently, reaching first for a knife to scrape away the blotted words, and then for a pumice stone to smooth the erasure. So intent was she upon her task that it was several moments before she glanced up, saw Caitlin standing in the doorway.

Although Caitlin had rejected every opportunity Ellen had given her to talk about Hugh, Ellen was not surprised to see her now, for she'd been sure that sooner or later Caitlin would need a confidante. Rising swiftly, she held out her hand, beckoned the girl into the chamber.

Caitlin did not know how to begin. She bit her lip, and then blurted out, "It hurts so much."

Ellen slipped her arm around Caitlin's slender shoulders, drew her toward the settle. "I know, lass," she said and sighed, wondering why there were so many salves and balms for a bruised and battered body, but none for a wounded heart.

"Do you?" Caitlin did not mean her question to sound so skeptical, but she had no experience in confiding secrets of the soul. "Do you?" she repeated, puzzled. "How? Was there another man in your life ere you wed my uncle?"

"No. Llewelyn is my first—and last—love. But I know what it is like to lose a loved one. Be it a father's death or a lover's loss, the pain is no different. Any time that one we love is taken from us, it leaves a jagged hole in the heart. I know about loss, Caitlin . . . and about living with the fear of loss. My aunt Joanna and her Llewelyn were blessed with a long, fruitful marriage, nigh on thirty-one years, and my parents . . . they were together for twenty-eight years. But Llewelyn and I . . . how many years can we hope to have? Not enough, not nearly enough. So much time squandered, stolen from us . . ."

Caitlin was quiet, considering. "Yes, you do understand," she said at last. "I feel so empty . . . and so angry. No, not at Hugh—at myself. If only I'd been forthright with him, let him know how I felt! But it was easier to wait, to give him the time he needed, time to discover that he cared for me, too. I knew he saw me as a little girl, a little sister. I was sure, though, that one day he'd look up and see me as I truly was, as a woman who loved him. So I . . . I kept silent, I kept my pride intact, and now my pride is all I have left . . ."

It was the longest speech that Ellen had ever heard Caitlin utter. It was heartening to learn that she'd been able to win the girl's trust so completely, but what was she to say? What comfort could she offer?

"The worst of it, though, is that I know she'll not make him happy. She is wrong for Hugh, all wrong. Oh, I know I'm not pretty, not like her. Eluned—even her name sounds musical. But a fair face and a honeyed name may not be enough—not for Hugh." Caitlin looked up then, green eyes darkening. "I realize how that makes me sound," she said defensively. "But it is not just jealousy, Aunt Ellen, that I swear!"

Ellen surprised her, then. "I know that, Caitlin, for I agree with you. I do not think Eluned is right for Hugh, either. She seems to have a sweet nature. But she also seems—for want of a better word—very giddy."

"You see it, too! I feared I was the only one. Hugh is not a man to be content with . . . with a butterfly, not for long. What happens when her chatter begins to pall, when her beauty no longer takes his breath away? Then what? I find it hard to see him so happy with Eluned, I'll not deny that. But how much harder it will be to see him unhappy . . ."

Ellen's hopes for Hugh's marriage were not much more sanguine than Caitlin's, but that was a worry to be confronted in the future, if and when their fears were borne out. Her immediate concern was Caitlin, and how to staunch the girl's bleeding. What she needed was to get away for a while, away from Hugh and Eluned's newlywed bliss. A pity she had no maternal kindred, for she'd sooner turn to the Devil than to Davydd.

"Caitlin, do you remember my cousin Hawise? You met her at my wedding. She is kin to you, too, for her mother was Llewelyn Fawr's daughter. I am sure she would be delighted to have you visit, to stay as long as—"

"Leave Wales?" Caitlin's eyes were wide; that was obviously an option she'd never considered, and one too outlandish to be taken seriously. "I could never leave Wales."

Ellen lapsed into a pensive silence. "Caitlin . . . have you given any thought at all to marriage?"

The girl nodded. "Of course I have, Aunt Ellen. What other solution is there for me? I want Uncle Llewelyn to find me a husband. But not yet, not until my grieving is not so raw. It would not be fair—to the man or to me—to wed whilst I still mourned what might have been."

Ellen could see the wisdom in that. But before she had a chance to say so, a sudden warning shout came echoing up from the gatehouse. Rising, Ellen moved to the window, with Caitlin just a step behind. The riders were not yet within recognition range. As they drew nearer, Ellen's eyes focused upon the bright, fluttering banner, for the arms—four quartered lions, countercharged—were very similar to Llewelyn's own. But the colors were wrong, silver and blue, not gold and red. "Oh, no," Ellen said, and Caitlin, leaning out the window, gave a gasp as she, too, saw the windblown banner.

"It is my father!" She turned a dismayed face toward Ellen. "What is he doing here?"

"Who knows?" Ellen watched morosely as a challenge was issued, answered, and the drawbridge began its creaking descent. "Davydd sent word last month that he would be crossing into Llewelyn's lands, not exactly asking permission, but as much as we could expect from him, I suppose. He said he and Elizabeth were bringing their sons to see Owain, who has been ailing. He also asked if we could offer a night's lodging at Castell y Bere. Why he should be in Meirionydd at all is beyond me, since it lies well to the south of Owain's lands in Llŷn, but ask he did, and we could not very well refuse. Not when the poorest Welsh hovel is open to travelers, every table is set for unexpected guests, and Lucifer himself could count upon a meal and a bed by the hearth on his sojourns in Wales."

"But why did you say nothing of this to me?"

"It seemed better to wait, at least until after Hugh's wedding. Davydd said they would be coming into Meirionydd the week after St Bartholomew's Day, and so we thought you had no need to know yet, not until the time drew nigh for his arrival."

Caitlin's mouth twisted. "Leave it to my father," she said bitterly, "to come a full fortnight early. Aunt Ellen . . . I do not think I can face him now."

Ellen knew exactly how she felt. "I shall tell them you are ailing," she said, and braced herself to offer Lucifer a meal and a bed by the hearth.

"LLELO, no!" Elizabeth thrust her baby at Ellen, hastily crossing the hall to corral her firstborn, just as he was about to take a swig from an untended wine flagon. Although caught in the act, he gave his mother a grin as unrepentant as it was contagious. As young as he was, he'd already learned that he would be called to account only for truly awesome misdeeds: the time he deliberately dropped a lit candle into the floor rushes, the time he put a frog in his mother's bath, the time he put a cat in his brother's cradle to watch it suck the baby's breath, as his nurse said cats did. His cockiness proved justified now; instead of scolding, Elizabeth could not help grinning back at him, and he got a hug, not a swat on his bottom.

Across the hall, Ellen was unable to take her gaze from the boy, her husband's nephew and potential heir. Llelo might bear Llewelyn's Christian name, even his childhood nickname, but he was the mirror image of his father. To Ellen, it was a bit unsettling to see Davydd's glinting green eyes in the chubby-cheeked face of a two-year-old. The baby in her arms hiccuped, began to whimper, and she rocked him gently until he quieted. He looked up at her, as solemn as a little owl.

Never had she seen such feathery golden lashes; never had she touched skin so soft. "Shall I sing you to sleep, Owain? I know a song sure to please a darling lad like you—"

Ellen's head jerked up, warned as much by instinct as by the approaching steps. For a moment, she and Davydd looked at each other, and then she summoned up a brittle, self-conscious smile. "You have a handsome son," she said, and held Owain out to him. Davydd looked as nonplussed as if he'd been handed hot coals, and after failing to spot the baby's wet nurse, gave Owain hurriedly back to Ellen.

A gleeful shriek now drew their attention again to Llelo. He'd coaxed Elizabeth into a game of tag, and she had begun to chase him around the table. Flushed and breathless, she looked like a child herself at that moment, careless of her dignity, intent only upon pleasing her small son. Ellen glanced quickly at Davydd, curious as to his reaction, for she knew many men would not approve of such unladylike antics; highborn wives were not expected to be such doting mothers, at least not in public. But Davydd was watching with an indulgent smile, a smile that vanished as soon as he turned back to Ellen.

"I hope," he said, "that Caitlin will at least make an appearance at dinner."

Ellen gave him a look of polite surprise. "Surely you have not forgotten so soon? Caitlin is ailing, confined to bed with a fever."

"Yes, so you said. But it must have come upon her right suddenly, for as we rode into the bailey, I saw her standing beside you at the solar window."

Damn his hawk's eye! Was there nothing he missed? "Mayhap I made more of it than I ought, for you are right; Caitlin is not bedridden. But she truly is unwell," Ellen insisted, in good conscience, for was not an aching heart an ailment, too? "She did not feel fit for company."

"But Elizabeth and I are not 'company,'" Davydd pointed out coolly, "we are kin. Moreover, I have something of importance to discuss with her. She is about sixteen now, no? I think it is time I found her a husband."

Ellen was stunned by his audacity. "That is for Llewelyn to do!"

"Caitlin is my daughter, not his," Davydd snapped, and Ellen's temper took fire, too fast for her to consider the consequences.

"You may have sired her," she snapped back, "but Llewelyn is more of a father to that girl than you could ever hope to be!"

No sooner were the words out of her mouth than she'd have given anything to recall them, for she realized at once what a weapon she'd just handed Davydd. How could she have been so rash, she who was always so prudent? She raised her chin, looked into Davydd's angry eyes, and waited for the blow to fall.

It did not come, though, the taunt she so dreaded about barren wives, princes without heirs. Davyyd gave her a cold, measur-
ing look, but then he shrugged, said, "Caitlin would likely agree
with you."

Ellen was amazed by the reprieve, feeling as if an arrow had just
been deflected, whizzing harmlessly over her head when it had been
aimed right at her heart. She hesitated, wanting to let Davydd know
that Caitlin's refusal to see him was not personal, not this time, feeling
that she owed him that much after his unexpected and inexplicable
forbearance. But she could not betray Caitlin's confidence, and she was
seeking a way to reconcile these conflicting needs when a man burst
into the hall with a startling message, that Llewelyn had just ridden into
the bailey.

Davydd was frowning. "I thought you said Llewelyn was hunting?"

"He was." Ellen was just as baffled as Davydd by Llewelyn's early
return, and more than a little uneasy, for men never cut the hunt short
unless the weather turned foul or there was a mishap of some sort.
Beckoning to Juliana, she handed her the sleeping child, for she did not
want Llewelyn to see her holding Davydd's son. She was turning toward
the door when it opened and her husband strode into the hall.

Even before she saw the injured—one man cradling his arm in a
makeshift sling, another whose tunic was torn, whose hair was matted
with blood—Ellen knew something had gone amiss. The men were grim-
faced, oddly silent, with none of the raucous boasting that normally
heralded a hunting party's return. Llewelyn stopped abruptly at sight
of Davydd and Elizabeth, but he recovered swiftly, and made a credible
attempt to meet the demands of hospitality, to make them welcome at
his hearth. He greeted them politely, sidestepped their queries without
overtly appearing to do so, and then excused himself so he might change
out of his muddied hunting clothes. His young squire started to follow,
then stopped, uncertain, for he'd been told that Llewelyn never wanted
servants hovering about when he was angry or in a hurry. But he was
newly come to Llewelyn's service, and he did not want his lord to think
he was shirking his duty. He dithered for a moment or so, not sure
what to do, and was relieved when Ellen made the decision for him,
drawing him aside to ask:

"Trevor? What happened on the hunt?"

"It began so well, my lady, to have ended so badly. Almost at once
the lymer hound sniffed out fresh tracks, and when we uncoupled the
running hounds, they flushed a prize stag, a ten pointer! Cynan got off
an arrow shot, but it did not bring him down, and as we gave chase,
Morgan's stallion stumbled and threw him. By the time we'd seen to
him and retrieved his horse, the dogs were out of sight, and when we

caught up with them, they'd lost the scent. We concluded the stag must have gone into the river, so we swam our mounts across."

Ellen felt a sudden chill, for the lands across the River Dyfi were now Crown lands; Edward had claimed the commote of Geneu'r Glyn as spoils of war. "The river . . . it was the Dyfi?"

The boy nodded. "What else could we do?" he asked, a question Ellen knew to be rhetorical, for she also knew it was a point of honor with hunters that once an animal was wounded, it must be slain.

Davydd had joined them by now, but she kept her eyes on Trevor. "Go on," she said. "What happened then?"

"Some of us went downstream, the others upstream, seeking to find where the stag had come ashore. I rode with Dion and Selwyn, and our dogs soon picked up the trail again. We decided to follow them a short way ere we summoned the others, to be sure they were on the right scent. But we'd gone no more than half a mile when we came upon the beast, down and foundering. We saw then why we'd seen no blood, for Cynan had gut-shot him. We sounded the horn, and Selwyn hamstrung him and gave the coup de grace."

Ellen had been listening with mounting impatience. She appreciated Trevor's slow, deliberate Welsh, for her grasp of her husband's language was still a tenuous one, but she wished he did not feel the need to relate a moment-by-moment account of the hunt. She'd been about to urge him to cut to the bone when he threw in that sudden French phrase, looking so proud of himself that she did not have the heart to rein him in.

Davydd was not so tolerant, however. "Do you suppose, lad, that you could pick up the pace a bit? I'm sure Lady Ellen never meant you to make this tale your life's work."

Ellen glared at him, and Trevor blushed. "I'm sorry, my lord. I was just trying to be sure I left out nothing of importance. They sent me then, to find our lord and fetch him back to the kill. Whilst I was gone, the others came—the King's men, who'd heard the horn. Dion and Selwyn identified themselves as Prince Llewelyn's huntsmen, explained that they'd chased the stag across the river. But the King's officers paid no heed. They claimed the stag, and when our lads tried to stop them, they were set upon and beaten. The knaves even clubbed one of the dogs!"

Trevor finally paused for breath. "By the time we reached the clearing, they were gone, the stag was stolen, and Dion and Selwyn lay bruised and bleeding upon the ground. How could that happen, my lady? How could they dare to treat our Prince like a trespasser in his own country?"

LLEWELYN had stripped off his muddied tunic and sweat-stained shirt. He was standing at the laver, splashing water onto his face and chest as Ellen entered. "I'll get you a clean shirt," she said, crossing to a coffer. For the second time that day, she found herself at a loss for words. She could not heal his wounds any more than she could Caitlin's. But she had to try. However feeble her offering—sympathy and indignation when what he wanted was retribution—she had to try.

Llewelyn reached for a towel dangling from a wall pole. "You know?"

She nodded. "England has very harsh forest laws, darling, and it may—"

"Geneu'r Glyn is in Wales, not England!"

Ellen flinched. "I know that, Llewelyn. I meant only that it may not have been a deliberate attempt to demean you or undermine your authority. It might well be that these men were mere lackeys, short-sighted hirelings seeking to curry favor by enforcing the law no matter who—"

"English law?" he said in a dangerously soft voice, and tears came suddenly to her eyes, more from frustration and helplessness than hurt.

"I am sorry," she whispered. "I wanted only to comfort you, but I seem to be making an utter botch of it . . ."

There was silence then, until he said wearily, "No, I am the one who is sorry, lass," and as she held out the shirt, his hand closed over hers. "My men wanted to hunt them down, take back our kill, and avenge Dion and Selwyn. Do you have any idea, Ellen, how much I wanted to let them?"

"Yes," she said, as the memory came flooding back, with unnerving intensity, that moment when she stood in the cabin of the *Holy Cross* and surrendered to Thomas the Archdeacon the knife she so wanted to thrust into his jugular. "I think I do."

"It was men from Geneu'r Glyn who raided into Meirionydd during Lent. Had I been able to punish them as they deserved instead of having to seek justice from the English King, this would never have happened. The whoresons would not have dared—"

The door opened before they could respond to the perfunctory knock. The surprise was in that opening door, not in the identity of the intruder; they were instinctively expecting to see Davydd, for who else would have dared to enter Llewelyn's chamber uninvited?

"If my memory serves," Davydd said abruptly, "your lands in Meirionydd were plundered not long ago by Edward's Welsh lapdog, Rhys ab Einion, and when your men followed his bandits into Geneu'r Glyn to complain, they were attacked, some severely wounded."

"Yes," Llewelyn said tersely, "your memory serves."

"I also heard that you'd lodged a complaint at Edward's Easter Parliament. But I have not heard that the culprits were brought to justice. Were they?"

"No . . . not yet."

"Now why does that not surprise me?"

"What do you want, Davydd?"

"I'd rather talk about what Edward wants. When any two Welshmen get together these days, their conversation is not about the vile Welsh weather. They swap stories about English double-dealing and thievery. You are shielded by Eryri and the River Conwy, are not harassed unless your men venture beyond your own borders. But my lands abut those seized by Edward, and rarely does a week go by without some sort of confrontation with English bailiffs and sheriffs and their minions. My woods have been cut down, I've been accused of harboring outlaws, and Edward has yet to respond to my request for a writ of certiorari against that Cheshire wretch who sued me in shire court. And my complaints can be multiplied a hundredfold all over Wales. I'd wager there is nary a Welshman to be found who does not nurse some grievance against the King's men."

"You think I do not know that? That you would dare to preach to me about Welsh suffering at English hands, you of all—"

"You're twisting my words! I am not the enemy, Llewelyn, not this time. It is becoming very clear that Edward wants war, that he means to provoke us into rebellion. Well, I've always been an obliging sort. I say we give the man what he wants."

Ellen had mastered enough Welsh to get the gist of what was being said, and at that, she could not suppress a gasp. But neither man noticed; they were intent only upon each other.

"What would you have me do, Davydd? Go to war over a stolen stag?" Llewelyn asked, with an angry smile, one sardonic enough to burn hot color into Davydd's face.

"Do not mock me, Llewelyn!"

"Do you truly think you're telling me anything I do not already know? Do you honestly think I am blind to Edward's predatory nature? Or his plans for Wales?"

Davydd started to speak, stopped, and then mustered up a tight smile of his own. "Some things never change, do they? I did not mean to offend you—for once—and I well know that you're the last man in Christendom to be taken in by the English King. I am just not sure if you realize yet how very close the day of reckoning is."

Turning, he took Ellen by surprise, catching her hand and raising it to his lips. "My apologies, Sister-in-law mine, for breaking into your bower. But we both know how bad-mannered I am." As an exit line, he did not think it could be improved upon, and he headed then for the door, wondering all the while if Llewelyn would summon him back, and yet knowing that Llewelyn would not.

Glancing down at the shirt he still held, Llewelyn discovered that he'd crumpled it in his fist, rendering it unwearable. "Where are my shirts, Ellen, in which . . . Ellen?"

She'd been staring at the door, now looked at him so blankly that he reached out, put his hands on her shoulders. "What is it? You've heard Davydd and me quarrel before . . ."

Ellen was shaking her head. "Not like this. I've never trusted your brother, that you well know. But he never frightened me—until now."

"Because you do not believe he is sincere?"

"No . . . because I do believe he is. His outrage was very real and very raw; not even Davydd could feign that. He sees now what you always saw, and it scares him. And that is what scares me, Llewelyn. A man burdened with so many regrets is not going to rest until he gets rid of them. Other sinners seek redemption in church, but Davydd seems to think it is to be found on the battlefield."

Llewelyn bent his head, kissed her on the forehead. "There is truth in what you say, cariad. But there was some truth in what Davydd said, too."

Ellen stepped back so she could see his face. "Then you also think that Edward wants war?" she asked anxiously, and was very relieved when he shook his head.

"No," he said, "I do not think he wants war." And then he added, "But he does want Wales. He lusts after an island empire, which means that he thinks Wales and Scotland are his for the taking. It is enough that he wants a thing; he needs no more justification than that, for never have I known anyone who so confused appetite with entitlement. But he is as far from a fool as any man can get, and he would much rather whittle away Wales piecemeal than pay an honest price for it in English blood. Davydd is wrong; he wants no rebellion. But he'll keep taking more and more, insisting all the while that he acts in good faith, mayhap even believing it. And he'll not understand until it is too late, that men pushed to a cliff's edge have nothing left to lose."

Ellen's mouth was suddenly very dry. "Llewelyn . . . would you be willing to fight a war you could not hope to win?"

Llewelyn did not want to answer her. She saw that at once, and turned away to gaze blindly out the window at a sky oddly empty of clouds, not a Welsh sky at all. After a moment, she said, "Guy told me that my uncle Henry pleaded with my father to surrender at Evesham, insisting that it was sheer madness to offer resistance when defeat was certain. My father said . . . he said, 'I pity a man who has nothing in his life worth dying for.' "

She felt Llewelyn's hand on her arm then, and she spun away from the window, into his embrace. She could hear his heart beating against her ear, feel the faint tickle of his chest hair against her cheek, and through her lashes she could see the thin white line of an old scar, slanting across his collarbone, along his shoulder. "I would not want to live without you," she said, so softly that Llewelyn could not be sure if she'd even meant for him to hear.

Because it was so likely that one day she would have to live without him, no matter what Edward did or did not do, and because there was so much pain in her voice, he almost made a grave mistake, almost fell back upon his last line of defense, his instinctive response to what he most dreaded. But if he had long ago taken his grandfather's credo as his own—that there were in this world some troubles so great, some dangers so menacing, that all a sensible man could do was mock them—he'd soon learned that his way was not his wife's way. Her sense of humor was flawed in two areas; she was not in the least amused when he jested about death or the gap in their ages.

If he could not joke away her fears, neither could he lie them away. He could not offer her false hope, could not promise her a future free of shadows. She would not have believed him even if he could, for she'd learned about Armageddon at a very early age.

And so he told her what he'd once told Caitlin, that "Sufficient unto the day is the evil thereof," switching from French to his own tongue to call her his "heart's joy," for he felt more comfortable expressing endearments in Welsh, and raising her face up so he could kiss her gently upon the eyelids, lashes, and mouth.

He'd meant the kiss as reassurance, but no sooner did their mouths meet than she entwined her arms around his neck, clung tightly. He suspected that her urgency had as much in it of despair as it did desire, but his body was already responding to her soft curves, hot mouth. He pulled off her wimple, and she shook her hair loose, an erotic, silken swirl against his skin, a sunset color so vivid that he never tired of looking at it, admiring it. They were halfway toward the bed when the rapping sounded at the door.

Ellen leaned against the table as Llewelyn crossed the chamber. She could not see who was outside, for he'd not opened the door all the way. As the fever faded, all the fear came back, and she found herself bitterly resenting whoever it was who'd interrupted, brought them back to reality. It was then that Llewelyn glanced over his shoulder, saw the lost look on her face. "Later," he said, and closed the door. As Ellen watched, he slid the bolt into place, and—for a brief while—shut out the rest of the world.

26

SHERBORNE CASTLE, DORSETSHIRE, ENGLAND

March 1281

THE mild, fair days so prized by most people could be a cruel kindness for captives. There had been times when Amaury de Montfort had actually prayed for rain, for weather so vile that only a lunatic would have willingly ventured from his hearth. Never did he feel so trapped, so fettered and shackled, as when he stood at an open window, gazing out upon the sunlit, seductive world beckoning just beyond the walls of Sherborne Castle.

This spring ought to have been to his liking, therefore, for it could not have gotten off to a soggier, chillier start. Instead, he found himself yearning for the merest glimpse of blue sky, for the faintest flicker of cheer. He'd suffered bouts of depression before, of course, but he'd always been able to check his fall, to grab a handhold, however precarious. Now . . . now he felt as if he were spiraling down into darkness, into a pit so deep that he'd never be able to climb out.

He was not even sure why he'd so suddenly lost his balance, his emotional equilibrium. He supposed that the Pope's death had played a part. For more than six months now, there'd been no hand on the papal helm, no one to pressure the English Crown on his behalf. And even worse might lie ahead. When the cardinals finally got around to electing a new Vicar of Christ, what if they anointed a man indifferent to his plight? He well knew that if he were ever to regain his freedom, it would only be at the Pope's behest. Should he lose his papal ally, he would languish for the rest of his wretched days as Edward of England's prisoner.

That was a daunting prospect to a man of five and thirty years. If it came to that, he knew he'd rather die. But his cousin the King was not about to put an end to his suffering, and if he found a way to do it himself, he'd be swapping a lifetime's misery for an eternity's damnation. Amaury was not yet so desperate that he could not see the drawbacks in such a deal.

It shocked him, though, that he'd even considered it, that he was so close to abandoning all hope. But as he began his sixth year of confinement, he was discovering that hope had become as slippery and elusive as the greased pigs he'd seen chased at village fairs. And now he'd gotten word that he was to be moved from Sherborne; within the week, he would be taken under guard to yet another prison. He'd never been to Taunton Castle, but he could see it clearly in his mind's eye— a bleak, secluded fortress looming over the barren, treeless moors of the West Country, well away from towns and roads and the memories of men.

He was lodged in the upper chamber of the keep, with a window overlooking one of the castle's three gateways. The window lacked glass panes, but the castellan had gotten an oiled linen screen to fit into the frame, and Amaury had moved his table to take advantage of that filtered light. Sometimes, unless it was truly frigid, he removed the top half of the screen, willing to endure the cold for the sake of the view. But today he had not even bothered to unlatch the shutters, much less monitor the bailey below. He still lay on his bed in the shadowed gloom, although it was almost noon.

He was taken by surprise, therefore, by the sudden entrance of John de Somerset, Sherborne's castellan. John was in an ambiguous position, for he was more than Amaury's gaoler; in the past three years, he'd also become Amaury's friend. That often required him to balance competing needs, as now, when he knocked briskly, according Amaury a privacy to which a prisoner was not entitled, and then entered without waiting for a response.

"Lord, lad, if you're not turning into a sluggard! But you've no more time for lying abed. You'd best hurry and make yourself presentable, for you've got company waiting out in the stairwell."

Amaury's mood took an abrupt, dramatic upswing. A man who'd once wanted fame and wealth and power, his hungers had diminished as his world had contracted; these days he craved only freedom and companionship. He was already dressed, had hastily combed his hair in those moments before John ushered his visitor into the chamber.

"Hugh!" Amaury could not have been more delighted, for the faithful young Englishman was his link to Ellen.

Hugh grinned. "Do not be squandering your welcome on me, my lord. This time I'm not the company, merely the escort."

Amaury tensed, afraid to take Hugh's words at face value, afraid to risk so bitter a disappointment. But Hugh's grin had widened; he looked so joyful that Amaury no longer doubted. He started forward just as Hugh stepped aside, revealing the woman in the doorway. Amaury had time only to say Ellen's name before she was in the room, in his arms.

AMAURY watched in amusement as his sister surreptitiously inspected his surroundings. Her relief at what she found was so obvious that he realized she'd not allowed herself to believe Hugh's optimistic reports, and he felt regretful that she'd become so wary, so like him. He also felt very thankful that she'd never seen his Spartan cell at Corfe Castle.

"So tell me," he joked, "you just happened to be passing by?"

"Something like that," she said, but when he asked, only half-playfully, whom she'd had to bribe, she lost her smile. "Not a bribe," she said, "a bone thrown to a starving dog."

Amaury understood. "You went to Ned," he said. "You entreated him to free me, and he refused."

Ellen nodded. "I paid a visit last month to our cousin's court at Windsor. Ned made me welcome, seemed honestly gladdened to see me. Mayhap he even was, for I've never known anyone blessed with such a selective memory. Sometimes I think he truly does see me just as Harry's little sister . . ."

"Until you made mention of me," Amaury said, and again she nodded, reluctantly this time.

"He seemed so friendly, Amaury, so encouraging, even fond. But as soon as I brought up your name, he stopped listening. I might as well have been speaking in Welsh. He heard me out, politely, patiently, and then he said no, regretfully, of course, for all the world as if your imprisonment for the past five years was no doing of his!"

Ellen had not meant to let her bitterness get away from her like this, but her sense of failure was still too raw to bear the slightest touch. "I am so sorry, Amaury," she said. "There must have been a way to reach him. But I could not find it, and it was all for naught . . ."

"No, not all for naught. You're here, are you not? A sop to his conscience, a bone from his table, whatever you want to call your visit, I just thank the Lord for it," Amaury said fervently, before adding, with a thinly astringent smile, "the 'Lord' in question being the One Who rules the Kingdom of Heaven, not the realm of England."

Ellen was much heartened by that barbed aside; her secret fear, not even shared with her husband, was that captivity might break her brother's spirit. "I did not come empty-handed," she said. "I bring glad tidings. Whilst I was at Windsor, the Archbishop of Canterbury sent word that the cardinals have finally chosen a new Pope, to be known henceforth as Martin IV. But you know him as Simon de Brion, former Chancellor to the French King."

Amaury, usually so self-contained, gave a jubilant shout. "God has not forsaken me then, and for certes, neither will the new Pope. I know him well, Ellen. Not only was he a friend of our father, he has close ties to Guy's patron, Charles of Sicily."

The castellan had sent up a flagon of spiced red wine, and they drank to Martin's accession, to the resurgence of hope. "Now," Ellen said, "I have other news for you, too parlous to commit to a letter. Last year a rumor reached Ned that Guy was in Norway. He at once wrote to the Norwegian Crown, seeking to have the man arrested and turned over to English agents. The Norwegian King complied, but the unlucky soul suspected of being Guy was eventually able to prove his identify. As for Guy's actual whereabouts, he is still in Italy, and openly back in Charles's favor. It must have given him a jolt, though, to learn that Ned was casting his nets even as far as the lands of the Norsemen."

Amaury did not want to talk about his brother's return to royal favor. He did not blame Guy for his troubles, at least not consciously, but he preferred not to dwell upon the ironic inequities of their respective circumstances. "Tell me," he said, "about the nets Ned has been casting in Wales. From what your letters say—and all you leave unsaid—I gather that the Welsh are not yet reconciled to their new lives as inferior Englishmen?"

In just one succinct, memorable sentence, he had gone to the heart of the Welsh dilemma, summed up the troubled state of affairs in her husband's unhappy homeland. Ellen was impressed, but not at all surprised; she'd often suspected Amaury of being the cleverest of all the de Montforts. " 'Inferior Englishmen,' " she said somberly. "Not even Llewelyn could have put it better than that."

Amaury poured them both more wine. "And by balking, they do but confirm the worst of Edward's suspicions, that they are a reckless, rebellious, vexatious people who need to be tamed, broken to the royal will—for their own good, of course."

"You understand exactly how it is," she marveled, "and yet you've never set foot in Wales!"

"I know Edward, know how he thinks," he said simply.

"Life in Wales these days . . ." Ellen hesitated, fumbling for the right words. "It is like waiting for a storm to break, Amaury. We go about our daily tasks with an eye ever on those clouds looming on the horizon, feeling the wetness on the wind, wondering how much time we'll have ere it hits."

Amaury was chilled as much by her matter-of-fact tones as by the bleakness of her vision. "It is truly as bad as that, Ellen?"

"Yes," she confided, "God help us, it is. With every day that passes, the Welsh are becoming more and more aggrieved and resentful, for Edward's crown officials are exercising power with a heavy hand, indeed. It may be that Edward is not fully aware of the extent of their arrogance, their insufferable contempt for all things Welsh. But he is certainly aware of Llewelyn's own grievances, and he has yet to redress any of those wrongs."

Amaury prodded his memory to recall her past letters. "You mean those men hanged at Oswestry? And the attack upon Llewelyn's huntsmen?"

"And the raid into Meirionydd. And the seizure of Llewelyn's goods in Chester. And Arwystli, always Arwystli. And . . . well, I see no need to burden you with the rest. But each time the result is the same. Llewelyn protests to the King, and Edward assures him that he will investigate Llewelyn's complaints, see that justice is done. And that is the last we ever hear of it."

Ellen drank too deeply, began to cough. "I do not think I wrote to you about the distraints, did I? Briefly put, Welsh law gives its princes the same rights over shipwrecks that the English kings enjoy. A few years ago a prosperous English merchant, Robert of Leicester, lost a ship in Welsh waters, and Llewelyn claimed the cargo that washed ashore. But after the Treaty of Aberconwy was signed, this merchant brought suit against Llewelyn in an English court for restitution. Llewelyn did not even know about it, not until some of his men rode into Chester to buy honey, and the Justiciar not only seized the honey, he confiscated their horses, too. Since then, he has continued to distrain Llewelyn's goods whenever the opportunity arises. Llewelyn complained to Edward. He got a most sympathetic reply, too. Edward offered his apologies for the misunderstanding, and promised Llewelyn that he would order the Justiciar to return the seized goods. I saw that letter myself. Yet he then wrote to his Justiciar and approved the seizures. Is it any wonder that Llewelyn feels such anger and frustration when confronted with such bad faith? No man can long endure being made to feel helpless, least of all, mine."

"What about his suit against Gruffydd ap Gwenwynwyn? Has that not been settled yet?"

Ellen's laugh held little humor. "It has been more than three years since Llewelyn first brought suit, and they have yet even to decide the first issue, whether Welsh or English law should apply. Llewelyn is sorely vexed by all the delays, and who can blame him?"

"Jesú forfend that I sound as if I am defending our right beloved cousin," Amaury said, and grinned. "But in truth, sweetheart, I can see why he is so loath to allow it to be litigated. From what you've said in your letters, Llewelyn has a good claim under Welsh law. But Ned owes Gruffydd ap Gwenwynwyn too much to let him lose. At the same time, he'd not want to risk pushing Llewelyn into rebellion. So delay must seem like the only road open to him."

"But it is unjust!" Ellen said sharply, and Amaury hid another grin, thinking that his little sister might not look like their late, lord father, but she for certes sounded like him.

Curbing her indignation, Ellen continued with the tangled tale of the Arwystli suit. "It has been adjourned more times than I can remember. Then, at Ned's Easter Parliament last year, it was decided to appoint a commission to inquire into Welsh laws and customs. They did not even choose the members until December, and when they did, surprise of surprises, all three happened to be English, and one was a man greatly loathed by the Welsh, Reginald de Grey. But even so, they'll have no choice but to find that Welsh law applies. The Treaty says so, Amaury, in most unambiguous terms, says that if Llewelyn brings claim against any lands occupied by others than the lord King, the King will do him full justice according to the laws and customs of those parts in which the lands lie. And," she concluded triumphantly, "not even Edward can deny that Arwystli is in Wales!"

Amaury felt no surprise that she should take such an active interest in the politics of her husband's realm; theirs had never been a family in which women dutifully deferred to the greater wisdom of their menfolk. The very thought amused Amaury no end, for he doubted that his lady mother would have deferred to the Devil himself; Simon had even entrusted her with the wartime defense of Dover Castle. Ellen's impassioned partisanship on Llewelyn's behalf was no less than he'd have expected of Nell de Montfort's daughter.

"Moreover," Ellen said, with a sudden, unexpected grin, "we have a most unlikely ally in the Arwystli suit, even if that's not his intent, none other than that misbegotten hellspawn, Roger de Mortimer. You see, Gruffydd ap Gwenwynwyn sued de Mortimer for thirteen vills in Cydewain, and when de Mortimer did not respond, Gruffydd sought a judgment in default. But de Mortimer is now contesting that, arguing that since the land is in Wales, Welsh law should apply, for Welsh law happens to allow three defaults!"

"Well, it does sound as if Llewelyn has both law and logic on his side," Amaury admitted. "So why, then, are your nerves so on the raw? Why borrow trouble ere the debt is due, Ellen?"

"Is that what I am doing, Amaury? I wish I could be sure that was so, wish I could be more like Elizabeth . . ."

"Elizabeth? Our de Ferrers cousin?"

She nodded. "I have not told you all, have not told you about Davydd. He and Elizabeth and their young sons stayed briefly with us at Castell y Bere last summer. It was not a pleasant visit, but it was a revealing one. Davydd has his own grievances against the English Crown, and he seems, too, to have developed a conscience of late. I know that sounds unlikely, but I do not know how else to explain his turnaround. He wants war, Amaury, mayhap for the novelty of being on the Welsh side for once. I know I sound uncharitable, but he frightens me. He is so . . . so unpredictable, so irresponsible, and he has caused Llewelyn so much pain . . ."

"But you mentioned Elizabeth. How does she come into this? Do you not like her, Ellen?"

"As a matter of fact, I do. I admire her pluck and I like her forthrightness, although I'll admit to being baffled by her inexplicable devotion to Davydd. I could not endure being wed to a man I could not respect. But I do not doubt that she loves him, even if I cannot understand it. I only wish she could influence him to the good, provide the voice of reason that he seems so utterly to lack. Instead, she indulges his every whim, no matter how outrageous. I believe that a wife ought to defer to her husband, of course, but Elizabeth is truly besotted with the man, and it has blinded her to the dangers we face. I tried to talk to her, but she is serenely sure that all will be well, that her darling Davydd will always prevail, that he is invincible merely because she wills it so."

Ellen paused, but Amaury was an attentive listener, clever at coaxing confidences, able to loosen tongues by his very silence. "I would that I could share her certainty, Amaury. Blessed Lady, how I wish it! It is not that I lack faith in Llewelyn. It is just that . . . that I cannot help remembering that Mama was as trusting as Elizabeth—once. She, too, believed that God would always favor the just, that our father would always triumph over his enemies. She believed that right up to the moment we stood together in the great hall of Dover Castle and heard a weeping man tell her, 'They are dead, my lady. They are all dead.' "

A silence fell between them. Amaury reached across the table, clasped his fingers around hers. After a while, she said, "I was there, Amaury, at Evesham. We stopped at the abbey on our way to Windsor. The Abbot was very kind, escorted me into the church and then left me alone. I prayed for Papa and for Harry, but I could not stop thinking of Bran, risking his life to make that reckless, desperate pilgrimage to Evesham, to make his peace with Papa . . ."

She looked up then, into bright hazel eyes very like her own. "I thought I'd find comfort there, but I did not. It was a disappointment to Hugh, too, for the monk who'd befriended him, Brother Damian, was gone, having been sent to another of the Benedictine Houses, the one at Shrewsbury. Hugh had so looked forward to their reunion, though, that I shall have to find some errand that needs doing in Shrewsbury."

"I doubt that you'd be doing the lad much of a favor," Amaury said impishly. "I'm sure he'd much rather be snug in his young wife's bed than chasing about Shrewsbury after a monk he's not laid eyes upon in ten years!" He was very adroit at reading faces, and after studying Ellen's, he sat back in surprise. "Trouble in Eden so soon? They've been wed less than a year, hardly time enough, I would think, for them to have grown bored with each other."

"It is lucky that you're a priest, for any man so cynical would have made a most unsatisfactory husband! But you're quick, I'll grant you that. Indeed, all is not well betwixt Hugh and Eluned. Not that he'd ever admit it, not our Hugh. I daresay he'd endure trial by fire ere he'd speak ill of her. But I know he is hurting, Amaury, and I think I know why. There is no way I can say this without sounding cruel, but the truth is that although the Lord bestowed beauty in plenitude upon Eluned, He was not as generous in His other gifts. She is a good-hearted lass, but not, I fear, at all clever or quick-witted. To some men, that would not matter, to others it would. From what I've heard, her first husband felt no lack in her; he was older than she, proud to have such a desirable wife, amused by her child-like ways. But what so charmed him no longer charms Hugh, and the poor lass does not know why. I do feel sorry for her, Amaury; she truly wants to please, and senses that she is disappointing Hugh somehow, but does not understand how she is failing him. And Hugh . . . he breaks my heart, for he is wretched, and I suspect he's likely blaming himself for his discontent. Llewelyn's people have a saying, 'Hir amod ni ddaw yn dda,' or 'A long betrothal is not lucky.' But in this case, it might have saved Hugh and Eluned a lifetime of misery."

"A pity," Amaury said, and meant it; his flippancy notwithstanding, his fondness for Hugh was quite genuine. "But if a man is a fool to wed for love, he must be utterly daft to wed for lust. No one with sense would expect a candle to burn forever, so why should a flame kindled in bed?"

Ellen laughed. "To hear you talk, if you'd been in Eden, you'd have sided with the snake! Speaking for myself, my marital candle is burning quite merrily, thank you, and I have every confidence that it shall stay lit, too. They are not as rare as you seem to think. You cannot deny that our parents found a candle to last the life of their marriage. It's quite obvious to anyone with eyes to see that Ned and Eleanora do not lack for light or heat in their marriage bed. And Edmund and Blanche can kindle a fire without flint or tinder, too. The best part of my English sojourn—until now—was the time I had with them—"

Breaking off, she entreated, "Ah, Amaury, do not look like that! I know you begrudge Edmund Papa's earldom, but would you rather it had gone to that whoreson de Mortimer or to Gloucester or that Judas, John Giffard? Edmund and Blanche have been good friends to me, and I am right glad that they have found such contentment in their marriage. They have a second son now, did you know? Blanche gave birth to a fine, healthy lad a fortnight after Christmas, christened him Henry."

Amaury gave his sister a discerning look. He didn't say anything, but he didn't have to, for they understood each other as few people ever did. Ellen smiled sadly, shook her head. "No," she said quietly, "it did not hurt as much as you think—or I feared. In truth, I found it much harder to look upon Davydd and Elizabeth's little lads. I do not envy Blanche her sons, would not begrudge her a nursery-full. Hers was a loss no mother should ever have to suffer—"

"What are you talking about? What loss?"

"Surely you could not have forgotten? Not a death so bizarre, so— But then, you never knew! How could you, for you were in Italy when it happened, whilst Blanche was still wed to her first husband, the King of Navarre. Their young son was killed in a dreadful accident. His nurse was walking with him upon the battlements of their castle at Estrella, and somehow she tripped, dropped the baby over the wall, down into the bailey."

"Jesus wept!"

"I doubt that a wound like that could ever truly heal. Blanche has never spoken to me about it, and I would never ask. I just hope that the sons she has borne Edmund give her joy in full abundant measure, for she deserves nothing less."

"So do you, lass. Will you tell me the truth, Ellen? Does Llewelyn ever blame you for your failure to conceive?"

"No," she said, "no, dearest, you may set your mind at rest. Llewelyn has never reproached me for my barrenness, never. Indeed, he has done all he could to comfort me, to reassure me that if I cannot give him a son, he will see that as God's Will, not as my failing. I may not be blessed with a fertile womb, but I have been truly blessed in my marriage."

Amaury was vastly relieved. "I think," he said, "that I could get to like that husband of yours, Little Sister."

Ellen laughed. "I'm somewhat fond of him myself. Now I want you to promise me that you'll stop fretting about me. No man on God's green earth could take better care of me than Llewelyn does. And I have by no means given up my hopes of motherhood, shall do my best to make you an uncle. I still have time, for a woman of twenty and eight ought to have another twelve childbearing years at the very least, mayhap more. In fact, I have a plan in mind."

Ellen's eyes shone in the candle light. She leaned toward him, eager to share her secret. "There is a holy well in North Wales, close by Basingwerk Abbey. It is dedicated to a Welsh saint, Gwenfrewi, and its waters are said to have wondrous healing powers, especially for women unable to conceive. Upon my return home, I shall make a pilgrimage to her well, Amaury, beseech St Gwenfrewi to heed my prayers, that I may give Llewelyn a son."

"God grant it so," he said, and never had he meant any prayer more.

"Ere I forget, I have something for you." Ellen reached into the bodice of her gown, drew out a thin gold chain. "Papa's ring. I've kept it safe for you, as I promised. But I think it is time now for you to have it back."

As she held the ring out to him, Amaury caught her hand. "No," he said, "not yet. You hold on to it a while longer, until I am freed, until I can come into Wales to fetch it back—and to see your son."

Ellen's eyes searched his face, and then she nodded slowly. Clutching the ring so tightly that the sapphire dug into her palm, clutching it as if it were a holy relic, she echoed softly, "God grant it so."

THAT cold, wet spring eventually yielded to a rainy, cool summer. The Welsh had almost given up hope of seeing the sun again when, without warning, the second Saturday in June dawned to vividly blue skies, an all-but-forgotten warmth, and a mild, southerly breeze. The inhabitants of Llewelyn's seacoast manor at Aber and the village that had grown up in its shadow soon found plausible excuses to escape into that dazzling white-gold light, to make the most of Nature's sudden reprieve.

Ellen loved their times at Aber. She loved to walk upon the beach and gaze across the straits toward Llanfaes. She loved to follow the shallow, meandering river that flowed through a deeply wooded glen, and she loved to watch for that flash of silver amidst the trees ahead, anticipating her first glimpse of the surging waterfall that splashed over a sheer cliff in a narrow ribbon of white water. She loved lying beside

Llewelyn at night in the same chamber where Joanna had once slept with her Llewelyn. Aber was the heart of her husband's realm; it was here that she felt the pull of the past most strongly, and she never came back to Abergwyngregyn—musical Mouth of the Whiteshell River— without feeling as if she were coming home.

Ellen was an avid gardener, and she'd lavished loving care upon the gardens at Aber. Accompanied by Juliana and Edwyn, an aged gardening wizard whose plant-lore was legendary, Ellen prepared to survey her verdant, flowering domains. They went first to the small vegetable plot; the Welsh were no more keen for vegetables than were the English, and Edwyn's kitchen garden held only onions, leeks, garlic, and cabbage. Ellen's inspection was rather cursory, and they soon moved on to the evenly spaced rows of the herb garden. Here were grown the medicinal plants used to make ointments and potions. The scent of rue wafted toward them upon the balmy summer air, and all about them was the evidence of Edwyn's industry, his Merlin's touch.

Juliana watched a fragile white butterfly dance upon the breeze while Ellen and Edwyn discussed his strategy for repelling the moles that were every gardener's scourge. But Ellen's usual enthusiasm was oddly lacking today; in a surprisingly short time, Edwyn was free to resume his other duties and the women were entering the flower garden that was Ellen's Welsh Eden.

Enclosed by neatly trimmed hawthorn hedges, the garden had been laid out with exacting care, for symmetry and proportion and uniformity were the gardener's goal; it would have been unheard-of to allow flowers to grow in the helter-skelter disorder to be found in Nature. The rectangular, raised beds were bordered by low wattle fences, and the centerpiece was a flowery mead, a sea of billowing Welsh grass adrift with daisies. Turf benches were scattered about, and a small fountain bubbled beside a trellised arbor, a shaded haven besieged by climbing roses and entwining honeysuckle.

Setting down her watering pot, Ellen took the scissors Juliana was proferring, began to gather an eclectic bonquet of Madonna lilies, blue columbines, and peonies. "If you take these," she said, "I'll cut some roses."

"Ellen . . . I do not mean to pry. But I'd have to be blind not to see that you're troubled. Would it help to talk?"

Ellen shook her head, a moment later let out an unladylike oath. With Juliana's help, she managed to extract the thorn embedded in her thumb. Picking up a dropped rose, its ivory-white petals smeared with blood, she hesitated, then said, "I suppose I have been distracted this morn. It is just that . . . that Llewelyn and I quarrel so rarely. It was so needless, too, an argument that blew up like a summer storm, with no warning, no sense to it. I know I am making more of it than I ought. But this was the first time that we'd quarreled and then gone to bed angry . . ."

Juliana plucked a red rose, held it out to Ellen. "Send him a peace offering."

Ellen reached for the flower. "I know the rose is a token of love, but I think Llewelyn might be won over more quickly by a roast carp, rice savory, and those angel-bread wafers he so fancies."

"Well, then, why are we tarrying in the garden when we ought to be seeking out the cooks?" Juliana prompted, and within moments they were on their way to the kitchens. Taking action had done much to raise Ellen's spirits, and by the time they returned to her bedchamber, she was discussing her planned "peace dinner" with a resurgence of enthusiasm. As they set about putting their cut flowers in clay pitchers, it was Juliana who first noticed the white cloth trailing from the bed canopy. Puzzled, she walked over for a closer look. "Ellen, what is this doing here?"

But Ellen was a soldier's daughter. One glance at that makeshift white banner and she began to laugh, for she understood its significance at once. Flying over her marriage bed was a flag of truce.

ELLEN was alone in their bedchamber when Llewelyn entered, sitting in a window-seat as she embroidered a linen altar cloth. She was an accomplished needlewoman, had been laboring that summer upon a new set of vestments for the priest of Dolwyddelan's parish church. Nestled beside Ellen in the window-seat, Hiraeth gave Llewelyn an intent, faintly suspicious stare; although the little dog was resigned by now to this intruder's presence in its mistress's life, it had yet to offer him more than a grudging tolerance. Fortunately, he got a warmer welcome from his wife. Putting aside her sewing, she rose at once, facing him with just the hint of a smile.

The white flag had been taken down, folded neatly, and laid upon Llewelyn's pillow. "Does that mean," he asked, "that you reject my offer of a truce?"

"No, my lord husband. It means that you've no need of a truce, for I would make an unconditional surrender."

"Without even knowing my terms? How very brave of you," he said, and they both laughed, moved into each other's arms. When they turned toward the settle, they discovered, though, that Hiraeth had already anticipated them, and was comfortably curled up on the cushions, regarding them with regal forbearance, a queen deigning to share her domain. "Never doubt that I love you," Llewelyn said wryly, "for only a man hopelessly smitten would put up with that beast of yours. Now . . . I have a suggestion, Ellen. If the Truce of God can forbid shedding of blood on holy days or in the Lord's House, why can we not consecrate our marriage bed, too, as a place where no quarreling shall be permitted?"

Ellen laughed, agreed that henceforth the boundaries of their bed would be as hallowed as the church threshold, and they sealed their pact with a kiss. "I wanted to make a proper, formal surrender," she confided, "but as a woman, I was at a distinct disadvantage, having no sword to offer up to you, my lord." To her amusement, he gallantly promised her free use of his sword, and she agreed, with mock gravity, to accept his offer that very night. But as much as she delighted in their erotic banter, she felt that she owed him a genuine apology, one she tendered now in all sincerity, for it was a wife's duty to keep harmony in the home.

"My ill temper was even more inexcusable," she said, "for I well knew why you were so testy these past few days. Is the tooth any better, my love—the truth now?"

"Much better," he said, so emphatically that she knew he lied, and decided to ask Edwyn for feverfew, since the cloves did not seem to be helping. Dislodging Hiraeth, she insisted that he stretch out upon the settle and pillow his head in her lap, all the while marveling that a man so conversant with the perils of the battlefield would yet go to such stubborn lengths to avoid having a tooth pulled.

"Just lie back," she coaxed. "The world will not come to an end because you take your ease for a brief while." She stroked his hair, gently caressing his temples, a smile hovering about her mouth, for their jesting about swords had triggered an old memory.

"My parents quarreled far more frequently than we do," she said, "but it never seemed to poison the pleasure they took in each other . . . mayhap because they both thrived upon chaos! I remember one quarrel in particular, when I was eleven. My father had broken his leg in a fall from his horse, and it could not have happened at a worse time, for he'd been about to sail for France, where the French King had agreed to mediate his dispute with the English Crown. Instead of arguing his cause in Paris, he found himself bed-ridden at Kenilworth Castle, in a truly vile temper. On the day in memory, he'd had a blazing row with my mother, and she'd stalked out, leaving him to lie alone in bed and fume. When I came into the bedchamber, he demanded to know why his squire had not answered his summons, and I explained that the rest of the household were loath to face him when he was in such a foul mood. He seemed surprised, asked if he was such a bad patient, and was quite taken aback when I told him he'd been a truly dreadful patient so far!"

Ellen laughed softly, and Llewelyn reached up, traced the curve of her cheek. "You were not afraid to be so plain-spoken, cariad?"

"Afraid—of my father?" Ellen laughed again, this time incredulously. "Not ever! He was always gentle with me, more than I doubtless deserved, for looking back, I can see I was more indulged than I ought to have been. My brothers, too. Papa demanded so much of all others, especially himself, and not enough of us. But to return to Kenilworth Castle, he said that I'd convinced him that he'd best make amends with Mama, and he needed my help. He sent me back to the great hall, Llewelyn, proudly bearing his battle sword to surrender to my mother!"

This was a pastime they both enjoyed, swapping memories of the yesterdays they'd not shared, for their marriage was still new enough that they had much to learn about each other. Ellen in particular liked reliving her past and delving into his, although it saddened her to discover that her childhood had been so much happier than his. The de Montfort family's binding cords had been hammered out of finely tempered steel, like the best swords almost impossible to break, but Llewelyn could not recall a time when his family had not been torn asunder by conflicting loyalties, by the estrangement between his father and grandfather. Ellen found it a little easier to understand the puzzling, often inexplicable contradictions in his troubled relationship with Davydd after getting glimpses into her husband's storm-buffeted boyhood. And the more she learned, the more she yearned to give him children.

"They are all too rare," she said regretfully, "our quiet moments together like this," and indeed, the words were no sooner out of her mouth than her sentence was punctuated by a discreet knock. Llewelyn gave Ellen a rueful look, shrugged, and within moments was gone, hastening back to the great hall to receive a courier from the English King.

By now, Ellen was accustomed to such abrupt disappearances. Fetching her sewing from the window-seat, she resumed working upon the altar cloth. But Eluned and Juliana soon entered, and she put it aside for more secular concerns—making herself ready to preside with Llewelyn over the evening's meal. She would not normally have changed clothes, for they entertained no guests at Aber that night. But her reconciliation with her husband still had a final act to be played out, later, in the privacy of their newly sanctified marriage bed, and she wanted to look as pleasing as possible for him.

With her ladies' help, she donned a softly draped gown of emerald silk, Llewelyn's favorite shade, and over it, a pale green surcote. Although the Church constantly preached against the use of cosmetics, earnestly deplored the sin of vanity, Ellen found herself squarely on the side of majority opinion, that there was nothing wrong in seeking to enhance God's gifts, which she proceeded to do with powder, lip rouge, perfume, and a mouthwash of honey and myrrh. She was already anticipating her private time alone with Llewelyn much later that night, and as she turned away from her mirror, she laughed suddenly, remembering Amaury's skepticism about bonfires and beds, thinking that a priest, even a priest as clever as Amaury, could not hope to understand the bond that could be forged between a man and a woman, if they truly committed themselves to their marriage vows, if they were reasonable in their expectations—and if they were very lucky.

Ellen's high spirits lasted as long as it took her to cross the bailey and enter the great hall. Even before she reached the dais, the silence in the hall had alerted her that something was very wrong. The King's courier was nowhere in sight, but Llewelyn held in his hand a parchment bearing the royal seal of the English Crown. "Here," he said, as Ellen drew near. "Edward's commission has issued its findings about Arwystli."

There was not yet need for torches; the light lingered well into the evening hours during Welsh summers. Ellen took the writ, read that the royal commission had determined by inquest which laws and customs had been recognized in the reigns of Edward's predecessors, and by these laws, so would justice be rendered unto the Prince of Wales. Ellen had grown up at court, was familiar with the deliberate ambiguities of diplomatic jargon. But even by those lax standards of clarity, this document was hopelessly obscure, so cryptic as to seem incomprehensible to her. "What exactly does this mean, Llewelyn?"

"It means," he said tersely, "that we'll not be using Welsh law," and when his suspicions would later be proved correct, there was no surprise; by then, she had concluded, as he had done, that Edward would have no need for such deceptive equivocation if he meant to adhere to the Treaty, to let Welsh law control. Now, though, she could only look up into her husband's face in dismay, seeing a man standing at the cliff's edge.

NINE days after the findings of Edward's commission were published, his court ruled that Gruffydd ap Gwenwynwyn's suit against Roger de Mortimer must be decided by Welsh law, as the lands in issue were situated in Wales.

27

HAFOD-Y-LLAN, NANHWYNAIN, WALES

September 1281

LLEWELYN often stayed at Nanhwynain, the largest of Aberconwy's abbey granges, for its twelve thousand alpine acres encompassed some of the most scenic vistas in all of Gwynedd. From the open window, he could see the mountains he so loved, Eryri's awesome "Haunt of Eagles." Stars had begun to glimmer through the twilight, and he could hear the distant baaing of the sure-footed sheep that were the grange's greatest resource. It was a peaceful, pastoral scene, but for once he was blind to the beauty of his homeland, so preoccupied was he with political strategy and statecraft, so intent upon his next move in his high-stakes chess game with England's King.

Turning from the window, he said, "I wanted to speak with you both ere the council meets, to let you know what I shall propose to them. I have attempted to abide by the English King's treaty, and what has it gotten me but mockery and insults? For a Welshman seeking justice, the least likely place to look must be in an English court. He'd have better luck hunting virgins in the bawdy-houses of the Southwark stews, tracking fabled beasts like the centaurs of ancient Greece, or the monster that is said to lurk in a lake on Cader Idris."

Dai smiled at that, and Goronwy laughed outright, but their amusement was grim; these days, most humor in Wales had sharp edges. Llewelyn took a swallow of cider, regarding them intently as he drank. "We have," he said, "been playing a game in which Edward provides the dice, keeps score, makes up the rules as he goes along, and has the power to cry 'forfeit' should he somehow lose. Well, I think it is time to teach him about Welsh games of chance. I mean to invite a new player into the game."

Dai and Goronwy exchanged speculative glances. But Goronwy was, as always, too impatient to wait, and blurted out, "A Marcher lord?"

Llewelyn smiled. "Yes," he said, "what better place to look for an ally than in the Marches? That stratagem served my grandfather well, for never did his power burn so bright as in those years after he'd allied himself with the Earl of Chester. Only time will tell if it works as well for me, but it is the only trail still open."

Both Dai and Goronwy were nodding appreciatively, offering Llewelyn a foretaste of the approval he expected to get from his council. "Who, my lord? The Earl of Gloucester?" The guess was Goronwy's, and it was a shrewd one, for Llewelyn and Gloucester had been allied together once before. But Llewelyn, still smiling, shook his head.

"No," he said, "not Gloucester. My cousin, Roger de Mortimer."

They looked startled, then dubious. "None would deny that Gloucester is about as affable as a cornered badger," Dai said slowly, "but he does have a few scruples. Whereas de Mortimer would cut his own grandmother's throat if you made it worth his while."

Llewelyn didn't dispute it. "Fortunately for me," he said dryly, "I am not the man's grandmother. If we begin to tally up all his flaws of character, we'll still be talking come Judgment Day. But he has certain attributes that make him an ideal ally for my purposes. He is clever, ambitious, ruthless, and"—Llewelyn paused—"Gruffydd ap Gwenwynwyn's neighbor."

DAI had gone, Goronwy still lingered. Dai had seen the advantages of Llewelyn's scheme, but he'd seen the dangers, too. If Goronwy did, he must have dismissed them as negligible, for his imagination was soaring, unencumbered by any earthly tethers. His zestful enthusiasm was contagious, appealing, a very likable aspect of his personality. But it was also why Llewelyn had chosen Dai as his Seneschal. Goronwy's opinions were always interesting, often amusing, occasionally ingenious, but never objective, never balanced. Now his partisan passion was at full flame, so pleased was he that Llewelyn was laying plans to hold on to Arwystli, that he was not going to let it be stolen away in an English court. If these plans risked war, so be it; Goronwy tended to look upon war as he did the coming of winter: as unwelcome, onerous, and inevitable.

Draining his cider cup, Goronwy said suddenly, "I must confess, my lord, that one thing about this alliance does trouble me."

"Only one?" Llewelyn asked, but Goronwy was impervious to irony, and nodded vigorously.

"How can we be sure," he asked, "that de Mortimer shall be willing?"

That was the least of Llewelyn's worries. "I know the man," he said, with enough certainty to satisfy Goronwy. But his was an easy face to read. Llewelyn waited, then prompted, "Well? What else bothers you?"

"What of your lady?"

Goronwy's query was so unexpected, so presumptuous, that Llewelyn realized almost at once that it could only be motivated by a very genuine concern. It was an undeniable familiarity, but one spurred on by friendship, and Llewelyn acknowledged it as such with the candor it deserved.

"I would to God there was another way, Goronwy," he conceded quietly, "for she would sooner see me in league with Lucifer than allied with Roger de Mortimer. But my wife is a reasonable woman. She will understand."

LLEWELYN was awakened by the screeching of gulls. The raucous clamor puzzled him at first, until he remembered that they were no longer at the mountain grange of Hafod-y-Llan. He'd moved his household to his coastal castle at Cricieth, where Ellen was to remain while he journeyed south to meet with Roger de Mortimer.

The squabbling of the gulls had grown louder; it sounded as if they were fighting over a fish right under his window. It had been left unshuttered, open to the night air, for the weather had been unusually mild that September, as if Nature seemed set upon making amends for such a chill, rain-sodden spring and summer. Llewelyn lay still for a few moments, breathing in the tangy salt air. Almost lulled back to sleep by the rhythmic sound of ocean waves breaking upon the rocks below the castle, he reached drowsily for Ellen. But his seeking hand encountered only the rumpled folds of the bed sheets.

Fully awake now, he raised himself on his elbow. Ellen was awake, too, reclining upon a pillow propped against the headboard, with the breadth of the bed between them. As he stirred, her lashes quivered, but her eyes stayed downcast. So close to the edge of the mattress was she that a careless move could have sent her tumbling onto the floor. She looked pale and tired in the dawn light, and Llewelyn felt a sudden surge of tenderness. It was time to heal this foolish rift, to make things right between them. The first overtures would have to be his, but that was fair, for her grievance was a real one. He'd not begrudged her right to anger, had just not expected that she would cling to it so stubbornly.

Leaning across the bed, he reached for her long braid, entwining its tip around his fingers. "It is lonely over here by myself, Ellen," he murmured coaxingly. "I am accustomed to finding you beside me when I awake, and I've missed that, cariad, missed your warmth, the feel of your breath on my skin as you slept. You once said our marriage bed was a haven, but in this past week, it has begun to resemble a kingdom split in twain and under siege. If I could tempt you into venturing into my half of our disputed domain, I feel sure we could find a way to mend this breach, to make our peace."

Having offered her an olive branch, he felt a sense of relief; he ought to have done this days ago, spared them both some unquiet nights. Her lashes flickered again, no longer hovered along her cheeks, and he found himself looking into eyes utterly opaque and inscrutable. He could see color rising in her face and throat. She glanced away, then, sat up, and slid over onto his side of the bed.

Llewelyn did not want to talk, for he realized there was nothing he could say to ease her discontent; only time could do that. He knew she'd never like it, his association with Roger de Mortimer. But she'd learn to accept it; what other choice had she? "I have a confession to make," he said, gently smoothing back the stray tendrils of hair framing her face. "Nothing under God's sky disheartens me more than quarreling with you." Her lashes had veiled her eyes again; he brushed his lips against her eyelids and temples before seeking her mouth.

Ellen offered no resistance, but neither did she respond. She simply lay there, let him kiss and caress her as he wished, and when he pulled back, ended the embrace, he was as angry as she'd ever seen him. "How long," he demanded, "is this going to continue?"

She did not pretend to misunderstand him. "I am not refusing you, Llewelyn," she pointed out coolly. "I am ready to perform all of my wifely duties when and as you will."

"How very noble," he snapped. "And what am I supposed to do— just wake you when it's over?"

"I would suggest that you take what is offered, because duty is about all I can muster up at the moment!"

Llewelyn could have been looking at a stranger. "Of a sudden," he said, "I do not feel as if I know you at all."

"I can return the compliment, my lord, for I do not think I know you either, not anymore. I would have wagered my life that you'd never willingly hurt me—and I'd have been wrong!"

"Christ Jesus, woman, must we get into this again? What more is there to say? You know why I am doing this—"

"And you know what Roger de Mortimer did to my father! We stood in our bridal chamber at Worcester Castle and you listened as I told you what I'd never told another living soul, how that evil, ungodly man maimed and mutilated my father's body—need I repeat all the vile, disgusting details? De Mortimer and his cut-throats butchered my father, hacked him into bloody pieces, threw what was left of him to the dogs. And this is the man you would have me break bread with! You tell me how, my lord husband, how do I do that? As I sit across the table and smile at him, how do I not think of Wigmore Castle . . . and my father's head rotting above the gateway?"

"Stop it, Ellen! That would never happen, and you know it. Did I not promise you that you'd not have to lay eyes upon the man, much less make him welcome at our hearth? Is my word no longer enough for you?"

"I am neither a fool nor a child, Llewelyn. You can offer me a plenitude of promises today—and mean each and every one of them. But should the day ever come when your new ally arrives unexpectedly at your gate, wanting to conspire with you against Gruffydd ap Gwenwynwyn, we both know you'll not turn him away, you'll not risk offending him to spare my feelings."

"For God's sake, Ellen, you're more important to me than Roger de Mortimer!"

"Am I? Prove it to me, then. Give up this accursed idea."

What hurt her the most was that he did not even hesitate. "I cannot do that. There is too much at stake."

She'd already gone further than she'd intended, but the utter matter-of-factness of his answer goaded her on. "So you're saying, then, that avenging yourself upon Gruffydd ap Gwenwynwyn matters more than our marriage."

"No . . . but the survival of Wales does," he said, with a bluntness that took her breath away, and after that, there was nothing left to be said. Rising from the bed, Llewelyn strode to an open coffer, pulling out garments more or less at random. Ellen reached for her bedrobe, began to unbraid her hair with fingers that shook. They summoned neither his squires nor her ladies, dressed themselves in utter and suffocating silence. Llewelyn was still fumbling with his belt as he reached the door. There he paused, glancing back at his wife.

"You think I do not understand your anger," he said abruptly, "and you are wrong, for I do." Ellen put her hairbrush down, watching him warily, for although his words sounded conciliatory, his voice did not; it seemed edged in flint. "You have every reason to loathe de Mortimer, and your loyalty to your father is both natural and commendable. But we owe a greater loyalty to the living than to the dead, and you seem to have forgotten that. You are more than Simon de Montfort's daughter. You are also my wife, and that, too, you seem to have forgotten. I can only hope that your memory improves, Ellen—for both our sakes."

Ellen did not reply, and he jerked the door open, barely resisting the urge to slam it behind him. She sat very still, long after he'd gone, staring blindly at that closed door. The dawn mist had burned off by now, and a patch of sapphire-blue sky shimmered within the window's framed opening. The day was promising all the false, lulling warmth of a Michaelmas summer, but only the innocent would be taken in, those who'd not yet learned that such brief, bittersweet respites too often led to killing frost and the bone-crippling cold of an early winter.

LLEWELYN spared no time for breakfast, plunged at once into the day's work. He dictated letters to Madog Goch ap Iorwerth, constable of Penllyn, to the Abbot of Aberconwy, and the Justiciar of Chester. He got a report about storm damage to the Menai ferry. He discussed with his chamberlain the collection of court amercements, a major source of princely revenue. He agreed to preside over a perjury case during his Christmas court at Dolwyddelan. He authorized a Michaelmas payment due upon the thousand marks owed to his brother Rhodri. And he interrogated the eye-witness to a brawl that had broken out when one of his rhingylls had attempted to confiscate the goods of a man convicted of receiving stolen property.

To all appearances, he'd passed a busy and productive morning. But he was finding it unexpectedly difficult to concentrate upon the matters at hand. He struggled against the tide until noon, refusing to admit that the husband's distraction could prove stronger than the Prince's will. But eventually he gave up, sent Trevor to fetch his sword and scabbard from his bedchamber, and ordered his horse saddled.

His departure was delayed by the strenuous objections of his teulu, but Llewelyn's need for solitude was increasingly urgent, and he prevailed. His stallion was young and spirited, eager to run. He gave the animal its head, setting so swift a pace that Cricieth Castle soon disappeared into the distance.

He was riding into the wind and it whipped his hair about wildly, burned his face. He barely felt it, though, was equally oblivious to the low-lying hills and marshes stretching along either side of the road. He forded the River Dwfor at the commotal settlement of Dolbenmaen, and the tenants tending its desmesne lands stopped their work to gape as he passed, astonished that their Prince should suddenly appear in their midst like this, alone, accompanied by none of his household guard.

Llewelyn had not planned to depart for his meeting with Roger de Mortimer until Friday of the following week, for he'd wanted to be with Ellen on her twenty-ninth birthday. Now, though, he was reconsidering. Mayhap it might be for the best if he left early, if they had some time apart. He realized what an inadequate solution that was, but he was unable to come up with a better one. And underlying his anger and frustration was a new and unsettling anxiety. For the first time, he found himself thinking what would have been unthinkable even hours ago. What if Ellen did not come to her senses? Or when she did, what if, by then, it was too late? Once a foundation cracked, it put the entire building at risk. Was that true, as well, for a marriage?

Llewelyn's stallion shied as a hare broke from the bushes, flashed in front of them. Reining in, he stroked the horse's neck. It was lathered with sweat, and only then did he realize just how far they'd come. He had to go no more than twenty feet from the road to find water; Llŷn was crisscrossed with serpentine streams and shallow, muddy rivers. As the horse drank, he stretched his stiff muscles, measured the westward slide of the sun. He'd forgotten a flask, now knelt, cupped his hands, and drank, too. But he was also hungry and tired, and as he gazed at the road winding its way south, he knew suddenly that he did not want to make that long, wearying ride back to Cricieth—and Ellen.

Llewelyn studied the surrounding terrain, needing but a few moments to get his bearings, for he carried a mental map of his Welsh domains. Off to the southwest lay Bwlch Mawr; he'd once fought a battle within its shadow, scored a sweeping victory over the invading army led by his brothers, Owain and Davydd. He was only a few miles, then, from the monastery at Clynnog. His uncle Einion had a manor just south of Clynnog. Why not ride over, stay the night? Einion's health was failing, and he kept close to his own hearth these days; it would be good to pass some time together. It was an easy decision for Llewelyn to make; Einion's manor was far closer than Cricieth. But so reluctant was he to face Ellen while he was still so angry with her that he'd have found a way to justify his choice had the distance been twice as great. Mounting his horse again, he abandoned the road and headed west, cutting cross-country toward the ocean.

He knew when he was nearing the sea, alerted by the soft glow of light that hovered upon the horizon. Reaching the coast road, he drew rein, passed a few moments savoring the view. But as he was about to start south toward Clynnog, he heard the sound of approaching riders. A small group of horsemen were coming from the north, from the direction of Caer yn Arfon. Even at such a distance, Llewelyn could tell that they were well armed and well mounted. Curious, he wheeled his stallion, waited for them.

It would have been difficult to say which one was the more startled, Llewelyn or Davydd. Davydd was certainly the more pleased. After reining in abruptly at sight of his brother, he did a deliberately comic doubletake, then spurred his stallion forward, laughing. "I rarely see apparitions without a fair helping of wine, but I'd hardly expect to find the Lord Prince of Wales and Eryri loitering on the Clynnog Road—and alone, too, by God! If I had a suspicious mind, Llewelyn, I'd think you must have a tryst planned with some local lass. Of course you could have been waiting patiently by the roadside to bid me a personal, warm welcome, but even I find that far-fetched!"

It may have been Davydd's cocky grin. Or that recent ride through Bwlch Mawr Pass, where a lifetime's conflict with Davydd had begun. Or simply that he was tired, his nerves on edge. But suddenly Llewelyn heard himself saying belligerently, "What are you doing in Llŷn, Davydd? Do you think you can come and go in my domains as you will?"

Davydd lost his smile in a hurry. "I wrote last month," he said, "to let you know I'd be coming into Llŷn to see Owain. I thought that would be sufficient. Should I have asked for a safe-conduct?"

Llewelyn almost lashed back with the obvious retort, that in light of their history, he was the one likely to be in need of a safe-conduct. But he caught himself in time, for he was remembering now that Davydd had indeed written as he claimed. And Davydd's stiff, prideful tone did not completely camouflage what he'd never admit, that Llewelyn's angry rebuff had stung.

"It is my memory that is at fault," Llewelyn said reluctantly, "not you. I've much on my mind, and I forgot about your letter."

Had it been anyone but Davydd, Llewelyn would have gone further, offered a genuine apology rather than a hinted one. With Davydd, though, this was the best he could do. It was still more than Davydd had expected, and he nudged his mount closer, his eyes searching Llewelyn's face.

"What are you really doing out in the middle of nowhere by yourself, Llewelyn?"

"I'm sorry to disappoint you, but the explanation is not a sinister one. I was out riding, went farther than I'd meant to, and rather than riding all the way back to Cricieth, I decided to beg a meal and a bed from Einion."

Davydd was not buying that, but he let it drop, for the moment. "Is that why you look so careworn . . . hunger pangs? Lucky for you that I happened along when I did." Glancing back toward his waiting men, he waved them forward. "We'll stop here for a while, rest the horses, and eat."

Llewelyn started to protest, then stopped. Why not? In truth, he was ravenous, for he'd not had a morsel since yesterday. Davydd's men were already dismounting, unpacking the food, throwing flasks and insults about with equal abandon. Davydd gave his retainers a lot of leeway, but the only ones who lasted long in his service were those who learned early on that Davydd would overlook a great deal—provided that they were competent and discreet. Now, despite the rowdiness and tomfoolery, they soon found an alder tree, which could usually be relied upon to take root near water. This one was no exception, and, having tethered the horses by the brook, they then withdrew to eat just out of earshot of their lord and his brother.

Davydd picked up a basket, walked over into the shade cast by the alder. "Will this do?" he asked innocently, as if unaware of the widespread belief that evil spirits lurked in the shadow of alder trees. Llewelyn knew just how suspect was Davydd's innocence if any man did, but he accepted the challenge, and joined his brother under the alder. Davydd tossed him a wineskin, tore a loaf of bread in half, and threw that his way, too. Llewelyn was not surprised to find that Davydd had included a vial of salt, even napkins, for Davydd had always liked his comforts, unable to see any virtues in abstinence. "Here," Davydd said, "catch," and a leg of roast capon came sailing through the air. Llewelyn caught it just before it splashed into the stream, and then gave Davydd an accusing look.

"This is chicken," he said.

"Yes . . . so? I'm sure your lordship would rather have venison, but—"

"It is Wednesday, Davydd," Llewelyn said impatiently. "You know full well that the Church forbids the eating of meat on Wednesdays."

"Wednesday—are you sure?" Davydd's bluff faltered under Llewelyn's skeptical gaze, and he said grudgingly, "Aye, I know. But it was a choice between sinning and eating salted herring, and I chose the lesser evil. I do hope you're not going to lecture me now about my impious eating habits?"

Llewelyn shook his head. "No . . . I daresay you'll have such spectacular sins to answer for on Judgment Day that the question of salted herring will never even come up."

Davydd could not help grinning. "Jesú, but I walked right into that thrust, with shield down and sword sheathed!" Lounging back on the grass, he raised his own half-eaten chicken leg, gesturing toward the one Llewelyn held. "Life is full of hard choices, Brother. You can be sated and sinful, or righteous and hungry. Do not keep me in suspense; which will it be?"

He was being melodramatic, for Llewelyn's confessor would cheerfully absolve so small a sin with an easy penance. But he'd just given Llewelyn his first real smile of the day. Glancing thoughtfully at the chicken, Llewelyn said, "I could be wrong. It does look like capon. But I suppose it might be barnacle goose."

Davydd's eyes widened. Few myths were as popular as that of the barnacle goose, a wondrously strange beast said to hatch in the sea, for this belief allowed people to eat it in good conscience on fast days. But Llewelyn was the last man Davydd would have expected to put credence in so fishy a fable, and he eyed his brother now in some surprise. "Do you really believe that the barnacle goose is a sort of fish?" he asked, and Llewelyn shrugged.

"I will if you will," he said, and Davydd burst out laughing.

"I took that bait quick enough, never even felt the hook." Passing Llewelyn the salt, he said, "Well . . . what shall we talk about? We can always swap family gossip. I'll tell you what I heard about Rhodri's English bride if you—"

"Rhodri got married?"

"I take it you were not invited to the wedding either. Yes, our little brother snared himself an English heiress, crumbs from Edward's table. More than crumbs, actually, for Beatrice de Malpas brought Rhodri a manor in Surrey and lands in Cheshire . . . not to mention the God-given opportunity to live amidst English gentry. I'd wager that in no time at all he'll be quaffing ale and dining before noon and calling himself Sir Roderick."

Llewelyn gave Davydd a curious look. "Do you not think you're being rather hard on him? The both of us have English wives, too."

"Yes . . . but it is different with Rhodri. He's the worst sort of fool, Llewelyn, for he lacks the sense to value the only thing he truly has to be proud of—his Welsh blood."

Llewelyn had to defer to Davydd on that, for he simply did not know Rhodri well enough to say if Davydd's scathing assessment was correct or not. "At least that is one charge that can never be lain at your door. Whatever else men might say to you, no one could ever accuse you of not being utterly Welsh!"

That earned him an amused, faintly sardonic smile. "I assume you mean that I'm fully as contrary and fickle as the English expect us to be. But you ought to have a care, for that almost sounded approving. Llewelyn . . . I heard about Edward's latest sleight of hand. There is not a jongleur alive who'd not barter his soul for Edward's bag of tricks. The best of them can only hope to make a dove disappear, whilst Edward plucks an entire cantref right out of Wales, waves his sceptre, and lo, Arwystli is of a sudden located in England. Why did he not spare Christendom all those lives lost striving to free Jerusalem from the infidels? Would it not have been easier had he just declared it to be English, too, like Arwystli?"

Llewelyn would have sworn that he'd never be able to find any humor in Edward's Arwystli double-dealing, but as usual, he'd reckoned without Davydd's sense of the absurd. Laughing, he reached for another piece of chicken. "Simon de Montfort used to contend that serving King Henry put him in mind of an ancient Greek King, the one condemned to push a boulder up a hill for all eternity, only to have it roll down each time he reached the top. Well, we start rolling that damnable rock up the hill again next week, when my attorneys argue my case once more before Edward's English justices at Montgomery."

Davydd could not hide his dismay. "Christ, Llewelyn, you do not still believe you can get justice in Edward's court, do you?"

In truth, Llewelyn had never fully believed that, and he'd long ago begun to prepare for the day that his suspicions were borne out; for more than three years, he'd had a secret understanding with Gruffydd ap Gwenwynwyn's Seneschal. But he was not about to share that with Davydd.

"No," he said, "of course I do not believe it, Davydd. That is why I am going to Radnor next week to meet with Roger de Mortimer."

"De Mortimer?" Davydd's surprise was fleeting, giving way almost at once to jubilant comprehension. "Of course—his lands in Maelienydd border upon Arwystli! This is a masterful stratagem, Llewelyn. A seemingly straightforward pact of alliance, right? Ah, but with so much left unsaid, so much left to Gruffydd ap Gwenwynwyn's fevered imagination. The potential for conspiracy and mischief-making is truly awesome here. Even if you never call upon de Mortimer for battlefield aid, the mere fact that you could is sure to rob men of sleep. I just cannot decide if you're being forthrightly devious, or overtly underhanded, but whichever, I like it—a lot."

Llewelyn grinned. "Yes, I thought you might."

"Wait until Gruffydd ap Gwenwynwyn hears about this . . . By the Rood, how I'd love to be the one to tell him!" Davydd laughed, and Llewelyn wondered if he even remembered just then that he and Gruffydd had once been linked together in a murder plot. "I tell you, Llewelyn, this idea of yours is inspired, is good enough to be mine! With this one pact, you'll vex Edward beyond measure, rattle Gruffydd down to his very bones, and set tongues wagging from Wales to Westminster. There is even a chance, however remote, that Edward might allow his court to try your case on the actual merits, once he understands that you're willing to go to war against Gruffydd to hold on to Arwystli. Not that I'd want to wager my life's last breath on it! Still, though, it is not beyond the realm of possibility."

Davydd's enthusiasm was running away with him, but he seemed to be thoroughly enjoying the ride. "Of course if it does come to war, de Mortimer will expect a portion of the spoils, but you're more than a match—"

He stopped so abruptly that Llewelyn glanced up in surprise. "De Mortimer—of course! Cousin Roger is doing double duty here, making ready to sow discord amongst your enemies whilst wreaking havoc in your marriage!" Davydd's grin was triumphant; he could never abide a mystery, and he was pleased by how quickly he'd solved this one. "That is it? Why you're out here on your own—"

"Davydd," Llewelyn said sharply, warningly.

"I know I'm right, Llewelyn. It makes perfect sense. Now I may be high up on your wife's list, but Roger—"

"What list?"

"Men she'd like to see end their days as galley slaves. In all modesty, though, I cannot hold a candle to de Mortimer. Ellen likes me not, but she'd thank God fasting for the chance to do old Roger an ill turn. Not that I blame her. Our de Mortimer cousin gets his enemies the honest way; he earns them, each and every one. She'd never embrace de Mortimer as an ally . . . and I daresay she's no longer keen on embracing you! Women may not be the most logical of God's creatures, but they do know how to wield the weapons He gave them—"

"You are wasting your breath and my time, Davydd. That door is locked and bolted. What happens between my wife and myself is no one else's concern, least of all, yours."

Davydd was unfazed. "If you admit it, then I can help. You've already made your first mistake, but—"

"Have I, indeed?"

"Yes, you have, for certes. You told her about it!"

Llewelyn gave his brother an astonished look, then an incredulous laugh. "You cannot be serious? You expect me to believe that if you were in my place, you'd not have told Elizabeth about the pact?"

"Nary a word."

Llewelyn felt the same morbid fascination that drew people to fires and public hangings. "Let's take this madness a bit further. You make the alliance, and you tell Elizabeth nothing about it. What in God's Name do you then, when she eventually finds out?"

"Well, first of all, I'd not worry about it until she did. She might not, after all. But if the worst did happen, I'd trust that I'd come up with something."

Llewelyn shook his head. "I will go to my grave," he said, "never understanding how a man so clever can be so indifferent to consequences."

Davydd had begun to root around in the basket again. But he looked up quickly at that. "I'm not indifferent," he said. "Sometimes consequences just do not turn out as we expected them to . . ."

There was an unexpectedly poignant, unfinished quality to that sentence. It seemed to hang in the air between them, fraught with all that had been left unsaid. Their eyes caught, held. And then, by common consent, they let the moment go, too wary to venture further. Davydd was the first to look away. He passed out the last of the chicken, making another jest about barnacle geese, and they moved on to safer ground, back to the familiar banter and verbal sparring, but not quite as barbed as before, not quite as guarded. Some yards away, Davydd's escort sprawled comfortably in the sun, joking amongst themselves, looking over occasionally toward the alder tree, hearing laughter and marveling that these two men could sound so relaxed with each other, so oddly at ease.

EINION had been delighted by the unexpected arrival of his nephews. He'd welcomed them joyfully, tactfully concealing his surprise that Llewelyn should turn up without his bodyguards and in Davydd's company, and they had passed an amicable evening together. Llewelyn was shocked, though, to see how rapidly Einion's strength was waning. Suffering from "heart-pain" and shortness of breath, he seemed to have aged years in a matter of months. Davydd had confided that Owain, too, was ailing again, stricken by the crippling "joint-evil" that brought such misery to so many. Watching as Einion made a gallant attempt to mask his discomfort, thinking of Owain, Llewelyn and Davydd exchanged glances, sharing the same thought, that death was not to be feared as much as those maladies that left a man alive but enfeebled, a still strong will entrapped within an infirm body.

Davydd departed early the next morning for Owain's lands to the south, but Llewelyn lingered, enjoying Einion's company, not yet ready to face his wife. A night's sleep had changed nothing, provided no new insights into his dilemma. He'd long known that Ellen had an idealized, visionary view of her father. Hers was the uncritical, adoring devotion of an innocent, for time had frozen for her as well as for Simon on that August day at Evesham. It was easy for Llewelyn to understand, and equally easy to accept—until now, until Roger de Mortimer robbed him of the woman that young girl had become, and he found himself unable to get past the daughter, to reach his wife.

It was late afternoon when he bade Einion farewell, and with an escort provided by his uncle, began his reluctant journey back to Cricieth. They set an unhurried pace, and were traveling with lit lanterns by the time the castle loomed up against the darkening sky, high above the sea, its towering battlements crowned in mist.

Trevor darted forward as Llewelyn dismounted, materializing so swiftly that Llewelyn knew he must have been keeping vigil. Llewelyn spared some moments for the boy, for he was well aware that Trevor was convinced he could walk on water if he had a mind to, but all the while his eyes kept straying across the bailey, toward the lights flooding the upper windows of the southwest tower, where Ellen awaited him.

She was standing by a window as he entered, clad in one of her favorite gowns, a flattering shade of sapphire. But tonight the vivid color only served to accentuate her pallor, to call attention to the shadows smudged under her eyes.

"I did not know when to expect you," she said, "for Einion's messenger said you might not be returning till the morrow. Are you hungry? I can rouse the cooks . . ."

"Thank you, but that will not be necessary. We stopped and ate by the roadside."

She nodded. "Well, then . . . are you thirsty? What would you like . . .?"

"Mayhap some wine."

"Red? White?"

"Either one will do. Thank you." He watched as she moved to the door to summon a servant. This was intolerable. Not even beggars seeking alms were as polite as this. But what she wanted to hear, he could not say.

Ellen returned to the chamber more quickly than he expected, or desired. She hovered nearby while he unbuckled his scabbard, hung it on a chair. As he pulled his dusty, travel-stained tunic over his head, she took it from him, carried it across the chamber, and stuffed it into a sack for their laundress.

"You've torn the sleeve of your shirt," she said. "I'll see that it is mended." And then, "Llewelyn . . . I hate this. I can hardly breathe, feel as if a weight were pressing against my chest. How did things go so wrong between us, and . . . and what if we cannot get them right again?"

"I hate it, too, Ellen," he admitted. "But I am not sure that now is the time to try to sort it all out. I've been in the saddle for hours, am bone-weary . . ."

"I am, too," she said. "I lay awake till dawn, thinking. In truth, that is all I've done for these past two days. I thought about us, about my father, about Roger de Mortimer, about what you said to me yesterday morn, and the way you looked at me then, as if you did not like me very much at that moment."

He seemed about to speak, and she shook her head. "Please . . . hear me out. I did not mean that as a reproach." She found for him a very wan smile. "You see, I did not like you very much at that moment, either. And it scared me, that I did not."

"I know," he said quietly, for he did.

"I was so wroth with you, Llewelyn. But I was wretchedly unhappy, too, so unhappy I feared I'd sicken on it. I knew you thought I was being unreasonable, and so I forced myself to go over it in my mind, to remember all I've ever been told about Evesham."

She drew a deep, hurtful breath, then gestured toward her swollen, bloodshot eyes. "I know you can tell I've been weeping. But my tears were not all for you. I wept, too, for my father and for the brutal way he died. I made myself think about how it must have been for him, and about what they did to him, all the shameful, loathsome cruelties . . . Roger de Mortimer's cruelties. And when I was done, I knew that I could never forgive de Mortimer, never. And I knew, too, that I had the right to hate him. As Simon de Montfort's daughter, I need make no apologies for that, nor will I."

She saw him stiffen, and said quickly, "I am not done yet. There is more. I realized that you, too, had right on your side, for what you said was true. I had indeed forgotten what I owed to you, and for that, I do seek your pardon. Nothing in my life has given me greater joy than being your wife. In this past week, I let myself forget that, forget that my loyalties are pledged to you, just as my heart is. But I promise you that it will not happen again."

Llewelyn crossed the space between them. "And you'll be able to accept my alliance with Roger de Mortimer?"

She nodded somberly. "I shall have to, shan't I?"

He felt no triumph; there was too much pain in her eyes for that. But he did feel an intense relief, overwhelming enough to render him speechless. Taking her in his arms, he held her close, for he now knew— they both knew—that marital vows might bind them unto death, but love was far more fragile, love could be lost.

ON the 9th of October in God's Year, 1281, a "treaty of peace and indissoluble concord" was entered into by Llewelyn ap Gruffydd, Prince of Wales, and Roger de Mortimer, Lord of Wigmore, in which they pledged to support each other, both in time of war and peace, against all men, save only the King of England, his brother, and heirs.

IN early December, Llewelyn had a clandestine meeting with the man who was Seneschal to Gruffydd ap Gwenwynwyn, but privately pledged to Llewelyn. Their secret colloquy was cut short, however, by the inclement winter weather. It had been, all would agree, an odd, unpredictable year, heavy spring and summer rains yielding to a brief, beautiful autumn, and now ending in an unseasonably early cold spell. There had been one major snowstorm already, even before November was done. The roads were mired in frigid mud, sleet pelted the last leaves from the trees, and the wretched people huddling before their hearths knew that the worst still lay ahead. As the second week of Advent began, the sky was flying such storm warnings that Llewelyn and his covert ally agreed they'd best hasten their departure; it would, they joked grimly, ill serve their conspiracy to be snowbound together.

Llewelyn left Beddgelert Priory at dawn, raced the snowclouds north. He won, by the narrowest of margins. Snow had begun to fall by the time he reached the Lledr Valley, but Dolwyddelan was soon in sight, a torch-lit beacon beckoning from the crest of its high, rocky hill.

Trevor bolted from the great hall as they rode into the bailey. He'd not even paused to collect his mantle, so thankful was he that his lord had come safely back from his mysterious mission. He stood shivering in the snow as Llewelyn sent his men into the hall to thaw out, and squirmed in pleased embarrassment when Llewelyn chided him for courting frostbite. But when Llewelyn started for the keep, beckoning him to follow, he backed away in confusion.

"My lord, I . . . I cannot go up to your chamber. Your lady wife . . . she is taking a bath!"

Llewelyn arched a brow. "And just how do you know that?"

Trevor flushed bright red, began to stammer that he'd seen the servants lugging buckets of water up the stairs. But then he looked more closely into his lord's face, gave an abashed smile. "Oh! You were jesting!"

"Yes, lad," Llewelyn said patiently, "I was jesting." Llewelyn had grown fond of Trevor, whose devotion to duty even Hugh might envy. But the boy insisted upon taking Llewelyn's lightest utterances as Holy Writ, and Llewelyn sometimes suspected that Trevor had been cheated of one of life's strongest shields, a sense of humor. He smiled now at his squire—young, eager, turning blue with cold—and ordered him back into the hall before he froze those body parts he would least like to lose. Trevor grinned shyly, trotted off through the snow. It was falling faster now; Llewelyn quickened his step, grateful that he would not be out on the roads this night, but snug before his own hearth.

He encountered a servant on the stairs, laden with a flagon and ginger-filled wafers. Taking the tray himself, Llewelyn crossed the fore-building drawbridge, knocked briskly on his bedchamber door. Fortunately, it was not Eluned who opened it, for Hugh's young wife would have spoiled his surprise then and there. But Juliana needed no prompting. She bit back the cry that rose to her lips, gave Llewelyn a co-conspirator's grin, and then she was gone, snatching up her mantle and making a discreet departure for the hall. Llewelyn spared a moment to bless both her tact and her timing, and then shut the door upon the storm, slid the bolt into place.

Ellen's back was to the door. The tub had been dragged so close to the hearth that she risked being singed by its heat, but she liked to linger over her bath until the water began to cool. Llewelyn had never known anyone who took such sensual delight in bathing, and once he'd learned of her secret vice, he'd been quite willing to indulge it. The wooden tub had been custom-made to his specifications, twice the usual size, round and deep and well sanded to protect her skin from splinters, the rim padded so she could lie back in comfort. By now Llewelyn knew the rituals she would follow, knew that the water would be scented with rosemary and chamomile, that she would lather herself with liquid French soap, and as she soaked, she would slowly sip a goblet of wine. Then, when she was done and dried off, she would dust herself lavishly with a fragrant powder. The routine never varied, and he had yet to tire of watching it, especially on a night like this, when the wind was rising, and the castle lay under a white, silent siege.

Ellen's hair had been swept up, but a few long strands were defying their pins. They trailed in the water, lay wet and gleaming against her breasts, giving her the look of a modest mermaid, one who happened, however, to be singing a song bawdy enough to have made her confessor blush. Llewelyn would have lingered a moment longer by the door, enjoying the flickering play of firelight upon her skin. But she interrupted her song to ask Juliana if that had been the wine, and he crossed the chamber, reached down for her out-stretched, waiting hand, and pressed a kiss into her palm.

Ellen's eyes snapped open; she sat up with a splash. "Llewelyn!" More water splashed, but as quickly as she rose from the tub to fling her arms around his neck, just as quickly did she recoil, for his mantle was glazed with unmelted snow.

Llewelyn laughed, freed the clasp, and let the mantle fall to the floor. "Let's try that again," he said, and Ellen came back into his arms, warm and wet and smelling of rosemary. The tub was so full that her movements sent water sloshing over the sides, onto the floor and Llewelyn's boots. He got even wetter as he lifted her out of the tub, but he did not care. Plucking the pins from her hair, he kissed her mouth, then her throat.

"When a mortal man catches a mermaid, does she not have to pay a forfeit for her freedom? If memory serves, I think he gets to keep her tail."

"That is a scandalous way to talk to your wife," Ellen scolded, but she would have been more convincing had her voice not quivered with laughter. "We did not expect you back until Thursday, at the earliest. I had such a special welcome planned," she said and sighed regretfully. "We were going to have all your favorite foods, Gruffydd ab yr Ynad Coch was composing a song for your pleasure, and I was going to wear my newest gown, the crimson one with the lace—"

She got no further; he kissed her again. "Actually," he said, "I like you better like this, soft and slippery."

"And shivering," she added with a smile, and began to wrap herself in a towel, deftly sidestepping his attempt to snatch it away.

"Are all mermaids so skittish? Why are you in such a hurry to put your clothes on? It would make more sense if I got rid of mine, joined you in the bath. Generous lass that you are, you've shared half of it with me, already."

Ellen giggled. "The last time we tried that, we flooded the room! But if you really want to risk drowning again, I am willing. Not yet, though. First we must talk, beloved. I have a gift for you, and I would give it now."

"A New Year's gift? But that is still more than a fortnight away."

"I know, but I cannot wait any longer, not another moment. And it is not just a New Year's gift. It is also a very early birthday gift, a belated anniversary gift."

"One gift in lieu of all that? I think I am sure to come out on the losing side here, for how could any one gift possibly be as wondrous as . . . as that?"

She caught the telling pause, so quickly covered up, knew exactly what he'd found himself thinking at that moment, and it hurt her to see how swiftly he'd rejected it, as if hope had become the enemy.

"Say it, my love," she entreated. "Say what we both know to be true—that only one gift could be as great as that—a son and heir."

"Ah, Ellen . . ." he said softly, and she reached up, gently laid her fingers to his lips.

"You do not understand, not yet. That is what I am telling you, Llewelyn, that is my gift. I am with child."

Llewelyn's breath stopped. "You are sure?"

Ellen nodded. "Yes, my darling, yes . . . oh, yes!" She laughed up at him, and there was on her face a look of such pure and perfect happiness that he no longer doubted.

"I kept telling myself it was not to be, and I tried to accept it, God Above, how I tried!" He touched his fingers to her cheek. "I've loved no woman as I've loved you," he said huskily, "and now you have given me what no other woman could . . ." She thought she saw the glint of tears, but before she could be sure, he'd caught her up in his arms, carrying her across the room and putting her down upon the bed, all the while looking at her with such tenderness that she felt sure she'd never know such intense, abiding joy again—not until that moment when she held her son for the first time.

She'd lost her towel on the way to the bed, and he amused her now by insisting she get under the covers at once, not sitting beside her until he had positioned pillows behind her back. "How far along are you, Ellen?"

"Last week I missed my flux again—for the third time."

"Three!" Llewelyn was taken aback. "Why did you not tell me ere this . . . and how were you able to hide it?"

"Why is obvious, beloved. I would not raise your hopes only to see them cruelly dashed down. I wanted to tell you so much, Llewelyn, but I had to be sure first. I could not bear to break your heart with a false hope. As for how, that was rather easy. I missed my first flux in October, whilst you were at Radnor with Roger de Mortimer. That was as hard a thing as I've ever done, keeping silent when you returned! And then, I missed again in Martinmas week. I did not lie, my love, just said nothing. I knew you did not keep track of my monthly flux on your own, not since the first months of our marriage, and as you were away twice in November, I felt sure you'd assume it must have come during one of your absences . . . and you did, no?"

He nodded, and she caught his hand, pressed it between her breasts. "Can you feel my heart, Llewelyn? I hope it is not sinful to be so happy! Last week, when again my flux failed to come, I began to count the hours until you got home, until I could tell you. On Sunday I had Hugh take Juliana and me up the road to Trefriw, and I consulted secretly with Dame Blodwen, for I'd heard she is one of the best midwives in all of Gwynedd. She confirmed what I already knew, that I am indeed pregnant."

Llewelyn could not stop touching her, stroking her damp, disheveled hair, following the golden gleam of her crucifix chain. "When, cariad?"

"Mid-June. When I told the midwife that my last flux had been whilst we were at Hafod-y-Llan in September, she said I conceived in the following fortnight—during our time at Cricieth, during one of those nights after we'd made our peace and ere you left for Radnor." She smiled suddenly, wickedly. "Remember what I told you, that those were nights I'd not soon forget?"

"If we are picking one in particular when the deed was done," he said with a grin, "I'd put my money on that Thursday, the night I came back from Einion's." June . . . a good time to bring a child into the world. Summer babies, he knew, had an easier time of it than those born during the dark, bleak days of a Welsh winter.

"Llewelyn . . . can we pick a name tonight?"

"We can do whatever you like, cariad. I have an uneasy suspicion that the balance of power has suddenly shifted in this marriage," he said, and laughed.

Ellen laughed, too, for laughter came to them both as easily as breathing this night. "I know better than that, my lord Prince of Wales, and I shall mercifully refrain from holding you to those rash words once you sober up!"

He realized there was truth in her teasing, for he knew now that it was indeed possible to get as drunk on joy as on mead. Sliding his arm around her shoulders, he drew her in against his chest. "If my lady wants to talk of names, then we shall. How about Siwan for a girl and—" He stopped in surprise, for Ellen was already shaking her head. "I thought you would fancy that one for certes. You do know, cariad, that Siwan is Welsh for Joanna?"

"Yes, I do. But we have no need to consider names for a lass. I am carrying a son."

"God grant it so. But how can you be so sure?"

"I just know," she said simply, with such utter conviction that he found it very easy to believe her, to believe that mayhap women truly could tell such things.

"I want you to choose the name, Llewelyn. I ask only that it be a name I can pronounce . . . and that it not be Davydd. I know he is the patron saint of the Welsh, but I think one Davydd in your family is more than enough! The Welsh do not often name sons after the fathers, do they? What of Gruffydd, then, after your own father?"

"No, lass, I have another name in mind. A name that the Welsh will like well, for it belonged to a man whose exploits were celebrated in our Mabinogi. And one that will please you, too, Ellen, for it will be a living link between your past and our future." Raising her face up to his, he said, "Should you like to name our son Bran?"

He had just betrayed himself, for the name came too rapidly to his lips, a name born of long hours of wishful yearning, of a hunger so deep it burned to the bone, but one he'd denied again and again in these past three years—for her sake, for a beloved, barren wife. Tears filled Ellen's eyes. She nodded mutely, the words catching in her throat, and reached for his hand. Drawing it under the covers, she laid it against her belly.

"My lord husband," she said, "meet Bran ap Llewelyn. Meet your son."

28

DOLWYDDELAN, WALES

December 1281

THE brutal winter weather had not kept the lords of Wales from braving the high mountain passes. From North Powys came Llewelyn Fychan ap Gruffydd Maelor, Lord of Nanheudwy and Cynllaith, and his brother Gruffydd Fychan, Lord of Ial. From the south came Cynan ap Maredudd and Rhys Fychan, Lords of Ceredigion, and Rhys Wyndod, Lord of the Vale of Tywi, and his younger brother, Llewelyn ap Rhys of Is Cennen. And from the Perfeddwlad came the most surprising arrival of all, the Lord of Dinbych and Yr Hob, Llewelyn ap Gruffydd's brother Davydd.

And as word spread of their presence at Dolwyddelan, Llewelyn's troubled countrymen began to converge upon his court, bearing their grievances against the English Crown like Christmas offerings for their Prince. One by one they rose to speak in the great hall, to reveal their wrongs, their rage, and their yearning for vengeance.

Some of their complaints spoke to affronted pride, others struck at the heart, but through them all echoed a common cry, one of loss—of lands, of dignity, of hope.

Men whose lands had been seized to build Edward's castle at Flynt charged that the royal promises of compensation were never honored. Men who'd brought goods to sell in the new borough of Rhuddlan told how they were compelled to sell only to the English, at prices set by the English, and those who balked were gaoled and beaten. Their woods were cut down, without recompense. Their laws were mocked. And as each man came forward to bare his wounds, the hall fell silent; here at least their voices would be heard.

Einion ab Ithel claimed that because he drove his oxen through the streets of Oswestry, he was beaten and both of his oxen taken from him. Ithel ap Gwysty was fined a vast sum for a crime committed by his father forty years before. Iorwerth ap Gwrgwneu was fined for escaping from an English prison during the war. Others spoke of the harshness of the English forest laws, so alien to the Welsh; three men lost all they owned for one foot of a stag found in a dog's mouth. The church of St Davydd at Llangadog was used by the English as a stable, the priest stabbed and left bleeding before the altar, and none were called to account for it. The new Justiciar of Chester, Reginald de Grey, claimed the lands of the men of Merton without cause and bestowed them upon the Abbot of Basingwerk.

There were many hated officials of the English Crown—Bogo de Knovill, Roger Clifford, John Giffard, Roger Lestrange—but none were loathed as much as de Grey. Again and again his name was heard in the hall, until by repetition alone it began to sound like a curse. De Grey had forced free Welshmen to plough his lands like English serfs. English masons from Rhuddlan Castle assaulted a Welshwoman passing by, attacking her husband when he sought to defend her, and when the family of the slain woman captured the killers and brought them to de Grey for justice, he set them free, then arrested the complaining kinsmen. He accused the men of Rhos and Tegeingl of trespasses committed in the reign of the present King's late father, and demanded money to forgo prosecution. He violated the terms of his King's own treaty and harassed the Welsh so shamelessly that they despaired of ever finding justice in his courts. How long must they endure his tyranny? How long must they deal with the Devil?

Later, when Llewelyn and his highborn guests were at ease in the great chamber of the castle's new West Tower, those were questions that trailed after them, lurking unanswered beneath their guarded courtesies, shadowing their occasional silences.

There was much that lay unspoken between these men, for most of them had abandoned Llewelyn four years ago to save their own lands. But there was also between them an affinity that could not be disavowed, one of blood. Rhys Wyndod, his brother Llewelyn, Rhys Fychan, and Cynan ap Maredudd were cousins, great-grandsons of the Lord Rhys, most renowned of all the southern princes. Rhys Wyndod and his brothers were also nephews of the Prince of Wales, son of Llewelyn's long-dead sister. The Lords of North Powys, Llewelyn Fychan and Gruffydd Fychan, were his kinsmen, too, albeit much more distant ones. Llewelyn no longer trusted kinship, if ever he did; if a blood bond could not bind his brother to him, how could it hold fast nephews or cousins? But theirs was still a common heritage, a shared history in which regrets, resentments, ambitions, and jealousies all existed in uneasy accord.

Servants stoked the hearth, refilled mead cups, and discreetly withdrew. The silence that had fallen as the servants entered lingered after they departed, a silence that was speculative, wary, and yet expectant. Llewelyn had been awaiting just such an opening. "I think it is time," he said, "to speak of our own grievances against the English King."

There was a moment more of quiet, and then the chamber was reverberating with the sounds of anger. Voices were raised, chairs shoved back, fists slammed down upon the oaken table with enough force to alarm Nia, Llewelyn's canine shadow. Llewelyn made no attempt to exert control, let them vent their rage as they pleased, interrupting one another in their haste to share the injustices each had suffered at English hands.

None of their complaints were unfamiliar to Llewelyn; he'd kept a close watch upon all of their dealings with the English Crown, knew their wrongs as he did his own. His cousin of North Powys had seen his lands raided by the Marcher lord John Fitz Alan, had been feuding for several years now with the constable of Oswestry, Roger Lestrange. He had also endured the humiliation of being abducted by the sons of Gruffydd ap Gwenwynwyn, and then of being unable to avenge himself afterward upon his assailants, for none stood higher in royal favor than the Lord of South Powys. Llewelyn's nephew, Rhys Wyndod, had lost his castles at Dinefwr, Carreg Cennen, and Llandovery, and when he'd sought to defend his rights in Hirwryn against the claims of John Giffard, he'd discovered that no Welsh quagmire could bog men down as hopelessly as an English court case. Cynan ap Maredudd and his absent brother had been deprived of their lands in Geneu'r Glyn and Creuddyn. And these were all men who'd yielded to Edward, lain down their swords in a vain attempt at self-preservation. Those who'd spurned accommodations had paid an even greater price; Rhys Wyndod's brothers had been stripped of all they'd once held for their failure to forsake Llewelyn in those desperate months of 1277.

Davydd had so far kept silent. But once some of their passion had been spent; once their fury no longer burned at full flame, he said, "Let Goronwy ap Heilyn be heard now, for I know no one who has greater grievances against Reginald de Grey, not even myself."

Davydd had been attracting more than his share of suspicious glances, for most men saw distinct differences between surrender and collaboration. But Goronwy commanded both liking and respect, and none begrudged him a chance to speak of his wrongs.

Goronwy was not disconcerted to find himself the focus of all eyes. "I hardly know where to begin," he said, "but I will confine myself to the most arrant offenses. One of my tenants was brought before the King's court on a false charge, and although I sought to testify on his behalf, he was fined twenty-seven pounds, a sum so great he'd need three lifetimes in which to pay it. Then a man whose friendship I held dear, one whom I'd trusted to foster my son, was slain. His kinsmen brought the killer to Rhuddlan, demanding justice. But they were the ones cast into prison, whilst the killer went free. De Grey took away the bailiwick given to me by the King and sold it for his own profit. Then there was the trouble over Maenan and Llysfayn, lands I'd leased for a four-year term. Sir Robert Cruquer, a knight of de Grey's household, attempted to evict me from these lands by force, and when I resisted, de Grey summoned me to answer in court. There he had men at arms ready to seize me, and would have done so had I not been warned beforehand, come accompanied by an armed force of my own. He even dared threaten to have me beheaded, and only the presence of the Bishop of St Asaph stayed his hand."

Goronwy's dark eyes glinted with remembered rage, but he kept his voice even, as if recounting another man's misfortunes, for so great was his sense of outrage that he'd been forced to distance himself from it. "Three times," he said, "I traveled to London, seeking justice from the English King. Three times I came away with nothing but empty, hollow promises, promises that were never kept. I'll not go a fourth time, that I swear upon the soul of my son."

There was not a man present who could not identify with Goronwy's complaints, but their commiserations were cut short by Davydd, who said, "Now it is my turn. I'll concede straightaway that my legal troubles with that whoreson de Vanabeles are less entangled than Rhys Wyndod's lawsuit against John Giffard, and as for Arwystli . . ." Here he gave his brother a sudden, sideways grin. "Do they know yet, Llewelyn? Tell them about the latest twist in a road already as crooked as Edward's ethics!"

Llewelyn's smile was almost amused, for he'd had more than a month to come to terms with Edward's latest ploy. "Gruffydd ap Gwenwynwyn is now claiming that my case against him cannot proceed without the King's writ. And Edward has informed me—brace yourselves for a great surprise—that they just cannot seem to find the original writ. Since they cannot, he is most regretful, but we'll have to begin the case all over again, as if the past four years had never been. Who would have guessed that an English lawsuit could have as long a lifespan as any man's? It gives a whole new meaning to the concept of perpetuity, does it not? The next time that I grant a charter 'forever and aye,' mayhap I ought to add, 'or the end of the Arwystli lawsuit, whichever occurs first.' "

There was laughter at that, but not from Rhys Wyndod, who could find no humor in the subject of lawsuits, not after being yoked to John Giffard in an English court for the past two years. "How can you jest about it?" he asked in genuine bemusement, and Llewelyn shrugged.

"Because," he said, "I'll not let Edward rob me of laughter, too." Glancing toward his brother, he said, "Go on, Davydd. Say what you will."

There were some startled looks, for few could remember the last time he'd addressed Davydd so affably. But if Davydd was surprised, too, he hid it well.

"I could set forth my grievances in just three words: Reginald de Grey. But the truth is that he's merely the puppet, doing the bidding of the royal puppeteer at Westminster. They've harassed my men, cut down my woods at Llyweny and Caergwrle, and refused to make good my losses. Nigh on four years ago I agreed to an exchange of manors with my wife's stepson, provided that I would be compensated for the difference in value, but I've yet to receive so much as a farthing. And then there are the vills in Dyffryn Clwyd. They were held for life by my aunt, Gwenllian de Lacy. I never met the lady, for Llewelyn Fawr had wed her to one of the de Lacys ere I was even born, and she lived out all her days in Ireland. But I hold Dyffryn Clwyd now, and when she died last month, those vills ought to have passed to me. Instead Edward claimed them, proving once again that thievery and statecraft are but two sides of the same English coin."

He had their attention, but Davydd could see thinly veiled satisfaction on some faces, a so-what skepticism on others. "When I learned that outlaws were lurking in the woods near my castle at Caergwrle and preying upon travelers," he said in sudden anger, "I had them hunted down and hanged. My reward was to have de Grey accuse me of harboring them all along and warn me that my sons could always be held as hostages until I mended my manners!"

There were murmurings at that, and even a few glances of surprised sympathy. "Yes," Davydd said, still angrily, "at the moment I wanted to kill him, I admit it. But for what? For doing what he's told? To hear men talk today, he might well be the true Prince of Darkness. But he's not; he's merely Edward of England's lackey. And when he strews sun-dried straw about and then saunters by with a lit flame, it's because Edward bloody well wants him to!"

Davydd checked himself with an effort, ignored the others, and gave Llewelyn a probing look. "Is it your wish to speak now?" he asked, with a deference that was not entirely free of challenge. "Why did you summon us to Dolwyddelan?"

"To talk," Llewelyn said, "of war."

There was a stir among the men, but no real surprise, for that was what they were expecting—even hoping—to hear. Rhys Wyndod made an emphatic, involuntary gesture of assent, balling a fist and driving it into the palm of his hand, while the aggrieved Lord of North Powys nodded in grim satisfaction, and his brother sat up straight in his chair, squaring his shoulders with an odd mixture of bravado and resignation. Goronwy looked somber but approving, a few looked dubious, a few more, pleased. But no reaction was as spontaneous or as revealing as Davydd's; he gave a loud, ringing laugh in which triumph vied with relief.

"I knew it," he exulted, "knew you'd come to see that there is no other way, that we have to fight!"

Llewelyn regarded him impassively for a moment. "I doubt that there is a Welshman breathing who does not know war is coming," he said. "But not yet. Not until we've done our part, for this will not be a war to leave to Fortune or Fate or even the manifold mercies of the Almighty. Against a foe like Edward, we shall have to make the most of every advantage, to turn to our benefit time and weather and random chance itself, and even then we'll still need the luck of the angels, the blessings of every Welsh saint in martyrdom, and the prayers of all our people, both the living and the dead."

That was not what they'd wanted from him. Llewelyn saw it on their faces, saw their disappointment, and a stray, subversive thought came shooting from the back of his brain, came perilously close to escaping into speech: Just where were all these firebrands four years ago when an English army was starving Gwynedd into submission?

Davydd was frowning. "That was eloquently said, vividly expressed. But what does it mean? That we continue to let the English treat us like serfs and bondsmen? How much offal can we swallow ere we choke on it? I'm not saying I do not understand your caution, Llewelyn. But if a wolf was raiding your flock, would you comfort yourself that he was only taking one sheep at a time? No, by God, you'd put a stop to it whilst you still had sheep left to steal!"

Llewelyn lost all patience. "In case it has escaped your notice, we are not facing a lone, marauding wolf! One of the worst mistakes a man can make is to hold his enemies too cheaply. Edward Plantagenet is one of the greatest soldiers in Christendom, and we forget that at our peril. You'd best bear in mind that he not only out-fought Simon de Montfort at Evesham, he outwitted him first. And this 'wolf' of yours, Davydd, has all the resources of the English Crown at his command, wealth and men we cannot hope to match. Lastly, we need to remember that he truly believes he is doing God's work in bringing Wales under his control, and a man with a sense of divine mission is a very dangerous foe, indeed."

"What are you saying, that we are bound to lose?"

"I am saying, Davydd, that we can make no mistakes, none at all. We cannot afford to plunge ahead heedlessly, to be rash or reckless, not with so much at stake. We owe our children—and their children— better than that, for they, too, would have to pay the price for our failure, a price higher than most of us could imagine."

They were listening intently now, but with some resentment. Llewelyn knew why, knew the risks of lecturing proud men. But he could not help himself; his sense of urgency was too great, overriding all else, even political acumen.

"So what, then, would you have us do, Uncle?"

Llewelyn glanced thoughtfully at Rhys Wyndod, then let his gaze shift to take in the others, moving slowly from face to face. "We can begin," he said, "by talking of iron and salt and cloth and corn and wine, all the goods that we buy from England. Our people have to be ready for a long, drawn-out siege. Our larders must be stocked and our coffers filled, for Edward's fleet will enforce an embargo we cannot hope to break."

"That does make sense," Cynan ap Maredudd said grudgingly. "But whilst we lay plans for the morrow, what about today? What about the abuses and injustices heaped upon us now? Do we just endure it all as best we can?"

His tone was incredulous, that of a man suggesting a tactic he'd already dismissed as ludicrous. His shock was all the greater, therefore, when Llewelyn said, with brutal candor, "Yes, that is exactly what we do."

"I doubt that I can do that," Llewelyn Fychan said, and mutterings of agreement went rustling around the table. "I've had a bellyful of English insults, do not think I can force down another morsel. You make it sound so easy, Cousin, but it is not, is—"

"Easy?" Llewelyn echoed. "You think it was easy for me to come to Edward at Rhuddlan, to seek a pardon from the man who had ravaged my lands and abducted my wife? Easy to humble myself before the English court at Westminster? But I did it, and you will, too, all of you, for it's not a matter of choice!"

It was the throb of raw fury in his voice that stopped Llewelyn. He regained control by resorting to Ellen's trick, drawing several deep, deliberate breaths, giving other tempers a chance to cool, too. "I know how much I ask," he said. "But there is no other way. You must not let them goad you into rebellion ere we are ready, for this war must be fought on our terms. Our people's suffering will not be for naught. Each time that a man is abused because he is Welsh, each time that our laws are denied us and our traditions mocked, we strengthen our grip upon the hearts of our people. Edward may not know it yet, but not a day passes that he does not convert new rebels to our cause. And thank God for that, for too often Welsh unity has been the first casualty of our wars. This time it must be different. This time we must recognize the enemy and hold fast against him."

In the silence that followed, very few could meet Llewelyn's eyes, for too many of them had the blood of that Welsh unity on their own hands. He'd won no friends by reminding them of that, but none could refute what he'd just said, either.

"It is writ in Scriptures that he who is not with me is against me. Never has that been more true than now. There can be no forgiveness for those who aid and abet the English. When the war comes, the lords of Wales must stand together. Those few who would whore after English favors—Rhys ap Gruffydd, Rhys ap Maredudd, and above all, Gruffydd ap Gwenwynwyn—must learn that there is a debt due for past treacheries. This time Edward will not be able to claim he seeks to end a civil war, to bring peace to a primitive, quarrelsome people warring amongst themselves. This time he'll have no Welsh pawns to play, to flaunt as false allies. We must see to that."

Although Llewelyn did not look toward Davydd as he spoke so scathingly of Welsh pawns, all the others did. Davydd's color had deepened, but he said nothing, kept his eyes upon his brother. It was Goronwy who asked the question uppermost in their minds. "When do we rise up against our oppressors, my lord? How long must we wait?"

"I do not know, Goronwy," Llewelyn admitted, "for I am no soothsayer, cannot foresee what might occur in the coming months. There is this to consider, though, that it has been five years since Edward swore that he would lead another crusade to the Holy Land. My sources at the papal court tell me that ere long, the new Pope will urge him to make good that vow. What better time to throw off the English yoke than whilst their King is half-way to Palestine? But even if that never comes to pass, Edward is soon to visit his cousin, the French King, to occupy himself in French matters, just as he did two years ago."

"I see," Davydd said at last. "You would have us lay our plans and then bide our time, awaiting that moment when Fortune is most likely to favor us."

Llewelyn nodded bleakly. "I know that is not what some of you wanted to hear. I know, too, that it will not be an easy road to travel. We all agree that this is a war we must fight." He let a pause develop then, to give his words more impact, before adding with quiet, compelling conviction: "But above all, it is a war we cannot lose."

CAITLIN gave a joyful cry, jumped to her feet, and embraced Ellen. "How I bless the day you came to us! I could see at once that you made my uncle happy, and I loved you for it, but now . . . a child! He rarely spoke of it, but I knew how much he wanted a son, we all knew, and—"

It was not Caitlin's enthusiasm that ran out, it was her breath. Ellen laughed and hugged her back, giving her a chance to regain her composure. "I could not help noticing that Uncle Llewelyn's spirits were soaring sky-high this past week, but I never suspected . . . No one else knows yet?"

"Very few, just Juliana and Dame Blodwen, the midwife. Oh, and Hugh, for he was my escort, but he swore he'd tell no one, not even Eluned."

Caitlin thought that was a prudent promise, for confiding in Eluned was the quickest way to get word out and about; it was her private conviction that Hugh's wife could not have kept a secret unless she was bound and gagged. But she said nothing, for even with Ellen she was circumspect, resolutely denying herself the dubious comfort of snide slurs and gibes, as much to safe-guard her own self-respect as to spare Hugh's feelings.

"Caitlin, I would like you to have this length of topaz velvet. It would suit your coloring perfectly, and we still have a few days, can make it into a dazzling Christmas gown. No, lass, do not thank me, not until you've heard the bad news, too. You know that Rhys Wyndod has stayed over for the festivities. Goronwy will be coming back, as will Dai, and the Abbot of Aberconwy is expected, and so is Brother Gwilym and Tudur's son and numerous others . . . including Davydd and Elizabeth."

Caitlin's fingers froze upon the velvet folds, then clenched into a small fist. "I suppose I ought not to be surprised," she said, "for he delights in thrusting himself into places where he is not wanted."

"In truth," Ellen admitted, "I am no longer sure that is so. Llewelyn was rather vague about it, which leads me to wonder if this invitation might not be his doing. I doubt that there could ever be a true reconciliation between them, but having said that, I do sense something different when I see them together. I cannot pretend that I'd understand or approve if Llewelyn did choose to make peace with Davydd, but I would accept it, Caitlin, for his sake."

Caitlin knew what was being asked, ever so subtly, without the risk of words, and she felt a flicker of envy, wishing she had just a portion of Ellen's tact. "So would I, Aunt Ellen," she said quietly, "so would I."

Just then, the door swung open, letting in a rush of frigid air. "It is only me," Juliana said cheerfully. "But Eluned is on her way up, too. She wants you to meet her brother, Ellen."

Eluned's brother was living, breathing proof that her beauty was no fluke, for Hywel ab Iago was handsome enough to turn most female heads, and Ellen, Juliana, and Caitlin all eyed him appreciatively as Eluned made the introductions. But his polished courtesy was devoid of charm, for it was devoid of warmth, and he cut short the amenities with the brusque assurance of a man accustomed to getting his own way. "I am here, Madame," he said, "to take my sister home."

Ellen was surprised, for Hugh had said nothing to her of these plans. But she was heartily in favor of a Christmas visit to Eluned's family, hoping this was an indication that they were finally thawing toward Hugh. "By all means," she said, and smiled at Eluned. "Take as much time as you like. Shall you be leaving as soon as Hugh gets back from Beddgelert?"

Although the question was directed at Eluned, it was her brother who answered. "You do not seem to understand, Madame. Eluned will not be returning. This marriage of hers was a great mistake. My sister sees that now, and she wants to end it."

Ellen stared at them. "Eluned, I fear you have been misled. The process of dissolving a marriage is very lengthy, very expensive, and such pleas are rarely granted. The Church will not end a marriage. It will declare one void from the outset, but only if there existed a prior plight troth, kinship within the fourth degree, or the sort of spiritual consanguinity that results from acting as godparent. Eluned, you can claim none of those impediments, so how can you hope to end the marriage?"

Hywel did not interrupt, heard Ellen out, but with obvious impatience. As soon as she was done, he said, "You are not one of us, Madame, so it is to be expected that you'd be ignorant of our ways. Whether the Church agrees or not is immaterial, for Welsh law provides a number of grounds for dissolving a marriage, one of which is mutual assent of the husband and wife. If the Englishman is as chivalrous as he would have us believe, he will do the decent thing, let my sister go."

"I think you are the one who should go," Ellen said icily. "So far you've done all the talking. Now I would hear Eluned speak for herself. You may wait in the great hall whilst we talk."

Hywel was furious, but he was not so foolhardy as to defy his Prince's wife. As soon as he had gone, Ellen swung about toward Caitlin. "What he said of Welsh law . . . is it true?"

"Yes," Caitlin said, "it is. A wife can divorce her husband if he brings his harlot under their roof, if he is incapable in bed, is stricken with leprosy, or . . . Well, this is not the time for a lesson in Welsh law. But Eluned is quite within her rights as a Welshwoman in seeking to end her marriage."

"I see," Ellen said grimly. "But is this what you truly want, Eluned? I know your family opposed this match. If they have put pressure upon you to disavow Hugh, you need only say so."

Eluned had yet to meet Ellen's gaze. But now silky, sable lashes fluttered upward, revealing eyes of a remarkable lavender-blue. "It is not like that, my lady. Hywel and my other brothers have always been protective of me, for I was the youngest and the only lass . . . like you. But they want only what is best for me. I ought to have heeded them when they warned me that it was folly to wed an Englishman," she said, quite ingenuously, for her insults were always unintentional. "Once I abandoned the pretense, admitted how miserable I was in this marriage, Hywel came to fetch me home."

"I thought you loved Hugh." This from Juliana, who could no longer hold her indignation in check.

"I thought I did," Eluned said simply.

"Eluned, listen to me." Ellen often found herself talking to the girl in the overly patient tones one would use with a child, but now she was hard put to keep her anger from surfacing. "You have only been wed a brief while, little more than a year—"

"Seventeen months, my lady."

"Seventeen months, then. But that is not very long, not in the life of a marriage. If you and Hugh commit yourselves anew to each other, I am sure you can find contentment together. Wait a while, do not do anything rash."

"Wait till what, my lady? Till I get with child?"

"I think Eluned is right," Caitlin said suddenly, ignoring the withering, warning look Ellen shot her way. "Marriage is a sacred trust to us, too, Aunt Ellen. We take it no less seriously than do other Christians. But we understand that men and women are flawed, often impetuous, not always steadfast. We can make mistakes, our needs can change. Why yoke a couple for life if they'd both rather be free of each other? No sensible person would drink from a salted well, but a marriage gone sour is just as poisoned, and our laws merely recognize the reality of that. In truth, I could never see the logic in the Church's insistence that marriage must last from the altar to the grave. Why is it that there is forgiveness for sins, but not for mistakes?"

Eluned was favoring Caitlin with a dazzling smile, grateful to have an advocate who could plead her case so persuasively. Ellen was considerably less pleased with Caitlin, but her niece met her eyes with studied innocence. Turning back to Eluned, Ellen said abruptly, "And what of Hugh? Does he, too, want to end your marriage?"

Eluned shook her head. "No . . . he is being very stubborn, very English, with his talk of duty and honor and binding vows. I've tried to make him understand, my lady, truly I have." She sighed, looking, for that moment, quite forlorn. "I thought . . . hoped that you might talk to Hugh, my lady, make him see it is the only way. Hywel has written him a letter, and if you could give it to him . . . ?"

Ellen blinked. "Hywel wrote it?"

"Well, I told him what I wanted to say. I do not know how to write myself." Eluned was eager to be gone, uncomfortably aware of Ellen's disapproval. Not sure how to extricate herself, she looked to Caitlin for guidance, and the other girl stepped forward, saying:

"If you like, Eluned, I can help you pack?"

"Yes, please." Eluned made a hasty, graceful curtsy to Ellen, looked apologetically at the stony-faced Juliana, and then said softly, "I want Hugh to be happy, too, my lady. He is a good man, and I wish him well. This is for the best, you'll see."

Juliana had been seething, and as the door closed, she snatched up a cushion, flung it across the chamber. "That bitch," she said succinctly.

Ellen watched glumly as her dog pounced on the cushion, began to drag it through the floor rushes. "I suppose we ought to be thanking God that Hugh no longer loves her. It will still leave a lasting scar, though. And the blow to his pride will not be the worst of it. I think he is bound to feel a secret sense of relief, and he's sure to be guilt-stricken over it. He's likely to forgive Eluned long ere he forgives himself. . . ."

Juliana called Eluned another harsh name, rescued the cushion from Hiraeth. Ellen sat down on the settle, beckoned the disappointed dog up into her lap. She understood now why Llewelyn was so often at odds with the Bishops of Bangor and St Asaph; in no other Christian land was Church law subordinate to secular law, and the Church was never so zealous as in defense of its own prerogatives. But at the moment her concerns were personal, not political. "Poor Hugh," she said, and then, "Well, at least I know now why Caitlin has been balking every time we spoke of finding her a husband."

"You think she truly expected this to happen, Ellen?"

"She obviously had hopes that it might. That girl was much too knowledgeable about Welsh divorce law for it to be pure chance."

As Juliana took this new complication in, she shook her head in dismay. "Hugh has enough on his plate at the moment, needs no more grief. Surely Caitlin must know that she could have no future with Hugh? Your husband would never give his consent."

"No," Ellen agreed sadly, "he would not . . . and he would be right. Hugh is very dear to me, but Caitlin is a daughter of the Welsh royal House, for illegitimacy counts for naught amongst Llewelyn's people. If she still has her heart set upon a landless English knight, she's going to get it broken, for certes."

It was quiet then, as both women considered the multitude of troubles Eluned had inadvertently set loose upon them all. Ellen was the first to rebel. "No," she said, "this time I shall prove Amaury wrong. He swears I cannot keep from seeking trouble out, but for once I shall wait for it to find me, if indeed it can. Eluned might even be right, and this may well be for the best. Hugh will need time to mourn his marriage, but at least he'll be free of Eluned. As for Caitlin, we'll just have to wait and watch. Hugh is the last man to dally with a girl both highborn and innocent. And I am no less confident that Caitlin would never willingly put Hugh in peril. So it may well be that we need do nothing at all, Juliana." When Juliana did not reply, Ellen gave her a curious glance. "You do not think so?"

"What I think is that you've been raiding your hope coffer again," Juliana said wryly. "I know you seem to have hope in amazing abundance these days, but it might still be prudent to store some of it away for leaner times."

Ellen grinned, putting up her hand to fend off Hiraeth's questing tongue. "I'll admit that my garden now grows hope in lavish profusion, leaving little room for anything else. I suppose it has squeezed out more practical plants like caution and common sense. Still, though, hope does not flourish in every garden, and I feel thankful that it has taken root in mine," she said lightly, beginning to laugh. "But then, I've proved myself to be a superior gardener, for am I not soon to harvest a genuine miracle?"

ELIZABETH could not remember a colder winter. It had been a fortnight since the last snowfall, but the ground was still hidden under a treacherous glaze, snow packed-down and dirty where paths had been dug across the bailey, frozen in deep drifts wherever walls came together. The Christmas Eve sky was clear of clouds, but the stars glittered without warmth, piercing the blackness like scattered shards of ice. The comparison was a natural one for Elizabeth to make, for ice had come to symbolize the worst of winter suffering. Davydd had told her of forest trails splattered with blood, of deer foundering in the snow, legs cut and gashed after breaking through the ice. Most rivers were frozen solid; the Thames had iced over all the way from Lambeth to Westminster, and five arches of London's great bridge had cracked under the weight of so much snow. Even the wind put her in mind of an icy blade, for it slashed and thrust at her as she scurried across the open space separating Dolwyddelan's hall and West Tower. Never had spring seemed so far away.

Elizabeth's sons were almost invisible under the pile of blankets heaped upon their pallet. Although stacked kindling still fed the hearth's flames, the air was chill. Davydd would probably want to make love once the revelries were done, but afterward she'd take their lads into bed with them, where it was warm and snug. Their nurse dozed in a chair by the fire; Elizabeth tiptoed around her, bent over the boys. They were in familiar poses, creatures of habit even in sleep, Llelo sprawled on his back, Owain curled up like a cat, head ducked down under the covers; she used to worry that he might somehow suffocate, and even now her eyes lingered upon his chest until reassured by its rhythmic rise and fall. Her fingers brushed Llelo's cheek, gentle as a breath, and she carefully tucked Owain's stuffed dog into the crook of his arm before departing the chamber.

She knew she'd done Ellen no kindness by bringing Llelo and Owain, and she was sorry for that. But she was not willing to be separated from them, for a mother's time with her sons was all too brief. The sons of English gentry were sent off to serve as pages at as young an age as seven. The Welsh were more flexible, but she knew their sons were often fostered in noble households, and she suspected that the time would come when Davydd would entrust Llelo into Llewelyn's keeping, to be raised at his court as Caitlin had been. And she would not object, for such a sojourn might one day make her Llelo Prince of Wales. But she would miss him with every breath she drew, fret that he was not eating as he ought, worry that he might be homesick or fevered or risking life and limb in the sort of rash foolhardiness little boys found so irresistible, for motherhood was both burden and blessing; once her sons were born, she'd realized that she would never again be free of fear.

Slipping inconspicuously back into the great hall, Elizabeth was pleased to see that her absence seemed to have passed unnoticed, for she knew Davydd thought she coddled their sons. Although she deferred willingly to Davydd in most matters, she did not think he was all that reliable a judge of maternal behavior, for his own mother's affections had been doled out in unequal, sparing portions, with the lion's share going to Owain, her firstborn. Shedding her mantle, Elizabeth looked about the hall with keen interest. Candle light, scented evergreen, silver-stringed harps, lively carols, and later, a dalliance with Davydd: Elizabeth could not have have envisioned a more perfect Christmas Eve. She was still shivering, had started toward the hearth when an arm snaked suddenly about her waist and a familiar voice breathed against her ear, "You're lucky I have such a trusting nature, or I might have suspected you of sneaking out of the hall to meet a lover."

Elizabeth smiled sheepishly. "I just wanted to make sure the lads were settled down for the night, love. Ah, Davydd, you should have seen them; they looked so sweet, almost angelic."

"So they were asleep, then?" Davydd murmured, and Elizabeth laughed, let him lead her over to the center hearth.

"I did not miss the surprise, did I?"

Davydd looked puzzled. "What surprise?"

"It might be nothing; I could be wrong. But I've been watching Ellen and Llewelyn all evening and they seem . . . I do not know, somehow expectant, as if something were afoot. I thought they might have a special sort of entertainment planned: mayhap a shepherd's play or a rope dancer like the one we saw at Westminster, who balanced high above the hall whilst juggling daggers . . . remember?"

She'd caught Davydd's interest; nothing intrigued him like secrets. "I think you might be right, Elizabeth. Look over there," he said, and turning, she saw that Ellen had approached her husband, was whispering a few words in his ear. A moment later they were heading toward the oaken partition that blocked off the far end of the hall. Grabbing Elizabeth's hand, Davydd began an oblique stalking maneuver, ignoring his wife's half-hearted protest that "We cannot spy on them, Davydd, for pity's sake!"

"Of course we can," he said, drawing her into a window recess, which gave them a partial view of the screened-off section of the hall. They were just in time to see Llewelyn and Ellen embrace. "We dashed madly across the hall for this," Davydd demanded, "to watch a man snatch a quick kiss from his own wife? I'm beginning to pity Llewelyn's confessor, for any account of his sins must put the poor man straightaway to sleep!"

Elizabeth took the bait. "I think it is very romantic," she insisted. "I noticed tonight how often Llewelyn's gaze kept straying toward Ellen, even whilst he was talking to others. What woman would not want a husband so devoted that he truly cannot keep his eyes off her?"

"Or his hands, either," Davydd joked, for teasing Elizabeth was a temptation he could rarely resist. Elizabeth's nature was such an incongruous mix of salt and sugar that she was not always predictable, a trait many men would have found undesirable in a wife, but one Davydd relished.

Just then, Ellen took Llewelyn's hand, pressed it against the velvet skirt of her surcote. It was a private moment not meant to be witnessed by other eyes, and as he watched, Davydd's amusement vanished in the span of seconds, in the time it took a memory to surface. Ellen's gesture was familiar to him, for Elizabeth had often done that when she was pregnant with Llelo and then Owain, putting his hand upon her belly so he might feel the baby kicking.

"Davydd? You look so odd, love. Is something amiss?"

"No," he said. "It was just that . . . that for a moment, I found myself wondering if Ellen could possibly be with child."

Elizabeth had a face that mirrored her every mood. He watched now as the emotions chased across it, like sun and shadow, first joy, giving way to dismay as she realized that Ellen's pregnancy would put her own sons' prospects at risk, followed by shame that she could begrudge her cousin the child Ellen so desperately wanted. "Do you truly think it may be so?" she asked hesitantly, and he shook his head, bent down and brushed his mouth to hers.

"It was a daft notion, lass. Think no more on it."

Elizabeth was quite willing to heed him, for she was acutely uncomfortable with ambivalence, usually dealt with it by denying it. "I've been thinking about babies a lot lately," she confided. "Now that Owain is into his second year, it would be a good time to have another one. I just hope the Almighty agrees with me! I'd dearly love a lass next time. Would that please you, Davydd? Would you not want a daughter?"

Davydd already had six daughters, and he almost reminded her of that. But he caught himself in time; the most conclusive proof of his fondness for Elizabeth was that he had learned to do for her what he'd never done for anyone else: exercise a mild form of self-censorship. "Yes, I'd fancy a little lass," he said, "as long as she looked like you, cariad."

Elizabeth smiled, shook her head. "No, love, I'd want her to have your coloring . . . like Caitlin." She came close to adding, "only prettier," but did not, for that would have been unkind, and tonight, at least, not altogether true, for she'd noticed earlier that evening that Caitlin was looking unusually appealing. In part, it was the gown, a rich dusky gold that set off her slender figure to its best advantage. But it was more than velvet and moonstones. Elizabeth had never seen the girl so animated, so quick to laugh. Her green eyes were glowing, catching the candle light like emeralds. Unfortunately, she was casting that glow where she oughtn't, Elizabeth thought, gazing across the hall at Davydd's daughter and that young English knight, the married one.

It would not do for her to talk to the girl, for Caitlin would take it badly. But she might ask Ellen to have a word with her. What an odd little creature she was, at one and the same time as skittish as a woodland fawn and as stubborn as a Spanish mule. Her rudeness to Davydd was irksome, indeed, but still she ought to be alerted to the risks of the real world, warned about gossip and jealous Welsh wives.

"Davydd . . . have I met Hugh de Whitton's wife? Which one is she?"

"I forgot to tell you, then? Can you not see it in Hugh's face? He's been moping about the hall all night like a puppy that lost a bone, only in his case, it was a wife. She left him last week, packed up and went home to her kinfolk in Meirionydd."

Elizabeth was not surprised that Davydd should be so well informed about Hugh's marital woes; he had an uncanny knack for smoking out choice gossip. But she was so shocked by what she'd just heard that she could only stare at Davydd in disbelief. "A Welsh wife can do that? What a fool she must be! Most women would barter their hopes of salvation for a husband like Hugh, good and kind and faithful—"

"If that is what women want, would it not be easier just to buy a dog? I admit Hugh does look rather pitiful, but let's spare a few crumbs of sympathy for the runaway wife. I'd wager that life with St Hugh was about as much fun as a Lenten fast. The poor lass probably never got a good night's sleep, for do haloes not glow in the dark?"

Elizabeth could not help laughing. "You have such a wicked tongue!"

He arched a brow, gave her so suggestive a look that color rose in her cheeks, much to his amusement. "I cannot believe," he said, "that I can still make you blush! Anyone would think you were still a virgin maid instead of a wife almost five years wed."

Elizabeth was unperturbed, both by her blushing and his teasing; she sometimes feigned a modesty she'd long ago outgrown, simply because she knew it beguiled Davydd. "I do not often feel like a wife," she confessed, "more like an unrepentant sinner sharing her bed with a wayward, wanton lover, never knowing if he'll still be there in the morning."

She'd revealed more than she realized, but Davydd was so pleased with the compliment that he never noticed. Taking her hand, he pressed a hot kiss into her palm, then ushered her across the hall. Elizabeth tensed once she saw that he meant to intercept Hugh and Caitlin. But Hugh looked so despondent that Davydd could not bring himself to joke at the Englishman's expense, and to Elizabeth's relief, he soon showed that he was on his good behavior, deftly piloting the conversation away from the shoals of marriage, divorce, and flighty, fickle wives.

There was only one awkward moment, occurring as Hugh went to flag down a passing servant and bring them back wine. Davydd took advantage of his brief absence to subject his daughter to a discerning scrutiny. "You are very loyal, Caitlin. I hope that you are also prudent."

Caitlin had been unexpectedly cordial—so far. But now her eyes narrowed, and her chin jutted up, surprising Elizabeth by how much she suddenly looked like Davydd in one of his tempers. Before she could respond, though, people began to turn toward the dais, where Llewelyn was signaling for silence.

"My chaplain has informed me that time is drawing nigh for the Midnight Mass." Llewelyn paused; for a moment his eyes sought out Ellen, standing by the steps of the dais. "Ere we depart for the chapel, I have something to say. Tonight, when you give thanks to the Almighty for His bounty and divine mercy, for giving us His Only Begotten Son that we might have life everlasting, I ask you to pray, too, for the health of my beloved wife and the child she carries."

There were a few seconds of silence, no more than that, and then, pandemonium. Elizabeth spoke very little Welsh, not enough to follow what Llewelyn had said. But she understood almost at once, for the joy surging through the hall needed no translation. Spinning around, cat-quick, she flung her arms around Davydd's neck and kissed him on the mouth, shielding him from the stares that would soon be winging his way, giving him the time he needed to master his shock.

That Davydd was shocked, she did not doubt, and she was right. He was as stunned by his own emotional turmoil as he was by Llewelyn's impending fatherhood. This was a possibility he'd long ago relegated to the far reaches of supposition, until it had seemed no less improbable to him than unicorns or winged dragons or the chance that he might fail to get all he wanted from this life. He was shaken now by his overwhelming sense of loss, as if something vital and valuable had been taken from him, something that went beyond the fading, golden glimmer of a crown.

"Well . . . mayhap Simon de Montfort is a saint, after all. For certes, someone wrought a miracle here." These bitter words were for Elizabeth's ear alone. For the hall, the world, and Llewelyn, he found a taut smile, still ragged around the edges. Llewelyn was besieged by well-wishers. Never had Davydd seen him look so jubilant, so un-guarded. Had it not occurred to him that this miracle babe might be a lass? Davydd stepped back, loosening his hold upon Elizabeth, and only then, when he was able to fake both his smile and his swagger, did he walk across the hall to congratulate his brother.

29

LLANFAES, WALES

March 1282

THE bitter cold spell lingered on. January and February were so frigid and wind-lashed that the roads had rarely been as deserted, or as safe, for even the bandits were holed up by their own hearths. Few had high hopes for March, the most mercurial of months, but this year it ushered in an early spring thaw. By Passion Week, the skies were clear, the snows had melted, and budding primroses had begun to adorn the high mountain meadows. And the people of England and Wales, starved for sun and warmth, gloried in it all.

To the casual eye, Caitlin, too, seemed to have succumbed to the spring fever sweeping Wales. She danced through her days with a light, nimble step, lavished smiles and pleasantries upon all who crossed her path, and thanked the Almighty fervently and frequently, for Hugh was free and, at last, beginning to heal.

She'd feared for a time that he wouldn't, that his grieving might outlast his marriage. It frightened her at first, for she'd convinced herself that he'd never truly loved Eluned. So why, then, was he so troubled by her departure? But she'd soon supplied her own answer. Hugh was English; it was as simple as that. The laws that seemed so natural and sensible to her were alien to him, and he was afraid to trust them. Once Caitlin understood that, she sought out the Bishop of Bangor, for although he was no friend to her uncle, she knew no one so knowledgeable about Church law or history. Puzzled but pleased by her sudden interest in subjects so dear to his heart, he'd unwittingly given her the information—and ammunition—she needed.

It had taken a bit of coaxing on her part, but she'd gotten Hugh to confirm her suspicions, that it was the Church's shadow, not Eluned's, that was preying upon his peace. Under her gentle, insistent prodding, he blurted out his doubts, his unease of mind. If the Church said marriage was for life, how could Welsh law say it nay?

Indeed, Caitlin agreed readily, marriage was a bond eternal and unbroken. Of course Lady Ellen's grandfather, the English King John, had divorced his first wife to wed a beautiful young heiress, Isabelle d'Angoulême. And then there was John's remarkable mother, that most illustrious lady, Eleanor of Aquitaine. She'd been fifteen years wed to the King of France, mother to his two daughters, when the Pope granted them a divorce because they were third cousins once removed, a kinship known but ignored until the marriage had become inconvenient. Once Eleanor was free, she straightaway wed Henry Plantagenet, he who would soon be England's King, although Henry was her cousin, too! Did Hugh not think it odd that the Church would wink at the second marriage whilst declaring the first one null and void?

She'd given him no chance to answer, plunged ahead. Did Hugh know how often the highborn sought divorce . . . and how often the Church accommodated them? It was true that popes occasionally balked, as when Philippe Auguste tried to disavow his Danish bride the morning after their wedding; Ingeborg had been more fortunate, though, than many rejected wives, for her brother had been a King, too. But what of

Philippe's brother sovereigns? Every French king in the span of a hundred and half years had gotten at least one divorce, and King Robert the Pious had even been granted two! And what of the Earl of Gloucester and— But by then, Hugh was grinning, holding up his hand in mock surrender.

They'd not talked of it again. In the days and weeks that followed, though, she could see the shadow receding, and she sensed that he was no longer at war with himself, no longer denying that Eluned's rejection was in reality a reprieve. Wounds—be they of the body or spirit— needed time to heal, and Caitlin was willing to be patient, content to give him that time, so sure was she that this was meant to be. Nothing could penetrate the shield of her utter certainty, not even Ellen's well-intentioned words of warning. Caitlin had, like Ellen, become a devout believer in miracles.

The bailey was dappled in sun and shadow, the sky patterned with drifting cotton clouds. Standing in the doorway of the great hall, Caitlin paused to adjust her soft, gossamer veil; although many Welshwomen had adopted the English fashion and wore wimples like their Prince's lady, Caitlin clung to the old, Welsh style. Having secured the pins anchoring her veil, she stepped out into the sunlight and almost bumped into Trevor, just rounding the corner. He was precariously balancing a cumbersome platter, piled so high with bread and dried figs and a brimming goblet that he was sloshing cider with every step. Reaching out, Caitlin steadied the goblet. "I did not know you fancied noonday dinners, like the English do," she teased.

Trevor smiled diffidently. "Oh, this is not for me, Lady Caitlin. Lord Llewelyn's roan mare is foaling."

"Well . . . I think she might prefer carrots over brown bread, Trevor." Caitlin's attempts at levity were hesitant, for they took her into unfamiliar terrain. But her jokes were wasted upon Trevor, who knew even less than Caitlin about the mysteries of humor.

"This is not for the mare, my lady," he said gravely. "Dion was up all night with her, and I . . . I thought to bring him something to eat . . ." He shrugged self-consciously, and Caitlin wondered why men seemed so uncomfortable when caught doing good deeds; even Hugh acted at times as if kindness was something to be done under cover of darkness, and he with a heart so soft he could not let a kitten be drowned.

"I think I'd best take this," she said, reaching again for the cup, "whilst you still have cider left to spill." Brushing aside his thanks, she fell into step beside him. "I owe Dion more than a breakfast, Trevor. He may well have saved my life." She smiled at Trevor's look of surprise. "It happened a long time ago, nigh on ten years. I was trying to rescue a cat caught up in the stable rafters, and I fell. It was Dion who found me. He even went back afterward for the cat! So I would right gladly—"

Not only did she cut herself off in mid-sentence, she stopped so abruptly that cider splashed onto the skirt of her gown. There was such a stricken look on her face that Trevor's puzzlement gave way to concern. But a glance about the bailey revealed nothing to cause her distress. People were strolling about in the sun. Dogs sprawled in the spring grass. Laundresses were soaking sheets in a solution of wood ashes and caustic soda. Several friars from the nearby friary were chatting with Llewelyn's chaplain and the parish priest. And Hugh de Whitton was engaging in a playful tug of war with a lass from the village, insisting upon taking her basket of eggs, ignoring her demure protests. Such gallantry did not seem out of the ordinary to Trevor, not for Hugh, especially since the girl was very pretty; he'd have been quite happy to tote her basket himself. At the moment, though, he had eyes only for his lord's niece and the unknown threat lurking unseen in the sunlit bailey.

"My lady, what is it? What is wrong?"

Caitlin did not appear to have heard him; he saw now that her gaze was locked upon Hugh and the village lass, but that provided no enlightenment. Hugh and the girl were laughing, so intent upon each other that they did not notice Caitlin and Trevor, not until they were almost upon them. Hugh smiled then, at Caitlin, just scant seconds before she flung the contents of the cider cup at him.

Hugh recoiled with an astonished oath, the girl gave a muffled scream, and Trevor was so startled that he dropped the platter, carpeting the ground with bread and figs. For a stunned moment, no one moved, not even Caitlin, who seemed shocked herself by what she'd done. But then she threw the goblet into the grass at Hugh's feet, spun around, and began to walk swiftly away. That brought Hugh out of his disbelieving daze. "Caitlin, wait!" She did not look back, and within a few steps, she was running. As Trevor and the girl and a score of intrigued eye-witnesses watched in fascination, she fled into the stable, with Hugh in close pursuit.

Coming from sun to shadow, Caitlin collided with Dion, drawn by the clamor out in the bailey. She staggered backward, grabbing the nearest post for support, not even hearing his apologies for the blood thudding in her ears.

"Caitlin!" Hugh filled the doorway, blocking out the light. He sounded out of breath, perplexed, and angry, and Caitlin squeezed her hands together to still their trembling.

"Go away," she said. "I have nothing to say to you."

"Yes, you do, by God! You owe me an explanation, if not an apology, and I mean to have it."

"You'll have a long wait!"

They glared at each other, never even noticing the embarrassed Dion, who was in hasty retreat back into the foaling stall. Hugh swung around and slammed the door shut behind him. But Caitlin knew there was another door, one leading out into the stable yard. By the time Hugh turned toward her again, she was already in flight. Ignoring Hugh's shout, she raced for the rear of the stable. As quick as she was, though, Hugh was faster. He overtook her before she could reach the door, and grabbed for her arm. Whirling, she tried to pull free, but lost her balance, lurched against Hugh, and they both went sprawling over a bale of hay, tumbling down into the straw of the nearest stall.

Hugh got his breath back first. "Are you all right, Caitlin?" Not trusting her voice, she nodded, wishing she could lie there forever in the sheltering, shadowy gloom, never have to face anyone ever again. But Hugh was already sitting up.

"At least," he said, "you had the foresight to fall into a stall without a horse in it." To Caitlin's dismay, he was beginning to sound amused. What would she do when he asked her again, quietly and calmly this time, to explain herself? Blessed Lady, what could she tell him?

When she didn't move, Hugh reached over, put his arm around her shoulders and gently drew her up beside him. She'd lost her veil in their struggle and her hair was tumbling down her shoulders in disarray, tickling the back of his hand. He'd never seen it wild and loose like this, started to brush it away from her face, but stopped just before his fingers touched her skin, for that suddenly seemed too intimate a gesture. "I do not know what I did to make you so vexed with me, but I'd not hurt you for the world, Caitlin, that I swear. Tell me so I may make it right."

Caitlin drew a constricted breath, and suddenly she was angry again, angry with herself, with that wretched girl and her rotten eggs, with all those avid spectators out in the bailey, but above all, with Hugh, whose blue eyes were blinder than any bat's.

"I was willing to wait for you," she said, in a voice both hot and husky, "to wait as long as it took for you to see that I was no longer a child, was a woman grown. I was so sure you would, so sure . . . But no, you had to let yourself be snared by Eluned, Eluned who could not outwit Nia, my uncle's greyhound! So then I waited for you to come to your senses, to realize what a mistake you'd made. And for these past three months, I've waited again, whilst you mourned your marriage. But no more. I am done with waiting for you, Hugh de Whitton!"

With that, she leaned over, awkwardly sought his mouth with hers.

It was her first kiss, and that was obvious; it was also a decided disappointment. When she drew back, tears had begun to well in the corners of her eyes, slowly spilled down her cheeks. Hugh wiped them away with his fingers, and then somehow they were kissing again, and this time it was different, was all she imagined it would be, for this time he was the one kissing her.

IT was customary to select maidens and young widows as attendants and companions for women of high birth, for life in a noble household offered numerous advantages, not the least of them being enhanced opportunities for marriage. But Ellen had broken with tradition in choosing Eluned's replacement. Gwynora was a widow of fifty-one, the mother of eight children, a woman so knowledgeable in the ways of childbirth and pregnancy that even midwives sought her out. In the two months since she'd entered Ellen's service, she'd proved to be a patient, good-natured guide, taking Ellen on a day-by-day tour of the unknown realm of pregnancy.

On this third Wednesday in March, they were sitting side by side in a window-seat in Ellen's bedchamber, needles flashing, Gwynora stitching the hem of a blanket for the baby's cradle, Ellen at work upon a christening cloth of linen and lace, embroidering it with Llewelyn's Welsh lions and the fork-tailed lion of the House of de Montfort. When she paused suddenly, laying a hand upon her abdomen, Gwynora gave her a knowing smile. "The little one is stirring, is he?"

Ellen nodded. "At first it felt as if I'd swallowed a butterfly, but these days I'd swear he is playing a game of football in there!" Picking up her needle again, she stitched in contented silence for some moments. "Are you sure, Gwynora, that a babe does not quicken until the fourth month?"

"Quite sure, my lady. I've never heard of it happening earlier than that."

"Well, I'll know better what to expect with the next one," Ellen said, and then laughed. "But I'd as soon you not mention that to my lord husband. I swore to him, you see, that I felt the babe quicken on Christmas Eve!"

Gwynora laughed, too, was holding up her handiwork for Ellen's approval as Juliana entered the chamber. Ellen's needle froze in mid-air. "You have the queerest look on your face, as if you cannot decide whether you want to laugh or cry. Whatever is amiss?"

"Do you remember, Ellen, saying that you'd wait for trouble to find you? Well . . . you'd best make ready to welcome it to Llanfaes. I saw none of this myself, but there was no lack of witnesses. It seems Caitlin caught our Hugh flirting with a local lass, and she doused him with cider, then fled into the stables, with Hugh but a stride or two behind. As if that were not enough to start tongues wagging, they did not emerge from the stable for the longest time, and when they did, they had straw in their hair and dazed, lovesick looks on their faces!"

ELLEN had a special fondness for the friary of the Franciscans at Llanfaes. It was here that she felt closest to Joanna, in the tranquil stillness of the church that was Llewelyn Fawr's last gift to a well-loved wife. The candle she'd just lit for Joanna's peace burned with a clear, bright flame. "I think you'd be so happy for me, Aunt Joanna, if you knew," she said softly. "But then, you do know . . ."

Footsteps sounded in the nave. But she felt no embarrassment, for talking to the beloved dead seemed very natural to her, a way to make life's losses more bearable until that blessed reunion at God's great throne. Turning away from the High Altar and Joanna's marble tomb, she met Juliana on the other side of the rood screen.

"Brother Gwilym told me you were here, Ellen. I could stand the suspense no longer. Did you talk to Caitlin yet?"

"This morn, but it served for naught. When love comes in the door, common sense flies out the window."

" 'Common sense,' " Juliana echoed glumly. "Why did we ever assume that Hugh had any? This is the man, after all, who set his heart upon wedding Eluned ere he even knew her name! So why should we be surprised that he now claims he's been in love with Caitlin all along and just never realized it until yesterday?"

"Hugh is not our real problem. Even if we cannot rely upon his common sense, or the lack thereof, I still believe we can depend upon his sense of honor. But Caitlin . . . Caitlin is another matter altogether. And to think I once saw her as shy! That girl has a reckless streak to rival Davydd's . . . and has, as well, his irksome ability to turn an argument upon its head. Do you know what she said to me, Juliana? She said that if she and Hugh ran away together, got married in England, Llewelyn would be furious, but he'd eventually forgive her . . . and of course she was right. We both know there are men capable of cutting off a son or daughter the way a doctor would amputate a festering arm, but Llewelyn is not one of them. So why, then, Caitlin asked, should she and Hugh be punished because they chose to do the honorable thing, to ask his permission?"

"She truly believes that she and Hugh will be permitted to wed?"

Ellen nodded. "She asked me to speak to Llewelyn on their behalf." She was no longer meeting Juliana's eyes. "I told her that I'd have to think about it."

Juliana was taken aback. "Ellen? Surely you do not believe this to be a suitable match?"

"No," Ellen said quietly, "of course I do not. If Caitlin is too young and headstrong to think of her children's future, we must do it for her. It is foolhardy and even dangerous to wed one of a lower rank. It is true that many felt my father had overreached himself when he wed a King's daughter, but he did hold an earldom, and his House was one of France's proudest. My mother knew he'd be able to provide for their children, that there'd be a title for their eldest son. But Hugh is no earl, not even a baron, and there is hardly a soul in Christendom who would see him as a fit husband for Caitlin."

Ellen paused, seemed to sigh. "But . . . but I am finding it so hard, Juliana, to heed my head and not my heart. I love them both, and I cannot bear to see them hurt . . ."

Juliana sighed, too, for she feared they'd all be hurt before this storm had blown over. "Hugh is very dear to me," she said, "but if he had to go stark, raving mad like this, why could he not have waited until after your baby was born?"

That brought back Ellen's smile; thoughts of her baby always did. By now they'd reached the door. As they emerged onto the cloister path, Ellen headed for one of the wooden benches bordering the grassy inner garth. She tired quite easily these days, for her pregnancy was now into its sixth month. They were still sitting there in the sun when Caitlin and Hugh found them.

"Aunt Ellen, we've been searching everywhere for you. Please . . . you must help us! I tried to convince Hugh to wait, but he said he could not, that he owed it to my uncle to be honest with him, and now—"

Ellen sat up straight on the bench, ignoring her aching back. "Llewelyn would not give his consent."

"No," Hugh said, sounding as miserable as he looked. "I knew there was a likelihood that he might refuse me, but . . . My lady, he never hesitated, not for a moment, just said no straightaway, and that was all. In truth, it was almost as if he were not even listening to me."

Ellen had heard enough. "Help me up, Hugh," she said, holding out her hand. "I have to get back to the manor, for something is wrong." When they still showed no comprehension, she said impatiently, "I realize you have naught on your minds but each other, but you ought to have seen it. Llewelyn holds you in high esteem, Hugh. I do not mean that he'd think you a suitable husband for his niece; indeed, I warned you that he would not. But he would be fair, and he would try to be kind. He would hear you out, and he would seek to make you understand why it could not be. He would never shame you, never—"

Breaking off, she began to walk up the cloister path, as briskly as her girth would allow. Juliana was quick to follow, and after a moment, so did Hugh and Caitlin, clasping their hands together in a despairing, defiant act of faith.

ELLEN watched her husband closely during dinner that night. He smiled occasionally, responded whenever she spoke to him, showed no overt anger, no unease. But Ellen knew him as no one else did. She noticed that he'd been pushing his food around on the trencher, eating only a few mouthfuls at most. She noticed that he did not really listen when his bard approached the dais to sing of Llewelyn Fawr's fame. And she noticed that in quiet moments, his eyes focused upon the hearth's flames with an unnerving intensity, taking him far from the hall, far from her.

They retired early to their own chamber, at Ellen's urging. She'd rarely seen Llewelyn so restless. As she removed the pins binding her hair, he prowled aimlessly about the room, picking up and discarding books at random, fingering a quill pen so absently that it snapped in two. But he came back to the settle when Ellen reached for a brush, took it from her hand, and began to draw it through her hair.

"Llewelyn . . . did you talk to Hugh this afternoon?"

"I may have," he said, sounding so dubious that her hand clenched upon his arm. Jesú, Hugh was more right than he knew! But what had distracted him to such an extent? What dark spectre was he seeing?

"I heard that you had an unusual visitor today, a shabbily dressed stranger, very ill at ease, who begged to see you alone. Hugh said this man was being ushered out just as he was given entry into your chamber. My love, I can see how troubled you are. Did this man bring you evil tidings?" When he hesitated, she said urgently, "Llewelyn, I entreat you to tell me the truth. Your silence cannot protect me, can only stoke my fears higher."

Llewelyn laid the brush down, took her hand in his. "It first struck me as odd when my nephew, Rhys Wyndod, paid a Lenten visit to my cousin in North Powys, Llewelyn Fychan. They were the last two men I'd have expected to find together, for there has long been bad blood between them. And then I learned that my constable in Penllyn, Madog Goch, has had at least two clandestine meetings with Llewelyn Fychan since Candlemas. That seemed more than odd. Call it a sixth sense if you will, but it is one I've come to trust. Still, though, I had nothing but suspicions . . . until today."

"I was right, then, about that man?"

"Yes. He brought me a right strange story, gotten from a cousin deep in his cups. Mayhap it was the mead talking, mayhap not. But the man was boasting that he knew a valuable secret, one that the English would pay well to hear, that plans were being laid to steal lead from the King's mine at Flynt."

Ellen understood the significance of that at once, for dinner-table talk in the de Montfort household had focused more often than not upon sieges, wars, and weaponry. "Lead for mangonels and trebuchets," she said, and Llewelyn nodded. "Did this braggart reveal who was planning the theft?"

"Indeed, he did," Llewelyn said, with a twisted, mirthless smile. "Me."

"What? I do not understand!"

"Neither did I, lass . . . at first. But what better way to reassure would-be rebels than to make the rising mine? The irony of it is that is why our good samaritan rode for Llanfaes in such haste, to warn me that my plans were being put in peril by his cousin's bragging. Did I mention yet that this cousin is a man of Powys, having lived all his life in the commote of Maelor Cymraeg?"

Ellen gasped. "Llewelyn Fychan's lands," she said, and again he nodded grimly. "I remember you telling me that he was one of the lords most stubbornly set upon war. But would he dare to defy you, Llewelyn? Would he dare to make use of your name like this?"

"Not if left to his own devices. He does not lack for courage, but neither is he a man to seize the moment. If he truly is laying plans for a rebellion against the English Crown, we can be sure he is following, not leading."

"Who, then? Rhys Wyndod?"

"He is a more likely suspect than Llewelyn Fychan. But I do not think he'd dare to defy me like this, either, not after our December meeting at Dolwyddelan." He looked at her somberly, the strain and exhaustion showing clearly now in his face. "In truth, Ellen, I can think of only one man who would."

Ellen swallowed. Jesus God. "Your brother?"

"Who else? I found myself remembering something at dinner to-night. My cousin of Powys was one of the first Welsh lords to surrender to the English Crown, within weeks after Edward declared war upon us. Can you guess who accepted his surrender, who most likely talked him into it?"

"Davydd," Ellen whispered. Dear God Above, no, not now. Her sudden pallor alarmed Llewelyn. He reached out swiftly, drew her into his arms.

"You must not be afraid, cariad. If these are indeed straws in the wind, I'll soon know for certes. I've already taken measures to deal with this, have summoned Madog Goch to Llanfaes, and sent men to find out more about that theft at the Flynt mine. If need be, I'll confront Davydd with my suspicions, too. I cannot do that yet, beloved, not without proof that he is the cat amongst the pigeons. But this I swear to you, that if something is afoot, I'll put a stop to it. I'll not let any man put at risk what I've worked all my life to protect. And I'll let no harm come to you or our son. I promise you that, Ellen," he said, and kissed her gently upon the mouth. "Now I want you to make a promise in return, that you'll put this from your mind, that you'll not let your peace be poisoned by shadows and suspicions."

Ellen entwined her fingers in his. "I promise," she said, and they smiled at each other, as if they did not know she lied.

30

LLANFAES, WALES

March 1282

By midnight, the storm had spent its fury. The last echoes of unseasonal thunder were dying away in the distance, and the wind no longer banged relentlessly against creaking shutters or sent roof shingles spiraling up into the black, cloud-choked sky. Quiet cloaked the Welsh countryside, and soon, so did sleep.

But for Llewelyn, sleep was becoming harder and harder to catch, and then, to keep. He'd dozed fitfully, jerking awake at every thunderclap. Even after the storm passed over, he tossed and turned restively, unable to shut out the sounds ricocheting about in his head, the instinctive inner voices that whispered of dire forebodings, that argued for action. Dawn was still three hours away when he made the decision to yield to them.

It had been two days since he'd learned of the planned theft at the Flynt mine. Two days since he'd sent for his constable, Madog Goch. But he could wait no longer; already his nerves were stretched as taut as a hide staked out for scraping. Madog Goch was not the only key to this puzzle. Llewelyn Fychan would also have the answers he sought, and he meant to have them with no more delay. He had no doubts whatsoever that in any clash of wills with his cousin, he would prevail.

If only it were not a holy day, he'd leave at first light. But this dawning Sunday was one of the most sacred on the Church calendar. Yew and willow would be blessed in lieu of palm, and triumphantly borne round churchyards throughout England and Wales, and the rood, veiled during this bleak season of penitence and self-denial, would be revealed for the eyes of the faithful, from morning Mass till evensong. Lent was at last ending. Holy Week was upon them, and the time for rejoicing was nigh. No, he could not ride out on Palm Sunday, for then Ellen would know how truly troubled he was.

He shifted so he could see his wife's face. Her breathing was even, peaceful; he could only hope that so were her dreams. Carefully lifting the corner of the sheet, he let his eyes wander over her body, lingering upon her swollen belly. As he watched, he saw the skin ripple, like the surface of a pond, and he smiled, thinking Bran was wakeful, too, this night. The wonder of it had yet to fade, that he could actually see his son moving within Ellen's womb. He'd always assumed that intimacy was to be found in bed. But now he knew better. Naked bodies could entwine like ivy and oak without souls ever touching; he'd coupled with women whose names he could not even remember afterward. There could be no greater intimacy than this, watching as his wife grew large with child, nurturing within her body a life sprung from his seed. How could men take such a marvel for granted? Why seek out miracles and yearn after holy relics when God's greatest blessing was bestowed so close to home?

Ellen stirred in her sleep and he drew the coverlets up over her shoulders, gently extricated her long night plait from under his arm. In past wars with the Crown, he'd feared defeat, not death. It had been easy enough to say "Thy Will be done" when his life alone was at stake. But now the scales were out of balance, and he found himself haunted by the greatest dread of all, the fear of those who loved. If he died fighting the English King, what would befall his wife and son?

Eventually, though, his exhaustion muffled his internal voices, and he slept. When he awoke again, the room was still dark, he'd lost all sense of time, and his name was being whispered in an urgent undertone. Opening his eyes, he saw a worried face peering through the bed hangings.

"Goronwy ap Heilyn has just ridden in, my lord, insists upon seeing you straightaway—"

"What time is it?"

"Very early, my lord, a good two hours yet till dawn. But he swore by all the saints that his news could not wait."

"Tell him," Llewelyn said softly, "that I'll meet him in the great hall after I dress—"

"Llewelyn." Ellen's hand slid along his arm. "I am awake," she said, "and I would hear, too, what brought Goronwy to you at such an ill-omened hour . . . if I may?"

He was deceived neither by her quiet question nor her calm demeanor, could gauge in her eyes the depths of her fear. "Fetch Goronwy here," he said, and when Goronwy was ushered into the bedchamber, he dispelled the younger man's doubts with a brusque, "You may speak freely in front of my wife."

Goronwy was mantled in wet wool, unshaven, bleary-eyed. One glance at him was enough to confirm Llewelyn's suspicions, that he'd ridden all night to bring his "news that could not wait." He made a perfunctory obeisance, politely averted his gaze from his lord's lady, even though Ellen had the coverlets drawn up to her chin, and said, without any preamble whatsoever, "This past week your brother sought me out, swore me to secrecy, and then confided that he and your kinsmen in Powys and Ceredigion were soon to rise up against the English King. He said he knew how raw my own grievances were, and he thought I deserved a chance to throw my lot in with them."

"What did you tell him?"

"The truth, that my heart would be with them, but I could not break faith with my Prince." Goronwy was trembling with fatigue and cold, for although the rain had ended hours ago, he was soaked to the skin. Without waiting for Llewelyn's permission, he slumped down upon the closest stool. "For three days now, I've been at war with myself, and it was not until yesterday that I knew what I must do. I never thought I'd be one for disavowing my sworn oath, but I came to understand that I'd rather betray my honor than betray you, my lord."

"You've served Wales well this day," Llewelyn said, no more than that, but for a man chary of praise, sparing with accolades, it spoke volumes, and Goronwy flushed with pleasure. "This rising, Goronwy . . . can you tell me when or where?"

"Alas, no, my lord. Only that Davydd said 'soon.' "

There was a bell-rope by the bed. Llewelyn grasped it, yanked, and when a servant appeared, he gave terse instructions to rouse the cooks, bestir the men asleep in the hall, and saddle every horse in the stables. After that, he sent Goronwy off to the hall under orders to eat a hearty breakfast and steal an hour's sleep if he could. And then, he was once again alone with his wife.

They looked at each other in silence. Llewelyn covered her hand with his own. "I'll put a stop to it," he said, in what was both a prayer and a promise, and Ellen nodded somberly.

"My lord husband," she said, "go with God."

LLEWELYN delayed his departure just long enough to gather as many men to his banners as he could on such brief notice. He had, of course, his teulu, the men of his household guard, and those of his Seneschal, as well, for Dai was already at Llanfaes, having been summoned as soon as Llewelyn's first suspicions had begun to smolder. Goronwy, too, had brought an armed escort of his own, and as word spread, the island tenants of Llewelyn's desmesne manors hastened to buckle their scabbards, to saddle their horses. The friary church bells had not yet rung for Morrow Mass as Llewelyn spurred his stallion into the waters of the narrow, perilous strait that separated Môn from the Welsh mainland. They headed east at first, following the coast until they reached the Conwy estuary. Spurning the abbey ferry as too slow, they forded the river at Cymryd, then swung inland.

Goronwy guessed that they had at least thirty miles to cover, over roads still muddy in stretches. For a time, too, they were battling against a stiff headwind. But Llewelyn's unspoken urgency had communicated itself to his men, and every last one of them was determined to ride until he could no longer stay in the saddle. The miles and hours blurred behind them. By late afternoon, they had reached Davydd's lands in Rhufoniog, and the sky was still streaked with fading light as Dinbych Castle came into view.

Dinbych was a formidable presence, set upon a high hill, the chief jewel in Davydd's crown. Smoke curled up from chimneys, lights flickered at the upper windows of the apsidal towers, and armed men patrolled the walkways of the outer curtain walls. Llewelyn exchanged grim looks with Dai and Goronwy, sharing the same thought, that this was a castle garrisoned for war. For a moment, he wondered if Davydd would dare to deny him entry. But he soon saw there was no need even to demand admittance, for the drawbridge was coming down, the barbican going up. Llewelyn swiftly divided his men, taking with him enough to discourage treachery, leaving some behind to bear witness as a further precaution. His banner was known on sight throughout Wales; he passed without challenge into the heart of his brother's citadel.

As they strode into the great hall, they were greeted not by Davydd, though, but by his wife. Elizabeth seemed unnerved by their arrival, for her smile was brittle, her welcome overly effusive. The tension in the hall had affected her small son, too. Llelo had always struck Llewelyn as a cocky, inquisitive child. Yet now he hung back at their approach, shadowing his mother's footsteps, a little fist tightly entwined in the folds of her skirt.

"Elizabeth, I cannot afford the indulgence of good manners, not this day," Llewelyn said abruptly, cutting off her prolonged queries about Ellen's health. "I must speak with Davydd straightaway."

"He is not here, Llewelyn."

"Where is he?"

Elizabeth averted her eyes. She had no qualms about lying to a man she mistrusted, but she did not want to lie to Llewelyn, and her reluctance showed in her face. Llewelyn stepped forward, caught her hand in his. "Tell me where he is, Elizabeth. You must not lie to me, lass. There is far too much at stake for lies."

"So you know," she said softly. "And you are enraged. Davydd said you would be. But you must not think he was plotting against you, Llewelyn, not this time. He wants you at his side, God's truth, he does. He told me so, even quoted me a Welsh proverb, that stronger is the bowstring twisted than single . . ."

She had rehearsed an eloquent plea upon her husband's behalf, but she forgot it now as she gazed up into Llewelyn's face. "Davydd said . . . he said this war would be unlike the last one, for this time the Welsh would be united against the English. Llewelyn . . . he is right? This is a war the Welsh can win?"

Llewelyn's hand tightened upon hers. "Tell me where he is, Elizabeth, ere it is too late."

Elizabeth's mouth had gone dry. "It is already too late, Llewelyn. Hawarden Castle has been under siege for hours . . ."

Llewelyn sucked in his breath; behind him, he heard someone swear. "Davydd began his war today? On Palm Sunday?"

He sounded so incredulous that Elizabeth flushed. But she was too loyal to admit how distressed she was by Davydd's sacrilegious strategy. "Davydd said . . . said it was the best time to launch an attack, for they'd never be expecting it, not on such a holy day . . ." She faltered for a moment. "I know how sinful that must sound, but Davydd explained to me about a Church doctrine called the 'just war.' He said that a just war could be waged even during God's Truce—"

But Llewelyn was no longer listening. He was half-way to the door.

❦

HAWARDEN Castle was less than twenty miles from Dinbych, but their horses were winded and lathered, had to be rested and watered and cooled down. Darkness had fallen by the time their journey was nearing its end. They'd ridden, for the most part, in a disquieted silence. Goronwy was berating himself for letting Davydd outwit him so easily. How well Davydd had known him, not disclosing his plot until the eleventh hour, until it would too be late for Llewelyn to thwart it. Dai was still grappling with his disbelief, his outraged piety. Battles were sometimes fought on holy days. He knew it was not always practicable to observe God's Truce in the midst of war. Dai was deeply shocked, though, by this deliberate, calculated decision to shed blood on so blessed a Sunday. Even from Davydd, he'd not have expected such profane cynicism. Llewelyn had been taken aback, too, by Davydd's willingness to exploit canon law, perverting men's faith into a weapon to be used against them. But his own flawed judgment troubled him more than Davydd's brazen breach of God's Truce. What a fool he'd been, for he'd almost begun to believe that his brother's betrayals were in the past. And as they spurred their horses toward Hawarden, there rode with them an unseen spectre, the looming shadow of Davydd's war.

The sun had set more than an hour ago, but there was an odd glow along the horizon. Halting his men, Llewelyn dispatched a scout to investigate. The man was soon back. "Well?" Llewelyn demanded tensely, still holding to a shredded hope, that Elizabeth might be wrong. "Is there a fire ahead? Is Hawarden under siege?"

"Nay, my lord. The siege is over, the castle fallen!"

LLEWELYN had a very personal knowledge of Hawarden, for he'd destroyed the castle more than fifteen years ago, only to see it rebuilt in defiance of treaty terms. Boasting a large, circular stone keep situated upon a steep motte, its curtain wall was bolstered by a deep double ditch, and it had acted as a magnet for English settlers from nearby Cheshire. Although Hawarden had been granted no borough charter, houses had soon sprung up under the castle's imposing silhouette, like small pilot fish shadowing a shark. But the settlers had paid a high price for their reliance upon English might. Their thatched roofs and timbered beams had been easy targets for Welsh fire arrows, and all that remained now of those clustered cottages were smoldering shells, the unlucky occupants either having fled or lying dead within the smoking ruins.

Llewelyn saw no siege engines, other than a lone mangonel, for Davydd had not needed them, gambling, instead, upon the lethal weapon of stealth, trusting to the storm and darkness to camouflage his army's approach. Scaling ladders leaned against the curtain walls, and the drawbridge was down. The door to the gatehouse stood wide open, still intact, for they'd not needed to take a battering ram to it. The first intruders over the wall had swiftly overpowered the unsuspecting sentries, then opened the gates. The guards posted now at intervals along the walls were Welsh, and they raised no outcry at sight of Llewelyn. They showed neither surprise nor alarm at their Prince's sudden appearance before the castle walls, and Llewelyn wondered bitterly just what they'd been told by Davydd. Dispatching some of his men to wait, as at Dinbych, he led the others forward, over the drawbridge and on into the bailey of the captured castle.

There they abruptly reined in their mounts, transfixed by the scene that met their eyes, for it was bloody enough to startle even men well inured to violent death. Bodies were everywhere, sprawled in doorways, propped against walls, crumpled in the trampled grass of the inner bailey. Some wore chain mail, others just the clothes they'd snatched up as they rolled out of bed in those first chaotic, panicked moments of the assault. A whimpering dog cowered by the body of a youth with bloodied yellow hair and a shattered skull. Another corpse crouched, half-hidden, behind a horse trough, a spear protruding from his chest. Wherever Llewelyn looked, he saw bodies, so many he soon lost count. The stench of death overhung the bailey, a stench once encountered, never forgotten—the acrid odor of smoke mingling with the smell of pooled blood and the stink of voided bowels and bladders.

"Christ Jesus," Goronwy said hoarsely, "we've ridden into a charnel house!" Llewelyn nodded, glanced then at the others, battle-seasoned soldiers who, nevertheless, could not hide their surprise, for although it was not unheard-of to put an enemy garrison to the sword, it was not a commonplace, either.

SUMMONED by one of his men, Davydd approached the hearth, stood looking down at the man shivering upon a wooden bench. Roger Clifford's fear and hatred had ebbed away in the hours since their last confrontation. Now his flickering eyelids, contorted mouth, and clenched fists testified to pain, not defiance.

"See, my lord? He's hurt worse than we first thought. What would you have us do?"

Davydd gazed impassively upon Clifford's blanched face, noting the profuse sweating, the trickle of blood oozing from a bitten lip, the rasping sound he made as he gulped for air. He was quite unmoved by the other man's suffering; what pity had Clifford ever shown the Welsh? "I'll tell you what I'd like to do, Brychan, hang the whoreson from the rafters in his own great hall. But his day of reckoning must wait, for he might be of some use alive. Tend to his wounds ere he bleeds to death."

"What ought we to do with the chaplain, my lord? He's so scared and—"

It sounded as if he'd suddenly swallowed his own tongue. Davydd glanced up, curious, and saw that Brychan was staring over his shoulder. Turning quickly, he saw his brother standing in the doorway, flanked by Goronwy and Dai. He was surprised, but their confrontation was inevitable, and might as well be now as later. Moreover, he was not displeased that Llewelyn should arrive in time to witness the fall of the English fortress. Taking a castle like Hawarden in a matter of hours was a feat any battle commander might envy, even Llewelyn. Aye, let Llewelyn see for himself what his younger brother could accomplish on his own, let Llewelyn see that his was not the only voice to be heeded in Wales.

"You're just in time, Llewelyn. I've been trying to decide if I ought to make Clifford a hostage . . . or a corpse. Which do you fancy?"

Llewelyn did not even glance toward the captive Englishman, kept his eyes riveted upon Davydd's face. "I would talk with you—now," he said, and hardly recognized the voice as his, so husky with fatigue was it, so slurred with rage, for his fury had been burning down to bedrock despair—until he'd reached Hawarden, until he saw what Davydd had wrought for Wales.

Davydd had been braced for Llewelyn's anger, and was prepared to appease it. But he still found himself bridling at his brother's peremptory tone, for he invariably reacted badly to commands, especially Llewelyn's. "I'm rather busy at the moment, Brother. You have noticed, I assume, that I've just captured an English castle? Mayhap later—"

"It matters little to me whether there are witnesses or not. It might matter to you."

It did, and Davydd gave in with as much grace as he could muster up for the benefit of their audience. "That door over there, Brychan . . . where does it lead?"

"To the chapel, my lord."

"Perfect," Davydd said, stepping aside with exaggerated deference so Llewelyn could precede him. He was well aware how foolhardy it was to jest with a man who had such reason for rage, but still he couldn't keep from adding wryly, "Quite convenient, too, for the survivor can seek absolution on the spot."

It was an ill-advised joke, and a moment later, turned very sour, indeed, for Llewelyn slammed the chapel door shut, shoved him roughly back against it. "I ought to kill you now, right where you stand!"

The words themselves did not trouble Davydd unduly, for he often said things he did not mean. What sobered him so swiftly was the look upon his brother's face, and the fact that Llewelyn's hand had dropped to the hilt of his sword. Wrenching free, he snapped, "You can try!"

The chapel had been ransacked by Davydd's men, the altar overturned, prayer cushions slashed open and strewn about the floor rushes, the candlesticks and chalices taken for use in Welsh churches. A rushlight still burned in a wall sconce, casting an eerie, flickering light upon the chapel debris, upon the taut, shadowed faces of the two men. Davydd was the first to recover his composure, to remember the need for conciliation.

"I knew you'd be wroth, Llewelyn, and I do not begrudge your anger, but—"

"Do you not, by God? How magnanimous of you!"

"Will you at least hear me out?" Davydd was growing impatient again; playing the penitent was not a role that came easily to him. "I assume you do want to know why I—"

"The whys and wherefores count for naught. Words always come easily to you, feathers on the wind. But all that matters now is this—" With a sweeping gesture that encompassed the devastation that lay beyond the chapel walls. "The destruction you have loosed upon us!"

"Those are English bodies out in the bailey, Llewelyn, and this blood on my sword," Davydd said hotly, jerking his blade half-way out of its scabbard, "is English, not Welsh!"

"Today the dying was done by the English. But what of the morrow? Or do you expect Edward to surrender because you captured one castle in the middle of the night? Christ, Davydd, do you not realize what you've done? Almost I might believe you possessed, or in the pay of the English Crown, for you have played right into Edward's hands! Damn you to Hell, you knew better! You are no fool, are too clever by half. And you were at Dolwyddelan, you heard me give my reasons why we must wait—"

"Ah, yes, I heard your reasons: we all did. But did it ever occur to you that we might not agree with them? No, of course not, for you gave us the Gospel according to the Lord God Llewelyn, and what more could we ask than that? Well, I tried to tell you then, and I tell you now—that you are wrong. Delay accomplishes nothing, it but serves to let the English entrench themselves even further in Wales."

"And what did you accomplish this day? You began a war at Eastertide, thus giving Edward all spring and summer in which to quell the rising, giving him six months or more ere he need worry about fighting a war during a Welsh winter. You chose a day sure to outrage the Pope, the Church, and all of Christ's faithful, and you struck at a time when Edward was at Devizes, less than two days' ride from the Welsh border, when just a few months hence, he'd have been in France!"

"You can never see any point of view but your own, can you? Because you do not want war with England, any man who argues otherwise must be crazed or an English pawn! I suggest, my lord Prince, that you scrutinize your own motives ere you be so quick to cast aspersions upon the motives of other men!"

"Just what does that mean?"

"That your reasons for seeking to stave off war were not all political, were personal, too. You're not going to like what I'm about to say, but it needs to be said. You're past fifty, you've got a young wife who dotes on you like you're the Lord Christ come down to earth again, and at long last, there is a loaf in the oven. I do not mean that you should not be gladdened by Ellen's pregnancy. How could you not be? But you've let this babe shackle you to the nursery at a time when your people have need of you on the battlefield. Can you deny it, Llewelyn? Can you in all honesty tell me that you'd still be so loath to challenge Edward if there were no child?"

"I think it must be a remarkable child, indeed, who can act both as my anchor and your goad!"

"You're talking in riddles!"

"Am I? I think not. For fifteen years or more, you expected to be my heir. Even after you became impatient enough to give murder a try, you still thought to claim my crown, for who would deny your right once I was dead? Not Owain, and for certes, not Rhodri. But if I should ever have a son . . . Are you going to tell me they are unrelated happenings, connected by pure chance, my wife's pregnancy and your sudden haste to take the field against England? When did you decide upon a spring campaign, Davydd—at Dolwyddelan on Christmas Eve?"

"No! The one had naught to do with the other!"

"You cannot stop lying, can you? Even to yourself!"

"I'll say this once more, and only once. You were not the target, not this time. Whatever mistakes I've made in the past, I know full well who the enemy is. Not you, Llewelyn . . . Edward!" Davydd spat out the English King's name as if it were a curse, and striding to the window, jerked back the shutters. "Those bodies down in the bailey . . . you saw them?"

"They were hard to miss."

"Jesú, how quick you are to judge! I did not give the command to spare none. I would have, but there was no need for it. For nigh on five years, my men have been cheated and mocked and treated like aliens, like intruders in their own homeland. They had years of abuse to avenge, avenge it they did, and who can blame them? For certes, not me. That is what we should be discussing, Llewelyn, not our rivalry— their rage. This is not my war, it is theirs, and we both know it. I may have been the one to strike the first spark, but flint cannot ignite without tinder. The kindling had to be there, awaiting that spark, and it was, in abundant measure."

Llewelyn was silent. He had stepped into the wavering range of the rushlight, and such exhaustion showed now in his face that Davydd could almost believe he was bleeding from a hidden wound. But the hollowed dark eyes threw back the light like splinters of ice; they held such a glazed, unforgiving glitter that Davydd felt a stirring sense of disquiet. Llewelyn was proving to be harder to placate than he'd expected.

"Who else, Davydd? Who helped you to stoke this fire?"

Davydd was quite willing to reveal the rest, for he was proud of the breadth and reach of his conspiracy, a masterwork of timing and forethought and clandestine communication. "Our cousins in Powys were my first converts. Llewelyn Fychan and his brothers and your constable, Madog Goch, were to assault Oswestry this morn, to coincide with my attack upon Hawarden. Gruffydd ap Maredudd and the men of Ceredigion are allies, too. We came up with a strategy for taking the King's castle at Aberystwyth, and he'll soon put it to the test. Rhys Wyndod wanted to throw in with us, but not without you. Once he hears that you are now with us, he'll be right eager—"

"What makes you think I am willing to fight your war?"

Davydd blinked. "You cannot be serious," he said warily. "Of course you'll be with us. That was always part of the plan."

"Your plan, not mine."

Davydd moved hastily from the window. "You do not mean that, Llewelyn. Blame me if you will, but we cannot win this war without you!"

Llewelyn did not answer. Davydd's words hung in the air between them, even as Llewelyn turned away. As Davydd watched in disbelief, he walked out and did not look back.

"BUT why? Why must you involve yourself in this madness? Davydd began this war, not you. Let him be the one to fight it!"

"Ellen, I cannot do that. On the ride back from Hawarden, I sought to convince myself that I could, but I knew better, knew I had no choice but to make Davydd's war mine." Llewelyn silenced her protest then by grasping her shoulders, compelling her to look up into his face.

"My love, you must listen," he said. "I have sworn allegiance and fealty to Edward as my King and liege lord. Once he learns that Wales is in rebellion, he will summon his vassals to put down this rising, and he will expect me to be amongst them. English law gives him that right, and he will exercise it. But do you truly think I could answer that summons? That I could fight with Edward against my own people?"

Ellen's throat had closed up. She shook her head mutely, leaned for a moment within his embrace, resting her cheek against his chest. "No," she said, almost inaudibly, "of course you could not . . ."

Llewelyn held her close for a heartbeat or two. "You'd best sit down," he said, thinking that Davydd deserved damnation for this alone, for the look on his wife's face.

His solicitude usually amused her, for she'd been unable to convince him that a pregnant woman was not made of gossamer and glass, likely to break if breathed upon. Now, though, she needed his support, and let him lead her toward a chair. "What if Edward did not summon you to aid him, Llewelyn? Surely he'd rather have you remain neutral than allied against him. If he could be made to see what he risked, mayhap he'd be willing to let you be . . ."

"He would not, lass. Even if he did, how could I stand aloof whilst Wales went up in flames? If I played no part in the war, and the Welsh lost, they would blame me for that loss—justly so. And if Davydd somehow managed to defeat Edward, who, then, would have the better claim to be Prince of Wales? Do you not see how much is at stake? A lifetime's travail and the legacy I would leave my son . . . mayhap even the survival of Wales. For if Edward wins this war—"

He stopped, looked sharply down into her averted face. "Ah, Ellen, do not weep," he entreated, "lest you break my heart. I know how much you fear for our child, but you must be strong, you must try to understand. Cariad, I cannot fight you and Edward both."

"I do understand," she whispered. "That is why I weep, because you are right. This war must be won, and you are the one man who can win it. I'll not deny that I am afraid. But I have faith in you, faith in the Almighty, and I know you will prevail."

Llewelyn tilted her face up to his, kissed her tears, and then her mouth, with sudden urgency, with passion indistinguishable from despair. "I promise you," he said, "that I'll be with you when our babe is born."

He left her then, as late as it was, for he had much still to do before he could sleep. She knew his writs would soon be going out across

Wales, summoning men to fight the English King. To fight his brother's battle, she thought, dry-eyed now, bitter beyond words, for never had she hated anyone so much as she hated Davydd ap Gruffydd at that moment. She supposed she ought to go to the chapel, offer up prayers for her husband, her son, and Wales. But she could not find the energy to move from the chamber, from the chair.

"How did you do it, Mama?" she murmured. "During that last dreadful year, you never once lost faith, you never begged Papa to seek safety in France. You never asked him to choose between his honor and his life. Where did you get the strength?"

She paused, then, almost as if she were expecting a ghostly response. She already knew the answer, though. Her mother had never doubted that Simon would win. How often she'd told him what Ellen had said to Llewelyn just moments ago, that right would triumph, justice would prevail. "But you truly believed it, Mama," Ellen said softly, "whilst I . . . I lied. . . ."

THE Wiltshire castle of Devizes had long been a favorite fortress of the English Crown. Situated on a hillside just west of the town, it possessed spacious living accommodations, formidable defenses, and the most powerful lure of all, a pallisaded deer park. It was at Devizes that Edward had planned to celebrate Easter, and it was at Devizes that he learned of the Palm Sunday attack upon Hawarden Castle and the town of Oswestry.

April was an unreliable escort, heralding spring's approach one day, signaling its retreat the next. The sun seemed to have caught the same contagion. For more than a week now, its appearances were hesitant, fitful, each flash of blue sky soon clouding over, every sunlit interlude followed by brief, drenching downpours. This Saturday of Easter Week was no different, for it had begun in drizzle, hinted at clearing skies, then reneged with clouds gathering low upon the horizon, sweeping in from Wales.

It was mid-day, but the great hall at Devizes was already lit with torches, wall rushlights, and an overhead candelabra. The hearth was ablaze, too, as was the temper of England's King. Edward was striding back and forth, dictating rapidly to a harried scribe. The man's task was a thankless one, for Edward was too angry to frame his thoughts in coherent form, and it was up to the scribe to capture the gist of his King's outpouring, then recast it into the conventional, formal mold used for letters, even a letter such as this one, going to the King's brother, Edmund, in France.

It had taken just three days for news of the Welsh rebellion to reach

Edward, and he had acted with his usual dispatch, swiftly establishing three military commands to contain the rising until he could take the field himself. The war-lord for mid-Wales was now slouched in a window-seat, watching his sovereign with alert interest, guarded amusement, and some degree of wariness.

Roger de Mortimer was not an easy man to impress, and a crown alone did not bedazzle him, for he'd grown up during the haphazard reign of Edward's feckless father. The de Mortimers had been a power in the Marches for generations, had clashed with one king after another, wheeling and dealing with impunity, for their family had been blessed with an abundance of audacity and a dearth of scruples. But the rules of the game had changed in the years since Evesham. A man played such games with Edward at his own peril, and de Mortimer had thought it prudent to hasten to Devizes and pledge anew his loyalty, lest Edward cast a jaundiced eye upon his erstwhile alliance with Llewelyn ap Gruffydd.

For the same reason, de Mortimer did not confide his own suspicions, that this war was not of Llewelyn's doing. It did not make sense to him that Llewelyn should launch a war until he'd accomplished the aim of their alliance, the elimination of the threat posed by Gruffydd ap Gwenwynwyn. De Mortimer had a strong hunch that any hunt for blame would lead to Davydd's door, for Davydd thrived upon double-dealing, and this would have been a rare temptation, indeed, a chance to impale Edward and Llewelyn upon the same lance. But de Mortimer kept these speculations to himself, for rage against the Welsh was running high at Devizes, and angry men were often quick to imbue even innocuous words with sinister significance.

Edward had not yet begun his letter to Edmund, having interrupted himself to greet John Giffard, newly arrived for the morrow's council of war. There was but one topic of conversation at court these days, the perfidy of the Welsh, and although de Mortimer caught only an occasional word, it was easy enough to fill in the blank spaces. At a burst of particularly vigorous and vivid cursing from Edward, he concluded that Davydd was the one under discussion, for he had noticed that Edward reserved his most scathing condemnation for his one-time ally. For Llewelyn and the Welsh people, Edward employed such stinging terms of contempt as "disloyal, lawless, faithless, and false." But Davydd was more than a traitor, he was an ingrate as well, and whenever Edward began to blister the air with "misbegotten, treacherous son of Satan" and "accursed, fork-tongued Welsh Judas," de Mortimer knew Davydd was the likely target of Edward's wrath.

De Mortimer agreed wholeheartedly with Edward's vitriolic assessment of Davydd's character, and he was entertained, as well, by Edward's colorful turn of phrase. But he was puzzled by the genuine echoes of indignation in Edward's voice. To hear Edward tell it now, he'd welcomed Davydd at his court out of sheer Christian kindness, moved by pity for Davydd's woeful plight. It amused de Mortimer enormously to hear Davydd described as an orphan of the storm, instead of a sword leveled at Llewelyn's throat. It was true that Edward had shown Davydd considerable favor. It was also true that Edward would have let Davydd starve by the roadside had he not been so useful a weapon to the English Crown. So why then, did his outrage sound so sincere when he decried Davydd's ingratitude?

De Mortimer was willing to wager his hopes for salvation that self-interest was the one drink no man refused, but he had never understood why most men must sweeten it so lavishly ere they could swallow it. It seemed, though, that even a King had need of sugar, and he felt a faint flicker of the contempt that weakness of any kind always aroused in him. But he took care to keep such dangerous thoughts safely buried in the back of his brain, for a king could afford the luxury of lying to himself—if he was also the greatest soldier in Christendom.

Dismissing Giffard, Edward turned back to his patiently waiting scribe. "This next letter goes to my brother, the Earl of Lancaster. You add his other titles. I believe he is still at La Ferté Milon. The usual greetings. Say then, that I would advise him of recent happenings in Wales; he already knows of their Palm Sunday treachery. Tell him that two days afterward, the Welsh lured the constable of Aberystwyth Castle away, under the pretext of inviting him to dine with them. Instead, they seized him, and then attacked the town, killing English citizens and taking the castle. That same week—Holy Week it was, too, for the Welsh are as impious and ungodly as even the Jews and Saracens—the Welsh captured castles at Llandovery and Carreg Cennen. And on Good Friday, they attacked Oswestry again, left it in flaming ruins."

Edward paused, staring past the scribe with blind, inward eyes. The man squirmed uneasily under the intensity of that blue-white gaze, and Edward eventually came back to the moment, back to the hall.

"Tell Edmund that I have called upon my vassals and the shire levies. I have also engaged fifteen hundred Gascon crossbowmen, and I shall be laying claim to the services of the ships of the Cinque Ports. Gruffydd ap Gwenwynwyn has vowed to hold fast for the Crown, and I have received pledges of loyalty from Rhys ap Gruffydd, Rhys ap Maredudd, and the least of Llewelyn ap Gruffydd's brothers. But the rest of Wales is rallying to Llewelyn. And their treachery has so far been rewarded with unholy success."

Edward had begun to pace. "Davydd ap Gruffydd now holds Ruthin and Dinas Bran as well as Hawarden, and indeed, his bloody forays took him almost to the gates of Chester itself. He then hastened south to stir the flames of rebellion in Ceredigion. Llewelyn is said to be commanding the sieges of my castles at Flynt and Rhuddlan. They will not fall to him, though. They cannot be taken by force, nor can they be starved into submission, for when I built them, I made sure they could be victualed from the sea. So they ought to be able to hold out until I can raise the sieges."

Edward paused again. This letter to Edmund, when done, would be full of facts, but it would offer no glimpse into his mind, his heart. He would to God Edmund was here now, for with Edmund, he could be honest, with Edmund, he could reveal more than rage. Eleanora would try to understand. He knew that. But as much as he loved his wife, he did not think women could comprehend issues of honor. More-over, she had always looked upon Davydd with loathing; it would never even occur to her that his betrayal could hurt. Edward's jaw muscles clenched, for Davydd's very name tasted foul to him now. He'd been fair to both brothers, more than fair. He'd not sought Llewelyn's de-struction, offered terms, instead, let the man keep his crown and Ellen, too. As for Davydd . . . what had he not given Davydd? Lands in Cheshire, royal favor, a rich wife, and she his own kinswoman, even his friendship. And they repaid his generosity with treason.

He'd not realized how long his brooding silence had lasted, not until he glanced up, saw that they were all watching him. "Pick up your pen," he told the scribe. "End the letter thus. Say that the Welsh are an accursed, willful, and vexatious people, enemies of the King's Peace, shameless violators of God's Holy Truce. Again and again they have rejected English laws, disavowed their sworn oaths, and spilled the blood of innocents. But no more. They shall pay and pay dear for their latest treachery, for Scriptures say that those who sow the wind, reap the whirlwind."

Edward was no longer speaking just to the scribe. His eyes were sweeping the hall, moving from face to face. "There can be but one writ recognized in this isle of ours, one government, one sovereign lord. I know that is God's Will, just as surely as I know this turmoil and defiance must cease. This is not the first war English kings have had to fight with the Welsh, but I swear, upon the surety of my soul, that it shall be the last."

31

TAUNTON CASTLE, ENGLAND

April 1282

Amaury's memories of the years he'd passed in English prisons were blurred, grey, and indistinct. But his seventh year of captivity had begun in a blaze of brightness, with word of his sister's pregnancy. His own future had seemed more promising, too, for Pope Martin IV had sent a papal nuncio to England, charged with one task—securing Amaury's release. He had been well received by the English clergy, and on February 5th, an assembly of Bishops was convened at London, where the Bishops earnestly entreated their King on Amaury's behalf. So insistent were their voices that Edward reluctantly agreed to consider Amaury's fate when Parliament met on April 2nd.

Amaury kept his hopes tethered, though, afraid to let them soar. And his caution served him well, for in March, Wales was engulfed in flames. Ellen had kept her wits about her, dispatching a letter within hours after learning of Davydd's treachery, a letter that reached him before the castellan of Taunton Castle knew Wales and England were at war. Amaury was rereading it now, wondering bleakly when he'd get another one. How would he even know when her babe was born? How would he know if evil befell her?

He'd left a window unshuttered, as was his habit. Taunton Castle had been a pleasant surprise, not at all the remote and foreboding moorland fortress he'd been dreading. Rising up on the south bank of the River Tone, this ancient castle built by Bishops overlooked the Augustinian priory of St Peter and St Paul and a thriving small town that traced its beginnings back to the Saxon kingdom of Wessex. Even the persistent April rain could not diminish the beauty of the Somerset countryside, and Amaury often spent time at the window, gazing out upon the emerald-green tranquillity of the Vale of Taunton. But today his thoughts and his fears were focused far to the west, upon Wales and his pregnant sister's peril.

Amaury had often heard that the blind were compensated for the loss of their sight by the enhancement of their other senses, and he'd come to believe that it was true, as well, for prisoners. Never had his hearing been more acute, and he heard the footsteps long before they approached his door. He was on his feet, waiting, when it opened and John de Somerset entered.

Amaury was pleased. "Well, this is a surprise for certes. Who is keeping Sherborne safe from enemy attack?"

"Ah, but I am no longer its castellan, not since April fifth, when the King bade me turn it over to the Sheriff of Dorsetshire. I've a new and more interesting duty at hand, have brought you a visitor, an archdeacon no less, come on behalf of the Bishop of Bath and Wells."

"Edward's Chancellor?" Amaury was intrigued, but wary, for Robert Burnell was Edward's other self, far more loyal to Edward than to the Pope. "Where is he, then, this archdeacon of Burnell's?"

"He wanted to change his wet clothes. You'd think he was in danger of melting like sugar, the way he's been griping about the rain. And I'll wager he's likely to want a nap, too, as soon as he sees a bed. Old bones chill easily, it seems. But I was glad of it, for I wanted to be the one to tell you. Your days at Taunton are done. You'd best start gathering up your books and such, for we leave on the morrow."

Amaury's face did not change, but beneath his surface calm, fear was stirring. Blessed Lady Mary, not back to Corfe! "Where are we going?" he asked, once he was sure his voice would not give away his inner agitation.

"To London. And then . . . Dover, I expect. After that . . ." But John could no longer keep a straight face. "I seem to remember you telling me that you bought a house in Paris after your lady mother died. Unless you want to go first to Italy and thank the Pope in person?"

Amaury stared at the other man. "I'm to be freed? You swear it is so, John? This is not one of your jests?"

"By the Rood, no! I fancy a joke as well as the next lad, but I'd not jest about this. God's holy truth, the King has agreed to set you free. We're to escort you to the Chancellor in London, where you must swear never to return to English shores. Then we hand you over to the papal nuncio, and off you go—with nary a regret, I'll wager!"

"I cannot believe it," Amaury said softly, more to himself than to John. "I'd just about given up hope of it ever happening, for no less than three Popes have sought to gain my freedom. What made Edward relent? Why now?"

"Judging from what the archdeacon said, and he'd talk the ears off a rabbit, give him half a chance, you owe your freedom to the Pope's persistence and the rebellion of that Welsh brother-in-law of yours. The King has but one thought in mind these days—to bring the wrath of God down upon the Welsh—and he wants the Church to support him whilst he does it. According to the archdeacon, the Pope knows this full well, and was canny enough to exact a price for that support—you. It may be, too, that the King was growing weary of fighting with his own clergy about you, for the Archbishop of Canterbury has been right keen on getting you freed, lad, going to Devizes to argue your case. He's another one who likes to talk, and when you're wearing a mitre, even a king has to hear you out."

John was a talker, too, and Amaury rarely resisted an opportunity to twit him about his babbling brook of a tongue. But now John's cheerful patter rained about him unaware, for he was caught up in the diabolic irony of it all, that the Welsh war could restore his world at the same time that it threatened Ellen's. He looked so somber that John unfastened a wineskin from his belt, poured for them both, and then sloshed a wet wine cup into his hand.

"I remembered that you've a taste for malmsey. Drink up, lad, for you'll not have a better reason for rejoicing. So tell me, what is the first thing you mean to do once you're free?"

The corner of Amaury's mouth twitched. "If you'd been locked away from the world for more than six years, what is the first thing you'd do?"

John choked on his wine, then laughed so hard that he choked again. "That sounds suspiciously like sinning to me, and you a man of God!"

Amaury grinned. "And precisely because I am a priest, I well know the cleansing power of confession and contrition," he said, sending John off into another spasm of irreverent mirth. He'd strolled over to the window, stood looking out at the misted hills. "How far are we from Bristol, John, about fifty miles? Why could I not take ship from there?"

John's amiable manner cloaked a sharp wit. He frowned thoughtfully, and was not long in remembering that only a narrow stretch of water separated Bristol from the Welsh border. "Jesus God, lad, you'd best banish that notion straightaway! Even if you were free to wander off into Wales at your will, the country is up in arms against the English. Nor are we just going to shove you across the drawbridge on the morrow and wish you Godspeed. You'll be in the custody of the Church until you have abjured the realm, and, to speak bluntly, the last thing you want is to give the King a reason—any reason—to change his mind. I understand your wish to bid your sister farewell. But your only concern now must be getting safe aboard the papal nuncio's ship, watching Dover's white cliffs fade into the distance."

"You're right, of course," Amaury admitted. "It was indeed a mad whim." Turning back to the window, he watched the clouds drifting across the vale, as white as those chalk cliffs of Dover. "But it suddenly occurred to me that I might never see my sister again."

LLEWELYN had moved his household across the strait to Aber, for memories were still raw of the last English invasion of Môn. He would have preferred to ensconce Ellen deep within the defenses of Eryri, but he'd hesitated to subject her to that long ride through the mountains to Dolwyddelan. It was easier, too, for him to return to Aber from the sieges of Flynt and Rhuddlan; he knew how much she needed him with her in these last months of her pregnancy. Torn betwen Ellen's unspoken fears and the unrelenting demands of wartime command, he expended his energy and efforts with reckless abandon, seeking to give strength to his men, encouragement to his troubled subjects, and hope, the most finite of all his resources, to his wife.

MAY had dawned in such summery, sunlit warmth that Ellen's garden was soon ablaze with white and purple violets. Juliana was artistically arranging delicate blossoms in a glazed clay pitcher, but her eyes kept straying to the window-seat, where Ellen was intent upon her baby's christening cloth.

"I saw Hugh and Caitlin going into the chapel," she said. "They may have been planning to pray, but I think it more likely that they were seeking a lovers' sanctuary, a few stolen moments together. Are you sure, Ellen, that nothing need be done about them?"

"Quite sure," Ellen said, with an unaccustomed edge to her voice; she was discovering that exhaustion and impatience went hand in glove. "We had a long talk, and they agreed with me that Llewelyn has enough cares at the moment, needs no more burdens thrust upon him. Caitlin promised me that they would wait ere they sought Llewelyn's permission to wed. She may love Hugh, but she loves Llewelyn, too, and now his need must come first."

"I do not mean to question their good faith, but they are very young, Ellen, and for the young, love can burn hotter than any fever. Do you truly think their resolve will hold if this war drags on?"

"If you are asking whether I think they would lay together, no, I do not. Hugh would never dishonor my niece. Let them snatch a tryst or two, have some private moments in a quiet chapel, a walk on the beach. We both know that this brief time is all they'll ever have."

Juliana nodded, then sighed. "But they are not discreet, look upon each other with far too much fondness for others to miss. Already there is talk, Ellen, and it will get worse."

Ellen shrugged, snapped her thread in two. "Gossip," she said tersely, "is the least of my worries these days."

"Do you think Llewelyn might return to Aber this week?"

"I do not know, Juliana. He could return on the morrow, or not for a fortnight. It depends upon the fortunes of war. I know that he will come if he can, and I must take comfort in that."

Ellen let her sewing drop onto the seat beside her, leaned back wearily against the cushions. "When Llewelyn promised me that he would not take the field until after Bran was born, I knew he meant it. But I knew, too, that circumstances of war might make his promise impossible to keep. So far, though, he has held to it, has left the fighting in the south to Davydd, and not an hour passes that I do not thank God for it. One of Llewelyn's bards once said of him, 'Pan el i ryfel nid ymgyddia'—'When he goes to war, he hides not himself.' "

Juliana groped hastily for comfort, aware how lame her offering was even as she said, "But he is not fighting now in battles, Ellen. He is commanding a siege. That must be safer, surely?"

"I keep telling myself that, too, Juliana. And I try not to remember that my grand-uncle, the King the English call 'Lionheart,' died whilst besieging a paltry, insignificant castle at Châlus."

Juliana moved to the table, poured for Ellen the rest of her posset, for that concoction of spiced milk and wine was known to benefit those ailing or heavy with child. "Have you heard from Llewelyn since you sent him word of his brother's death?"

"No, not yet. I know he loved Owain not, but even so . . ." Ellen accepted the posset, took several dutiful sips, then essayed a smile and a joke, one that held more raw honesty than humor. "You have no idea, Juliana, how often I've wished Llewelyn were an only child!"

"And if God had to give him a brother, a pity it could not have been Edmund. Better yet, why could the Almighty not have grafted Davydd upon Edward's family tree?"

Ellen's laughter was half-hearted, hollow. "A perfect pairing that would be, a match made in Hell," she said, striving gamely to echo Juliana's bantering tone. But Juliana did not look convinced, and Ellen gave up the pretense. "You should have made your escape whilst you could, Juliana, for I'm not fit company for man or beast these days. I'm not sleeping as I ought, and when I do . . . I've been having this dreadful dream. It is always the same. I am alone on this dark, unfamiliar road.

I can sense danger ahead, but I cannot go back, so I keep on, getting closer and closer, until the ground starts to slip under my feet, and I've nothing to hold on to . . ."

Juliana crossed swiftly to the window-seat, truly alarmed now, for she knew that such morbid fancies might well harm Ellen's babe; some people claimed that disfiguring birthmarks were the result of a bad scare whilst the child was still in the womb. But as she leaned over, her eye was caught by movement behind Ellen's head. Straightening up, she peered through the thick, greenish glass, and then laughed, out of sheer relief. "How about holding on to your husband? He has just ridden into the bailey."

"THE sieges still go on, then?"

Llewelyn nodded, shifting so he could slide his arm around Ellen's shoulders. "Nothing has changed. They cannot get out, we cannot get in. But as long as they are penned up behind the walls of Rhuddlan and Flynt, they are not able to prey upon the Welsh countryside."

Ellen moved closer on the seat. When they'd been apart for a time, she usually liked to sit on his lap, but that was not a comfortable position now, not with just six weeks until the baby was due. "I had a Requiem Mass said for the repose of Owain's soul," she said, and Llewelyn gave her a quick, grateful kiss.

"Thank you, lass. I knew he'd been ailing, so it was not such a surprise. Nor can I say that I grieved for him, although Davydd might. But I was glad, nonetheless, that he'd not died at Dolbadarn."

"Llewelyn . . . how long can you stay this time?"

"Only a few days," Llewelyn said reluctantly. "This was not the best time for me to return to Aber, for I'd ordered several trebuchets to be built, and they'll be done any day. But I got news last night from England, and I had to come back, for I had to be the one to tell you."

He saw her flinch, then brace herself to be brave, and he said hastily, "Ah, no, my love, the news need not always be bad! This is news to give you great joy, and I had to see your face when you heard it, for you've been waiting six years and more for this day. Your brother has been freed from Edward's prison."

He heard her indrawn breath, saw her eyes widen, and then she was in his arms, her breath warm upon his neck, and the words echoing in his ear were the same ones, over and over, a starkly simple "thank God, oh, thank God!"

AMAURY had been turned over to the papal nuncio, Raymond Nogeriis, Dean of Le Puy, on the 21st of April. They sailed at once for France. On the 22d of May, Amaury wrote to Edward from Arras, in northern France, thanking his royal cousin for his "grace," pledging fidelity, and asking for the liberty to sue Edmund in an English court for the recovery of the earldom of Leicester. The letter infuriated Edward, as it was clearly meant to do.

32

ABER, WALES

June 1282

LLEWELYN awakened to the sweet, heavy scent of honeysuckle, for Ellen had filled their bedchamber with blooming woodbine. It was just after dawn; light had begun to filter through the window glass, and the night shadows were in retreat. He shifted his position carefully, not wanting to disturb Ellen. But when he glanced over, he found himself gazing into clear hazel eyes. Leaning toward her, he brushed his lips against her cheek. "I'd hoped to let you sleep."

"I've been awake for a while," Ellen said and smiled at him. "I think this might be the day."

To her amusement, her drowsy husband shot up in bed as if stung. "Why did you not wake me, Ellen? Thank Christ the midwife is already at Aber!" He was flinging aside the covers when she caught his arm.

"Llewelyn, there is no need for haste. The baby will not pop out like a cork from a bottle!" Laughing, she drew him back into bed beside her. "I am not even sure yet, for I've been having pains come and go for days now. Gwynora did say, though, that the true pangs start in the back, and that is where I am feeling these, so . . ." She smiled again. "We'll know soon enough. But for now, I'd like to stay here in bed with you, for this is the last time we'll be alone until the babe is born. Once my lying-in begins, you'll not be able to set foot across this threshold, Prince or no!"

She let Llewelyn prop pillows behind her, let him cradle her within the safe circle of his arms. When her next pain came, he massaged the small of her back until it passed, then confessed, "It does not seem real to me yet."

"I know," she confessed. "To me, either. It is so odd, for never have I longed for any happening, not even our wedding, as I've longed for this day. Yet now that it is nigh, I almost wish it were not . . ."

His fingers had been caressing the nape of her neck, now were suddenly still. "Are you afraid, Ellen?"

She shook her head. "No. Well . . . maybe a little. A woman's first birth is said to be the hardest. But my mother was brought to bed of seven healthy babies, a right reassuring family tradition. And I have faith in Dame Blodwen. I also will have Gwynora with me, and Elizabeth and Juliana. If I would hold time back, it is not that I am fearful. It is because once our child is born, you'll leave me, ride off to war."

From the corner of her eye, she saw him wince, and was at once contrite. "Ah, love, I am sorry! I ought never to have said that, for I know you have no choice. Do what you must, and your son and I will be here to welcome you home once this war is done."

"You need never apologize for saying what you think, lass. I understand. How could you ever forget that Evesham summer, waiting with your mother at Dover Castle for word of your father's fate? But it will not be like that this time, Ellen. A letter a day—I promise—delivered by swift-riding couriers whose only duty will be to keep you informed of my whereabouts, my well-being, and, of course, my triumphs!"

"You know me so well," she said softly. "I shall hold you to that vow, too. Llewelyn . . . I've seen a change in you during these past few weeks. You seem more at ease, more at peace with yourself. Even after Reginald de Grey was able to raise your sieges at Flynt and Rhuddlan, you did not appear much troubled by it. Will you answer me honestly? Will you tell me if you truly believe you can win this war?"

He'd have lied without any qualms whatsoever, if that would give her the strength she needed to face the ordeal that lay ahead of her. But he did not have to lie, for she'd read him correctly; he was indeed more hopeful now than at any time since Davydd's Palm Sunday betrayal. "Yes," he said slowly, "I do believe it is a war we can win. Never have my people been so united, so determined to hold fast against the English invaders. Edward has accomplished what I never could, lass, brought us together. Who knows, one day far in the future men might well see him as the patron saint of Welsh unity."

Ellen smiled at that, as he'd hoped she might. "Edward is a superior soldier, cariad, but he is also a King, with a King's far-reaching concerns, and too much common sense to let himself be caught up in battlefield bravado. If we can make this war costly enough and bloody enough, he'll offer terms, settle for what he can get. It will not be easy and it will not be soon. We'll have to pay a high price for victory, Ellen. But it's within our reach. God willing, it is also within our grasp."

Ellen pillowed her head in the crook of his shoulder. "Why should God not will it? You've fought three wars with Edward, have won two. I do—" She jerked suddenly in his embrace, then expelled an uneven breath. "Well, it is no longer in doubt," she said, and began to laugh. "Bran is definitely knocking on the door!"

THAT Tuesday, the 16th of June in God's Year, 1282, did not at first appear out of the ordinary. It was warm, skies overcast, an erratic breeze wafting seaward from the inland mountains. Those at Aber did not seem to be aware of its odder aspects. Only Llewelyn—and possibly Hugh— had guessed the truth, that it somehow held more hours than those allotted to other days.

As the morning ebbed away, Llewelyn began to revise all his ideas of eternity. He paced and waited and blazed a path from the hall to Ellen's lying-in chamber, each time getting the same impatient answer, that the babe would come in God's own time and not sooner. He made such a nuisance of himself that Elizabeth finally promised to seek him out every hour without fail, even if there was naught to report. After that, he waited and paced, and he and Hugh took turns reassuring each other that Ellen would soon be delivered of a healthy, handsome son.

In mid-afternoon, Dai and Goronwy arrived, bearing unwelcome news. The English had burned the town of St Asaph, not sparing even the cathedral. Anian, St Asaph's Bishop, had long been at odds with Llewelyn, but he'd refused to obey the Archbishop of Canterbury's command, refused to publish the edict that excommunicated Llewelyn, and he'd now paid a great price for his defiance.

But not even the vivid image of a town in flames could keep Llewelyn's thoughts from straying across the bailey, and Dai and Goronwy gallantly conceded Ellen the victory, no longer tried to talk to Llewelyn of strategy and his coming campaign in the south. Instead, they began to make the heavy-handed, well-meaning jokes that people inevitably inflicted upon first-time fathers. Llewelyn did not mind, though; he was grateful for any distraction, for anything or anyone who could stop him from dwelling upon his wife's ordeal, upon all that could go wrong in a birthing.

Elizabeth kept her word, and when she did not come herself to the hall, she sent Juliana or Caitlin. Whoever the messenger was, though, the message seemed woefully inadequate to Llewelyn, that all was going as it ought. But soon after dusk Elizabeth brought more encouraging word. Ellen's waters had broken, she reported cheerfully, a sure sign that the babe would soon be delivered.

The evening hours passed. Dinner was served. Dai and Goronwy ate heartily, Llewelyn very little. Juliana had assured him they were feeding Ellen honey and wine to keep her strength up, insisted that her spirits were good. He found himself marveling more and more at the quiet, unsung courage of women. And he'd begun to wish fervently that he knew more about the female mysteries of the birthing chamber. By his reckoning, Ellen had been in labor now for eighteen hours, but he did not know if that was what the midwives termed a "lingering" delivery. By prodding boyhood memories, he seemed to remember his mother giving birth to Davydd in ten hours or so; he could stir up no recollection of Rhodri's birth. The women continued to offer vague, evasive assurances that he no longer believed. As the night advanced, so, too, did his sense of foreboding.

Llewelyn could not sleep, lay watchful and tense upon a pallet in the great hall. All around him, men were snoring, fumbling for blankets as the hearth burned low. Dogs prowled about amidst the sleepers, scratching fleas, sniffing out food dropped into the floor rushes. Out in the dark beyond the hall, an owl screeched, and Llewelyn raised his head, listening uneasily, for that was an ill omen for certes; all his life he'd heard it said that owls, like howling dogs, heralded an impending death. When he could endure neither the solitude nor his own thoughts any longer, he rose and, trailed by Nia, crossed the hall, stepped out into the bailey.

He'd begun to think the night would never end, but the sky was slowly greying to the east. He stood for a time gazing across the bailey; the shutters of Ellen's lying-in chamber were in place, but a few glimmers of light escaped through the cracks. The owl cried again, and he hesitated no longer, began to walk toward the silent, darkened chapel.

The door was ajar. As Llewelyn moved into the shadows of the nave, he saw a lantern flickering upon the altar. A woman was kneeling within its feeble glow. She was cloaked in a long, full mantle, and it was not until she turned at sound of his footsteps that he recognized his sister-in-law. He looked into the pale, tear-streaked face upturned to his, and then he reached down, pulled Elizabeth to her feet.

"You've been lying to me," he said. "Why?"

"Ellen made us promise not to tell you. She said it would serve for naught, that you were anxious enough about the birthing, needed no more cares thrust upon you, and she would not be denied."

Llewelyn was silent for a moment. "More fool I, for not expecting
that of Ellen." Grasping Elizabeth by the elbow, he steered her back
into the lantern light. "Now I'd have the truth," he said. "Why is the
birth taking so long? What has gone wrong?"

"Only the Almighty could answer that with certainty. All we can
do is guess. Ellen's pains are sharp and too frequent for her to get any
rest, but the mouth of her womb has not dilated as it ought by now.
Dame Blodwen said she has seen this happen when the babe is large
and the mother narrow across the hips—like Ellen. It may be—"

"Christ! Are you saying she cannot deliver the baby?"

"No!" Elizabeth's cry, shrill and scared, focused Llewelyn's attention fully upon her for the first time, and he saw now the toll Ellen's
travail was taking upon Elizabeth. Her eyes were red-rimmed, her lips
bitten raw, and she looked even younger than her twenty-four years,
looked like a weary, bewildered child kept up past her bedtime.

"You're about done-in, lass," he said, in a gentler voice. "Just tell
me the truth. No more lies. How bad is it?"

"You must not despair, Llewelyn. I'll not deny that she's suffering,
or that the midwives are very disquieted, but they have not given up
hope, I swear they have not. It is just so hard to see her in such pain
and not be able to help her . . . If only her waters had not broken!"

"But you said that was a good sign! Or was that a lie, too?"

"No! When the waters break, that usually means the birth is drawing
nigh. But sometimes it does not happen, and then the risk to the mother
and baby is much greater. Her pains become more severe, you see, and
if the labor lingers on too long, she loses heart, her strength bleeds
away . . ." Elizabeth's voice faltered, then steadied again. "But not Ellen!
I've never seen a woman so set upon giving her husband a son, and
she will, Llewelyn, I know she will!"

Llewelyn loosened his grip upon her arm, turned away as he sought
to master his fear. By now it ought to have been a familiar foe, a presence
sensed if not seen since Ellen's lying-in began, hovering close at hand
these long hours past, awaiting its chance. But Elizabeth had just given
it legitimacy, infused it with enough raw power to gain the upper hand,
to become the only voice he heeded, and he swung around abruptly,
started for the door. Elizabeth had seen his face, though, and she darted
forward, her small, slender body a barricade thrust into his path, arms
outstretched.

"No," she cried, "you cannot do that, Llewelyn! You cannot go to
her, not now, not until the babe is born."

"I have to do something! Can you not see that?"

"I understand," she said, "I truly do, for you're more like Davydd
than either of you know. Nothing is harder for you than waiting, but

that is all you can do for Ellen now. It would not help to go to her, for you could not ease her pains, you could not make the babe come a blessed moment sooner. All you could do would be to burden her with your fear, and she is not strong enough to bear it. Men are always barred from the birthing chamber, always. You take but one step into that room and Ellen will know the truth, that you think she's dying."

Llewelyn started to speak but the words wouldn't come, for there was no way to refute her argument, and even half-crazed with fear, he knew it. "You'll tell me how she is faring?"

She nodded, tears brimming over again. "I'll hold nothing back," she promised. "I swear it upon the souls of my own sons." He was too tall for her to kiss. Instead, she took his hand, pressed it against her cheek. "God will not abandon Ellen in her time of need," she said, and then she was gone, dark mantle blending into the shadows, her steps too light and quick to linger long on the quiet air. She'd forgotten her lantern, and the candle's fluttering white flame drew Llewelyn back to the altar.

Thy Will be done. The Christian's greatest test of faith. Llewelyn knew the words by heart, the prayer of the Saviour at Gethsemane just before His betrayal. "Father, all things are possible to Thee. Remove this cup from me. Yet not what I will, but what Thou wilt." He knew the words by heart. But they caught in his throat. He could not say "Thy Will be done" if that meant Ellen might die in childbirth. Instead, he pleaded and he bargained, offered up to God all that he had, his soul, his tomorrows, hopes of salvation, if only the Almighty would save his wife and son.

AT Gwynora's urging, Ellen would try to swallow a spoonful of honey. Juliana kept wiping her hot face with a wet cloth, massaging her legs when they cramped. Caitlin fanned her, brushed her hair, rubbed her temples with rosewater. They gave her feverfew, and wine mixed with the bark of cassia fistula. Elizabeth found an eaglestone for her to hold when the pain got too bad. And they offered their hope and cheer in abundant measure, assuring her that she had nothing to fear, that the child was coming soon.

Ellen knew better, knew she and her baby were in grave danger. The chamber was stifling, dimly lit, the shutters still latched. It was unexpectedly disconcerting, not knowing day from night, and she kept asking what time it was. Wednesday, love, mid-morning. Nigh on noon, lass. Mayhap about four, my lady. Over Ellen's head, their eyes met in the same silent, frightened query. Thirty-six hours. How much longer could her strength hold out?

Ellen could deny her fear, but not her fatigue. She was no longer able to walk across the room to the privy chamber; they had to bring her the chamber pot now. Exhaustion was becoming as great an enemy as the pain, and her brain had begun to play queer tricks. She got it into her head that Blanche was on her way to Aber, could not understand when they told her Blanche was in France. She would ask about Llewelyn, receive Elizabeth's assurances that he was enduring the waiting as well as men ever did, forget she asked, and ask again. And she suddenly had to have her dog, would not rest until Caitlin brought the little creature into the chamber, where it huddled by the birthing stool, whining and getting underfoot.

Dame Blodwen was again lowering herself onto her knees before the birthing stool. She was a statuesque woman, full figured, and stiff in the joints, but she managed the awkward maneuver without losing her dignity. She held out her hands, and Gwynora poured thyme oil into her cupped palms. Reaching for the hem of Ellen's chemise, she raised the skirt, uttering a polite "By your leave, my lady" that Ellen thought preposterous under the circumstances. The next contraction came then, and she forgot Dame Boldwen's probing fingers, forgot all but the pain. When it was over, she slumped back upon the stool, just in time to catch the troubled look that passed between Dame Blodwen and Gwynora.

"Is it the baby? Is he dead? Is that why I have not been able to bring him forth—because he is dead?"

"Ah, no, my lady! The babe is not dead!"

But now that Ellen had at last asked the unspeakable, she was not to be so easily satisfied. Gwynora saw her disbelief, and leaned over, catching Ellen's hand in her own. "Listen to me, child," she said, forgetting that Ellen was her mistress, seeing only a young woman urgently in need of comfort. "Dame Blodwen spoke true; the babe is not dead. If he were, you'd not be feeling him move in the womb, your nipples would be contracted, your eyes sunken, and your skin cold as ice—and none of that is true, is it now?"

She'd been specific enough to prevail over Ellen's doubts, aided by Ellen's desperate desire to believe her. "What is wrong, then? Why is it taking so long, Gwynora? Is it that . . . that he is positioned wrong in the womb?"

Dame Blodwen started to deny it, but Gwynora risked offending the midwife's professional pride by cutting her off. They should have been honest with Ellen from the very first; she'd known that, for she knew Ellen. "We do not think so, lass, but we'll not know for sure until the birth is nigh. If the babe is not coming head first as it ought, Dame Blodwen will reach up into the womb, try to turn it.

But even if it does come feet first, it can still be safely delivered."

Gwynora paused; she'd given Ellen the truth, but not all of it, for if the child lay crosswise in the womb, both mother and babe were doomed. Before Ellen could question her further, she brought a wine cup to the younger woman's lips, waited while Ellen drank.

"Listen to me, child," she said again. "You've had a rough time of it, and the worst lies ahead. I'll not lie to you about that. You asked why Dame Blodwen and I were so troubled just now. It is because the mouth of your womb is still not fully opened. All these hours and still not opened. But it is dilating, lass. It is slow, slow enough to break your heart—if not your spirit. Your babe may be a mite shy about making his entrance, but make it he will—as long as your courage does not fail you."

Ellen's eyes were fastened unwaveringly upon Gwynora's face. "It will not," she said, then gasped, her body contorting upon the stool. When the pain had passed, she was drenched in sweat, but as soon as she got her breath back, she repeated, "It will not . . ."

It was dusk before Ellen's cervix had fully dilated. Soon thereafter, she was stricken with recurring, severe bouts of nausea and vomiting, and then, odd shivering fits, although she was hot and flushed and soaked in sweat. The midwives insisted that these were proofs that the birth was near, but it was still alarming to Juliana, and Elizabeth, who had not suffered such extreme symptoms in either of her pregnancies.

By now the strain was telling upon all the women. Only Caitlin's temper showed no signs of fraying. Gwynora had been opposed at first to Caitlin's presence, for she did not think the birthing chamber was a proper place for a young, impressionable virgin maid. But Caitlin had proved to be a godsend. Neither Elizabeth nor Juliana spoke much Welsh, Dame Blodwen and Gwynora spoke no French, and they could hardly expect Ellen to translate between contractions. Caitlin had been more successful, too, at hiding her fears than either Elizabeth or Juliana, and she seemed to know instinctively how best to comfort Ellen.

It was Caitlin who began to rummage through Ellen's jewelry coffer as Ellen's sweating, shivering tremors persisted. The other women saw a flash of coral and gold as she pressed an object into Ellen's hand, and they nodded approvingly, the midwives because coral was known to aid in childbirth travails, and Juliana because she knew the pater noster was a gift from Llewelyn. Ellen clutched the rosary tightly each time the pain came, held fast until it passed. "Hail Mary, full of grace. The Lord is with thee. Blessed art thou amongst women . . ." But soon the familiar, formal words of entreaty gave way to a far more simple prayer. "Blessed Lady Mary, do not let my baby die . . ."

"Soon, my lady, soon." The midwives had a litany of their own, one they murmured at soothing intervals . . . soon, soon now, lass. Until Gwynora gave a triumphant cry. "I can see the head!"

Removing Ellen's soiled chemise, Juliana moved behind her, sought to brace her body as she writhed and twisted upon the stool. Dame Blodwen was pressing upon her abdomen as each contraction hit. Ellen bit down until she tasted blood, Dame Blodwen pressed even harder, there was a burning sensation, pain greater than any that had come before, and then she could see her child's head, a cap of wet, scanty, dark hair. But it was not over yet. Urged on by the midwives, Ellen called upon her remaining strength, bore down, until at last the baby's shoulders came free, and the puckered, red, and bruised little body slid out in a gush of blood and mucus, into Gwynora's waiting hands.

Ellen sagged back against Juliana, too weak to feel anything yet, even relief. She was so tired, so very tired, and it was so peaceful now, dark and soothing and quiet . . . A jolt of sheer terror arrested her drift, brought her back, the realization that she'd yet to hear the baby cry. As she struggled to sit up, her abrupt movement sent pain surging through her abused, exhausted body, but she barely felt it, aware only of the utter silence and the dismayed looks upon the faces of the women.

"No . . . he cannot be dead! No!"

"The babe is not dead, my lady!"

"I do not believe you! Why do you look like that, then? Unless . . . is he whole? Crippled?" Ellen tried to reach out, but her arms were suddenly leaden, too heavy to lift. "Give him to me," she insisted. "Let me see . . ."

Their obvious reluctance only fed her fears. Alarmed by her increasing agitation, Elizabeth said hastily, "We will, Ellen, we will. But first I must tell— Dear God!"

The horror in Elizabeth's voice was puzzling to Ellen, intent only upon her child. But she followed Elizabeth's downward gaze, and gasped, for blood was everywhere, spurting out upon her thighs, splattering the skirts of the midwives, running down into the floor rushes.

Not even Caitlin, in her innocence, could convince herself this was just the afterbirth coming. If she'd harbored any doubts, the urgent actions of the other women soon showed how great was Ellen's peril. The next few moments were chaotic. Elizabeth snatched up the baby, even in her panic taking care not to jerk upon the umbilical cord still bound to Ellen. Dame Blodwen had begun to knead Ellen's abdomen, gesturing for Caitlin to elevate her legs. And Gwynora was holding a cup to her lips, urging her to swallow.

Ellen obeyed, and Gwynora reached over, pinched the baby's foot until it began to cry. "Do you hear that?" she said, digging her fingers into Ellen's shoulders. "This is your baby crying, your baby that needs you! You listen to that crying, lass, and you hold on!"

Ellen tried. She clung to that thin, reedy wail as if it were a life-line. But it was already growing weak, faint and far away. Someone was crying out her name. Then that, too, faded, and she heard nothing more.

ELIZABETH stood in the darkness before the door of the great hall, dreading to cross that threshold as she'd never dreaded anything before. But the baby had begun to whimper, and she knew she could delay no longer. Pray God she'd find the right words. She reached for the latch before she could lose her nerve, swung the door open.

Llewelyn was sitting in one of the window-seats, looking so haggard and hollow-eyed that Elizabeth felt pity twist like a knife. Hugh was the first to notice her. He half-rose from his seat, but his cry died on his lips, for one glance at Elizabeth's face was enough to warn him that something was very wrong. Others saw her now, too; there were uneasy murmurings, then an odd hush. It was the sudden silence that alerted Llewelyn. He glanced up and his breath stopped.

"Elizabeth?" He was on his feet now, his eyes shifting from the small blanketed bundle in her arms to her white, drawn face. "Ellen . . . ?"

"She . . . she is abed." Elizabeth swallowed with difficulty; never had her mouth felt so dry. "Llewelyn . . . you have a daughter."

Llewelyn stared at her, and for a moment, her words had no meaning. A daughter. A lass. Why? God in Heaven, why?

The other men had drawn near enough to hear, and they looked on in sympathetic silence, stunned by the unfairness of it all. Their lord had fought a lifetime to win and then keep a crown, but with no one now to leave it to. Not a lass for certes; Welsh law did not recognize female heirs, not where a principality was at stake. They glanced surreptitiously at their Prince and then away, not knowing what to say. Later they could offer hope, and not false hope, either, for mayhap the next time his lady would be luckier. But even the most undiscerning of them realized this was not the time to talk to Llewelyn of future birthings, not after his wife's childbed had come so close to being her deathbed.

Llewelyn was thinking of that, too, thinking of Ellen's ordeal. Two days suffering the torments of the damned, and all for a lass. "The ways of the Almighty," he said huskily, "can be beyond mortal understanding. This is like to break Ellen's heart, for she was so sure it would be a son, so sure . . ." What could he say to her? How could he convince her that it did not matter, that this was a disappointment he could live with? She'd know it was a lie, for them both, a lie. Turning back to Elizabeth, he made himself ask. "How did she take it?"

Elizabeth began to fuss with the baby's blanket, for she could not bear to watch his face as she told him. "She does not know yet, Llewelyn. After the babe was born, she began to bleed . . ."

In two strides, he was at her side. "She bled? But you did stop it? She will recover? Elizabeth, tell me!"

Elizabeth's eyes filled with tears. "She is in a bad way, Llewelyn," she said softly, "very bad . . ." She swayed suddenly, sick with fatigue and grief and remorse, for it haunted her now, remembering how she'd hoped Ellen might bear a daughter. Someone grasped her arm, led her toward a bench, and she sank down upon it gratefully, for she'd begun to tremble. She braced herself, then, to tell him the rest, the worst. But when she looked up, Llewelyn was gone.

JULIANA was huddled in the window-seat, weeping bitterly, oblivious of Caitlin's ineffective attempts at consolation. The midwives were both preoccupied with the woman in the bed, and neither one looked up until Llewelyn let the door slam shut. The smell of blood was still so strong that he almost gagged. The rushes were soaked, and so were several crumpled towels. Llewelyn was no stranger to bloodshed, but this blood was different, it was Ellen's. "Jesus God," he whispered, and then Caitlin was at his side. She'd meant to offer comfort, but she began to cry, and he was the one to reassure her. He held her close for a moment, neither one speaking, kept his arm around her shoulders as they approached the bed.

What he saw so far exceeded his worst fears that he was momentarily rendered speechless. Ellen's eyes appeared badly bruised, so sunken and shadowed were they. Her face had a waxen pallor that terrified him, for he'd seen that odd, ashen shade in too many coffins. Even her coppery red-blonde hair had lost it lustre; it lay limp and lifeless upon the pillow. So did her hand; her skin was cold, her fingers inert, unmoving in his. When he said her name, there was no response, not even a flicker of her lashes. He slid his fingers along her wrist, searching feverishly until he found a weak, rapid pulse. Only then did he straighten up, turn to face the waiting women.

"She's not come to her senses yet?"

Dame Blodwen slowly shook her head. "No, my lord, and we've not been able to bring her around. We've put a burned feather under her nose, rubbed her wrists with vinegar, to no avail."

Gwynora moved around the bed. "At least she is still breathing," she said bluntly, saw his face change, and drew a sharp, dismayed breath. "I am indeed sorry, my lord, but I assumed Lady Elizabeth would have told you all."

"She said that Ellen bled after the birth. There is more?"

"We almost lost her, my lord . . . twice. The first time she flooded, we were able to stop it, praise God, by massaging her belly until her womb tightened up again, and by getting her to swallow powdered root of dragonwort mixed with blackthorn. We'd prepared it before-hand . . . just in case. That is when she fainted, and no surprise, after what the poor lass had been through. But we had to get the afterbirth out, else she'd die for certes. And when we did, she bled again. The second time it was harder to stop. Nothing helped until we bled her at the ankle. But her strength bled away, too, my lord. I felt Death hovering right over our shoulders, never thought we'd be able to stave him off, and that is God's truth."

Llewelyn looked down at his wife, then back at Gwynora. "Will she live?" he asked at last, very low.

"She is in God's Hands, my lord. If only she were not so weak . . ." But as her eyes met Llewelyn's, Gwynora found she had to give him more than that, at least a hint of hope. "She might recover, my lord, as long as childbed fever does not set in . . ." She hesitated, not sure how much she should tell him. "That is an infection of the womb, my lord, which oft-times afflicts women who've just given birth or miscarried of a baby—"

"He understands," Caitlin interrupted hastily, for she knew what Gwynora did not, that Llewelyn had watched his favorite aunt die of childbed fever, another Elen. Her uncle had gone so pale that she was once again fighting back tears. "Uncle Llewelyn . . . I am going to fetch some servants, put them to cleaning up the bl— cleaning up the chamber. That way it will be neat and tidy when Aunt Ellen wakes up."

Llewelyn said nothing, and she began to wonder if he'd even heard her. But just as she reached the door, he said, "Tell them to bring flowers from her garden. Roses . . . Ellen loves roses."

LLEWELYN was dozing in a chair by his wife's bed. He jerked upright at sound of the closing door, then swiftly leaned over the bed, and Elizabeth flinched, for she knew he was reassuring himself that Ellen still breathed. "How does she?" she asked quietly.

"She awakened briefly after midnight, and then again near dawn. I am not sure if she knew me, though, for she soon slept again." Llewelyn straightened up and winced, for his muscles were aching and cramped, his body starved for sleep. "In the past hour or so, she's become more restless, tossing and turning. I think that is a good sign."

Optimism came as naturally to Elizabeth as breathing, and she agreed readily with Llewelyn that Ellen's increasing restiveness was very hopeful. He asked then what time it was, and she told him it was midmorning, apologizing for having been gone so long. "But I had to check on my lads, make sure their poor nurse was not going mad, trying to keep them out of mischief. And I wanted to look in on the baby. She's still uncommonly quiet for a newborn, but the wet-nurse says she has a right healthy appetite." She paused, waiting for Llewelyn to ask about his daughter. But he did not, and she sighed, watching as he moved his chair closer to the bed. He'd not left Ellen's side for the past twelve hours, sometimes talking softly to her, sometimes just holding her hand, but never more than an arm's length away. Elizabeth sighed again, and bent down to capture Ellen's dog, who sneaked into the room at every chance.

"Let her stay," Llewelyn said, then half-turned in his seat, for the door was opening again. Coming from morning sun into the shuttered sick-room, Caitlin and Hugh had to grope their way into the candlelit dimness. Hugh was carrying a tray; it had occurred to Caitlin that Llewelyn had eaten virtually nothing for the past two days. But as they came forward into the chamber, a sudden murmuring drew them all toward the bed.

"Llewelyn . . ."

"I'm here, cariad, right here."

Ellen's lashes flickered, giving Llewelyn a brief glimpse of glazed greenish eyes, pupils shrunk to slits. "I'm so cold," she whispered. "Why am I so cold?"

Llewelyn sat on the edge of the bed, gathered her into his arms. She was already beginning to tremble, and he reached hastily for the blanket at the foot of the bed. "Fetch the midwives," he said, with enough urgency in his voice to send Caitlin whirling toward the door. But she'd taken only a few steps before coming to an abrupt halt, for it was then that the tray of food slipped from Hugh's fingers, went clattering down into the floor rushes.

Caitlin stared at the broken crockery, then looked up at Hugh. He'd gone the color of chalk; even his mouth was rimmed in white. "Hugh? What is it?" He did not seem to hear her, continued to look blindly toward the bed, where Llewelyn and Elizabeth were wrapping Ellen in blankets. Ellen was shivering so violently now that her teeth were chattering, and it was then that Caitlin understood. Hugh was no longer in Wales; he was back in the Maremma, that accursed Tuscan marsh, watching helplessly as Ellen's brother was stricken with chills and then fever, unable to save Bran . . . or Ellen.

❧

ELLEN's chill lasted an hour, was followed by fever. Her temperature rose rapidly; by that Thursday afternoon, it was consuming her body in lethal heat. The midwives did what they could. They bled her again at the ankle, put hot poultices on her inflamed abdomen, tried to lower her fever with cold compresses, vervain, and sage. But their efforts were futile, and they knew it. Llewelyn's bedside vigil had become a death watch. He alone held on to hope.

The speed of Ellen's decline testified to the virulent nature of her infection. Gwynora and Dame Blodwen privately thought it a blessing that death would be so quick, for they'd tended too many women who died in agony, after suffering for days. But they said nothing to Llewelyn, understanding that he was not yet ready to face the truth, that his wife was dying. And so they did their best to ease Ellen's last hours, and they did not protest when Llewelyn insisted upon summoning a doctor, although they knew it was for naught.

The doctor arrived at nightfall. He listened intently to their recital of Ellen's symptoms—the raging fever, swollen, painful abdomen, extreme weakness, delirium—and gravely echoed the midwives' diagnosis: childbed fever. He was hampered by his inability to conduct a personal examination of the patient, but it was unthinkable for a woman to reveal her private female parts to a man not her husband. He did take Ellen's weak, racing pulse, noted her pallor, her hot, dry skin, her labored breathing, carefully studied a vial of her urine, and expressed his approval when the midwives assured him that they'd bled Ellen twice since the onset of the fever.

His arrival was well-timed, he said, for although men could be classed as choleric, sanguine, melancholic, or phlegmatic, all women were known to be melancholic, and the best time for bleeding a melancholic was during the evening hours. But he recommended the use of leeches rather than a lancet. Green leeches, taken from a frog pond and starved for a day first, were preferable, and fortunately he had been foresighted enough to bring some with him. Since they were to be applied to the Lady Ellen's belly, he had to rely upon the midwives to act for him, and he tutored them in the art of leeching at great length, instructing them how to place the leeches, rubbing the skin raw first, afterward sprinkling salt to break their grip.

The doctor was so sure that the leeching would benefit Ellen that Llewelyn let himself believe it, too. But she showed no improvement afterward. In fact, she seemed worse to Llewelyn. She'd been drifting in and out of delirium for hours, mumbling incoherently, breaking out in sweats, her breathing burdened now by intermittent coughing spells. Sometimes she seemed to know Llewelyn was there; too weak to talk, she'd give his hand a feeble squeeze. At other times, she'd cry out his name, but when he'd bend over the bed, he could find no recognition in the depths of those fever-bright, hollowed eyes.

The doctor admitted to being baffled by her failure to rally. There was one more treatment he could try, though. Good health was dependent upon the proper equilibrium of the four basic humors: blood, phlegm, white bile, and black bile. Lady Ellen's ailment was due to the imbalance in her womb of three of these humors. But they could be balanced by use of the cauter. Brandishing a slender needle-like rod for Llewelyn's inspection, he said proudly that it was made of beaten gold. Once it was heated and then applied hot to the lady's belly, the blisters it raised would not only adjust the imbalance of humors, they might also draw out some of the infection.

"Of course I could not do the blistering myself, for that would not be seemly. But I could show one of the women how to do it, if that meets with your approval, my lord?"

Llewelyn was looking at him with odd intensity; without knowing why, he found himself increasingly uncomfortable under that unblinking scrutiny. But he was still unprepared for what happened next. "Get out," Llewelyn said, "now." He did not raise his voice, but the doctor, stunned, indignant, yet thoroughly intimidated, snatched up his medical satchel, made a hasty retreat.

As soon as the doctor had fled, Llewelyn crossed to the bed. "Ellen? Ellen, can you not hear me?" He smoothed her hair, stroked her cheek, and linked his fingers in hers, but she did not respond, either to his touch or the sound of his voice, and he slowly knelt by the side of the bed. He had leaned forward, his head resting upon his arms, when he heard someone hesitantly clearing a throat.

"I beg your pardon, my lord, for intruding . . ." His chaplain was standing in the doorway; behind him, Llewelyn could see Caitlin and Elizabeth. Getting stiffly to his feet, he beckoned them into the room, then drew back into the camouflaging night shadows that spilled from every corner.

"My lord, I must speak with you about your daughter. We ought not to wait any longer, ought to christen her as soon as possible. Jesú forfend that evil should seek out an innocent, but if it did happen ere she was baptized, her soul would be lost to God, forever condemned to limbo."

"Do it, then, without delay."

"But my lord, we . . . we do not know what to name her!"

Llewelyn focused upon the priest with an effort. "We never picked a name, not for a lass. Ellen was so sure we'd not need one . . ."

His voice trailed off. The priest waited patiently, until he realized that Llewelyn was not going to offer up a name. "Well, then . . . suppose we name the little lass after her mother?"

"No!" The vehemence in Llewelyn's voice took them all aback. "She has taken Ellen's life, but not her name, too!"

There was a shocked silence. Elizabeth seemed about to speak, but Caitlin caught her eye and shook her head. "What about . . . Gwenllian, Uncle Llewelyn? That is a name I've always fancied," she lied; it was merely the first name that came into her head.

Llewelyn's throat had closed up, making speech impossible. He nodded, staying where he was, safe in the shadows, until he heard their footsteps receding, the door closing behind them. Only then did he move back to the bed. Sitting down beside Ellen, he gently lifted her off the pillows, took her into his arms. Her head lolled against his chest; her breath was hot upon his hand, as ragged and shallow as her pulse. After a time, he wept.

ELLEN knew she was dying. But it was a muted awareness, for in the twilit world she now inhabited, regrets and fears had lost their edge. Nothing was as she'd known it. Her fevered dreams recognized no boundaries, brought back her dead, merged her past and present in a hot haze of shifting color and light. But sometimes the heat receded. When it did, the pain became sharper, more acute. So did her wits, though. It was then that her fear would come flooding back, a fear all the greater for being unfocused. All she knew was that it somehow concerned Bran, her brother. He was in grave danger. Yet it puzzled her, too, for she sensed she'd forgotten something, something important. But each time she seemed about to remember, the fever got in the way.

She was so thirsty, so very thirsty. But she could not get her parched tongue to form the words. It seemed miraculous when a cup was suddenly tilted to her swollen lips. She drank gratefully, greedily, then opened her eyes, squinting against the light. The face above hers was dark, familiar, loved. Llewelyn. So good to have him here, so sad to die alone . . . like Bran. And then she gasped, for she remembered. Bran was long dead. He'd died in Italy. It was her baby, his namesake, the baby who was dead, her baby. Her heart had begun to pound, and her head was filled with silent screaming. "No . . . he cannot be dead, no!" But all that emerged from her lips was a weak whisper, a no as soft as any sigh.

"Ellen?" Llewelyn's face was closer now. Another face was hovering over the bed, too . . . Juliana. She tried to speak, but all she could get out was a broken breath, an almost inaudible "dead."

Juliana choked back a sob. "No, Ellen, no, you're not dying!"

But Llewelyn was leaning forward. Her lips were almost at his ear, and she tried again. "Bran . . ." He pulled back then and she did not think he'd heard her; tears welled up, spilled from the corners of her eyes into her hair.

"Bran," he echoed. And then he understood. "Ah, no, Ellen! The baby is not dead!"

She did not believe him, not at first. He saw her doubt, and turned away. She heard him say, "Fetch the child," and then he was back, sliding his arm around her shoulders, lifting her up so she could see. She closed her eyes as another memory broke through, a memory of Gwynora entreating her to "hold on, hold on for your baby." She would, and she did, and at last Elizabeth was there, and Llewelyn was reaching out for the baby, putting him down on the bed beside her. Dark hair like Llewelyn, like Bran. She yearned to touch it, and Llewelyn seemed to know, for he took her hand, placed it on the little head, and her fingers felt the silky, feathery wisps. Llewelyn had brought up the corner of the sheet, was blotting her tears. She hadn't realized that she was still crying. She found it so hard to take her eyes away from the baby, but for a moment she sought her husband's face. So much to tell him, and no time. But he knew. He did not need the words. He knew. "Bran," she whispered again, and the baby whimpered, squirmed closer, instinctively seeking her warmth.

Above their heads, Llewelyn's eyes met Elizabeth's; a message passed between them. Swallowing her own tears, she slipped quietly from the chamber, went to fetch the priest.

DAVYDD's scouts kept the English under close surveillance, and he had plenty of warning when Reginald de Grey led an army out of Chester, toward his castle at Caergwrle. Abandoning the castle, Davydd withdrew without haste to safety at Dinbych. But before retreating, he dismantled Caergwrle's walls, filled in its wells, did all he could to render the castle a worthless prize. It gave him a certain grim amusement to envision Reginald de Grey's bitter disappointment once he discovered his prey had eluded him. The English were born fools, and their chief failing was that they assumed their enemies were fools, too. As if he'd hole up in Caergwrle like a fox run to earth, wait tamely for the English to starve him out. The slowest-witted Welshman had more sense than that! Let de Grey have his fun trying to put Caergwrle right; it had been only half-done, anyway, for the war had overtaken his ambitious building plans. And he still held Dinbych, Dinas Bran, and Hawarden. He was winning his war; he knew it even if Edward did not . . . yet.

Night had fallen by the time they were approaching Aber. However much he sought to deny it, Davydd was vaguely uneasy about seeing his brother. They'd had but two brief, tense meetings since their confrontation at Hawarden, and Davydd was not looking forward to another one. It baffled him a bit that Llewelyn had not come around by now, for the war was going their way, just as he'd known it would. Most likely Lady de Montfort was doing all she could to poison the well. He could only hope that she'd be too busy with the birthing to muddy the waters on this visit; by his reckoning, she was due any day now.

They were almost upon Aber when he had a stroke of good luck, the sort of fortunate happenchance that so often came his way. They encountered a hard-riding courier from Rhys Wyndod, bringing Llewelyn word of a great Welsh victory in the south. The Earl of Gloucester had succeeded in retaking Carreg Cennen Castle, was on his way to Dinefwr when he was ambushed by Rhys Fychan and Rhys Wyndod. The ensuing battle ended in an utter rout of the English. Gloucester barely escaped with his life, and among the dead was the son of the much-loathed Earl of Pembroke. It was an enormous setback for Edward, and Davydd was delighted that he should be the one to give the news to Llewelyn. The Welsh triumph at Llandeilo Fawr would go far toward melting Llewelyn's icy anger, and he meant to take full advantage of the thaw.

But from the moment he drew rein in the inner bailey at Aber, Davydd knew something was amiss. He'd always been sensitive to atmosphere, and here the very air seemed charged with tension. The faces of the men in the bailey confirmed his suspicions, for he'd seen more cheer at hangings. He'd just dismounted when his wife came running across the bailey, flung herself into his arms.

"Davydd, thank God! Never have I needed you more!" Burying her face against his chest, she burst into gasping, convulsive sobs.

Davydd had never seen her so distraught. "Elizabeth, what has happened? For Christ's sake, tell me?!"

"Ellen . . . she is dying!"

Davydd's shock was genuine. Although he'd known, of course, how risky childbirth could be, he'd always lived his life as if he and his were somehow invulnerable to the every-day dangers that struck down others. He'd borne no liking for Ellen, but he'd still included her within his charmed circle, for she belonged to his brother. "How? What went wrong?"

"Everything. She was in travail for nigh on two days, and when the babe was born, she bled heavily. All night she lay senseless, and by yesterday morn, she was afire with fever . . ."

"And the babe?"

"A lass."

Davydd felt a shamed sense of relief. "Llewelyn must be . . ." He slowly shook his head, for he could not begin to imagine his brother's grieving; nor did he even want to, in truth.

Elizabeth had regained some of her composure by now. Clinging tightly to his arm, she said, "Come, I'll take you to him." They crossed the bailey in silence, but as they neared the door of Llewelyn's chamber, Davydd's steps began to lag. Elizabeth had been about to reach for the door latch. "Davydd?"

He was staring at the door, and the expression on his face was one she was not familiar with. It was the first time she'd seen her husband flustered, utterly at a loss. "Llewelyn was besotted with that woman," he said. "What do I say to him, Elizabeth? What can I say?"

THE chamber was deep in shadows. Llewelyn was alone with his wife, sitting very still in a chair by the bed. He did not look up as they entered, not until Elizabeth said his name. He showed no surprise at sight of Davydd, showed no emotion at all. Davydd stepped forward, still not knowing what he would say. "Llewelyn . . ." He stopped, started again. "I'm sorry. Christ, but I'm so sorry . . . How does she?"

Llewelyn was holding Ellen's hand in his, staring down at the jeweled wedding band, the ring she'd called her talisman, her luck. Just when Davydd had decided he was not going to answer, he said tonelessly, "She is dead."

ELEANOR DE MONTFORT died on Friday, June 19th, feast day of St Gervasius and Prothasius, less than four months from her thirtieth birthday. She was buried beside Joanna in the Franciscan friary at Llanfaes, following her kinswoman in death as she had in life.

JOANNA had been buried on a raw day in February. Llewelyn had been just a boy, only eight, but more than four decades later, the memory was still vivid, sharply etched; he had only to close his eyes to see his grandfather standing alone by Joanna's marble tomb. Now it was his turn to bury a wife at Llanfaes, and as the day dragged on, it began to seem as if his grieving and his grandfather's pain had become inextricably entwined, much like their lives. Each time he looked up, saw the soft June sunlight spilling through the window, he felt a dulled sense of surprise, expecting to see the panes streaked by a frigid February rain.

On their return to Aber, Llewelyn remained for a time in the great hall, accepting condolences, acknowledging the expressions of sympathy and regret. Some of those who'd come to mourn their Prince's lady were impressed by his composure; he was bearing up well, they agreed among themselves. Others knew better.

Davydd was standing in a window recess, watching his brother. After a time he was joined by Goronwy, and then, Elizabeth. Goronwy was the first to put it into words, the fear that all three shared. "I do not think," he said, "that he is going to get over this."

Davydd frowned. "I never thought to find myself tongue-tied, but I do not know what to say to him. I keep thinking there must be something I can do, something that will help. But mayhap not. Mayhap there is nothing anyone can do."

"I think there is," Elizabeth said, after a long silence. The two men looked at her curiously, but she did not elaborate, and the moment passed. They continued to watch as Llewelyn moved among the mourners, as he did what was expected of him.

LLEWELYN was standing before his bedchamber door. He'd not crossed that threshold since Ellen's death, and he was still not sure if he could do it now. His fist tightened on the latch, and then he was shoving the door inward.

The room was bright with sun, scrubbed clean and scented with fragrant incense. The smell of death was gone, lingered only in his memory. He'd been dreading to see Ellen's perfume vials and hairbrush on the table, her bed slippers in the floor rushes, her gowns hanging neatly from wall poles, as if she'd just stepped out for a moment, would soon be back. But Caitlin and Elizabeth had obviously anticipated that, for the chamber had been cleared of his wife's possessions. Clothes, books, even her favorite silver candlesticks—all had been whisked from sight, hidden away. It was as if Ellen had come into his life and gone and left no trace of her passing. And that was infinitely worse than finding a room awaiting her return.

As he moved toward the center of the chamber, not yet ready to approach the bed, he caught movement from the corner of his eye. Ellen's little dog was crouched on the window-seat, watching him warily. "Hiraeth," he said, "come, lass." But it retreated as he advanced, scrambled down and hid under the bed. "Contrary to the last," he said ruefully, and then drew a breath sharp enough to hurt, for he'd recognized the crumpled cloth the dog had dragged up onto the window-seat. It was one of Ellen's stockings.

He never knew how long he stood there, staring down at that scrap of bright scarlet. Eventually he became aware of the knocking on the door. "Enter," he said, and Elizabeth came into the chamber, carrying the baby.

Elizabeth halted a few feet away. "I have never suffered a loss like yours," she said, "but I think I can understand a little of your pain, for I'd go stark mad if evil ever befell Davydd or my sons. I know it is no comfort now, not yet, but Ellen left you more than memories. She left you part of herself, Llewelyn."

She crossed the chamber then, thrust the baby toward him. For a moment, she feared he would refuse, but although he hesitated, he did take the child from her. "As Gwenllian grows into girlhood, there will come a day when you'll look at her and you'll see Ellen. It might be the tilt of her head, or her laugh, or mayhap the color of her eyes, but you'll know then that you've not lost Ellen, after all, that she lives on in your daughter."

Llewelyn turned toward the light. This was the first close look that he'd gotten at his daughter. She seemed frighteningly fragile, a tiny little doll, not quite real. She had long, golden lashes, which she raised now as the sun warmed her skin. He was startled to see that she had blue eyes. But then he remembered something Ellen had told him, that all babies had blue eyes, at first.

He did not hear the door closing quietly behind Elizabeth, continued to gaze down at his daughter. "Gwenllian," he said, and realized with a shock that this was the first time he'd said her name. Her face was blurring, for tears had begun to burn his eyes, too hot to hold back. "Ellen was cheated of so much," he said softly. "But you've been cheated, too, lass, cheated of your mother."

33

ABER, WALES

June 1282

Llewelyn held his daughter until she began to cry. He handed her then to his sister-in-law. Elizabeth stroked the baby's dark, downy hair, all the while looking up intently at Llewelyn. "You need not fear for Gwenllian whilst you are gone," she said earnestly. "She will want for nothing, that I promise you."

"I know," he said, and embraced her briefly, then did the same to Caitlin. Watching from the window-seat, Davydd rose as the women departed the chamber.

"Are you ready?" he queried, but Llewelyn shook his head.

"Not yet. I have to bid farewell to Hugh and Juliana."

The words were no sooner out of his mouth than Trevor was on his way to fetch them. Davydd settled down again in the window-seat, wondering if his brother realized just how much his people loved him, grieved for his pain. It was hard to tell; never had Llewelyn seemed so remote to him, so distant, as in these days after Ellen's death.

As Hugh and Juliana were ushered into the chamber, Llewelyn moved forward to meet them. "Are you still sure this is what you want to do?" he asked, and Juliana nodded.

"I must, my lord," she said, speaking so softly that Davydd barely heard her. "I was with . . ." She faltered, for even now she could not bring herself to say Ellen's name. ". . . With my lady for sixteen years, nigh on half my life. I could not bear to be here without her. . . ."

"I understand. I've written to Edward, asking him to grant you both a safe-conduct into England. Once it comes, my men will escort you under a flag of truce to Chester."

Hugh cleared his throat. "What if the English King will not consent?"

"He will. He'll do it for . . . for Ellen." Llewelyn found it no easier than Juliana to say his wife's name. A silence fell. It seemed to Davydd as if hours passed before Llewelyn reached out, handed Hugh a leather pouch. "For your lodgings, and your passage to France. I think this should cover your expenses."

Hugh thought so, too; the pouch lay heavy in his hand. He started to thank Llewelyn, then saw that the Welsh Prince was holding out something else; a sealed letter and a small casket.

"I would be grateful, Hugh, if you could deliver these to Amaury de Montfort."

Hugh's jaw muscles clenched as he fought to keep his emotions under control. He nodded wordlessly, knowing what the casket contained: Simon de Montfort's sapphire-star ring.

Llewelyn was turning toward the table. "I am holding Ellen's jewelry for Gwenllian. But I know she would want you each to have something of hers, for she loved you both."

When Juliana saw what he was offering her, Ellen's gold-and-coral rosary, she could no longer blink back her tears. She wanted to assure him that she'd cherish it, but her composure was fast shredding. She managed a choked "Thank you," then fled the chamber before her sobs could overtake her; she was determined not to break down in front of Llewelyn, determined not to salt his grief anew by seasoning it with hers.

"I should like you to have her psalter, Hugh," Llewelyn said, and the young Englishman reached out blindly for his lady's prayer book, clutching it close against his chest as he backed toward the door. There he halted, saying hoarsely:

"God keep you safe, my lord Llewelyn."

It was quiet after Hugh left. Davydd waited what he thought was a discreet interval, and then got to his feet again. Llewelyn's venture into South Wales had been long in the planning, long before Ellen died. He was to lead his army across the River Dyfi, penetrate into Cyfeiliog and Ceredigion, even into Ystrad Tywi, while Davydd guarded the mountain passes of Eryri. But Davydd was discovering that he had conflicting feelings about his brother's campaign. He thought a military command might prove to be Llewelyn's salvation in the difficult weeks that lay ahead; he'd have little time for grieving, that was for certes. But how trustworthy was the judgment of a man numbed and heartsick? Might he not be likely to take more chances, run greater risks?

Llewelyn had buckled his scabbard, was starting for the door. "Llewelyn, wait!" He did, turning back to face Davydd. Their exchanges were invariably polite now. He showed no signs of the anger that had burned so hot in the weeks after Hawarden. What Davydd did sense, though, was an emotion far more chilling than rage, the one

emotion he'd never gotten from Llewelyn in even the worst of times—
indifference.

"Yes?" Llewelyn said, without impatience. But without much interest, either, Davydd thought bleakly.

"I just wanted to say . . . to tell you to . . . to take care of yourself,"
he concluded lamely, thwarted as much by his own confusion as by
Llewelyn's reticence, for in truth, he did not know himself what he'd
wanted to say.

Trevor had brought up Llewelyn's stallion. The other men were
already mounted, waiting. Llewelyn was surprised to find the bailey so
crowded. Elizabeth was standing a few feet away, holding his daughter.
Caitlin was nearby, too, as was Hugh. Dai stood in the shade by the
hall, smiled as their eyes met, but Goronwy was astride a restive chestnut, having made an eleventh-hour decision to accompany Llewelyn
south. And Trevor was making haste now to mount, too.

It touched Llewelyn to see so many familiar faces, to realize that all
of Aber had turned out to see him off; even Davydd was there, lingering
in the doorway as if by chance. The spectators cheered as he emerged
into the sunlight, wished him Godspeed and farewell and great victories
over the English. But as Llewelyn swung up into the saddle, the only
voice he heard was Ellen's. "Do what you must, and your son and I
will be here to welcome you home once this war is done:"

Llewelyn's men were taken aback when he so suddenly spurred
his horse forward, and had to urge their own mounts to catch up with
him. As soon as they were through the gateway, Llewelyn gave his
stallion its head, not easing the rapid pace until they were well onto the
road south, until Aber had receded into the distance.

"I DO NOT understand." Caitlin stopped so abruptly that her shoe slid
on the wet grass, and she stumbled, had to catch Hugh's arm for support. "It was all agreed between us. You'd escort Juliana safe home to
France, seek out Ellen's brother, and then you'd come back. Hugh, we
agreed!"

"I know," he conceded. "But it was a fool's bargain, for certes. I
ought to have known better, suppose my wits were addled by my grieving. Wait, Caitlin, hear me out! You'll see that I'm right, that we did
not think this through. Getting Juliana safe to her brother's manor ought
not to be too hard a task now that we've got the King's safe-conduct.
But suppose Lord Amaury is not in Paris? What if he has gone on to
Rome? Is it not likely that he'd want to thank the Pope personally for
gaining his freedom?"

To Caitlin, the solution to that was obvious. "Well, then you'd leave the ring and letter with Juliana. Then you could . . . Hugh? Are you saying that you'd feel honor-bound to go to Italy after him?''

He nodded somberly. "I'd have to, lass. I have to be the one to tell him. Surely you see that?''

She did not, but neither did she argue; she'd long ago learned that his devotion to the de Montforts was the lodestar of his life. "So you do what you must, then,'' she said. "I will wait.''

"I would that it were so simple. But it is not. If I must journey to Italy, it will take me at least six weeks from Paris, mayhap much longer, for I'd rather take the sea route from Marseilles than brave the Alps again. So I'd not get to Rome till summer's end. And coming back, even if I encountered no unexpected delays, no bandits or pirates or storms at sea, I'd still not be able to reach France until the first frost. And then what? I could not take ship for Wales, not with the English King's fleet prowling the Channel for prey. I'd have to sail for an English port like Bristol, try to slip across the border into Wales, then make my way north into Gwynedd, at risk from English and Welsh alike. The King's men would be right quick to suspect an Englishman wandering about in the midst of a Welsh war, and the Welsh would never take me for one of their own, not with this yellow hair of mine, would likely shoot first and ask afterward.''

They had walked well up the glen, following the stream toward Aber's white waterfall in their quest for privacy. Now Caitlin leaned back against the closest tree, for her knees had begun to tremble. This could not be her Hugh talking; he was never one to dwell upon danger, accepted risks as matter-of-factly as he did air to breathe. And then she understood. "You do not want to come back, do you?''

"No,'' he admitted, and she felt pain that was physical. "You are right, lass. I do not want to return to Wales. This is your homeland, Caitlin, not mine, and now that my lady is dead, there is nothing here for me. That is why I want you to come with me.''

"What?''

"I said I want you to come with me, Caitlin.'' Hugh had been pacing back and forth by the stream bank, but at that, he crossed swiftly to her, reached for her hand. "Why do you sound so surprised? What did you think I meant?''

"Hugh, I . . . I cannot!''

"Of course you can, sweetheart, and you must, for it is the only way. We can be wed in France, but here . . . here it could never be. We'd best face the truth, lass, that our one chance of winning over your uncle died with my lady. He will never give his consent now.''

"We do not know that for certes!''

"Yes,'' he insisted, "we do. Let's say it straight out. In Wales, I'll never be good enough for you. But this is a land at war, and who knows what the future holds? In France, at least you'd be safe, and I know I could make you happy." He put his arms around her then, but she stood stiff and rigid in his embrace, and he said gently, "I understand, lass, truly I do. What I ask is not easy. I know you'd miss Wales to the end of your days. But that is often a woman's fate, for it is the wife who follows the husband, and your uncle might have chosen to wed you to an Englishman or a Scot or—"

"No! No, you do not understand. It would tear a hole in my heart to leave Wales, but I would do it for you. I have thought about this, too, you see, long and hard. You are right, Hugh. Ellen's death does change everything, and I would go with you to France if that were the only way we could be together. But not now. Later, mayhap, but never now. How could I possibly leave my uncle with his wife just in her grave?"

"Caitlin, I know how much you love him. But—"

"He is fighting for the survival of his homeland, Hugh! And he's not drawn an easy breath since Ellen died, not one. Do you truly think I could forsake him in the midst of a war? Jesú, you were there, you saw what Ellen's death did to him! How could I give him more pain when he's had so much? How could you even ask that of me?"

"I know it is not fair. But if you love me, you must make a choice, Caitlin. God help us, that is never the way I wanted it, but it is the way it must be."

"What of your choice, Hugh? If I accepted yours, why can you not accept mine?"

"What choice? What do you mean?"

"When you told me that you must get Juliana safe back to France, did I try to talk you out of it? You know I did not! And when I now learn that you mean to chase off to Italy after Amaury de Montfort, what did I say? Go and Godspeed! I understand your loyalty to the de Montforts. Why can you not understand my loyalty to my uncle?"

"I do! But if you insist upon staying in Wales, we'll not have another chance. Can you not see that? For God's sake, Caitlin, think what you do, what you'll be throwing away! You say you love me. Prove it then, come with me."

She stepped back and slowly shook her head. "I cannot do that."

Hugh was stunned, for he'd been sure she would agree. "I see," he said huskily, but then pride came to his rescue, offering him a way to hide his hurt. "If that is your choice, I shall have to abide by it. I think, though, that you shall come to regret it, Caitlin. But by then, it will be too late. I'll be gone."

"If I asked you to stay, if I promised to go away with you once this accursed war is done . . . But no, you could not do that, could you? As long as there is a de Montfort to beckon, off you'll go, even unto the ends of the earth! Bran, the Lady Nell, our Ellen, now Amaury. You're running out of de Montforts, Hugh. What if evil befalls Amaury, too? Who, then, will be left for you to serve so blindly—Guy?"

"You've said enough!" Hugh was too angry now to risk remaining, for if he did, they'd cut each other to pieces with rash, reckless words, say what could not be forgotten or forgiven. Instead, he turned on his heel, strode off, and left her there in the quiet glen.

Caitlin let him go. "So be it," she cried after his retreating back. "Go, then, to Italy, chase your de Montfort ghosts! Go to Persia, Cathay, or even to Hades, and see if I care! If you do not love me enough to stay, I'll shed no tears for you, Hugh, nary a one!"

That was a lie, though, for her eyes were already burning. She sank down on the grass, wiping away tears with the back of her hand. "Why did you have to die, Ellen?" she whispered. "Why did God take you when we all needed you so much?"

ITALY was in turmoil during the summer of 1282. The long-smoldering feud between the Guelphs and Ghibellines had heated up again, and the Pope had so far been unable to put down a Ghibelline rebellion in the papal state of Romagna. Charles, French-born King of Naples and Sicily, was facing the greatest challenge to his authority in his sixteen-year reign. An Easter Monday uprising in Palermo, known as the Sicilian Vespers, sent shock waves across Europe, for the rebellious Sicilians offered their island crown to the King of Aragon, and he accepted, landing at Trapani in late August. But Charles was not a man to be daunted by either royal rivals or insurgent subjects, and as he made ready to defend his disaffected realm, peace seemed as far from Italy as it did Wales.

Caught up in these dangerous currents was a mild-mannered, affable Frenchman, Simon de Brion, now His Holiness, Martin IV, Vicar of Christ. He'd been a reluctant Successor of Peter, for he was that rare man, one who knew his own limitations, and his misgivings were soon borne out; many of the Italians saw him as a French pawn, as Charles's puppet. He'd been unable to be crowned at St. Peter's, for the Romans denied him entry into the city, and eighteen months after his election, he was still at Orvieto, had yet to set foot in the Vatican.

But for one man, the political strife was a godsend. Guy de Montfort was once more in high favor, with both his King and his Pope, for in such turbulent times, a brilliant battle commander could name his own price. Blood spilled eleven years ago in a Viterbo church no longer mattered much—except to England's King.

THE Torre delle Milizie rose up over the slopes of the Quirinal, the northernmost of Rome's seven hills. A formidable structure, dominating the quarter called the Biberatica, visible for miles, the Torre was presently in the custody of the powerful Annibaldi family, one of whom was Amaury's host. Standing now at an open window, he looked out upon a breathtaking panorama of Rome.

Amaury had long had a special fondness for Rome. He'd heard it said that thirty-five thousand people dwelled within its ancient moss-covered walls, which made it a large city, indeed, by English standards, but not by Italian ones, for Florence, Genoa, and Naples all had populations in excess of a hundred thousand.

Nor was Rome one of the most vital or prosperous of Italian cities. But Amaury had never seen a place in which the past seemed so close, so real. Rome had the same labryinth of narrow, crooked streets to be found in any town in Italy, France, England. It also had triumphal arches built for long-dead emperors, broken aqueducts, crumbling public baths overgrown with grass, ruined stone bridges rising from the yellow waters of the Tiber, decaying marble monuments to heathen gods, remarkable relics of a vanished civilization. A pagan one, of course, Amaury knew. But an extraordinary one for all that, still casting a spell a thousand years after its glory had gone to dust.

The day was nearly done, but the sun still hovered above the horizon. It glinted upon the dome of Amaury's favorite temple, the Pantheon, beat down upon the Market of Trajan at the foot of the hill, upon the houses scattered below the Torre, each with its thatched or shingled roof, outside staircase leading to the upper floor, its small courtyard boasting an apple or olive tree. Farther on, it bedaubed the Tiber with a dull, tawny sheen. The riverbanks were crowded, as always, with Romans dipping drinking water from the muddy depths, collecting eel pots, dumping garbage, gossiping and joking in the fading glow of the September sun.

A triumphant laugh now drew Amaury's attention back into the solar, where Raymond Nogeriis, Dean of Le Puy, had claimed yet another victim. Amaury was not surprised, for he'd had ample opportunity to test Raymond's mettle during their journey from London. He was himself a superior chess player, but he'd been hard pressed to hold his own against Raymond, and he knew Adam Fourrier was no match for the papal legate.

Adam grimaced, saying tersely, "I yield." He had never been one to lose with grace, as Amaury well knew, for their friendship stretched back to his university days at Padua. One of the many transplanted Frenchmen who'd followed Charles to Italy, Adam had seen his fortune turn golden in the years since Amaury had last encountered him; he now held the prestigious post of Rector of the papal Patrimony of Tuscany. He had arrived just that morn, having missed Amaury at Orvieto, bearing a wealth of rumor and gossip and a letter from Amaury's brother Guy.

Raymond rose, stretched, and gave Adam a complacent compliment upon a game "well played." Noticing then that Amaury had begun to reread his brother's letter, he queried, "What says Guy?"

"He regrets not being able to come to Orvieto to greet me, but the Pope sent him into Romagna with reinforcements for John d'Eppe. He says the campaign is not going well, which likely means he thinks he ought to be directing the siege at Meldola instead of d'Eppe."

"He may well get his chance," Adam predicted. "Rumor has it that the Pope grows daily more discontented with d'Eppe, especially after his failure at Forli. My source tells me he's thinking of giving d'Eppe's command to Guy."

"Captain-general of the papal army," Amaury said softly, then flashed a smile that was sudden and sardonic. "What I would not give to see Edward's face when he hears that!" he said, and the other men laughed.

Picking up his brother's letter again, Amaury said, "Guy also tells me that I'm an uncle. Margherita bore him a daughter last year, whilst I was still caged at Taunton."

"A belated congratulations, then," Raymond said heartily, "twice-over!" Seeing Adam's puzzlement, he explained, "Amaury's sister is wed to a Welsh Prince, and when we left England, she was great with child. Due in June, did you not say, Amaury?"

"It must be vexing," Adam sympathized, "that here it is September, and still you know not if it is a lad or lass. But then, you're not likely to hear from her till the war's done, are you?"

"I keep hoping," Amaury admitted. "If Ellen could smuggle a letter into England, there are friends of our lord father who'd right gladly find for her a pilgrim or merchant bound for Rome. It would not be easy, but it could be done, and my sister has never lacked for mother-wit. She'll find a way."

They were interrupted then, by a young servant, bearing brimming, gilded goblets of a Tuscan red wine that Amaury fancied. He also brought a bowl of pears, Amaury's favorite fruit. Raymond and Adam watched in amusement as the boy hovered at Amaury's elbow, shyly waiting to see if he could be of further service, not withdrawing until Amaury dismissed him with a smile and a "Grazie, Giovanni."

"This is the second time he's brought us wine, unbidden," Adam marveled. "Who does this lad think you are, Amaury—his long-lost father?"

Amaury grinned. "I may have sired a by-blow or two in my wilder days, but Giovanni is not one of them. The lad suffered a nasty mishap a few days ago, was trying to break up a fight down in the kitchens, and fell into the hearth. I happened to notice his blistered arm, gave him an aloe salve that eased his pain, and I've been fending off his gratitude ever since!"

"That medical training of yours can be right useful at times. A pity you're so set upon returning to France, for we can never have enough doctors in these pestilent parts. Roman air is as unhealthy as can be found anywhere in Christendom, and fevers and agues strike down more people than—" Adam caught himself, too late, and gave Amaury an apologetic look. "Damnation, me and my flapping tongue! I forgot for the moment that your brother died of a tertian fever . . . sorry."

"That is no longer a raw wound, Adam. I—" Amaury turned then, toward the door, for Giovanni was back, breathless and excited.

"My lord . . . for you, a visitor," the boy stammered, managing at last to convey, in his very faulty French, that one of Amaury's countrymen, "un inglese rubio," was seeking him out, on a matter most urgent.

His journey to Rome had been an unending ordeal for Hugh. It had stirred up all his buried memories of Bran, and at times he felt as if he were reliving that nightmare odyssey from Tuscany to Montargis, bearing Nell de Montfort word of her son's death. Grieving for Ellen, haunted by Bran, wretchedly unhappy at having failed to reconcile his differences with Caitlin, he raced his ghosts and his regrets through the stifling summer heat, pushed himself to the limits of his endurance as he tracked Amaury to the papal residence at Orvieto, then on to Rome. And now he was here, after so many weeks, and so many miles, and he still did not know how he was going to tell Amaury that his sister was dead.

But he'd forgotten how quick-witted Amaury was. As Raymond and Adam looked on, puzzled, Amaury got slowly to his feet, staring at the dusty, disheveled Englishman with disbelief that gave way almost at once to comprehending horror. Only death could have torn Hugh from Ellen's side, and Amaury knew that, even as he made one desperate attempt at denial. "No! Oh, Christ Jesus, no . . ."

Hugh's eyes filled with tears. Pulling a leather pouch from his tunic, he stumbled forward, spilling its contents onto the table in front of Amaury: a frayed, folded letter that bore the royal seal of Wales and a sapphire ring cut in the shape of a cross.

34

ABER, WALES

October 1282

LLEWELYN struck deep into South Wales during that war-shadowed summer, where he exacted a high price from Rhys ap Maredudd, one of the few Welsh lords to support the English Crown. The skies over Ystrad Tywi were soon fire scorched and smoke blackened.

Farther south, John Giffard was having some notable successes, although Roger de Mortimer was just holding his own in skirmishing along the Upper Severn. But in the North, Edward was now able to take the field himself, and by July, he'd reached Rhuddlan Castle. He'd called upon the Cinque Ports, and soon had forty ships and two great galleys patrolling the waters of the Menai Straits, awaiting his planned invasion of Môn. By late August, he was ready, dispatched Luke de Tany with a large force to occupy the island and seize its harvest. The loss of Môn had been a devastating blow to the Welsh in the last war, and when Edward learned of de Tany's landing, he exulted, "I've just plucked the finest feather in Llewelyn's tail!"

But Edward had even more ambitious plans in mind for Môn. It was his intent to build a bridge from Môn to the mainland, thus enabling him to strike at Llewelyn's rear at the same time that he crossed the River Conwy, advanced upon Aber. Timber, iron, and nails were dispatched from Chester; so were carpenters and blacksmiths. It was an audacious undertaking, but by no means an easy one, and de Tany's men suffered their share of setbacks, the worst occurring when it was discovered that the pontoon boats they'd ordered were too large to be transported to the island by ship; local replacements had to be hastily built.

They were handicapped as well by the erratic Welsh weather, and the Welsh themselves did all they could to sabotage the construction; the harassed workers found themselves performing their hazardous tasks under guard and often under fire. But Edward's will was not to be thwarted, and slowly the bridge took shape, three lines of barges attached to one another with heavy chains, anchored against the strait's treacherous currents, covered by a wooden platform wide enough for sixty men to cross abreast. Day by day, the bridge moved closer and closer to the Welsh shoreline.

But before Edward could launch his assault upon the Welsh heartland, he had to win back the four cantrefs of the Perfeddwlad, lands defended by Davydd's castles at Hawarden, Dinbych, Ruthin, and Dinas Bran. To this end, he brought to bear the full might of the English Crown, an army that numbered no less than seven hundred fifty cavalry, a thousand archers, and eight thousand foot soldiers. It took him three months to prevail, but eventually, he did. Davydd was forced to evacuate Hawarden. In early September, Ruthin Castle fell to Reginald de Grey. By mid-October, Dinas Bran and Davydd's stronghold at Dinbych were in English hands, too. Davydd was so hard pressed that Llewelyn had to abandon his campaign in the South, hasten back to his brother's aid. Together, they made ready to defend Gwynedd.

"LLEWELYN!" Davydd burst into the great hall, bore down upon his brother, and all but dragged him away from his guest, an astonished Franciscan friar.

Llewelyn was irked and made no attempt to hide it once they'd reached the privacy of a window recess. "If you'd given me half a chance to introduce you to Brother John, you'd have realized the significance of his—"

"I already know too many monks and priests, and my news could not wait. You'll not guess which of our enemies has been called to God . . . or more likely, the Devil. Roger de Mortimer is dead!"

"Are you sure? Was he struck down in battle? A fall from his horse?"

"Brace yourself for a surprise. Our de Mortimer cousin, a man born to hang if ever there was one, actually died in bed! I do not yet know what ailment killed him, but he was not sick for long. Now . . . is this news not important enough to justify my lapse of manners?"

Llewelyn admitted that it was. De Mortimer's death was both a blow to the English and a blessing to the Welsh, for his lands would likely be in turmoil for some time to come. His vassals and tenants were bound to be disturbed by this sudden upheaval in their lives, for loyalties were personal, and for most men, their local lord mattered more than a distant, unknown king. There was opportunity here for fishing in troubled waters, and Llewelyn and Davydd exchanged gratified glances, already thinking of lures and baited hooks. But first Llewelyn had news of his own to impart.

"Come on back to the hearth," he said. "I want you to meet Brother John. He is Welsh, his name notwithstanding, a respected Franciscan theologian . . . and the Archbishop of Canterbury's personal peace emissary."

"You cannot be serious! Edward would sooner beg by the roadside ere he'd seek peace terms. He's not ready, not yet, for he's ever been one for learning lessons the hard way."

"This is Peckham's doing, not Edward's . . . or so he says. He claims Edward balked like a mule at first, but it seems our lord Archbishop's zeal to be a peacemaker would not be denied, and Edward reluctantly agreed to let him try to bring his erring sheep—that's us— back to the fold."

" 'Reluctantly agreed,' " Davydd echoed derisively. "How witless do they think we are? If Peckham's an impartial mediator, I'm bidding fair to become the next Pope! How long did it take him to excommunicate us at Edward's behest . . . and for what godless sin? 'Disturbers of the King's peace,' not one of the Holy Commandments the last time I looked. This peace mission is Edward's Trojan Horse, a clumsy attempt to distract us whilst they get that accursed bridge completed."

"The bridge is well nigh done already. Nor are we likely to be caught off guard, for we have them under such close watch that if someone drops a hammer into the water, we know about it by the time it hits bottom."

Davydd looked thoughtfully at his brother. "You're even quicker than me to suspect the English of double-dealing. Yet you seem to be saying that you believe Peckham's peace overture is sincere . . . why? What do you know that I do not?"

Llewelyn's smile was fleeting, but it held a hint of approval, for whatever Davydd's other failings, his fast thinking made him a useful ally. "You are right, there is a piece missing from this puzzle. It so happens that the Archbishop has offered to come to Aber, to discuss peace terms in person."

Davydd's jaw dropped. "He'd actually do that, make a journey through a land at war to break bread with men he himself had excommunicated? Jesus God above! I never heard of a prelate who'd even cross the path of one under the Church anathema! If he would truly come to us, no one could doubt his good faith—not even me! You will agree to see him?"

Llewelyn nodded. "In truth, I do not expect anything to come of it. But if the Archbishop would make such a remarkable concession, then I think we ought to hear him out. I owe him that much," he said, suddenly sounding very tired, "for he did all he could to free Ellen's brother from Edward's gaol."

A TRUCE was declared, and John Peckham, Archbishop of Canterbury, passed three days at Aber, earnestly seeking to convince the Welsh that the salvation of their souls depended upon submission to England's King. They had sinned grievously in shedding blood on one of God's holiest days, he told them, and the best proof of their repentance would be their readiness to make peace. They listened, accorded him the respect due his rank, and Llewelyn said that he would be willing to yield to the English King, but only if Edward agreed to honor their ancient customs and liberties. He would not surrender without such assurances from the Crown, for his people looked to him for protection, and he could not fail them. The Archbishop could offer no such assurances, though, for Edward's terms were not open to interpretation, as simple as they were inflexible—"the entire and unconditional surrender of Llewelyn ap Gruffydd and his people"—terms utterly unacceptable to the Welsh. Bitterly disappointed, the Archbishop prepared to return to Rhuddlan Castle on the morrow, knowing that when this brief truce ended, the killing would begin again.

Brother John watched as the Archbishop restlessly paced the chamber's length, then its breadth. He had expected their mission to fail, for Peckham was as tactless as he was well intentioned, and he had scant sympathy for the people he'd come to convert. Brother John knew that the Archbishop, like most of his fellow countrymen, believed the Welsh to be lazy, immoral, and untrustworthy. It was not surprising, then, that when the Welsh argued that they should be governed by their own laws, he turned a deaf ear. How could it be otherwise when he was convinced that Welsh law was contrary to reason and Holy Writ?

And yet Brother John knew, too, that the Archbishop's dismay was genuine. He might loathe Welsh law, distrust the Welsh leadership, and scorn Welsh custom, but he truly cared about the salvation of Welsh souls. He'd been quite sincere when he called the Welsh his "lost sheep," vowed to make his body "a bridge to bring them back to the safety of the Holy Church." Now their souls would be lost to God, and even as he fumed at their intransigence, he grieved for their damnation.

The Archbishop suddenly stopped his pacing, shot Brother John a look that managed to be both accusatory and defensive. "I suppose," he said tartly, "that you think I ought to have coddled them more,

sugared the truth for the sake of good manners, pretended that I'd
forgotten what Scriptures say, that rebellion is as the sin of witchcraft."

Brother John hesitated, for his master was easy to respect, not so
easy to serve. He had a prickly integrity of spirit that Brother John had
found in few others, but he was also exceedingly thin-skinned, not a
man to take kindly to criticism.

"It is not my place to judge you, my lord. I cannot help thinking,
though, that candor is verily like salt. We need them both to season our
conversations and our meals, but in moderation, my lord. Mayhap a
whit less salt might have made your offer more palatable?"

Peckham's mouth twitched in what was almost a smile. "What an
odd pair we are, John. I use words like nails, forthrightly hammering
them home, whilst yours flit about like butterflies, always offering a
moving target. You're referring, I assume, to my comments about Hywel
Dda, the so-called giver of their laws?"

"Well, my lord, your remarks were somewhat . . . intemperate . . .
might possibly have given offense—"

"Their very laws give offense," the Archbishop snapped. "Mayhap
I was too plain-spoken, but they were hardly blameless. Have you forgotten their response when I relayed the King's message? When I told
them what he said, that if they'd had reason to complain of any Crown
official, they ought to have come to him, for he was always ready to do
justice to all of his subjects, they . . . they laughed!"

"I never claimed, my lord, that the Welsh were blameless," Brother
John said mildly, and the Archbishop was forced to concede this was
so, for he prided himself upon his sense of fairness.

"I did not mean to take out my foul temper on you, John. It is just
so hard to accept failure when so much is at stake. Christian warring
upon Christian . . . it is wrong, grieves our Holy Father and delights
the Devil. I truly thought I could make them see reason . . . How can
they hold this wretched barren land so dear, their souls so cheaply?"

Brother John moved to the table, piled high with testaments. "These
Welsh petitions we are bringing back to the King . . . have you read any
of them yet, my lord?"

"No, not yet. You think I should?"

"I think you might find them informative, possibly even illuminat-
ing, my lord."

The Archbishop considered, then nodded. "I shall, then," he said
briskly, and upon retiring took the unwieldy stack of parchments to
bed with him. The complaints spoke of Welsh laws flouted, but also of
justice denied. The complainants were both highborn and of humble

rank. They testified to lands unjustly confiscated and to oxen seized, to wrongs great and small, to a troubling abuse of royal power. The Archbishop frowned over these testaments as his candle dimmed, splattered wax onto the parchments. He read far into the night.

The Archbishop still rose early the next morning, as was his custom. He eschewed breakfast, for he was a man of austere habits, and soon after dawn, he was standing in the doorway of the great hall, bidding farewell to Llewelyn and Davydd.

"It is not yet too late," he said. "I urge you to think upon what I've said, for this is not a war you can win. The King is expecting Gascon mercenaries any day now. As for myself, it would be with the greatest reluctance that I would lay all Wales under Interdict, but if I must—"

He got no further, drowned out by the sudden clamor from the bailey. As the gates swung open, a rider came racing through, shouting for Llewelyn even as he reined in his lathered, heaving stallion, flung himself from the saddle. Llewelyn pushed past the Archbishop, hastened out into the bailey, with Davydd but a stride behind.

"The English whoresons have broken the truce, my lord, are making ready to cross their bridge!"

The Archbishop spoke no Welsh, but the reaction of the men warned him that something was very wrong. Brother John gasped, whispered a few words in his ear. The Archbishop paled noticeably, and when Llewelyn and Davydd swung back to confront him accusingly, he said hoarsely, "I knew nothing of this! As God is my witness, I did not know!"

THE Prior of the Dominican friary at Bangor was the grandson of the great Ednyved Fychan. But he was not loyal to his Prince; his sympathies were pledged to Llewelyn's old adversary, the Bishop of Bangor. Two of his brothers were already in the English camp; Rhys ap Gruffydd, bearing a grudge for his months in Llewelyn's gaol, had gone over to the English at the start of the war, and their younger brother Hywel was among those who'd landed upon Môn with Luke de Tany. But the Prior stayed behind in Bangor, where he and a few of his fellow friars secretly plotted with the English.

On this cold, clear Friday in early November, they sent Luke de Tany the signal he'd been awaiting, and he gave the order to secure the mainland side of the bridge, which was done with grapnels, massive grappling hooks that bit deep into the ground. The bridge was now ready and waiting.

They began to cross at dawn, under a sky so blue it might have been summer, although the brisk, gusting wind let no one forget it was actually November. Even at low tide, it was not an easy crossing. The horses had to be blindfolded and led across, and the boats pitched and tossed upon the swirling current, causing men to stumble and swear uneasily. One clumsy youth tripped and dropped his pike into the water, much to the amusement of his comrades. But they all eventually made it over, men and horses both, a score of knights, twice that many squires, and a large number of foot soldiers, thankful that the worst was behind them, for now they were safe on dry land again, and ahead lay the chance for plunder and looting, for the rich prizes that a man could hope to gain in war, a hope that would have gone aglimmering if the Archbishop succeeded in his peace mission.

It had been decided beforehand to avoid the narrow coast road, where they'd be more likely to encounter Welsh who'd raise the alarm. Their Dominican allies had told them of an inland road, built long ago by the Romans but still in use, which would enable them to approach Bangor undetected, perhaps even to risk a raid upon Aber itself, for both targets were well within striking distance, Bangor only three or four miles to the east and Aber just six miles farther on. Flying a multitude of banners, for among the knights were scions of some of England's proudest Houses, they left the beach behind, headed inland toward the Roman road.

Some of the men were battle-scarred veterans of the last Welsh war, a few had fought in skirmishes in Gascony or the Holy Land, and others were raw youths about to get their baptism by fire. One of the latter was a young foot soldier in the service of Sir Roger Clifford, son of the lord held hostage since the capture of Hawarden Castle. The Cumbrian village of Appleby seemed very far away indeed to Thomas, a good-natured, affable lad who bore with equanimity the inevitable teasing about his bright red hair, profusion of freckles, and rustic North Country accent. He missed Appleby dearly, missed the security of knowing what each day held, a comfort he'd not valued until he'd lost it. But he was still enormously proud to be serving a lord like Sir Roger, who claimed the lordship and Honour of Appleby through his wife, Tom's liege lady.

Not that Tom saw much of Sir Roger, a brusque, impatient man who had no time to spare for underlings. But he had struck up a tentative friendship with Gervaise Fitz Alan, one of Sir Roger's squires, for they'd discovered that their difference in rank seemed somehow less significant on the occupied Welsh island; that they were both seventeen, homesick, and facing their first battle mattered more. Now Tom tried to keep close to Gervaise, his eyes locked upon Clifford's checkered blue-and-gold banner as they began their march into the Welsh interior.

The hills were not high, not yet, but the horizon was shadowed by the formidable peaks of Snowdon; Gervaise had told him that the Welsh called the mountains Eryri, and Tom tried to say it under his breath, but had trouble trilling his r's. He was very glad that they'd not have to brave those redoubtable heights, for he found these lowlands daunting enough. He had never seen a country so heavily wooded. He'd heard that King Edward had cut wide swathes through the Welsh forests, but these towering trees had never known an axe. Winter had not yet stripped them bare, and Tom felt as if he were trapped in a tunnel, for the trail was walled in on each side by high hedges, brambles, and camouflaging clouds of brown, brittle leaves.

It took little imagination to envision a Welsh archer lurking behind every tree trunk, and Tom looked enviously at his lord's chain-mail armor. He knew it did not render its wearer invulnerable; it could not ward off broken bones, nor save a man if the metal links broke under pressure. And he was not without protection himself. His gambeson, a thickly padded leather tunic, was surprisingly effective at absorbing a blow's impact, and not all that easy to pierce—so he'd been told. But he'd still have traded it in the blink of an eye for Sir Roger's hauberk and great helm.

Tom knew very little about the Welsh, and what he did know was bad; he'd been told that they were despoilers of churches, that they had neither honor nor courage. Tom secretly hoped that they were as craven as Gervaise claimed, that they hid in the hills, leaving their houses and goods and livestock for the soldiers to share. For as excited as he was about this chance to make his fortune, Tom did not really want to kill anyone. He'd been given a mace, for Sir Roger spared no expense in outfitting his men, but he could not truly imagine himself splitting a man's head open, gouging out an eye, maiming or murdering. Gervaise assured him that it would be different in battle, that men's blood heated up so that killing became easy, but Tom could not help wondering how Gervaise knew that for certes; he was a battlefield virgin, too.

They'd advanced several miles inland, had almost reached the Roman road when it happened. They had no warning whatsoever, were suddenly under attack. Shrill yells erupted all around them, and a spear went hurtling through the trees, buried itself in an English chest. The man fell to his knees, almost close enough for Tom to touch. Other spears were finding targets now, the knights and crossbowmen were shouting and cursing, fumbling for swords and crossbows, Welsh arrows were fanning the air, aimed with lethal accuracy, and the men around Tom began to die.

The Welsh had picked an ideal spot for ambush, for there were boulders and thick cover on both sides of the narrow trail, and the English found themselves caught in a deadly cross-fire. Luke de Tany saw at once that they could not defend themselves against an unseen enemy, and he hastily ordered them back to the beach. The Welsh followed, forest phantoms who continued to fire upon them, picking off stragglers one by one. Several times they turned on their tormentors, daring them to come out into the open, but they raged in vain. Mocking laughter floated from the woods, and then another hail of arrows.

De Tany sought to maintain some order, shouting commands, trying to stop his men from panicking. Tom was breathless and bruised, for he'd taken a jolting fall. Fortunately, Gervaise had pulled him roughly to his feet, for those who could not keep pace were easy prey for the pursuing Welsh. Tom had never been so scared, had never been so glad to see anything as he was that beckoning blue sheen of the Menai Straits. But it was then that a group of Welsh horsemen came galloping up the coast road.

Tom stood rooted, gaping at these new arrivals. "Jesú, it's him!" Gervaise was pointing at the red-and-gold banner. "It's their Prince!" Tom had no time to react to that, for Luke de Tany and the other knights were trying hastily to close ranks, to stave off this new threat. But Llewelyn gave them no chance. Spurring their horses forward, the Welsh careened into the English, and a wild mêlée broke out there upon the beach.

What followed was utter horror for Tom. All around him were plunging horses and grappling, struggling men. Swords clashed, blood spurted, and the trampled sand was soon splattered with crimson. As a Welsh horseman bore down upon him, Tom swung his mace in a haphazard arc. His blow never connected, and the stallion then swerved into him, sent him sprawling. For several terrifying seconds, there was nothing in his world but flailing hooves. By some miracle, though, the horse did not step on him. Rolling clear, he got shakily to his feet, just in time to be knocked flat by a Welsh lord upon a huge roan stallion, so intent upon crossing swords with the nearest English knight that he hadn't even a glance to spare for Tom. Once again the boy scrambled to his feet, half-dazed by the fall. And then Gervaise was jerking at his arm, shouting at him to run, and he stumbled after the others, joined the desperate dash for the bridge.

It was a retreat that almost at once became a rout. It was chaos then, as men sought only to save themselves, reeling and gasping as they splashed into the shallows. Llewelyn led his men in close pursuit, cut off some of the knights and men-at-arms, and another bloody clash took place within yards of the bridge. Breaking free, the surviving English knights forced their horses right onto the end of the bridge, trampling a few of their own men, those not quick enough to jump out of the way. The Welsh pursued them to the water's edge, then turned back to deal with those still trapped upon the beach. Those fortunate enough to have gotten onto the bridge shoved and pushed as they sprinted for the far shore. But they were not out of arrow range, and at Llewelyn's signal, Welsh bowmen sent arrows winging across the water at eye-blurring speed, finding such easy targets that several of the knights soon had multiple arrow shafts caught in the links of their chain mail, much like bristling porcupine quills.

"Llewelyn!" Davydd reined in his roan beside his brother, sending up a wild spray of sand. Welsh warfare, so dependent upon hit-and-run tactics, was not suited to the cumbersome English armor. Like Llewelyn himself, Davydd shunned the heavy great helm for an old-fashioned kettle-style helmet with nose guard, for the Welsh preferred to take greater risks rather than to squint blindly at the enemy through slitted eye sights. Davydd's face was streaked with sweat and a smear of blood that did not appear to be his; his eyes were blazing with excitement, greener than any cat's. "I've an idea," he panted. "Let's see if we cannot set fire to the bridge!"

That same thought had occurred to Llewelyn, and he'd just put some of his bowmen to the task; several men were searching for wood that would be quick to kindle, as others hastily improvised makeshift fire arrows, knotting them with cloth that could be ignited. Turning in the saddle now to see if they would have time before the English reached the safety of the island, Llewelyn caught his breath, transfixed by what had just occurred out in the straits. "There is no need," he said, "not now. Look!"

Davydd swung his mount around to see. "Jesus God," he murmured softly, almost reverently, for the bridge was breaking up.

The calamity began with a terrified horse. Balking suddenly, it reared up, unseating its rider and creating panic, for the bridge then pitched and rolled alarmingly, sending men to their knees, grabbing for handholds. Other horses started to snort and fight the bit, lashing out in fear. The bridge had not been built to withstand such strain; it was meant to accommodate an orderly, measured passage, not this wild, frenzied mob, and it was dangerously overloaded. Moreover, it was now high tide, and the powerful ocean currents were at war with the anchors, surging against the sides of the barges, already riding too low in the water, in danger of swamping.

Now, as the horses kicked and plunged, the wooden platform finally gave way. Planks split asunder, collapsing a large section of the deck, and men were thrown about as the bridge seemed to fall out from under them. The sinking boats rapidly took on water, dragging the others down, too, and within moments, the icy straits were filled with floundering men and horses. Those who'd not yet reached the gap clutched at the chains, the heaving platform, one another, trying desperately to stay on the tossing, crippled bridge.

It was then that the Welsh sealed the bridge's doom, for now that the fighting was done, they could turn all their attention to it. Racing to the grappling hooks, they began struggling to dig them up. One by one they were pried loose, and when the last grapnel was pulled from the earth, the bridge snapped sideways as if shot from a bow, whip-lashed with such violence that some of the anchors were dragged up and the remaining soldiers were flung into the water.

THE water was freezing. Sputtering and choking, Tom fought his way back to the surface, kicking to keep afloat. Unlike most of the men, he knew how to swim, but the water was so cold that his body was rapidly going numb, and he was encumbered by his clothing; he knew instinctively that he'd never be able to make the shore. Gervaise had been beside him when the bridge capsized, but now he was nowhere in sight. All around Tom, though, men were thrashing about in the water, screaming for help. The knights drowned first, their own armor dragging them down like anchors. Tom saw one flailing about just a few feet away, trying frantically to remove his great helm. As the boy looked on in horror, the man sank below the surface, did not come back up. A few of the knights had somehow managed to stay astride their mounts, and they would be among the small number of survivors, for their horses were swimming for the island. The others were on their own.

There were no longer as many men in the water with Tom; one by one, they were going under. Just then a riderless horse came within reach, and Tom mustered the last of his strength for a wild lunge. He swallowed so much salt water that he began to gag, and his groping hand fell just short of the saddle pommel. The horse veered away, and he sobbed. But then he saw a silvered streamer whipping through the water. He grabbed for it, his fingers entangling in the horse's long, trailing tail. He sobbed again, held tight to that wet, blessed life-line as the stallion struck out for shore.

The screaming did not continue for long; the water was too cold. An eerie hush slowly settled over the straits, for the Welsh, too, had fallen silent by now, awed by the utter magnitude of their victory.

HAD there been any eye-witnesses to the scene in the solar at Rhuddlan Castle, they'd have been hard pressed to say who was angrier, the Archbishop of Canterbury or England's King.

"Such treachery was unforgivable, my liege. This shameful use of my peace mission made me an unwitting accomplice to their perfidy, might well have put our lives at risk, too. If the Welsh had not believed me—"

"Surely you are not suggesting, my lord Archbishop, that it was my doing?"

Peckham was not intimidated. "I would indeed hope not, my liege," he said coldly.

"Of course it was not! What sort of fool do you take me for? After finally mending fences with the Church by freeing Amaury de Montfort, do you truly think I'd sacrifice all that papal good will by using you as bait?"

Edward wheeled, stalked over to the window, while he made a futile attempt to get his temper under control. "What a botch, what a bloody botch! All my plans set at naught, and for what? That hellspawn de Tany was to wait for word from me. Nothing was to happen until I was ready to cross the Conwy and move against Llewelyn at Aber . . . nothing!"

Whirling back to face the Archbishop, he said tautly, "Do you know what this crazed folly of his has cost me? I lost all chance of making a two-pronged assault upon the Welsh, lost my chance to put a quick end to this war. I had to send the fleet back to the Cinque Ports, for the towns were bemoaning the absence of their ships, vowing it would be the ruination of their trade. This means that what's left of de Tany's army is stranded on that accursed island!"

It was then that Edmund hastened into the chamber. "Ned, a courier had just arrived from the island!"

Edward was startled into a mildly sacrilegious retort. "However did he get here . . . walk on water?"

"A brave lad, this one. He waited until dark, swam his mount across the strait, then rode by night to elude capture, and somehow got to Rhuddlan without falling over a Welsh cliff or running into a Welsh spear. He's about done-in, though. I sent him into the hall to get a meal and some sleep, told him that you'd question him at length later."

Edward nodded. "See that he is amply rewarded, for that was a deed well done. Now . . . tell me the worst of it. What of de Tany? Was he amongst the dead?"

"Yes," Edmund said, "he drowned when the bridge broke apart."

"If he had not, I might have hanged him. What of the others? Were there many dead?"

"All England will mourn," Edmund said bleakly. "The losses were . . . were beyond belief. How often does a lord die in battle? If his chain mail does not save him, his ransom price will. But fully fifteen knights died on Friday, most of them drowning. Lord Clifford's son and heir. Lord Audley. The two sons of your Chancellor. Peter de la Mere. Rhys ap Gruffydd's brother. At least thirty-two squires, mayhap more, and God alone knows how many men-at-arms, as many as a hundred and a half . . ."

Edward shook his head in disbelief. "The fools, the poor stupid fools! Did they never think to send out scouts? They ought to have known that Llewelyn would be watching that bridge like a cat at a mouse hole!"

The Archbishop listened impatiently as Edward launched into another scathing denunciation of the foolhardy de Tany, for he had no further interest in the man, although he did hope, of course, that de Tany had died in God's Grace. But he had far more important matters to discuss now with the King, for the last faint hope for peace was about to be snuffed out like an unneeded candle.

"I ask you, my liege, to convene your council on the morrow, that we may talk further of peace terms."

"What is there left to say, my lord Archbishop? You said they refused to surrender, did you not?"

"How could they not refuse, my lord, when you offered them nothing, gave them no reason not to fight on?"

"I do not bargain with traitors and rebels!"

"Ned . . . we do it all the time," Edmund contradicted him calmly. "There were no mass executions after Evesham. What was the Dictum of Kenilworth if not an offer to bargain? You wanted the de Montfort rebels to lay down their arms, and so you made it worth their while to do so. If it made sense then, why not now?"

Edward glared at his brother, who was quite unfazed. "I agree with my lord Archbishop, think we ought to be seeking a way to end this war. I know you can win . . . eventually. But is it worth the price you'll have to pay? You yourself told me that the Exchequer has estimated that the costs might well run as high as a hundred fifty thousand pounds if the war drags on long enough . . . as it seems likely to do. A hundred and fifty thousand pounds, Ned . . . that is seven times the cost of the last Welsh war!"

Edward's smile was sour. "Remind me not to confide in you so freely in the future, Little Brother." But Edmund merely shrugged, and waited. Edward paced to the window again, then back to the hearth, where he stopped abruptly, spun around to confront them. "I will not yield those four cantrefs; they are Crown lands now. A fortnight ago I granted Dyffryn Clwyd to Reginald de Grey, and let Davydd be damned! As for the island—Anglesey, Môn, whatever you want to call it—it is mine!"

They both nodded, for these were Crown Commandments, carved in stone; none who heard him could doubt that. "Well, then," Edmund said thoughtfully, "if that is what the Welsh must swallow, what we need to do is sugar it enough for them to get it down. But ere we begin to speak of inducements, we ought to discuss . . . retribution. How set are you, Ned, upon punishing them for their rebellion? For alas, if you are—"

"Ere you answer that, my liege," the Archbishop said quickly, "there is something I would say. Rebellion is a grave offense against God and man, for it violates the natural order of things. Nevertheless, I am inclined to urge you to show mercy to the Welsh. I do not know if you've yet read the testaments I brought back from Aber, but I found them troubling, my liege. If the allegations they make are true, they have indeed been ill used by certain officials of the Crown. I am not saying that excuses their sedition or their sacrilege, but it may be that these mitigating circumstances do argue for clemency."

Edward was scowling, but he had not interrupted, and they considered that a good sign. After a long silence, he said, "From what I've been hearing, it may be that Llewelyn ap Gruffydd was goaded into this war by that Judas brother of his. And God has already seen fit to punish him grievously for his sins, for I do not doubt that he truly loved my cousin. If he agrees to submit to the Crown, he will not find me unmerciful."

The Archbishop favored Edward with one of his infrequent smiles, but he still thought it best to act at once, lest the King change his mind. "Might the council meet this day, my liege? We have much to do, after all, for we must somehow find a way to make the Welsh Prince realize that it is in his own best interest to end this accursed war. Our task will not be an easy one, but this I can assure you, that you'll not regret your generosity."

Edward looked skeptical. "That," he said, "will depend upon Llewelyn ap Gruffydd."

35

ABER, WALES

November 1282

You are welcome, of course, at Aber," Llewelyn said. "But I must admit, Brother John, that your return is a surprise. The English King demanded our surrender, and we refused. That does not leave much to discuss."

"I bring you an offer, my lord, from King Edward," Brother John said, lowering his voice so the others in the hall would not hear. "But it is not one I can present to your council. May I see you alone . . . you and your brother?"

Llewelyn and Davydd traded startled glances. Llewelyn did not like the sound of it, and he was inclining toward a refusal. But nothing attracted Davydd like intrigue. Leaning over, he murmured, "We have to hear him out, Llewelyn. If not, it'll haunt me till the end of my days, wondering what devil's brew Edward was stirring up! How can you not be at all curious?"

Llewelyn's mouth curved. "So I am curious," he conceded, and turned back to the waiting friar. "Let's go."

Waiting until a servant had poured wine and then withdrawn, Llewelyn waved the friar into a seat across the table. "Well, Brother John? Suppose you tell us what the English King would like to offer me?"

"An English earldom, my lord."

Davydd was close enough for Llewelyn to hear his indrawn breath. The look they exchanged this time was one of utter astonishment. Llewelyn set his wine cup down upon the table, very carefully. "What?"

Brother John smiled; if it had been exciting before to be a witness to history, how much more exhilarating it was to be a participant, to make peace happen. "I do not blame you for doubting, my lord, for rarely—if ever—has a king made so generous an offer to a rebel vassal. But it is genuine, I can assure you. King Edward is willing to grant you lands in England worth a thousand pounds a year. He will also provide honorably for your daughter, his cousin. And if you should wed again and your new wife gives you a male heir, your son can inherit the earldom. For all this, you need only submit to the Crown, and then put the King in peaceful possession of Snowdon, what you call Eryri, those lands west of the River Conwy."

Llewelyn said nothing, leaning back in his chair, his face unreadable to the friar. But Davydd could see how Llewelyn's hands had clenched upon the arms of his chair. Reaching for his wine cup, he raised it in a mock salute. "Amazing," he said, "truly amazing. But do not keep me in suspense, Brother John. After hearing what Edward has just offered Llewelyn, I cannot wait to hear what he has in mind for me!"

A flicker of distaste crossed the friar's face, and was quickly gone. "If you agree, my lord Davydd, to go on crusade to the Holy Land, and not to return except upon the King's pleasure, he will then undertake to provide for your wife and children."

Brother John paused for a response, but Davydd was no more forthcoming now than his brother. "The Archbishop bade me, my lords, to assure you that he will do all in his power to secure merciful and just treatment for the King's Welsh subjects if you agree to these terms."

He was becoming uncomfortable with their continuing silence. "It was my intent to return to Rhuddlan on the morrow with your answers. But if you need more time, my lord Llewelyn, I will be glad to wait—"

"No," Llewelyn said, "I need no more time." He pushed his chair back then, and the friar took the hint, got to his feet.

"I shall leave you now, my lords," he said politely, "for I am sure you wish to discuss this between yourselves." He got all the way to the door before he could bring himself to convey the rest of the royal message, for he was at heart a man of peace, and he found it both demeaning and disturbing to have to resort to threats, even if it was at the King's behest.

"My lords . . . I would that I did not have to say this to you, but there is too much at stake for discretion. My lord Archbishop would be loath to do it, but if this war continues, he will have no choice but to lay all Wales under Interdict. And the King wants you to understand that this is your last chance to save yourselves. If you spurn his generosity, he will bring to bear all the manifold power and resources of the English Crown in the conquest of Wales. It will be war to the utmost, a war of extermination. Forgive me for putting it so bluntly, my lords, but those were the King's very words."

Davydd shoved aside his wine cup, stood up, and followed the friar to the door, shouting for a servant, returning in a few moments with another flagon. "I thought," he said, "that we needed a stronger drink than this watered-down French wine," and he proceeded to empty their cups into the rushes, refilling them to the brim with mead.

They drank in silence for a time. "I have been trying to decide," Llewelyn said at last, "which of us received the greater insult."

"Well, they think I can be scared into submission and you can be bribed. If insults were horses and this a race, I'd venture that they'd reach the finish line in the same stride," Davydd said, and as they looked at each other, they began to laugh, laughter that held echoes of outrage and disbelief and even a few mordant traces of a very bitter humor.

EDWARD was so reluctant to be separated from Eleanora that he'd taken her with him into Wales, even though she was heavily pregnant at the time. And when Edmund arrived from France at the end of July, he, too, brought his wife, eloquent testimony to English self-confidence, and irrefutable proof that a marriage of state could be more than a practical, political alliance, much more.

Blanche was sitting in a window-seat in the great hall at Rhuddlan. The new castle was not yet completed, and living accommodations there were not as comfortable as she was accustomed to enjoying. But that was not the reason why she yearned to return to England; for Blanche, Wales was haunted. She had a book open upon her lap, a French version of the story of the star-crossed lovers Tristan and Iseult, but she was not reading. She was inconspicuously daubing at the corner of her eye, did not hear the approaching footsteps until it was too late.

Edward was surprised to catch a glimmer of tears, for his sister-in-law was not a woman who wept easily. "Is the book as sad as that, Blanche?"

Blanche looked up at him. "I was thinking of Ellen."

Edward stiffened, hesitated, and then sat down across from her in the window-seat. "I know," he said, "I know, lass. We are taught that the Almighty always has a divine purpose in mind, but sometimes it is hard to see . . ." He murmured a low "Thy Will be done," crossed himself, and Blanche thought he would depart then.

He stayed there in the window-seat, though, and after a brief silence, said, "I never fretted much about Eleanora's confinements. Birthings always came easily for her, even if the babe was too often sickly or stillborn. I suppose that after so many, childbirth had become too familiar, for I just took it for granted that nothing would go wrong. But then . . . then I learned about Ellen, may God assoil her, the poor lass.

That last month, Blanche, till the babe was born, I'd lie in bed beside Eleanora, and all I could think about was what my life would be like without her . . ."

Blanche was both surprised and touched by his confession; it was the first time that Edward had given her a glimpse into any of the secret corners of his soul. "But you did not lose her," she said. "Instead, she bore you a healthy baby girl. I've been meaning to ask you, Ned, about that. Why Elizabeth? That is not a common name, nor is it one from your family . . . is it?"

He smiled, shook his head. "I just fancied it, and after twelve babies, we were running out of names! I hear the servants are calling her 'the Welshwoman.' I imagine she'll go through life as Elizabeth of Rhuddlan, for my daughter born in the Holy Land is known to one and all as Joanna of Acre."

"I've heard rumors that you are thinking of wedding Joanna to the Earl of Gloucester?"

"Nothing is settled as yet, but yes, I am considering it. There are a few obstacles to be overcome . . . Gloucester's wife, for one! They have been living apart for nigh on twenty years, but he never got around to petitioning the Pope to annul the marriage. Joanna is still a little lass, though, barely ten, so a year or two's delay will not matter—" Edward broke off at that, for he'd noticed his brother entering the hall.

"Ah, there's Edmund." He grinned suddenly. "Alas, he just got himself snared by Rhodri ap Gruffydd . . . poor lad!"

Blanche craned her neck to see, for she was quite curious about Rhodri, the man Edward cruelly called "the least of Llewelyn's brothers." She could not help wondering what Rhodri thought about in his quiet hours, when he was alone. Did he ever think of his brothers at Aber? Had he any regrets?

"He is not at all like Llewelyn, is he? I see no resemblance whatsoever, and for certes he has not Llewelyn's . . . whatever it is that enables a man to command others. Mayhap there is truth, after all, in those folk tales of changelings!"

"You are still fond of Llewelyn."

It was not a question, not quite an accusation. Blanche made no attempt to deny it. "Yes," she said, meeting her brother-in-law's eyes squarely, "I am."

She was not sure what his reaction would be, for there was an unpredictable streak in his nature that made him both interesting and dangerous. She waited now to see if he would be angered or amused by her candor.

Amusement won out, for he found boldness hard to resist—most of the time. "Such a shy, timid lass," he said, but with a smile. "You must be right pleased, then, with the offer we made to Llewelyn. How often is a rebel awarded with an earldom?"

"Do you truly expect Llewelyn to accept?" Blanche asked, as neutrally as she could, and Edward shrugged.

"He is a fool if he does not," he said, and then Edmund had reached them. Blanche made room for him on the seat, and he slid in. But his greeting for her was preoccupied, his attention focused upon his brother.

"Ned, we just got word from Roger de Springhouse. The sheriff of Shropshire," he added, just for Blanche's benefit; he knew Edward's memory was far too keen to need any prompting about Crown officials. "As you ordered, he put Thomas de la Hyde in charge of de Mortimer's castle at Clun. But that did not please de Mortimer's widow. The Lady Maude complained to him right sharply, saying that her husband's vassals would not welcome Crown meddling in de Mortimer lands. And there's some truth to that, I'm sorry to say. This past week de Springhouse rode to Clun to confer with de la Hyde. When he arrived, the constable came out beyond the walls to greet him, and the castle garrison promptly locked him out."

Edward cursed, fluently and so freely that Blanche knew he'd forgotten her presence. "That sort of unease is a contagion that can spread, Edmund. The sheriff had warned me that he found de Mortimer's people to be 'fickle and haughty,' saying openly that they 'have no lord now.' I had not realized, though, that it was as bad as this."

"I think you ought to invest de Mortimer's eldest son with his lands as soon as possible, Ned."

Edward nodded. "Let's hope that will help, for if Maelienydd catches fire, you can be sure the Welsh will be right there to fan the flames. Of course, if Brother John was persuasive enough to make Llewelyn see reason, I can deal with de Mortimer's discontented vassals at my leisure, and still be back in London in time for Christmas."

"I would not rely on that," Blanche said, and Edward gave her a cool glance, no longer amused.

"What makes you say that, Blanche? Has your fondness for Llewelyn ap Gruffydd given you some special insight into the man's mind?"

"No insight," she said composedly, "and not second sight, either. But the Archbishop of Canterbury is coming our way, and he does not look like a man with good news to share."

"The Welsh are an accursed, insolent people, and I rue the day I ever tried to bring them back to God's Grace!" The Archbishop halted in front of the window-seat, brandishing several pages of parchment. "I should have heeded you, my liege, for they are indeed beyond salvation."

"Llewelyn refused the earldom?" Edward was incredulous.

"He said that your offer was neither safe nor honest, and he could never consent, for it would mean the destruction of his people." The Archbishop thrust the letters at Edward. "See for yourself. He says that even if he'd been willing to agree to his own disinheritance, his council would never permit him to renounce his birthright . . . and he adds that they marveled such a proposal would even be made. The second letter is from his council. They say that these terms are utterly unacceptable, that they will never again do homage to strangers, to those whose tongue, manners, and laws are alien to them."

Edward's eyes glittered. "Will they not, indeed? And Davydd?"

"His was the most offensive answer of all. He says that if he is ever disposed to go to the Holy Land, he will do so for God, not for the English King. He even dares to say that he was amazed I should sanction an enforced pilgrimage, which could have no merit in God's eyes. And he casts vile aspersions upon my neutrality and good faith, insists that they will win this war, that God would never reward English cruelty and treachery with victory."

Edward began, then, to read the letters, and Edmund shifted position so he could see over his brother's shoulder. The Archbishop was too angry to wait patiently, striding back and forth before the window-seat, his robes flaring out behind him. "I should have expected this, for they know no more of gratitude than they do of honor. Their priests are too often unlettered rustics who are ignorant of Latin and take wives or hearth-mates in defiance of Church law. Their own laws are a scandal throughout Christendom, for they permit divorce and they accord bastards the same rights as heirs born in holy wedlock, and they even claim that Church law should be subordinate to the laws of Hywel Dda. Assuming this law-giver of theirs ever lived, he quite clearly took his instructions from the Devil himself!"

Peckham paused for breath. "The whole of Welsh history is a shameful tale of treachery, massacres, arson, and other unspeakable crimes. I ought to have studied it ere I risked so much to save them, for I'd have realized that my efforts were doomed to fail. Why a people so slothful and wanton and faithless should take such pride in their pitiful heritage is truly beyond the comprehension of reasonable men. After reading these letters, my liege, I can say only that an English conquest of Wales would be a blessing for these people, belatedly bringing them the benefits of Christian civilization."

Edward put the letters down, got to his feet. "So be it," he said, no more than that, but Blanche felt a chill, and she reached hastily for her husband's hand. Edmund gave her fingers a reassuring squeeze, but his smile could not banish the vision that Edward's words had conjured up: Wales in flames, a land stalked by death, and Edmund in the midst of it all, dying for his brother on a Welsh battlefield, in an ambush on a snow-shrouded hillside of Eryri.

Edmund had risen now, too. "You mean then, to wage the war throughout the winter?" he asked, and Edward nodded.

"As long," he said grimly, "as it takes."

The men did not linger, for Edward's council must be told that the Welsh had chosen the sword over the olive branch. Blanche sat where she was, watching them go. "God keep you safe, Edmund," she whispered, and God help Llewelyn ap Gruffydd. Mayhap Ned was right, and the Almighty had been merciful in taking Ellen when He did.

As he was about to enter the great hall at Aber, Llewelyn came to a sudden halt. "Go on in," he told his companions, Dai and Goronwy and his cousin of Powys, "and I'll join you soon."

Crossing the bailey then, he stopped before the cradle. Caitlin was bending over the baby, and looked up, startled, as his shadow fell across the blankets. "Uncle Llewelyn! Is it all right to have Gwenllian out here? Elizabeth probably would not approve, but it's not that cold today, and she's well wrapped up . . . see?"

"She looks quite content, lass." Llewelyn had noticed signs of strain between his niece and sister-in-law since his return to Aber, and now he understood why. Elizabeth, a mother of two, would naturally assume she knew best where Gwenllian was concerned, but her proprietary attitude clearly did not sit well with Caitlin. He was not sure what he could do about it, though, for he'd be gone again by week's end; they'd just have to settle it themselves. Reaching down, he gave Gwenllian his finger to hold, and she blinked up at him curiously, began to make soft, cooing sounds.

"Her eyes are getting cloudier," he said. "Will they be brown, do you think?"

"Elizabeth says so. I hope they will stay this shade, for it is such a pretty color, a pale gold-brown, lighter than your eyes, darker than Aunt Ellen's."

"Yes," he agreed, "it is," and then he smiled, for he'd just noticed the small dog curled up at Caitlin's feet. "How did you ever win Hiraeth over, lass?"

"It took time and patience and a prayer or two. But I'd heard that dogs like Hiraeth, the sort that loved but one master, have been known to pine away, and I was not going to let that happen to Aunt Ellen's dog."

"I'm glad," he said, "that you were so persistent. It could not have been easy, though, for she loved Ellen and only Ellen. I'd tried halfheartedly to befriend her at first, for I am fond of dogs, even one that looks like a barking ball of yarn. But she never accepted me except on sufferance . . . although she did seem more tolerant of Hugh; at least she never bit him!" He saw his niece's lashes flicker, saw her react to Hugh's name, and he said quietly, "You miss him, I think . . . very much."

Caitlin's eyes flew to his face, but she did not find what she'd feared. He did not know! She spared a moment for a swift, silent prayer of thankfulness, for he already had trouble and griefs enough to last a lifetime and more. "Yes," she said, "I do miss Hugh, for he was a good friend. Uncle Llewelyn . . . is it true that you are again going south?"

"Yes," he said. "The Welsh down in Ceredigion and Ystrad Tywi are in danger of losing heart, for their resistance seems to have waned once I returned to Gwynedd. Moreover, since Edward means to continue his campaign during the winter months, we'll need to take some of the pressure off Gwynedd, and what better way to do it than to give Edward trouble elsewhere? Lastly, Roger de Mortimer's death has shaken Maelienydd to its very core, and if we are to take advantage of that unrest, I need to be there."

"I suppose," she said grudgingly, but she could not keep from adding, "I still wish you'd send Davydd instead, whilst you stayed in Gwynedd."

"I've done more fighting down in those cantrefs than Davydd has, know the lay of the land better than he does." Leaving unsaid what she knew to be an equally important consideration, that he could encourage the faithful, embolden the wavering, as Davydd could not.

She looked so somber, so forlorn that Llewelyn found himself fumbling for comfort. "Ere I depart, we shall have a great feast at Aber, to rejoice in the favor the Almighty has shown us and to celebrate last week's triumph over the English invaders. I would be beholden to you, Caitlin, if you would plan the meal, consult with my bard, undertake all that must be done, and act as my hostess at the high table . . . as Ellen did whenever we had guests."

Her eyes widened. "Truly, Uncle? You are sure you want me to do that? Not Elizabeth?"

"Quite sure," he said, and was rewarded with a smile bright enough to blind. It had been a long time, he thought, since he'd seen her smile like that, since he'd seen her smile at all.

THE feasting at Aber had gone on for hours. The Welsh drank to their victory upon the shores of the Menai Straits. They listened raptly as Llewelyn's court bard sang of past glories. They dined upon roast venison, sturgeon pie, egg custard, stewed capon, hot sugared wafers filled with fruit, and wine and mead in spiced abundance. Llewelyn withdrew when the dancing began, for he rode south at first light, and the sound of the music followed him back to his own chamber, floating for miles upon the quiet night air.

Llewelyn was not tired, though, knew it would be hours before he could sleep. He roamed the chamber restlessly, then abruptly insisted that Trevor return to the festivities, and as soon as the boy had gone, he, too, left the chamber.

It was cold, but the wind was still, and the sky spilling over with stars. The gatehouse guards looked startled, but something in Llewelyn's face kept them quiet, and they watched in puzzlement as he passed through. He told himself a walk would help him sleep, clear his head of mead, and he would have insisted that he was merely wandering at random, with no set destination in mind. But his steps took him unerringly into the darkness, until his boots were scuffed with sand and he no longer heard the harp music from the hall, heard only the sounds of waves breaking upon the beach.

He stopped at the water's edge and glanced over his shoulder, half expecting to see a sleek shadow racing toward him across the sand; Nia had loved the shore more than any dog he'd ever had. But Nia, two months dead, ran now only in memory.

He was gazing across the strait when he heard a sudden crunch, the sound a boot might make stepping upon a shell. He swung around and saw that his instincts had served him well, for he was no longer alone. A figure was emerging from the darkness, not yet close enough to recognize. But he had no need of moonlight or lanterns, somehow knew—how he was not even sure himself—who it had to be. He waited, and a few moments later Davydd sauntered out of the shadows, whistling softly, as if he took a midnight stroll along Aber's beach every eve of his life.

"I never knew you numbered night tracking amongst your talents, Davydd."

"Actually, I do not." Davydd picked up a shell, examined it in painstaking detail, then pitched it into an incoming wave. "I stopped by your chamber to chat, what with you leaving in the morn, and found you gone. So . . . I came looking for you."

"How," Llewelyn asked, genuinely surprised, "did you guess that I'd be here?"

"Where else would you be on a night when you could not sleep?" Davydd said, and they both turned at that, looked across the water toward Llanfaes.

A wave splashed upon the beach, almost at their feet. Davydd glanced around, spotted a log not far away, moss-grown, half-buried in sand. "Have a seat, my lord Prince," he invited, deftly spreading the folds of his mantle to make himself as comfortable as possible. Llewelyn did, but he could not sit still for long, was soon up on his feet again, back at the water's edge.

"I thought I was doing the right thing, burying Ellen at Llanfaes. I thought she would have wanted that, being with Joanna. So I picked the friary over the abbey at Aberconwy, and now I cannot even visit her grave."

Davydd pushed himself off the log, slowly crossed the sand until he stood by Llewelyn's side. "It is not getting any better, is it?" he asked, sounding as hesitant as he felt, for this was new and troubling territory, and he was not sure he wanted to venture too far into it.

Llewelyn shook his head. Keeping his eyes upon the black silhouette that was Môn, he said, "I kept telling myself that if I could just get through October, if I could do that, the worst would be over. October was so full of ambushes—her birthday, our wedding anniversary. It is behind me now, and I suppose I should be thankful. But I'd forgotten about December; I'd forgotten about Christmas."

Davydd bit his lip, not knowing what to say. He'd never lost anyone he'd loved, had never been bereaved. He did not even remember his father, had never forgiven his mother for offering him up so readily as a hostage, and while he'd been saddened by Owain's death, it had been neither unexpected nor tragic; for Owain, it had been a release. His silence seemed to be blanketing the beach, so thick they were like to smother in it; for certes, Llewelyn must be wondering why he did not at least make an attempt at consolation. He frowned, started to speak, stopped, and then saw that Llewelyn was not even aware of him at that moment, was alone with a dead woman and a wound that would not heal.

"Llewelyn . . ." He reached out, his hand almost brushing Llewelyn's sleeve. "Are you not ready to go back? You do have to get up ere the sun does . . . remember?"

"Soon," Llewelyn said. "You go on, ere Elizabeth starts to worry."

Davydd nodded, backed away a few feet, then turned toward Aber. He'd not gone far, though, before he stopped again, swung around to face his brother. "The battle at the bridge last week," he said abruptly. "That was the first time we fought together. Being on the same side . . . I found I liked it."

Llewelyn looked at him across the shadowed expanse of sand. It was too dark for Davydd to see his face. "Enough to make it a habit?"

"In a world where you get offered an English earldom, I'd say anything is possible," Davydd said wryly, but he was smiling in the darkness. Starting to whistle again, he moved back into the shadows, heading home.

It was then that he caught it from the corner of his eye, a sudden streak of light. Stopping in his tracks, he swiftly scanned the heavens. All agreed that a comet was a harbinger of doom, blazing across the sky to foretell the coming death of a great lord or king. But people were more ambivalent about shooting stars, some convinced they were ill omens, too, others sure that they heralded good fortune for those lucky enough to spot them. Davydd was firmly in the latter camp, and he tracked the star's plunging fall with delight, then spun around, eager to share this with Llewelyn. But as he did, he saw that his brother had missed the shooting star. Llewelyn had turned back toward the strait, toward Llanfaes.

36

CWM-HIR ABBEY, WALES

December 1282

My lord!" Trevor leaned over the bed. "Wake up, my lord!" Llewelyn's eyes opened at that, but they were still sleep-clouded, not yet focused. "You were having a bad dream. I heard you cry out . . ."

Llewelyn remembered now. He sat up slowly, feeling as if he'd not been to bed at all. His exhaustion was obvious; his eyes were bloodshot and smudged with shadows, his dark hair shot through with glints of silver, and in the cold, greying light of this December dawn, he looked like a man long past his youth, a man with too many cares, too few joys. Trevor started to speak, emboldened by anxiety, but the words caught in his throat.

He yearned to tell Llewelyn that he understood. During the day, memories could be held at bay, but at night, dreams became the Devil's own accomplices. He knew his lord's haunted dreams as if they were his own—dreams of the Lady Ellen's death. Just as he knew that the other dreams were even worse, the ones in which she still lived, the ones that gave Llewelyn back all he'd lost, so that when he awakened, there was always a moment when he forgot, when he thought his world was still whole.

Llewelyn had yet to move, and Trevor hesitated no longer. "I know about death dreams," he blurted out, plunging ahead before he could lose his nerve. "You see, my lord, I had a brother. There were just eleven months between us, and people oft-times mistook us for twins, so alike were we. One day, not long past Tegan's thirteenth birthday, we were playing the fool as lads will, and I chased him into the stables, where he stepped upon a rake. It seemed a minor mishap, no more than that. But it festered, and soon he could no longer swallow. When he went into spasms, the doctors could do nothing for him. It . . . it was a hard death, my lord."

Llewelyn felt pity stir; how little he'd known about this steadfast, earnest youngster. "Ere we depart Cwm-hir," he said, "I think you and I ought to seek out Abbot Cadwgan, ask him to say a Mass for my lady and your brother."

Trevor's face lit up. "That would be a deed well done," he said, and smiled. "What I wanted to tell you, my lord, is that it does get better in time. Now, when Tegan comes to me in dreams, it is a comfort." Suddenly shy then, fearing he'd over-stepped, he turned away, made haste to bring Llewelyn his clothes, that their day might begin.

Llewelyn was soon standing by the unshuttered window, heedless of the cold air invading the chamber. Winter had come early to mid-Wales; the abbey grounds were carpeted in deep drifts of glistening white, and the River Clywedog was glazed with patches of brittle, sun-blinding ice. Cwm-hir meant "long valley" in Welsh, and the abbey was ringed by nature's own battlements, densely wooded hills, dusted now with December snow. Llewelyn had often marveled at his homeland's wild beauty, but few vistas had pleased him as much as this peaceful glen, a jewel hidden away from the world within the mountains of Maelienydd.

Turning reluctantly from the window, he took the razor from Trevor, waited for the boy to fetch a mirror. It was small and round and made of polished brass; as he held it up, Trevor wondered what had become of the magical, silvered mirror his lord had given the Lady Ellen. Llewelyn always insisted upon shaving himself, joking that his was the only hand he trusted to wield a blade against his throat, but Trevor knew he'd sometimes let his wife shave him. It seemed unfair indeed that even the most commonplace of tasks could salt a wound anew, and he spoke up quickly now, before his Prince's memories could get past his defenses. She was a loving ghost, the Lady Ellen, too loving; it was time she let his lord go.

"Lord Goronwy told me that there is much bad blood amongst the Marchers. He says that when you put so many tomcats in the same sack, they're bound to come out spitting and clawing. Is he right, my lord? Is it possible that they might start squabbling amongst themselves?"

Llewelyn shrugged, then winced, for he'd nicked his chin. "Possible, lad, but not likely. Oh, they're all ones for tending a grudge the way a shepherd looks to his lambs. Gruffydd ap Gwenwynwyn has been feuding with the Corbets and de Mortimers for years. The Corbets also loathe the Lestranges, and none of them can abide John Giffard. But however much they detest one another, Trevor, they fear Edward more. The days are gone when the Marchers could play the Welsh off against the King, at least as long as the King happens to be one of the best battle commanders in Christendom." He smiled then, wryly. "I'd wager, lad, that there are times when they miss poor hapless King Henry even more than we do!"

Trevor removed the shaving basin, slopping soapy water into the floor rushes. "We've had great success in Powys, men flocking to your banners. Where do we go next?"

"Fetch me the map and I'll show you," Llewelyn offered, and together they unrolled the parchment, held it toward the light. "It is my intent to venture as far south as Brycheiniog, Trevor. On the morrow, we'll move on into Gwerthrynion, and then into Buellt. These lands were once mine; men will remember." He gestured with the razor, and water splattered the map, dripping down the winding trail of the River Gwy, onto the Crown castle that rose up on its south bank.

ON Friday morning, the 11th of December, Llewelyn and the Welsh were on the hills northwest of that royal riverside fortress. An English town had sprung up around the castle, called by the Welsh Llanfair-ym-Muallt, the Church of St. Mary in Buellt. A brisk wind was blowing; it dispersed the drifting smoke of hearth fires, unfurled the banner flying from the castle keep, revealing the arms of its new castellan, John Giffard. It was just past dawn, and there was little stirring below, either in the streets or upon the castle battlements; they did not yet know the Welsh were on the heights above them.

At first light, Llewelyn began to divide his army, for they had agreed that his Seneschal would continue on to accept the homage of the men of Brycheiniog on his behalf, while he met with the local Welsh, sought to win them away from their enforced allegiance to the Crown. As soon as Dai departed, Llewelyn deployed his remaining men along the high ground between the River Gwy and its tributary, the Irfon. A narrow bridge spanned the latter river, and he wasted no time in dispatching an armed force to seize and hold it. Once that was done, the military advantages lay with the Welsh. Safe behind the barriers of the Gwy and Irfon, Llewelyn had the upper hand, for as long as he controlled the bridge, he could determine when or if battle would be joined.

John Giffard was not the only Marcher lord they faced across the width of the Irfon. Roger de Mortimer's sons were known to be at Buellt Castle with Giffard, as were two sons of Gruffydd ap Gwenwynwyn. They were not long in discovering the presence of the Welsh, and soon sallied forth to assault the bridge. Although they were soundly repulsed, they were not convinced and launched a second attack, only to be beaten back again. After that, they withdrew into the castle while they considered their next move.

Just before noon, Llewelyn received reinforcements from the western reaches of Buellt. Rhosier ap Gruffydd had been Llewelyn's steward in the years when the cantref had been under his rule; he was also a friend, one Llewelyn was well pleased to see. Llewelyn was already in good spirits, for the day had so far gone exactly as they'd planned. Moreover, he'd had a heartening encounter with a White Monk from Ystrad Fflur Abbey.

"He was on his way," Llewelyn explained, "to their grange at Aberduhonw. He offered to say Mass for me in Llanganten Church, and when I felt honor-bound to remind him that I was excommunicate, he laughed scornfully. 'That,' he said, 'was the English King's doing, not the Almighty's!' "

Rhosier grinned. "Why does that surprise you? The English can claim from now till Judgment Day that God is on their side; indeed, they seek to make him a veritable partner in their crimes! But what Welshman would ever believe it?" They were gathered in Llewelyn's command tent; Rhosier moved closer to the fire, stripped off his gloves, and warmed his hands. "Well?" he queried. "What happens next? Do we fight this day . . . or not?"

"Not," Llewelyn said. "I've agreed to meet with some of the local Welsh, men whose hearts are with us, but who are too wary of their English overlords to come openly into my camp, lest they be left to face Giffard's wrath once I'm no longer here to protect them. I'm putting Goronwy and my cousin, Llewelyn Fychan, in command whilst I'm gone, but I'd as soon have you at my side, Rhosier. You know these men, and I trust your judgment."

At that, Goronwy started to speak, stopped himself just in time.

He'd already made his objections known to Llewelyn, to no avail. It was not that he disagreed with Llewelyn's aims. He, too, thought it worthwhile to meet with the local Welsh, and was willing to overlook their timidity, for Buellt was occupied territory, and King's men like Giffard would be quick to suspect, quicker to strike. But he did not want his Prince to be the one to seek them out.

This was an old grievance between them, for he'd long worried that Llewelyn was far too casual when it came to his own safety, too quick to take risks better left to others. In that, he was much like Davydd; Goronwy thought the brothers had more in common than they realized, or were willing to admit. But like Davydd, too, Llewelyn shrugged off unwelcome advice, deflecting with sarcasm what he did not want to hear. Goronwy's remonstrances had fallen on deaf ears.

And so now he kept silent as Llewelyn picked a mere handful of men to accompany him, knowing Llewelyn would only have pointed out—with some justification—that a clandestine meeting would become conspicuous right quickly if he brought an army along. But as Llewelyn swung up into the saddle, he could not help himself. "You'll not be gone long? Dusk comes early in December, and you're not familiar with these roads, my lord."

Llewelyn shot him a look that was both amused and irked. "What are you asking, Goronwy? That I do not play after dark?"

The other men were grinning widely. Goronwy managed a sheepish smile of his own, and as Llewelyn and Rhosier rode out of their encampment, they were followed by the cheering echoes of laughter.

THERE was little laughter, however, in the English castle at Buellt. Roger Lestrange, commander of the King's forces in mid-Wales, was stalking about the great hall as if it were a cage. He had little space for pacing, though, for it was overflowing with men, women, and wide-eyed children; the townspeople had sought refuge in the castle upon learning that there was a Welsh army positioned above them at Llanganten. The younger children had quickly grown bored, and they were playing a noisy game of tag; the castle dogs had eagerly joined in, and the hall was soon a scene of sheer bedlam, much to Lestrange's annoyance.

He was not usually so thin-skinned, but he bore a heavy burden these days, as Roger de Mortimer's successor, and he well knew that all were watching him closely, wondering if he'd be up to the task at hand; de Mortimer, whatever his vices, had cast a long shadow. The sudden appearance of the Welsh Prince in their midst was the sort of opportunity that might not come again, and God save him if he botched it, as he seemed likely to do.

His frustration intensified as the day wore on. Just one wretched bridge lay between him and what might be the decisive battle of the war. But the Irfon was running high with snow-melt, and they had no hope of crossing it unless they could take the bridge, as they'd conclusively proved they could not do. So now they waited, and Llewelyn ap Gruffydd, damn his soul to Hell, took his ease behind the Irfon, Lestrange thought sourly, laughing at them.

The continuing clamor was one aggravation too many in a day so full of disappointments, and when Lestrange spotted John Giffard's wife, he went over to complain. He'd meant to speak sharply to her; after all, she was the lady of the manor, and responsible for maintaining some semblance of order. But as he looked into Maude's tired, troubled face, he found himself softening his words.

Lestrange had known Maude Clifford in her youth, remembered her as a handsome lass, flirtatious and given to giggling, but that was before her abduction and marriage to John Giffard. This woman was a stranger, a pitiful, drab creature, wan as a ghost, timid as a hedge-sparrow. Her oldest daughter by Giffard, a girl of ten, clung to her skirts. Katherine had inherited Maude's dark coloring, but none of her father's swagger; she seemed unwilling to leave Maude's side for even a moment. Lestrange was not normally one for speculating about what went on in women's heads, but he found himself recalling now that Maude was a kinswoman of the Welsh Prince; which one, he wondered, did she pray for—husband or cousin?

When he suggested, far more kindly than he'd intended, that Lady Maude ought to quiet the hall, Maude hastily complied—or tried to. Watching as she attempted to restore calm, Lestrange soon saw how ineffectual her efforts were. She might be a great heiress and John Giffard's lady wife, but she seemed unable to daunt a single soul in the hall, even the youngest ones. Lestrange turned away, stopped a servant, and ordered a flagon of hippocras.

It was then that John Giffard strode into the hall. Coming to an abrupt halt, he scowled, and shouted, "Quiet!" Children froze where they were, and the babble of voices subsided, gave way to subdued hush. Giffard paused just long enough to locate Lestrange. "Roger! I need to talk to you!"

Lestrange did not appreciate the other man's peremptory tone, but Giffard never even noticed. He was close enough now for Lestrange to see how flushed he was. His eyes had a glazed, blue glitter that Lestrange associated with too much wine, but Giffard was quite sober. "What was it you said, Roger . . . that we needed a miracle? Well, I've brought you one." Turning, he beckoned to a man who'd trailed him into the hall.

"Meet your miracle, also known as Helias Walwyn. Go on, Helias, tell him."

The man was not known to Lestrange, but his name identified him as a fellow countryman; the English had been settling in Wales in ever growing numbers, lured by their King's promises of profit and opportunity. Helias Walwyn seemed to be relishing the attention. He grinned, brushed back a shock of blond hair, letting the suspense build, like a child about to share a secret.

"I know of a way to cross the Irfon, my lord. There is a ford not far from where the Wye and Irfon meet. It will be a hazardous crossing, what with the water running so high. But if we are willing to risk it, we can hit the Welsh defenders from the rear, take the bridge, and then fall upon Llewelyn ap Gruffydd ere he realizes his danger."

JUST as Goronwy had predicted, December dusk descended swiftly upon the wooded hills and valleys of Buellt. The last light had begun to fade from the winter sky as Llewelyn rode back toward Llanganten. Somewhere in the distance, Vespers was being rung. "Llanynys Church, most likely," Rhosier concluded, tilting his head to listen. "A pity that it is on the wrong side of the Irfon, or we could have stopped for the service. I had no obliging White Monk to say Mass for me today," he said, casting Llewelyn a sideways glance of mock reproach.

"Ah, but you've led such a sinless life that you're always in a state of grace," Llewelyn said blandly, although the corner of his mouth gave him away, twitching as he sought to suppress a grin. The other men hooted loudly at that, but Rhosier was not offended, for he was a man quick to laugh, even at his own expense.

Only Llewelyn and Rhosier had attended the meeting in a secluded grange barn. Their escort had waited at a discreet distance, out of hearing range, and they were quite curious about the outcome. One youth was especially eager to know the particulars, and as Robyn ap Gwern seized control of the conversation, Trevor fought back a disapproving frown. Robyn was a newcomer to his lord's household, a well-born youth who was connected by marriage to Llewelyn's nephew, Rhys Wyndod. But Trevor found him to be insufferably cocky and brash, and it vexed him now to hear Robyn interrogating his lord as if they were equals; that Llewelyn did not seem to mind only irritated him all the more.

"Well . . . what happened? Did they pledge you their support, my lord? Or swoon dead away at the mere thought of committing themselves?"

"I hope," Llewelyn said, "that the Almighty is more forgiving of men's failings than you are, Robyn." Although Trevor could not see his face, it sounded as if he was smiling. "It has not been easy for them, living in the shadow of the Crown. Edward's lackeys have ruled Buellt with a heavy hand these five years past. They've had to learn caution, to embrace it as an article of faith. In fact, so skittish have they become that the letter they gave me is so cryptic and obscure it reads as if it were in code!"

Robyn was too young, though, to empathize with those who were half-hearted, apprehensive, or downtrodden. "That just proves what I've been saying, that I've seen field mice with more backbone. If they lack courage enough even to seek you out in daylight, how likely is it that they'd take up arms on your behalf? If I may be blunt, my lord, this is one quest that will yield no Holy Grail!"

"Mayhap not, but I gained information from them that might well save our lives," Llewelyn said, and Robyn turned sharply in the saddle to stare at him. The others urged their mounts closer to hear, too; Llewelyn had their undivided attention now. "I knew Edward had appointed Roger Lestrange to de Mortimer's command, and I knew, too, that he was on his way to join Giffard at Buellt Castle. But what I did not know was that he'd already arrived, and with a large force from Montgomery and Oswestry." Llewelyn paused, then added dryly, "With half our army on their way to Brycheiniog with Dai, I suppose it's rather obvious that I did not know!"

There was a silence after that, until Robyn gave voice to the thought uppermost in all their minds. "Thank God," he said, "that we hold the bridge!"

"Speaking of the bridge," Llewelyn said, "we might as well take care of it now. Morgan, you and Andras ride on ahead to the camp, tell Goronwy and my cousin what we learned about Lestrange, and that we've gone to check upon the bridge. We'll set it afire, and bring our men back with us to the camp. The day of reckoning with Giffard and Lestrange will have to wait."

It had snowed earlier in the day, and they were studying the sky as they rode, attempting to gauge the chances of snow on the morrow. But Robyn soon brought his stallion up to ride beside Llewelyn and Rhosier. "Whilst we were at Cwm-hir, I got to talking with one of the monks. He was almost as old as God, having reached his full three score years and ten, and he told me about an ambush that had taken place fifty years ago or more, involving Llewelyn Fawr and a monk of Cwm-hir. Do you know about that, my lord?"

Trevor had been bristling over this new evidence of Robyn's presumption, but at the mention of Llewelyn Fawr, he no longer minded so much. His lord could not yet bear to talk of his wife; that wound was

still too raw. But he took great pleasure in reminiscing about the grandfather he'd so loved, and Trevor was glad to see those memories evoked
now, even if it was Robyn's doing. Already he could hear the laughter
in his lord's voice, just beneath the surface, as Llewelyn said, "Indeed,
I do, lad. That was a story my grandfather loved to tell. It happened
during one of his campaigns against the English King, Edward's father.
Henry's men came upon a White Monk, who offered to show them a
way to ford the Gwy. Instead he led them into a marsh, where they
were soon bogged down and easy prey for the Welsh. Henry was so
wroth with Cwm-hir that he burned one of their barns, levied a fine of
three hundred marks—"

They heard it, too, then, sounds echoing through the trees. As
Llewelyn drew rein, he saw sudden fear on the faces of his men, fear
for him. "Let me scout ahead," Robyn urged. For once, though, Trevor
was the bolder of the two youths; he was already in motion.

But there was no need to seek out danger; it found them. Trevor
had not yet reached the bend in the trail when he ran into a band of
English horsemen. There was no knight among them, for they wore
hooded coifs and leather gambesons, not the great helms and mail hau-
berks too costly for men-at-arms. They were clearly no novices to warfare
and battlefield surprises, for they recovered swiftly and surged forward,
confident that they would prevail; they easily outnumbered their Welsh
foes.

None of this mattered to Trevor; none of it even registered with
him. He knew only that his Prince was in grave peril. Shouting over his
shoulder, "My lord, save yourself!" he spurred his horse forward.

Trevor barely had time to draw his weapon. As soon as a target
was within range, he lashed out wildly with his sword, too frantic to
feel any fear. The first man he encountered seemed startled by the
ferocity of his attack, and veered off. Another swung at Trevor as he
galloped past, but his battle axe just sliced through the air, harmlessly.
Trevor's rush had carried him into the very midst of the enemy ranks.
As he tugged at his horse's reins, seeking to turn it about, he risked a
quick glance back, and what he saw took his breath like a blow. His
lord had not fled. He was unsheathing his sword, making ready to
defend himself.

"No," Trevor cried, "no!" He jerked again on the reins, wheeled
his mount, and careened into the nearest rider. His sword struck the
Englishman's shield, glanced off. As the other man counter-thrust,
Trevor twisted in the saddle to avoid the blow. But it was then that his
horse's hooves came down upon a patch of ice. It scrabbled to keep its
footing, slid sideways, and went down heavily. Trevor was thrown clear,
rolling over and over until he slammed into a tree. But his opponent

was more interested in claiming Trevor's floundering stallion than in confirming a kill, and paid no more heed to the boy sprawled in the snow, dazed and defenseless, under a barren alder tree.

Trevor put his hand up to his head; his fingers came away bloodied. He tried to sit up, sagged back against the trunk of the tree. His vision was slow to clear. When it did, he saw Rhosier's body crumpled nearby. Robyn was unhorsed, struggling to hold off a soldier armed with a deadly chained mace. But it was Llewelyn whom the boy sought, Llewelyn alone who filled his world. He was some yards away, but Trevor heard the shivering sound his sword made as it deflected his enemy's slashing blade. The other man was bleeding, and when Llewelyn struck again, the Englishman's sword went spinning out of his grip, fell into the trampled snow between their horses. But Llewelyn did not see the second rider bearing down upon him, lance couched and at the ready. Lurching to his knees, Trevor screamed, "My lord, beware! Look to your left!"

Llewelyn heard his warning. Turning in the saddle, he started to bring up his shield. But it was too late, for the man was coming fast, was already upon him. The chain mail of his hauberk proved no protection against the penetrating power of a lance. It hit him in the side, with the full weight of horse and rider behind it, chain links breaking apart as the weapon plunged into his flesh, thrust up under his ribcage. The impact of the blow sent him reeling against the saddle cantle. There was a burning pain as the lance blade tore free, and unable to catch himself, he went over backward into the snow. The rider followed, reined in, and for a moment, the lance hovered above Llewelyn's throat, splattering him with his own blood. But then it was withdrawn. Satisfied that there was no need for a second strike, the Englishman set off in pursuit of Llewelyn's stallion.

Llewelyn sought to raise himself up on his elbows, only to sink back, defeated. It was as if his body no longer belonged to him, obeyed no more orders from his brain. He was bleeding heavily, and the snow was rapidly turning crimson. He put the palm of his hand over the wound and pressed. That caused fresh pain, but the blood continued to drain away, and his strength with it. He watched in disbelief as it soaked his glove, seeped through his fingers, a river of red that showed no signs of stopping. How could it end like this? Was this where God had been leading him, to this December dusk and a thrusting lance? What of Wales?

The English were riding off, triumphant. Trevor reached Llewelyn first, and then Robyn. Blood was still streaming down Trevor's face, and Robyn's right arm hung useless at his side, at an odd angle. But neither youth seemed even aware of his own injuries. Their faces ashen, their eyes filled with horror, they knelt beside their Prince, saying his name in unison, almost like a prayer.

It was Robyn who took control. Jerking off his mantle, he said tautly, "Help me wrap this about the wound, Trevor, and hurry! If we do not stop the bleeding . . ." Trevor still seemed to be in a state of shock, but he did as Robyn bade, and then took off his own mantle, made of it a pillow for his Prince's head.

"Rhosier?" Llewelyn's voice was slurred and breathless, but Trevor had never heard a sound more welcome to his ears. The question, though, was one he did not want to answer, and he felt a surge of gratitude when Robyn did it for him.

"Rhosier has gone to get help, my lord." They could not tell if Llewelyn believed the lie, for he'd closed his eyes again. Robyn was finding it harder to ignore the dull throbbing of his broken arm, but he knew he could not give in to it, not yet. "I'll bring back men and horses," he told Trevor quietly. "Stay with him."

Alone with Llewelyn in the twilit clearing, Trevor gently removed his coif, smoothing his lord's hair with fingers that shook. Llewelyn's skin was cold to the touch, and almost as pale as the surrounding snow. Their makeshift bandage seemed to have slowed the gush of blood, but not enough. Not, he knew, nearly enough.

"Are you thirsty, my lord?" It was all he could offer, and he was thankful when Llewelyn nodded, so desperate was he to do something for his Prince, anything. He had no wineskin or flask, but after several moments of hurried searching, he found a small stream amidst a grove of alder trees. Dipping Rhosier's helmet into the icy water, he hastened back to Llewelyn. After he poured water into his cupped hands, Llewelyn managed to swallow a little. But when Trevor looked again at the bandage, the stain had spread, and he was unable to choke back a sob.

Llewelyn's lashes flickered, his eyes searching the boy's tear-streaked face. "Do not grieve so, lad," he said huskily, "for there are far worse ways to die. Think of Simon . . ."

He saw that Trevor did not understand, but talking was too much of an effort, and he could not explain that he was thinking of Simon de Montfort, who'd died knowing that his dreams for reform died with him on Evesham Field. But his war would go on without him. Almighty God would not forsake Wales. Never had his people been so united. They'd mourn his death, but they'd not lose heart. They'd hold fast for Davydd.

It was easier than he'd ever expected, accepting that his wound was mortal. There was almost a relief in letting go, in knowing that he'd done all he could, that it was now up to others, up to Davydd. No, he was far luckier than Simon. He left no grieving widow, no sons who might suffer for his sins. How Simon must have feared for Nell, for his family as he rode out to die. But Ellen awaited him at God's Throne, and Gwenllian was a little lass, safe as a son might not be, whilst Wales . . . Wales was Davydd's now.

It was becoming more and more difficult for Llewelyn to focus his thoughts. The pain was not as intense as he'd have imagined it would be, but he was cold, so very cold, even though sweat had broken out on his face and throat. Trevor was saying his name, entreating him not to die, but he was hearing other voices now, for his dead were close at hand. He was drifting again. Making a great effort, he said weakly, "Tell Davydd . . ."

Trevor leaned over. "What, my lord? Tell him what?"

"I commend Gwenllian to his care," Llewelyn said, very low. "And Caitlin . . ." He'd had her for a lifetime, only fair to give her back. Davydd must look after them both, as he must look after Wales. A great burden, a great trust. God All-merciful, let him prove worthy of it. "All in his keeping now . . ."

"I will tell him, my lord, I promise. Is there . . . is there nothing else I can do for you?" the boy pleaded, and Llewelyn nodded.

"Pray for me, lad," he said, and Trevor sobbed again. He had no crucifix, and Llewelyn's sword, which held a holy relic within its hilt, had been taken by the English soldiers. But he remembered then that Llewelyn's dagger hilt was fashioned in the shape of the Holy Cross, and he unsheathed it, put it in Llewelyn's hand, and closed his fingers around the haft.

"Dear Lord God and Father Everlasting, into Thy Hands and those of Thy Blessed Son, now and forever I commit to Thee the body, soul, and spirit of Thy servant, Llewelyn. Grant him remission of all his sins, Lord . . ."

Trevor's tears were flowing faster now. He drew a strangled breath, and then his head jerked up sharply. "Oh, Christ Jesus, the English . . . they are coming back!"

"Go, then, and go quickly, whilst you still can!"

Trevor shook his head vehemently. "I'll not leave you!"

"Trevor, I command you!"

But the youth shook his head again. "My lord, I . . . I cannot!"

"What is the worst they can do, cheat me of a few final breaths? If you love me, go and go now. Would you make me watch you die?"

Still, Trevor hovered beside him, in his face so much anguished indecision that Llewelyn feared he'd not obey, even now. Only at the last possible moment did he snatch up Llewelyn's hand, press it to his lips, and disappear into the darkness.

Tears of relief welled in Llewelyn's eyes. The sounds were growing louder; he heard the jangling of spurs, the snorting of horses, and then the wind brought to him the voices.

"But why do you think it was a lord that Stephen struck down, Rob? He said the man's shield was plain, not emblazoned."

"Mayhap not, but Stephen showed me that stallion. In all my born days, I've rarely seen a finer animal, one even a king would not scorn to ride. And there was a garnet set in the man's sword hilt, one that seemed real to these eyes. He must be a lord of some sort, and at the least, worth a second look."

The first voice was eager now. "Think you that he might have a gold ring, then?"

"You can be sure I did not ride back to see that he gets a Christian burial!" There was laughter at that, and then they were there, for from the corner of his eye, Llewelyn could see the snow kicked up by their horses.

"Did I not tell you this was the place? Look, there is the body!" A horse was reined in a few feet away, and then a soldier was bending over Llewelyn. Reaching down, he grasped Llewelyn's wrist and started to strip off the glove, only to recoil suddenly. "Jesú, he is still alive!"

"They're a tough breed, God rot them. Send him to Hell, and let's get on with this."

The first soldier rose to his feet, unsheathing his sword. He was, Llewelyn now saw, quite young, only a few years older than Trevor. He brought the sword up, then slowly lowered it again. "He's already dying, Rob."

"If you are not as squeamish as a maid! Get out of the way, then, and I'll do it."

Someone had a lantern. Night-blinded, Llewelyn averted his eyes from its glare, and braced himself for the sword's rending thrust.

But it did not come. Instead, it was a voice that cut through the darkness, amazed, urgent. "Rob, wait! I know him! Mother of God, it's their Prince!"

"You're daft!"

"I tell you it's him! I've seen him often enough, for certes, for did I not serve my lord de Mortimer for twenty years and more? Just last year he came to Radnor Castle, signed that pact with my lord, and as close to me then as he is now. It is Llewelyn ap Gruffydd, no mistake!"

"I think Fulk is right, Rob. I've seen the man, too, and by God, it does look like him!" There was a moment of awed silence, and then they all began laughing and talking at once, unable to believe their good fortune. They were made men, every one of them, for no reward would be too much for those who could deliver Llewelyn ap Gruffydd into the King's hands.

Robert Body had the command, and began, then, to snap out orders. "Get a few blankets from your bedrolls. Fulk, you and Harry start cutting down some branches, for we're going to need a litter. The King's joy will be all the greater if we can keep him alive."

They scattered, under his prodding. The first youth claimed the lantern, raised it so he could look into Llewelyn's face. "Is it true?" he asked. "Are you the Welsh Prince?"

Llewelyn labored to draw enough air into his lungs. "I am Llewelyn, son of Gruffydd, son of Llewelyn Fawr, Prince of Wales and Lord of Eryri," he said, softly but distinctly, "and I have urgent need of a priest."

The young Englishman seemed momentarily nonplussed. "I'd fetch one," he said hesitantly, "if it were up to me." Kneeling in the snow, he unhooked his flask, supported Llewelyn's head while he drank. "There will be a doctor at the castle," he said, and then, surprisingly, "I'm Martin."

"Thank you, Martin," Llewelyn whispered, and drank again. He was almost amused by their solicitude, their determination to keep him from dying. He could envision no worse fate than to be handed over, alive and helpless, to Edward. But he did not fear it, for he knew it would not come to pass. He'd be dead ere they reached Buellt Castle, mayhap much sooner. He measured his life now not in hours or even moments, but in breaths, and he would answer for his sins to Almighty God, not the English King.

Another of the soldiers was coming back. "Here, Martin, put this about him."

Martin took the blanket. "He's in a bad way, Fulk," he murmured, as if Llewelyn ought not to hear. Fulk picked up the lantern, and swore under his breath at the sight of the blood-soaked snow.

"Christ," he said, and then, to Llewelyn, almost fiercely, "You hold on, hear? We're going to get you a doctor, for the King wants you alive!"

Llewelyn gazed up at him, marveling. "Indeed," he said, "God forbid that I should disoblige the English King by dying." It was only when he saw that Fulk and Martin were uncomprehending that he realized he'd lapsed into Welsh. But he made no effort to summon back his store of Norman-French. A man ought to die with his own language echoing in his ears.

The English soldiers were discussing his wound in troubled tones. But their voices seemed to be coming now from a distance, growing fainter and fainter until they no longer reached Llewelyn. He heard only the slowing sound of his heartbeat, and he opened his eyes, looked up at the darkening sky.

"Well," Fulk said finally, "we have to try. You watch over him whilst I help get that litter put together." As he swung the lantern about, its flickering light fell across Llewelyn's face, and he stiffened, then bent swiftly for a closer look at the Welsh Prince. Blood was trickling from the corner of Llewelyn's mouth, and the dark eyes staring up at Fulk were blind. Fulk reached hastily for Llewelyn's throat, fumbling to find a pulse.

"Hellfire and furies!" Straightening up, he shook his head in disgust. "Too late, Martin. He is dead, damn him."

Trevor had retreated only as far as a copse of trees on the far side of the clearing. Fulk's words struck at his heart, and he jammed his fist up against his mouth, bit down upon his glove to keep from crying out. His throat closed up, his chest heaved, and so great was his grief that he honestly thought he might die of it. Snatches of conversation came to him, but he did not really hear them, his ears still ringing with Fulk's blunt, brutal avowal, "He is dead."

The English soldiers were keenly disappointed, but Robert Body now reminded them that Llewelyn ap Gruffydd's death was sure to please the King mightily, even if he was cheated of the chance to take his enemy alive. He would be open-handed, with bounty enough for all who'd played a part in the Welsh Prince's downfall. They nodded among themselves, cheering up as they realized he spoke the truth, and when Trevor looked up again, he discovered that they were searching Llewelyn's body.

If Trevor had almost given himself away in his grieving, he was even more endangered by his rage. As he watched them treat his lord so callously, rolling him over in the snow, stripping off his hauberk, and ripping his clothing in their hunt for valuables, Trevor's hatred swept him to the very brink of reason. He grasped a low-hanging branch, held on to it as if it were an anchor, while he fought back his fury that these English hellspawn would dare to lay hands upon his Prince.

Their search was productive, and they gathered around to examine the results: two gold rings and a silver mantle clasp, Llewelyn's privy seal, a small wooden comb, a lock of reddish-blond hair tied with a scrap of ribbon, a dagger with an ivory hilt, and a letter in Welsh. But it occurred then to Martin that they had a problem.

"How are we going to get him back, Rob? We do not have an extra horse."

"So? We have to prove his identity, but we do not need his body for that." And he strode over to Llewelyn, drawing his sword from its scabbard.

As Trevor watched, aghast, the blade came up, started on its downward swing. He averted his eyes just in time, and thus spared himself the sight of Robert Body lifting his Prince's head up by the hair, brandishing it like a trophy for the others to see. "Take it over to the stream, Fulk, and wash away all this blood. I'd not have thought he had any more to lose!"

Trevor saw none of this. Crouching close to the ground, he wrapped his arms around his drawn-up knees, and wept, silently and hopelessly. Soon afterward, the soldiers rode off, for they had momentous news to deliver. Getting stiffly to his feet, Trevor stumbled out into the clearing. They'd left a blanket behind, blood-drenched by the decapitating. Trevor reached for it, began to drape it over Llewelyn's body, taking great care. By the time it was done to his satisfaction, he'd gotten blood all over himself, too, but he did not mind, for it was his lord's blood. Sitting down in the snow beside the body, he said, "I'll not leave you, my lord. I'll not leave you."

And that was how Goronwy found them, long after the battle of Llanganten had been fought and lost.

37

DOLWYDDELAN, WALES

December 1282

Iт pains me to say this, my lord, but I am beginning to believe you might be cheating."

About to reach for the dice, Davydd gave his wife a look of wounded innocence. "Why ever should you think that?"

"I daresay it is just my suspicious nature. But this wanton game was your idea, the dice are yours, and after four throws, you've yet to forfeit so much as a belt buckle, whilst I am sitting here clad only in my chemise."

Davydd shrugged. "Clearly," he said, "God is on my side." Getting off the bed, he stretched, then suggested, "Whilst I fetch us some wine, you can be deciding what to give up next."

Elizabeth reclined against the pillows, watching as he crossed to the table. "Davydd, have you written to Llewelyn yet . . . about our baby?"

"No, not yet."

"Dear heart, you cannot wait much longer. When Llewelyn left, I'd not begun to show yet. But I'm now past my fourth month. If you do not tell him soon, you risk him finding out from others."

"I know," Davydd conceded. "And I'll tell him, I will. I just have not got around to it yet."

Elizabeth let it go, for Davydd would balk all the more if pushed. She knew full well why he was so loath to tell Llewelyn about her pregnancy; it was bound to remind Llewelyn of all he'd lost. She only wished Davydd could admit as much. But if he could not, so be it. She'd long ago learned that she could not hope to change him, could only love him as he was. Fortunately, she thought, that was not difficult.

Davydd was coming back now with a brimming cup. Passing it to her, he said, "Well? I believe you still have a debt to pay, cariad. You are going to honor it, I trust?"

Elizabeth smiled demurely. "I always pay my debts," she said, gesturing toward the foot of the bed, where her shoes, surcote, and blue wool gown were neatly piled. "I shall forfeit my stockings." She was reaching for the hem of her chemise when Davydd caught her hand.

"Let me, my lady fair," he said, with such mock gallantry that Elizabeth could not help giggling. Putting the wine cup down on the floor, she lay back, closing her eyes. His hand lingered on her ankle, moved up toward her knee, then began an unhurried exploration of her thigh.

"You have over-shot your target," she pointed out. "My stockings are gartered at the knee."

"I know," he murmured. "But have you never heard of a scouting expedition?"

Elizabeth burst out laughing. "Ah, Davydd, I do adore you!"

"Words," he said, "are cheap," and she hit him with a pillow. He grabbed her wrist, pulled her into his arms, and they rolled to the very edge of the bed. Drawing out the last of her pins, Davydd let her hair fall free. It spilled over into the floor rushes, as soft as silk and as pale as moonlight. Davydd loved the silvered fairness of it, loved the feel of it against his skin, and made a flaxen rope of it now, entangling them both in its coils as he began to kiss her mouth, her throat. They heard neither the knock nor the opening door.

"My lord Davydd, you must—"

Davydd looked up with a scowl. "You may not have noticed, Math, but I am about to ravish my wife." He could feel Elizabeth's body quivering under him, shaking with silent mirth, and said flippantly, "Come back later—mayhap in a fortnight."

That provoked another smothered giggle from Elizabeth, muffled against his shoulder. But from Math, it drew not even a smile. "You must come, my lord," he repeated. "Goronwy ap Heilyn has just ridden into the bailey."

BY the time Davydd crossed the bailey, men were converging upon the great hall, stumbling, groggy and bleary-eyed, into the torch-light spilling out into the snow. Caitlin had just reached the doorway. She had a mantle modestly wrapped around her, but her hair hung over her shoulder in a long night plait, braided for sleep. She was shivering, and as Davydd glanced down, he saw why; beneath the folds of her mantle peeped a pair of embroidered bed slippers, soaked with snow. At sight of Davydd, she halted, looked up intently into his face.

"Do you know what has happened?" she asked, and Davydd shook his head. Elizabeth had caught up with him by then, for she'd tarried just long enough to retrieve her shoes and fling a mantle over her chemise. The wind was whipping her hair about untidily, and she would normally have been the focus of most male eyes, for a women with free-flowing, unbound hair was rarely seen outside the intimacy of the bedchamber. But now Elizabeth received only the most cursory of glances. The men heading for the hall were too preoccupied to pay heed to a pretty woman, even one with blonde hair. They knew that their Prince would never have dispatched so important a lord as Goronwy with a mundane message. The news he brought was sure to be significant.

"Trevor, you've been hurt!" Caitlin started forward, only to stop in bewilderment when he shrank back, refusing to meet her eyes. Davydd glanced at the bloodied bandage swathing the boy's head, then at Goronwy, so haggard and fatigued that his mantle might well conceal a wound of his own.

"I think," he said, "that what you've come to tell us, we'll not want to hear."

"No," Goronwy said slowly, "no, you will not. On Friday eve, there was a battle fought at Llanganten, two miles west of the castle at Buellt. It . . . it was not planned. We held the bridge, believed ourselves to be secure behind the Irfon. In the afternoon hours, Llewelyn left us, rode off to meet with some of the Welsh who dwelled in the cantref. But whilst he was gone, the English found a way to ford the Irfon. They captured the bridge, crossed the river, and took us by surprise."

Someone now handed Goronwy a goblet, and he drank, not even

aware of what he was swallowing. He'd not meant to begin with the battle. But he was not yet ready to tell them of Llewelyn's death, and he found himself putting off the moment as long as he could, hoping that one of them would guess the truth and spare him this terrible task, sure to break his heart anew in the telling.

But as he looked about the hall, he saw that it was not to be. They were listening to him in a hushed silence, not needing to be told that the battle had gone against them, that their homeland would soon be echoing with the cries of Welsh widows and orphans, bewailing their losses on Llanganten's bloody field. But no one yet realized where his dark, twisted tale was taking them, Davydd no more than the others. They waited patiently for him to continue, and he knew that they would not see the blow coming, not until it was too late.

"We were out-numbered," he said, "and unmanned by our lord's absence. But our men acquitted themselves well. They fought bravely, and they died. By the hundreds, they died, until both the Gwy and the Irfon ran red, and there were bodies beyond counting . . ." His voice hoarsened, pitched so low now that they had to crowd in closer to hear.

"They died," he said, "not knowing that the battle had been lost ere it ever began, not knowing that Llewelyn was already dead."

THEY had not believed Goronwy, not at first. They fought against belief, for they sensed, even then, just what had been lost. Their grieving, when it came, was raw, frenzied. Men wept and cursed, women sobbed brokenly, and Llewelyn's chaplain was too stunned himself to be of any comfort. When they learned that Llewelyn had been beheaded, rage briefly vanquished pain. But the lamentations soon began again, until Davydd could endure the hall not another moment. Striding toward the closest door, he plunged out into the December darkness.

It was a frigid night, too cold for snow. He had no idea where he was going, although he knew full well where he ought to be—back in the hall, assuring those bereft, fearful men and women that Wales could survive his brother's death. Or if not there, up in his bedchamber, consoling his wife. Elizabeth had a generous heart, but he knew her tears were not just for Llewelyn; she wept, too, for her lost faith. She'd truly believed in miracles and mercy and God's blessed justice, and not even Ellen's death had shaken her little girl's trust in happy endings. He must make sure that she got through this grief, too, with her hope intact; he could not let her innocence die with Llewelyn. And he would go to her, but later, later, ignoring the inner voice that whispered she had need of him now.

Davydd was not the only one who'd fled the hall. There were others, too, who needed to be alone, keeping to the deeper shadows of the bailey. He was vaguely aware of them as he passed by, ghostly figures who did not seem quite real to him; but then, nothing about this night did. He was nearing the stables when a man lurched from the darkness, so unsteady on his feet that they almost collided.

"Have a care," Davydd snapped, and the man swerved just in time, tear-blinded, mumbling an apology. He was holding an open flagon, but seemed to have spilled as much as he'd drunk, for his mantle reeked of mead. Recognizing him now—Dolwyddelan's blacksmith—Davydd put out a supportive hand.

The blacksmith sucked in his breath, his eyes narrowing upon Davydd's face. "You!" He recoiled in such haste that he staggered, almost fell. "It was a long wait—eight years—but you finally got what you wanted. My congratulations!"

For a moment, Davydd honestly did not know what he meant. When he did, he grabbed the man by the neck of his tunic, shoved him roughly back against the stable wall. The blacksmith grunted in pain, and Davydd slowly unclenched his fist. Wheeling about, he walked rapidly away.

The chapel was deserted, dimly lit. As he moved into the choir, Davydd found himself unexpectedly remembering another empty chapel, the one at Hawarden Castle, where Llewelyn had so angrily confronted him. "The destruction you have loosed upon us!" Llewelyn's words seemed to echo in the air; so vivid was the memory that it was almost as if he were still hearing his brother's voice. But he knew better. Death takes and restores not.

He moved restlessly toward the altar, where candles still burned. Fool priest, to court fire like this. He began to snuff them out, until the only light left was the one smoldering in a wall sconce by the door. Had Llewelyn realized how much his people loved him? Had they even realized it themselves? His mouth twisted into a sardonic smile; there were none like the Welsh for learning a lesson too late. He slumped wearily against the edge of the altar, as an image formed behind his closed eyelids, that of his daughter's stricken face. God pity the lass, for she'd truly believed Llewelyn's every breath was blessed. What could he say to her? What comfort could he offer?

He'd never had many thoughts to spare for Caitlin, might as well admit it. But she needed him now . . . or did she? What if she shared that dolt of a blacksmith's suspicions? If she, too, thought he'd welcomed Llewelyn's death? That was a troubling thought, but what followed it was far worse. Had Llewelyn believed that, too?

Pushing away from the altar, Davydd began to pace. That accursed plot with Gruffydd ap Gwenwynwyn, the worst mistake of his life. He'd told Owain how much he'd regretted it, but he'd not told Llewelyn. Christ, why had he never told Llewelyn?

Davydd stretched out his arm, leaned for a moment against the chapel wall. "Damn you, Llewelyn," he said suddenly, "damn you!" And then he was slamming his fist into the wall, again and again, until his knuckles were scraped and raw and the whitewash splotched with blood. When he heard footsteps in the nave, he spun around, snarling, "Get out!"

The footsteps slowed, but did not retreat. They grew louder then, until Goronwy emerged from the shadows, out into the flickering light cast by the wall sconce. "I've been looking for you," he said, and Davydd shrugged.

"Well, now you've found me." He started to tell Goronwy to go, but instead, heard himself saying, "You told us that you buried Llewelyn at Cwm-hir. But what of the monks? They knew he was excommunicate. They did not object?"

"Object?" Goronwy's smile was sad. "They pleaded for the privilege! But we dared not bury him in the abbey itself, for we remembered how the Evesham monks buried Simon de Montfort in their church, only to have his enemies dig his body up, deny him a Christian burial. So we laid Llewelyn to rest where he would be safe and at peace, with the Welsh sky for his ceiling and the snow for his shroud."

Davydd frowned. "But still in hallowed ground?"

Goronwy nodded. "He loved Cwm-hir, Davydd, told me that more than once."

He sounded as if that was supposed to be a comfort. Davydd's frown deepened; why were men such fools about death? What did it matter if Llewelyn had thought Cwm-hir was Eden on earth? He'd never heard of a grave with a view.

"Did he know?" he said abruptly. "Did he know he was dying?"

"He knew."

"What of the battle? Did he know of that?"

"Trevor thinks not," Goronwy said, and only then did Davydd see the boy hovering in the shadows.

Trevor came forward at sound of his name, saying softly, "It happened so fast, my lord. When we ran into that English patrol, we had no time to wonder how they'd gotten across the Irfon, for they were upon us at once . . ."

Davydd had discovered that swallowing was becoming painful. His mouth was parched, and he'd have bartered his soul for a drink, ought to have taken the flagon from that besotted blacksmith. "I know we need to talk, Goronwy," he said. "But not tonight. Seek me out on the morrow."

Goronwy did not argue, turned to go. But Trevor stood his ground. "I have a message for you, my lord Davydd."

Davydd stiffened. "From Llewelyn?"

"Yes. He said—" Trevor got no further, breaking off in bewilderment as Davydd flung up his hand, bade him be silent.

Gronowy looked no less puzzled than Trevor. Davydd felt their eyes upon him, and he would have choked his cry back if only he could. But it was too late. He could hear his heart hammering wildly, hear the uneven, rapid rhythm of his own breathing. Llewelyn's message . . . what had he been thinking as he watched his life bleed away? That this war was not of his making? Had he drawn his last breath out in a curse? So much left unsaid between them, and the final words now to be Llewelyn's. Jesú, what an unfair advantage the dead had over the living, for there could be no rebuttal, no denial, nothing but the accusing silence of the grave.

"So be it," he said then, defiantly. "Tell me!"

"He entrusted you with his daughter, my lord, and with the Lady Caitlin."

Davydd reached out, grasped Trevor's wrist. "That is truly what he said? You swear it?"

"Yes, my lord. He was quiet after that, for talking was an effort, and I thought he was done speaking. But then he said, so low I barely heard him, '. . . in his keeping now.' "

"He meant . . . Gwenllian?"

Trevor shook his head. "No, my lord. I think he meant Wales," he said, and his face blurred then, for Davydd, in a haze of hot tears.

EDMUND dressed in the dark, with the help of a sleepy squire, shunning the candle light that might have awakened Blanche. She stirred once, and he bent over the bed, grazed her cheek with a kiss. "Sleep well, sweet," he said, "and I'll be back soon."

He hoped that would indeed be so, hoped the noise that had awakened him did not herald disaster. Coming on the heels of Luke de Tany's calamity in the Menai Straits, another defeat would be dangerously disheartening for their men. Not that it would shake his brother's resolve. Ned would have victory, no matter the cost. Even if that meant— God help them—a winter campaign in the Welsh mountains. Edmund gave his sleeping wife one last, lingering look, then moved into the cold, dark stairwell.

The King's hall was situated along the north-west side of Rhuddlan Castle's inner courtyard. Unlike the Queen's apartments, which were still dark, light was flooding the glazed glass windows of Edward's hall, and when Edmund opened the door, he came to a surprised halt. All around him were men recently roused from sleep, men who were laughing and drinking and joking, rejoicing. Spotting the Earl of Gloucester a few feet away, Edmund headed in that direction. He'd known the temperamental Earl all his life, a man so soured in his outlook that Edward claimed he must have vinegar, not blood, running through his veins. Yet now that man was beaming, looking upon the chaos around him with a benevolent air. Marveling, Edmund bore down upon the Earl. The noise level was considerable, and he had to shout to make himself heard. What he heard in return was so unexpected that he stared at Gloucester in disbelief, and then turned, began to shove his way across the hall, toward the stairwell leading up to his brother's solar.

Edward was alone in the chamber, standing by the hearth. Edmund paused in the doorway, just long enough to catch his breath. "Ned, is it true? Is Llewelyn ap Gruffydd dead?"

"Yes." Edward gestured toward the table. "See for yourself."

The letter bore the seal of Roger Lestrange. Holding it up toward the lamp light, Edmund began to read:

Sire, know that the stout men whom you assigned to my command fought against Llewelyn ap Gruffydd in the region of Buellt on the Friday next after the feast of St. Nicholas, and that Llewelyn ap Gruffydd is dead, his army vanquished, and the whole flower of his army killed, as the bearer of this letter will tell you, and have credence in what he will tell you on my part.

Edmund read it a second time, then a third. "But can you be sure this is true, Ned? Did Lestrange offer proof?"

"Irrefutable proof, Little Brother—Llewelyn's head." Edward's smile was grim. "Lestrange hoards his words like a miser does coins, and that is a lean epitaph, indeed. But an epitaph it is, for Llewelyn and for the rebellion that doomed him."

"You think then, that the war is over? That Davydd will surrender now?"

Edward shook his head. "I know that he will not. But any chance the Welsh had of winning this war died on Friday eve with Llewelyn ap Gruffydd." Moving toward the table, he said, "I was just going to send someone to fetch you, for this is a moment to be shared, Edmund. The Welsh have for too long been a burr under the Crown's saddle. What an opportunity we now have, lad, to make our world anew!"

There was a flagon on the table, and Edmund poured for them both. "Your luck," he said, "never fails to amaze me."

"It was not luck, Edmund. I had right on my side, for I am doing the Almighty's bidding. If Scriptures say a house divided against itself cannot stand, how can an island kingdom?"

"Ned . . . what will you do with Llewelyn's head?"

"Show it to my army, then send it on to London, put it on a pike above the Tower so all may look upon it and learn what befalls rebels."

Edmund had expected as much. "You're not planning, then, to display it first at Rhuddlan?"

Edward shrugged. "I might . . . why?"

"I'd rather you did not, Ned. I'd as soon Blanche not see it."

Edward said nothing, but managed to convey quite a bit by the upward slant of his brow, silent sarcasm not at all to Edmund's liking. "I should think," Edmund said, with a hint of coolness, "that you would not want Eleanora to see it, either. Llewelyn may have been an enemy of the Crown, but she did dance at the man's wedding, after all!"

"You may be right," Edward admitted. "I did not think of it that way, and mayhap I should have, for women can be queasy about such sights." He straddled a chair, then, reaching for his wine cup. "Edmund . . . you are gladdened by my triumph?"

"I am, indeed. Why do you even ask?"

"Because it gives off a right feeble glow, this joy of yours," Edward said reproachfully, and Edmund acknowledged the thrust with a rueful smile.

"I did not mean to cast a shadow upon your victory. You are my brother and my King. Of course I wanted you to win! But I'll not deny that I think it a pity Llewelyn would not come to terms with you. I'd found in the man much to respect, and I suppose I do feel he deserved a better death than he got."

"Would it surprise you if I said I agreed? I, too, found him a worthy foe. It was meant to be, Edmund, that Wales should come under the control of the English Crown. But Llewelyn ap Gruffydd need not have died as he did. I gave him a chance to save himself. Did I not offer him an English earldom?" Edward shook his head slowly. "And I will never understand," he said, "why he did not accept."

As Elizabeth entered the bedchamber, the nurse rose to meet her. "I just wanted to look in on them once more," Elizabeth whispered. "Have they been sleeping?"

"Owain, yes. But Llelo is still restive, keeps waking up."

Elizabeth frowned. "He may be too young to understand about death, but not about fear," she said, and sighed. He was too clever by half, her firstborn, picked up much more than people realized. Crossing to the bed, she leaned over, began to tuck the blankets about them. As she did, Llelo opened his eyes.

"What is the matter, love? Another bad dream?" When he nodded, Elizabeth sat beside him on the bed. "Do you want to talk about it? No? Well, suppose I tell you about a bad dream I had? In it, I was scared and alone, and it was so dark I did not know where I was. Does that sound like your dream, Llelo? It does? Would you like to know how my dream ended? Your father came looking for me, not at all daunted by the dark or the wolves. Did I forget to mention the wolves?"

"I'm not afraid of wolves."

"You are braver then, than I am, love, for I am very much afraid of them."

"Did Papa find you?"

"Yes, he did, and guess what? I was not scared anymore, then." Elizabeth smoothed back his hair from his eyes. "Llelo . . . there is no reason for you to be scared, either. We are all very sad about your uncle Llewelyn, and we will miss him very much. But the Welsh are so lucky, for in their time of need, they could turn to your father. Uncle Llewelyn's council met and all agreed that your father should be Prince of Wales now. They know he will keep Wales safe. So . . . the next time you get scared, I want you to remember that Papa would never let harm befall us."

Llelo kept his eyes upon her face, green eyes, like Davydd's. It was hard to tell what he was thinking; Elizabeth was learning that a four-year-old's mind could take some unexpected turns. "If Papa is Prince of Wales, does that make you a Princess, Mama?"

Elizabeth smiled. "Yes, love," she said, sounding faintly surprised, for that had not yet occurred to her, "I suppose it does."

She was still thinking of this later, as she hastened across the snow-bound bailey, back toward the great hall. Davydd had told her, upon their first meeting, that she might one day wear a crown, but she'd not believed him. Had he believed it? Probably so; she'd never known anyone so sure of himself. It was a wondrous blessing, Davydd's confidence, a shield to deflect her own doubts and fears, a well that never ran dry.

The night was overcast and bitter-cold, but her steps began to slow as she neared the hall. She'd sworn she'd not do this, would not let herself think of last December at Dolwyddelan. But memories knew no more of mercy than men, came whether she willed them or not: Ellen pulling Llewelyn behind the hall screen, laughing up at him, pressing his hand to her belly so he could feel their babe. Tears were stinging Elizabeth's eyes. They must see that Gwenllian wanted for naught in her life, not ever. How hard it was at times to understand the ways of the Almighty.

She was approaching the hall when the door suddenly swung open. Caitlin brushed past, unseeing, stopping only when Elizabeth reached out and caught her arm. "Caitlin? What is it?"

The girl's mouth trembled, but her eyes were dry, beyond tears. "Gruffydd has written a tribute to my uncle," she said. "I thought I could stay, listen to it. But I cannot, I'm sorry, I cannot—" She pulled away, then, from Elizabeth's grasp, fled into the darkness.

Gruffydd could only be Gruffydd ab yr Ynad Goch—Gruffydd, son of the Red Judge—Llewelyn's court bard. Elizabeth had heard him perform occasionally, but was unable to assess his talent, for she had only the most rudimentary knowledge of Welsh. She hesitated, then decided it would be a greater kindness to let Caitlin go, and turned back toward the hall.

Davydd was seated on the dais, with Goronwy standing close by, befitting his new eminence, for Davydd had chosen him as his Seneschal. Like all the others in the hall, they were listening intently to Gruffydd's requiem for his slain Prince.

Not wanting to draw attention away from his performance, Elizabeth took a circuitous path to the dais, as inconspicuously as possible. In the past, she'd made a few half-hearted attempts to master her husband's language, to no avail. But as she looked out now upon the hushed hall, she vowed to try again, for she felt suddenly like an intruder, an outsider unable to appreciate the grieving eloquence of Llewelyn's bard. That it was a work of extraordinary power, crafted and polished by pain, she never doubted, for many in the audience were weeping openly, while others were slipping away, too overcome to risk remaining.

Taking her place beside Davydd on the dais, Elizabeth did not like what she saw. His face was pale and set, his jaw muscles so tightly clenched that she yearned to reach out, caress away those signs of strain. If only he could untether his emotions like Goronwy, who was unselfconsciously wiping away tears. Leaning over, she laid her hand upon her husband's arm, squeezed gently.

Davydd did not notice, his eyes riveted upon the solitary figure in the center of the hall. Gruffydd's elegy was, in some ways, a traditional song of lament, a harmonious weave of alliteration and rhyme, relying upon the familiar imagery of sceptre and sword. It eulogized Llewelyn as a "hawk free of reproach," the "strong lion of Gwynedd," and "lord of the red lance." But it held depths of emotion rarely found in such formalized, epic verse. In language all the more affecting for being so stark, Gruffydd was giving voice to the anguish of an entire people, and there were many who found his impassioned artistry too much to bear.

When he'd avowed that it was for him to rave against God, for him to pass all his lifetime sorrowing for his lord, Trevor had bolted the hall in tears, and others soon followed. Davydd had expected nothing like this, not so much a tribute as a rending cry from the heart. He groped hastily for his wine cup, drank deeply.

Gruffyd had paused, and there was a slight stirring, some thinking he was done. But he was not, and in a voice that carried clearly throughout the hall, he demanded of them all:

> *See you not the rush of wind and rain?*
> *See you not the oaks lash each other?*
> *See you not the ocean scourging the shore?*
> *See you not the truth is portending?*
> *See you not the sun hurtling the sky?*
> *See you not that the stars have fallen?*
> *Have you no belief in God, foolish men?*
> *See you not that the world is ending?*

By now, sobbing was audible throughout the hall. The poet had to halt, briefly, as he struggled to keep his own composure. After a few moments, he was able to continue, and eventually concluded with a conventional expression of hope for Llewelyn's eternal peace: "King right royal of Aberffraw, may Heaven's fair land be his home." But Davydd, listening incredulously from the dais, knew full well that what men would remember was the haunting cry, "Ah, God, that the sea would cover the land! What is left us that we should linger?"

There was no applause; those in the hall paid Gruffydd a far greater compliment, with their silence and their tears. He stood motionless, shoulders slumping, revealing what an ordeal it had been for him, too. And then he started slowly toward the dais, in answer to Davydd's summons.

Davydd did not care if Goronwy heard or not, and he knew Elizabeth's Welsh was meagre enough to speak safely in front of her. Beckoning Gruffydd up onto the dais, he said in a voice low-pitched and filled with fury, "How dare you? That was no lament for Llewelyn. That was for Wales!"

The poet met his gaze and his anger, unflinching. He looked for a long moment into Davydd's accusing eyes, his own bright with unshed tears. "Yes," he said at last, "it was."

He did not wait for Davydd's response, turned away. Davydd watched him go, then took a hard, probing look around the hall. On every face he saw grief, which was only to be expected. He saw fear, too, and that was also to be expected. But he refused to accept the other, the utter despair. No, by God, he vowed silently, it is not over. Let them mourn you, Llewelyn; I'll not begrudge it. I might even mourn you, too, though you're not likely to believe that. But you are not Wales, Llewelyn. Wales will survive without you.

FROM the Welsh chronicle, Brenhinedd Y Saesson, having related the death of Llewelyn ap Gruffydd near Llanganten on the eleventh day of December: "And then all Wales was cast to the ground."

38

PARIS, FRANCE

January 1283

THE weather had been cold and wet for weeks, and spring had begun to seem very far away. On this rain-drenched evening in late January, Amaury's great hall was filled with guests, some of them friends, others fellow clerics who found the accommodations of his town house far more comfortable than the lodgings offered by local inns. Several chess games were in progress; so was a lively dice game, for the Church's exhortations against gambling were little heeded. Another group had gathered near the settle, where a Franciscan friar was reading aloud from the Arthurian chronicle, Wace's *Roman de Brut*. But Amaury was not tempted by any of these entertainments. Crossing the hall, he put his hand on the shoulder of a young man seated close by the hearth.

Hugh had been staring intently into the flames, unaware of Amaury's approach. He jerked around in surprise, then smiled sheepishly. Amaury claimed a chair, stretching his legs toward the fire's warmth. "It has been a long drought, but it has broken at last. I actually have some good news to share. I've a letter here from Juliana, inviting us to a wedding."

"Hers?" Hugh asked hopefully, and beamed when Amaury nodded. "Who?"

"A neighbor of her brother's. He holds a manor in Artois, is liege-man to a cousin of the Count, so he sounds like a man of some substance. And he has a need, for certes; he lost his wife in childbed last year, leaving him with two small sons to raise, boys who seem to have stolen Juliana's heart. Oh, she speaks well of her betrothed, too, says he is good-natured and open-handed and a man of his word. But I suspect it is those little lads who are the true lure."

Hugh nodded. "Juliana has ever had a fondness for children. I often thought it a pity that she had none of her own. Well, God willing, now she may, for she is still young enough. I'd wager that she'll soon have all three—husband and stepsons—utterly smitten." He paused then, giving Amaury an approving look. "Men have always been drawn to Juliana. Like bees to the honey hive, they kept buzzing around, to no avail. But she'd not have gotten a wedding ring, my lord, for all her charms, if not for that generous marriage portion you gave her."

Amaury shrugged. "If I had not," he said, "Ellen would have haunted me to the grave." Looking around, he beckoned for wine. "Let's drink to Juliana and her tomorrows. It would indeed have been folly to mourn all her life for a man who did not love her. But then, what Bran needed, no woman could give—absolution."

Hugh had not realized that Amaury knew about Bran and Juliana. He felt no surprise, though, for he well knew that the youngest de Montfort son turned upon the world an aloof, ironic gaze that, never-theless, missed very little. Amaury had passed him Juliana's letter, waited until he'd read it before saying, "Now . . . let's talk of your plight. I do understand, Hugh, how difficult it is for you, not knowing what is happening in Wales. But by now, the French King will have gotten my letter. If anyone is likely to have word about the Welsh war, it will be Philippe."

"God grant it so," Hugh said, so fervently that Amaury's eyes narrowed thoughtfully on the younger man's face.

"You are not still thinking of going back, Hugh? We agreed that would be madness." Hugh said nothing, but his silence spoke for him, and Amaury frowned. "It is your choice, for it is your life you'd be risking. But I think you'd be making a great mistake, mayhap a fatal one. Let us assume that you do get from England into Wales, somehow avoiding English patrols and Welsh archers. How are you going to find your lass in the midst of a war? But we'll assume again that God once more favors you with your own personal, private miracle, and you do. What then? If she would not leave Llewelyn last summer, why would she do so now? And if you stayed with her, and the war turned against them, as I fear it must, you might well end up facing a charge of treason—and a gallows."

"Treason?" Hugh echoed, sounding startled.

"You are English, Hugh, owe your allegiance to the King. Do you truly think Edward would overlook that?"

"No," Hugh admitted reluctantly, "I do not suppose he would. But you do not know what it is like, my lord, to feel so helpless, so cut off—" He stopped, color flooding his face. Who would know such feelings better than Amaury de Montfort?

Amaury charitably forbore to say so. "I know that if you set your mind upon this, I'll not be able to talk you out of it. I ask only that you think long and hard ere you decide, and that you do nothing till the spring. You cannot possibly hope to survive a war and a Welsh winter, too."

Hugh could not deny the common sense of that. Unfortunately, the inner voice counseling him these days was one more attuned to passion than reason. He soon excused himself, went up to bed, and as Amaury watched him go, he knew that his advice was not apt to prevail. All he could do was to delay Hugh as long as possible, and hope that the Welsh—like Hugh—might find for themselves an unlikely miracle or two.

Moving over to the trestle table, Amaury sent a servant for an ink horn, quill pen, and parchment—but not his scribe, for the letter was confidential, its contents too provocative to risk sharing them with a clerk. "To the Dean of Le Puy, Raymond Nogeriis, greetings." Was Raymond still with the Pope in Orvieto? Well, if not, the courier would track him down. "I have a favor to ask of you, my friend. I want you to find out if it would be possible for me to sue Edmund, the English King's brother, in the Court of Rome, demanding the restitution of the earldom of Leicester."

Amaury could not help grinning as he wrote. Not that such a lawsuit could succeed, of course. But nothing would be as likely to have Edward so outraged that he'd be raving and ranting and all but foaming at the mouth. Amaury poised the pen over the parchment, laughing quietly to himself.

"My lord, a Cistercian monk is seeking entry. Shall we admit him?"

"Of course. We can always find another bed for the night." Amaury was reaching for the pen when the servant explained that the monk sought an audience, not a night's lodging. Amaury hesitated, but curiosity won out. "I'll see him."

The traditional white tunic of the Cistercians was hidden by a muddied black travel mantle, so long it swept the floor rushes. Pulling back his hood, the monk now revealed a tousled cap of reddish-brown hair, cropped at ear level, but lacking the tonsure, the shaven crown that proudly proclaimed a monk had taken his final vows. Amaury had already guessed, though, that his petitioner was a novice, for the monk's extreme youth made that a certainty. So undersized he might have been taken for a child at first glance, with skin too smooth to have known a razor yet, he looked so bedraggled, so tense, and so obviously exhausted that Amaury felt a twinge of pity, made up his mind to grant the youngster's plea, if he could.

The monk's companion wore the plain brown habit of the conversi, the lay brothers of the Cistercian order. He seemed fatigued and uneasy, too, and very young himself, for he had the barest beginnings of a beard, so pitifully skimpy and scraggly that only a youngster's misplaced male pride could have endured it.

But what intrigued Amaury the most was the dog. No bigger than a cat, wrapped in a blanket and cradled in the monk's arms as if it were a baby, it peered suspiciously up at Amaury through rain-soaked tufts of dripping white fur, looking so comically belligerent that Amaury was hard put not to laugh. The Church was constantly scolding its brethren for keeping pets, but that was more of a problem in convents, where nuns stubbornly lavished love upon cats, spaniels, and caged birds, bishops' edicts notwithstanding. Monasteries tended to have more serious disciplinary breaches, those involving the sins of the flesh, and the sight of this wet, shivering little dog only underscored the monk's tender years. Watching this odd trio bear down upon him, Amaury was suddenly glad that he'd agreed to see them, for they promised an encounter that would be out of the ordinary.

"You wish to see me?" he asked encouragingly, and then, seeing how the monk was trembling, he steered the youth over to a bench near the hearth. "You're half-frozen, lad. This matter of yours must be urgent, indeed, for you to venture out on a night like this."

The monk was staring up at Amaury with a compelling intensity. "I was so afraid that you'd still be in Rome . . ."

Amaury's interest sharpened. "I was," he said, "did not return to Paris until last month. What do you want of me?"

"It . . . it is my heartfelt hope that you can tell me the whereabouts of Sir Hugh de Whitton."

"He is above-stairs," Amaury said slowly. "Ranulf . . . fetch Hugh for me." The monk's French was excellent, but the intonations were slightly off, just enough to suggest that French might not be his native tongue. Amaury moved closer for a more critical scrutiny, remembering now what Ellen had told him, that the Welsh White Monks were devoted to Llewelyn.

"Are you bringing Hugh a message from Wales?" he demanded, so unexpectedly that the monk, caught off balance, nodded. But when Amaury pressed him further, he merely shrugged, never taking his eyes from the far door, so still of a sudden that he scarcely seemed to be breathing. Amaury studied the boy's profile, noticing the long sweep of his lashes, noticing, too, how slender and delicate were the fingers twisting in the dog's wet fur, and he was struck by an extraordinary suspicion, one so outlandish that he was not sure how to confirm it, for if he was wrong, he'd be offering the young monk an unforgivable insult.

He was still mulling it over as Hugh emerged from the stairwell. Hugh had a strained expression on his face, one that managed to be both eager and apprehensive, for it had occurred to him, too, that this mystery monk might be a messenger from Caitlin, but he was afraid to let himself hope, lest it be for nothing. He paused, eyes searching the hall, then started toward them. Almost at once, though, he came to an abrupt halt. The monk had risen at sight of him, took a hesitant step forward. And then Hugh was moving again, very fast this time. As Amaury watched in delight and the others in amazement, he startled and scandalized the hall by gathering the monk into his arms, into an exuberant, impassioned embrace.

It was several moments before Hugh became aware of their exceedingly attentive audience. "This would be an ideal time," Amaury suggested cheerfully, "to reassure all these good priests and friars that you are not about to commit a most grievous mortal sin. Assuming, of course, that I am right and we have just met the Lady Caitlin?"

Hugh laughed. "Indeed you have, my lord!" But he had eyes only for the girl in his arms. "However did you get here, sweetheart? Never again will I ask the Almighty for anything, never again will I . . . Caitlin?" His joyful rush of words ebbed away as he got his first real look into her face. "Caitlin, what is it? What is wrong?"

Tears had begun to burn Caitlin's eyes, the first tears she'd been able to shed since that moment when she'd stood in Dolwyddelan's great hall and heard Goronwy say that Llewelyn was dead. Her grieving had been all the more painful for that. She'd lain awake into the early hours of dawn, night after night, dry-eyed, her tears catching in her throat, until she'd feared she might choke on them, until nothing seemed real to her anymore. It was then that she'd known what she must do. But her flight had not seemed real to her, either. It was as if she'd become trapped within a terrifying daytime dream, one that would not end. How could her uncle be dead? How could God have forsaken him, forsaken Wales?

"He is dead," she whispered, and then she was crying at last, clinging to Hugh, sobbing as if she'd never stop, telling him again and again, as if saying it would somehow make it believable, "My uncle is dead . . ."

CAITLIN looked lost in the vastness of the bed. Her eyes were bruised and bloodshot, her lids drooping. But she was fighting off sleep, as a child might, and her lashes flickered as Hugh drew the sheets up over her bared shoulders. He leaned still closer, brushed his lips to the corner of her mouth, provoking a low growl from Hiraeth, muffled under the covers. "Try to sleep, sweetheart," he entreated, but she stubbornly shook her head.

"Trevor?"

"We made him up a bed in the great hall, close by the hearth, and he slept as soon as his head touched the pillow."

Caitlin's lashes fluttered downward. "Hugh . . . stay with me."

"Of course I will. I'll be right here in this chair whilst you sleep, and I'll be here when you awake," he promised, and touched his fingers gently to her cheek. When they strayed into her hair, she stirred, opened her eyes again.

"My hair looks dreadful," she said drowsily. "I ought not to have minded cutting it off, but I did . . ."

Hugh found himself blinking away tears. "It will grow back."

"Hugh . . ." Caitlin raised herself on her elbows, looking intently into his face. "You do still want me?"

Hugh sat beside her upon the bed, ignored Hiraeth's muted protest, and took her in his arms. "I want you so much," he said, "that I was going back to Wales for you, even though it might mean my death."

Caitlin groped for his hand, held tight, and soon, she slept.

"HOW is she faring this morn?"

Hugh dropped down into a chair before the hearth, gave Amaury a tired smile. "Still sleeping."

"No surprise, not after the ordeal she's been through."

"The worst of it, she said, was her fear that you'd still be in Italy, for she admitted to me that she had no idea what she would have done then. Her flight was," Hugh said wonderingly, "truly an act of faith."

"God was obviously with her all the way. Of course she did her part, too, made it easy for the Almighty to get her safely to France. A monk . . ." Amaury shook his head admiringly. "What better way for a woman to travel?"

"The credit belongs to Llewelyn, for he thought of it first, when we were trying to figure out how I could get into Corfe Castle to see you. Thank God that Caitlin remembered!" Hugh's smile was fleeting, for Llewelyn's name seemed to linger on the air. "I cannot believe it," he said, "cannot believe he is dead. I wish you'd known him, my lord. He was a remarkable man, in truth, and your sister . . . she loved him so."

Amaury's eyes darkened. "They did not have much time together, not long at all. They ought to have had more, her years of confinement at Windsor Castle. Edward cheated Ellen of those years, Hugh. Whenever I think of her death, I cannot help thinking, too, of that stolen time, and what might have been—if not for my cousin the King, may he rot in Hell."

It was not often that Hugh heard Amaury reveal such bitterness; his were hidden currents, surging well beneath the surface. A silence fell, a mourning silence, broken after a time by Amaury. "How long," he asked, "do you mean to make me wait, Hugh? When do I get to hear of your Caitlin's perilous quest?"

"She was so clever, my lord," Hugh said proudly, "for she sought out the White Monks at Aberconwy Abbey. Abbot Maredudd died last year, but there was no dearth of monks willing to help their Prince's niece. They at once begged a safe-conduct from Edward, contriving a reason why they had to visit their brother monks at Vale Royal, across the border in Cheshire."

"Vale Royal? Is that not Edward's new abbey? My memories are somewhat dim, but I seem to recall that Edward was caught in a storm at sea, feared he was going to drown, and swore to found an abbey in honor of the Blessed Virgin if only he were spared. Unfortunately, he was, and eventually, he did. I suppose even Edward thinks it prudent to keep his word to the Almighty. Vale Royal, a very shrewd choice, indeed. I'd wager the monks got their safe-conduct in the barest blink of an eye!"

Hugh grinned. "They did, and Caitlin crossed into England with them, just one more sheep in the flock. It was agreed that Caitlin and Trevor would then take ship for Ireland, where they'd arrange passage to France. But the monks talked it over amongst themselves, decided that such a long winter sea voyage held too many dangers, and they insisted upon escorting Caitlin all the way to Southampton."

Hugh grinned again. "I suspect that they were relishing their new-found freedom, and wanted to savor it whilst they could, ere they'd have a new abbot to answer to. But bless them, each and every one, for Caitlin could not have been safer in their midst. At Southampton, she and Trevor sailed on the first ship for France, changed to a smaller river craft at Rouen, and anchored yesterday at the Paris wharves. She then set about finding you and—"

Cutting himself off in mid-sentence, Hugh excused himself, hastening around the other side of the hearth, where Trevor was just starting to stir upon his pallet. "I've been waiting all morning to talk to you, to thank you. I will be in your debt till the day I die, Trevor."

Trevor sat up stiffly. "I was glad to help Lady Caitlin, need no thanks for it." He looked at Hugh, then said softly, "It was the last service I could do for my lord."

Amaury watched as the two young men talked quietly for several moments. Hugh then spoke briefly with a servant, and headed back across the hall as Trevor began to pull his habit on, under cover of the blankets. "I am sorry, my lord," Hugh explained, "but I owe Trevor more than I could ever repay, and I wanted to tell him so. Then I had to order him a meal from the kitchen, for Lord knows what they might have made of his Welsh!"

"The lad speaks no French? Did that not pose a risk whilst they were still in England?"

"It might have, but Caitlin saw to that, too. She told people that Trevor was a mute, and whenever they were in sight of others, he took care to communicate only with signs."

Amaury leaned back in his chair, beginning to laugh. "A lass pretending to be a monk, a youth feigning to be mute, and lest we forget, a powderpuff disguised as a dog—by God, Hugh, I do like your lady's style!"

"She could not leave the dog behind, my lord," Hugh said earnestly. "Hiraeth belonged to Lady Ellen."

Amaury stopped laughing. "I think," he said, "that it is time to talk about your plans. Have you had a chance to make any yet? No? Well, I have. You know that I was my mother's heir, and that she left me her share of her own mother's lands in Angoulême. They've been much neglected these eight years past, thanks to Edward. I need a man I can truly trust to look after them for me, to act as my agent, to make sure the revenues keep coming in. It would be a great responsibility, Hugh, one not lightly undertaken. In return for such valuable services, you'd hold one of the manors as my liege-man, and like any vassal, you'd then have the right to pass the manor on to your firstborn son. That is, of course, assuming you accept the offer?"

Hugh was stunned, and all but speechless. "My lord," he stammered, "I . . . I do not know what to say! Your generosity is . . ."

As he fumbled for words, Amaury provided them: ". . . no more than you deserve. For all you've done for my family in the past twelve years, you have earned yourself an earldom, at the very least. Regrettably, an earldom is not in my power to bestow, and if it were," Amaury continued, with just the faintest glimmer of a smile, "I'd most likely keep it for myself."

Hugh laughed. "Can I at least thank you?"

"If you insist. But I'm also doing this for Caitlin. She is Ellen's niece, and therefore my kinswoman, too. Despite all that Evesham and Edward have taken from us," Amaury said, suddenly quite grim, "the de Montforts still look after their own."

"My lord . . . Caitlin and I want to wed. We would be honored if you'd say the marriage Mass for us."

"It would be my pleasure. When? Before Lent . . . or after?"

"As soon as possible. On the morrow?"

"You're truly willing to wait that long?" Amaury smiled then, at sight of the girl just entering the hall, clad in the only clothes she had, an over-sized white habit and black scapular. "I think," he said, "that we'd best consult Caitlin about this. Whilst I'm perfectly willing to preside over a wedding in which the bride could be mistaken for a monk, I suspect that she might not find the prospect so pleasing!"

RAIN fogged the solar windows, and even a blazing candelabra could not dispel the gloom. Caitlin was seated closest to the candles, and as she talked, Amaury watched the light play across her face. Hugh had told him she'd been born not long before the battle of Lewes, which made her almost nineteen. It may have been the feathery short hair curling about her face, or the thin little wrists half-hidden by the hanging sleeves of her habit, or the faint scattering of freckles across her nose, but she seemed much younger to him than that . . . unless he looked into her eyes.

She'd been talking for much of the afternoon, mainly about Llewelyn. Tears had streaked her face at times, but she'd kept her voice steady, even as she told them how her uncle had died, alone amidst his English enemies, bleeding to death in a cold, December dusk as Edward's soldiers looked on, and the Welsh waited for him in vain upon the heights of Llanganten.

She told Amaury, too, about Gwenllian, assured him that Elizabeth truly loved the baby as if she were her own. Reaching then for a pouch at her belt, she drew out a wisp of soft black hair, neatly clipped by a yellow ribbon. "I cut two locks," she said, "one for me and one for you, my lord," and Amaury wrapped the gossamer curl around his finger, knowing this was as close as he'd ever get to his sister's child.

"It hurt to leave her," Caitlin confessed, "but I had no choice, could never have brought her with me. Even if it had not been so dangerous, I did not have the right to take away her birthright, to take away Wales."

Amaury nodded in agreement, although he suspected that was likely to happen anyway, for if Edward won—when Edward won—the war, he would probably send Gwenllian into England to be raised at his court and, in time, married off to an English husband of his choosing. Ellen would never have wanted that for her daughter, but there was not a blessed thing he could do about it, just hope that the fates would be kind to this de Montfort daughter of Wales, the niece he'd never get to see.

Caitlin fell silent as a servant entered, bringing mulled wine flavored with cinnamon and a platter of hot angel's-bread wafers. And as he looked at the girl, it occurred to Amaury that there had been one glaring omission in Caitlin's account of her escape from Wales. Not once had she mentioned her father.

He knew, from Hugh, that she and Davydd were long estranged. And he knew, too, again from Hugh, that she had not confided in Davydd or Elizabeth, concocted an excuse for leaving Dolwyddelan, arranging with the Cistercian monks to send back a letter once she'd gotten safely into England. But he still thought it odd that she would not have made even a passing reference to the man who'd sired her, who now ruled Wales, confronting two formidable foes: the English King and the larger-than-life shadow cast by his slain brother.

"So the war goes on," he said, and Caitlin nodded. For a moment, their eyes caught; then she glanced away. But in the brief look that passed between them, Amaury had seen that Caitlin knew the truth, knew that the war would never be won without Llewelyn, knew that Wales was already lost, and Davydd doomed.

39

SHREWSBURY, ENGLAND

October 1283

EDWARD was sure that Llewelyn ap Gruffydd's death guaranteed an English victory. But even he was surprised by how fast it happened. Welsh resistance seemed to collapse overnight. Davydd was not long in making the bitter discovery that he could succeed his brother, but not supplant him. Men who'd have laid down their lives for Llewelyn were not willing to die for Davydd. Disheartened and demoralized by the loss of their Prince—the loss of hope—they began to surrender.

Edward was quick to seize his advantage. Crossing the Conwy, he pushed into the very heart of Gwynedd and laid siege to Dolwyddelan. It fell to the English on January 18th, with enough speed to suggest a secret capitulation by the garrison. The capture of Llewelyn's favorite castle sent shock waves throughout Wales, convincing the stricken Welsh that God had indeed turned His Face away from them. And with each day that passed, Edward flexed the might of the English Crown, strengthened by the arrival of Gascon mercenaries. Their second attempt to bridge the Menai Straits was successful; under Otto de Grandison's command, English troops secured Bangor, marched along the coast to take Caer yn Arfon, and penetrated as far as Harlech. And as his army advanced at will into Llewelyn's bleeding realm, Edward made ready to send in architects, masons, carpenters, men to build great stone fortresses for the Crown, castles to last a thousand years.

The English called it "Davydd's war" now, and none doubted the outcome. Davydd had withdrawn to Dolbadarn Castle once Dolwyddelan was imperiled. But he was soon forced to abandon Eryri for the mountain fastness of Meirionydd. In March he and his dwindling band of supporters took shelter at Castell y Bere, where Elizabeth gave birth, a month early, to a daughter, whom they named Gwladys. The wild beauty of the Dysynni Valley could offer refuge, though not for long. The English followed. After a ten-day siege, Castell y Bere fell on April 25th. Narrowly escaping capture, Davydd retreated back to Dolbadarn. But the noose was tightening, the end inevitable.

It came on June 21st. Betrayed by Welsh seeking to curry favor with the English King, Davydd, his wife, and children were trapped, sent in chains to Edward at Rhuddlan Castle.

Davydd's capture quenched the last flickers of rebellion. Some of his allies had already surrendered. Others—Goronwy ap Heilyn and Dai ab Einion—were dead. The rest—Rhys Wyndod and his brothers, Rhys Fychan, Gruffydd ap Maredudd—now yielded, and were promptly cast into English prisons.

But Davydd would not be joining them. Not for him a swift and ignominious disappearance into one of the Tower dungeons. For Davydd, Edward had other plans. Writs soon went out across England, summoning earls, barons, and knights to a parliament at Shrewsbury on the morrow after Michaelmas. Edward even summoned the citizens from each of twenty-one towns, a reform he'd resisted fiercely during Simon de Montfort's time. But no prelates, no priests, no members of the clergy were called, for it was not thought seemly that clerics should take part in the purpose of this parliament—the shedding of blood.

IT was over, for the trial had taken but a day. Edward had mapped it out with his usual precision, as meticulously as he did his military campaigns, leaving nothing to chance. Under English law, a prince—even a Welsh one—had the right to be tried by his peers. And so Edward had summoned eleven earls and ninety-nine barons to Shrewsbury. The King could not act both as accusor and judge. He'd circumvented that inconvenience, though, by asking his parliament if Davydd's crimes could be considered treasonous. When they agreed, not surprisingly, that it was so, he was then free to pass judgment through his justices.

It was, Davydd thought, like watching a play in which the chief actor never set foot upon the stage, directing all the action from Acton Burnell, his Chancellor's manor not far from Shrewsbury. This was the second time that Edward had refused a face-to-face confrontation, for he'd done the same at Rhuddlan Castle. And he'd gotten what he wanted—a guilty verdict on a charge of high treason. They were waiting now for his justices to reconvene the court, to pass sentence. But there was no suspense. Davydd knew that the English King would again get what he wanted—the death penalty.

The trial had been held in the Chapter House of the Benedictine abbey of St Peter and St Paul. The chamber seemed vast to Davydd after three months in small prison cells, first at Rhuddlan and then Shrewsbury Castle. He wished the windows were not patterned with colored glass, for he would have enjoyed gazing up at the sky; the pleasures he'd always taken utterly for granted were those he'd missed the most in confinement.

The chamber was half empty; a number of the men had wandered off, having grown tired of waiting. A pity, Davydd thought, that he could not do the same. But Shrewsbury's two bailiffs were watching him like hungry hawks, ready to pounce at his slightest move. They seemed to think he might vanish verily like Merlin if given half a chance; indeed, if they'd had their way, he would be shackled now at both wrists and ankles. Much to Davydd's surprise, though, he'd gotten some unexpected support from the sheriff of Shropshire, for Roger de Springhouse had brushed aside the bailiffs' protests, saying curtly that wrist manacles would be enough.

The sheriff was an unlikely ally. Davydd could only guess that his defiant stance had won de Springhouse's grudging respect. For months now, he'd been under siege, sorely beset on all sides by English loathing.

At Rhuddlan Castle. In the streets of Shrewsbury. Above all, in this parliament summoned to decree his doom. But some of the men taking part in his trial had been reluctantly impressed by his bravado. He'd even overheard a few of them marveling at his courage in the face of certain death. God's greatest fools were English, for certes. They thought he feared death? Christ, he was counting upon it!

Noticing that the nearest bench was now vacant, Davydd turned toward it, seeing no reason why he should not be comfortable while awaiting the justices' return. He was at once challenged, though, by John le Vileyn, the more vigilant of the two bailiffs. "Halt right there! Just where do you think you're going?"

Davydd gave the man a shrug, a look of weary contempt. "I thought I'd pass some time at the local ale-house, mayhap drop by the whore-house over in Grope Lane. Does your wife still warm a bed above-stairs?"

The bailiff gaped, then sputtered an outraged oath. It never failed to amaze Davydd how quickly they rose to the bait, each and every time. But the other bailiff had reached them, and Thomas Champeney had a cooler head. "Do not give him what he wants, John. Let him sit on the bench, no harm in that."

But as Champeney steered his infuriated colleague away from temptation, laughter suddenly rustled through the hall, and both men instinctively looked to Davydd as the source. Their suspicions were justified, for Davydd had stretched out on the bench, shading his eyes with his arms, like a man about to take a nap. That was too much for le Vileyn. Striding back toward his prisoner, he snapped, "Get up from there! This is the King's court and you'll show some respect for it!"

Davydd opened one eye. "And if I do not? What will you do—hang me?"

Le Vileyn flushed, then grabbed for Davydd's chains. But Davydd's indolent pose was deceptive. He came swiftly to his feet, making sure that the bench was between them. By now, though, they'd attracted attention; the sheriff of Shropshire was already bearing down upon them.

"Let it be, man," he said, in a tone that brooked no argument. But le Vileyn was too angry to heed common sense. When the sheriff turned away, he followed.

"That misbegotten Welshman has been goading me all day. Let me teach him a lesson, Sir Roger! Why do you keep coming to his defense?"

"Because I—" The sheriff caught himself just in time, shaken by how close he'd come to blurting out the truth, that he did pity the Welshman. Holy Jesus, how could he not, though, now that he knew what the King had in mind for the man? "Do what you're told!" he said, then stalked away.

Le Vileyn waited, seething, until the sheriff was out of hearing range. "Go on," he taunted Davydd, "laugh whilst you can. For I've never yet heard of a man laughing as they dragged him up the steps of the gallows!"

"Wake me up when the justices come back," Davydd said, settling himself upon the bench again. Did they truly think they could scare him with talk of gallows and ropes? Not that any man would choose hanging of his own free will. Scriptures called it a shameful death. Moreover, it was a painful, lingering one, for unless a man was lucky enough to be hanged on horseback, he slowly choked to death. But Davydd could think of a far worse fate than hanging—being entombed alive in an English prison.

Thank God Edward was so set upon his death, for he was forty-five, could have survived for years in one of the Tower dungeons. Never again to see the sun or sky. Never again to feel a woman's soft body writhing under him in bed. Never again to race a horse after a bolting stag. Never again to hear the hunting cry of a hawk, or the rising wind that foretold a coming storm, or the sound of Welsh. What man in his senses would not prefer death to that? The worst of it was the solitude, the silence. Being alone in the dark with rats and regrets and ghosts and memories no man could long abide, not without going mad.

Davydd sat up abruptly, the affectation of indifference forgotten. Jesú, no, not now, the memories could not come now. He'd had a lot of practice in fending them off, and he deliberately bit down on the inside of his mouth, focusing on the pain and only the pain. He could endure whatever the English might devise for him. He could endure knowing that Edward meant to turn Wales into another English shire. He could even endure thoughts of Elizabeth. But what he could not endure was the memory of the last time he'd seen her, the day they'd taken their sons away. He bit down harder, until he bled. And then men were turning toward the door; judgment was at hand.

JOHN DE VAUX was a justice of the eyre, a former sheriff, a man whose loyalty to Edward stretched back a quarter century. Davydd knew him slightly, having encountered him occasionally over the years at the English court. But he'd never seen de Vaux look as somber, as grim, as he did now. He seemed in no hurry to proceed, waiting with unwonted patience for the chamber to quiet, and then waiting for Davydd to be brought forward. When he finally began to speak, he was no less deliberate, pausing often, choosing his words with care.

"You stand convicted of the most serious of crimes: treason, rebellion, sacrilege, murder. You have grievously offended your King and liege lord, a man who showed you naught but kindness. He received you as an exile, nourished you as an orphan, and endowed you with lands and honors, his own kinswoman, an English barony. And you repaid his generosity with treachery and betrayal. You led your people astray, you violated your sworn oath, and sinned against Almighty God by shedding blood on one of the holiest of His days. There can be no forgiveness for you, and no mercy. It is the King's will that your punishment match your crimes, that your fate serve as a warning to all who'd dare to defy the Crown. The King would have men remember how you died, Davydd ap Gruffydd."

There was a stirring throughout the chamber, quickly stilled. Men leaned forward, intent upon the justice's words, morbidly curious as to what form the King's vengeance would take. Davydd was chilled by de Vaux's ominous pronouncement, but he hid it well, as always, and said scornfully, "I am no English baron, and calling me one does not make it so. I am Prince of Wales, and I do not recognize this court's right to judge me. Let your King do his worst, for I would rather face the Almighty with my sins than with his."

His insolence provoked some angry muttering, but de Vaux remained impassive. "Davydd ap Gruffydd," he said solemnly, "it is the judgment of this court that on the morrow, the second day of October in this, the tenth year of our sovereign lord's reign, you are to suffer the penalty reserved for those found guilty of treason. It is hereby decreed that you be dragged behind a horse through the streets of Shrewsbury, from the castle to the gallows set up by the High Cross."

There was no surprise in that; the sounds behind Davydd evidenced general satisfaction. De Vaux signaled for silence. "For the crime of murder, you are to be hanged. But you are to be cut down whilst you still live."

Davydd stiffened, staring at the justice in disbelief. The murmurings grew louder; no one had been expecting this. De Vaux paused until it again grew quiet. "For the crime of sacrilege, you are to be disemboweled alive, and your entrails burned before your eyes. Then, for the crime of plotting the King's death, you are to be beheaded and your body hacked into four quarters, which shall be sent to cities throughout the realm, to be put on public display so that people may know what befalls traitors and rebels."

There was a hush now throughout the Chapter House. De Vaux paused again. "Have you anything to say?"

Davydd's throat was too tight for speech. He shook his head, tasting blood in his mouth.

De Vaux hesitated, for now he always evoked God's pity upon the poor wretches he'd just condemned. The Welsh Prince was excommunicate, though, one damned for all eternity. But as he looked upon the silent, stunned man before him, the words came of their own volition, and he added, "May God have mercy upon your soul."

DAVYDD gasped, jerking upright on the blanket, for he remembered at once where he was and what he faced on the morrow. How could he have fallen asleep? And how long had he slept? They had brought him a candle with supper, but it wasn't notched, so he had no way of knowing how much time had passed, how much time he had left to live.

His last meal lay untouched by the door. They'd given him a double helping of some sort of fish stew and a full flagon of ale—execution eve charity. He'd brought the flagon back to the bed, and he reached for it now, swallowed and grimaced at the flat, tepid taste. The cell was damp and chilly, but his tunic was splotched with sweat; although he could not remember his dream, he'd wager it held a gallows and a grave. But no . . . not a grave. Passing strange, for he'd not wanted to be buried in England, and now Edward had seen to it. Even the Saracens did not deny a man decent burial. Only the most Christian King of England would think of that.

He'd never doubted his courage, not ever. Until today, it had not even crossed his mind that his nerve might fail him. But how could flesh and blood and bone not shrink from such deliberately drawn-out suffering? How could he be sure that he'd be able to face it without flinching?

He was not accustomed to asking hard questions; that had never been his way. But he'd had three months and more of solitary confinement, time in which he'd been forced to confront the consequences of his actions, after a lifetime of evading them. There was no room to run in a prison cell.

He'd always gotten his strength from his utter confidence, from his faith in his own abilities. What could he fall back on now? The Almighty was said to be deaf to the pleas of an excommunicate. Even though he did not believe that God was on England's side, divine mercy might well be as scarce as Edward's. Those charges flung at him in the Chapter House were crimes only in English eyes, not in his. But he had no lack of sins to answer for, a lifetime's worth if truth be told. How could he be sure that God would understand? Llewelyn never had.

When he'd prayed in these past months, it was usually to the Blessed Mary, for he'd always had better luck with women, a thought that bordered on blasphemy and well he knew it. But he could not suppress an uneasy suspicion that God no longer heard his prayers. He'd not even tried to get his excommunication lifted, for only the

Archbishop of Canterbury or the Pope could do that, and he knew he could never have satisfied Edward's Archbishop. Absolution required contrition, confession, and penance, none of which he was willing to offer to an English prelate.

Never, though, had he so needed the solace of the Church, and he fervently wished he still had the Croes Naid, Llewelyn's fragment of the True Cross. But Edward held it now, just as he held the crown of Arthur, the coronet that was once Llewelyn's and—so briefly—his. Reaching for the flagon, he drank again. Well, if God would not get him through the morrow's ordeal, that left only pride. He smiled bleakly at that, seeing the twisted humor in it. For if pride was to be his deliverance, it had also been his downfall. If not for pride and jealousy, would the bond between brothers have frayed so badly? If not for pride, it might have held fast—and Wales with it.

Leaning back against the wall, he made a careless move, almost knocking the flagon over with his chain; he righted it just in time. "I'll admit it," he said, "I got more than I bargained for. But fair is fair, Llewelyn. Even you cannot deny that it is also more than I deserved."

He could not remember when he'd begun to talk to his brother. It had been a joke at first, a self-mocking attempt to deny his pain, and perhaps, too, an expression of his hunger to hear a voice, even his own, to escape the smothering burden of silence, for he'd never been utterly alone before, not like this. But although he jeered at his own need—telling himself that confiding in the dead offered distinct advantages over confessing to the living—it had given him an odd sort of comfort, and he was fast learning to take comfort anywhere he could find it.

"If you happen to be free on the morrow, Llewelyn, if nothing is going on at God's Throne, I'd not mind if you wanted to hover close by the gallows," he said, and then gave a shaken laugh. Christ keep him, he was beginning to babble, and did not even have the excuse of being drunk, not on this weak, English ale. If only he knew the time! Midnight? Matins? Or nigh unto dawn?

He lay down on the blanket again, closed his eyes. But sleep wouldn't come, and he swore suddenly, savagely. "So I lied, Llewelyn! Mayhap I do deserve it. Is that what you'd have me say? You want me to confess my sins? For that, I'd need more time than I've got, much more . . ."

He was lying again, though. There was time. So be it, then. Wales, the greatest casualty of his war. Just as Llewelyn had foreseen. "We'd become aliens in our own land," he'd warned, "denied our own laws, our own language, even our yesterdays, for a conquered people are not allowed a prideful past. Worst of all, we'd be leaving our children and grandchildren a legacy of misery and loss, a future bereft of hope."

More than a prophecy. An epitaph for Wales, for Llewelyn's doomed principality. Davydd knew it had never been his, not truly. He'd ruled over a domain in its death throes. But if he could not be blamed for losing the war, he could be for starting it.

He still believed war would have come, eventually. But it need not have come when it did. Mayhap if he'd heeded Llewelyn, if he'd agreed to wait, if . . . He sat up angrily. "What if" was a game for fools. What if Edward had died of that poisoned dagger in Acre? Or if the Welsh had not lost the will to fight? If they'd only shown some faith, if they'd given him but one measure of the loyalty they'd given Llewelyn? No, there was blame and more to go around, and not all of it his.

He raised his head then, waiting. He knew what Llewelyn would say to that. What right had he to complain that the Welsh had let him down? What of all those he'd let down, those he'd failed? What of Llewelyn's daughter? His brother's dying plea was that he keep Gwenllian safe. But he had not been able to do it. And when he faced Llewelyn in the Hereafter, what could he say? For Edward had seized Llewelyn's little lass, sent her into England, where she would live out her life behind convent walls, deep in the flat, marshy Fenlands, far from Wales. And his own babe. Gwladys, still suckling at Elizabeth's breast, taken away, too, pledged to God ere she could talk, because the English King would have it so.

No, if the Welsh must bear some of the burden for their own ruin, and if Llewelyn, too, was not blameless, that could not be said for Gwenllian, for Gwladys. Or Elizabeth. What was her sin? Falling in love with the man she'd been forced to marry. What was it she'd said to Edward that November night at Worcester? "I'll not be yoked to another rebel. I'll not wed a Welsh malcontent whose only loyalty is to himself, for, sooner or later, he'll fall . . . and drag me down with him!"

And yet she'd never thrown that up to him, not once in all those hellish months. If she had regrets, he never knew it. And after their betrayal and capture, when they'd been brought under guard to Rhuddlan Castle, she'd flung herself into his arms for the last time, clinging tightly before the soldiers pulled her away, again no recriminations, no accusations, just his name, over and over. Better for her if she'd died in childbed at Castell y Bere, like Ellen. He did not doubt that she would come to wish it had been so; mayhap she already did.

Elizabeth, I'm so sorry, lass, so sorry. . . . His eyes were stinging, his breathing grown ragged and hurtful. Where was she? Still held at Rhuddlan Castle? What would happen to her now? Would Edward convent-cage her like Gwenllian and Gwladys? Or would he think it safer to shackle her with another wedding band? Marry her off to a man of his choosing, lock her away in some remote English keep until the world forgot about her, and she alone remembered that she'd once been the wife of a Welsh Prince.

He'd known, of course, that if he fell into English hands, he was a dead man. But he'd not expected Edward to take vengeance upon Elizabeth or his daughters. He'd thought his sons would be spared too, that their youth would save them, for Owain was only three and Llelo five. The worst he'd feared was that they'd be taken as hostages, reared at the English court, as he and Rhodri had been. Merciful Christ, if only he'd realized what Edward had intended!

Slumping against the wall again, he watched as the candle burned closer and closer to the wick, nerving himself to relive one last memory, the worst of all.

He'd never known what day it was, sometime in July. When they'd brought him up from his dungeon, he'd thought that Edward had decided to confront him at last, and he was looking forward to it. At least he'd have the satisfaction of flinging the truth in Edward's face. And— although it was not easy now to admit it—there'd even been a flicker or two of hope, for a lifetime of being able to talk his way out of trouble lay behind him.

But it was not Edward who'd summoned him to the solar. The man awaiting him was his old enemy, the Justiciar of Chester, Reginald de Grey. He learned now that Edward was no longer at Rhuddlan. It seemed he was at Caer yn Arfon, for Sir Richard de Boys had just arrived that morn with a royal writ. Davydd had not liked the sound of that, and when he'd asked—warily—why this writ should matter to him, de Grey had pointed to the window, told him to see for himself.

The top half of the window was glazed with glass, and after weeks in darkness, Davydd was dazzled by the light. It took him several moments before he could focus upon the sun-bright bailey below. A goodly number of horsemen were milling about; they wore the red-and-white colors of the King, and he assumed the man in command must be this Sir Richard de Boys. But then he caught his breath, for his wife and sons were emerging from a corner tower. Whirling to face de Grey, he'd demanded to know where they were being taken. And where was Gwladys? Elizabeth could not be long apart from the baby, for she was still suckling. Did they not know that?

De Grey had not answered him, and he'd swung back to the window. It was only then that he noticed there was no horse for Elizabeth. Even then, he was slow to comprehend, for as much as he hated Edward, it had never occurred to him that the English King would separate Elizabeth from their sons. But Elizabeth was embracing the boys now in a tearful farewell, and then Llelo was being lifted by one of the guards, up into the outstretched arms of a waiting rider. When it was Owain's turn, though, he balked, clung to his mother, and began to cry. That was too much for Elizabeth. Her tenuous control shattered and she started to sob, too, as Davydd sought frantically to get the window open. He was still not used to the manacles, had not yet learned to compensate for their clumsiness, and by the time he'd worked the latches, soldiers had stepped in, dragging Elizabeth away from her son, forcing her back toward the tower. Owain was squirming in a soldier's grip, screaming for "Mama." But it was Llelo's wail that froze Davydd at the window. Llelo had begun to struggle, too, and in his panic, he called out to the most powerful person in his small world, the only saviour he'd ever known. "Papa! Papa!" Each cry a dagger thrust into Davydd's heart.

The rest of Davydd's memories of that afternoon were blurred. He remembered very little beyond that moment, watching helplessly from the window as his sons were sent off to confinement at Bristol Castle. Elizabeth had been taken back inside by soldiers obviously discomfited with their duty, for several of them appeared to be making awkward attempts at consolation. Just before she vanished into the tower, she had looked up toward the window, but Davydd was never to know if she saw him through her tears. Reginald de Grey had begun then to twist the blade deeper, for Davydd had accumulated a lifetime of debts now due and payable. De Grey's taunts were wasted, though; Davydd was beyond caring.

Not long afterward, they'd taken Gwladys and Gwenllian away from Elizabeth, dispatched them to nunneries in Lincolnshire. Reginald de Grey had made sure Davydd knew about that, too, and that Gwladys was not the only one of his daughters to be made a nun against her will, for the English King was casting a wide net. Davydd did not see Elizabeth again. In September, sixty archers had escorted him from Rhuddlan to Shrewsbury for his trial, and he would go to his death never knowing his wife's fate.

The candle light was waning. A mouse bolder than most had ventured out to feed from his plate, then scurried back into the shadows when Davydd got to his feet. He had no memories of his own father, who'd died in that Tower fall when he was six, and even after siring two sons and seven daughters, he'd never given fatherhood a high priority; he'd always had too many other irons in the fire. He'd probably spent more time with his sons in their six-month odyssey to elude Edward's troops than in all the years of their young lives. That they were bedazzled by him, he'd taken for granted; he'd found children as easy to charm as women, although the latter had held his interest far more than the former. But he'd been proud of them both, amused by Llelo's sprouting sense of mischief, flattered by their total trust. And he did not doubt that they still clung to that childish faith, sure he'd soon come for them, even after two months' captivity in Bristol Castle. They were too young yet to comprehend how utterly and unforgivably he had failed them.

Edward would never let them go. They would grow to manhood behind the walls of Bristol Castle. They would not know the joys and dangers and temptations that life could offer a man. They would learn naught of friendship or the urgency and sweetness of bedding a woman. They'd never have sons of their own. They would never see Wales again, and as their memories faded, they'd forget the world they'd known before Bristol Castle. They would forget him, forget Elizabeth, and not even know why they were doomed to live out their days as prisoners of the English King.

"Well? Are you satisfied, Llewelyn?" he said huskily. "You wanted a full confession, and by God, you got it, save for a few sins of the flesh, too minor to mention. What do you want to know now? If I'll shame you on the morrow? You'll just have to stop by the High Cross and see for yourself, like the rest of Shrewsbury."

There were a few swallows left in the flagon. He drained it dry and then flung it into the darkness beyond the candle. It made a metallic clang as it struck the wall, another as it bounced off onto the floor, dented but still intact; prisoners were not trusted with breakable crockery. God forbid, Davydd thought, that some poor soul might cheat the hangman, and then he was turning, straining to hear, his heart beginning to thud wildly in his ears as the sound grew louder, more distinct: footsteps approaching the door.

There were four of them, all known to Davydd, all hostile, for his barbed tongue had won him no friends at Shrewsbury Castle. In the lead was a tall, heavyset man with a soldier's bearing and skin like leather, browned by twenty years' exposure to blazing sun and desert heat, for he'd seen long service in the Holy Land. It was that service which had given him his odd name, for he'd been at Jaffa when it fell to Sultan Baibars, talked about it so often that his fellow guards had dubbed him "Jaffa." He was the first into the cell, raking Davydd with glittering eyes, a jeering smile.

"Surprised to see me, Welshman? I asked for today's duty, would not have missed it for all the whores in Babylon. I heard that they are paying your executioner right well—a full pound for his labors. A pity they did not know I'd have taken on the job for free!"

When Davydd said nothing, Jaffa feigned astonishment. "Can you truly be at a loss for words? What is the matter, you did not sleep well? I see you did not eat much. A little queasy, no?"

One of the other guards frowned, said impatiently, "Come on, Jaffa. Let's get this over with."

"Oh, I'm in no hurry. What about you, Welshman? I'd wager you're in no hurry, either. So . . . shall I tell you what you've got to look forward to this morn? I'm sorry to say that it was decided you're to be dragged to the gallows on a hurdle. I suppose they wanted to make sure they'd not be delivering a corpse to the hangman, but I'd have let you take your chances. By the way, you've drawn quite a crowd, for it looks like half of Shrewsbury has turned out to watch you die. Now . . . where was I? Ah, yes, hanging you alive. I've never seen this done, can only guess they'll cut you down once you start to turn blue in the face."

"Jaffa, let it be."

Jaffa ignored the protest, kept his eyes on Davydd. "Then they'll hold you down and heat a knife. They'll start by cutting off your cock, then take out your guts, your heart, your—"

"Christ Jesus, Jaffa, enough!" The speaker was not the only one glaring at Jaffa now. The other guards were beginning to look uncomfortable, and when the youngest of them happened to make eye contact with Davydd, he hastily glanced away.

"But I'm not done yet. I'm sure he wants to know how eager the towns all were to claim a portion of the prize. After all, they took him back to the castle ere the bickering began. Only the delegates from Lincoln balked, and I hear the King was right vexed by that, means to levy a goodly fine upon the town as punishment. But the others . . . ah, they were hot to have a piece of your carcass, Welshman. The Mayor of London will be taking your head back with him, to feed the ravens atop the Tower next to your hellspawn brother. York gets the right arm, having won out over Winchester. Northampton gets the right leg and hip. I believe Bristol claimed the left arm, and the left leg goes to Hereford. Let's see . . . did I leave any part out?"

Davydd's mouth was very dry. He swallowed with difficulty, but his voice held steady, held a hard, mocking edge as he said, "It sounds like they'll be wasting the best part. But then, I keep forgetting that you English know nothing of manhood. They could nail my cock up over the dais in Westminster Hall and none of you would even know what it was—least of all, Edward."

Jaffa was big, but not fast. When he swung, Davydd sidestepped and the blow missed him altogether, grazed the wall behind him. Jaffa swore, swung again, but by then the other guards were between them. A brief scuffle broke out, and then they were backing away, warily eying the man in the doorway.

Jaffa was deeply flushed. He gave Davydd a murderous look before turning to face the sheriff. "He asked for it, Sir Roger, I swear he did! He said—"

"I heard." Roger de Springhouse moved forward into the dungeon, stopped in front of Davydd. "That tongue of yours would put a viper to shame. A pity you never learned to curb it."

"I know," Davydd said. "I expect it will get me into trouble one of these days."

The corner of de Springhouse's mouth twitched, and then he startled them all by unfastening the flask of his belt, offering it to Davydd. "I'll say this for you, that you do not lack for nerve."

Davydd took the flask, drank deeply. The wine was strong, heavily spiced, burned his throat. He drank again, then handed the flask back to the Englishman. "Are you going to be there?"

The sheriff nodded slowly. "Yes."

"Good. I want you to watch, to watch closely, to miss nothing. And then," Davydd said tautly, "you go back to Acton Burnell, and you tell your whoreson English King how a Welsh Prince died!"

40

SHREWSBURY, ENGLAND

October 1283

Aʙʙᴏᴛ ᴊᴏʜɴ has sent someone to fetch Brother Damian. We do not have a guest parlor at the abbey, but you may await him in here." Smiling, the hospitaller ushered them into the Chapter House, left them alone.

Hugh followed the monk to the door, made sure he'd truly gone. It was not in his nature to be so suspicious, but his sense of foreboding had become too strong to ignore. He'd known from the first that they ought never to have returned to England. But Caitlin had been adamant, deaf to reason, entreaty, his most impassioned arguments. It was not that he'd feared for her safety. The war was over. But he did fear for

Caitlin's welfare; her grieving for Llewelyn was still raw, unhealed. How would she deal with Davydd's death, too?

He was sure that she'd not be permitted to see Davydd. He even thought it might be for the best if she were not. After years of silence, what could be said in an English gaol, in the shadow of the gallows? But once they'd learned of Davydd's capture and upcoming trial for treason, Caitlin had insisted she must go back, she must see her father ere he died. And so Hugh had reluctantly acquiesced, booked passage for them from Harfleur.

But upon their Michaelmas arrival in Bristol, he'd discovered that the stakes were far higher than he'd realized. Almost by chance, he'd learned that Davydd's small sons—Caitlin's half-brothers—were incarcerated at Bristol Castle. Stunned, he'd made some discreet queries, soon learned that Gwenllian and Davydd's daughters had been taken into England, too, disappeared into the cloistered seclusion of Gilbertine nunneries at Sempringham, Sixhills, and Alvingham.

Hugh would have sailed for France with the next tide. But Caitlin would not agree, and—not for the first time—Hugh found that his wife's will was stronger than his own. Her urgent desire to see her father had by now become a compulsion. She could not explain it, other than to say over and over that she must make peace with Davydd ere he was executed by the English King. But Hugh sensed that her need owed as much to her uncle's death and the Welsh defeat as it did to Davydd's peril.

Caitlin knew that Hugh was acting against his better judgment, and she'd done what she could to ease his mind, pointing out how unlikely it was that any Englishman would recognize her as Davydd's daughter, for she'd crossed the border only to attend her uncle's wedding at Worcester, and then to flee in disguise. But Hugh remained wary, insisting they proceed with the utmost caution. To placate him, Caitlin promised to do nothing foolhardy, to do nothing without his consent. She even conceded that it was not likely she'd succeed in seeing Davydd, whatever the stratagem they hit upon. Yet she had to try; surely Hugh could see that she had to try?

And so they'd come to Shrewsbury on this second Friday in October, had gone straight from their Mardevol Street inn to the Benedictine abbey of St Peter and St Paul. They'd decided to rely upon the ruse that had served them both so well in the past, but first Hugh wanted to know the lay of the land, and what better scout could he have than Brother Damian? It boded well for them, he'd told Caitlin, that God had seen fit to send Damian to Shrewsbury, and as he assured her of that again, the door opened.

Damian looked just as Hugh remembered, blinking a little as he left the sunlight behind, a quizzical smile on his face. "Abbot John said you wanted to see me?" He came closer, still smiling, still showing no signs of recognition. But then Hugh grinned and conjured up for Damian a ghost, twelve years gone, not yet forgotten. "No," he cried, "it cannot be! Hugh de Whitton? Is it truly you, lad?"

Hugh laughed. "It can be and is!"

Brother Damian was almost smothered in Hugh's hug, for the gangling youngster he'd befriended at Evesham Abbey now topped his own height by at least half a foot. "Look at you, lad," he marveled. "Tall as an oak and just as sturdy! Ah, Hugh, how the sight of you gladdens my eyes. I thought of you often over the years, wondered where you were, how you were faring."

"I'd hoped to see you two years ago," Hugh said, "when my lady Ellen and I stopped at Evesham. But by then you were already at Shrewsbury. I always meant to find my way here and pay a visit, but somehow I never did. I got married, and then the war . . ." He let the rest of the sentence go, for Damian was smiling at Caitlin, making the natural assumption that she was the wife in question. Hugh saw no point in correcting him; how could he ever explain about Eluned?

Damian acknowledged the introductions with enthusiasm, then puzzled Caitlin by dropping diffident hints about "blessings" and "boons." When she realized he was talking about babies, she said forthrightly, "No, not yet, but we hope to have a bevy of them ere we're done." Remembering to add, "God willing," for she did not want Damian to think her brazen; many monks, she knew, saw women only as Delilahs and Jezebels, weak vessels born to do the Devil's bidding.

But Damian did not share the darker suspicions of some of his brethren and was delighted by Caitlin's candor. "Fortune has indeed favored you, Hugh . . . and I was not at all sure it would be so, was not even sure you were still amongst the living."

"I've never been much for writing letters," Hugh said apologetically, and Damian laughed.

"Indeed not, lad! What did I get—two in twelve years? One telling me you were not coming back to the abbey, that you were off to Italy with Bran de Montfort. Then a seven-year silence until, lo and behold, I learn you're at Worcester, about to go into Wales with Eleanor de Montfort and her Welsh Prince! I thought of you when war broke out, Hugh, said many a prayer for your safe-keeping."

Hugh was feeling more remorseful by the moment that he'd been so neglectful a friend. "After my lady died in childbed, I left Wales," he explained, "and returned to France, to Lord Amaury de Montfort's service." Now that Wales had been introduced into the conversation, he didn't want to let the opportunity slip away, and said hastily, "As hard as it was to lose my lady, I am grateful she did not live to see Prince Llewelyn slain, her baby stolen away by the English King. It is only to be expected, though, that people saw it differently on this side of the border. I suppose there was great rejoicing when the war was won and Davydd ap Gruffydd taken by the King's soldiers."

"There was, indeed, and with good reason, Hugh. Whenever Wales goes up in flames, we in Shrewsbury are like to get scorched, too. I pray to God that this was the last war we'll ever fight with the Welsh, may they learn to live in peace." But Damian was at heart still Simon de Montfort's disciple, and he then continued rashly, "Though I'll admit to feeling some sympathy for the Welsh Prince, as I would for any man going up against Edward Plantagenet. He may well be blessed by God on the battlefield, but I still believe that England's honor died with Earl Simon at Evesham."

"Ah, Damian, you've not changed at all, courting calamity with every breath you draw," Hugh said wryly. But Caitlin was growing impatient, and he saw it. "The Welsh Prince—you mean Llewelyn? Not Davydd?"

"Llewelyn, of course. That brother of his was a bold knave, for certes, but a knave nonetheless."

Hugh frowned, but Caitlin did not catch it, Damian's use of the past tense. "The trial is to be held here, is it not? In Shrewsbury?"

"Done and over with, Lady Caitlin, here in our Chapter House. He stood right there," Damian said, pointing toward the lectern, "and mocked them all. He showed no contrition, no repentance, I'm sorry to say, went to his death defiant to the last, sacrificing his immortal soul for the sake of his accursed pride."

"He . . . is dead?"

"Oh, yes, my lady. The execution was done the very next morn . . . last Saturday at the High Cross. But I was glad of the haste, for it was a mercy that there was no delay, that he did not have days to dwell upon the horror awaiting him."

Caitlin had moved away from them. Hugh started to follow, saddened but not surprised that it should end like this. But Damian's last words stopped him in his tracks. Caitlin was already turning back to face the monk. "What do you mean?" she asked, and there was a tremor in her voice that belied the matter-of-fact way she added, "He was . . . hanged, was he not?"

Damian sighed. "Hanging is indeed the punishment for treason, but that was not enough for the King. He took a truly terrible vengeance upon the Welshman, my lady. Trust me when I say you do not want to hear more."

"I have to know," Caitlin said, with enough intensity to baffle

Damian, to make him uneasy. He looked to Hugh for guidance, and when Hugh nodded grimly, he told them—as briefly as he could—how Davydd had died.

When he was done, Hugh whispered, "Jesus God." Caitlin said nothing at all, but as she listened to Damian, the blood drained from her face. When Hugh would have embraced her, she pulled away, shaking her head. Hugh let her go . . . until she stumbled against the lectern, unable to see it for her tears. He reached her then, in two strides, gathered her into his arms, and held her close as she wept. But he was learning to know her as he'd known no one else. "Do you want to be alone for a while, lass?" And as he expected, she nodded. With Caitlin, sometimes the best way he could show his love was to step back, to wait. But it was also—for him—the hardest way.

Clouds had begun to gather overhead, and the cloisters had lost the sun; the sky above Hugh's head was mottled in grey-and-blue patches. He stared up at it, blindly, and then Damian was beside him, saying in quiet reproach, "I fear, Hugh, that you have not been entirely honest with me. What was Davydd ap Gruffydd to your wife?"

He'd not meant to confide in Damian; silence seemed safer for them all. But he could not lie to the other man, owed the monk a half-truth at the very least. "I ought to have told you," he admitted. "They were . . . kin."

Damian looked so stricken that Hugh felt a pang of guilt; he had no right to involve Damian in this, no right at all. The monk sat down abruptly on one of the carrel benches. "God forgive me," he said. "But I did not know . . ."

CAITLIN was sitting on the floor by the lectern. She'd feared for a time that she'd be sick, but it had passed. She still felt hollow, shaken to the very depths of her soul, and she sensed that nothing would ever be quite the same again. She no longer wept, and when Hugh came back, she let him lift her to her feet, lead her toward a bench. She was glad when he did not try to talk, for what was there to say?

"My lady . . ." She'd not noticed Damian, but he was there now, too, offering a cup filled with dark liquid. She did not want it, but it seemed to matter to him, and so she let him put the cup in her hands. "I am so sorry, my lady, so very sorry! Had I only known you were Welsh, I would never have spoken of his death. If it is of any comfort, he . . . he did die well. He showed great courage, Lady Caitlin. I know that must not matter much now, but—"

"It matters," Caitlin said. "It mattered to him."

Damian nodded slowly. "Again, I do regret being the one to tell you. I would to God you never had to know. Hugh said that he was . . . was your kinsman?"

Caitlin looked up at the monk. She'd thought her weeping was done, but tears were suddenly streaking her face again. "He was my father," she said.

THEY stopped on Bridge Street, stood gazing across at the castle's formidable defenses, its soaring towers and battlements. The moment was finally upon them, but not as they'd planned it would be. It was to have been Caitlin, posing as a nun to get into Shrewsbury Castle. But now it was Hugh who wore the disguise, the black cowl of the Benedictines, Damian's contribution to their quest. And the citadel rising up before them was the royal castle of Chester, the prisoner within, Davydd's widow.

"Hugh . . ." Caitlin was frowning, fighting the urge to reach up and adjust his hood; that was too intimate a touch for broad daylight on a busy Chester street. "Make sure you keep your hair hidden," she fretted, "lest they see you lack the tonsure. Cariad, it is not too late to change your mind . . ."

"Caitlin, we agreed that it was to be me. There is no way on God's earth that I'd let you enter one of Edward's castles, not now that we've seen into the darkness of his soul." Her frown deepened, but she did not argue, for she knew it would be futile. Hugh brushed his fingers against her hand in a brief, surreptitious caress before looking over at the third member of their enterprise. "Trevor, will you take my lady back to the inn? It is safer that you await my return there, not here on the street."

Caitlin began to protest, saw it was useless; both men were united against her in this. "Go with God, Hugh," she said, and she and Trevor watched then, as he started across the street, dodging carts and dogs and small boys playing tag, heading for the castle.

Hugh and Caitlin had concocted a plausible pretext, that he'd been sent by the King's lady mother, now residing at the Benedictine nunnery at Amesbury. Elizabeth was the King's cousin, after all. Was it not reasonable that the pious dowager Queen might pity her plight, at least enough to offer her the spiritual solace of the Church? As he approached the drawbridge, Hugh hoped fervently that it would seem so to the deputy constable of Chester Castle.

He was well aware that he was now deep in enemy territory, for Chester's Justiciar was Reginald de Grey and the castle constable the Earl of Lincoln, new master of Davydd's stronghold at Dinbych. But his fears proved needless. His mission was accepted without question, even approved. Whether the King's mother pitied Elizabeth or not, it was soon apparent to Hugh that the men guarding her did. He had heard disquieting tales of Elizabeth's earlier captivity; it was said she'd been brought to Rhuddlan Castle in chains, and he was thankful that she seemed to have found a kinder confinement here at Chester.

He did not know what to expect, sure only that Caitlin must be spared this encounter, and not just for her safety's sake. His first reaction was one of relief, for the room was decently furnished, a small chamber, but one with a window and a hearth. Highborn prisoners were usually allowed such basic amenities; even Amaury had not been denied a bed and charcoal brazier at Corfe Castle. But Damian had told him of the harsh conditions of Davydd's confinement, and he'd needed to see for himself that Elizabeth was not being held in a dungeon. Why, though, was she being held at all?

Hugh had not known Elizabeth well. He did remember her age— twenty-five—having learned by chance that she was just two years and one day younger than he. He was braced now to find that she'd aged years in a matter of months, for how many women ever suffered the losses that had been hers? But he found, instead, a lost child. She wore no wimple or veil, and her long fair hair trailed down her back, loose and limp like a little girl's. Her gown seemed to have been made for another woman, swallowing her up in billowing folds, for she'd not had weight to spare in the best of times. Hugh had once heard Davydd call her "angel," and thought it an apt endearment, even in jest. But she was earthbound now for certes, far from Heaven's grace, and as his eyes took in her pallor, her frailty, her betrayed faith, Hugh understood why she'd roused the protective urges of the castle garrison.

"It was kind of you to come, Brother Mark," Elizabeth said politely, but her blue eyes were blank, without hope or even curiosity.

Hugh mumbled the first piety to come to mind as the guard headed for the door. As soon as they were alone, he pulled back his hood. "I am no monk, my lady. Do you not recognize me? Hugh de Whitton, one of Lady Ellen's household knights."

Elizabeth showed no surprise at his revelation, and not much interest, either. "Did I know you?" she asked.

Hugh was momentarily at a loss. "My lady, may we sit down?"

"Of course," she said, looking vaguely about the chamber as if she'd never before noticed its accommodations. Hugh touched her elbow, guided her toward the lone bench. She startled him then, by saying, "I do remember you. You're Caitlin's lover."

"No," he said gently, "her husband." He could not tell, though, if Elizabeth understood. She did not seem dazed, just distant. As if she'd sought sanctuary, he thought, but not in a church, in some secret, inaccessible corner of her soul. He was not sure how to coax her out, not even sure if he should. And so they sat by the smoldering hearth, and he told her about his marriage to Caitlin, about their manor in Angoulême, about any topic that seemed safe, far removed from the life she'd lost.

It was to be an afternoon that would haunt his memory for years. Slowly, hesitantly, she'd begun to venture out of her sheltering silence, to talk, in fits and starts at first, of her broken family. She could not speak of her sons. She tried, once, and the words would not come. But eventually she did talk to him of her daughter and Gwenllian. The nuns would be kind to them, she said, surely they would? And Hugh assured her quite truthfully that Gwladys and Gwenllian would likely become the convent darlings, pampered and cosseted by nuns who did not see themselves as gaolers or their tiny charges as prisoners of the Crown.

"And at least they will grow up together, will be company for each other," Elizabeth said, "the last daughters of the royal House of Wales."

Hugh knew better, for he knew Gwenllian had been taken to Sempringham and Gwladys to Sixhills. But he agreed again, did what he could to feed Elizabeth's malnourished hopes. She had risen by now, was moving restlessly about the chamber. He remembered then, to give her the few comforts he'd smuggled in under his habit: a small metal mirror, a comb, and a pater noster.

Elizabeth gazed intently into the mirror, as if seeing a stranger. She fingered the rosary beads. And then she asked softly, "Is it true that Davydd is dead?"

This was the moment Hugh had been most dreading. "Yes, my lady. They told you, then?"

"Yes," she said, "the deputy constable and the chaplain. They said Davydd had been hanged in Shrewsbury on the Saturday after Michaelmas. That is so, Hugh? They did not lie to me?"

Mute, he could only shake his head. She did not know! His relief was so intense, so overwhelming that he was slow to realize she'd been given a reprieve, no more than that, one to last only as long as her confinement did. And there was no longer any reason to hold her captive now that Davydd was dead. For Hugh never doubted that Elizabeth's maltreatment was done to punish her husband. Now that Davydd was beyond Edward's vengeance, Elizabeth would eventually be set free. Then she would learn the truth about Davydd's death, and God help her when she did. But she could never have borne it now, and Hugh felt a rush of gratitude toward the men who'd lied to her, who'd shown more mercy than their King.

"They told me Davydd died bravely. But I knew that already."
Elizabeth sought to smile at Hugh, not convincingly. "Davydd . . .
Davydd would have laughed at the Devil on his way to Hell."

"Yes," Hugh said hoarsely, "he would, indeed, my lady." Her
composure made him uneasy, for it put him in mind of ice skimming
over a pond, too brittle to bear weight. He was amazed that she could
bring herself to speak of Davydd so soon after his execution. But then
he realized that this widow of a fortnight had been mourning Davydd
for months. And as he watched Elizabeth pacing before the hearth, he
understood, too, why her eyes were dry; she had no more tears left to
shed.

"Lady Elizabeth . . . is there nothing I can do for you?" He
comprehended the emptiness of his offer as soon as it was made, but
he could no longer bear witness to her pain, not without seeking to
alleviate it.

Elizabeth stopped, stood unmoving for a long moment. "You can
tell me why," she said at last. "I would to God that someone could tell
me why!"

"My lady, if only I could! I can tell you that the war was bound to
come, for Wales was too small a land to share a border with England.
I can even tell you when the war was lost, on the eleventh of December
at dusk. But I cannot tell you why God let it happen—"

"No," Elizabeth said, "that is not what I want to know. Why did
Edward take my sons away? Can you tell me that, Hugh? Can anyone?"

He shook his head again, unable to meet her eyes. "I knew,"
Elizabeth said, in a voice no longer steady, "that Davydd was doomed.
We both knew it, toward the last. But I could not leave him. Even if my
babe had not been due . . . How could I ever have forsaken him when
he needed me the most? But I did not knowingly sacrifice my sons for
him, I swear I did not! When they get older, will they understand that?
Or hate me for failing them?"

"Lady Elizabeth, no! You have nothing to reproach yourself for!"

"I truly did not believe they were at peril. What threat could a five-
year-old boy pose to a King? Or his three-year-old brother? I never once
thought that he'd imprison them, for were they not his own cousins?
Had I not made this marriage at his command?"

It was all spilling out, in a scalding surge. But even now, there were
no tears. "If Edward was not willing to set them free, could he not have
pledged them to God as he did my daughter? Or raised them at his
court? They were just little boys, would have learned whatever lessons
he chose to teach them. I've thought about it, you see, I've thought
about it until I feared I'd go stark mad, with the questions chasing round

and round in my head, never stopping. Why did he do it, Hugh? Even if he truly believed that he had no choice but Bristol Castle, why did he not let me go with them, then? Why?"

Hugh could think of only one reason why Edward would have torn Elizabeth away from her sons, and it was one that he believed was deserving of damnation. But he did not want to dwell upon the English King's vengefulness, for that would only intensify Elizabeth's fears for Llelo and Owain. Instead, he told her now of his arrival in Bristol, and then he began to lie, he who'd always scorned falsehoods, telling her that the boys had been seen playing in the castle bailey, that he'd heard they had comfortable lodgings and indulgent attendants. Elizabeth listened, saying little, and thanked him when he was done, but whether that meant she believed him, he did not know.

When it was time for him to go, he found himself delaying his departure, reluctant to leave her alone with her grieving, her ghosts. The King's brother and his lady were often in France, he told her, and when next they came to their lands in Champagne, he would seek them out, beseech them on her behalf. The Lord Edmund had a good heart, and if he and his lady spoke up for her, the King might heed them, might hasten her release. "And once you are free, Lady Elizabeth, you will have a home in Angoulême with Caitlin and me, for as long as you like."

"You are the one with the good heart, Hugh. But I cannot accept your kind offer, for I cannot leave England. You see," Elizabeth said, "the King might relent. He might let me see my children."

Hugh nodded wordlessly and kissed her hand, marveling that she had somehow held on to a few shreds of faith. But as he reached the door, she said suddenly, urgently, "You take care of Caitlin, Hugh. Keep her safe. Keep her far from Edward's England!"

THE rain had ceased, but not for long. November was always a wet month in Wales. The nights were cold now, the grass silvered with frost, the valleys and glens adrift in early morning fog, and the bracken mantling the hills was brown and sere. But those hills were still snow-free. Hugh hoped they'd stay that way for a few more days, time enough for them to get back across the border.

He still could not quite believe that they'd ventured into Wales, for that was the last place in Christendom he'd have chosen to be. When Caitlin first broached the idea, pleading that she wanted to thank the Aberconwy monks for her deliverance, he'd been appalled, for he was convinced that Caitlin was far safer in England than in Wales, where she was known. He could not forget that Davydd had been betrayed by men of his own tongue, and argued that all it would take was one craven wretch eager to earn English blood money, just one. But Caitlin had persisted, and for the first time in their marriage, they could find no common ground.

It was Trevor who'd made peace between them, Trevor who understood Hugh's fear and Caitlin's need. Let him go first into Gwynedd, he offered, let him see if the abbey was safe. While he was gone, Caitlin reluctantly nerved herself to cut her hair again, for she knew Hugh would insist upon cowled camouflage. But she never wielded her scissors, for Trevor returned to Chester with shocking news, news that ended her hopes of seeing Gwynedd one last time.

The English King wanted to build a great castle on the west bank of the River Conwy, Trevor told them, but the site he had in mind was already taken—by Aberconwy Abbey. And so he meant to move it— the entire monastery—seven miles to Maenan. The first construction order had been issued that past March, even before Davydd was captured, and in September he'd secured the consent of the Cistercian chapter-general. The abbey was overrun with English, he reported, was in a state of chaos and confusion, was for certes no place for Davydd ap Gruffydd's daughter to be found.

Hugh was vastly relieved, but Caitlin was devastated. Aberconwy was their Westminster Abbey, royal tomb to their princes. If Edward could uproot it at his will, what could he not do to her downtrodden countrymen, her conquered homeland? How could she turn away from their suffering? Hugh would give her Angoulême, would give her his heart, his world. But what of Wales?

Hugh had shared Caitlin's grieving in the past, had consoled her as she mourned for her uncle, then for her father. But now she mourned for her country, and he did not know how to help her. Again, it was Trevor who came to their aid. She needed, he explained, to say farewell. By then, Hugh's good nature was being rubbed raw by his frustration, and he'd snapped that he'd not known Trevor was one for belaboring the obvious. How could she lay her dead to rest at a distance? Trevor was untroubled, though, by Hugh's unwonted sarcasm. Gwynedd was indeed too dangerous, he agreed. But Lady Caitlin had never been in Maelienydd, did not risk recognition there. Hugh had been puzzled. What was in Maelienydd to give Caitlin comfort? And Trevor had said gravely, with just a trace of triumph in his voice, "Cwm-hir Abbey."

And so they left Chester behind, rode south again into Shropshire, and when they reached the border castle of Ludlow, they turned west, followed the sun into Wales. They were deep now in Maelienydd, the Welsh lands of the de Mortimers, and Hugh sensed a change in his wife, a change for the better. Just crossing the border seemed to have lifted her spirits, and he began to hope that this mad quest of theirs might truly recover the Grail, help her to heal.

Hugh and Caitlin were in agreement that they owed Trevor more than they could ever repay. But the quiet Welsh youth was to do them one last great service, for when they finally reached Cwm-hir Abbey, it seemed for a time that their pilgrimage was to end—unfulfilled—there in the Abbot's parlor. He received them with the utmost courtesy, but when they confided their mission, he responded with polite puzzlement. He was indeed sorry that they had traveled so far in vain, but they had been misled. The Cwm-hir monks knew naught of Llewelyn ap Gruffydd's grave. And nothing they said could shake his certainty. Caitlin's impassioned claims of kinship were not denied, but neither were they heeded. The Abbot smiled upon this unknown young woman and her English husband, sadly shook his head. They were mistaken. What more could he say?

But it was then that Trevor joined them in the Abbot's lodgings, Trevor who had helped to dig his Prince's grave. The monks remembered him well, embraced him in heartfelt welcome, as one of their own, and only then were they willing to admit that they were, indeed, keepers of the flame.

Abbot Cadwgan at once offered them his own hospitality, promising that on the morrow Brother Madog would guide them to the grave. That night at dinner he explained, quite unapologetically, that they dared not take people on faith alone, not when the sanctity of their Prince's grave was at risk. There were many amongst the English, he said, who would deny Prince Llewelyn a resting place in hallowed ground, just as his enemies had once done to Simon de Montfort.

The Archbishop of Canterbury had even authorized an investigation, rumors having reached him of the burial at Cwm-hir. In fairness, though, to the English prelate, he'd been trying to ascertain if there was reason for lifting Llewelyn's excommunication. The Lady Maude Clifford had pleaded with him on Llewelyn's behalf, and a brave act that was for the wife of John Giffard. But the Archbishop had concluded, not surprisingly, that Llewelyn could not be absolved unless it could be proved that he showed true repentance ere he died. And so, the Abbot said with a thin smile, we are baffled by the persistent rumors of a burial at Cwm-hir, and we can only tell the English to seek elsewhere for the grave of our Prince.

The Abbot held to his word, and the next morning Brother Madog led them into a grove of trees, within sight of the river. As soon as they stepped from the sunlight into the shadowed stillness of the clearing, Caitlin saw the grave, for although it bore no cross, it was sheltered beneath a blanket of flowers: golden gorse blossoms, fragrant yarrow, a scattering of red campion, and even a funeral wreath of glossy green holly, adorned with berries as bright as blood.

Brother Madog shook his head ruefully. "The worst-kept secret in Wales! We keep clearing them away, and people keep bringing more." Glancing at Caitlin, he saw the sudden shine behind her lashes, and said, "You need not fear, my lady. Men will remember Llewelyn ap Gruffydd."

As Caitlin moved forward, the men stopped, let her go on alone. Kneeling by the grave, she touched the wilted grass, the last autumn flowers, and she could not help thinking that even this small comfort would be denied to Elizabeth. Slowly she made the sign of the cross, and then she began to pray for her uncle, her father, Ellen, Elizabeth, Gwenllian, her little brothers at Bristol Castle, her sisters in distant English nunneries, for all on both sides of the border who'd come to grief in God's Year, 1283.

Trevor had leaned back against a gnarled, ageless oak, and although his face was in shadow, Hugh thought he caught a glimmer of tears. "Coming back could not have been easy for you," he said quietly, "for at this time last year, you were here with Lord Llewelyn."

"I am still here with Lord Llewelyn," Trevor said. "Last night was the first peaceful sleep I've had in nigh on a year, for I'd come home." He was quiet for a moment, his eyes moving past Hugh to the kneeling girl, the flower-strewn grave. "When you depart on the morrow, I will not be going back with you," he said. "My place is here."

Although they'd never discussed it, Hugh had known Trevor would not be leaving Wales. "I was expecting as much," he admitted. "But does this mean you'll not be returning to Gwynedd? You'll be staying in Maelienydd?"

"Here . . . at Cwm-hir. I talked to the Abbot last night, and he agreed to let me find out if my need is a true one, strong enough to last a lifetime. I should like a chance to serve God. I know," he said flatly, "that I could never serve the King of England."

"Ah, Trevor . . . we shall miss you. But our loss is God's gain."

"Hugh . . . when you return to England, take ship from Southampton. Do not bring Lady Caitlin back to Bristol."

Hugh was perplexed for a moment or so. And then he remembered that Bristol was one of the English cities to claim a portion of Davydd's butchered body for public display. He nodded bleakly. "I'll take care of her, Trevor. I would die for her if need be."

That elicited one of Trevor's rare smiles. "Better you should live for her," he said.

Caitlin had risen, and they started toward her, only to stop at sound of her voice. When she turned, Hugh said, "We're sorry, lass. We thought your prayer was done."

"It was. I was talking to Uncle Llewelyn, telling him how it broke my heart to see the English King's banner flying over Wales. But I then told him what you'd said to me, that beneath his banner, people were still speaking Welsh. And I told him, too, how that reminded me of a story he'd liked to tell, one he'd gotten from his grandfather, Llewelyn Fawr of blessed memory. It seems that an English King once asked a Welsh sage if he'd win his war. The old man said that on the Day of Direst Judgment, no race but the Welsh would give answer to the Almighty for this small corner of the earth."

A silence fell after that. Caitlin bent down, picked up a sunlit gorse bloom, and then she reached for Hugh's hand.

Trevor watched them go, lingering a few moments more by Llewelyn's grave. "She is right, my lord Prince," he said softly. "Wales will endure. Scriptures tell us so, tell us that one generation passeth away, and another generation cometh, but the earth abideth forever. We must remember that in the dark days that lie ahead."

AFTERWORD

Edward I continued to rule England and Wales for another twenty-four years. He was devastated by the death of his Queen, Eleanora, in November 1290, and did not marry again for nine years. Despite the vast difference in their ages—he was sixty, his French bride was just twenty—his second marriage seems to have been a successful one. Edward grew increasingly autocratic in the remaining years of his reign. In March 1284, he issued the Statute of Rhuddlan, which imposed English law upon the conquered lands of Wales. In July 1290, he ordered the expulsion of all Jews from England. In February 1301, he conferred the title Prince of Wales upon his eldest surviving son; it has been reserved ever since for the heir to the English Crown. Edward died of dysentery on July 7, 1307, at age sixty-eight, while campaigning against the Scots, and was succeeded by his ill-starred, inept son, Edward II.

Edmund, Earl of Lancaster, died on June 5, 1296. His wife, Blanche, survived him by seven years. Their eldest son was accused of treason during the political turmoil of Edward II's reign, and beheaded in 1322.

The grandson and namesake of Roger de Mortimer achieved lasting notoriety as the lover of Edward II's Queen, Isabella of France, and as the man responsible for Edward's murder in 1327. He was executed by Edward's son in 1330.

Maude Clifford died in the same month as her cousin, Llewelyn ap Gruffydd, soon after she'd courageously pleaded with the Archbishop of Canterbury on Llewelyn's behalf. Her husband, John Giffard, lived long and prospered.

❧

IN 1283, the Pope appointed Guy de Montfort as captain-general of the papal forces in Romagna. But on June 23, 1287, Guy was captured during a sea battle with the Aragonese admiral, Roger Loria, and cast into a Sicilian dungeon. His family and friends offered the vast sum of eight thousand ounces of gold for his release, but all attempts to ransom him came to naught; it is believed that Edward I exerted influence upon the King of Aragon. Guy never regained his freedom. He was dead by March 1292; one Sicilian chronicle reported that he'd committed suicide. While Guy was imprisoned, his wife, Margherita, took a lover, whom she subsequently married; she was eventually to wed no less than five times. Guy's daughters, Tomasina and Anastasia, married into the Italian nobility. Guy was to have a dubious immortality conferred upon him by Dante, who consigned him to one of the outer rings of Hell for the murder in Viterbo.

Amaury de Montfort sued Edward's brother, Edmund, in the Court of Rome for the return of the earldom of Leicester, a suit as futile as it was audacious. He moved permanently to Italy in 1286, and died between 1292 and 1300. One chronicle claimed that he renounced his priestly vows and took part in the same battle in which Guy was captured, but the truth of this cannot now be substantiated.

LLEWELYN's uncle, Einion ap Caradog, disappeared from the Welsh records in 1277, which seems to indicate that he either died or was incapacitated by illness prior to the outbreak of the war in 1282. Goronwy ap Heilyn and Llewelyn's Seneschal, Dai ab Einion, died fighting the English Crown. Llewelyn's nephews, Rhys Wyndod and his brother, died in English prisons. His other Welsh allies were imprisoned and then impoverished, forfeiting all but their lives. The once-proud Lords of Ceredigion were among the five thousand Welsh who fought for Edward's wages during the war in Flanders.

Llewelyn's daughter, Gwenllian, lived out her days as a nun at Sempringham priory in the Lincolnshire Fens; she died in June 1337, just before her fifty-fifth birthday. Her cousin, Davydd's daughter Gwladys, died at the convent of Sixhills in 1336.

Llewelyn's brother Rhodri lived on in quiet, safe obscurity upon his English manor, dying in 1315. But his grandson, Owain Lawgoch, achieved fame as a battle commander in France, and was assassinated by an agent of the English Crown in July 1378.

Nothing is known of Elizabeth de Ferrer's subsequent fate. One historian contends that Edward eventually allowed her a portion of her first husband's dower lands. She is said to have been buried in the ancient church of St Michael's in Caerwys, Wales, in the shadow of the castle that had once been Davydd's. That seems to argue against her having married or taken the veil after Davydd's execution. It is not known whether she ever saw any of her children again.

Her eldest son, Llewelyn, or Llelo, as he is known in *The Reckoning*, died in captivity at Bristol Castle in March 1288; Edward paid for his burial in the Dominican church at Bristol. Davydd and Elizabeth's second son, Owain, survived into the reign of Edward II. In October 1305, Edward I dispatched a chilling order to the constable of Bristol Castle: henceforth, Owain was to be kept at night in a wooden cage bound with iron. According to the Bristol Record Society, Owain was still alive in August 1325, still a prisoner of the English Crown.

AUTHOR'S NOTE

As I have continued to write about people who led highly improbable lives, once again I feel the need to reassure my readers that I've been following medieval chronicles, not a Hollywood script. Edward's dramatic encounter with a would-be assassin comes from contemporary accounts of the time. For those of you who are familiar with the legend that Eleanora sucked the poison from her husband's wound, I'm sorry to say it is just that, a legend, with no basis in fact. According to an English chronicle, Bran de Montfort did make a reckless, secret pilgrimage to Evesham in 1271. And Davydd really did have his rebellion "rained out" by the Candlemas storm that kept Owen de la Pole's assassins from reaching Llewelyn's court.

Above all, I want to vouch for the historical accuracy of the "pirate" episode, the capture of Ellen de Montfort by Thomas the Archdeacon. It is not surprising that Edward's contemporaries were so convinced he had God on his side, not with luck like this. The chapter was great fun to write; I suspect that even if they won't admit it, most writers secretly harbor a wayward desire to do a pirate scene! And as proof that governments have changed very little down through the centuries, the Calendar of the Close Rolls contains an order from Edward to the sheriff of Cornwall, instructing him to reimburse Thomas the Archdeacon the sum of twenty pounds, for expenses he incurred "about the expedition of certain of the King's affairs in those parts, as the King has enjoined upon Thomas by word of mouth." Who, upon reading that, would ever guess it referred to a kidnapping on the high seas?

As always, I like to utilize the Author's Note to alert my readers to any historical liberties I've taken with known facts. I'm guilty of geographical tampering in chapter 26. Amaury de Montfort had already been moved to Taunton Castle at the time of the scene I set in Sherborne.

But I did not discover this until after I'd done a considerable amount of research on Sherborne, including a brief inspection of the castle ruins, and I just could not bring myself to see all that labor go to waste. As for Ellen de Montfort's purported visit to England in early 1281, historians cite as the source for this Mary Anne Everett Green's *Lives of the Princesses of England.* I've concluded that Ms. Green was in error on this point, attributing to 1281 a safe-conduct that actually refers to January 1278, while Ellen was still a prisoner at Windsor Castle. By the time I reached this conclusion, however, I already had the chapter firmly rooted in my imagination, and after some soul searching, the novelist's need prevailed over the historian's misgivings. And in an attempt to avoid unnecessary confusion in a book that—like a Cecil B. deMille movie—had a cast of thousands, I changed the name of Llewelyn ap Gruffydd's last Seneschal from Davydd to Dai, the latter being a form of Davydd in South Wales. For the same reason, I renamed Llewelyn's steward at Buellt; the man who died with Llewelyn that December day near Llanganten was Rhys ap Gruffydd, temporarily christened Rhosier ap Gruffydd so as not to confuse him with Llewelyn's enemy of the same name.

For the benefit of new readers, I would like to explain that I used Welsh spellings and place names wherever possible, e.g., the medieval Buellt instead of today's Builth Wells. Bearing in mind, though, that the majority of my readers do not speak Welsh, I chose the slightly anglicized "Llewelyn" over the pure Welsh of "Llywelyn," and I again used the medieval *v* for phonetic reasons, e.g., Davydd, Eva, Trevor, rather than the modern Welsh spelling of Dafydd, Efa, Trefor.

With just three exceptions, all of my major characters actually lived and died in medieval England and Wales. Caitlin alone is a creation utterly of my imagination; since some accounts credit Davydd with as many as six illegitimate daughters, I saw no reason not to make Caitlin one of them. Hugh and Juliana were both members of Ellen de Montfort's household; nothing is known of them, though, but their names, and so I felt free to give each one a "history." There are definite advantages in writing of people who really lived. At the very least, it gives me a road map. But there were times in *The Reckoning* when that map took me places I would rather not have gone.

Sharp-eyed readers of *Falls the Shadow* may have noticed a discrepancy between the two books as to the number of children I attribute to Edward and Eleanora. There is a simple, surprising explanation for that: medieval chroniclers could be careless in noting the birth of a baby, even a royal baby. Eleanora gave birth to at least fourteen children, possibly as many as sixteen or seventeen, most of whom died young. Some history buffs may have been puzzled by my portrayal of Eleanora as a woman little liked by her English subjects, for she is one of the best-loved of the English queens. But this is a verdict rendered by subsequent generations, influenced, perhaps, by the magnificent Eleanor crosses that her grieving husband erected to honor her memory. In her own lifetime, Eleanora was not a popular Queen; she was too "foreign" to win over the medieval English, and unfortunately she soon earned herself a deserved reputation for being avaricious and unscrupulous in her business dealings. She and Edward appear to have been more devoted to each other than to their vast brood of children; when their six-year-old son lay dying at Guildford, neither Eleanora nor Edward made the day's journey from London to be at his deathbed. Theirs was undoubtedly, though, one of the most successful royal marriages, a political union that developed into a genuine and lasting love match.

For those readers who may have been disturbed by the Archbishop of Canterbury's vitriolic anti-Welsh outburst in chapter 35, I can only say that the Archbishop's actual diatribe was even more poisoned with prejudice than his fictional tirade. But history owes him a great debt, for his records proved to be a treasure-trove for scholars of later ages. The Welsh grievances set forth in chapters 28 and 34 come from the Archbishop's archives; so do Llewelyn and Davydd's responses to the English Crown's offer of an earldom for Llewelyn, a crusade for Davydd. For such riches, the Archbishop can be forgiven much.

Over the past few years, I've gotten letters from readers curious as to how much history tells us about the color of a king's eyes or the length of his hair. In most cases, we unfortunately know nothing about the physical appearance of people so long dead, and novelists have to rely upon the imagination to fill in those crucial blanks. Occasionally, though, we find a tantalizing clue, a dropped hint, even a fleeting glimpse into a medieval mirror. We have excellent, vivid descriptions of many English kings, even down to such intriguing details as Edward I's slight lisp or Henry II's bloodshot grey eyes. We often have effigies, too, of historical figures, e.g., the regal likeness of Queen Eleanora upon her tomb at Westminster Abbey. And because the Victorian historians had no qualms about disturbing the dead, we even have the dimensions of some royal skeletons. Sometimes a man's name itself offers evidence: Owain Goch, Owain the Red. A son of Llewelyn Fawr's Seneschal, Ednyved ap Cynwrig, called Iorwerth the Leper. Red Gilbert, the flaming-haired Earl of Gloucester. Llewelyn Fawr's daughter, known as Gwladys Ddu in tribute to her dark coloring. But the chronicles are a novelist's best window to the past.

Pertinent, precious details often come to us by chance. We are told that when Gruffydd ap Llewelyn was attempting his reckless escape from the Tower of London, the sheets broke because he was such a big man, grown heavy and lethargic in captivity. The English Chronicle of Dunstable tells us that Llewelyn ap Gruffydd was a most handsome man, and testifies to the force of his personality by reporting that all Welshmen followed Llewelyn as if they were glued to him. No less than three chroniclers extol the beauty of his wife, Ellen de Montfort, which is not surprising, for her grandmother, Isabelle d'Angoulême, was one of the great beauties of her age, dubbed by later historians the Helen of the Middle Ages. So many of the women featured in my books were reputed to be beauties—Isabelle, Joanna, Nell and Ellen de Montfort, Blanche, Marguerite d'Anjou, Elizabeth Woodville—that I've occasionally wondered if the chroniclers were too easily dazzled by crowns. But then, they were not as kind to Richard I's Queen, Berengaria, who was depicted as virtuous yet plain, or to Henry I's Queen, Matilda, who was unenthusiastically described as "not ill favored." How reliable are these medieval monks? It is a difficult question to answer, and perhaps also an irrelevant one, for the chroniclers are all we have, and historical novelists soon learn to be grateful for small mercies.

I need now to discuss the fate of Llewelyn ap Gruffydd. Even after seven centuries, controversy still surrounds his last days. We cannot be sure what drew Llewelyn out of his mountain citadel. Was he motivated by military considerations? Or was he lured to his death? There were those who believed treachery was involved, those who blamed the sons of Roger de Mortimer, blamed the English King. There are those who still believe Llewelyn was betrayed. But I am not one of them. Throughout his life, Llewelyn evidenced an intense and abiding suspicion of the English Crown. I can conceive of no circumstances under which he would have trusted any of the Marcher lords. I think he moved south into Buellt for the strategic reasons I set forth in chapters 34 and 35, and I think he died because the luck of a lifetime ran out in that frigid December dusk—for him and for Wales.

Davydd ap Gruffydd courted controversy all his life, so it is not surprising that it should have followed him faithfully to the grave. It is sometimes said that Davydd was the first man to be drawn and quartered for treason. This is not strictly so. There are a few documented cases of this brutal penalty being imposed prior to Davydd's execution, but it was unquestionably viewed as an innovation by the medieval chroniclers, who much marveled at it; the Chronicle of Osney even claimed— erroneously—that it was a death of a type hitherto unknown. The true significance of the charges brought against Davydd—and the savage punishment inflicted—lies in the fact that here we find the origins of the state trial. It is not widely known that waging war against the king was not a crime in medieval England, not until Edward I chose to make it one, to classify it as high treason. There were no executions after

Evesham. But Davydd was far more vulnerable than the de Montfort partisans, for there were none to speak for him. As J. G. Bellamy points out very succinctly in *The Law of Treason in England in the Middle Ages*, "The King could make an example of Davydd with impunity." And at Shrewsbury, he did. Nine years later, another Welsh rebel suffered the same fate as Davydd. So, too, did the celebrated Scots patriot, William Wallace. By the end of Edward's reign, at least twenty political rivals had been executed for treason, and for the rest of the Middle Ages, those found guilty of defying the Crown would be drawn, quartered, and disemboweled—as Davydd ap Gruffydd was on that early October morning in the border town of Shrewsbury.

Ironically enough, Edward's merciless vengeance gave Davydd in death what he'd never gotten in life—the respect of his countrymen. The Welsh were outraged, did not forget how Llewelyn's brother died. But not even in death could he escape Llewelyn's shadow. Davydd ap Gruffydd was the last Welsh-born Prince of Wales. But it is Llewelyn ap Gruffydd whom the Welsh call *Ein Llyw Olaf*—Our Last Leader.

S.K.P.
January 1991

ACKNOWLEDGMENTS

I would like to thank the following people for their encouragement and assistance: My parents. My American editor, Marian Wood, of Henry Holt and Company. My American agent, Molly Friedrich, of the Aaron M. Priest Literary Agency. My British editor, Susan Watt, of Michael Joseph Ltd. My British agent, Mic Cheetham, of Sheil Land Associates. Valerie LaMont, for her consistent candor and her passion for medieval Wales. Joan Stora, for her unflagging enthusiasm—and for Viterbo. Cris Reay, for her help in filling in the tragic blanks of Elizabeth de Ferrer's life. Jan Barnes, secretary to the Dean of Worcester Cathedral. Above all, Stephen Owen, for his valuable translation of J. Beverley Smith's *Llywelyn ap Gruffydd, Tywysog Cymru*. And last, the staffs of the National Library of Wales, the British Library, the University College of North Wales Library at Bangor, the University of Pennsylvania, the Caernarfonshire Archives, and the research libraries at Shrewsbury, Bristol, Worcester, and Builth Wells.

HERE BE DRAGONS
introduced a world of darkness

FALLS THE SHADOW lit the way . . .

And then came THE RECKONING

Don't miss Sharon Kay Penman's
dramatic Medieval trilogy

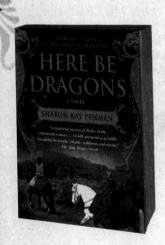
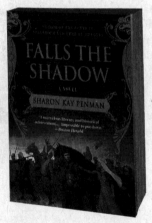

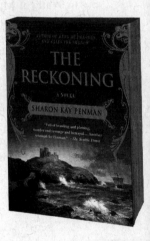

"Penman's characters are so shrewdly
imagined, so full of resonant human feeling
that they seem to breathe on the page."
— *SAN FRANCISCO CHRONICLE*

AVAILABLE WHEREVER BOOKS ARE SOLD

St. Martin's Griffin   www.stmartins.com

IF YOU THINK YOU KNOW THE STORY OF SHAKESPEARE'S RICHARD III, THINK AGAIN...

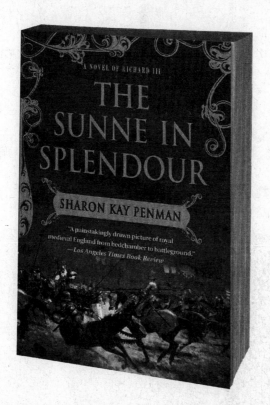

A NOVEL OF RICHARD III

THE SUNNE IN SPLENDOUR

SHARON KAY PENMAN

"A painstakingly drawn picture of royal medieval England from bedchamber to battleground."
—*Los Angeles Times Book Review*

"An uncommonly fine novel, one that brings a far-off time to brilliant life."

—*CHATANOOGA DAILY TIMES*

In her brilliant first novel, which has become a modern classic since it originally appeared in 1982, Sharon Kay Penman redeems Richard III from his maligned place in history as an evil, scheming, murderous hunchback. With a dazzling combination of research and storytelling, Penman paints a picture of a gifted man far more sinned against than sinning.

AVAILABLE WHEREVER BOOKS ARE SOLD

St. Martin's Griffin

www.stmartins.com